THOMAS HARDY

THE WOODLANDERS

THE WOODLANDERS (1887) was Thomas Hardy's own favorite among his stories, and no other book of his more fully represents the many sides of his genius. This portrait of five people in an English village who are tangled in a drama of passion, betrayal, poverty, and pride of place richly demonstrates all of Hardy's distinguishing qualities – his intimacy with rural England, his feeling for nature, his frankness about physical desire, and his gift for rendering, in the most specific way, the mystery at the heart of things.

EVERYMAN'S LIBRARY

EVERYMAN,
I WILL GO WITH THEE,
AND BE THY GUIDE,
IN THY MOST NEED
TO GO BY THY SIDE

THOMAS HARDY

The Woodlanders

with an Introduction by
Margaret Drabble

EVERYMAN'S LIBRARY
Alfred A. Knopf New York Toronto
233

THIS IS A BORZOI BOOK

PUBLISHED BY ALFRED A. KNOPF, INC.

First included in Everyman's Library, 1997

Typography by Peter B. Willberg

 Published in the United States by Alfred A. Knopf, Inc., New York, and simultaneously in Canada by Random House of Canada Limited, Toronto. Distributed by Random House, Inc., New York

ISBN 0-375-40082-6

Book Design by Barbara de Wilde and Carol Devine Carson

Printed and bound in Germany
by Graphischer Grossbetrieb Pössneck GmbH

THE WOODLANDERS

CONTENTS

INTRODUCTION

Thomas Hardy wrote most of *The Woodlanders* in the upstairs study of his new redbrick villa at Max Gate, which lay just outside Dorchester on the Wareham Road. He had purchased the land freehold from the Duchy of Cornwall for the considerable sum of £450, and had supervised the construction work: he and his wife Emma slept there for the first time on 29 June 1885. He had become a property owner, secure in his own dwelling place. Serialization of the novel began in May 1886 in *Macmillan's Magazine*, and, as Hardy noted in his diary, he finished work on the book at 8.20 p.m. on 4 February 1887. The contrast between the world he describes in the novel and the atmosphere of his new home could hardly be more striking.

Max Gate was built by his father and his brother Henry, both of them stonemasons and small builders. Hardy himself had trained and achieved some success as an architect, and they worked to his own (not wholly adequate) design. Some have detected the gentle, unambitious qualities of a Gabriel Oak or a Giles Winterborne in Henry Hardy, and Thomas Hardy's own social aspirations may be read into the new structure, described by John Fowles as 'a brick mediocrity, more suitable to a successful local merchant' than to a great writer. The immediate impression that the new house gave to visitors was one of rawness. It seemed arbitrarily superimposed on a windy bare upland: the trees which now surround it, some of which he himself had planted on New Year's Eve, 1884, took years to mature.

Yet the house was built on ancient ground. Below the foundations, disturbed during digging, lay the sites of a neolithic stone circle and a Romano-British cemetery; a neolithic 'Druid' or sarsen stone still stands in its garden. H. G. Wells and Rebecca West, visiting in 1919, noted somewhat irreverently what they saw as Hardy's morbid delight in living on top of his own 'skelingtons', but in fact, when human remains and urns were found, Hardy's first response had been of some dismay. He feared they would prove bad omens.

Hardy was peculiarly, even painfully sensitive to echoes of the past: the scientific discoveries of the Victorian era had immensely extended geological and evolutionary time and space, and Hardy's poetic consciousness took in stars, fossils, and prehistory as well as recorded history. So it was fitting that Max Gate itself should span the centuries.

Hardy wrote revealingly of the early days at his new villa in his poem, 'Everything Comes':

The house is bleak and cold
Built so new for me!
All the winds upon the wold
Search it through for me;
No screening trees abound,
And the curious eyes around,
Keep on view for me.

My love, I am planting trees
As a screen for you...

(*Moments of Vision*, 1917)

Interesting, then, that the first work he wrote there should be the most shaded, secret and leafy of all his novels, which celebrates the modest, quiet, hidden life of its woodland inhabitants. It is a book of holes and hollows and valleys. While Max Gate was being built, and while he was still writing his Dorchester novel, *The Mayor of Casterbridge*, Hardy was to be found haunting the woods round his birthplace, where his parents still lived. In winter he heard the noise as of 'the creaking of withy-chairs' that the birds made as they roosted in the hollies, in what the Hardy children used to call 'The Birds' Bedroom'. In June 1884 on his forty-fourth birthday, 'alone in the plantation', he noted: 'Holm leaves shine like human eyes, and the sky glimpses between the trunks are like white phantoms and cloven tongues...' Despite his new elevation – perhaps partly because of it – he felt himself drawn back to the secret places of his boyhood.

The Woodlanders is a work of Hardy's maturity: he was already well-established as a novelist, and had by this time laid out the landscape of his mythic Wessex, the region that provided the setting for his major novels. But it had not been a foregone conclusion that he would settle in what he perhaps ironically termed 'benighted Dorset'. He had made various attempts to escape from it, with a fictional foray into Cornwall, where in real life he had met and wooed Emma Gifford: this romance provided the setting for *A Pair of Blue Eyes*, published in 1873. He had ventured, with a characteristic mixture of diffidence and ambition, into London society, and written of it in a satirical vein, partly from a servant's viewpoint, in *The Hand of Ethelberta* (1876). He had travelled in Europe and described his visits to Rouen, Heidelberg, Étretat, and other continental attractions with evident delight – see the hectic itinerary of *A Laodicean: A Story of Today* (1881), which rushes its heroine from one beauty spot to another. But his own region continued to call upon him, and, like the native Clym Yeobright, he returned. Doris Lessing has written (in *African Laughter*, 1992) of the need of writers for what she calls 'myth-countries': some, she believes, are compelled to revisit these places, and others need to fence them off forever. Hardy retained a peculiarly close attachment to Wessex, which remained the source of his inspiration. He found he could not live away from it, though there are signs that his decision to return was accompanied by some doubt and uneasiness.

Hardy was to live at Max Gate for the rest of his life, but he did not become a recluse and isolate himself there, as some accounts have suggested: he received many visitors, if at times reluctantly, and always spent several months of the year in London, enjoying theatres, dinners, club nights, Platonic flirtations. The woodlanders of his novel belong to the age of carriage, cart and waggon, but Hardy himself took eagerly to the railway, the bicycle, and eventually to the motor car. The railway plays a prominent part in many of his plots, offering liberation, threatening disruption, but *The Woodlanders* is a novel of bridle-paths and tracks, in which even the turnpike road seems a novelty. Dr Fitzpiers, the incomer, travels by train – and he is, significantly, ill at ease on horseback – but the region remains remote, indeed backward and behind the times: strangers lose themselves in it, and find it hard to penetrate. Even barber Percomb, in the opening chapter, loses himself on the way to Little Hintock, and has to ask for directions – 'I am at fault about the small village', he has to admit, although he knows the neighbourhood well.

Hardy's new home lay only a few miles from his birthplace in the hamlet of Higher Bockhampton, in the parish of Stinsford: Stinsford had appeared as Mellstock in *Under the Greenwood Tree*, his first attempt at a naturalistic portrayal of rustic life. The cottage had been built at the turn of the century by his grandfather John Hardy on land leased from the Morton Pitt family. Low and thatched, it was (and is) the last building on a lane leading up to heathland past woodland, and it seems today a natural outcrop of its surroundings. Yet it too had once been exposed and new. One of Hardy's earliest recovered poems, 'Domicilium', describes his grandmother's memories of it in its early days:

> 'Our house stood quite alone, and those tall firs
> And beeches were not planted. Snakes and efts
> Swarmed in the summer days, and nightly bats
> Would fly about our bedrooms. Heathcroppers
> Lived on the hills, and were our only friends;
> So wild it was when first we settled here.'

This interpenetration of outdoor and indoor sounds and creatures is a recurrent motif in Hardy's work: in *The Woodlanders* he describes the young village woman Marty South at five in the morning listening to 'the sparrows walking down their long holes in the thatch above her sloping ceiling to their exits at the eves', and we know he is describing one of the familiar sounds of his own childhood. The proximity of beast and man, of man and nature, is stressed again and again – a proximity which seems at times benign, at times threatening. The invasive ivy which makes its way into a shed, pushing in with such force that it lifts shelves from their supports, signals both energy and destruction: human structures are fragile and temporary compared with vegetable force. Grace Melbury's timber-merchant father warns Grace's lover Giles Winterborne that he must tidy up himself and his gig before going to collect her at Sherton Abbas: 'We, living here alone, don't notice how the whitey-brown creeps out of the earth over us; but she, fresh from a city – why, she'll notice everything!'

And notice she must: we do not see at firsthand her reaction to finding a well-boiled slug in her winter-greens at Winterborne's Christmas party, but Creedle's defence of the slug to his master speaks volumes: the cabbage, he insists, was the slug's 'native home', and anyway he was only a little green slug, which must surely be harmless – 'for they were born on cabbage, and they've lived on cabbage, so they must be made of cabbage'. Towards the end of the novel, when Grace finds herself taking cover in Winterborne's single-roomed cot, the sense of the natural world's inquisitive imminence is overwhelming, as 'creatures of hair, fluff, and scale; the toothed kind and the billed kind; underground creatures jointed and ringed' eye the hut with 'a view to winter quarters'.

Most of the action takes place within the space of a few miles, but its precise location has proved curiously hard to establish. As in other works, Sherton is clearly Sherborne, Ivell is Yeovil, Shottsford Forum is Blandford Forum, Budmouth is Weymouth, and Abbot's Cernel is Cerne Abbas. The arched vaults and crocketed capital of the picturesque ruins of Sherton Castle, debased into a cattle shelter where calves cool 'their thirsty tongues by licking the quaint Norman carving', represent the ruins of Sherborne Old Castle, once the seat of the Digbys. The Digby Hotel in Sherborne, opened in 1869, and now a boarding-house of Sherborne School, becomes, with a little alteration, the Earl of Wessex: here Edred Fitzpiers, who claims descent from the Baxbys (i.e. the Digbys) through the maternal line, takes his bride Grace on their return from their honeymoon.

But many, like barber Percomb, have lost themselves in the search for Little and Great Hintock. The confusion arises from Hardy's own alterations to his text, which in later editions relocated the villages further east, in a composite landscape. It has been suggested that Hardy deliberately shifted and obscured the origins of the Hintocks and Hintock House because he was worried that the Ilchester family of Melbury House at Melbury Samford, already sensitive about his treatment of their family legends, would suspect an unwelcome connection with the doubtful Mrs Charmond: he had become friendly with the Ilchesters and he and his wife wished to stay on good terms with the local aristocracy. His replies in later years to queries about the Hintocks (see his own prefaces of 1895 and 1912) were evasive. But the choice of the name of Melbury for his heroine is certainly significant here. His maternal grandmother, Elizabeth (Swetman) Hand, came from Melbury Osmond, and had been supported there in her widowhood by the Poor Law Overseers. Some have confidently identified Great Hintock as Melbury Osmond, a view confirmed by a letter and postcard (April 1887) from Hardy to his friend Edmund Gosse, and by a deleted manuscript reference to Little Hintock's old name being 'Hintock St Osmond'. It is likely, as biographer Robert Gittings argues, that one of the reasons why, in 1912, re-reading the proof for the Wessex edition, Hardy spoke so warmly of *The Woodlanders* – 'I think I like it, *as a story*, the best of all' – was because, in its earliest versions, it was strongly associated with his mother's childhood, in a locality of which he said he was 'very fond'.

The novel gives an affectionate portrait of the onetime manor of Little Hintock, now untidily surrounded by the many sheds and outhouses in which George Melbury carries on his trade. It too, like Sherton Castle, has been debased in usage over the years. Landowner Mrs Charmond lives in the much grander, damp, low-lying, lichen-covered, vegetation-threatened Hintock House, presented in a birds'-eye view and in much precise architectural detail from its grey lead roofs 'with their gutters, laps, rolls, and skylights' to its Elizabethan mullioned windows of 'rich snuff-coloured freestone from Ham-hill quarries'. Hintock House has been identified as Turnworth House (demolished in 1959), which lay some miles from the Melburys: Hardy knew Turnworth well, for in his career as an architect he had been responsible for supervising the rebuilding of its church, and had designed its Early Gothic foliage capitals.

Hardy's use of place names for surnames served him well: thus he simultaneously avoided libel and suggested a deep-rooted natural order. There are several Melburys and many Winterbornes and Winterbournes in the county – Hardy's friend and mentor, the poet William Barnes, had been curate of Winterbourne Whitcombe and became rector of Winterborne Came, and Hardy was much attached to the little church of Winterborne Tomson, described by Frederick Treves in *Highways and Byways in Dorset* (1906) as 'the deserted church', with birds roosting in its pews, rats tugging at its altar cloth, and a churchyard hidden in wild undergrowth. (This church was restored in 1931 by money raised from the sale of Hardy manuscripts.) Melbury means a 'multi-coloured fortified place', and a Winterborne is a winter stream: both names are more or less unknown to the parish register. As surnames, they are Hardy coinages, but they belong to old England. Not so the Norman name of the disruptive invader Edred Fitzpiers, who in an early version of the text had appeared as Edgar Fitzpayne. Fitzpiers, like Fitzpaine, has an aristocratic and philandering ring – Hardy revived an echo of it in Jocelyn Pierston, the fickle and susceptible hero of his last work of fiction, *The Well-Beloved.* The unlikely name of the novel's other principal character, Felice Charmond, is pure invention, suggestive of her alien origins: she has come from further afield than Fitzpiers, and although she is a powerful landowner she has no liking for the Hintocks, and 'was never in the county till my husband brought me here'.

The naming of names is always important in Hardy: names may hold in themselves the history of the decline and fall of old families, much as buildings hold history in their changes of use and in their ruins. It is the very name of d'Urberville that sets the tragedy of Tess Durbeyfield in motion. Hardy seems to have wished, somewhat curiously, to insist that the Hardys were a family in decline, rather like the Melburys, who had once been lords of the manor: 'So we go down, down, down,' he remarked of the Hardys, with some satisfaction. Yet at the same time he was keenly aware of the comedy of false aspirations: in *A Laodicean* he mocks the *nouveau-riche* Paula Power's weakness for the aristocracy, a weakness which he seems nevetheless to have shared. In this novel, one might also note, he amuses himself by housing the railway magnate's daughter in the ancient castle, and the impoverished aristocrat de Stancy in a 'genteel and modern' streaked brick residence called 'Myrtle Villa'.

So where did Hardy's sympathies lie? With the labourer,

the yeoman, the craftsman, the tenant farmer, the aspiring professional man, or the lord? With the old order, or with the new? Or was he an impassive observer of life's little ironies and sombre tragedies?

Much praise has rightly been given to Hardy's accurate portrayal of the life of the Dorsetshire labourer. Dorset was then one of the poorest and least industrialized counties in England, and Hardy had observed at firsthand pursuits which are now preserved only in tableaux in agricultural museums. He had seen sharp-toothed man-traps, which had been banned as long ago as 1829: Mrs Charmond displays them as antiquarian relics, along with suits of armour, but Hardy knew that they still lay dangerously rusting in outhouses and barns. In other novels he describes the working lives of corn merchants, millers, dairy farmers and sheep farmers: in *The Woodlanders* we enter the world of copsework, where we meet timber-fellers, bark-strippers, tanners, hurdle-makers and hollow-turners, as well as cider-makers from the apple orchards of Blackmoor Vale.

Hardy knew the terminology of these trades from boyhood. In his preface of 1912 he asserted that 'the adoption of iron utensils and implements in agriculture, and the discontinuance of thatched roofs ... have almost extinguished the handicrafts classed formerly as "copsework"'. He might have been surprised to see how many of these traditional skills survive. A century later, wattle and gate hurdles are widely used in farming and landscaping, and baskets are still handmade in the willow wetlands of the south-west. The hazel spars which we see Marty South preparing are used in thatching today, and although many thatchers cultivate their own hazel coppices, the demand for these small handcrafted objects is so considerable that spar-making is now a small industry in some areas.

Many of the customary sights of the woodland have, however, gone forever. Saw pits, for example, have vanished, with the advent of the power saw: a saw pit such as Mr Melbury's consisted of a hole in the ground, over which a tree trunk was positioned on a frame. Two sawyers would work on the trunk with a two-handled saw, the one standing on top of the trunk being known as the 'top sawyer' and the man standing in the pit as the 'bottom sawyer'. So familiar a sight was this in Hardy's day that the phrase 'top sawyer' was used to mean 'top dog'; in *The Mayor of Casterbridge* Mr Tubber rightly predicts that Farfrae will overtake his master Henchard in power and popularity – 'He'll be top-sawyer soon of you two, and carry all afore him.'

Some of the copsework was relatively unskilled, and could be carried on with only half one's attention. Marty learns to make spars expertly in a matter of hours, to Winterborne's surprise. But other tasks required sensitivity as well as dexterity, and Marty has natural gifts which, Hardy suggests, could have been trained for a higher calling. Fitzpiers notices that Marty South outstrips all the men at barking, as she mounts to the tree's upper parts, where she stood 'encaged amid the mass of twigs and buds like a great bird, running her ripping-tool into the smallest branches, beyond the furthest points to which the skill and patience of the men enabled them to proceed'. She and Giles Winterborne are in tune with the woodland, and, unlike Fitzpiers and Mrs Charmond, can read its 'hieroglyphs': in one of the most haunting scenes of the novel Marty and Giles show their own unfulfilled and unspoken affinity as they silently plant young fir trees together in a clearing. He has a 'marvellous power of making trees grow', 'a sort of sympathy' with their roots, 'a gentle conjurer's touch' as he lays out the delicate fibres in the right direction for growth. He has a nurturing, almost maternal delicacy, a gift which he is to show again in his self-sacrificing domestic care for Grace.

Yet Hardy does not romanticize the country life. As Marty helps Winterborne by holding the trees upright in their holes she notices that they sigh 'as if they sigh because they are very sorry to begin life in earnest – just as we be', and during this scene Marty herself is silently perishing with cold. The stoic misery of many country people, who will go on stubbornly planting in sodden garden plots with a 'curious mechanical regularity ... in the face of hopelessness' is not glosssed over: nor is their dependence on the whims of the gentry, a dependence which Hardy's family knew at firsthand.

The plot of the novel turns in part on Marty and Winterborne's loss of their homes through the death of Marty South's father: their cottages had been held for life – that is, they were 'lifehold' rather than held by the more secure 'copyhold' or 'tenure by copy of court roll', and, unless formally renewed, tenure expired with the life of the last tenant of three lives named in the lease. Lifeholding was a survival of a medieval form of land-holding, and although leases were often renewed without question (as was the Hardys' own at Bockhampton), agreements could prove precarious. The Hardys maintained their respectability, and considered themselves socially superior to the landless labourer, but their position was tenuous: they too might have been displaced, like Giles Winterborne. As Hardy explains in the opening paragraph of Chapter 13, when South dies his and several other cottages, including Winterborne's, will 'fall in and become part of the encompassing estate'. (How villagers had in the past been persuaded to exchange copyhold for lifehold was, Hardy says, inexplicable: country people were not good at protecting their own interests, and were easily exploited.)

The loss of a long-occupied family home was becoming a common event. With the growing mechanization of agriculture, and the subsequent decline in the need for labour, landowners became increasingly unwilling to pay for repairs, and like Mrs Charmond preferred to pull property down rather than incur the expense of maintaining it. In the first chapter of *The Mayor of Casterbridge* Henchard, who is on the road looking for work as a hay-trusser, asks if there are any cottages available in the neighbourhood, and is told 'Pulling down is more the nater of Weydon. There were five houses cleared away last year, and three this; and the volk nowhere to go – no, not so much as a thatched hurdle' – and towards the end of the novel, Hardy describes the plight of respectable 'families from decayed villages – families of that once bulky, but now nearly extinct, section of village society called "liviers" or lifeholders', who are compelled to resort to the hedgerow, or to the vicious poverty of Casterbridge's Mixen Lane. Similarly, a chorus of witnesses to Winterborne's loss echoes 'Pulling down is always the game.'

William Barnes wrote a dialect poem on the theme: 'The Hwomstead A-Vell Into Hand' is the lament of a cottager who foresees the loss of a property very similar to that of the Souths, with 'elem trees a-growen round', and an apple orchard, and two strips of land, on which the family have maintained themselves for generations. All this will be swallowed up into 'the squiër's wide estëate' because no life can be put in for his when he is gone. His home will disappear, like those in the village that have gone already:

> An' all the happy souls they ved
> Be scatter'd vur an' wide.
> An' zome o'm be a'wanten bread,
> Zome, better off, ha' died . . .*

Hardy was familiar with the problems of the displaced: writing to social reformer Percy Bunting on 5 November 1883, in response to an invitation to submit an article to the *Contemporary Review* on the subject of the rural vote (a topic to which 'labourers as a body have (as far as I see) given no thought at all'), he affirms:

> You ask me if I am clear about the labourer's dread of being turned out of his house. There is no doubt that what weighs most heavily upon the farm labourer's mind is the general insecurity of his position: this oppresses him much more than the question of so many shillings a week; and the knowledge that his house is a mere tent for his use while working in the fields of any given farmer, is a great portion of his feeling of insecurity. It is obvious that there is no remedy for this growing disassociation with localities – this complete reversal of the old condition of things – but some system by which he could have a personal interest in a particular piece of land.

In *The Woodlanders*, Hardy powerfully dramatizes the effects of this insecurity. Marty attempts to appease fate and to prevent the disaster of losing her home by the sale of her chestnut hair to Mrs Charmond, persuaded to do so when she is reminded by barber Percomb that it would be 'as well to oblige' the woman who may soon have the power to dislodge her: however, Winterborne stubbornly and disastrously offends Mrs Charmond when the heavy timber-waggon he is escorting

*From *Poems of Rural Life in the Dorset Dialect*, First Collection, 1879.

meets her carriage on a dark night and he and his carter refuse to back off.

Critics have complained about the improbable coincidences or 'ingenuities' of Hardy's plots – unlikely encounters, lost letters, missed appointments. *The Woodlanders* is not free of such intrusions, which appear notably in the convenient figure of Mrs Charmond's old admirer: however, Winterborne's ill-timed affront to Mrs Charmond and his failure (by a few days) to renew his lease do not fall into this category. They are integral to the mood of the novel. Winterborne's fatalistic and superstitious fear of the worst seems all too plausible: his reluctance to inspect the terms of his lease (which he keeps in a canvas bag under his mattress) may surely be recognized by many more sophisticated readers who dread and sometimes foolishly postpone reading the small print of a contract.

Hardy had an understanding of this inertia in the face of fate – 'paralysis' and 'listlessness' are other words that he uses for it. The labourer and the yeoman were not given to energetic defence of their own interests. The agricultural depression of the 1820s and 1830s had indeed led to a strongly-resisted attempt to form a union, and to the forced deportation to Australia in 1834 of the Tolpuddle Martyrs, but this defeat was followed by decades of apathy. (Tolpuddle lies some five miles east of Bockhampton, so for Hardy this was a local and living memory.) The scale of emigration continued to increase throughout the century, reaching a peak in 1881–90, when over two and a half million left the British Isles. This was the route taken by Winterborne's aunt and, somewhat reluctantly, by Suke Damson and Tim Tangs. One might note that in the second half of the century many of the parishes Hardy knew best suffered a slow but seemingly inexorable decline in population – Cerne Abbas, for example, dropped from 1,342 in 1841 to 834 in 1891, and over the same period Tolpuddle fell from 368 to 288, and Okeford Fitzpaine from 675 to 557.

Despite this background of distress, displacement and difficulty, however, the prevailing mood of *The Woodlanders* is not one of unremitting bitterness, nor is Hardy's purpose sociological. 'The "simply natural" is interesting no longer,' he had reminded himself, in January 1887, just before finishing the novel – a remark prompted by a revealing comparison between the calm and scenic landscapes of Bonington and wild late Turner. He himself was now seeking 'the deeper reality underlying the scenic, the expression of what are sometimes called abstract imaginings'.

The Mayor of Casterbridge, the work which immediately precedes *The Woodlanders*, is perhaps Hardy's harshest and bleakest: it is a hard, dry, urban, money-driven book, in which even a natural product like corn is seen in actuarial terms as a dusty commodity. The 'skimmity-ride' which leads to Lucetta Farfrae's death shows peasant superstition at its most ignorant and vindictive. In *The Woodlanders*, Hardy's mood seems to have softened. This 'woodland story', which he had set aside in 1875 in order to write his light-hearted comedy, *The Hand of Ethelberta*, must be classed with his tragedies, and it is true that it presents some powerful illustrations of ill health, obsession, and vegetable decay. By selective quotation, one could certainly introduce the novel as an exposition of Hardy's own obsession with the theme of Nature's Unfulfilled Intention. Yet it also rejoices in equally powerful images of fruitfulness and abundance, of moisture and juice and oozings of 'prodigal' bounty. Man may fall into apathy, but in April the sap continues 'to heave with the force of hydraulic lifts inside all the trunks of the forest' – an extraordinarily vivid representation of overpowering energy. Spring in the cider country of Blackmoor Vale, with its 'blaze of pink bloom', gives way to 'gardens and orchards now bossed, nay encrusted, with scarlet and gold fruit, stretching to infinite distance under a luminous lavender mist'. Autumn brings both decay and fruition. Two of the most famous passages in the book celebrate Winterborne as 'Autumn's very brother', who rises upon Grace's memory 'as the fruit-god and the wood-god in alternation: sometimes leafy and smeared with green lichen, as she had seen him amongst the sappy boughs of the plantations: sometimes cider-stained and starred with apple-pips . . .'

We see here Hardy's gift for lifting his narrative above the 'simply natural', for moving from microcosm to macrocosm: he had set himself not merely to record Dorsetshire life, but also to compose tragedy on a classic scale, to write a drama 'of a grandeur and unity truly Sophoclean'. His story is embossed with references that extend far beyond the small world of the Hintocks: Giles is a god, a faun, an Arcadian figure; Marty South is tempted like Faustus by Mephistopheles, and even the fire in Winterborne's bakehouse expands to 'a vast scorching Sahara, with red-hot boulders lying about everywhere'. Quotations from Shakespeare, Bunyan and the Bible mingle with allusions to Norse mythology, and there are frequent invocations of Italian, Dutch and British artists. Some have found this insistent display of scholarship self-conscious and intrusive, the tell-tale mark of a self-educated man, but Hardy's own pictorial sense is so strong that it overrides these objections. And may one not detect a note of self-mockery when Fitzpiers rhapsodizes from Shelley and addresses Winterborne on the subject of Spinoza? For Hardy shows himself to be fully aware that neither Fitzpier's sensibilities nor his morals have been improved by his book-learning.

'A little learning is a dang'rous thing,' declared Pope, and this could be a motto for many of Hardy's plots and sub-plots. His novels are populated by characters who have been educated or who have educated themselves out of contentment, but not into achievement. Jude the Obscure is the archetype of all such failures, and Clym Yeobright in *The Return of the Native* treads a dangerously similar path: many more hover between two worlds, as Hardy must at times have felt himself to do, in a painful state of incomplete evolution. Grace Melbury goes to boarding-school and travels to Bath, Cheltenham and the Continent: Hardy's sisters and his cousin Tryphena Sparks, like Fancy Day in *Under the Greenwood Tree* and Sue Bridehead in *Jude*, became teachers. These young women were torn between differing allegiances, as are Tess and Henchard's daughter Elizabeth-Jane, both of whom are forced to learn to speak two dialects of their own tongue. The Wiltshire writer Richard Jefferies, in *Hodge and his Masters* (1880), writes with sympathy of the farmer's daughter, who, like Grace Melbury, is sent away to be educated, and returns home dissatisfied with her lot: 'You cannot blame these girls . . . for thinking of something higher, more refined and elevating than the cheese-tub or the kitchen. It is natural, and it is right, that they should wish to rise above that old, dull, dead level in which their mothers and grandmothers worked from youth to age ...'

The theme is familiar enough in the fiction of the period, a period marked by increasing mobility and the rapid expansion of state education, but Hardy dramatizes it with a peculiar and personal intensity. The social gulf he had himself crossed was unusually wide – a gulf which he crossed and recrossed, as he moved between Max Gate and his relatives in Higher Bockhampton and Puddletown. For Fancy Day, the story ends well, if a little ambiguously, as she rejects the tempting overtures of the vicar of Mellstock and settles for her village lover and a little deceit: for Grace, Fancy's tragic counterpart, there can be no happy ending, for neither of her lovers can satisfy her. In losing Winterborne, she loses her continuity with her past, and although Hardy allows her to be reunited with Fitzpiers it is clear that her husband will not be faithful to her, nor she content with him.

Yet, as has been said, the tone of this novel is not punitive: it has at times a wryness and lightness more in keeping with Hardy's minor fictions than with his major tragedies. There are no villains here, and one must suspect that although Hardy mocks Fitzpiers, he also feels some sympathy with his inconstancies: Hardy himself was highly susceptible both to female beauty and to social graces. He did not blame those who succumbed to either, though he sometimes wrote with relish of their overthrow. But he did blame critics and publishers who attempted to censor his exploration of sexual attraction: the textual variations in different editions of *The Woodlanders* make interesting reading here. Hardy, although he himself was (twice) respectably married, was a firm advocate of divorce reform, which provides an important strand in the plot of this novel: it is Mr Melbury's misunderstanding of a new liberal divorce law (presumably that of 1878, though some have suggested Hardy refers to an earlier reform of 1857) that precipitates the final catastrophe. Hardy also strongly opposed the customary bowdlerization which forbade expletives, censored bawdy country songs, and attempted (sometimes successfully) to impose conventional morals and marriages upon his characters.

Hardy was, for his period, remarkably open-minded about the power of sexuality. Fitzpiers is barely condemned for his dalliance with Suke Damson, and the tone of the scene in Chapter 35 in which the three women, Suke, Felice Charmond, and Grace attend him after he had been attacked by his father-in-law is frankly comic: Grace opens his chamber door with a brave 'Wives all, let's enter together!' Comic, too, is the tone of Grace's eventual reunion with Fitzpiers: she steps out into the garden to get a little parsley, or so her father thinks, and ends up in bed with Fitzpiers in the Earl of Wessex hotel.

Hardy's attitude to marriage was unorthodox, though he seems to have found it easier to express himself more freely on the topic in verse than in prose. In a little poem called 'Over the Coffin', from *Satires of Circumstance* (1914), he describes two wives meeting over the body of their dead husband: the first wife tells the second that although she divorced him

> '... because of you –
> It seemed I must do it, boundenly;
> But now I am older, and tell you true,
> For life is little, and dead lies he;
> I would I had let alone you two!
> And both of us, scorning parochial ways,
> Had lived like the wives in the patriarchs' days.'

Perhaps, Hardy may hint, it is largely convention that obliges Grace to condemn Fitzpiers's infidelity.

It is not always easy to tell whether Hardy is aware of the sexually suggestive nature of some of his scenes: take, for instance, the passage in which Grace and the fur-clad Felice cuddle and embrace one another when lost in the woodland, which is in itself an echo of an even more erotic scene in bed between young Cytherea Gray and her older mistress Miss Aldclyffe in his first published novel, *Desperate Remedies.* Female relationships intrigued Hardy – see also the friendship and rivalry between Lucetta and Elizabeth-Jane in *The Mayor of Casterbridge* – and his treatment of sexuality, flirtation, fetishism and frigidity remind us that he was a near contemporary of Freud and Havelock Ellis. Havelock Ellis, the pioneer sexologist, in an essay on Hardy in the *Westminster Review* (published in 1883, before *The Woodlanders* appeared), noted Hardy's 'lingering echoes of the old tree-worship': it would not be too fanciful to elaborate a connection between Hardy's love of the damp vegetable hollows of his mother's country, the thirsty sucking earth of young dry Max Gate, and his own planting of trees. And what of that phallic red tower he designed for his new home?

All ages are transitional, but some are more transitional than others. One of Hardy's great strengths – a strength which cost him dear at times – lay in his ability to negotiate between extremes. He was an atheist who restored churches and attended sermons: he was a progressive thinker who wrote warmly of a deeply traditional past. His father was a builder, his mother had been a cook and domestic servant, yet Hardy learned to mix with lords and ladies, with men and women of letters. He saw life from above and below stairs, through town eyes and country eyes. A great social and educational chasm separated Thomas Hardy from his brother Henry, who continued all his life to speak with a broad Dorset accent. Yet Henry's world provided Thomas with his subject matter, and the two brothers saw one another regularly. As Thomas sat writing *The Woodlanders*, in the house that Henry built, he knew he had escaped from the insecurity which is one of the themes of the novel. He had elevated himself above it. Had he become, as biographer Martin Seymour-Smith suggests, 'an artificial countryman, mocking his most loved ones'? His best work belonged not to his new life, but to his old. Dispossession and decay, not advancement and restoration, were his themes.

The final image of the novel is, appropriately, of the utterly lonely, sexless figure of young Marty South, in her solitary vigil, speaking to the dead. Nobody can take the dead from her. The tone of loneliness and tenderness is an elegy not only for the man she loved, but for a way of life which Hardy knew to be passing even as he wrote, and from which he was forever exiled. 'None can plant as you planted,' Marty proudly laments. And the squirrels have vanished from the plantation.

Margaret Drabble

SELECT BIBLIOGRAPHY

There are several biographies of Hardy, including one published under the name of his second wife, Florence Emily Hardy, but in fact largely prepared by himself. This appeared in two volumes in 1928 and 1930, published by Macmillan. A more reliable witness is Robert Gittings, whose *Young Thomas Hardy*, Heinemann Educational, 1975, and *The Older Hardy*, Heinemann, 1978, offer a different (and more critical) portrait. See also Michael Millgate's *The Life and Work of Thomas Hardy*, Macmillan, 1985, and Martin Seymour-Smith's *Hardy*, Bloomsbury, 1994, both of which add new information and insights.

The *Collected Letters*, edited by Richard Little Purdy and Michael Millgate, were published in 1978–9 by the Clarendon Press.

For Hardy's topography, see Hermann Lea's *Thomas Hardy's Wessex*, Macmillan, 1913, and *Hardy's Wessex Reappraised* by Denys Kay-Robinson, David and Charles, 1972. F. B. Pinion's *A Hardy Companion*, Macmillan, 1978, is also useful. *Thomas Hardy's England* by Jo Draper, introduced and edited by John Fowles, Jonathan Cape, 1984, gives a good account of the rural background.

The manuscript of *The Woodlanders* is held in the Dorset County Museum.

M.D.

MARGARET DRABBLE's many novels include *The Millstone, The Waterfall, The Radiant Way,* and *The Witch of Exmoor.* She is also the editor of *The Oxford Companion to English Literature.*

CHRONOLOGY

DATE	AUTHOR'S LIFE	LITERARY CONTEXT (up to 1897)
1837		
1840	2 June: Thomas Hardy born, Upper Bockhampton, Dorset. Younger siblings: Mary, Henry, Katherine, to whom he remained close.	
1846		
1846–60		
1847		Thackeray: *Vanity Fair*.
1848		Dickens: *Dombey and Son*. Elizabeth Gaskell: *Mary Barton*.
1848–56	Schooling in Dorset.	
1849–50s		
1850		Dickens: *David Copperfield*.
1851		
1852		Thackeray: *Henry Esmond*.
1853		Dickens: *Bleak House*. Elizabeth Gaskell: *Cranford*. Elizabeth Gaskell: *Ruth*.
1854		Dickens: *Hard Times*.
1854–6		
1855		Elizabeth Gaskell: *North and South*. Anthony Trollope: *The Warden*; followed by other Barchester novels: *Barchester Towers* (1857); *Doctor Thorne* (1858); *Framley Parsonage* (1861); *The Small House at Allington* (1864); *The Last Chronicle of Barset* (1867).
1856	Hardy watched the hanging of Martha Browne for the murder of her husband.	
1856–60	Articled to Dorchester architect, John Hicks.	
1857		Dickens: *Little Dorrit*. Gustave Flaubert: *Madame Bovary*.

HISTORICAL EVENTS

Accession of Queen Victoria.

'Railway Mania Year': 272 Railway Acts passed.
England became Free Trade country.

Pre-Raphaelite Brotherhood.

Great Exhibition.

Crimean War.

Matrimonial Causes Act, which permitted husbands to divorce wives on grounds of adultery. Wives also had to prove desertion or cruelty.

DATE	AUTHOR'S LIFE	LITERARY CONTEXT
1859		Dickens: *A Tale of Two Cities.* George Eliot: *Adam Bede.*
late 1850s	Important friendship with Horace Moule who became his intellectual mentor and encouraged his self-education.	
1860s		Lurid 'sensation' novels such as M. E. Braddon, *Lady Audley's Secret* (1862).
1860		George Eliot: *The Mill on the Floss.*
1861		George Eliot: *Silas Marner.* Dickens: *Great Expectations.*
1862	London architect, Arthur Blomfield, employed him as draughtsman. Self-education continued.	
1864–80		Anthony Trollope's political 'Palliser' novels: *Can You Forgive Her?* (1864); *Phineas Finn* (1869); *The Eustace Diamonds* (1873); *Phineas Redux* (1876); *The Prime Minister* (1876); *The Duke's Children* (1880).
1865		Dickens: *Our Mutual Friend.*
1867	Returned to Dorset as jobbing architect.	
1868	His first novel, *The Poor Man and the Lady*, rejected for publication.	
1869		
1870	After many youthful infatuations, met his first wife, Emma Lavinia Gifford, on a professional visit to St Juliot in Cornwall.	Dickens: *The Mystery of Edwin Drood.*
1870–1900		
1871	*Desperate Remedies.*	
1872	*Under the Greenwood Tree.*	George Eliot: *Middlemarch.*
1873	*A Pair of Blue Eyes.* Horace Moule committed suicide.	

CHRONOLOGY

HISTORICAL EVENTS

Charles Darwin: *The Origin of Species*. Hardy was an early enthusiast.

Josephine Butler leads nationwide campaign against Contagious Diseases Acts (1864–9), an attempt to control prostitution both ineffective and degrading to women (repealed 1886).

First Women's Suffrage Committee formed in Manchester.

J. S. Mill: *The Subjection of Women*, a classic rejection of unequal treatment of the sexes.
Death of Charles Dickens.

Economic depression.

DATE	AUTHOR'S LIFE	LITERARY CONTEXT
1874	*Far from the Madding Crowd.* Hardy married Emma and set up house in London. They had no children, to Hardy's regret.	
1875	The Hardys returned to Dorset.	
1876	*The Hand of Ethelberta.*	George Eliot: *Daniel Deronda.* Henry James: *Roderick Hudson.*
1877		Henry James: *The American.*
1878	*The Return of the Native.* The Hardys moved back to London.	
1880	*The Trumpet Major.* Hardy ill for many months.	
1881	*A Laodicean.* The Hardys returned to Dorset.	Henry James: *The Portrait of a Lady.*
1882		
1884–92		
1885	The Hardys moved for the last time, to a house designed by Hardy and built by his brother: Max Gate.	George Moore: *A Mummer's Wife.*
1886	*The Mayor of Casterbridge.*	
1887	*The Woodlanders.*	
1888	*Wessex Tales.*	
1889		George Gissing: *The Nether World.*
1890		Henry James: *The Tragic Muse.*
1890s		
1891	*A Group of Noble Dames* (tales). *Tess of the d'Urbervilles.*	George Gissing: *New Grub Street.* George Gissing: *The Odd Women.*
1892	Hardy's father, Thomas, died. Serialized version of *The Well-Beloved.* Growing estrangement from Emma.	
1893	Met Florence Henniker, one of several society women with whom he had intense friendships.	
1894	*Life's Little Ironies* (tales).	George Moore: *Esther Waters.*
1895	*Jude the Obscure*, a savage attack on marriage which worsened relations with Emma.	

CHRONOLOGY

HISTORICAL EVENTS

First exhibition of Impressionist paintings.

Fiftieth anniversary, Stockton & Darlington Railway.
Principle of all children receiving elementary education established by law.

Matrimonial Causes Act, which enabled courts to make an order that a wife be no longer bound to cohabit at risk of her own safety.
Death of George Eliot.

'Otto' bicycle patented; Hardy and Emma became keen cyclists.

Death of Anthony Trollope.
Parliament repeatedly vetoed votes for women.

Death of Robert Browning.

Decline of circulating libraries and weakening of literary censorship.
Free elementary education. US International Copyright Bill: improved authors' finances.

Death of Alfred, Lord Tennyson. International Railway Congress, St Petersburg.

Founding of Independent Labour Party.

DATE	AUTHOR'S LIFE	LITERARY CONTEXT
1890s		Much-discussed 'New Women Novels' including Grant Allen, *The Woman Who Did* (1895).
1895–6	First Collected Edition of novels: *Wessex Novels.*	
1897	*The Well-Beloved* (rewritten) published as a book. From now on Hardy published only the poetry he had been writing for most of his life. **No more novels.**	Henry James: *What Maisie Knew.*
1898	*Wessex Poems.* Hardy and Emma continued to live at Max Gate but 'kept separate'.	
1899–1902		
1900s		
1901	*Poems of the Past and the Present.*	
1902	Macmillan became Hardy's publishers.	
1903		
1904	Hardy's mother, 'the single most important influence in his life', died. Part 1 of *The Dynasts* (epic-drama in verse on Napoleon).	
1905	Met Florence Emily Dugdale, his future second wife. Soon a friend and secretary.	
1906	Part 2 of *The Dynasts.*	
1908	Part 3 of *The Dynasts.*	
1909	*Time's Laughingstocks.*	
1910		
1912	Awarded Order of Merit. Major collected edition of works, revised by Hardy: *The Wessex Edition.* Emma died still estranged. This triggered the writing of Hardy's finest lyrics about their early time in Cornwall.	
1913	*A Changed Man and Other Tales.*	

HISTORICAL EVENTS

Non-militant 'suffragists': National Union of Women's Suffrage Societies. Hardy wanted votes for women but refused an active role.

Boer War.

Reversion to protectionism in trade.
Death of Queen Victoria; accession of Edward VII.

Emmeline Pankhurst's militant 'suffragettes': Women's Social and Political Union.

Death of Edward VII; accession of George V.
Sinking of the *Titanic* with 1,500 deaths; Hardy wrote 'The Convergence of the Twain' – a poem on the disaster.

DATE	AUTHOR'S LIFE	LITERARY CONTEXT
1914	Married Florence Dugdale (already hurt by his poetic reaction to Emma's death).	
1914–18		
1914	*Satires of Circumstance.*	
1915	Mary, Hardy's sister, died.	
1916	*Selected Poems.*	
1917	*Moments of Vision.*	
1918		
1919–20	*Mellstock Edition.*	
1922	*Late Lyrics and Earlier.*	
1924	Dramatized *Tess* at Dorchester. Hardy infatuated with local woman, Gertrude Bugler, who played Tess.	
1925	*Human Shows.*	
1928	Hardy died. *Winter Words* published posthumously. Hardy's brother, Henry, died.	
1928–30	Hardy's autobiography published under his second wife's name (as he wished).	
1937	Florence Hardy (his second wife) died.	
1940	Hardy's last sibling, Kate, died.	

CHRONOLOGY

HISTORICAL EVENTS

World War I. Hardy's young relative, Frank George, killed at Gallipoli.

Vote given to women over thirty.

P R E F A C E

In the present novel, as in one or two others of this series which involve the question of matrimonial divergence, the immortal puzzle – given the man and woman, how to find a basis for their sexual relation – is left where it stood; and it is tacitly assumed for the purposes of the story that no doubt of the depravity of the erratic heart who feels some second person to be better suited to his or her tastes than the one with whom he has contracted to live, enters the head of reader or writer for a moment. From the point of view of marriage as a distinct covenant or undertaking, decided on by two people fully cognizant of all its possible issues, and competent to carry them through, this assumption is, of course, logical. Yet no thinking person supposes that, on the broader ground of how to afford the greatest happiness to the units of human society during their brief transit through this sorry world, there is no more to be said on this covenant; and it is certainly not supposed by the writer of these pages. But, as Gibbon blandly remarks on the evidence for and against Christian miracles, 'the duty of an historian does not call upon him to interpose his private judgment in this nice and important controversy'.

The stretch of country visible from the heights adjoining the nook herein described under the name of Little Hintock, cannot be regarded as inferior to any inland scenery of the sort in the west of England, or perhaps anywhere in the kingdom. It is singular to find that a worldwide repute in some cases, and an absolute famelessness in others, attach to spots of equal beauty and equal accessibility. The neighbourhood of High-Stoy (I give, as elsewhere, the real names to natural features), Bubb-Down Hill, and the glades westward to Montacute; of Bulbarrow, Hambledon Hill, and the slopes eastward to Shaston, Windy Green, and Stour Head, teems with landscapes which, by a mere accident of iteration, might have been numbered among the scenic celebrities of the English shires.

September 1895

I have been honoured by so many inquiries for the true name and exact locality of the hamlet 'Little Hintock', in which the greater part of the action of this story goes on, that I may as well confess here once for all that I do not know myself where that hamlet is more precisely than as explained above and in the pages of the narrative. To oblige readers I once spent several hours on a bicycle with a friend in a serious attempt to discover the real spot; but the search ended in failure; though tourists assure me positively that they have found it without trouble, and that it answers in every particular to the description given in this volume. At all events, as stated elsewhere, the commanding heights called 'High-Stoy' and 'Bubb-Down Hill' overlook the landscape in which it is supposed to be hid.

In respect of the occupations of the characters; the adoption of iron utensils and implements in agriculture, and the discontinuance of thatched roofs for cottages, have almost extinguished the handicrafts classed formerly as 'copsework', and the type of men who engaged in them.

The Woodlanders was first published complete, in three volumes, in the March of 1887.

April 1912 T.H.

THE WOODLANDERS

'Not boskiest bow'r,
When hearts are ill affin'd,
Hath tree of pow'r
To shelter from the wind!'

CHAPTER 1

THE rambler who, for old association's sake, should trace the forsaken coach-road running almost in a meridional line from Bristol to the south shore of England, would find himself during the latter half of his journey in the vicinity of some extensive woodlands, interspersed with apple-orchards. Here the trees, timber or fruit-bearing as the case may be, make the wayside hedges ragged by their drip and shade, their lower limbs stretching in level repose over the road, as though reclining on the insubstantial air. At one place, on the skirt of Blackmoor Vale, where the bold brow of High-Stoy Hill is seen two or three miles ahead, the leaves lie so thick in autumn as to completely bury the track. The spot is lonely, and when the days are darkening the many gay charioteers now perished who have rolled along the way, the blistered soles that have trodden it, and the tears that have wetted it, return upon the mind of the loiterer.

The physiognomy of a deserted highway expresses solitude to a degree that is not reached by mere dales or downs, and bespeaks a tomb-like stillness more emphatic than that of glades and pools. The contrast of what is with what might be, probably accounts for this. To step, for instance, at the place under notice, from the edge of the plantation into the adjoining thoroughfare, and pause amid its emptiness for a moment, was to exchange by the act of a single stride the simple absence of human companionship for an incubus of the forlorn.

At this spot, on the louring evening of a bygone winter's day, there stood a man who had thus indirectly entered upon the scene from a stile hard by, and was temporarily influenced by some such feeling of being suddenly more alone than before he had emerged upon the highway.

It could be seen by a glance at his rather finical style of dress that he did not belong to the country proper; and from his air, after a while, that though there might be a sombre beauty in the scenery, music in the breeze, and a wan procession of coaching ghosts in the sentiment of this old turnpike-road, he was mainly puzzled about the way.

He looked north and south, and mechanically prodded the ground with his cane.

At first not a soul appeared who could enlighten him as he desired, or seemed likely to appear that night. But presently a slight noise of labouring wheels, and the steady dig of a horse's shoe-tips became audible; and there loomed in the notch of sky and plantation a carrier's van drawn by a single horse.

The vehicle was half full of passengers, mostly women. He held up his stick at its approach, and the woman who was driving drew rein.

'I've been trying to find a short way to Little Hintock this last half-hour, Mrs Dollery,' he said. 'But though I've been to Great Hintock and Hintock House half a dozen times, on business with the dashing lady there, I am at fault about the small village. You can help me, I dare say?'

She assured him that she could – that as she went to Abbot's Cernel her van passed near it – that it was only up the lane branching out of the road she followed. 'Though,' continued Mrs Dollery, ' 'tis such a little small place that, as a town gentleman, you'd need have a candle and lantern to find it if ye don't know where 'tis. Bedad! I wouldn't live there if they'd pay me to. Now at Abbot's Cernel you do see the world a bit.'

He mounted and sat beside her, with his feet outwards, where they were ever and anon brushed over by the horse's tail.

This van was rather a movable attachment of the roadway than an extraneous object, to those who knew it well. The old horse, whose hair was of the roughness and colour of heather, whose leg-joints, shoulders, and hoofs were distorted by harness and drudgery from colthood – though if all had their rights he ought, symmetrical in outline, to have been picking the herbage of some Eastern plain instead of tugging here – had trodden this road almost daily for twenty years. Even his subjection was not made congruous throughout, for, the harness being too short, his tail was not drawn through the crupper, and the breeching slipped awkwardly to one side. He knew every subtle incline of the ten miles of ground between Abbot's Cernel and Sherton – the market town to which he journeyed – as accurately as any surveyor could have learnt it by a Dumpy level.

The vehicle had a square black tilt which nodded with the motion of the wheels, and at a point in it over the driver's head was a hook to which the reins were hitched at times, forming a catenary curve from the horse's shoulders. Somewhere about the axles was a loose chain, whose only known function was to clink as it went. Mrs Dollery, having to hop up and down many times in the service of her passengers, wore, especially in windy weather, short leggings under her gown for modesty's sake; and instead of a bonnet a felt hat tied down with a handkerchief, to guard against an ear-ache to which she was frequently subject. In the rear of the van was a glass window, which she cleaned with her pocket-handkerchief every market-day before starting. Looking at the van from the back the spectator could thus see, through its interior, a square piece of the same sky and landscape that he saw without, but intruded on by the profiles of the seated passengers, who, as they rumbled onward, their lips moving and heads nodding in animated private converse, remained in cheerful unconsciousness that their mannerisms and facial peculiarities were sharply defined to the public eye.

This hour of coming home from market was the happy one, if not the happiest, of the week for them. Snugly ensconced under the tilt they could forget the sorrows of the world without, and survey life and discuss the incidents of the day with placid smiles.

The passengers in the back part formed a group to themselves, and while the newcomer spoke to the proprietress they indulged in a confidential chat about him, which the noise of the van rendered inaudible to himself and Mrs Dollery sitting forward.

' 'Tis Barber Percomb – he that's got the waxen woman in his window,' said one. 'What business can bring him out here at this time, and not a journeyman haircutter, but a master-barber that's left off his pole because 'tis not genteel?'

The barber, though he had nodded and spoken genially, seemed indisposed to gratify the curiosity that he had aroused; and the unrestrained flow of ideas which had animated the inside of the van before his arrival was checked thenceforward.

Thus they rode on, and High-Stoy Hill grew larger ahead. At length could be discerned in the dusk, about half a mile to one side, gardens and orchards sunk in a concave, and, as it were, snipped out of the woodland. From this self-contained place rose in stealthy silence tall stems of smoke, which the eye of imagination could trace downward to their root on quiet hearthstones, festooned overhead with hams and flitches. It was one of those sequestered spots outside the gates of the world where may usually be found more meditation than action, and more listlessness than meditation; where reasoning proceeds on narrow premisses, and results in inferences wildly imaginative; yet where, from time to time, dramas of a grandeur and unity truly Sophoclean are enacted in the real, by virtue of the concentrated passions and closely-knit interdependence of the lives therein.

This place was the Little Hintock of the master-barber's search. The coming night gradually obscured the smoke of the chimneys, but the position of the wood-environed community could still be distinguished by a few faint lights, winking more or less ineffectually through the leafless boughs and the undiscernible songsters they bore, in the form of balls of feathers, at roost among them.

At the corner of the lane which branched to the hamlet the barber alighted, Mrs Dollery's van going onward to the larger place, whose superiority to the despised smaller one as an exemplar of the world's movements was not particularly apparent in its means of approach.

'A very clever and learned young doctor lives in the place you be going to – not because there's anybody for'n to cure there, but because they say he is in league with the devil.'

The observation was flung at the barber by one of the women at parting, as a last attempt to get at his errand that way.

But he made no reply and without further pause plunged towards the umbrageous nook, and paced cautiously over the dead leaves which nearly buried the road or street of the hamlet. As very few people except themselves passed this way after dark, a majority of the denizens of Little Hintock deemed window curtains unnecessary; and on this account their visitor made it his business to stop opposite the casements of each cottage that he came to, with a demeanour which showed that he was endeavouring to conjecture, from the persons and things he observed within, the whereabouts of somebody or other who resided here.

Only the smaller dwellings interested him; one or two houses whose size, antiquity, and rambling appurtenances signified that notwithstanding their remoteness they must formerly have been, if they were not still, inhabited by people of a certain social standing, being neglected by him entirely. Smells of pomace, and the hiss of fermenting cider, which reached him from the back quarters of other tenements, revealed the recent occupation of some of the inhabitants, and joined with the scent of decay from the perishing leaves underfoot.

Half a dozen dwellings were passed without result. The next, which stood opposite a tall tree, was in an exceptional state of radiance, the flickering brightness from the inside shining up the chimney and making a luminous mist of the emerging smoke. The interior, as seen through the window, caused him to draw up with a terminative air and watch. The house was rather large for a cottage, and the door, which opened immediately into the living-room, stood ajar, so that a riband of light fell through the opening into the dark atmosphere without. Every now and then a moth, decrepit from the late season, would flit for a moment across the outcoming rays and disappear again into the night.

CHAPTER 2

In the room from which this cheerful blaze proceeded he beheld a girl seated on a willow chair, and busily working by the light of the fire, which was ample and of wood. With a bill-hook in one hand and a leather glove much too large for her on the other, she was making spars, such as are used by thatchers, with great rapidity. She wore a leather apron for this purpose, which was also much too large for her figure. On her left hand lay a bundle of the straight, smooth hazel rods called spar-gads – the raw material of her manufacture; on her right a heap of chips and ends – the refuse – with which the fire was maintained; in front a pile of the finished articles. To produce them she took up each gad, looked critically at it from end to end, cut it to length, split it into four, and sharpened each of the quarters with dexterous blows, which brought it to a triangular point precisely resembling that of a bayonet.

Beside her, in case she might require more light, a brass candlestick stood on a little round table curiously formed of an old coffin-stool, with a deal top nailed on, the white surface of the latter contrasting oddly with the black carved oak of the sub-structure. The social position of the household in the past was almost as definitively shown by the presence of this article as that of an esquire or nobleman by his old helmets or shields. It had been customary for every well-to-do villager, whose tenure was by copy of court-roll, or in any way more permanent than that of the mere cotter, to keep a pair of these stools for the use of his own dead; but changes had led to the discontinuance of the custom, and the stools were frequently made use of in the manner described.

The young woman laid down the bill-hook for a moment and examined the palm of her right hand which, unlike the other, was ungloved, and showed little hardness or roughness about it. The palm was red and blistering, as if her present occupation were as yet too recent to have subdued it to what it worked in. As with so many right hands born to manual labour, there was nothing in its fundamental shape to bear out the physiological conventionalism that gradations of birth show themselves primarily in the form of this member. Nothing but a cast of the die of destiny had decided that the girl should handle the tool; and the fingers which clasped the heavy ash haft might have skilfully guided the pencil or swept the string, had they only been set to do it in good time.

Her face had the usual fulness of expression which is developed by a life of solitude. Where the eyes of a multitude continuously beat like waves upon a countenance they seem to wear away its mobile power; but in the still water of privacy every feeling and sentiment unfolds in visible luxuriance, to be interpreted as readily as a printed word by an intruder. In years she was no more than nineteen or twenty, but the necessity of taking thought at a too early period of life had forced the provisional curves of her childhood's face to a premature finality. Thus she had but little pretension to beauty, save in one prominent particular – her hair.

Its abundance made it almost unmanageable; its colour was, roughly speaking, and as seen here by firelight, brown; but careful notice, or an observation by day, would have revealed that its true shade was a rare and beautiful approximation to chestnut.

On this one bright gift of Time to the particular victim of his now before us the newcomer's eyes were fixed; meanwhile the fingers of his right hand mechanically played over something sticking up from his waistcoat pocket – the bows of a pair of scissors, whose polish made them feebly responsive to the light from within the house. In her present beholder's mind the scene formed by the girlish spar-maker composed itself into an impression-picture of extremest type, wherein the girl's hair alone, as the focus of observation, was depicted with intensity and distinctness, while her face, shoulders, hands, and figure in general were a blurred mass of unimportant detail lost in haze and obscurity.

He hesitated no longer, but tapped at the door and entered. The young woman turned at the crunch of his boots on the sanded floor, and exclaiming, 'O, Mr Percomb, how you frightened me!' quite lost her colour for a moment.

He replied, 'You should shut your door – then you'd hear folk open it.'

'I can't,' she said; 'the chimney smokes so. Mr Percomb, you look as unnatural away from your wigs as a canary in a thorn hedge. Surely you have not come out here on my account – for—'

'Yes – to have your answer about this.' He touched her hair with his cane, and she winced. 'Do you agree?' he continued. 'It is necessary that I should know at once, as the lady is soon going away, and it takes time to make up.'

'Don't press me – it worries me. I was in hopes you had thought no more of it. I can *not* part with it – so there!'

'Now look here, Marty,' said the other, sitting down on the coffin-stool table. 'How much do you get for making these spars?'

'Hush – father's upstairs awake, and he don't know that I am doing his work.'

'Well, now tell me,' said the man more softly. 'How much do you get?'

'Eighteenpence a thousand,' she said reluctantly.

'Who are you making them for?'

'Mr Melbury, the timber-dealer, just below here.'

'And how many can you make in a day?'

'In a day and half the night, three bundles – that's a thousand and a half.'

'Two and threepence.' Her visitor paused. 'Well, look here,' he continued with the remains of a computation in his tone, which reckoning had been to fix the probable sum of money necessary to outweigh her present resources and her woman's love of comeliness; 'here's a sovereign – a gold sovereign, almost new.' He held it out between his finger and thumb. 'That's as much as you'd earn in a week and a half at that rough man's-work, and it's yours for just letting me snip off what you've got too much of.'

The girl's bosom moved a very little. 'Why can't the lady send to some other girl who don't value her hair – not to me?' she exclaimed.

'Why, simpleton, because yours is the exact shade of her own, and 'tis a shade you can't match by dyeing. But you are not going to refuse me now I've come all the way from Sherton on purpose?'

'I say I won't sell it – to you or anybody.'

'Now listen,' and he drew up a little closer beside her. 'The lady is very rich, and won't be particular to a few shillings; so I will advance to this on my own responsibility – I'll make the one sovereign two, rather than go back empty-handed.'

'No, no, no!' she cried, beginning to be much agitated. 'You are tempting me. You go on like the Devil to Doctor Faustus in the penny book. But I don't want your money, and won't agree. Why did you come? I said when you got me into your shop and urged me so much that I didn't mean to sell my hair!'

'Marty, now hearken. The lady that wants it wants it badly. And, between you and me, you'd better let her have it. 'Twill be bad for you if you don't.'

'Bad for me? Who is she, then?'

The wig-maker held his tongue, and the girl repeated the question.

'I am not at liberty to tell you. And as she is going abroad soon it makes no difference who she is at all.'

'She wants it to go abroad wi'?'

He assented by a nod.

The girl regarded him reflectively. 'Now, Mr Percomb,' she said, 'I know who 'tis. 'Tis she at the House – Mrs Charmond!'

'That's my secret. However, if you agree to let me have it I'll tell you in confidence.'

'I'll certainly not let you have it unless you tell me the truth. Is it Mrs Charmond?'

The man dropped his voice. 'Well – it is. You sat in front of her in church the other day, and she noticed how exactly your hair matches her own. Ever since then she's been hankering for it, to help out hers, and at last decided to get it. As she won't wear it till she goes off abroad she knows nobody will recognize the change. I'm commissioned to get it for her, and then it is to be made up. I shouldn't have vamped all these miles for any less important employer. Now, mind – 'tis as much as my business with her is worth if it should be known that I've let out her name; but honour between us two, Marty, and you'll say nothing that would injure me?'

'I don't wish to tell upon her,' said Marty coolly. 'But my hair is my own, and I'm going to keep it.'

'Now that's not fair, after what I've told you,' said the nettled emissary. 'You see, Marty, as you are in the same parish, and in one of this lady's cottages, and your father is ill, and wouldn't like to turn out, it would be as well to oblige her. I say that as a friend. But I won't press you to make up your mind to-night. You'll be coming to market to-morrow, I dare say, and you can call then. If you think it over you'll be inclined to bring what I want, I know.'

'I've nothing more to say,' she answered.

Her companion saw from her manner that it was useless to urge her further by speech. 'As you are a trusty young woman,' he said, 'I'll put these sovereigns up here for ornament, that you may see how handsome they are. Bring the article to-morrow, or return the sovereigns.' He stuck them edgewise into the frame of a small mantel looking-glass. 'I hope you'll bring it; for your sake and mine. I should have thought she could have suited herself elsewhere; but as it's her fancy it must be indulged if possible. If you cut it off yourself, mind how you do it so as to keep all the locks one way.' He showed her how this was to be done.

'But I shan't,' she replied with laconic indifference. 'I value my looks too much to spoil 'em. She wants my curls to get another lover with; though if stories are true she's broke the heart of many a noble gentleman already.'

'Lord, it's wonderful how you guess things, Marty,' said the barber. 'I've had it from those that know that there certainly is some foreign gentleman in her eye. However, mind what I ask.'

'She's not going to get him through me.'

Percomb had retired as far as the door; he came back, planted his cane on the coffin-stool, and looked her in the face. 'Marty South,' he said with deliberate emphasis, '*you've got a lover yourself*, and that's why you won't let it go!'

She reddened so intensely as to pass the mild blush that suffices to heighten beauty; she put the yellow leather glove on one hand, took up the hook with the other, and sat down doggedly to her work without turning her face to him again. He regarded her head for a moment, went to the door, and with one look back at her departed on his way homeward.

Marty pursued her occupation for a few minutes, then suddenly laying down the bill-hook she jumped up and went to the back of the room, where she opened a door which disclosed a staircase so whitely scrubbed that the grain of the wood was well-nigh sodden away by cleansing. At the top she gently approached a bedroom, and without entering said, 'Father, do you want anything?'

A weak voice inside answered in the negative; adding, 'I should be all right by to-morrow if it were not for the tree!'

'The tree again – always the tree! O, father, don't worry so about that. You know it can do you no harm.'

'Who have ye had talking to 'ee downstairs?'

'A Sherton man called – nothing to trouble about,' she said soothingly. 'Father,' she went on, 'can Mrs Charmond turn us out of our house if she's minded to?'

'Turn us out? No. Nobody can turn us out till my poor soul is turned out of my body. 'Tis lifehold, like Giles Winterborne's. But when my life drops 'twill be hers – not till then.' His words on this subject so far had been rational and firm enough. But now he lapsed into his moaning strain: 'And the tree will do it – that tree will soon be the death of me.'

'Nonsense, you know better. How can it be?' She refrained from further speech, and descended to the ground floor again.

'Thank Heaven then,' she said to herself, 'what belongs to me I keep.'

CHAPTER 3

The lights in the village went out, house after house, till there only remained two in the darkness. One of these came from a residence on the hill-side – that of the young medical gentleman in league with the devil, of whom there is something to be said later on; the other shone from the window of Marty South. Precisely the same extinguished effect was produced here, however, by her rising when the clock struck ten and hanging up a thick cloth curtain. The door it was necessary to keep ajar in hers as in most cottages because of the smoke; but she obviated the effect of the riband of light through the chink by hanging a cloth over that also. She was one of these people who, if they have to work harder than their neighbours, prefer to keep the necessity a secret as far as possible; and, but for the slight sounds of wood-splintering which came from within, no wayfarer would have perceived that here the cottager did not sleep as elsewhere.

Eleven, twelve, one o'clock struck; the heap of spars grew higher, and the pile of chips and ends more bulky. Even the light on the hill had now been extinguished; but still she worked on. When the temperature of the night without had fallen so low as to make her chilly she opened a large blue umbrella to ward off the draught from the door. The two sovereigns confronted her from the looking-glass in such a manner as to suggest a pair of jaundiced eyes on the watch for an opportunity. Whenever she sighed for weariness she lifted her gaze towards them, but withdrew it quickly, stroking her tresses for a moment as if to convince herself that they were still secure.

When the clock struck three she arose and tied up the spars she had last made in a bundle resembling those that lay against the wall.

She wrapped round her a long red woollen cravat and opened the door. The night in all its fulness met her flatly on the threshold, like the very brink of an absolute void, or the ante-mundane Ginnung-Gap believed in by her Teuton forefathers. For her eyes were fresh from the blaze, and here there was no street lamp or lantern to form a kindly transition between the inner glare and the outer dark. A lingering wind brought to her ear the creaking sound of two overcrowded branches in the neighbouring wood, which were rubbing each other into wounds, and other vocalized sorrows of the trees, together with the screech of owls, and the fluttering tumble of some awkward wood-pigeon ill-balanced on its roosting-bough.

But the pupils of her young eyes soon expanded, and she could see well enough for her purpose. Taking a bundle of spars under each arm, and guided by the serrated line of tree-tops against the sky, she went some hundred yards or more down the lane till she reached a long open shed, carpeted around with the dead leaves that lay about everywhere. Night, that strange personality which within walls brings ominous introspectiveness and self-distrust, but under the open sky banishes such subjective anxieties as too trivial for thought, gave to Marty South a less perturbed and brisker manner now. She laid the spars on the ground within the shed and returned for more, going to and fro till her whole manufactured stock was deposited here.

This erection was the waggon-house of the chief man of business hereabout, Mr George Melbury, the timber, bark, and copse-ware merchant for whom Marty's father did work of this sort by the piece. It formed one of the many rambling outhouses which surrounded his dwelling, an equally irregular block of building whose immense chimneys could just be discerned even now. The four huge waggons under the shed were built on those ancient lines whose proportions have been ousted by modern patterns, their shapes bulging and curving at the base and ends like Trafalgar line-of-battle ships, with which venerable hulks, indeed, these vehicles evidenced a constructive spirit curiously in harmony. One was laden with sheep-cribs, another with hurdles, another with ash poles, and the fourth, at the foot of which she had placed her thatching-spars, was half full of similar bundles.

She was pausing a moment with that easeful sense of accomplishment which follows work done that has been a hard struggle in the doing, when she heard a woman's voice on the other side of the hedge say anxiously, 'George!'

In a moment the name was repeated, with 'Do come indoors! What are you doing there?'

The cart-house adjoined the garden, and before Marty had moved she saw enter the latter from the timber-merchant's back door an elderly woman sheltering a candle with her hand, the light from which cast a moving thorn-pattern of shade on Marty's face. Its rays soon fell upon a man whose clothes were carelessly thrown on, standing in advance of the speaker. He was a thin, slightly stooping figure, with a small, nervous mouth, and a face cleanly shaven; and he walked along the path with his eyes bent on the ground. In the pair Marty South recognized her employer Melbury and his wife. She was the second Mrs Melbury, the first having died shortly after the birth of the timber-merchant's only child.

' 'Tis no use to stay in bed!' he said, as soon as she came up to where he was pacing restlessly about. 'I can't sleep. I keep thinking of things.'

'What things?'

He did not answer.

'The lady at the Great House?'

'No.'

'The turnpike bonds?'

'No. Though I wish I hadn't got 'em.'

'The ghosts of the Two Brothers?'

He shook his head.

'Not about Grace again?'

'Yes. 'Tis she.'

(Grace was the speaker's only daughter.)

'Why worry about her always?'

'First, I cannot think why she doesn't answer my letter. She must be ill.'

'No, no. Things only appear so gloomy in the night-time.'

'Second, I have not invested any money specially for her, to put her out of the reach of poverty if my affairs fail.'

'They are safe. Besides, she is sure to marry well.'

'You are wrong. That's my third trouble. I have, as I have hinted to you a dozen times, that plan in my head about her, and according to my plan she won't marry well.'

'Why won't it be marrying well?' said his wife.

'Because it is a plan for her to marry that particular person, Giles Winterborne, and he is poor.'

'Well, it is all right. Love will make up for his want of money. He adores the very ground she walks on.'

(Marty South started, and could not tear herself away.)

'Yes,' said the timber-merchant; 'I know that well. There will be no lack of that with him. But since I have educated her so well, and so long, and so far above the level of the daughters hereabout, it is *wasting her* to give her to a man of no higher standing than he.'

'Then why do it?' she asked.

'Why, as you must surely see, it is in obedience to that solemn resolve I made.... I made it because I did his father a terrible wrong; and it has been a weight on my conscience ever since that time, till this scheme of making amends occurred to me through seeing that Giles liked her.'

'Wronged his father?' asked Mrs Melbury.

'Yes, grievously wronged him,' said her husband. 'I have spoken of it to you.'

'Well, don't think of it to-night,' she urged. 'Come indoors.'

'No, no; the air cools my head. I shall not stay long.'

He was silent awhile; then he reminded her that his first wife, his daughter's mother, was first the promised of Winterborne's father, who loved her tenderly, till he, the speaker, won her away from him by a trick, because he wanted to marry her himself. He went on to say that the other man's happiness was ruined by it; that though he married Winterborne's mother it was but a half-hearted business with him. Thus much Marty had heard before. Melbury added that he was afterwards very miserable at what he had done; but that as time went on, and the children grew up, and seemed to be attached to each other, he determined to do all he could to right the wrong by letting his daughter marry the lad; not only that, but to give her the best education he could afford, so as to make the gift as valuable a one as it lay in his power to bestow. 'I still mean to do it,' said Melbury.

'Then do,' said she.

'But all these things trouble me,' said he; 'for I feel I am sacrificing her for my own sin; and I think of her, and often come down here to look at this. I have come to-night to do so once more.'

He took the candle from her hand, held it to the ground, and removed a tile which lay in the garden-path. ' 'Tis the track of her shoe that she made when she ran down here the day before she went away all those months ago. I covered it up when she was gone; and when I come here to look at it, I ask myself again, why should she be sacrificed to a poor man?'

'It is not altogether a sacrifice,' said the woman. 'He is in love with her, and he's honest and upright. If she encourages him, what can you wish for more?'

'I wish for nothing definite. But there's a lot of things possible for her. Why, Mrs Charmond is wanting some refined young lady, I hear, to go abroad with her – as companion or something of the kind. She'd jump at Grace.'

'That's all uncertain. Better stick to what's sure.'

'True, true,' said Melbury; 'and I hope it will be for the best. Yes, let me get 'em married up as soon as I can, so as to have it over and done with.' He continued looking at the imprint while he added, 'Suppose she should be dying, and never make a track on this path any more?'

'She'll write soon, depend upon't. Come, 'tis wrong to stay here and brood so.'

He admitted it, but said he could not help it. 'Whether she write or no, I shall fetch her in a few days.' And thus speaking he covered the shoe-track, and preceded his wife indoors.

Melbury perhaps was an unlucky man in having the sentiment which could make him wander out in the night to regard the imprint of a daughter's footstep. Nature does not carry on her government with a view to such feelings; and when advancing years render the opened hearts of those that possess them less dexterous than formerly in shutting against the blast, they must inevitably, like little celandines, suffer 'buffeting at will by rain and storm'.

But her own existence, and not Mr Melbury's, was the centre of Marty's consciousness, and it was in relation to this that the matter struck her as she slowly withdrew.

'That, then, is the secret of it all,' she said. 'I had half thought so. And Giles Winterborne is not for me!'

She returned to her cottage. The sovereigns were staring at her from the looking-glass as she had left them. With a preoccupied countenance, and with tears in her eyes, she got a pair of scissors and began mercilessly cutting off the long locks of her hair, arranging and tying them with their points all one way as the barber had directed. Upon the pale scrubbed deal of the coffin-stool table they stretched like waving and ropy weeds over the washed white bed of a stream.

She would not turn again to the little looking-glass out of humanity to herself, knowing what a deflowered visage would look back at her and almost break her heart; she dreaded it as much as did her own ancestral goddess the reflection in the pool after the rape of her locks by Loke the Malicious. She steadily stuck to business, wrapped the hair in a parcel, and sealed it up; after which she raked out the fire and went to bed, having first set up an alarm made of a candle and piece of thread with a stone attached.

But such a reminder was unnecessary to-night. Having tossed about till five o'clock Marty heard the sparrows walking down their long holes in the thatch above her sloping ceiling to their exits at the eaves; whereupon she also arose and descended to the ground floor.

It was still dark, but she began moving about the house in those automatic initiatory acts and touches which represent among housewives the installation of another day. While thus engaged she heard the rumbling of Mr Melbury's waggons, and knew that there, too, the day's toil had begun.

An armful of gads thrown on the still hot embers caused them to blaze up cheerfully, and bring her diminished headgear into sudden prominence as a shadow. At this a step approached the door.

'Are folk astir here yet?' inquired a voice she knew well.

'Yes, Mr Winterborne,' said Marty, throwing on a tilt bonnet, which completely hid the recent ravages of the scissors. 'Come in!'

The door was flung back, and there stepped in upon the mat a man not particularly young for a lover, nor particularly mature for a person of affairs – each of which functions he in some degree discharged. There was reserve in his glance, and restraint upon his mouth. He carried a perforated lantern which hung upon a swivel and, wheeling as it dangled, marked grotesque shapes upon the shadier part of the walls and ceiling.

He said that he had looked in on his way down to tell her that they did not expect her father to make up his contract if he was not well. Mr Melbury would give him another week, and they would go their journey with a short load that day.

'They are done,' said Marty, 'and lying in the cart-house.'

'Done?' he repeated. 'Your father has not been too ill to work after all, then?'

She made some evasive reply. 'I'll show you where they be, if you are going down,' she added.

They went out and walked together, the pattern of the air-holes in the top of the lantern rising now to the mist overhead, where they appeared of giant size, as if reaching the tent-shaped sky. They had no remarks to make to each other, and they uttered none. Hardly anything could be more isolated or more self-contained than the lives of these two walking here in the lonely hour before day, when grey shades, material and mental, are so very grey. And yet their lonely courses formed no detached design at all, but were part of the pattern in the great web of human doings then weaving in both hemispheres from the White Sea to Cape Horn.

The shed was reached, and she pointed out the spars. Winterborne regarded them silently; then looked at her.

'Now, Marty, I believe—' he said, and shook his head.

'What?'

'That you've done the work yourself!'

'Don't you tell anybody, will you, Mr Winterborne?' she pleaded by way of answer. 'Because I am afraid Mr Melbury may refuse the work if he knows it is mine.'

'But how could you learn to do it? 'Tis a trade!'

'Trade!' said she. 'I'd be bound to learn it in two hours.'

'O no, you wouldn't, Miss Marty.' Winterborne held down his lantern, and examined the cleanly split hazels as they lay. 'Marty,' he said with dry admiration, 'your father with his forty years of practice never made a spar better than that. They are too good for the thatching of houses; they are good enough for the furniture. But I won't tell. Let me look at your hands – your poor hands!'

He had a kindly manner of quietly severe tone; and when she seemed reluctant to show her hands he took hold of one and examined it as if it were his own. Her fingers were blistered.

'They'll get harder in time,' she said. 'For if father continues ill I shall have to go on wi' it. Now I'll help put 'em up in waggon.'

Winterborne without speaking set down his lantern, lifted her like a baby as she was about to stoop over the bundles, dumped her down behind him, and began throwing up the bundles himself. 'Rather than you should do it I will,' he said. 'But the men will be here directly. Why, Marty – whatever has happened to your head? Lord, it has shrunk to nothing – it looks like an apple upon a gate-post!'

Her heart swelled, and she could not speak. At length she managed to groan, looking on the ground, 'I've made myself ugly – and hateful – that's what I've done!'

'No, no,' he answered. 'You've only cut your hair – I see now.'

'Then why must you needs say that about apples and gate-posts?'

'Let me see!' He moved to lift her bonnet.

But she ran off into the gloom of the sluggish dawn. He did not attempt to follow her. When she reached her father's door she stood on the step and looked back. Mr Melbury's men had arrived and were loading up the spars; and their foggy lanterns appeared from the distance at which she stood to have wan circles round them, like eyes weary with watching. She observed them for a few seconds as they set about harnessing the horses, and then went indoors.

CHAPTER 4

THERE was now a distinct manifestation of morning in the air, and presently the bleared white visage of a sunless winter day emerged like a dead-born child. The woodlanders everywhere had already bestirred themselves, rising this month of the year at the far less dreary time of absolute darkness. It had been above an hour earlier, before a single bird had untucked his head, that twenty lights were struck in as many bedrooms, twenty pairs of shutters opened, and twenty pairs of eyes stretched to the sky to forecast the weather for the day.

Owls that had been catching mice in the outhouses, rabbits that had been eating the winter-greens in the gardens, and stoats that had been sucking the blood of the rabbits, discerning that their human neighbours were on the move discreetly withdrew from publicity, and were seen and heard no more till nightfall.

The daylight revealed the whole of Mr Melbury's homestead, of which the waggon-sheds had been an outlying erection. It formed three sides of an open quadrangle, and consisted of all sorts of buildings, the largest and central one being the dwelling itself. The fourth side of the quadrangle was the public road.

It was a dwelling-house of respectable, roomy, almost dignified aspect; which, taken with the fact that there were the remains of other such buildings hereabout, indicated that Little Hintock had at some time or other been of greater importance than now. The house was of no marked antiquity, yet of a well-advanced age; older than a stale novelty, but no canonized antique; faded, not hoary; looking at you from the still distinct middle-distance of the early Georgian time, and awakening on that account the instincts of reminiscence more decidedly than the remoter, and far grander, memorials which have to speak from the misty reaches of mediaevalism. The faces, dress, passions, gratitudes, and revenges of the great-great-grandfathers and grandmothers who had been the first to gaze from those rectangular windows, and had stood under that keystoned doorway, could be divined and measured by homely standards of to-day. It was a house in whose reverberations queer old personal tales were yet audible if properly listened for; and not, as with those of the castle and cloister, silent beyond the possibility of echo.

The garden-front remained much as it had always been, and there was a porch and entrance that way. But the principal house-door opened on the square yard or quadrangle towards the road, formerly a regular carriage entrance, though the middle of the area was now made use of for stacking timber, faggots, hurdles, and other products of the wood. It was divided from the lane by a lichen-coated wall, in which hung a pair of gates, flanked by piers out of the perpendicular, with a round white ball on the top of each.

The building on the left of the inclosure was a long-backed erection, now used for spar-making, sawing, crib-framing, and copse-ware manufacture in general. Opposite were the waggon-sheds where Marty had deposited her spars.

Here Winterborne had remained after the girl's abrupt departure, to see that the loads were properly made up. Winterborne was connected with the Melbury family in various ways. In addition to the sentimental relationship which arose from his father having been the first Mrs Melbury's lover, Winterborne's aunt had married and emigrated with the brother of the timber-merchant many years before – an alliance that was sufficient to place Winterborne, though the poorer, on a footing of social intimacy with the Melburys. As in most villages so secluded as this, intermarriages were of

Hapsburgian frequency among the inhabitants, and there were hardly two houses in Little Hintock unrelated by some matrimonial tie or other.

For this reason a curious kind of partnership existed between Melbury and the younger man – a partnership based upon an unwritten code, by which each acted in the way he thought fair towards the other, on a give-and-take principle. Melbury, with his timber and copse-ware business, found that the weight of his labour came in winter and spring. Winterborne was in the apple and cider trade, and his requirements in cartage and other work came in the autumn of each year. Hence horses, waggons, and in some degree men, were handed over to him when the apples began to fall; he, in return, lending his assistance to Melbury in the busiest woodcutting season, as now.

Before he had left the shed a boy came from the house to ask him to remain till Mr Melbury had seen him. Winterborne thereupon crossed over to the spar-house where some journeymen were already at work, two of them being travelling sparmakers from Stagfoot Lane, who, when the fall of the leaf began, made their appearance regularly, and when winter was over disappeared in silence till the season came again.

Firewood was the one thing abundant in Little Hintock; and a blaze of gad-ends made the outhouse gay with its light, which vied with that of the day as yet. In the hollow shades of the roof could be seen dangling and etiolated arms of ivy which had crept through the joints of the tiles and were groping in vain for some support, their leaves being dwarfed and sickly for want of sunlight; others were pushing in with such force at the eaves as to lift from their supports the shelves that were fixed there.

Besides the itinerant journey-workers there were also present John Upjohn, Melbury's regular man; a neighbour engaged in the hollow-turnery trade; old Timothy Tangs and young Timothy Tangs, top and bottom sawyers at work in Mr Melbury's pit outside; Farmer Cawtree, who kept the cider-house, and Robert Creedle, an old man who worked for

Winterborne, and stood warming his hands; these latter having been enticed in by the ruddy blaze, though they had no particular business there. None of them calls for any remark, except perhaps Creedle. To have completely described him it would have been necessary to write a military memoir, for he wore under his smock-frock a cast-off soldier's jacket that had seen hot service, its collar showing just above the flap of the frock; also a hunting memoir, to include the top-boots that he had picked up by chance; also chronicles of voyaging and shipwreck, for his pocket-knife had been given him by a weather-beaten sailor. But Creedle carried about with him on his uneventful rounds these silent testimonies of war, sport, and adventure, and thought nothing of their associations or their stories.

Copse-work, as it was called, being an occupation which the secondary intelligence of the hands and arms could carry on without the sovereign attention of the head, allowed the minds of its professors to wander considerably from the objects before them; hence the tales, chronicles, and ramifications of family history which were recounted here were of a very exhaustive kind.

Winterborne, seeing that Melbury had not arrived, stepped back again outside the door; and the conversation interrupted by his momentary presence flowed anew, reaching his ears as an accompaniment to the regular dripping of the fog from the plantation boughs around.

The topic at present handled was a highly popular and frequent one – the personal character of Mrs Charmond, the owner of the surrounding glades and groves.

'My brother-in-law told me, and I have no reason to doubt it,' said Creedle, 'that she'll sit down to her dinner with a gown hardly higher than her elbows. "O, you wicked woman!" he said to hisself when he first see her, "you go to the Table o' Sundays, and kneel, as if your knee-jints were greased with very saint's anointment, and tell off your hear-us-good-Lords as pat as a business-man counting money; and yet you can eat your victuals a-stript to such a wanton figure as that!" Whether she's a reformed character by this time I can't say; but I don't care who the man is, that's how she went on when my brother-in-law lived there.'

'Did she do it in her husband's time?'

'That I don't know – hardly, I should think, considering his temper. Ah—!' Here Creedle threw grieved remembrances into physical form by resigning his head to obliquity and letting his eyes water. 'That man! "Not if the angels of heaven come down, Creedle," he said, "shall you do another day's work for me!" Yes – he would as soon take a winged angel's name in vain as yours or mine! Well, now I must get these spars home-along, and to-morrow, thank God, I must see about using 'em.'

An old woman now entered upon the scene. She was Mr Melbury's servant, and passed a great part of her time in crossing the yard between the house-door and the spar-shed, whither she had come now for fuel. She had two facial aspects – one, of a soft and flexible kind, which she used indoors; the other, with stiff lines and corners, which she assumed when addressing the men outside.

'Ah, Grammer Oliver,' said John Upjohn, 'it do do my heart good to see a old woman like you so dapper and stirring, when I bear in mind that, after fifty, one year counts as two did afore! But your smoke didn't rise this morning till twenty minutes past seven by my beater; and that's late, Grammer Oliver.'

'If you was a full-sized man, John, I might take notice of your scornful meanings. But really a woman couldn't feel hurt if such smallness were to spit fire and brimstone itself at her. Here,' she added, holding out a spar-gad to one of the workmen, from which dangled a long black-pudding, 'here's something for thy breakfast, and if you want tea you must fetch it from indoors.'

'Mr Melbury is late this morning,' said the bottom-sawyer.

'Yes. 'Twas a dark dawn,' said Mrs Oliver. 'Even when I opened the door, so late as I was, you couldn't have told poor men from gentlemen, or John from a reasonable-sized object. And I don't think maister's slept at all well to-night. He's anxious about his daughter; and I know what that is, for I've cried bucketfuls for my own.'

When the old woman had gone Creedle said –

'He'll fret his gizzard green if he don't soon hear from that maid of his. Well, learning is better than houses and lands. But to keep a maid at school till she is taller out of pattens than her mother was in 'em – 'tis a tempting o' Providence.'

'It seems no time ago that she was a little playward girl,' said young Timothy Tangs.

'I can mind her mother,' said the hollow-turner. 'Alway a teuny, delicate piece; her touch upon your hand was like the passing of wind. She was inoculated for the small-pox and had it beautiful fine, just about the time that I was out of my apprenticeship – ay, and a long apprenticeship 'twas. I served that master of mine six years and three hundred and fourteen days.'

The hollow-turner pronounced the days with emphasis, as if, considering their number, they were a rather more remarkable fact than the years.

'Mr Winterborne's father walked with her at one time,' said old Timothy Tangs; 'but Mr Melbury won her. She was a child of a woman, and would cry like rain if so be he huffed her. Whenever she and her husband came to a puddle in their walks together he'd take her up like a halfpenny doll and put her over without dirting her a speck. And if he keeps the daughter so long at boarding-school he'll make her as nesh as her mother was. But here he comes.'

Just before this moment Winterborne had seen Melbury crossing the court from his door. He was carrying an open letter in his hand, and came straight to Winterborne. His gloom of the preceding night had quite gone.

'I'd no sooner made up my mind, Giles, to go and see why Grace didn't come or write than I get a letter from her. "My dear father," says she, "I'm coming home to-morrow (that's today), but I didn't think it worth while to write long beforehand." The little rascal, and didn't she! Now, Giles, as you are going to Sherton market to-day with your apple-trees, why not join me and Grace there, and we'll drive home all together?'

He made the proposal with cheerful energy; he was hardly the same man as the man of the small dark hours. Even among the moodiest the tendency to be cheered is stronger than the tendency to be cast down; and a soul's specific gravity constantly re-asserts itself as less than that of the sea of troubles into which it is thrown.

Winterborne, though not demonstrative, replied to this suggestion with alacrity. There was not much doubt that Marty's grounds for cutting off her hair were substantial enough, if this man's eyes had been a reason for keeping it on. As for the timber-merchant, his invitation had been given solely in pursuance of his scheme for uniting the pair. He had made up his mind to the course as a duty, and was strenuously bent upon following it out.

Accompanied by Winterborne he now turned towards the door of the spar-house, when his footsteps were heard by the men as aforesaid.

'Well, John, and Robert,' he said, nodding as he entered. 'A rimy morning.'

' 'Tis, sir!' said Creedle energetically, for not having as yet been able to summon force sufficient to go away and begin work he felt the necessity of throwing some into his speech. 'I don't care who the man is, 'tis the rimiest morning we've had this fall.'

'I heard you wondering why I've kept my daughter so long at boarding-school,' said Mr Melbury, looking up from the letter which he was reading anew by the fire, and turning to them with the suddenness that was a trait in him. 'Hey?' he asked with affected shrewdness. 'But you did, you know. Well now, though it is my own business more than anybody else's, I'll tell ye. When I was a boy, another boy – the pa'son's son – along with a lot of others, asked me "Who dragged Whom round the walls of What?" and I said, "Sam Barret, who dragged his wife in a wheeled chair round the tower when she went to be churched." They laughed at me so much that I went home and couldn't sleep for shame; and I cried that night till my pillow was wet; till I thought to myself – "They may laugh at me for my ignorance, but that was father's fault, and none o' my making, and I must bear it. But they shall never laugh at my children, if I have any; I'll starve first!" Thank God I've been able to keep her at school at the figure of near a hundred a year; and her scholarship is such that she has stayed on as governess for a time. Let 'em laugh now if they can: Mrs Charmond herself is not better informed than my girl Grace.'

There was something between high indifference and humble emotion in his delivery, which made it difficult for them to reply. Winterborne's interest was of a kind which did not show itself in words; listening, he stood by the fire, mechanically stirring the embers with a spar-gad.

'You'll be ready, then, Giles?' Melbury continued, awaking from a reverie. 'Well, what was the latest news at Shottsford yesterday, Mr Cawtree?'

'Oh, well, Shottsford is Shottsford still – you can't victual your carcase there unless you've got money; and you can't buy a cup of genuine there, whether or no. . . . But as the saying is, "Go abroad and you'll hear news of home." It seems that our new neighbour, this young Doctor What's-his-name, is a strange, deep, perusing gentleman; and there's good reason for supposing he has sold his soul to the wicked one.'

' 'Od name it all,' murmured the timber-merchant, unimpressed by the news but reminded of other things by the subject of it; 'I've got to meet a gentleman this very morning, and yet I've planned to go to Sherton Abbas for the maid.'

'I won't praise the doctor's wisdom till I hear what sort of bargain he's made,' said the top-sawyer.

' 'Tis only an old woman's tale,' said Cawtree. 'But it seems that he wanted certain books on some mysterious black art, and in order that the people hereabout should not know anything about them he ordered 'em direct from London, and not from the Sherton bookseller. The parcel was delivered by mistake at the pa'son's; and as he wasn't at home his wife opened it, and went into hysterics when she read 'em, thinking her husband had turned heathen, and 'twould be the ruin of the children. But when he came he knew no more about 'em than she; and found they were this Mr Fitzpiers's property. So he wrote "Beware!" outside, and sent 'em on by the sexton.'

'He must be a curious young man,' mused the hollow-turner.

'He must,' said Timothy Tangs.

'Nonsense,' said Mr Melbury; 'he's only a gentleman fond of science and philosophy, and poetry, and, in fact, every kind of knowledge; and being lonely here he passes his time in making such matters his hobby.'

'Well,' said old Timothy, ' 'tis a strange thing about doctors that the worse they be the better they be. I mean that if you hear anything of this sort about 'em ten to one they can cure 'ee as nobody else can.'

'True,' said Cawtree emphatically. 'And for my part I shall take my custom from old Jones and go to this one directly I've anything the matter inside me. That last medicine old Jones gave me had no taste in it at all.'

Mr Melbury, as became a well-informed man, did not listen to these recitals, being moreover preoccupied with the business appointment which had come into his head. He walked up and down looking on the floor – his usual custom when undecided. That stiffness about the arm, hip, and knee-joint, which was apparent when he walked, was the net product of the divers sprains and over-exertions that had been required of him in handling trees and timber when a young man, for he was of the sort called self-made, and had worked hard. He knew the origin of every one of these cramps; that in his left shoulder had come of carrying a pollard, unassisted, from Tutcombe Bottom home; that in one leg was caused by the crash of an elm against it when they were felling; that in the other was from lifting a bole. On many a morrow, after wearying himself by these prodigious muscular efforts, he had risen from his bed fresh as usual; and confident in the recuperative power of his youth he had repeated the strains anew. But treacherous Time had been only hiding ill-results when they could be guarded against for greater effect when they could not. Now in his declining years the store had been unfolded in the form of rheumatisms, pricks, and spasms, in every one of which Melbury recognized some act which, had its consequences been contemporaneously made known, he would wisely have abstained from repeating.

On a summons by Grammer Oliver to breakfast he went to the kitchen, where the family breakfasted in winter to save house-labour; and sitting down by the fire looked a long time at the pair of dancing shadows cast by each fire-iron and dog-knob on the whitewashed chimney corner – a yellow one from the window, and a blue one from the fire.

'I don't quite know what to do to-day,' he said to his wife at last. 'I've recollected that I promised to meet Mrs Charmond's steward in Round Wood at twelve o'clock, and yet I want to go for Grace.'

'Why not let Giles fetch her by himself? 'Twill bring 'em together all the quicker.'

'I could do that – but I always have gone, without fail, every time hitherto; and perhaps she'll be disappointed if I stay away.'

'You may be disappointed, but I don't think she will, if you send Giles,' said Mrs Melbury dryly.

'Very well – I'll send him.'

Melbury was often persuaded by the quiet of his wife's words when strenuous argument would have had no effect. This second Mrs Melbury was a placid woman who had been nurse to his child Grace after her mother's death. Little Grace had clung to the nurse with much affection; and ultimately Melbury, in dread lest the only woman who cared for the girl should be induced to leave her, persuaded the mild Lucy to marry him. The arrangement – for it was little more – had worked satisfactorily enough; Grace had thriven, and Melbury had not repented.

He returned to the spar-house and found Giles near at hand, to whom he explained the change of plan. 'As she won't arrive till five o'clock you can get your business very well over in time to receive her,' said Melbury. 'The green gig will do for her; you'll spin along quicker with that, and won't be late upon the road. Her boxes can be called for by one of the waggons.'

Winterborne, knowing nothing of the timber-merchant's restitutory aims, quietly thought this to be a kindly chance. Wishing, even more than her father, to despatch his apple-tree business in the market before Grace's arrival, he prepared to start at once.

Melbury was careful that the turn-out should be seemly. The gig-wheels, for instance, were not always washed during winter-time before a journey, the muddy roads rendering that labour useless; but they were washed to-day. The harness was polished, and when the grey horse had been put in, and Winterborne was in his seat ready to start, Mr Melbury stepped out with a blacking-brush and with his own hands touched over the yellow hoofs of the animal.

'You see, Giles,' he said as he blacked, 'coming from a fashionable school she might feel shocked at the homeliness of home; and 'tis these little things that catch a dainty woman's eye if they are neglected. We, living here alone, don't notice how the whitey-brown creeps out of the earth over us; but she, fresh from a city – why, she'll notice everything!'

'That she will,' said Giles.

'And scorn us if we don't mind.'

'Not scorn us.'

'No, no, no – that's only words. She's too good a girl to do that. But when we consider what she knows, and what she has seen since she last saw us, 'tis as well to meet her views. Why, 'tis a year since she was in this old place, owing to her going abroad in the summer; and naturally we shall look small, just at first – I only say just at first.'

Mr Melbury's tone evinced a certain exultation in the very sense of that inferiority he affected to deplore; for this advanced and refined being, was she not his own all the time? Not so Giles; he felt doubtful. He looked at his clothes with misgiving; but said nothing.

It was his custom during the planting season to carry a specimen apple-tree to market with him as an advertisement of what he dealt in. This had been tied across the gig; and mounting in front he drove away, the twigs nodding with each step of the horse. Melbury went indoors. Before the gig had passed out of sight Mr Melbury reappeared and shouted after –

'Here, Giles,' he said, breathlessly following with some wraps, 'it may be very chilly to-night, and she may want something extra about her. And Giles,' he added, when the young man put the horse in motion once more, 'tell her that I should have come myself, but I had particular business with Mrs Charmond's agent which prevented me. Don't forget.'

He watched Winterborne out of sight under the boughs, where cobwebs glistened in the now clearing air, lengthening and shortening their shine like elastic needles; he saw the wood-pigeons rise as Giles drove past them; and said to himself with a jerk – a shape into which emotion with him often resolved itself – 'There now, I hope the two will bring it to a point, and have done with it! 'Tis a pity to let such a girl throw herself away upon him – a thousand pities! . . . And yet 'tis my duty, for his father's sake.'

CHAPTER 5

Winterborne sped on his way to Sherton Abbas without elation and without discomposure. Had he regarded his inner self spectacularly, as lovers are now daily more wont to do, he might have felt pride in the discernment of a somewhat rare power in him – that of keeping not only judgment but emotion suspended in difficult cases. But he noted it not.

Arrived at the entrance to a long flat lane, which had taken the spirit out of many a pedestrian in times when, with the majority, to travel meant to walk, he saw before him the trim figure of a young woman in pattens, journeying with that steadfast concentration which means purpose and not pleasure. He was soon near enough to see that she was Marty South. Click, click, click went the pattens; and she did not turn her head.

Yet she had seen him, and shrank from being overtaken by him thus; but as it was inevitable she braced herself up for his inspection by closing her lips so as to make her mouth quite unemotional, and by throwing an additional firmness into her tread.

'Why do you wear pattens, Marty? The turnpike is clean enough although the lanes are muddy.'

'They save my boots.'

'But twelve miles in pattens – 'twill twist your feet off. Come, get up and ride with me.'

She hesitated, removed her pattens, knocked the gravel out of them against the wheel, and mounted in front of the nodding specimen apple-tree. She had so arranged her bonnet with a full border and trimmings that her lack of long hair did not much injure her appearance; though Giles of course saw that it was gone, and may have guessed her motive in parting with it; such sales, though infrequent, being not unheard-of in that locality.

But nature's adornment was still hard by – in fact, within two feet of him. In Marty's basket was a brown-paper packet, and in the packet the chestnut locks which, by reason of the barber's request for secrecy, she had not ventured to intrust to other hands.

Giles asked, with some hesitation, how her father was getting on.

He was better, she said; he would be able to work in a day or two; he would be quite well but for his craze about the tree falling on him.

'You know why I don't ask for him so often as I might, I suppose?' said Winterborne. 'Or don't you know?'

'I think I do.'

'Because of the houses?'

She nodded.

'Yes. I am afraid it may seem that my anxiety is about those houses which I should lose by his death, more than about him. Marty, I do feel anxious about the houses, since half my income depends upon them; but I do likewise care for him; and it almost seems wrong that houses should be leased for lives, so as to lead to such mixed feelings.'

'After father's death they will be Mrs Charmond's?'

'They'll be hers.'

'They are going to keep company with my hair,' she thought.

Thus talking they reached the ancient town of Sherton Abbas. By no pressure would she ride up the street with him. 'That's the right of another woman,' she said with playful malice as she put on her pattens. 'I wonder what you are thinking of! Thank you for the lift in that handsome gig. Good-bye.'

He blushed a little, shook his head at her, and drove on ahead into the streets; the churches, the abbey, and other mediaeval buildings on this clear bright morning having the linear distinctness of architectural drawings, as if the original dream and vision of the conceiving master-mason were for a brief hour flashed down through the centuries to an unappreciative age. Giles saw their eloquent look on this day of transparency, but could not construe it. He turned into the inn-yard.

Marty, following the same track, marched promptly to the hairdresser's. Percomb was the chief of his trade in Sherton Abbas. He had the patronage of such county off-shoots as had been obliged to seek the shelter of small houses in that venerable town, of the local clergy, and so on; for some of whom he had made wigs, while others among them had compensated for neglecting him in their lifetime by patronizing him when they were dead, and letting him shave their corpses. On the strength of all this he had taken down his pole and called himself 'Perruquier to the aristocracy'.

Nevertheless, this sort of support did not quite fill his children's mouths, and they had to be filled. So behind his house there was a little yard, reached by a passage from the back street, and in that yard was a pole, and under the pole a shop of quite another description than the ornamental one in the front street. Here on Saturday nights from seven till ten he took an almost innumerable succession of twopences from the farm-labourers who flocked thither in crowds from the country. And thus he lived.

Marty, of course, went to the front shop, and handed her packet to him silently.

'Thank you,' said the barber quite joyfully. 'I hardly expected it after what you said last night.'

She turned aside, while a tear welled up in each eye at this reminder.

'Nothing of what I told you,' he whispered. 'But I can trust you, I see.'

She had now reached the end of this distressing business, and went listlessly along the street to attend to other errands. These occupied her till four o'clock, at which time she recrossed the market-place. It was impossible to avoid rediscovering Winterborne every time she passed that way, for standing, as he always did at this season of the year, with his specimen apple-tree in the midst, the boughs rose above the heads of the farmers, and brought a delightful suggestion of orchards into the heart of the town.

When her eye fell upon him for the last time he was standing somewhat apart, holding the tree like an ensign, and looking on the ground instead of pushing his produce as he ought to have been doing. He was, in fact, not a very successful seller either of his trees or of his cider, his habit of speaking his mind when he spoke at all militating against this branch of his business.

While she regarded him he lifted his eyes in a direction away from Marty, and his face kindled with recognition and surprise. She followed his gaze and saw walking across to him a flexible young creature in whom she perceived the features of her she had known as Miss Grace Melbury, but now looking glorified and refined to much above her former level. Winterborne, being fixed to the spot by his apple-tree, could not advance to meet her: he held out his spare hand with his hat in it, and with some embarrassment beheld her coming on tip-toe through the mud to the middle of the square where he stood.

Miss Melbury, as Marty could see, had not been expected by Giles so early. Indeed, her father had named five o'clock as her probable time, for which reason that hour had been looming out all the day in his forward perspective like an important edifice on a dull plain. Now here she was come, he knew not how, and his arranged welcome stultified.

His face became gloomy at her necessity for stepping into the road, and more still at the little look of shamefacedness she showed at having to perform the meeting with him under an apple-tree ten feet high in the middle of the market-place.

Having had occasion to take off the new gloves she had bought to come home in she held out to him a hand graduating from pink at the tips of the fingers to white at the palm; and the reception formed a scene, with the tree over their heads, which was not by any means an ordinary one in town streets.

The greeting in her looks and on her lips had a restrained shape, which perhaps was not unnatural. For true it was that Giles Winterborne, though well-attired and well-mannered for a yeoman, looked rough beside her. It had sometimes dimly occurred to him, in his ruminating silences at Little Hintock, that external phenomena – such as the lowness or height or colour of a hat, the fold of a coat, the make of a boot, or the chance attitude of a limb at the instant of view – may have a great influence upon feminine opinion of a man's worth, so frequently founded on non-essentials; but a certain causticity of mental tone towards himself and the world in general had prevented to-day, as always, any enthusiastic action on the strength of that reflection; and her momentary instinct of reserve at first sight of him was the penalty he paid for his laxness.

He gave away the tree to a bystander as soon as he could find one who would accept the cumbersome gift, and the twain moved on towards the inn at which he had put up. Marty made as if to step forward for the pleasure of being recognized by Miss Melbury; but abruptly checking herself she glided behind a carrier's van, saying dryly, 'No; I bain't wanted there'; and critically regarded Winterborne's companion.

It would have been difficult to describe Grace Melbury with precision, either then or at any time. Nay, from the highest point of view, to precisely describe a human being, the focus of a universe, how impossible! But apart from transcendentalism, there never probably lived a person who was in herself more completely a *reductio ad absurdum* of attempts to appraise a woman, even externally, by items of face and figure.

Speaking generally it may be said that she was sometimes beautiful, at other times not beautiful, according to the state of her health and spirits.

In simple corporeal presentment she was of a fair and clear complexion, rather pale than pink, slim in build and elastic in movement. Her look expressed a tendency to wait for others' thoughts before uttering her own; possibly also to wait for others' deeds before her own doings. In her small, delicate mouth, which had hardly settled down to its matured curves, there was a gentleness that might hinder sufficient self-assertion for her own good. She had well-formed eyebrows which, had her portrait been painted, would probably have been done in Prouts's or Vandyke brown.

There was nothing remarkable in her dress just now beyond a natural fitness, and a style that was recent for the streets of Sherton. But had it been quite striking it would have meant just as little. For there can be hardly anything less connected with a woman's personality than drapery which she has neither designed, manufactured, cut, sewed, nor even seen, except by a glance of approval when told that such and such a shape and colour must be had because it has been decided by others as imperative at that particular time.

What people therefore saw of her in a cursory view was very little; in truth, mainly something that was not she. The woman herself was a conjectural creature who had little to do with the outlines presented to Sherton eyes; a shape in the gloom, whose true quality could only be approximated by putting together a movement now and a glance then, in that patient attention which nothing but watchful loving-kindness ever troubles itself to give.

There was a little delay in their setting out from the town, and Marty South took advantage of it to hasten forward with the view of escaping them on the way, lest they should feel compelled to spoil their *tête-à-tête* by asking her to ride. She walked fast, and one-third of the journey was done, and the evening rapidly darkening, before she perceived any sign of them behind her. Then, while ascending a hill, she dimly saw their vehicle drawing near the lowest part of the incline, their heads slightly bent towards each other; drawn together, no doubt, by their souls; as the heads of a pair of horses well in hand are drawn in by the rein. She walked still faster.

But between these and herself there was a carriage, apparently a brougham, coming in the same direction, with lighted lamps. When it overtook her – which was not soon on account of her pace – the scene was much darker, and the lights glared in her eyes sufficiently to hide the details of the equipage.

It occurred to Marty that she might take hold behind this carriage and so keep along with it, to save herself from the patronage of being overtaken and picked up for pity's sake by the coming pair. Accordingly, as the carriage drew abreast of her in climbing the long ascent, she walked close to the wheels, the rays of the nearest lamp penetrating her very pores. She had only just dropped behind when the carriage stopped, and to her surprise the coachman asked her, over his shoulder, if she would ride. What made the question more surprising was that it came in obedience to an order from the interior of the vehicle.

Marty gladly assented, for she was weary, very weary, after working all night and keeping afoot all day. She mounted beside the coachman, wondering why this good fortune had happened to her. He was rather a great man in aspect, and she did not like to inquire of him for some time.

At last she said, 'Who has been so kind as to ask me to ride?'

'Mrs Charmond,' replied her statuesque companion.

Marty was stirred at the name, so closely connected with her last night's experiences. 'Is this her carriage?' she whispered.

'Yes; she's inside.'

Mary reflected, and perceived that Mrs Charmond must have recognized her plodding up the hill under the blaze of the lamp: recognized, probably, her stubbly poll (since she had kept away her face), and thought that those stubbles were the result of her own desire.

Marty South was not so very far wrong. Inside the carriage a pair of deep eyes looked from a ripely handsome face, and though behind those deep eyes was a mind of unfathomed mysteries, beneath them there beat a heart capable of quick, extempore warmth – a heart which could indeed be passionately and imprudently warm on certain occasions. At present, after recognizing the girl, she had acted on impulse, possibly feeling gratified at the denuded appearance which signified the success of her agent in obtaining what she had required.

‘ ’Tis wonderful that she should ask ’ee,’ observed the majestic coachman presently. ‘I have never known her do it before, for as a rule she takes no interest in the village folk at all.’

Marty said no more, but occasionally turned her head to see if she could get a glimpse of the Olympian creature who, as the coachman had truly observed, hardly ever descended from her clouds into the Tempe-vale of the parishioners. But she could discern nothing of the lady. She also looked for Miss Melbury and Winterborne. The nose of their horse sometimes came quite near the back of Mrs Charmond’s carriage. But they never attempted to pass it till the latter conveyance turned towards the park gate, when they sped by. Here the carriage drew up that the gate might be opened; and in the momentary silence Marty heard a gentle oral sound, soft as a breeze.

‘What’s that?’ she whispered.

‘Mis’ess yawning.’

‘Why should she yawn?’

‘Oh, because she’s been used to such wonderful good life, and finds it dull here. She’ll soon be off again on account of it.’

‘So rich and so powerful, and yet to yawn!’ the girl murmured. ‘Then things don’t fay with her any more than with we!’

Marty now alighted; the lamp again shone upon her, and as the carriage rolled on a voice said to her from the interior, ‘Good-night.’

‘Good-night, ma’am,’ said Marty, dropping a curtsey. But she had not been able to see the woman who began so greatly to interest her – the second person of her own sex who had operated strongly on her mind that day.

CHAPTER 6

MEANWHILE Winterborne and Grace Melbury had also undergone their little experiences.

As he drove off with her out of the town the glances of people fell upon them, the younger thinking that Mr Winterborne was in a pleasant place, and wondering in what relation he stood towards her. Winterborne himself was unconscious of this. Occupied solely with the idea of having her in charge he did not notice much with outward eye.

Their conversation was in briefest phrase for some time, Grace being somewhat disconcerted through not having understood till they were about to start that Giles was to be her sole conductor, in place of her father. When they had left Sherton Park and Castle nearly out of sight and were in the open country, he spoke.

'Don't Brownley's farm-buildings look strange to you, now they have been moved bodily from the hollow where the old ones stood to the top of the hill?'

She admitted that they did, though she should not have seen any difference in them if he had not pointed it out.

'They had a good crop of bitter-sweets; they couldn't grind them all.' He nodded towards an orchard where some heaps of apples had been left lying ever since the ingathering.

She said 'Yes,' but looking at another orchard.

'Why, you are looking at John-apple trees! You know bitter-sweets – you used to well enough?'

'I am afraid I have forgotten, and it is getting too dark to distinguish.'

Winterborne did not continue. It seemed as if the knowledge and interests which had formerly moved Grace's mind had quite died away from her. He wondered whether the special attributes of his image in the past had evaporated like these other things.

However that might be, the fact at present was merely this, that where he was seeing John-apples and farm-buildings she was beholding a much contrasting scene: a broad lawn in the fashionable suburb of a fast city, the evergreen leaves shining in the evening sun, amid which bounding girls, gracefully clad in artistic arrangements of blue, brown, red, and white, were playing at games with laughter and chat in all the pride of life, the notes of piano and harp trembling in the air from the open windows adjoining. Moreover they were girls – and this was a fact which Grace Melbury's delicate femininity could not lose sight of – whose parents Giles would have addressed with a deferential Sir or Madam. Beside this visioned scene the homely farmsteads did not quite hold their own from her present twenty-year point of survey. For all his woodland sequestration Giles knew the primitive simplicity of the subject he had started, and now sounded a deeper note.

' 'Twas very odd what we said to each other years ago; I often think of it. I mean our saying that if we still liked each other when you were twenty and I twenty-five, we'd—'

'It was child's tattle.'

'H'm?' said Giles suddenly.

'I mean we were young,' said she more considerately. That abrupt manner of his in making inquiries reminded her that he was unaltered.

'Yes. . . . I beg your pardon, Miss Melbury; your father *sent* me to meet you to-day.'

'I know it, and I am glad of it.' And she looked at him affectionately.

He seemed satisfied with her and went on – 'At that time you were sitting beside me at the back of your father's covered car when we were coming home from gipsying, all the party being squeezed in together as tight as sheep in an auction-pen. It got darker and darker and I said – I forget the exact words – but I put my arm round your waist, and there you let it stay till your father, sitting in front, suddenly stopped telling his story to Farmer Bollen, to light his pipe. The flash shone into the car, and showed us all up distinctly; my arm flew from your waist like lightning, yet not so quickly but that some of 'em had seen and laughed at us. Yet your father, to our amazement, instead of being angry, was mild as milk, and seemed quite pleased. Have you forgot all that, or haven't you?'

She owned that she remembered it very well, now that he mentioned the circumstances. 'But I must have been in short frocks,' she said slyly.

'Come now, Miss Melbury, that won't do! Short frocks indeed! You know better as well as I.'

Grace thereupon declared that she would not argue with an old friend she valued so highly as she valued him, but if it were as he said, then she was virtually no less than an old woman now, so far did the time seem removed from her present.

'But old feelings come to life again in some people,' she added softly.

'And in others they have never died!' said he.

'Ah – they are Love's very *ownest* and best, I suppose! I don't pretend to rank so high as they.'

'It's not a they – it's a he.'

Grace sighed. 'Shall I tell you all about Brighton or Cheltenham, or places on the Continent that I visited last summer?' she said.

'With all my heart.'

She then described places and persons, avoiding, however, what he most wished to hear – everything specially appertaining to her own inner existence. When she had done she said gaily, 'Now do you tell me in return what has happened in Hintock since I have been away.'

'Anything to keep the conversation away from her and me,' said Giles within him.

It was true; cultivation had so far advanced in the soil of Miss Melbury's mind as to lead her to talk of anything save of that she knew well, and had the greatest interest in developing: herself. She had fallen from the good old Hintock ways.

He had not proceeded far with his somewhat bald narration when they drew near a carriage that had been preceding them for some time in the dusk. Miss Melbury inquired if he knew whose carriage it was.

Winterborne, although he had seen it, had not taken it into account. On examination he said it was Mrs Charmond's.

Grace watched the vehicle and its easy roll, and seemed to feel more nearly akin to it than to the one she was in.

'Pooh – we can polish off the mileage as well as they, come to that,' said Winterborne, reading her mind; and rising to emulation at what it bespoke he whipped on the horse. This it was which had brought the nose of Mr Melbury's grey close to the back of Mrs Charmond's much eclipsing vehicle.

'There's Marty South sitting up with the coachman,' said he, discerning her by her dress.

'Ah, poor Marty! I must ask her to come to see me this very evening. How does she happen to be riding there?'

'I don't know. It is very singular.'

Thus these people with converging destinies went along the road together, till the track of the carriage and that of Winterborne parted, and he turned into Little Hintock, where almost the first house was the timber-merchant's. Pencils of light streamed out of the windows sufficiently to show the white laurustinus flowers, and glance against the polished leaves of laurel. The interior of the rooms could be seen distinctly, warmed up by the fire-flames, which in the parlour were reflected from picture and book-case, and in the kitchen from the utensils and ware.

'Let us look at the dear place for a moment before we call them,' she said.

In the kitchen dinner was preparing; for though Melbury dined at one o'clock at other times to-day the meal had been kept back for Grace. A rickety old spit was in motion, its end being fixed in the fire-dog, and the whole kept going by means of a cord conveyed over pulleys along the ceiling to a large stone suspended in a corner of the room. Old Grammer Oliver came and wound it up with a rattle like that of a mill.

In the parlour a colossal shade of Mrs Melbury's head fell on the wall and ceiling; but before the girl had regarded this room many moments their presence was discovered, and her father and stepmother came out to welcome her.

The character of the Melbury family was of that kind which evinces some shyness in showing strong emotion among each other; a trait frequent in rural households, and one curiously inverse to most of the peculiarities distinguishing villagers from the people of towns. Thus hiding their warmer feelings under commonplace talk all round, Grace's reception produced no extraordinary demonstrations. But that more was felt than was enacted appeared from the fact that her father, in taking her indoors, quite forgot the presence of Giles without, as did also Grace herself.

He said nothing; but took the gig round to the yard and called out from the spar-house the man who attended to these matters when there was no conversation among the spar-makers to particularly engage him. Winterborne then returned to the door with the intention of entering the house.

The family had gone into the parlour, and were still absorbed in themselves. The fire was as before the only light, and it irradiated Grace's face and hands so as to make them look wondrously smooth and fair beside those of the two elders; shining also through the loose hair about her temples as sun-light through a brake. Her father was surveying her in a dazed conjecture, so much had she developed and progressed in manner and in stature since he last had set eyes on her.

Observing these things Winterborne remained dubious by the door, mechanically tracing with his fingers certain time-worn letters carved in the jambs – initials of bygone generations of householders who had lived and died there.

No, he declared to himself, he would not enter and join the family; they had forgotten him, and it was enough for to-day that he had brought her home. Still, he was a little surprised that her father's eagerness to send him for Grace should have resulted in such indifference as this.

He walked softly away into the lane towards his own house, looking back when he reached the turning from which he could get a last glimpse of the timber-merchant's roof. He hazarded guesses as to what Grace was saying just at that moment, and murmured, with some self-derision, 'nothing about me!' He looked also in the other direction, and saw against the sky the thatched hip and solitary chimney of Marty's cottage, and thought of her too, struggling bravely along under that humble shelter, among her spar-gads and pots and skimmers.

At the timber-merchant's, in the meantime, conversation flowed; and as Giles Winterborne had rightly enough deemed, on subjects in which he had no share. Among the excluding matters there was, as chief, the effect upon Mr Melbury of the womanly mien and manners of his daughter, which took him so much unawares that it thrust back the image of her conductor homeward into quite the obscurest cellarage of his brain.

Another was his interview with Mrs Charmond's agent that morning, at which the lady herself had been present for a few minutes. Melbury had purchased some standing timber from her a long time before, and now that the date had come for felling it he was left to pursue almost his own course. This is what the household were actually talking of during Giles's cogitation without.

'So thoroughly does she trust me,' said Melbury, 'that I might fell, top, or lop, on my own judgment, any stick o' timber whatever in her wood, and fix the price o't, and settle the matter. But name it all, I wouldn't do such a thing. However, it may be useful to have this good understanding with her. . . . I wish she took more interest in the place and stayed here all the year round.'

'I am afraid 'tis not her regard for you, but her dislike of Hintock, that makes her so easy about the trees,' said Mrs Melbury.

When dinner was over Grace took a candle and began to ramble pleasurably through the rooms of her old home, from which she had latterly become well-nigh an alien. Each nook and each object revived a memory, and simultaneously modified it. The chambers seemed lower than they had appeared on any previous occasion of her return, the surfaces of both walls and ceilings standing in such near relations to the eye that it could not avoid taking microscopic note of their irregularities and old fashion. Her own bedroom wore at once a look more familiar than when she had left it, and yet a face estranged. The world of little things therein gazed at her in helpless stationariness, as though they had tried and been unable to make any progress without her presence. Over the place where her candle had been accustomed to stand, when she had used to read in bed till the midnight hour, there was still the brown spot of smoke. She did not know that her father had taken especial care to keep it from being cleaned off.

Having concluded her perambulation of this now uselessly commodious edifice, Grace began to feel that she had come a long journey since the morning; and when her father had been up himself, as well as his wife, to see that her room was comfortable and the fire burning, she prepared to retire for the night.

No sooner, however, had she extinguished her candle than her momentary sleepiness took itself off, and she wished she had stayed up longer. She amused herself by listening to the old familiar noises that she could hear to be still going on downstairs, and by looking towards the window as she lay. The blind had been drawn up as she used to have it when a girl, and she could just discern the dim tree-tops against the sky on the neighbouring hill. Beneath this meeting-line of light and shade nothing was visible save one solitary point of light, which blinked as the tree-twigs waved to and fro before its beams.

From its position it seemed to radiate from the window of a house on the hill-side. The house had been empty when she was last at home, and she wondered who inhabited the place now.

Her conjectures, however, were not intently carried on, and she was watching the light quite idly when it gradually changed colour, and at length shone blue as sapphire. Thus it remained several minutes, and then it passed through violet to red.

Her curiosity was so widely awakened by the phenomenon that she sat up in bed, and stared steadily at the shine. An appearance of this sort, sufficient to excite attention anywhere, was no less than a marvel in Hintock, as Grace had known the hamlet. Almost every diurnal and nocturnal effect in that woodland place had hitherto been the direct result of the regular terrestrial roll which produced the season's changes; but here was something dissociated from these normal sequences, and foreign to local knowledge.

It was about this moment that Grace heard the household below preparing to retire, the most emphatic noise in the proceeding being that of her father bolting the doors. Then the stairs creaked, and her father and mother passed her chamber. The last to come was Grammer Oliver.

Grace slid out of bed, ran across the room, and lifting the latch said, 'I am not asleep, Grammer. Come in and talk to me.'

Before the old woman had entered Grace was again under the bedclothes. Grammer set down her candlestick, and seated herself on the edge of Miss Melbury's coverlet.

'I want you to tell me what light that is I see on the hill-side,' said Grace.

Mrs Oliver looked across. 'Oh, that,' she said, 'is from the young doctor's. He's often doing things of that sort. Perhaps you don't know that we've a doctor living here now – Mr Fitzpiers by name?'

Grace admitted that she had not heard of him.

'Well, then, miss, he's come here to get up a practice. Though he belongs to the oldest, ancientest family in the country, he's stooped to make hisself useful like any common man. I know him very well, through going there to help 'em scrub sometimes, which your father said I might do if I wanted to in my spare time. Being a bachelor-man he've only lodgings. O yes, I know him very well. Sometimes he'll talk to me as if I were his own mother.'

'Indeed.'

'Yes. "Grammer," he said one day when I asked him why he came here where there's hardly anybody living, "I'll tell you why I came here. I took a map, and I marked on it where Dr Jones's practice ends to the north of this district, and where Mr Taylor's ends on the south, and little Jemmy Green's on the east, and somebody else's to the west. Then I took a pair of compasses, and found the exact middle of the country that was left between these bounds, and that middle was Little Hintock; so here I am." . . . But, Lord, there: poor young man!'

'Why?'

'He said, "Grammer Oliver, I've been here three months, and although there are a good many people in the Hintocks and the villages round, and a scattered practice is often a very good one, I don't seem to get many patients; and I'm not rich. And there's no society at all; and I'm pretty near melancholy mad," he said, with a great yawn. "I should be quite if it were not for my books, and my lab – laboratory, and what not. Grammer, I was made for higher things!" And then he'd yawn and yawn again.'

'Was he really made for higher things, do you think? Is he clever?'

'Well, no. How can he be clever? He may be able to jine up a broken man or woman after a fashion, and put his finger upon an ache if you tell him nearly where 'tis; but these young men – they should live to my time of life, and then they'd see how clever they were at five-and-twenty! And yet he's a projick, a real projick, and says the oddest of rozums. "Ah, Grammer," he said at another time, "let me tell you that Everything is Nothing. There's only Me and Not Me in the whole world."

And he told me that no man's hands could help what they did, any more than the hands of a clock. . . . Yes, he's a man of strange meditations, and his eyes seem to see as far as the north star.'

'He will soon go away, no doubt.'

'I don't think so.'

Grace did not say 'Why?' and Grammer hesitated. At last she went on, 'Don't tell your father or mother, miss, if I let you know a secret?'

Grace gave the required promise.

'Well, he talks of buying me; so he won't go away just yet.'

'Buying you – how?'

'Not my soul – my body, when I'm dead! One day when I was there cleaning, he said, "Grammer, you've a large brain – a very large organ of brain," he said. "A woman's is usually four ounces less than a man's; but yours is man's size." Well, then – hee, hee! – after he'd flattered me a bit like that, he said he'd give me ten pounds to have my head as a natomy after my death. Well, knowing I'd no chick nor chiel left, and nobody with any interest in me, I thought, faith if I can be of any use to my fellow-creatures after I'm gone they are welcome to me; so I said I'd think it over, and would most likely agree and take the ten pounds. Now this is a secret, miss, between us two. The money would be very useful to me; and I see no harm in it.'

'Of course there's no harm. But O, Grammer – how can you think to do it? I wish you hadn't told me.'

'I wish I hadn't – if you don't like to know it, miss. But you needn't mind. Lord, hee! hee! I shall keep him waiting many a year yet, bless ye!'

'I hope you will, I am sure.'

The girl thereupon fell into such deep reflection that conversation languished, and Grammer Oliver taking her candle wished Miss Melbury good-night.

The latter's eyes rested on the distant glimmer, around which she allowed her reasoning fancy to play in vague eddies that shaped the doings of the philosopher behind that light on the lines of intelligence just received. It was strange to her to come back from the world to Little Hintock and find in one of its nooks, like a tropical plant in a hedgerow, a nucleus of advanced ideas and practices which had nothing in common with the life around. Chemical experiments, anatomical projects, and metaphysical conceptions had found a strange home here.

Thus she remained thinking, the imagined pursuits of the man behind the light intermingling with conjectural sketches of his personality; till her eyelids fell together with their own heaviness, and she slept.

CHAPTER 7

Kaleidoscopic dreams of a weird alchemist-surgeon, Grammer Oliver's skeleton, and the face of Giles Winterborne, brought Grace Melbury to the morning of the next day. It was fine. A north wind was blowing – that not unacceptable compromise between the atmospheric cutlery of the eastern blast and the spongy gales of the west quarter. She looked from her window in the direction of the light of the previous evening, and could just discern through the trees the shape of the surgeon's house. Somehow, in the broad, practical daylight, that unknown and lonely gentleman seemed to be shorn of much of the interest which had invested his personality and pursuits in the hours of darkness, and as Grace's dressing proceeded he faded from her mind.

Meanwhile Winterborne, though half-assured of her father's favour, was rendered a little restless by Miss Melbury's own behaviour. Despite his shy self-control he could not help looking continually from his own door towards the timber-merchant's, in the probability of somebody's emergence therefrom.

His attention was at length justified by the appearance of two figures, that of Mr Melbury himself, and Grace beside him. They stepped out in a direction towards the densest quarter of the wood, and Winterborne walked contemplatively behind them till all three were soon under the trees.

Although the time of bare boughs had now set in there were sheltered hollows amid the Hintock plantations and copses in which a more tardy leave-taking than on windy summits was the rule with the foliage. This caused here and there an apparent mixture of the seasons; so that in some of the dells they passed by holly-berries in full red growing beside oak and hazel whose leaves were as yet not far removed from green, and brambles whose verdure was rich and deep as in the month of August. To Grace these well-known peculiarities were as an old painting restored.

Now could be beheld that change from the handsome to the curious which the features of a wood undergo at the ingress of the winter months. Angles were taking the place of curves, and reticulations of surfaces – a change constituting a sudden lapse from the ornate to the primitive on Nature's canvas, and comparable to a retrogressive step from the art of an advanced school of painting to that of the Pacific Islander.

Winterborne followed and kept his eye upon the two figures as they threaded their way through these sylvan masses. Mr Melbury's long legs, his gaiters drawn in to the bone at the ankles, his slight stoop, his habit of getting lost in thought and arousing himself with an exclamation of 'Hah!' accompanied with an upward jerk of the head, composed a personage recognizable by his neighbours as far as he could be seen. It seemed as if the squirrels and birds knew him. One of the former would occasionally run from the path to hide behind the arm of some tree, which the little animal carefully edged round *pari passu* with Melbury and his daughter's movement onward, assuming a mock manner as though he were saying, 'Ho, ho! you are only a timber-merchant, and carry no gun!'

They went noiselessly over mats of starry moss, rustled through interspersed tracts of leaves, skirted trunks with spreading roots whose mossed rinds made them like hands wearing green gloves; elbowed old elms and ashes with great forks, in which stood pools of water that overflowed on rainy days and ran down their stems in green cascades. On older trees still than these huge lobes of fungi grew like lungs. Here, as everywhere, the Unfulfilled Intention, which makes life what it is, was as obvious as it could be among the depraved crowds of a city slum. The leaf was deformed, the curve was crippled, the taper was interrupted; the lichen ate the vigour of the stalk, and the ivy slowly strangled to death the promising sapling.

They dived amid beeches under which nothing grew, the younger boughs still retaining their hectic leaves, that rustled in the breeze with a sound almost metallic, like the sheet-iron foliage of the fabled Jarnvid wood. Some flecks of white in Grace's drapery had enabled Giles to keep her and her father in view till this time; but now he lost sight of them and was obliged to follow by ear – no difficult matter, for on the line of their course every wood-pigeon rose from its perch with a continued clash, dashing its wings against the branches with well-nigh force enough to break every quill. By taking the track of this noise he soon came to a stile.

Was it worth while to go further? He examined the doughy soil at the foot of the stile, and saw amongst the large sole-and-heel tracks an impression of a slighter kind from a boot that was obviously not local. The mud-picture was enough to make him swing himself over and proceed.

The character of the woodland now changed. The bases of the smaller trees were nibbled bare by rabbits, and at divers points heaps of fresh-made chips, and the newly cut stool of a tree, stared white through the undergrowth. There had been a large fall of timber this year, which explained the meaning of some sounds that soon reached him.

A voice was shouting intermittently in a sort of human bark, reminding Giles that there was a sale of trees and faggots that very day. Melbury would naturally be present. Winterborne decided that he himself wanted a few faggots, and entered upon the scene.

A large group of buyers stood round the auctioneer, or followed him when, between his pauses, he wandered on from one lot of plantation-produce to another, like some philosopher of the Peripatetic school delivering his lectures in the shady groves of the Lyceum. His companions were timber-dealers, yeomen, farmers, villagers, and others; mostly woodland men, who on that account could afford to be curious in their walking-sticks, which consequently exhibited various monstrosities of vegetation, the chief being corkscrew shapes in black and white thorn, brought to that pattern by the slow torture of an encircling woodbine during their growth, as the Chinese have been said to mould human beings into grotesque toys by continued compression in infancy. Two women wearing men's jackets on their gowns conducted in the rear of the halting procession a pony-cart containing bread and cheese, with a barrel of strong ale for the select, and cider in milking-pails into which anybody dipped who chose.

The auctioneer adjusted himself to circumstances by using his walking-stick as a hammer, and knocked down the lot on any convenient object that took his fancy, such as the crown of a little boy's head, or the shoulders of a bystander who had no business there except to taste the brew; a proceeding which would have been deemed humorous but for the air of stern rigidity which the auctioneer's face preserved, tending to show that the eccentricity was a result of that absence of mind which is engendered by the press of affairs, and no freak of fancy at all.

Mr Melbury stood slightly apart from the rest of the Peripatetics, and Grace beside him, clinging closely to his arm; her modern attire looking almost odd where everything else was old-fashioned, and throwing over the familiar garniture of the trees a homeliness that seemed to demand improvement by the addition of a few contemporary novelties also. Grace seemed to regard the selling with the interest which attaches to memories revived after an interval of obliviousness.

Winterborne went and stood close to them; the timber-merchant spoke, and continued his buying; Grace merely smiled. To justify his presence there Winterborne began bidding for timber and faggots that he did not want, pursuing the occupation in an abstracted mood in which the auctioneer's voice seemed to become one of the natural sounds of the woodland.

A few flakes of snow descended, at the sight of which a robin, alarmed at these signs of imminent winter, and seeing that no offence was meant by the human invasion, came and perched on the tip of the faggots that were being sold, and looked into the auctioneer's face whilst waiting for some chance crumb from the bread-basket. Standing a little behind Grace, Winterborne observed how one flake would sail downward and settle on a curl of her hair, and how another would choose her shoulder, and another the edge of her bonnet, which took up so much of his attention that his biddings proceeded incoherently; and when the auctioneer said every now and then, with a nod towards him, 'Yours, Mr Winterborne,' he had no idea whether he had bought faggots, poles, or log-wood.

He regretted that her father should show such inequalities of temperament as to keep Grace tightly on his arm to-day, when he had quite lately seemed anxious to recognize their betrothal as a fact. And thus musing, and joining in no conversation with other buyers except when directly addressed, he followed the assemblage hither and thither till the end of the auction, when Giles for the first time realized what his purchases had been. Hundreds of faggots, and divers lots of timber, had been set down to him, when all he had required had been a few bundles of spray for his man Robert Creedle's use in baking and lighting fires.

Business being over, he turned to speak to the timber-merchant. But Melbury's manner was short and distant; and Grace too looked vexed and reproachful. Winterborne then discovered that he had been unwittingly bidding against her father, and picking up his favourite lots in spite of him. With a very few words they left the spot, and pursued their way homeward.

Giles was extremely blank at what he had done, and remained standing under the trees, all the other men having strayed silently away. He saw Melbury and his daughter pass down a glade without looking back. While they moved slowly through it a lady appeared on horseback in the middle distance, the line of her progress converging upon that of Melbury's. They met, Melbury took off his hat, and she reined in her horse. A conversation was evidently in progress between Grace and her father and this equestrian, in whom he was almost sure that he recognized Mrs Charmond, less by her outline than by the livery of the groom who had halted some yards off.

The interlocutors did not part till after a prolonged pause, during which much seemed to be said. When Melbury and Grace resumed their walk it was with something of a lighter tread than before.

Winterborne pursued his own course homeward. He was unwilling to let coldness grow up between himself and the Melburys for any trivial reason, and in the evening he went to their house. On drawing near the gate his attention was attracted by the sight of one of the bedrooms blinking into a state of illumination. In it stood Grace lighting several candles, her right hand elevating the taper, her left hand on her bosom, her face thoughtfully fixed on each wick as it kindled, as if she saw in every flame's growth the rise of a life to maturity. He wondered what such unusual brilliancy could mean to-night.

On getting indoors he found her father and stepmother in a state of suppressed excitement which he could not comprehend.

'I am sorry about my biddings to-day,' said Giles. 'I don't know what I was doing. I have come to say that any of the lots you may require are yours.'

'Oh, never mind – never mind,' replied the timber-merchant with a slight wave of his hand. 'I have so much else to think of that I nearly had forgot it. Just now, too, there are matters of a different kind from trade to attend to, so don't let it concern 'ee.'

As the timber-merchant spoke, as it were, down to him from a higher plane than his own, Giles turned to Mrs Melbury.

'Grace is going to the House to-morrow,' she said quietly. 'She is looking out her things now. I dare say she is wanting me this minute to assist her.' Thereupon Mrs Melbury left the room.

Nothing is more remarkable than the independent personality of the tongue now and then. Mr Melbury knew that his words had been a sort of boast. He decried boasting, particularly to Giles; yet whenever the subject was Grace his judgment resigned the ministry of speech in spite of him.

Winterborne felt surprise, pleasure, and also a little apprehension at the news. He repeated Mrs Melbury's words.

'Yes,' said paternal pride, not sorry to have dragged out of him what he could not in any circumstances have kept in. 'Coming home from the woods this afternoon we met Mrs Charmond out for a ride. She spoke to me on a little matter of business, and then got acquainted with Grace. 'Twas wonderful how she took to Grace in a few minutes; that freemasonry of education made 'em close at once. Naturally enough she was amazed that such an article – ha – ha! – could come out of my house. At last it led on to Mis'ess Grace being asked to the House. So she's busy hunting up her frills and furbelows to go in.' As Giles remained in thought without responding, Melbury continued: 'But I'll call her downstairs.'

'No, no; don't do that, since she's busy,' said Winterborne.

Melbury, feeling from the young man's manner that his own talk had been too much at Giles and too little to him, repented at once. His face changed, and he said, in lower tones, with an effort: 'She's yours, Giles, as far as I am concerned.'

'Thanks – my best thanks, sir. But I think since it is all right between us about the biddings, that I'll not interrupt her now. I'll step homeward, and call another time.'

On leaving the house he looked up at the bedroom again. Grace, surrounded by a sufficient number of candles to answer all purposes of self-criticism, was standing before a cheval glass that her father had lately bought expressly for her use; she was bonneted, cloaked, and gloved, and glanced over her shoulder into the mirror, estimating her aspect. Her face was lit with the natural elation of a young girl hoping to inaugurate on the morrow an intimate acquaintance with a new, interesting, and influential friend.

CHAPTER 8

The inspiriting appointment which had led Grace Melbury to indulge in a six-candle illumination for the arrangement of her attire carried her over the ground the next morning with a springy tread. Her sense of being properly appreciated on her own native soil charged her heart with expansive gratitude. She moved along, a vessel of emotion, going to empty itself on she knew not what.

Twenty minutes' walking through copses, over a stile, and along an upland lawn, brought her to the verge of a deep glen, in which Hintock House appeared immediately beneath her eye. To describe it as standing in a hollow would not express the situation of the manor-house; it stood in a hole. But the hole was full of beauty. From the spot which Grace had reached a stone could easily have been thrown over or into the birds'-nested chimneys of the mansion. Its walls were surmounted by a battlemented parapet; but the grey lead roofs were quite visible behind it, with their gutters, laps, rolls, and skylights, together with letterings and shoe-patterns cut by idlers thereon.

The front of the house was an ordinary manorial presentation of Elizabethan windows, mullioned and hooded, worked in rich snuff-coloured freestone from Ham-hill quarries. The ashlar of the walls, where not overgrown with ivy and other creepers, was coated with lichen of every shade, intensifying its luxuriance with its nearness to the ground till, below the plinth, it merged in moss.

Above the house to the back was a dense plantation, the roots of whose trees were above the level of the chimneys. The corresponding high ground on which Grace stood was richly grassed, with only an old tree here and there. A few sheep lay about, which as they ruminated looked quietly into the bedroom windows.

The situation of the house, prejudicial to humanity, was a stimulus to vegetation, on which account an endless shearing of the heavy-armed ivy went on, and a continual lopping of trees and shrubs. It was an edifice built in times when human constitutions were damp-proof, when shelter from the boisterous was all that men thought of in choosing a dwelling-place, the insidious being beneath their notice; and its hollow site was an ocular reminder by its unfitness for modern lives of the fragility to which these have declined.

The highest architectural cunning could have done nothing to make Little Hintock House dry and salubrious; and ruthless ignorance could have done little to make it unpicturesque. It was vegetable nature's own home; a spot to inspire the painter and poet of still life – if they did not suffer too much from the relaxing atmosphere – and to draw groans from the gregariously disposed.

Grace descended the green escarpment by a zigzag path into the drive, which swept round beneath the slope. The exterior of the house had been familiar to her from her childhood, but she had never been inside, and the first step to knowing an old thing in a new way was a lively experience.

It was with a little flutter that she was shown in; but she recollected that Mrs Charmond would probably be alone. Up to a few days before this time that lady had been accompanied in her comings, stayings, and goings by a relative, believed to be her aunt; latterly, however, the two had separated, owing, it was supposed, to a quarrel; and Mrs Charmond had been left desolate. Being presumably a woman who did not care for solitude this deprivation might account for her sudden interest in Grace.

Mrs Charmond was at the end of a gallery opening from the hall when Miss Melbury was announced, and saw her through the glass doors between them. She came forward with a smile on her face, and told the young girl it was good of her to come.

'Ah! you have noticed those,' she said, seeing that Grace's eyes were attracted by some curious objects against the walls. 'They are man-traps. My husband was a connoisseur in man-traps and spring-guns and such articles, collecting them from all his neighbours. He knew the histories of all these – which gin had broken a man's leg, which gun had killed a man. I don't like them here; but I've never yet given directions for them to be taken away.' She added playfully, 'Man-traps are of rather ominous significance where a person of our sex lives, are they not?'

Grace was bound to smile; but that side of womanliness was one which her inexperience felt no great zest in contemplating.

'They are interesting, no doubt, as relics of a barbarous time happily past,' she said, looking thoughtfully at the varied designs of the instruments.

'Well, we must not take them too seriously,' said Mrs Charmond with an indolent turn of her head, and they moved on inwards.

When she had shown her visitor different articles in cabinets that she deemed likely to interest her, some tapestries, wood carvings, ivories, miniatures, and so on – always with a mien of listlessness which might either have been constitutional, or partly owing to the situation of the place – they sat down to an early cup of tea.

'Will you pour it out, please? Do,' she said, leaning back in her chair, and placing her hand above her forehead, while her almond eyes – those long eyes so common to the angelic legions of early Italian art – became longer, and her voice more languishing. She showed that oblique-mannered softness which is perhaps seen oftenest in women of darker complexion and more lymphatic temperament than Mrs Charmond's; women who lingeringly smile their meanings to men rather than speak them, who inveigle rather than prompt, and take advantage of currents rather than steer.

'I am the most inactive woman when I am here,' she said. 'I think sometimes I was born to live and do nothing, nothing, nothing but float about, as we fancy we do sometimes in dreams. But that cannot be really my destiny, and I must struggle against such fancies.'

'I am so sorry you do not enjoy exertion – it is quite sad! I wish I could tend you and make you very happy.'

There was always something so sympathetic, so responsive in Grace's voice, that it impelled people to overstep their customary reservations in talking to her. 'It is tender and kind of you to feel that!' said Mrs Charmond. 'Perhaps I have given you the notion that my languor is more than it really is. But this place oppresses me, and I have a plan of going abroad a good deal. I used to go with a relation, but that arrangement has dropped through.'

Regarding Grace with a final glance of criticism she seemed to make up her mind to consider the young girl satisfactory, and continued:

'Now, I am often impelled to record my impressions of times and places. I have often thought of writing a new *Sentimental Journey*. But I cannot find energy enough to do it alone. When I am at different places in the south of Europe I feel a crowd of ideas and fancies thronging upon me continually; but to unfold writing materials, take up a cold steel pen, and put these impressions down systematically on cold smooth paper – that I cannot do. So I have thought that if I always could have somebody at my elbow with whom I am in sympathy, I might dictate any ideas that come into my head. And directly I had made your acquaintance the other day it struck me that you would suit me so well. Would you like to undertake it? You might read to me, too, if desirable. Will you think it over, and ask your parents if they are willing?'

'O yes,' said Grace. 'I am almost sure they would be very glad.'

'You are so accomplished, I hear; I should be quite honoured by such intellectual company.'

Grace, modestly blushing, deprecated any such idea.

'Do you keep up your lucubrations at Little Hintock?' the lady went on.

'O no. . . . Lucubrations are not unknown at Little Hintock; but they are not carried on by me.'

'What – another student in that retreat?'

'There is a surgeon lately come, and I have heard that he reads a great deal – I see his light sometimes through the trees late at night.'

'O yes – a doctor – I believe I was told of him. It is a strange place for him to settle in.'

'It is a convenient centre for a practice, they say. But he does not confine his studies to medicine, it seems. He investigates theology, and metaphysics and all sorts of subjects.'

'What is his name?'

'Fitzpiers. He represents a very old family, I believe, the Fitzpierses of Oakbury-Fitzpiers – not a great many miles from here.'

'I am not sufficiently local to know the history of the family. I was never in the county till my husband brought me here.'

Mrs Charmond did not care to pursue this line of investigation. Whatever mysterious merit might attach to family antiquity, it was one which her adaptable, wandering, *weltbürgerliche* nature had grown tired of caring about – a peculiarity that made her a piquant contrast to her neighbours.

'It is of rather more importance to know what the man is himself than what his family is,' she said, 'if he is going to practise upon us as a surgeon. Heaven send him skill! Have you seen him?'

Grace had not. 'I think he is not a very old man,' she added.

'Has he a wife?'

'I am not aware that he has.'

'Well, I hope he will be useful here. I must get to know him when I come back. It will be very convenient to have a medical man – if he is clever – in one's own parish. I get dreadfully nervous sometimes, living in such an outlandish place; and

Sherton is so far to send to. No doubt you feel Little Hintock to be a great change after watering-place life.'

'I do. But it is home. It has its advantages and its disadvantages.' Grace was thinking less of the solitude than of the attendant circumstances.

They chatted on for some time, Grace being set quite at her ease by her entertainer. Mrs Charmond was far too well-practised a woman not to know that to show anything like patronage towards a sensitive young girl who would probably be very quick to discern it was to demolish her dignity rather than to establish it in that young girl's eyes. So being violently possessed with her idea of making use of this gentle acquaintance, ready and waiting at her own door, she took great pains to win her confidence at starting.

Just before Grace's departure the two chanced to pause before a mirror which reflected their faces in immediate juxtaposition, bringing into prominence their resemblances and their contrasts. Both looked attractive as glassed back by the faithful reflector; but Grace's countenance had the effect of making Mrs Charmond appear more than her full age. There are complexions which set off each other to great advantage, and there are those which antagonize, one of such killing or damaging its neighbour unmercifully.

This was unhappily the case here. Mrs Charmond fell into a meditation, and replied abstractedly to a cursory remark of her companion's. However, she parted from her young friend in the kindliest tones, promising to send and let her know as soon as her mind was made up on the arrangement she had suggested.

When Grace had ascended nearly to the top of the adjoining slope she looked back, and saw that Mrs Charmond still stood at the door meditatively regarding her.

Often during the previous night, after his call on the Melburys, Winterborne's thoughts had run upon Grace's announced visit to Hintock House. Why had he not proposed to walk with her part of the way? Something told him that she might not, on such an occasion, have cared for his company.

He was still more of that opinion when, standing in his garden next day, he saw her go past on the journey with such a pretty pride in the event. He questioned if her father's ambition, which had purchased for her the means of intellectual light and culture far beyond those of any other native of the village, would not operate to the flight of her future interests above and away from the local life which was once to her the movement of the world.

Nevertheless, he had her father's permission to win her if he could; and to this end it became desirable to bring matters soon to a crisis. If she should think herself too good for him he must let her go, and make the best of his loss. The question was how to quicken events towards an issue.

He thought and thought, and at last decided that as good a way as any would be to give a Christmas party, and ask Grace and her parents to come as chief guests.

These ruminations were occupying him when there became audible a slight knocking at his front door. He descended the path, and looked out, and beheld Marty South, dressed for outdoor work.

'Why didn't you come, Mr Winterborne?' she said; 'I've been waiting there hours and hours, and at last I thought I must try to find you!'

'Bless my soul, I'd quite forgot!' said Giles.

What he had forgotten was that there were a thousand young fir trees to be planted in a neighbouring spot which had been cleared by the woodcutters, and that he had arranged to plant them with his own hands. He had a marvellous power of making trees grow. Although he would seem to shovel in the earth quite carelessly there was a sort of sympathy between himself and the fir, oak, or beech that he was operating on; so that the roots took hold of the soil in a few days. When, on the other hand, any of the journeymen planted, although they seemed to go through an identically similar process, one quarter of the trees would die away during the ensuing August.

Hence Winterborne found delight in the work even when, as at present, he contracted to do it on portions of the woodland in which he had no personal interest. Marty, who turned her hand to anything, was usually the one who performed the part of keeping the trees in a perpendicular position whilst he threw in the mould.

He accompanied her towards the spot, being inclined yet further to proceed with the work by the knowledge that the ground was close to the roadside along which Grace must pass on her way from Hintock House.

'You've a cold in the head, Marty,' he said as they walked. 'That comes of cutting off your hair.'

'I suppose it do. Yes; I've three headaches going on in my head at the same time.'

'Three headaches!'

'Yes, Mr Winterborne: a rheumatic headache in my poll, a sick headache over my eyes, and a misery headache in the middle of my brain. However, I came out, for I thought you might be waiting and grumbling like anything if I was not there.'

The holes were already dug, and they set to work. Winterborne's fingers were endowed with a gentle conjurer's touch in spreading the roots of each little tree, resulting in a sort of caress under which the delicate fibres all laid themselves out in their proper directions for growth. He put most of these roots towards the south-west; for, he said, in forty years' time, when some great gale is blowing from that quarter, the trees will require the strongest holdfast on that side to stand against it and not fall.

'How they sigh directly we put 'em upright, though while they are lying down they don't sigh at all,' said Marty.

'Do they?' said Giles. 'I've never noticed it.'

She erected one of the young pines into its hole, and held up her finger; the soft musical breathing instantly set in which was not to cease night or day till the grown tree should be felled – probably long after the two planters had been felled themselves.

'It seems to me,' the girl continued, 'as if they sigh because they are very sorry to begin life in earnest – just as we be.'

'Just as we be?' He looked critically at her. 'You ought not to feel like that, Marty.'

Her only reply was turning to take up the next tree; and they planted on through a great part of the day, almost without another word. Winterborne's mind ran on his contemplated evening-party, his abstraction being such that he hardly was conscious of Marty's presence beside him.

From the nature of their employment, in which he handled the spade and she merely held the tree, it followed that he got good exercise and she got none. But she was a heroic girl, and though her outstretched hand was chill as a stone, and her cheeks blue, and her cold worse than ever, she would not complain whilst he was disposed to continue work. But when he paused she said, 'Mr Winterborne, can I run down the lane and back to warm my feet?'

'Why, yes, of course,' he said, awakening to her existence. 'Though I was just thinking what a mild day it is for the season. Now I warrant that cold of yours is twice as bad as it was. You had no business to chop that hair off, Marty; it serves you almost right. Look here, cut off home at once.'

'A run down the lane will be quite enough.'

'No, it won't. You ought not to have come out to-day at all.'

'But I should like to finish the—'

'Marty, I tell you to go home!' said he peremptorily. 'I can manage to keep the rest of them upright with a forked stick or something.'

She went away without saying any more. When she had gone down the orchard a little distance she looked back. Giles suddenly went after her.

'Marty, it was for your good that I was rough, you know. But warm yourself in your own way; I don't care.' He took her hand kindly a moment, and then let her go.

When she had run off he fancied he discerned a woman's dress through the holly bushes which divided the coppice from the road. It was Grace at last, on her way back from the interview with Mrs Charmond. He threw down the tree he was planting, and was about to break through the belt of holly when he suddenly became aware of the presence of another man, who was looking over the hedge on the opposite side of the way upon the figure of the unconscious Grace.

The stranger appeared as a handsome and gentlemanly personage of six or eight and twenty, and he was quizzing her through an eyeglass. Seeing that Winterborne was noticing him he let his glass drop with a click upon the rail which protected the hedge, and walked away in the opposite direction.

Giles knew in a moment that this must be Mr Fitzpiers. When he was gone Winterborne pushed through the holly, and emerged close beside the interesting object of their contemplation.

CHAPTER 9

'I heard the bushes move long before I saw you,' she began. 'I said first, "It is some terrible beast"; next, "It is a poacher"; next, "It is a friend!"'

He regarded her with a slight smile, weighing, not her speech, but the question whether he should tell her that she had been flatteringly watched by a gentleman. He decided in the negative.

'You have been to the House?' he said. 'But I need not ask.' The fact was that there shone upon Miss Melbury's face a species of exaltation which saw no environing details; not even Giles's occupation, only his bare presence.

'Why need you not ask?'

'Your face is like the face of Moses when he came down from the Mount.'

She reddened a little and said, 'How can you be so profane, Giles Winterborne!'

'How can you think so much of that class of people! Well, I beg pardon, I didn't mean to speak so freely. How do you like her house and her?'

'Exceedingly. I had not been near the place since I was a child, when it used to be let to strangers, before Mrs Charmond's late husband bought the property. She is *so* nice!' And Grace fell into such an abstracted gaze at the mental image of Mrs Charmond and her niceness that it almost conjured up a vision of that lady to Giles himself.

'She has only been here a month or two it seems, and cannot stay much longer, because she finds it so lonely and damp in winter. She is going abroad. Only think, she would like me to go with her!'

Giles's features stiffened a little at the news. 'Indeed: what for? But I won't keep you standing here. Hoi, Robert!' he cried to a swaying collection of old clothes in the distance, which composed the figure of Creedle, his man, who was looking for him. 'Go on filling in there till I come back.'

'I'm a-coming, sir; I'm a-coming.'

'Well, the reason is this,' continued she as they went on together. 'Mrs Charmond has a delightful side to her character – a desire to record her impressions of travel, like Alexandre Dumas, and Méry, and Sterne, and others. But she cannot find energy enough to do it herself.' And Grace proceeded to explain Mrs Charmond's proposal at large. 'My notion is that Méry's style will suit her best, because he writes in that soft, emotional, luxurious way she has,' Grace said musingly.

'Indeed!' said Winterborne, sighing. 'Suppose you talk over my head a little longer, Miss Grace Melbury.'

'O, I didn't mean it!' she said repentantly, looking into his eyes. 'And as for myself, I hate French books. And I love dear old Hintock, *and the people in it*, fifty times better than all the Continent! But the scheme; I think it an enchanting notion, don't you, Giles?'

'It is well enough in one sense, but it will take you away,' said he, mollified.

'Only for a short time; we should return in May.'

'Well, Miss Melbury; it is a question for your father.'

Winterborne walked with her nearly to her house. He had awaited her coming mainly with the view of mentioning to her his proposal to have a Christmas party; but homely Christmas gatherings in the jovial Hintock style seemed so primitive and uncouth beside the lofty matters of her conversation that he refrained.

As soon as she was gone he turned back towards the scene of his planting, and could not help saying to himself as he walked that this engagement of his was a very unpromising business.

Her outing today had not improved it. A woman who could go to Hintock House, and be friendly with its mistress; enter into the views of its mistress, talk like her, and dress not much unlike her: why, she would hardly be contented with him, a yeoman, immersed in tree planting, even though he planted them well. 'And yet she's a true-hearted girl,' he said, thinking of her words about Hintock. 'I must bring matters to a point, and there's an end of it.'

When he reached the place of work he found that Marty had come back, and dismissing Creedle he went on planting silently with the girl as before.

'Suppose, Marty,' he said after a while, looking at her extended arm, upon which old scratches from briars showed themselves purple in the cold wind, 'suppose you know a person, and want to bring that person to a good understanding with you, do you think a Christmas party of some sort is a warming-up thing, and likely to be useful in hastening on the matter?'

'Is there to be dancing?'

'There might be, certainly.'

'Will He dance with Her?'

'Well, yes.'

'Then it might bring things to a head, one way or the other, I won't be the maid to say which.'

'It shall be done,' said Winterborne, not to her, though he spoke the words quite loudly. And as the day was nearly ended, he added, 'Here, Marty, I'll send up a man to plant the rest tomorrow. I've other things to think of just now.'

She did not inquire what other things, for she had seen him talking with Grace Melbury. She looked towards the western sky, which was now aglow like some vast foundry wherein new worlds were being cast. Across it the bare bough of a tree stretched horizontally, revealing every twig against the evening fire, and showing in dark profile every beck and movement of three pheasants that were settling themselves down on it in a row to roost.

'It will be fine to-morrow,' said Marty, observing them with the vermilion light of the sun in the pupils of her eyes, 'for they are acroupied down nearly at the end of the bough. If it were going to be stormy they'd squeeze close to the trunk. The weather is almost all they have to think of, isn't it, Mr Winterborne? And so they must be lighter-hearted than we.'

'I dare say they are,' said Winterborne.

Before taking a single step in the preparations, Winterborne, with no great hopes, went across that evening to the timber-merchant's to ascertain if Grace and her parents would honour him with their presence. Having first to set his nightly gins in the garden to catch the rabbits that ate his winter-greens, his call was delayed till just after the rising of the moon, whose rays reached the Hintock houses but fitfully as yet, on account of the trees. Melbury was crossing his yard on his way to call on some one at the larger village, but he readily turned and walked up and down with the young man.

Giles, in his self-deprecatory sense of living on a much smaller scale than the Melburys did, would not for the world imply that his invitation was to a gathering of any importance. So he put it in the mild form of 'Can you come in for an hour when you have done business, the day after to-morrow; and Mrs and Miss Melbury, if they have nothing more pressing to do?'

Melbury would give no answer at once. 'No, I can't tell you today,' he said. 'I must talk it over with the women. As far as I am concerned, my dear Giles, you know I'll come with pleasure. But how do I know what Grace's notions may be? You see, she has been away amongst cultivated folks a good while; and now this acquaintance with Mrs Charmond – well, I'll ask her. I can say no more.'

When Winterborne was gone the timber-merchant went on his way. He knew very well that Grace, whatever her own feelings, would either go or not go, according as he suggested; and his instinct was, for the moment, to suggest staying at home. His errand took him near the church, and the way to his destination was equally easy across the churchyard or outside it. For some reason or other he chose the former way.

The moon was faintly lighting up the gravestones, and the path, and the front of the building. Suddenly Mr Melbury paused, turned in upon the grass, and approached a particular headstone, where he read, 'In memory of John Winterborne,' with the subjoined date and age. It was the grave of Giles's father.

The timber-merchant laid his hand upon the stone, and was humanized. 'Jack, my wronged friend!' he said, 'I'll be faithful to my plan of making amends to thee.'

When he reached home that evening he said to Grace and Mrs Melbury, who were working at a little table by the fire, 'Giles wants us to go down and spend an hour with him the day after to-morrow; and I'm thinking, that as 'tis Giles who asks us, we'll go.'

They assented without demur; and the timber-merchant sent Giles the next morning an answer in the affirmative.

Winterborne, in his modesty, had mentioned no particular hour in his invitation to the Melburys, though he had to the inferior guests; therefore Mr Melbury and his family, expecting no other people, chose their own time, which chanced to be rather early in the afternoon, by reason of the somewhat quicker despatch than usual of the timber-merchant's business that day.

They showed their sense of the unimportance of the occasion by walking quite slowly to the house, as if they were merely out for a ramble, and going to nothing special at all; or at most intending to pay a casual call and take a cup of tea.

At this hour stir and bustle pervaded the interior of Winterborne's domicile from cellar to apple-loft. He had planned an elaborate high tea for six o'clock or thereabouts, and a good roaring supper to come on about eleven. Being a bachelor of rather retiring habits the whole of the preparations devolved upon himself and his trusty man and familiar Robert Creedle, who did everything that required doing, from making Giles's bed to catching moles in his field. He was a survival from the days when Giles's father held the homestead and Giles was a playing boy.

These two, with a certain dilatoriness which appertained to both, were now in the heat of preparation in the bakehouse, expecting nobody before six o'clock. Winterborne was standing in front of the brick oven in his shirt-sleeves, tossing in thorn-sprays, and stirring about the blazing mass with a long-handled, three-pronged Beelzebub kind of fork, the heat shining out upon his streaming face and making his eyes like furnaces; the thorns crackling and sputtering; while Creedle, having ranged the pastry dishes in a row on the table till the oven should be ready, was pressing out the crust of a final apple-pie with a rolling-pin. A great pot boiled on the fire; and through the open door of the back-kitchen a boy was seen seated on the fender, emptying the snuffers and scouring the candlesticks, a row of the latter standing upside down on the hob to melt out the grease.

Looking up from the rolling-pin Creedle saw passing the window first the timber-merchant, in his second best suit, next Mrs Melbury in her best silk, and behind them Grace in the fashionable attire which, lately brought home with her from the Continent, she had worn on her visit to Mrs Charmond's. The eyes of the three had been attracted through the window to the proceedings within by the fierce illumination which the oven threw out upon the operators and their utensils.

'Lord, lord! if they bain't come a'ready!' said Creedle.

'No – hey?' said Giles, looking round aghast; while the boy in the background waved a reeking candlestick in his delight.

As there was no help for it Winterborne hastily rolled down his shirt-sleeves and went to meet them in the doorway.

'My dear Giles, I see we have made a mistake in the time,' said the timber-merchant's wife, her face lengthening with concern.

'Oh, it is not much difference. I hope you'll come in.'

'But this means a regular randyvoo!' Mr Melbury accusingly glanced round and pointed towards the viands in the bakehouse with his stick.

'Well, yes,' said Giles.

'And – not Great Hintock band, and dancing, surely?'

'I told three of 'em they might drop in if they'd nothing else to do,' Giles mildly admitted.

'Now why the name didn't ye tell us afore that 'twas going to be a bouncing kind of thing? How should I know what folk mean if they don't say? Now, shall we come in, or shall we go home, and come back-along in a couple of hours?'

'I hope you'll stay, if you'll be so good as not to mind, now you are here! I shall have it all right and tidy in a very little time. I ought not to have been so backward; but Creedle is rather slow.'

Giles spoke quite anxiously for one of his undemonstrative temperament; for he feared that if the Melburys once were back in their own house they would not be disposed to turn out again.

' 'Tis we ought not to have been so forward; that's what 'tis,' said Mr Melbury testily. 'Don't keep us here in your best sitting-room; lead on to the bakehouse, man. Now we are here we'll help ye get ready for the rest. Here, mis'ess, take off your things, and help him out in his baking, or he won't get done to-night. I'll finish heating the oven, and set you free to go and skiver up them ducks.' His eye had passed with pitiless directness of criticism into yet remoter recesses of Winterborne's awkwardly built premises, where the aforesaid birds were hanging.

'And I'll help finish the tarts,' said Grace cheerfully.

'I don't know about that,' said her father. ' 'Tisn't quite so much in your line as it is in your stepmother's and mine.'

'Of course I couldn't let you, Grace!' said Giles, with distress.

'I'll do it, of course,' said Mrs Melbury, taking off her silk train, hanging it up to a nail, carefully rolling back her sleeves, pinning them to her shoulders, and stripping Giles of his apron for her own use.

So Grace pottered idly about while her father and his wife helped on the preparations. A kindly pity of his household management, which Winterborne saw in her eyes whenever he caught them, depressed him much more than her contempt would have done.

Creedle met Giles at the pump after a while, when each of the others was absorbed in the difficulties of a *cuisine* based on utensils, cupboards, and provisions that were strange to them. He groaned to the young man in a whisper, 'This is a bruckle het, maister, I'm much afeard! Who'd ha' thought they'd ha' come so soon!'

The bitter placidity of Winterborne's look hinted the misgivings he did not care to express. 'Have you got the celery ready?' he asked quickly.

'Now, that's a thing I never could mind; no, not if you'd pay me in silver and gold!' said Creedle. 'And I don't care who the man is, I says that a stick of celery that isn't scrubbed with the scrubbing-brush is not clean.'

'*Very* well, very well! I'll attend to it. You go and get 'em comfortable indoors.'

He hastened to the garden, and soon returned, tossing the stalks to Creedle, who was still in a tragic mood. 'If ye'd ha' married, d'ye see, maister,' he murmured, 'this calamity couldn't have happened to us!'

Everything being at last under way, the oven set, and all done that could insure the supper turning up ready at some time or other, Giles and his friends entered the parlour, where the Melburys again dropped into position as guests, though the room was not nearly so warm and cheerful as the blazing bakehouse. Others now arrived, among them Farmer Cawtree and the hollow-turner, and tea went off very well.

Grace's disposition to make the best of everything, and to wink at deficiencies in Winterborne's way of living, was so uniform and persistent that he suspected her of seeing even more deficiencies than he was aware of. That suppressed sympathy which had showed in her face ever since her arrival told him as much too plainly.

'This muddling style of housekeeping is what you've not lately been used to, I suppose?' he said when they were a little apart.

'No; but I like it; it reminds me so pleasantly that everything here in dear old Hintock is just as it used to be. The oil is – not quite nice; but everything else is.'

'The oil?'

'On the chairs, I mean; because it gets on one's dress. Still, mine is not a new one.'

Giles found that the boy, in his zeal to make things look bright, had smeared the chairs with some greasy furniture-polish, and refrained from rubbing it dry in order not to diminish the mirror-like effect that the mixture produced as laid on. Giles apologized and scolded the boy; but he felt that the fates were against him.

CHAPTER 10

SUPPER-TIME came, and with it the hot-baked meats from the oven, laid on a snowy cloth fresh from the press, and reticulated with folds as in Flemish Last-Suppers. Creedle and the boy fetched and carried with amazing alacrity; the latter, to mollify his superior, and make things pleasant, expressing his admiration of Creedle's cleverness when they were alone.

'I s'pose the time when you learnt all these knowing things, Mr Creedle, was when you was in the militia?'

'Well, yes. I seed the world that year somewhat, certainly, and mastered many arts of strange, dashing life. Not but that Giles has worked hard in helping me to bring things to such perfection to-day. "Giles," says I, though he's maister. Not that I should call 'n maister by rights, for his father growed up side by side with me, as if one mother had twinned us and been our nourishing.'

'I s'pose your memory can reach a long way back into history, Mr Creedle?'

'O yes. Ancient days, when there was battles, and famines, and hang-fairs, and other pomps, seem to me as yesterday. Ah, many's the patriarch I've seed come and go in this parish! There, he's calling for more plates. Lord, why can't 'em turn their plates bottom upward for pudding, as we bucks used to do in former days!'

Meanwhile in the adjoining room Giles was presiding in a half-unconscious state. He could not get over the initial failures in his scheme for advancing his suit; and hence he did not know that he was eating mouthfuls of bread and nothing else, and continually snuffing the two candles next him till he had reduced them to mere glimmers drowned in their own grease. Creedle now appeared with a specially prepared stew, which he served by elevating the little three-legged crock that contained it and tilting the contents into a platter on the table, exclaiming simultaneously, 'Draw back, gentlemen and ladies, please!'

A splash followed. Grace gave a quick involuntary nod and blink, and put her handkerchief to her face.

'Good heavens! what did you do that for, Creedle?' said Giles sternly, jumping up.

' 'Tis how I do it when they bain't here, maister,' mildly expostulated Creedle, in an aside audible to all the company.

'Well, yes – but—' replied Giles. He went over to Grace, and hoped none of it had gone into her eye.

'O no,' she said. 'Only a sprinkle on my face. It was nothing.'

'Kiss it and make it well,' gallantly observed Mr Cawtree.

Miss Melbury blushed.

The timber-merchant replied quickly, 'O, it is nothing! She must bear these little mishaps.' But there could be discerned in his face something which said, 'I ought to have foreseen all this, and kept her away.'

Giles himself, since the untoward beginning of the feast, had not quite liked to see Grace present. He wished he had not asked such people as Cawtree and the hollow-turner. He had done it, in dearth of other friends, that the room might not appear empty. In his mind's eye, before the event, they had been the mere background or padding of the scene; but somehow in the reality they were the most prominent personages there.

After supper they sat down to cards; Cawtree and the hollow-turner monopolizing the new packs for an interminable game of langterloo, in which a lump of chalk was incessantly used – a game those two always played wherever they were, taking a solitary candle and going to a private table in a corner with the mien of persons bent on weighty matters. The rest of the company on this account were obliged to put up with old packs for their round game, that had been lying by in a drawer ever since the time that Giles's grandmother was alive. Each card had a great stain in the middle of its back, produced by the touch of generations of damp and excited thumbs, now fleshless in the grave; and the kings and queens wore a decayed expression of feature, as if they were rather an impecunious dethroned dynasty hiding in obscure slums than real regal characters. Every now and then the comparatively few remarks of the players at the round game were harshly intruded on by the langterloo jingle of Farmer Cawtree and the hollow-turner from the back of the room:

'And I´ will hold´ a wa´ -ger with you´
That all´ these marks´ are thirt´ -y two!'

accompanied by rapping strokes with the chalk on the table: then an exclamation, an argument, a dealing of the cards; then the commencement of the rhymes anew.

The timber-merchant showed his feelings by talking with a reserved weight in his words, and by praising the party in a patronizing tone, when Winterborne expressed his fear that he and his were not enjoying themselves.

'O yes, yes; pretty much. What handsome glasses those are! I didn't know you had such glasses in the house. Now, Lucy [to his wife], you ought to get some like them for ourselves.' And when they had abandoned cards, and Winterborne was talking to Melbury by the fire, it was the timber-merchant who stood with his back to the mantel in a proprietary attitude; from which post of vantage he critically regarded Giles's person, rather as a superficies than as a solid with ideas and feelings inside it; saying, 'What a splendid coat that one is you have on, Giles. I can't get such coats. You dress better than I.'

After supper there was a dance, the bandsmen from Great Hintock having arrived some time before. Grace had been away from home so long, and was so drilled in new dances, that she had forgotten the old figures, and hence did not join in the movement. Then Giles felt that all was over. As for her, she was thinking, as she watched the gyrations, of a very different measure that she had been accustomed to tread with a bevy of sylph-like creatures in muslin in the music-room of a large house, most of whom were now moving in scenes widely removed from this, both as regarded place and character.

A woman she did not know came and offered to tell her fortune with the abandoned cards. Grace assented to the proposal, and the woman told her tale unskilfully, for want of practice, as she declared.

Mr Melbury was standing by, and exclaimed contemptuously, 'Tell her fortune indeed! Her fortune has been told by men of science – what do you call 'em? Phrenologists. You can't teach her anything new. She's been too far among the wise ones to be astonished at anything she can hear among us folks in Hintock.'

At last the time came for breaking up, Melbury and his family being the earliest to leave, the two card-players still pursuing their game doggedly in the corner, where they had completely covered Giles's mahogany table with chalk scratches. The Melburys walked home, the distance being short and the night clear.

'Well, Giles is a very good fellow,' said Mr Melbury, as they struck down the lane under boughs which formed a black filigree in which the stars seemed set.

'Certainly he is.' Grace spoke quickly, and in such a tone as to show that he stood no lower, if no higher, in her regard than he had stood before.

When they were opposite an opening through which, by day, the doctor's house could be seen, they observed a light in one of his rooms, although it was now about two o'clock.

'The doctor is not abed yet,' said Mrs Melbury.

'Hard study, no doubt,' said her husband.

'One would think that, as he seems to have nothing to do about here by day, he could at least afford to go to bed early at night. 'Tis astonishing how little we see of him.'

Melbury's mind seemed to turn with much relief to the contemplation of Mr Fitzpiers after the scenes of the evening. 'It is natural enough,' he replied. 'What can a man of that sort find to interest him in Hintock? I don't expect he'll stay here long.'

His thoughts then reverted to Giles's party, and when they were nearly home he spoke again, his daughter being a few steps in advance: 'It is hardly the line of life for a girl like Grace, after what she's been accustomed to. I didn't foresee that, in sending her to boarding-school and letting her travel and what not, to make her a good bargain for Giles, I should be really spoiling her for him. Ah, 'tis a thousand pities! But he ought to have her – he ought!'

At this moment the two chalk-marking, langterloo men, having at last really finished their play, could be heard coming along in the rear, vociferously singing a song to march-time, and keeping vigorous step to the same in far-reaching strides –

'. . . said she,
"A maid again I never shall be,
Till apples grow on an orange tree!"'

The timber-merchant turned indignantly to Mrs Melbury. 'That's the sort of society we've been asked to meet!' he said. 'For us old folk it didn't matter; but for Grace – Giles should have known better!'

Meanwhile, in the empty house from which the guests had just cleared out, the subject of their discourse was walking from room to room surveying the general displacement of furniture with no ecstatic feeling; rather the reverse indeed. At last he entered the bakehouse, and found there Robert Creedle sitting over the embers, also lost in contemplation. Winterborne sat down beside him.

'Well, Robert, you must be tired. You'd better get on to bed.'

'Ay, ay, Giles – what do I call ye? Maister, I would say. But 'tis well to think the day *is* done, when 'tis done.'

Winterborne had abstractedly taken the poker, and with a wrinkled forehead was ploughing abroad the wood-embers on the wide hearth, till it was like a vast scorching Sahara, with red-hot boulders lying about everywhere. 'Do you think it went off well, Creedle?' he asked.

'The victuals did; that I know. And the drink did; that I steadfastly believe, from the holler sound of the barrels. Good honest drink 'twere, the headiest drink I ever brewed; and the best wine that berries could rise to; and the briskest Horner-and-Cleeves cider ever wrung down, leaving out the spice and sperrits I put into it, while that egg-flip would ha' passed through muslin, so little criddled 'twere. 'Twas good enough to make any king's heart merry – ay, to make his whole carcase smile! Still, I don't deny I'm afeard some things didn't go well with He and his.' Creedle nodded in a direction which signified where the Melburys lived.

'I'm afraid, too, that it was a failure there.'

'If so, 'twere doomed to be so. Not but what that slug might as well have come upon anybody else's plate as hers.'

'What slug?'

'Well, maister, there was a little small one upon the edge of her plate when I brought it out, and so it must have been in her few leaves of winter-green.'

'How the deuce did a slug get there?'

'That I don't know no more than the dead; but there my gentleman was.'

'But, Robert, of all places, that was where he shouldn't have been!'

'Well, 'twas his native home, come to that; and where else could we expect him to be? I don't care who the man is, slugs and caterpillars always will lurk in close to the stump of cabbages in that tantalizing way.'

'He wasn't alive, I suppose?' said Giles, with a shudder on Grace's account.

'O no. He was well boiled. I warrant him well boiled. God forbid that a *live* slug should be seed on any plate of victuals that's served by Robert Creedle.... But Lord, there; I don't mind 'em myself – them green ones; for they were born on cabbage, and they've lived on cabbage, so they must be made of cabbage. But she, the close-mouthed little lady, she didn't say a word about it; though 'twould have made good small conversation as to the nater of such creatures; especially as wit ran short among us sometimes.'

'O yes – 'tis all over!' murmured Giles to himself, shaking his head over the glooming plain of embers, and lining his forehead more than ever. 'Do you know, Robert,' he said, 'that she's been accustomed to servants and everything superfine these many years? How, then, could she stand our ways?'

'Well, all I can say is, then, that she ought to hob-and-nob elsewhere. They shouldn't have schooled her so monstrous high, or else bachelor-men shouldn't give randys, or if they do give 'em, only to their own race.'

'Perhaps that's true,' said Winterborne rising, and yawning a sigh.

CHAPTER 11

‘’Tis a pity – a thousand pities!’ her father kept saying next morning at breakfast, Grace being still in her bedroom.

Here was the fact which could not be disguised: since seeing what an immense change her last twelve months of absence had produced in his daughter, after the heavy sum per annum that he had been spending for several years upon her education, he was reluctant to let her marry Giles Winterborne, indefinitely occupied as woodsman, cider-merchant, apple-farmer, and what not, even were she willing to marry him herself.

But how could he, with any self-respect, obstruct Winterborne’s suit at this stage, and nullify a scheme he had laboured to promote – was, indeed, mechanically promoting at this moment? A crisis was approaching, mainly as a result of his contrivances; and it would have to be met.

‘She will be his wife, if you don’t upset her notion that she’s bound to accept him as an understood thing,’ said Mrs Melbury. ‘Bless you, she’ll soon shake down here in Hintock, and be content with Giles’s way of living, which he’ll improve with what money she’ll have from you. ’Tis the strangeness after her genteel life that makes her feel uncomfortable at first. Why, when *I* saw Hintock the first time I thought I never could like it. But things gradually get familiar, and stone floors seem not so very cold and hard, and the hooting of owls not so very dreadful, and loneliness not so very lonely after a while.’

‘Yes, I believe ’ee. That’s just it. I *know* Grace will gradually sink down to our level again, and catch our manners and way of speaking, and feel a drowsy content in being Giles's wife. But I can't bear the thought of dragging down to that old level as promising a piece of maidenhood as ever lived – fit to ornament a palace wi', that I've taken so much trouble to lift up. Fancy her white hands getting redder every day, and her tongue losing its pretty up-country curl in talking, and her bounding walk becoming the regular Hintock shail-and-wamble!'

'She may shail; but she'll never wamble,' replied his wife decisively.

When Grace came downstairs he complained of her lying in bed so late; not so much moved by a particular objection to that form of indulgence as discomposed by these other reflections.

The corners of her pretty mouth dropped a little down. 'You used to complain with justice when I was a girl,' she said. 'But I am a woman now; and can judge for myself. . . . But it is not that: it is something else!' Instead of sitting down she went outside the door.

He was sorry. The petulance that relatives show towards each other is in truth directed against that intangible Cause which has shaped the situation no less for the offenders than the offended, but is too elusive to be discerned and cornered by poor humanity in irritated mood. Melbury followed her. She had rambled on to the paddock, where the white frost lay, making the grass rustle like paper-shavings under their feet, and where starlings in flocks of twenties and thirties were walking about, watched by a comfortable family of sparrows perched in a line along the string-course of the chimney, and preening themselves in the rays of the sun.

'Come in to breakfast, my girl!' he said. 'And as to Giles, use your own mind. Whatever pleases you will please me.'

'I am promised to him, father; and I cannot help thinking that in honour I ought to marry him, whenever I do marry.'

He had a strong suspicion that somewhere in the bottom of her heart there pulsed an old simple indigenous feeling favourable to Giles, though it had become overlaid with implanted tastes. 'Very well,' he said. 'But I hope I shan't lose you yet. Come in to breakfast. What did you think of the inside of Hintock House the other day?'

'I liked it much.'

'Different from friend Winterborne's?'

She said nothing; but he who knew her was aware that she meant by her silence to reproach him with drawing cruel comparisons.

'Mrs Charmond has asked you to come again – when, did you say?'

'She thought Tuesday; but would send the day before to let me know if it suited her.' And with this subject upon their lips they entered to breakfast.

Tuesday came, but no message from Mrs Charmond. Nor was there any on Wednesday. In brief, a fortnight slipped by without a sign, and it looked suspiciously as if Mrs Charmond was not going further in the direction of 'taking up' Grace at present.

Her father reasoned thereon. Immediately after his daughter's two indubitable successes with Mrs Charmond – the interview in the wood and the visit to the House – she had attended Winterborne's party. No doubt the out-and-out joviality of that gathering had made it a topic in the neighbourhood, and that every one present as guests had been widely spoken of – Grace, with her exceptional qualities, above all. What then so natural as that Mrs Charmond should have heard the village news, and become quite disappointed in her expectations of Grace at finding she kept such company?

Full of this *post hoc* argument Mr Melbury overlooked the infinite throng of other possible reasons and unreasons for a woman changing her mind. For instance, while knowing that his Grace was attractive he quite forgot that Mrs Charmond had also great pretensions to beauty.

So it was settled in his mind that her sudden mingling with the villagers at the unlucky Winterborne's was the cause of her most grievous loss, as he deemed it, in the direction of Hintock House.

‘’Tis a great sacrifice!’ he would repeat to himself. ‘I am ruining her for conscience’ sake!’

It was one morning later on, while these things were agitating his mind, that something darkened the window just as they finished breakfast. Looking up they saw Giles in person, mounted on horseback, and straining his neck forward, as he had been doing for some time, to catch their attention through the window. Grace had been the first to see him, and involuntarily exclaimed, ‘There he is – and a new horse!’

On their faces, as they regarded Giles, were written their suspended thoughts and compound feelings concerning him, could he have read them through those old panes. But he saw nothing: his features just now were, for a wonder, lit up with a red smile at some other idea. So they rose from breakfast and went to the door, Grace with an anxious, wistful manner, her father in a reverie, Mrs Melbury placid and inquiring.

‘We have come out to look at your horse,’ she said.

It could be seen that he was pleased at their attention, and explained that he had ridden a mile or two to try the animal’s paces. ‘I bought her,’ he added, with warmth so severely repressed as to seem indifference, ‘because she has been used to carry a lady.’

Still Mr Melbury did not brighten. Mrs Melbury said, ‘And is she quiet?’

Winterborne assured her that there was no doubt of it. ‘I took care of that. She’s twenty-one, and very clever for her age.’

‘Well, get off and come in,’ said Melbury brusquely; and Giles dismounted accordingly.

This event was the concrete result of Winterborne’s thoughts during the past week or two. The want of success with his evening party he had accepted in as philosophic a mood as he was capable of; but there had been enthusiasm enough left in him one day at Sherton Abbas market to purchase the mare, which had belonged to a neighbouring parson with several daughters, and was offered him to carry either a gentleman or a lady, and to do odd jobs of carting and agriculture at a pinch. This obliging quadruped seemed to furnish Giles with a means of reinstating himself in Melbury's good opinion as a man of considerateness, by throwing out equestrian possibilities to Grace if she became his wife.

The latter looked at him with intensified interest this morning, in the mood which is altogether peculiar to woman's nature, and which, when reduced into plain words, seems as impossible as the penetrability of matter – that of entertaining a tender pity for the object of her own unnecessary coldness. The imperturbable poise which marked Winterborne in general was enlivened now by a freshness and animation that set a brightness in his eye and on his cheek. Mrs Melbury asked him to have some breakfast, and he pleasurably replied that he would join them, not perceiving that they had all finished the meal, and that the tune piped by the kettle denoted it to be nearly empty; so that fresh water had to be brought in, and a general renovation of the table carried out. Neither did he know, so full was he of his tender ulterior object in buying that horse, how the morning was slipping away, nor how he was keeping the family from dispersing about their duties.

Then he told throughout the humorous story of the horse's purchase, looking particularly grim at some fixed object in the room, a way he always looked when he narrated anything that amused him. While he was still thinking of the scene he had described Grace rose and said, 'I have to go and help my mother now, Mr Winterborne.'

'H'm?' he ejaculated, turning his eyes suddenly upon her.

She repeated her words with a slight blush of awkwardness; whereupon Giles, becoming suddenly conscious, too conscious, jumped up, saying, 'To be sure, to be sure!' and wished them quickly good-morning.

Nevertheless he had upon the whole strengthened his position, with her at least. Time, too, was on his side, for (as her father saw with regret) already the homeliness of Hintock life was fast becoming lost to her observation as a singularity; as the momentary strangeness of a face from which we have for years been separated insensibly passes off with renewed intercourse, and tones itself down into identity with the lineaments of the past.

Thus Mr Melbury went out of the house still unreconciled to the sacrifice of the gem he had been at such pains in mounting. He fain could hope, in the secret nether chamber of his mind, that something would happen before the balance of her feeling had quite turned in Winterborne's favour, to relieve his conscience and at the same time preserve her on her elevated plane.

CHAPTER 12

It was a day of rather bright weather for the season. Miss Melbury went out for a morning walk, and her ever-regardful father, having an hour's leisure, offered to walk with her.

The breeze was fresh and quite steady, filtering itself through the denuded mass of twigs without swaying them, but making the point of each ivy-leaf on the trunks scratch its underlying neighbour restlessly. Grace's lips sucked in this native air of hers like milk. They soon reached a place where the wood ran down into a corner, and they went outside it towards comparatively open ground. Having looked round they were intending to re-enter the copse when a panting fox emerged with a dragging brush, trotted past them tamely as a domestic cat, and disappeared amid some dead fern. They walked on, her father merely observing after watching the animal, 'They are hunting somewhere near.'

Further up they saw in the mid-distance the hounds running hither and thither, as if the scent lay cold that day. Soon members of the hunt appeared on the scene, and it was evident that the chase had been stultified by general puzzle-headedness as to the whereabouts of the intended victim. In a minute a gentleman-farmer, panting with Actaeonic excitement, rode up to the two pedestrians, and Grace being a few steps in advance he asked her if she had seen the fox.

'Yes,' said she. 'I saw him some time ago – just out there.'

'Did you cry Halloo?'

'I said nothing.'

'Then why the devil didn't you, or get the old buffer to do it for you?' said the man as he cantered away.

She looked rather disconcerted, and observing her father's face saw that it was quite red.

'He ought not to have spoken to 'ee like that!' said the old man in the tone of one whose heart was bruised, though it was not by the epithet applied to himself. 'And he wouldn't if he had been a gentleman. 'Twas not the language to use to a woman of any niceness. You so well read and cultivated – how could he expect ye to go shouting a view-halloo like a farm tomboy! Hasn't it cost me near a hundred a year to lift you out of all that, so as to show an example to the neighbourhood of what a woman can be? Grace, shall I tell you the secret of it? 'Twas because *I* was in your company. If a black-coated squire or pa'son had been walking with you instead of me he wouldn't have spoken so.'

'No, no, father; there's nothing in you rough or ill-mannered!'

'I tell you it is that! I've noticed, and I've noticed it many times, that a woman takes her colour from the man she's walking with. The woman who looks an unquestionable lady when she's with a polished-up fellow, looks a tawdry imitation article when she's hobbing and nobbing with a homely blade. You shan't be treated like that for long, or at least your children shan't. You shall have somebody to walk with you who looks more of a dandy than I – please God you shall!'

'But, my dear father,' she said much distressed, 'I don't mind at all. I don't wish for more honour than I already have!'

'A perplexing and ticklish possession is a daughter', according to the Greek poet, and to nobody was one ever more so than to Melbury. As for Grace, she began to feel troubled; she did not perhaps wish, there and then, to devote her life unambitiously to Giles Winterborne, but she was more and more uneasy at being the social hope of the family.

'You would like to have more honour, if it pleases me?' asked her father, in continuation of the subject.

Despite her feeling she assented to this. His reasoning had not been without weight upon her.

'Grace,' he said, just before they had reached the house, 'if it costs me my life you shall marry well! To-day has shown me that whatever a young woman's niceness she stands for nothing alone. You shall marry well.'

He breathed heavily, and his breathing was caught up by the breeze, which seemed to sigh a soft remonstrance.

She looked calmly at him. 'And how about Mr Winterborne?' she asked. 'I mention it, father, not as a matter of sentiment, but as a question of keeping faith.'

The timber-merchant's eyes fell for a moment. 'I don't know – I don't know,' he said. ' 'Tis a trying strait. Well, well; there's no hurry. We'll wait and see how he gets on.'

That evening he called her into his room, a snug little apartment behind the large parlour. It had at one time been part of the bakehouse, with the ordinary oval brick oven in the wall; but Mr Melbury in turning it into an office had built into the cavity an iron safe, which he used for holding his private papers. The door of the safe was now open, and his keys were hanging from it.

'Sit down, Grace, and keep me company,' he said. 'You may amuse yourself by looking over these.' He threw out a heap of papers before her.

'What are they?' she asked.

'Securities of various sorts.' He unfolded them one by one. 'Papers worth so much money each. Now here's a lot of turnpike bonds, for one thing. Would you think that each of these pieces of paper is worth two hundred pounds?'

'No, indeed, if you didn't say so.'

' 'Tis so then. Now here are papers of another sort. They are for different sums in the three per cents. Now these are Port-Bredy Harbour bonds. We have a great stake in that harbour, you know, because I send off timber there. Open the rest at your pleasure. They'll interest 'ee.'

'Yes, I will, some day,' said she rising.

'Nonsense, open them now. You ought to learn a little of such matters. A young lady of education should not be ignorant of money affairs altogether. Suppose you should be left a widow some day, with your husband's title-deeds and investments thrown upon your hands—'

'Don't say that, father. Title-deeds; it sounds so vain!'

'It does not. Come to that, I have title-deeds myself. There, that piece of parchment represents houses in Sherton Abbas.'

'Yes, but—' She hesitated, looked at the fire, and went on in a low voice, 'If what has been arranged about me should come to anything, my sphere will be quite a middling one.'

'Your sphere ought not to be middling,' he exclaimed. 'You said you never felt more at home, more in your element, anywhere than you did that afternoon with Mrs Charmond, when she showed you her house, and all her knick-knacks, and made you stay to tea so nicely in her drawing-room, surely you did!'

'Yes, I did say so,' admitted Grace.

'Was it true?'

'Yes, I felt so at the time. The feeling is less strong now, perhaps.'

'Ah! Now, though you don't see it, your feeling at the time was the right one, because your mind and body were just in full and fresh cultivation, so that going there with her was like meeting like. Since then you've been staying with us, and have fallen back a little, and so you don't feel your place so strongly. Now, do as I tell you, and look over these papers, and see what you'll be worth some day. For they'll all be yours, you know; who have I got to leave 'em to but you? Perhaps when your education is backed up by what these papers represent, and that backed up by another such a set and their owner, men such as that fellow was this morning may think you a little more than a buffer's girl.'

So she did as commanded, and opened each of the folded representatives of hard cash that her father put before her. To sow in her heart cravings for social position was obviously his strong desire, though in direct antagonism to a better feeling which had hitherto prevailed with him, and had, indeed, only succumbed that morning during the ramble.

She wished that she was not his worldly hope; the responsibility of such a position was too great. She had made it for herself mainly by her appearance and attractive behaviour to him since her return. 'If I had only come home in a shabby dress, and tried to speak roughly, this might not have happened,' she thought. She deplored less the fact, however, than the contingencies.

Her father then insisted upon her looking over his cheque-book and reading the counterfoils. This also she obediently did, and at last came to two or three which had been drawn to defray some of the late expenses of her clothes, board, and education.

'I, too, cost a good deal, like the horses and waggons and corn!' she said, looking up sorrily.

'I didn't want you to look at those; I merely meant to give you an idea of my investment transactions. But if you do cost as much as they, never mind. You'll yield a better return.'

'Don't think of me like that!' she begged. 'A mere chattel.'

'A what? Oh, a dictionary word. Well, as that's in your line I don't forbid it, even if it tells against me,' he said good-humouredly. And he looked her proudly up and down.

A few minutes later Grammer Oliver came to tell them that supper was ready, and in giving the information she added incidentally, 'So we shall soon lose the mistress of Hintock House for some time, I hear, Maister Melbury. Yes, she is going off to foreign parts to-morrow, for the rest of the winter months; and be-chok'd if I don't wish I could do the same, for my wind-pipe is furred like a flue.'

When the old woman had left the room Melbury turned to his daughter and said, 'So, Grace, you've lost your new friend, and your chance of keeping her company and writing her travels is quite gone from 'ee!'

Grace said nothing.

'Now,' he went on emphatically, ' 'tis Winterborne's affair has done this. O yes, 'tis! So let me say one word. Promise me that you will not meet him again without my knowledge.'

'I never do meet him, father, either without your knowledge or with it.'

'So much the better. I don't like the look of this at all. And I say it not out of harshness to him, poor fellow, but out of tenderness to you. For how could a woman, brought up delicately as you have been, bear the roughness of a life with him?'

She sighed; it was a sigh of sympathy with Giles, complicated by a sense of the intractability of circumstances.

At that same hour, and almost at that same minute, there was a conversation about Winterborne in progress in the village lane, opposite Mr Melbury's gates, where Timothy Tangs the elder and Robert Creedle had accidentally met.

The sawyer was asking Creedle if he had heard what was all over the parish, the skin of his face being toned towards brightness in respect of it as news, and towards concern in respect of its bearings.

'Why, that poor little lonesome thing, Marty South, is likely to lose her father. He was almost well, but is much worse again; a man all skin and grief he ever were; and if he leave Little Hintock for a better land, won't it make some difference to your good man Winterborne, neighbour Creedle?'

'Can I be a prophet in Hintock?' said Creedle. 'I was only shaping of such a thing yesterday in my poor long-seeing way! It is upon John South's life that all Mr Winterborne's houses hang. If so be South die and so make his decease, thereupon the law ordains that the houses fall without the least chance of saving 'em into Her hands at the House. I told him so; but the words of the faithful be only as wind!'

CHAPTER 13

THE news was true. The life – the one fragile life – that had been used as a measuring-tape of time by law, was in danger of being frayed away. It was the last of a group of lives which had served this purpose, at the end of whose breathings the small homestead occupied by South himself, the larger one of Giles Winterborne, and half a dozen others that had been in the possession of various Hintock village families for the previous hundred years, and were now Winterborne's, would fall in and become part of the encompassing estate.

Winterborne walked up and down his garden next day thinking of the contingency. The sense that the paths he was pacing, the cabbage-plots, the apple-trees, his dwelling, cider-cellar, wring-house, stables, weathercock, were all slipping away over his head and beneath his feet as if they were painted on a magic-lantern slide, was curious. In spite of John South's late indisposition he had not anticipated danger.

Whilst he was here in the garden somebody came to fetch him. It was Marty herself, and she showed her distress by her unconsciousness of a cropped poll.

'Father is still so much troubled in his mind about that tree,' she said. 'You know the tree I mean, Mr Winterborne? the tall one in front of the house that he thinks will blow down and kill us. Can you come and see if you can persuade him out of his notion? I can do nothing.'

He accompanied her to the cottage, and she conducted him upstairs. John South was pillowed up in a chair between the bed and the window, exactly opposite the latter, towards which his face was turned.

'Ah, neighbour Winterborne,' he said. 'I wouldn't have minded if my life had only been my own to lose; I don't vallie it in much of itself, and can let it go if 'tis required of me. But to think what 'tis worth to you, a young man rising in life, that do trouble me! It seems a trick of dishonesty towards ye to go off at fifty-five! I could bear up, I know I could, if it were not for the tree – yes, the tree 'tis that's killing me. There he stands, threatening my life every minute that the wind do blow. He'll come down upon us, and squat us dead; and what will ye do when the life on your property is taken away!'

'Never you mind me – that's of no consequence,' said Giles. 'Think of yourself alone.'

He looked out of the window in the direction of the woodman's gaze. The tree was a tall elm, familiar to him from childhood, which stood at a distance of two-thirds its own height from the front of South's dwelling. Whenever the wind blew, as it did now, the tree rocked, naturally enough; and the sight of its motion, and sound of its sighs, had gradually bred the terrifying illusion in the woodman's mind. Thus he would sit all day, in spite of persuasion, watching its every sway, and listening to the melancholy Gregorian melodies which the air wrung out of it. This fear it apparently was, rather than any organic disease, which was eating away the health of John South.

As the tree waved South waved his head, making it his fugleman with abject obedience. 'Ah, when it was quite a small tree,' he said, 'and I was a little boy, I thought one day of chopping it off with my hook to make a clothes-line prop with. But I put off doing it, and then I again thought that I would; but I forgot it and didn't. And at last it got too big, and now 'tis my enemy, and will be the death of me. Little did I think, when I let that sapling stay, that a time would come when it would torment me, and dash me into my grave.'

'No, no,' said Winterborne and Marty soothingly. But they thought it possible that it might hasten him into his grave, though in another way than by falling.

'I tell you what,' added Winterborne; 'I'll climb up this afternoon and shroud off the lower boughs, and then it won't be so heavy, and the wind won't affect it so.'

'She won't allow it – a strange woman come from nobody knows where – she won't have it done.'

'You mean Mrs Charmond? Oh, she doesn't know there's such a tree on her estate. Besides, shrouding is not felling, and I'll risk that much.'

He went out, and when afternoon came he returned, took a bill-hook from the shed, and with a ladder climbed into the lower part of the tree, where he began lopping off – 'shrouding' as they called it at Hintock – the lowest boughs. Each of these quivered under his attack, bent, cracked, and fell into the hedge. Having cut away the lowest tier he stepped off the ladder, climbed a few steps higher, and attacked those at the next level. Thus he ascended with the progress of his work far above the top of the ladder, cutting away his perches as he went, and leaving nothing but a bare stem below him.

The work was troublesome, for the tree was large. The afternoon wore on, turning dark and misty about four o'clock. From time to time Giles cast his eyes across towards the bedroom-window of South, where, by the flickering fire in the chamber, he could see the old man watching him, sitting motionless with a hand upon each arm of the chair. Beside him sat Marty, also straining her eyes towards the skyey field of his operations.

A curious question suddenly occurred to Winterborne, and he stopped his chopping. He was operating on another person's property to prolong the years of a lease by whose termination that person would considerably benefit. In that aspect of the case he doubted if he ought to go on. On the other hand he was working to save a man's life, and this seemed to empower him to adopt arbitrary measures.

The wind had died down to a calm, and while he was weighing the circumstances he saw coming along the road through the increasing mist a figure which, indistinct as it was, he knew well. Grace Melbury was on her way out from the house, probably for a short evening walk before dark. He arranged himself for a greeting from her, since she could hardly avoid passing immediately beneath the tree.

But Grace, though she looked up and saw him, was just at that time too full of the words of her father to give him any encouragement. The years-long regard that she had had for him was not kindled by her return into a flame of sufficient brilliancy to make her rebellious. Thinking that she might not see him, he cried, 'Miss Melbury, here I am.'

She turned up her head again. She was near enough to see the expression of his face, and the nails in his soles, silver-bright with constant walking. But she did not reply; and dropping her glance anew went on.

Winterborne's face grew strange; he mused, and proceeded automatically with his work. Grace meanwhile had not gone far. She had reached a gate, whereon she had leant sadly and whispered to herself, 'What shall I do?'

A sudden fog came on, and she curtailed her walk, passing under the tree again on her return. Again he addressed her. 'Grace,' he said, when she was close to the trunk, 'speak to me.' She gazed straight up, shook her head without stopping, and went on to a little distance, where she stood observing him from behind the hedge.

Her coldness had been kindly meant. If it was to be done, she had said to herself, it should be begun at once. While she stood out of observation Giles seemed to recognize her meaning; with a sudden start he worked on, climbing higher into the sky, and cutting himself off more and more from all intercourse with the sublunary world. At last he had worked himself so high up the elm, and the mist had so thickened, that he could only just be discerned as a dark grey spot on the light grey zenith; he would have been altogether out of notice but for the stroke of his bill-hook, and the flight of a bough downward, and its crash upon the hedge at intervals.

It was not to be done thus, after all: plainness and candour were best. She went back a third time; he did not see her now, and she lingeringly gazed up at his unconscious figure, loth to put an end to any kind of hope that might live on in him still.

'Giles – Mr Winterborne,' she said.

His work so rustled the boughs that he did not hear.

'Mr Winterborne!' she cried again, and this time he stopped, looked down, and replied.

'My silence just now was not accident,' she said in an unequal voice. 'My father says it is better for us not to think too much of that – engagement, or understanding, between us, that you know of. I, too, think that upon the whole he is right. But we are friends, you know, Giles, and almost relations.'

'Very well,' he answered in an enfeebled voice which barely reached down the tree. 'I have nothing to say, Grace – I cannot say anything till I've thought a while!'

She added with emotion in her tone, 'For myself I would have married you – some day – I think. But I give way, for I am assured it would be unwise.'

He made no reply, but sat back upon a bough, placed his elbow in a fork, and rested his head upon his hand. Thus he remained till the fog and the night had completely inclosed him from her view.

Grace heaved a divided sigh with a tense pause between, and moved onward, her heart feeling uncomfortably big and heavy, and her eyes wet. Had Giles, instead of remaining still, immediately come down from the tree to her, would she have continued in that filial, acquiescent frame of mind which she had announced to him as final? If it be true, as women themselves have declared, that one of their sex is never so much inclined to throw in her lot with a man for good and all as five minutes after she has told him such a thing cannot be, the probabilities are that something might have been done by the appearance of Winterborne on the ground beside Grace.

But he continued motionless and silent in that gloomy Niflheim or fogland which involved him, and she proceeded on her way.

The spot seemed now to be quite deserted. The light from South's window made rays on the fog, but did not reach the tree. A quarter of an hour passed, and all was blackness overhead. Giles had not yet come down.

Then the tree seemed to shiver, then to heave a sigh: a movement was audible, and Winterborne dropped almost noiselessly to the ground. He had thought the matter out; and having returned the ladder and bill-hook to their places pursued his way homeward. He would not allow this incident to affect his outer conduct any more than the danger to his leaseholds had done, and went to bed as usual.

Two simultaneous troubles do not always make a double trouble; and thus it came to pass that Giles's practical anxiety about his houses, which would have been enough to keep him awake half the night at any other time, was displaced and not reinforced by his sentimental trouble about Grace Melbury. This severance was in truth more like a burial of her than a rupture with her, but he did not realize so much at present; even when he arose in the morning he felt quite moody and stern; as yet the second note in the gamut of such emotions, a distracting regret for his loss, had not made itself heard.

A load of oak timber was to be sent away before dawn that morning to a building whose works were in a town many miles off. The trunks were chained down to a heavy timber carriage with enormous red wheels, and four of the most powerful of Melbury's horses were harnessed in front to draw them.

The horses wore their bells that day. There were sixteen to the team, carried on a frame above each animal's shoulders, and tuned to scale, so as to form two octaves, running from the highest note on the right or offside of the leader to the lowest on the left or nearside of the shaft-horse. Melbury was among the last to retain horse-bells in that neighbourhood; for living at Little Hintock, where the lanes yet remained as narrow as before the days of turnpike-roads, these sound-signals were still as useful to him and his neighbours as they had ever been in former times. Much backing was saved in the course of a year by the warning notes they cast ahead; moreover, the tones of all the teams in the district being known to the carters of each, they could tell a long way off on a dark night whether they were about to encounter friends or strangers.

The fog of the previous evening still lingered so heavily over the woods that the morning could not penetrate the trees. The load being a ponderous one, the lane crooked, and the air so thick, Winterborne set out, as he often did, to accompany the team as far as the corner, where it would turn into a wider road.

So they rumbled on, shaking the foundations of the roadside cottages by the weight of their progress, the sixteen bells chiming harmoniously over all, till they had risen out of the valley, and were descending towards the more open route, sparks rising from their creaking skid as if they would set fire to the dead leaves alongside.

Then occurred one of the very incidents against which the bells were an endeavour to guard. Suddenly there beamed into their eyes, quite close to them, the two lamps of a carriage, haloed by the fog. Its approach had been quite unheard by reason of their own noise. The carriage was a covered one, while behind it could be discerned another vehicle laden with luggage.

Winterborne went to the head of the team, and heard the coachman telling the carter that he must turn back. The carter declared that this was impossible.

'You can turn if you unhitch your string-horses,' said the coachman.

'It is much easier for you to turn than for us,' said Winterborne. 'We've five ton of timber on these wheels if we've an ounce.'

'But I've another carriage with luggage at my back.'

Winterborne admitted the strength of the argument. 'But even with that,' he said, 'you can back better than we. And you ought to, for you could hear our bells half a mile off.'

'And you could see our lights.'

'We couldn't, because of the fog.'

'Well, our time's precious,' said the coachman haughtily. 'You are only going to some trumpery little village or other in the neighbourhood, while we are going straight to Italy.'

'Driving all the way, I suppose?' said Winterborne sarcastically.

The contention continued in these terms till a voice from the interior of the carriage inquired what was the matter. It was a lady's.

She was informed of the timber people's obstinacy; and then Giles could hear her telling the footman to direct the timber people to turn their horses' heads.

The message was brought, and Winterborne sent the bearer back to say that he begged the lady's pardon, but that he could not do as she requested; that though he would not assert it to be impossible, it was impossible by comparison with the slight difficulty to her party to back their light carriages. As fate would have it, the incident with Grace Melbury on the previous day made Giles less gentle than he might otherwise have shown himself, his confidence in the sex being rudely shaken.

In fine, nothing could move him, and the carriages were compelled to back till they reached one of the sidings or turn-outs constructed in the bank for the purpose. Then the team came on ponderously, and the clanging of its sixteen bells as it passed the discomfited carriages tilted up against the bank, lent a particularly triumphant tone to the team's progress – a tone which, in point of fact, did not at all attach to its conductor's feelings.

Giles walked behind the timber; and just as he had got past the yet stationary carriages he heard a lofty voice say, 'Who is that rude man? Not Melbury?' The sex of the speaker was so prominent in the tones that Winterborne felt a pang of regret.

'No, ma'am. A younger man, in a smaller way of business in Little Hintock. Winterborne is his name.'

Thus they parted company. 'Why, Mr Winterborne,' said the waggoner when they were out of hearing, 'that was she –

Mrs Charmond! Who'd ha' thought it? What in the world can a woman that does nothing be cock-watching out here at this time o' day for? Oh, going to Italy – yes, to be sure, I heard she was going abroad. She can't endure the winter here.'

Winterborne was vexed at the incident; the more so that he knew Mr Melbury, in his adoration of Hintock House, would be the first to blame him if it became known. He accompanied the load to the end of the lane, and then turned back with an intention to call at South's to learn the result of the experiment of the preceding evening.

It chanced that a few minutes before this time Grace Melbury, who now rose soon enough to breakfast with her father, in spite of the unwontedness of the hour, had been commissioned by him to make the same inquiry at South's. Marty had been standing at the door when Miss Melbury arrived. Almost before the latter had spoken Mrs Charmond's carriages, released from the obstruction up the lane, came bowling along, and the two girls turned to regard the spectacle.

Mrs Charmond did not see them, but there was sufficient light for them to discern her outline between the carriage windows. A noticeable feature in her tournure was a magnificent mass of braided locks.

'How well she looks this morning!' said Grace, forgetting Mrs Charmond's slight in her generous admiration. 'Her hair so becomes her worn that way. I have never seen any more beautiful!'

'Nor have I, miss,' said Marty drily, and unconsciously stroking her crown.

Grace watched the carriages with lingering regret till they were out of sight. She then learnt of Marty that South was no better. Before she had come away Winterborne approached the house, but seeing that one of the two girls standing on the doorstep was Grace he turned back again, and sought the shelter of his own home till she should have gone away.

CHAPTER 14

The encounter with the carriages forced Winterborne's mind back again to the houses of his which would fall into Mrs Charmond's possession in the event of South's death. He marvelled, as many have done since, what could have induced his ancestors at Hintock, and other village people, to exchange their old copyholds for life-leases. And he was much struck with his father's negligence in not insuring South's life.

After breakfast he went upstairs, turned over his bed, and drew out a flat canvas bag which lay between the mattress and the sacking. In this he kept his leases, which had remained there unopened ever since his father's death. It was the usual hiding-place among rural lifeholders for such documents. Winterborne sat down on the bed and looked them over. They were ordinary leases for three lives, which a member of the South family, some fifty years before this time, had accepted of the lord of the manor in lieu of certain copyholds and other rights, in consideration of having the dilapidated houses rebuilt by the said lord. They had come into his father's possession chiefly through his mother, who was a South.

Pinned to the corner of one of the indentures was a letter which Winterborne had never seen before. It bore a remote date, the handwriting being that of some solicitor or agent, and the signature the landholder's. It was to the effect that, at any time before the last of the stated lives should drop, Mr John Winterborne, or his representative, should have the privilege of adding his own and his son's life to the life remaining on payment of a merely nominal fine; the concession being in consequence of the elder Winterborne's consent to demolish one of the houses and relinquish its site, which stood at an awkward corner of the lane, and impeded the way.

The house had been pulled down years before. Why Giles's father had not taken advantage of his privilege to insert his own and his son's lives it was impossible to say. In all likelihood death alone had hindered him in the execution of that project, the elder Winterborne having been a man who took much pleasure in dealing with house property in his small way.

Since one of the Souths still survived there was not much doubt that Giles could do what his father had left undone, as far as his own life was concerned. This possibility cheered him much; for by those houses hung many things. Melbury's doubt of the young man's fitness to be the husband of Grace had been based not a little on the precariousness of his holdings in Little and Great Hintock. He resolved to attend to the business at once, the fine for renewal being a sum that he could easily muster.

His scheme, however, could not be carried out in a day; and meanwhile he would run up to South's as he had intended to do, to learn the result of the experiment with the tree.

Marty met him at the door. 'Well, Marty,' he said; and was surprised to read in her face that the case was not so hopeful as he had imagined.

'I am sorry for your labour,' she said. 'It is all lost. He says the tree seems taller than ever.'

Winterborne looked around at it. Taller the tree certainly did seem, the gauntness of its now naked stem being more marked than before.

'It quite terrified him when he first saw what you had done to it this morning,' she added. 'He declares it will come down upon us and cleave us, like "the sword of the Lord and of Gideon".'

'Well; can I do anything else?' asked he.

'The doctor says the tree ought to be cut down.'

'O, you've had the doctor?'

'I didn't send for him. Mrs Charmond before she left heard that father was ill, and told him to attend him at her expense.'

'That was very good of her. And he says it ought to be cut down. We mustn't cut it down without her knowledge, I suppose.'

He went upstairs. There the old man sat, staring at the now gaunt tree as if his gaze were frozen on to its trunk. Unluckily the tree waved afresh by this time, a wind having sprung up and blown the fog away; and his eyes turned with its wavings.

They heard footsteps – a man's, but of a lighter weight than usual. 'There is Dr Fitzpiers again,' she said, and descended. Presently his tread was heard on the naked stairs.

Mr Fitzpiers entered the sick chamber as a doctor is wont to do on such occasions, and pre-eminently when the room is that of the humble cottager; looking round towards the patient with a preoccupied gaze which so plainly reveals that he has well-nigh forgotten all about the case and the circumstances since he dismissed them from his mind at his last exit from the same apartment. He nodded to Winterborne, who had not seen him since his peep over the hedge at Grace, recalled the case to his thoughts, and went leisurely on to where South sat.

Edred Fitzpiers was, on the whole, a finely formed, handsome man. His eyes were dark and impressive, and beamed with the light either of energy or of susceptivity – it was difficult to say which; it might have been chiefly the latter. That quick, glittering, empirical eye, sharp for the surface of things if for nothing beneath, he had not. But whether his apparent depth of vision were real, or only an artistic accident of his corporeal moulding, nothing but his deeds could reveal.

His face was rather soft than stern, charming than grand, pale than flushed; his nose – if a sketch of his features be *de rigueur* for a person of his pretensions – was artistically beautiful enough to have been worth modelling by any sculptor not over busy, and was hence devoid of those knotty irregularities which often mean power; while the classical curve of his mouth was not without a looseness in its close. Either from his readily appreciative mien, or his reflective manner, his presence bespoke the philosopher rather than the dandy – an effect which was helped by the absence of trinkets or other trivialities from his attire, though this was more finished and up to date than is usually the case among rural practitioners.

Strict people of the highly respectable class, knowing a little about him by report, said that he seemed likely to err rather in the possession of too many ideas than too few; to be a dreamy 'ist of some sort, or too deeply steeped in some false kind of 'ism. However this may be, it will be seen that he was undoubtedly a somewhat rare kind of gentleman and doctor to have descended, as from the clouds, upon Little Hintock.

'This is an extraordinary case,' he said at last to Winterborne, after examining South by conversation, look, and touch, and learning that the craze about the elm was stronger than ever. 'Come downstairs, and I'll tell you what I think.'

They accordingly descended, and the doctor continued, 'The tree must be cut down; or I won't answer for his life.'

''Tis Mrs Charmond's tree; and I suppose we must get permission?' said Giles.

'O, never mind whose tree it is – what's a tree beside a life! Cut it down. I have not the honour of knowing Mrs Charmond as yet; but I am disposed to risk that much with her.'

''Tis timber,' rejoined Giles. 'They never fell a stick about here without its being marked first, either by her or the agent.'

'Then we'll inaugurate a new era forthwith. How long has he complained of the tree?' asked the doctor of Marty.

'Weeks and weeks, sir. The shape of it seems to haunt him like an evil spirit. He says that it is exactly his own age, that it has got human sense, and sprouted up when he was born on purpose to rule him, and keep him as its slave. Others have been like it afore in Hintock.'

They could hear South's voice upstairs. 'O, he's rocking this way; he must come! And then my poor life, that's worth houses upon houses, will be squashed out o' me. O! O!'

'That's how he goes on,' she added. 'And he'll never look anywhere else but out of the window, and scarcely have the curtains drawn.'

'Down with it, then, and hang Mrs Charmond,' said Mr Fitzpiers. 'The best plan will be to wait till the evening, when it is dark, or early in the morning before he is awake, so that he doesn't see it fall, for that would terrify him worse than ever. Keep the blind down till I come, and then I'll assure him, and show him that his trouble is over.'

The doctor departed, and they waited till the evening. When it was dusk, and the curtains drawn, Winterborne directed a couple of woodmen to bring a cross-cut saw; and the tall threatening tree was soon nearly off at its base. Next morning, before South was awake, they went and lowered it cautiously, in a direction away from the cottage. It was a business difficult to do quite silently; but it was done at last, and the elm of the same birth-year as the woodman's lay stretched upon the ground. The weakest idler that passed could now set foot on marks formerly made in the upper forks by the shoes of adventurous climbers only; once inaccessible nests could be examined microscopically; and on swaying extremities where birds alone had perched the bystanders sat down.

As soon as it was broad daylight the doctor came, and Winterborne entered the house with him. Marty said that her father was wrapped up and ready, as usual, to be put into his chair. They ascended the stairs, and soon seated him. He began at once to complain of the tree, and the danger to his life and Winterborne's house property in consequence.

The doctor signalled to Giles, who went and drew back the dimity curtains. 'It is gone, see,' said Mr Fitzpiers.

As soon as the old man saw the vacant patch of sky in place of the branched column so familiar to his gaze, he sprang up, speechless; his eyes rose from their hollows till the whites showed all round, he fell back, and a bluish whiteness overspread him.

Greatly alarmed they put him on the bed. As soon as he came a little out of his fit he gasped, 'O, it is gone! – where – where?'

His whole system seemed paralyzed by amazement. They were thunderstruck at the result of the experiment, and did all they could. Nothing seemed to avail. Giles and Fitzpiers went and came, but uselessly. He lingered through the day, and died that evening as the sun went down.

'Damned if my remedy hasn't killed him!' murmured the doctor.

Dismissing the subject he went downstairs. When going out of the house he turned suddenly to Giles and said, 'Who was that young lady we looked at over the hedge the other day?'

Giles shook his head, as if he did not remember.

CHAPTER 15

WHEN Melbury heard what had happened he seemed much moved, and walked thoughtfully about the premises. On South's own account he was genuinely sorry; and on Winterborne's he was the more grieved in that this catastrophe had so closely followed the somewhat harsh suggestion to Giles to draw off from his daughter.

He was quite angry with circumstances for so heedlessly inflicting on Giles a second trouble when the needful one inflicted by himself was all that the proper order of events demanded. 'I told Giles's father when he came into those houses not to spend too much money on lifehold property held neither for his own life nor his son's,' he exclaimed; 'but he wouldn't listen to me. And now Giles has to suffer for it.'

'Poor Giles!' murmured Grace.

'Now, Grace, between us two, it is very, very remarkable. It is almost as if I had foreseen this; and I am thankful for your escape, though I am sincerely sorry for Giles. Had we not dismissed him already we could hardly have found it in our hearts to dismiss him now. So I say, be thankful. I'll do all I can for him as a friend; but as a pretender to the position of my son-in-law, that can never be thought of more.'

And yet at that very moment the impracticability to which poor Winterborne's suit had been reduced was touching Grace's heart to a warmer sentiment in his behalf than she had felt for years concerning him.

He, meanwhile, was sitting down alone in the familiar house which had ceased to be his; taking a calm if somewhat dismal survey of affairs. The pendulum of the clock bumped every now and then against one side of the case in which it swung, as the muffled drum to his worldly march. Looking out of the window he could perceive that a paralysis had come over Creedle's occupation of manuring the garden, owing, obviously, to a conviction that they might not be living there long enough to profit by next season's crop.

He looked at the leases again and the letter attached. There was no doubt that he had lost his houses and was left practically penniless by an accident which might easily have been circumvented if he had known the true conditions of his holding. The time for performance had now lapsed in strict law; but why should not the intention be considered by the landholder when she became aware of the circumstances, and his moral right to retain the holdings for the term of his life be conceded?

His heart sank within him when he perceived that, despite all the legal reciprocities and safeguards prepared and written, the upshot of the matter was that it depended upon the mere caprice of the woman he had met the day before, in such an unfortunate way, whether he was to possess his houses for life or no.

While he was sitting and thinking a step came to the door, and Melbury appeared, looking very sorry for his position. Winterborne welcomed him by a word and a nod, and went on with his examination of the parchments. His visitor sat down.

'Giles,' he said, 'this is very awkward, and I am sorry for it. What are you going to do?'

Giles informed him of the real state of affairs, and how barely he had missed availing himself of his chance of renewal.

'What a misfortune! Why was this neglected? Well, the best thing you can do is to write and tell her all about it, and throw yourself upon her generosity.'

'I would rather not,' murmured Giles.

'But you must,' said Melbury. 'Much depends on it.'

In short, he argued so cogently that Giles allowed himself to be persuaded, firmly believing it to be a last blow for Grace.

The letter to Mrs Charmond was written and sent to Hintock House, whence, as he knew, it would at once be forwarded to her.

Melbury, feeling that he had done so good an action in coming as to extenuate his previous arbitrary conduct, went home; and Giles was left alone to the suspense of waiting for a reply from the divinity who shaped the ends of the Hintock population. By this time all the villagers knew of the circumstances, and being well-nigh like one family a keen interest was the result all round.

Everybody thought of Giles; nobody thought of Marty. Had any of them looked in upon her during those moonlight nights which preceded the burial of her father they would have seen the girl absolutely alone in the house with the dead man. Her own chamber being nearest the stair-top, the coffin had been placed there for convenience; and at a certain hour of the night, when the moon arrived opposite the window, its beams streamed across the still profile of South, sublimed by the august presence of death, and onward a few feet further upon the face of his daughter, lying in her little bed in the silence of a repose almost as dignified as that of her companion – the repose of a guileless soul that had nothing more left on earth to lose, except a life which she did not over-value.

South was buried, and a week passed, and Winterborne watched for a reply from Mrs Charmond. Melbury was very sanguine as to its tenor; but Winterborne had not told him of the encounter with her carriage, when, if ever he had heard an affronted tone on a woman's lips, he had heard it on hers.

The postman's time for passing was just after Melbury's men had assembled in the spar-house; and Winterborne, who when not busy on his own account would lend assistance there, used to go out into the lane every morning and meet the postman at the end of one of the green rides through the hazel-copse, in the straight stretch of which his laden figure could be seen a long way off. Grace also was very anxious; more anxious than her father, more perhaps than Winterborne himself. This anxiety led her into the spar-house on some pretext or other almost every morning whilst they were awaiting the answer.

Eleven times had Winterborne gone to that corner of the ride, and looked up its long straight slope through the wet greys of winter dawn. But though the postman's bowed figure loomed in view pretty regularly, he brought nothing for Giles. On the twelfth day the man of missives, while yet in the extreme distance, held up his hand, and Winterborne saw a letter in it. He took it into the spar-house before he broke the seal, and those who were there gathered round him while he read, Grace looking in at the door.

The letter was not from Mrs Charmond herself, but from her agent at Sherton. Winterborne glanced it over and looked up.

'It's all over,' he said.

'Ah!' said they all together.

'Her lawyer is instructed to say that Mrs Charmond sees no reason for disturbing the natural course of things, particularly as she contemplates pulling the houses down,' he said quietly.

'Only think of that!' said several. 'Pulling down is always the game.'

Winterborne had turned away, and said vehemently to himself, 'Then let her pull 'em down, and be damned to her!'

Creedle looked at him with a face of seven sorrows, saying, 'Ah 'twas that sperrit that lost 'em for ye, maister!'

Winterborne subdued his feelings, and from that hour, whatever they were, kept them entirely to himself. Yet assuming the value of taciturnity to a man among strangers, it is apt to express more than talkativeness when he dwells among friends. The countryman who is obliged to judge the time of day from changes in external nature sees a thousand successive tints and traits in the landscape which are never discerned by him who hears the regular chime of a clock, because they are never in request. In like manner do we use our eyes on our taciturn comrade. The infinitesimal movement of muscle, curve, hair, and wrinkle, which when accompanied by a voice goes unregarded, is watched and translated in the lack of it, till virtually the whole surrounding circle of familiars is charged with the reserved one's moods and meanings.

So with Winterborne and his neighbours after his stroke of ill-luck. He held his tongue; and they observed him, and knew that he was discomposed.

Encountering Melbury one day his manner was that of a man who abandoned all claims. 'I am glad to meet 'ee, Mr Melbury,' he said in a low voice whose quality he endeavoured to make as practical as possible. 'I am afraid I shall not after this be able to keep that mare I bought for the use of – a possible wife, and as I don't care to sell her, I should like, if you don't object, to give her to Miss Melbury. The horse is very quiet, and would be quite safe for her.'

Mr Melbury was rather affected at this. 'You sha'n't hurt your pocket like that on our account, Giles. Grace shall have the horse, but I'll pay you what you gave for her, and any expense you may have been put to for her keep.'

He would not hear of any other terms, and thus it was arranged. They were now opposite Melbury's house, and the timber-merchant pressed Winterborne to enter, Grace being out of the way.

'Pull round the settle, Giles,' said the timber-merchant as soon as they were within. 'I should like to have a serious talk with you.'

Thereupon he put the case to Winterborne frankly, and in quite a friendly way. He declared that he did not like to be hard on a man when he was in difficulty; but he really did not see how Winterborne could marry his daughter now without even a house to take her to.

Giles quite acquiesced in the awkwardness of his situation, but from a momentary gasp of hope – a feeling that he would like to know Grace's mind from her own lips – he did not speak out positively even then. He accordingly departed somewhat abruptly, and went home to consider whether he would seek to bring about a meeting with her.

In the evening while he sat pondering he fancied that he heard a scraping on the wall outside his house. The boughs of a monthly rose which grew there made such a noise sometimes, but as no wind was stirring he knew that it could not be the rose-tree. He took up the candle and went out. Nobody was near. As he turned the light flickered on the whitewashed rough-cast of the front, and he saw words written thereon in charcoal, which he read as follows: –

> 'O Giles, you've lost your dwelling-place,
> And therefore, Giles, you'll lose your Grace.'

Giles went indoors. He had his suspicions as to the scrawler of those lines, but he could not be sure. What filled his heart far more than curiosity about their authorship was a terrible belief that they were turning out to be true, try to regain Grace as he might. They decided the question for him. He sat down and wrote a formal note to Melbury, stating that he shared to the full Melbury's view of his own and his daughter's promise made some years before; he wished that it should be considered as cancelled, and they themselves quite released from any obligation on account of it.

Having fastened up this their plenary absolution he determined to get it out of his hands and have done with it; to which end he went off to Melbury's at once. It was now so late that the family had all retired; he crept up to the house, thrust the note under the door, and stole away as silently as he had come.

Melbury himself was the first to rise the next morning, and when he had read the letter his relief was great, for he knew that Giles could have made matters unpleasant if he had chosen to work upon Grace. 'Very honourable of Giles, very honourable,' he kept saying to himself. 'I shall not forget him. Now to keep her up to her own true level.'

It happened that Grace went out for an early ramble that morning, and to go in her customary direction she could not avoid passing Winterborne's house. The morning sun was shining flat upon its white surface, and the words, which still remained, were immediately visible to her. She read them. Her face flushed to crimson. She could see Giles and Creedle talking together at the back; the charred spar-gad with which the lines had been written lay on the ground beneath the wall. Feeling pretty sure that Winterborne would observe her action she quickly went up to the wall, rubbed out 'lose' and inserted 'keep' in its stead. Then she made the best of her way home without looking behind her. Giles could draw an inference now if he chose.

There could not be the least doubt that gentle Grace was warming to more sympathy with, and interest in, Winterborne than ever she had done while he was her promised lover; that since his misfortune those social shortcomings of his, which contrasted so awkwardly with her later experiences of life, had become obscured by the generous revival of an old romantic attachment to him. Though mentally trained and tilled into foreignness of view, as compared with her youthful time, Grace was not an ambitious girl, and might, if left to herself, have declined upon Winterborne without much discontent. Her feelings just now were so far from latent that the writing on the wall had quickened her to an unusual rashness.

Having returned from her walk she sat at breakfast silently. When her stepmother had left the room she said to her father, 'I have made up my mind that I should like my engagement to Giles to continue.'

Melbury looked much surprised.

'Nonsense,' he said sharply. 'You don't know what you are talking about. Look here.'

He handed across to her the letter received from Giles.

She read it and said no more. Could he have seen her write on the wall? She did not know. Fate, it seemed, would have it this way, and there was nothing to do but to acquiesce.

It was a few hours after this that Winterborne, who, curiously enough, had *not* perceived Grace writing, was clearing away the tree from the front of South's late dwelling. He saw Marty standing in her doorway, a slim figure in meagre black, almost without womanly contours as yet. He went up to her and said:

'Marty, why did you write that on my wall last night? It was you, you know.'

'Because it was the truth.'

'Having prophesied one thing, why did you alter it to another? Your predictions can't be worth much.'

'I have not altered it.'

'But you have.'

'No.'

'It is altered. Go and see.'

She went, and read that in spite of losing his dwelling-place he would *keep* his Grace. Marty came back surprised.

'Well,' she said. 'Who can have made such nonsense of it?'

'Who indeed?' said he.

'I have rubbed it all out, as the point of it is quite gone.'

'You'd no business to rub it out; I meant to let it stay a little longer.'

'Some idle boy altered it, no doubt,' she murmured.

As this seemed very probable Winterborne said no more, and dismissed the matter from his mind.

From this day of his life onward for a considerable time Winterborne, though not absolutely out of his house as yet, retired into the background of human life and action thereabout – a feat not particularly difficult of performance anywhere when the doer has the assistance of a lost prestige. Grace, thinking that Winterborne saw her write, made no further sign, and the frail barque of fidelity that she had thus timidly launched was stranded and lost.

CHAPTER 16

Dr Fitzpiers lived on the slope of the hill, in a house of much less pretension both as to architecture and as to magnitude than the timber-merchant's. The latter had without doubt been once the manorial residence appertaining to the snug and modest domain of Little Hintock, of which the boundaries were now lost by its absorption into the adjoining estate of Mrs Charmond. Though the Melburys themselves were unaware of the fact there was every reason to believe – at least so the parson said – that the owners of that little manor had been Melbury's own ancestors, the family name occurring in numerous documents relating to transfers of land about the time of the civil wars.

Mr Fitzpiers's dwelling, on the contrary, was small, box-like, and comparatively modern. It had been occupied, and was in part occupied still, by a retired farmer and his wife, who, on the surgeon's arrival in quest of a home, had accommodated him by receding from their front rooms into the kitchen quarter, whence they administered to his wants, and emerged at regular intervals to receive from him a not unwelcome addition to their income.

The cottage and its garden were so regular in their plan that they might have been laid out by a Dutch designer of the time of William and Mary. In a low, dense hedge was a door, over which the hedge formed an arch, and from the inside of the door a straight path, bordered with clipped box, ran up the slope of the garden to the porch, which was exactly in the middle of the house-front, with two windows on each side.

Right and left of the path were first a bed of gooseberry-bushes; next of currant; next of raspberry; next of strawberry; next of old-fashioned flowers; at the corners opposite the porch being spheres of box resembling a pair of school globes. Over the roof of the house could be seen the orchard on yet higher ground, and behind the orchard the forest-trees, reaching up to the crest of the hill.

Opposite the garden door into the lane, and visible from the parlour window, was a swing-gate leading to a field, across which there ran a footpath. The swing-gate had just been repainted, and on one fine afternoon, before the paint was dry, and while gnats stuck dying thereon, the surgeon was standing in his room abstractedly looking out at an occasional pedestrian who passed along that route. Being of a philosophical stamp he perceived that the character of each of these travellers exhibited itself in a somewhat amusing manner by his or her method of handling the gate.

In the men there was not much variety: they gave the gate a kick and passed through. The women were more contrasting. To them the sticky woodwork was a barricade, a disgust, a menace, a treachery, as the case might be.

The first that he noticed was a bouncing young woman with her skirts tucked up and her hair wild. Fitzpiers knew her as Suke Damson. She grasped the gate without looking, giving it a supplementary push with her shoulder, when the white imprint drew from her an exclamation in language not too refined. She went to the green bank and sat down and rubbed herself in the grass, cursing the while.

'Ha! ha! ha!' laughed the doctor.

The next was a girl with her hair cropped short, in whom the surgeon recognized the daughter of his late patient, the woodman South. Moreover, a black gown that she wore by way of mourning unpleasantly reminded him that he had ordered a tree-felling which had caused her parent's death. She walked in thought, and not recklessly; but her preoccupation led her to grasp without suspicion the bar of the gate, and touch it with her arm. Fitzpiers felt sorry that she should have soiled that new black frock, poor as it was, for it was probably her only one. She looked at her hand and arm, seemed but little surprised, wiped off the disfigurement with an unmoved face and as if without abandoning her original thoughts. Thus she went on her way.

Then there came over the green quite a different sort of personage. She walked as delicately as if she had been bred in town, and as firmly as if she had been bred in the country; she seemed one who dimly knew her appearance to be attractive, but who retained some of the charm of ignorance by forgetting self in a general pensiveness. She approached the gate.

To let such a creature touch it even with the tip of her glove was to Fitzpiers almost like letting her proceed to tragical self-destruction. He jumped up and looked for his hat, but was unable to find the right one; glancing again out of the window he saw that his assistance was unnecessary. Having come up she looked at the gate, picked up a little stick, and using it as a bayonet pushed open the obstacle without touching it at all.

He steadily watched her out of sight, recognizing her as the very young lady whom he had seen once before and been unable to identify. Whose could that emotional face be? All the others he had seen in Hintock as yet oppressed him with their crude rusticity; the contrast offered by this suggested that she hailed from elsewhere.

Precisely these thoughts had occurred to him at the first time of seeing her; but he now went a little further with them, and considered that as there had been no carriage lately in that spot she could not have come a very long distance. She must be somebody staying at Hintock House – probably Mrs Charmond, of whom he had heard so much; and this probability was sufficient to set a mild radiance in the surgeon's somewhat dull sky.

Fitzpiers sat down to the book he had been perusing. It happened to be that of a German metaphysician, for the doctor was not a practical man, except by fits, and much preferred the ideal world to the real, and the discovery of principles to their application. The young lady remained in his thoughts. He might have followed her; but he was not constitutionally active, and preferred a conjectural pursuit. However, when he went out for a ramble just before dusk he insensibly took the direction of Hintock House, which was the way Grace had been walking, her mind having run on Mrs Charmond that day; though Grace had returned long since by another route.

Fitzpiers reached the edge of the glen overlooking the manor-house. The shutters were shut, and only one chimney smoked. The mere aspect of the place was enough to inform him that Mrs Charmond had gone away, and that nobody else was staying there. Fitzpiers felt a vague disappointment that the young lady was not Mrs Charmond; and without pausing longer to gaze at a carcase from which the spirit had flown he bent his steps homeward.

Later in the evening Fitzpiers was summoned to visit a cottage-patient about five miles distant. Like the majority of young practitioners in his vicinity he was far from having assumed the dignity of being driven his rounds by a servant in a brougham that flashed the sunlight like a mirror; his way of getting about was by means of a gig which he drove himself, hitching the rein of the horse to the gate-post, shutter-hook, or garden-paling of the domicile under visitation, or giving pennies to little boys to hold the animal during his stay – pennies which were well earned when the cases to be attended were of a certain cheerful kind that wore out the patience of the little boys.

On this account of travelling alone the night-journeys which Fitzpiers had frequently to take were dismal enough, an apparent perversity in nature ruling that whenever there was to be a birth in a particularly inaccessible and lonely place that event should occur in the night. The surgeon, having been of late years a town man, hated the solitary midnight woodland. He was not altogether skilful with the reins, and it often occurred to his mind that if in some remote depths of the trees an accident were to happen, his being alone might be the death of him. Hence he made a practice of picking up any countryman or lad whom he chanced to pass by, and under the disguise of treating him to a nice drive obtained his companionship on the journey, and his convenient assistance in opening gates.

The doctor had started on his way out of the village on the night in question when the light of his lamps fell upon the musing form of Winterborne, walking leisurely along as if he had no object in life. Winterborne was a better class of companion than the doctor usually could get, and he at once pulled up and asked him if he would like a drive through the wood that fine night.

Giles seemed rather surprised at the doctor's friendliness, but said that he had no objection, and accordingly mounted beside Mr Fitzpiers.

They drove along under the black boughs which formed a tracery upon the stars. Looking up as they passed under a horizontal limb they sometimes saw objects like large tadpoles lodged diametrically across it, which Giles explained to be pheasants at roost; and they sometimes heard the report of a gun, which reminded him that others knew what those tadpole shapes represented as well as he.

Presently the doctor said what he had been going to say for some time:

'Is there a young lady staying in this neighbourhood – a very attractive girl – with a little white boa round her neck, and white fur round her gloves?'

Winterborne, of course, knew in a moment that Grace, whom he had caught the doctor peering at, was represented by these accessories. With a wary grimness induced by the circumstances he evaded an answer by saying, 'I saw a young lady talking to Mrs Charmond the other day; perhaps it was she.'

'It might have been,' said Fitzpiers. 'She is quite a gentlewoman – the one I mean. She cannot be a permanent resident in Hintock, or I should have seen her before. Nor does she look like one.'

'She is not staying at Hintock House?'

'No; it is closed.'

'Then perhaps she is staying at one of the cottages, or farmhouses?'

'O no – you mistake. She was a different sort of woman altogether.' As Giles was nobody Fitzpiers treated him accordingly, and rhapsodized to the night in continuation:

'She moved upon this earth a shape of brightness,
A power, that from its object scarcely drew
One impulse of her being – in her lightness
Most like some radiant cloud of morning dew
Which wanders through the waste air's pathless blue
To nourish some far desert: she did seem
Beside me, gathering beauty as she grew,
Like the bright shade of some immortal dream
Which walks, when tempest sleeps, the wave of life's dark stream.'

The charm of the lines seemed to Winterborne to be somehow the result of his lost love's charms upon Fitzpiers.

'You seem to be mightily in love with her, sir,' he said, with a sensation of heart-sickness, and more than ever resolved not to mention Grace by name.

'O no – I am not that, Winterborne; people living insulated, as I do by the solitude of this place, get charged with emotive fluid like a Leyden jar with electric, for want of some conductor at hand to disperse it. Human love is a subjective thing – the essence itself of man, as that great thinker Spinoza says – *ipsa hominis essentia* – it is joy accompanied by an idea which we project against any suitable object in the line of our vision, just as the rainbow iris is projected against an oak, ash, or elm tree indifferently. So that if any other young lady had appeared instead of the one who did appear, I should have felt just the same interest in her, and have quoted precisely the same lines from Shelley about her, as about this one I saw. Such miserable creatures of circumstance are we all!'

'Well, it is what we call being in love down in these parts, whether or no,' said Winterborne.

'You are right enough if you admit that I am in love with something in my own head, and no thing-in-itself outside it at all.'

'Is it part of a country doctor's duties to learn that view of things, may I ask, sir?' said Winterborne, adopting the Socratic *εἰρωνεία* with such well-assumed simplicity that Fitzpiers answered readily –

'O no. The real truth is, Winterborne, that medical practice in places like this is a very rule of thumb matter: a bottle of bitter stuff for this and that old woman – the bitterer the better – compounded from a few simple stereotyped prescriptions; occasional attendance at births, where mere presence is almost sufficient, so healthy and strong are the people; and a lance for an abscess now and then. Investigation and experiment cannot be carried on without more appliances than one has here – though I have attempted a little.'

Giles did not enter into this view of the case; what he had been struck with was the curious parallelism between Mr Fitzpiers's manner and Grace's, as shown by the fact of both of them straying into a subject of discourse so engrossing to themselves that it made them forget it was foreign to him.

Nothing further passed between himself and the doctor in relation to Grace till they were on their way back. They had stopped at a wayside inn for a glass of brandy-and-cider hot, and when they were again in motion Fitzpiers, possibly a little warmed by the liquor, resumed the subject by saying, 'I should like very much to know who that young lady was.'

'What difference can it make, if she's only the tree your rainbow falls on?'

'Ha, ha! True.'

'You have no wife, sir?'

'I have no wife; and no idea of one. I hope to do better things than marry and settle in Hintock. Not but that it is well for a medical man to be married; and sometimes, begad, 'twould be pleasant enough in this place, with the wind roaring round the house, and the rain and the boughs beating against it. I hear that you lost your lifeholds by the death of South?'

'I did. I lost by that in more ways than one.'

They had reached the top of Hintock Lane or Street, if it could be called such where three-quarters of the roadside consisted of copse and orchard. One of the first houses to be passed was Melbury's. A light was shining from a bedroom window facing lengthwise of the lane. Winterborne glanced at it, and saw what was coming. He had withheld an answer to the doctor's inquiry, to hinder his knowledge of Grace. But 'who hath gathered the wind in his fists? who hath bound the waters in a garment?' – he could not hinder what was doomed to arrive, and might just as well have been outspoken. As they came up to the house Grace's figure was distinctly visible, drawing the two white curtains together which were used here instead of blinds.

'Why, there she is!' said Fitzpiers. 'How in the name of Heaven does she come there?'

'In the most natural way in the world. It is her home. Mr Melbury is her father.'

'Indeed – indeed – indeed! How comes he to have a daughter of that sort?'

Winterborne laughed coldly. 'Won't money do anything,' he said, 'if you've promising material to work upon? Why shouldn't a Hintock girl, taken early from home and put under proper instruction, become as finished as any other young lady if she's got brains and good looks to begin with?'

'No reason at all why she shouldn't,' murmured the surgeon with reflective disappointment. 'Only I didn't anticipate quite that kind of origin for her.'

'And you think an inch or two less of her now.' There was a little tremor in Winterborne's voice as he spoke.

'Well,' said the doctor with recovered warmth, 'I am not so sure that I think less of her. At first it was a sort of blow; but, dammy, I'll stick up for her. She's charming, every inch of her!'

'So she is,' said Winterborne. . . . 'But not for me!'

From this ambiguous expression of the reticent woodlander Dr Fitzpiers inferred that Giles disliked Miss Melbury, possibly for some haughtiness in her bearing towards him, and had, on that account, withheld her name. The supposition did not tend to diminish his admiration for her.

CHAPTER 17

GRACE'S exhibition of herself in the act of pulling-to the window curtains had been the result of an unfortunate incident in the house that day – nothing less than the illness of Grammer Oliver, a woman who had never, till now, lain down for such a reason in her life. Like others to whom an unbroken career of health has made the idea of keeping their bed almost as repugnant as death itself, she had continued on foot till she literally fell on the floor; and though she had, as yet, been scarcely a day off duty, she had sickened into quite a different personage from the independent Grammer of the yard and spar-house. Ill as she was, on one point she was firm. On no account would she see a doctor; in other words, Fitzpiers.

The room in which Grace had been discerned was not her own but the old woman's. On the girl's way to bed she had received a message from Grammer to the effect that she would much like to speak to her that night.

Grace entered and set the candle on a low chair beside the bed, so that the profile of Grammer, as she lay, cast itself in a coal-black shadow upon the whitened wall, her large head being still further magnified by an enormous turban, which was really her petticoat wound in a wreath round her temples. Grace put the room a little in order, and approaching the sick woman said –

'I am come, Grammer, as you wish. Do let us send for the doctor before it gets later?'

' 'Ch woll not have him!' said Grammer Oliver decisively.

'Then somebody to sit up with you?'

'Can't abear it! No. I wanted to see you, Miss Grace, because 'ch have something on my mind. Dear Miss Grace, *I took that money of the doctor, after all!*'

'What money?'

'The ten pounds.'

Grace did not quite understand.

'The ten pounds er offered me for my head, because I've a large organ of brain. I signed a paper when I took the money, not feeling concerned about it at all. I have not liked to tell 'ee that it was really settled with him, because you showed such horror at the notion. Well, having thought it over more at length, I wish I hadn't done it; and it weighs upon my mind. John South's death of fear about the tree makes me think I shall die of this. . . . 'Ch have been going to ask him again to let me off, but I hadn't the face.'

'Why?'

'I've spent some of the money – more'n two pounds o't! It do wherrit me terribly; and I shall die o' the thought of that paper I signed with my holy cross, as South died of his trouble!'

'If you ask him to burn the paper he will, I'm sure, and think no more of it.'

''Ch have done it once already, miss. But er laughed cruel-like. "Yours is such a fine brain, Grammer," er said, "that science couldn't afford to lose you. Besides, you've taken my money." . . . Don't let your father know of this, please, on no account whatever!'

'No, no. I will let you have the money to return to him.'

Grammer rolled the head in question negatively upon the pillow. 'Even if I should be well enough to take it to him he won't like it. Though why he should so particular want to look into the works of a poor old woman's headpiece like mine, when there's so many other folks about, I don't know. I know how he'll answer me: "A lonely person like you, Grammer," er woll say; "what difference is it to you what becomes of 'ee when the breath's out of your body?" O, it do trouble me! If you only knew how he do chevy me round the chimmer in my dreams you'd pity me. How I could do it I can't think! But 'ch was always so rackless! . . . If I only had anybody to plead for me!'

'Mrs Melbury would, I am sure.'

'Ay; but he wouldn't hearken to she! It wants a younger face than hers to work upon such as he.'

Grace started with comprehension. 'You don't think he would do it for me?' she said.

'O, wouldn't he!'

'I couldn't go to him, Grammer, on any account. I don't know him at all.'

'Ah, if I were a young lady,' said the artful Grammer, 'and could save a poor old woman's skellington from a heathen's chopper, to rest in a Christian grave, I would do it, and be glad to. But nobody will do anything for a poor old woman but push her out of the way!'

'You are very ungrateful, Grammer, to say that. But you are ill, I know, and that's why you speak so. Now believe me, you are not going to die yet. Remember you told me yourself that you meant to keep him waiting many a year.'

'Ay, one can joke when one is well, even in old age; but in sickness one's gaiety falters; and that which seemed small looks large; and the far-off seems near.'

Grace's eyes had tears in them. 'I don't like to go to him on such an errand, Grammer,' she said. 'But I will, if I must, to ease your mind!'

It was with extreme reluctance that Grace cloaked herself next morning for the undertaking. She was all the more indisposed to the journey by reason of Grammer's allusion to the effect of a pretty face upon Dr Fitzpiers; and hence she most illogically did that which, had the doctor never seen her, would have operated to stultify the sole motive of her journey; that is to say, she put on a woollen veil which hid all her face except an occasional spark of her eyes.

Her own wish that nothing should be known of this strange and gruesome proceeding, no less than Grammer Oliver's own desire, led Grace to take every precaution against being discovered. She went out by the garden-door as the safest way, all the household having occupations at the other side. The morning looked forbidding enough when she stealthily edged forth. The battle between snow and thaw was continuing in mid-air: the trees dripped on the garden plots where no vegetables would grow for the dripping, though they were planted year after year with that curious mechanical regularity of country people in the face of hopelessness; the moss which covered the once broad gravel terrace was swamped; and Grace stood irresolute. Then she thought of poor Grammer, and her dreams of the doctor running after her, scalpel in hand, and the possibility of a case so curiously similar to South's ending in the same way; thereupon she stepped out into the drizzle.

The nature of her errand, and Grammer Oliver's account of the post-mortem compact she had made, lent a fascinating horror to Grace's conception of Fitzpiers. She knew that he was a young man; but her single object in seeking an interview with him put all considerations of his age and social aspect from her mind. Standing as she stood in Grammer Oliver's shoes, he was simply a remorseless Jehovah of the sciences, who would not have mercy, and would have sacrifice; a man whom, save for this, she would have preferred to avoid knowing. But since, in such a small village, it was improbable that any long time could pass without their meeting, there was not much to deplore in her having to meet him now.

But, as need hardly be said, Miss Melbury's view of the doctor as a merciless, unwavering, irresistible scientist was not quite in accordance with fact. The real Dr Fitzpiers was a man of too many hobbies to show likelihood of rising to any great eminence in the profession he had chosen, or even to acquire any wide practice in the rural district he had marked out as his field of survey for the present. In the course of a year his mind was accustomed to pass in a grand solar sweep throughout the zodiac of the intellectual heaven. Sometimes it was in the Ram, sometimes in the Bull; one month he would be immersed in alchemy, another in poesy; one month in the Twins of astrology and astronomy; then in the Crab of German literature and metaphysics. In justice to him it must be stated that he took such studies as were immediately related to his own profession in turn with the rest, and it had been in a month of anatomical ardour without the possibility of a subject that he had proposed to Grammer Oliver the terms she had mentioned to her mistress.

As may be inferred from the tone of his conversation with Winterborne he had lately plunged into abstract philosophy with much zest; perhaps his keenly appreciative, modern, unpractical mind found this a realm more in his taste than any other. Though his aims were desultory Fitzpiers's mental constitution was not without its creditable side; a real inquirer he honestly was at times; even if the midnight rays of his lamp, visible so far through the trees of Hintock, lighted rank literatures of emotion and passion as often as, or oftener than, the books and *matériel* of science.

But whether he meditated the Muses or the philosophers, the loneliness of Hintock life was beginning to tell upon his impressionable nature. Winter in a solitary house in the country, without society, is tolerable, nay, even enjoyable and delightful, given certain conditions; but these are not the conditions which attach to the life of a professional man who drops down into such a place by mere accident. They were present to the lives of Winterborne, Melbury, and Grace; but not to the doctor's. They are old association – an almost exhaustive biographical or historical acquaintance with every object, animate and inanimate, within the observer's horizon. He must know all about those invisible ones of the days gone by, whose feet have traversed the fields which look so grey from his windows; recall whose creaking plough has turned those sods from time to time; whose hands planted the trees that form a crest to the opposite hill; whose horses and hounds have torn through that underwood; what birds affect that particular brake; what bygone domestic dramas of love, jealousy, revenge, or disappointment have been enacted in the cottages, the mansion, the street or on the green. The spot may have beauty, grandeur, salubrity, convenience; but if it lack memories it will ultimately pall upon him who settles there without opportunity of intercourse with his kind.

In such circumstances, maybe, an old man dreams of an ideal friend, till he throws himself into the arms of any imposter who chooses to wear that title on his face. A young man may dream of an ideal friend likewise, but some humour of the blood will probably lead him to think rather of an ideal mistress, and at length the rustle of a woman's dress, the sound of her voice, or the transit of her form across the field of his vision, will enkindle his soul with a flame that blinds his eyes.

The discovery of the attractive Grace's name and family would have been enough in other circumstances to lead the doctor, if not to put her personality out of his head, to change the character of his interest in her. Instead of treasuring her image as a rarity he would at most have played with her as a toy. He was that kind of man. But situated here he could not go so far as amative cruelty. He dismissed all deferential thought about her, but he could not help taking her somewhat seriously.

He went on to imagine the impossible. So far, indeed, did he go in this futile direction that, as others are wont to do, he constructed dialogues and scenes in which Grace had turned out to be the mistress of Hintock manor-house, the mysterious Mrs Charmond, particularly ready and willing to be wooed by himself and nobody else.

'Well, she isn't that,' he said finally. 'But she's a very sweet, nice, exceptional girl.'

The next morning he breakfasted alone as usual. It was snowing with a fine-flaked desultoriness just sufficient to make the woodland grey without ever achieving whiteness. There was not a single letter for Fitzpiers, only a medical circular and a weekly newspaper.

To sit before a large fire on such mornings and read, and gradually acquire energy till the evening came, and then, with lamp alight and feeling full of vigour, to pursue some engrossing subject or other till the small hours, had hitherto been his practice since arriving here. But to-day he could not settle into his chair. That self-contained position he had lately occupied, in which his whole attention was given to objects of the inner eye, all outer regard being quite disdainful, seemed to have been taken by insidious stratagem, and for the first time he had an interest without the house. He walked from one window to another, and became aware that the most irksome of solitudes is not the solitude of remoteness, but that which is just outside desirable company.

The breakfast hour went by heavily enough, and the next followed in the same half-snowy, half-rainy style, the weather now being the inevitable relapse which sooner or later succeeds a time too radiant for the season, such as they had enjoyed in the late mid-winter at Hintock. To people at home there these changeful tricks had their interests; the strange mistakes that some of the more sanguine trees had made in budding before their month, to be incontinently glued up by frozen thawings now; the similar sanguine errors of impulsive birds in framing nests that were swamped by snow-water, and other such incidents, prevented any sense of wearisomeness in the minds of the natives. But these were features of a world not familiar to Fitzpiers, and the inner visions to which he had almost exclusively attended having suddenly failed in their power to absorb him, he felt unutterably dreary.

He wondered how long Miss Melbury was going to stay in Hintock. The season was unpropitious for accidental encounters with her out of doors, and except by accident he saw not how they were to become acquainted. One thing was clear – any acquaintance with her could only, with a due regard to his future, be casual, at most of the nature of a mild flirtation; for he had high aims, and they would some day lead him into other spheres than this.

Thus desultorily thinking he flung himself down upon the couch, which, as in many draughty old country houses, was a hood, being in fact a legitimate development from the settle.

He tried to read as he reclined, but having sat up till three o'clock that morning the book slipped from his hand and he fell asleep.

CHAPTER 18

GRACE approached the house. Her knock, always soft in virtue of her nature, was softer to-day by reason of her strange errand. However, it was heard by the farmer's wife who kept the house, and Grace was admitted. Opening the door of the doctor's room the housewife glanced in, and imagining Fitzpiers absent asked Miss Melbury to enter and wait a few minutes whilst she should go and find him, believing him to be somewhere on the premises. Grace acquiesced, went in, and sat down close to the door.

As soon as the door was shut upon her she looked round the room, and started at perceiving a handsome man snugly ensconced on the couch, like a recumbent figure within some canopied mural tomb of the fifteenth century, except that his hands were not exactly clasped in prayer. She had no doubt that this was the surgeon.

Awaken him herself she could not, and her immediate impulse was to go and pull the broad riband with a brass rosette which hung at one side of the fireplace. But expecting the landlady to re-enter in a moment she abandoned this intention, and stood gazing in great embarrassment at the reclining philosopher.

The windows of Fitzpiers's soul being at present shuttered he probably appeared less impressive than in his hours of animation; but the light abstracted from his material features by sleep was more than counterbalanced by the mysterious influence of that state, in a stranger, upon the consciousness of a beholder so sensitive. So far as she could criticize at all she became aware that she had encountered a specimen of creation altogether unusual in that locality. The occasions on which Grace had observed men of this stamp were when she had been far away from Hintock, and even then such examples as had met her eye were at a distance, and mainly of commoner fibre than the one who now confronted her.

She nervously wondered why the woman had not discovered her mistake and returned, and went again towards the bell-pull. Approaching the chimney her back was to Fitzpiers, but she could see him in the glass. An indescribable thrill passed through her as she perceived that the eyes of the reflected image were open gazing wonderingly at her. Under the curious unexpectedness of the sight she became as if spell-bound, almost powerless to turn her head and regard the original. However, by an effort she did turn, when there he lay asleep the same as before.

Her startled perplexity as to what he could be meaning was sufficient to lead her to abandon her errand precipitately. She crossed quickly to the door, opened and closed it noiselessly, and went out of the house unobserved. By the time that she had gone down the path and through the garden-door into the lane she had recovered her equanimity. Here, screened by the hedge, she stood and considered a while.

Drip, drip, drip, fell the rain upon her umbrella and around; she had come out on such a morning because of the seriousness of the matter in hand; yet now she had allowed her mission to be stultified by a momentary tremulousness concerning an incident which perhaps had meant nothing after all.

In the meantime her departure from the room, stealthy as it had been, had roused Fitzpiers; and he sat up. In the reflection from the mirror which Grace had beheld there was no mystery; he had opened his eyes for a few moments, but had immediately relapsed into unconsciousness, if indeed he had ever been positively awake. That somebody had just left the room he was certain, and that the lovely form which seemed to have visited him in a dream was no less than the real presentation of the person departed he could hardly doubt.

Looking out of the window a few minutes later, down the box-edged gravel-path which led to the bottom, he saw the garden-door open and through it enter the young girl of his thoughts, Grace having just at this juncture determined to return and attempt the interview a second time. That he saw her coming instead of going made him ask himself if his first impression of her were not a dream indeed. She came hesitatingly along, carrying her umbrella so low over her head that he could hardly see her face. When she reached the point where the raspberry-bushes ended and the strawberry-bed began she made a little pause.

Fitzpiers feared that she might not be coming to him even now, and hastily quitting the room he ran down the path to meet her. The nature of her errand he could not divine, but he was prepared to give her any amount of encouragement.

'I beg pardon, Miss Melbury,' he said. 'I saw you from the window, and fancied you might imagine that I was not at home – if it is I you were coming for?'

'I was coming to speak one word to you, nothing more,' she replied. 'And I can say it here.'

'No, no. Please do come in. Well then, if you will not come into the house, come so far as the porch!'

Thus pressed she went on to the porch, and they stood together inside it, Fitzpiers closing her umbrella for her.

'I have merely a request or petition to make,' she said. 'My father's servant is ill – a woman you know – and her illness is serious.'

'I am sorry to hear it. I will come and see her at once.'

'But I particularly wish you not to come.'

'O indeed.'

'Yes; and she wishes the same. It would make her seriously worse if you were to come. It would almost kill her. . . . My errand is of a peculiar and awkward nature. It is concerning a subject which weighs on her mind – that unfortunate arrangement she made with you, that you might have her skull after death.'

'O, Grammer Oliver, the old woman with the fine head. Seriously ill, is she?'

'And *so* disturbed by her rash compact! I have brought the money back – will you please return to her the agreement she signed?' Grace held out to him a couple of five-pound notes which she had kept ready tucked in her glove.

Without replying or considering the notes Fitzpiers allowed his thoughts to follow his eyes and dwell upon Grace's personality, and the sudden close relation in which he stood to her. The porch was narrow; the rain increased. It ran off the porch and dripped on the creepers, and from the creepers upon the edge of Grace's cloak and skirts.

'The rain is wetting your dress; please do come in,' he said. 'It really makes my heart ache to let you stay here.'

Immediately inside the front door was the door of his sitting-room; he flung it open, and stood in a coaxing attitude. Try how she would Grace could not resist the supplicatory mandate written in the face and manner of this man, and distressful resignation sat on her as she glided past him into the room – brushing his coat with her elbow because of the narrowness.

He followed her, shut the door – which she somehow had hoped he would leave open – and placing a chair for her sat down.

The concern which Grace felt at the development of these commonplace incidents was, of course, mainly owing to the strange effect upon her nerves of that view of him in the mirror gazing at her with open eyes when she had thought him sleeping, which made her fancy that his slumber might have been a feint based on inexplicable reasons.

She again proffered the notes; he awoke from looking at her as at a piece of live statuary and listened deferentially as she said, 'Will you then reconsider, and cancel the bond which poor Grammer Oliver so foolishly gave?'

'I'll cancel it without reconsideration. Though you will allow me to have my own opinion about her foolishness. Grammer is a very wise woman, and she was as wise in that as in other things. You think there was something very fiendish in the compact, do you not, Miss Melbury? But remember that the most eminent of our surgeons in past times have entered into such agreements.'

'Not fiendish – strange.'

'Yes, that may be, since strangeness is not in the nature of a thing, but in its relation to something extrinsic – in this case an unessential observer.'

He went to his desk, and searching a while found a paper which he unfolded and brought to her. A thick cross appeared in ink at the bottom – evidently from the hand of Grammer. Grace put the paper in her pocket with a look of much relief.

As Fitzpiers did not take up the money (half of which had come from Grace's own purse) she pushed it a little nearer to him. 'No, no. I shall not take it from the old woman,' he said. 'It is more strange than the fact of a surgeon arranging to obtain a subject for dissection that our acquaintance should be formed out of it.'

'I am afraid you think me uncivil in showing my dislike to the notion. But I did not mean to be.'

'O no, no.'

He looked at her, as he had done before, with puzzled interest. 'I cannot think, I cannot think,' he murmured. 'Something bewilders me greatly.' He still reflected and hesitated. 'Last night I sat up very late,' he at last went on, 'and on that account I fell into a little nap on that couch about half-an-hour ago. And during my few minutes of unconsciousness I dreamt – what do you think? – that you stood in the room.'

Should she tell? She merely blushed.

'You may imagine,' Fitzpiers continued, now persuaded that it had indeed been a dream, 'that I should not have dreamt of you without considerable thinking about you first.'

He could not be acting; of that she felt assured.

'I fancied in my vision that you stood there,' he said, pointing to where she had paused. 'I did not see you directly, but reflected in the glass. I thought, what a lovely creature! The design is for once carried out. Nature has at last recovered her lost union with the Idea! My thoughts ran in that direction because I had been reading the work of a transcendental philosopher last night; and I dare say it was the dose of Idealism that I received from it that made me scarcely able to distinguish between reality and fancy. I almost wept when I awoke, and found that you had appeared to me in Time, but not in Space, alas!'

At moments there was something theatrical in the delivery of Fitzpiers's effusion; yet it would have been inexact to say that it was intrinsically theatrical. It often happens that in situations of unrestraint, where there is no thought of the eye of criticism, real feeling glides into a mode of manifestation not easily distinguishable from rodomontade. A veneer of affectation overlies a bulk of truth, with the evil consequence, if perceived, that the substance is estimated by the superficies, and the whole rejected.

Grace, however, was no specialist in men's manners, and she admired the sentiment without thinking of the form. And she was embarrassed; 'lovely creature' made explanation awkward to her gentle modesty.

'But can it be,' said he suddenly, 'that you really were here?'

'I have to confess that I have been in the room once before,' faltered she. 'The woman showed me in, and went away to fetch you; but as she did not return, I left.'

'And you saw me asleep,' he murmured, with the faintest show of humiliation.

'Yes – *if* you were asleep, and did not deceive me.'

'Why do you say if?'

'I saw your eyes open in the glass, but as they were closed when I looked round upon you I thought you were perhaps deceiving me.'

'Never,' said Fitzpiers fervently. 'Never could I deceive you.'

Foreknowledge to the distance of a year or so, in either of them, might have spoilt the effect of that pretty speech. Never deceive her! But they knew nothing, and the phrase had its day.

Grace began now to be anxious to terminate the interview, but the compelling power of Fitzpiers's atmosphere still held her there. She was like an inexperienced actress who, having at last taken up her position on the boards and spoken her speeches, does not know how to move off. The thought of Grammer occurred to her. 'I'll go at once and tell poor Grammer of your generosity,' she said. 'It will relieve her at once.'

'Grammer's is a nervous disease, too – how singular,' he answered, accompanying her to the door. 'One moment: look at this – it is something which may interest you.'

He had thrown open the door on the other side of the passage, and she saw a microscope on the table of the confronting room. 'Look into it, please; you'll be interested,' he repeated.

She applied her eye, and saw the usual circle of light patterned all over with a cellular tissue of some indescribable sort. 'What do you think that is?' said Fitzpiers.

She did not know.

'That's a fragment of old John South's brain, which I am investigating.'

She started back, not exactly with aversion, but with wonder as to how it should have got there. Fitzpiers laughed.

'Here am I,' he said, 'endeavouring to carry on simultaneously the study of physiology and transcendental philosophy, the material world and the ideal, so as to discover if possible a point of contact between them; and your finer sense is quite offended!'

'O no, Mr Fitzpiers,' said Grace earnestly; 'it is not so at all. I know from seeing your light at night how deeply you meditate and work. Instead of condemning you for your studies I admire you very much!'

Her face, upturned from the microscope, was so sweet, sincere, and self-forgetful in its aspect that the susceptible

Fitzpiers more than wished to annihilate the lineal yard which separated it from his own. Whether anything of the kind showed in his eyes or not, Grace remained no longer at the microscope, but quickly went her way into the falling mixture of rain and snow.

CHAPTER 19

INSTEAD of resuming his investigation of South's brain Fitzpiers reclined and ruminated on the interview. Grace's curious susceptibility to his presence – though it was as if the currents of her life were disturbed rather than attracted by him – added a special interest to her general charm.

Fitzpiers was in a distinct degree scientific, being ready and zealous to interrogate all physical manifestations; but primarily he was an idealist. He believed that behind the imperfect lay the perfect; that rare things were to be discovered amidst a bulk of commonplace; that results in a new and untried case might be different from those in other cases where the material conditions had been precisely similar. Regarding his own personality as one of unbounded possibilities, because it was his own (notwithstanding that the factors of his life had worked out a sorry product for thousands), he saw a grand speciality in his discovery at Hintock of an altogether exceptional being of the other sex.

One habit of Fitzpiers, commoner in dreamers of more advanced age than in men of his years, was that of talking to himself. He paced round his room with a selective tread upon the more prominent blooms of the carpet and murmured: 'This phenomenal girl will be the light of my life while I am at Hintock; and the special beauty of the situation is that our attitude and relations to each other will be purely casual. Socially we can never be intimate. Anything like matrimonial intentions towards her, charming as she is, would be absurd. They would spoil the recreative character of such acquaintance. And, indeed, I have other aims on the practical side of my life.'

Fitzpiers bestowed a regulation thought on the advantageous marriage he was bound to make with a woman of family as good as his own, and of purse much longer. But as an object of contemplation for the present Grace Melbury would serve to keep his soul alive, and to relieve the monotony of his days.

His first lax notion (acquired from the mere sight of her without converse) – that of a vulgar intimacy with a timber-merchant's pretty daughter, grated painfully upon him now that he had found what Grace intrinsically was. Personal intercourse with such as she could take no lower form than seemly communion, mutual explorations of the world of fancy. Since he could not call at her father's, having no practical views, cursory encounters in the lane, in the wood, coming and going to and from church, or in passing her dwelling, were what the acquaintance would have to feed on.

Such anticipated glimpses of her realized themselves in the event. Rencounters of not more than a minute's duration, frequently repeated, will build up mutual interest, even warm confidence, in a lonely place. Theirs grew as imperceptibly as the twigs budded on the trees. There never was a particular moment at which it could be said they became friends; yet a delicate understanding now existed between two who in the winter had been strangers.

Spring weather came on rather suddenly, the unsealing of buds that had long been swollen accomplishing itself in the space of one warm night. The rush of sap in the veins of the trees could almost be heard. The flowers of late April took up a position unseen, and looked as if they had been blooming a long while, though there had been no trace of them the day before yesterday; birds began not to mind getting wet. In-door people said they had heard the nightingale, to which out-door people replied contemptuously that they had heard him a fortnight before.

The young doctor's practice being scarcely so large as a London surgeon's he frequently walked in the wood. Indeed, such practice as he had he did not follow up with the assiduity that would have been necessary for developing it to exceptional proportions.

One day, book in hand, he went to a part of the wood where the trees were mainly oaks. It was a calm afternoon, and there was everywhere around that sign of great undertakings on the part of vegetable nature which is apt to fill reflective human beings who are not undertaking much themselves with a sudden uneasiness at the contrast. He heard in the distance a curious sound, something like the quack of ducks, which though it was common enough here about this time was not common to him.

Looking through the trees Fitzpiers soon perceived the origin of the noise. The barking season had just commenced, and what he had heard was the tear of the ripping-tool as it ploughed its way along the sticky parting between the trunk and the rind. Melbury did a large business in bark, and as he was Grace's father, and possibly might be found on the spot, Fitzpiers was attracted to the scene even more than he might have been by its intrinsic interest. When he got nearer he recognized among the workmen John Upjohn, the two Timothys, and Robert Creedle, who probably had been 'lent' by Winterborne; Marty South also assisted. A milking-pail of cider stood near, a half-pint cup floating on it, with which they dipped and drank whenever they passed the pail.

Each tree doomed to the flaying process was first attacked by Upjohn. With a small bill-hook he carefully freed the collar of the tree from twigs and patches of moss which encrusted it to a height of a foot or two above the ground, an operation comparable to the 'little toilette' of the executioner's victim. After this it was barked in its erect position to a point as high as a man could reach. If a fine product of vegetable nature could ever be said to look ridiculous it was the case now, when the oak stood naked-legged, and as if ashamed, till the axe-man came and cut a ring round it, and the two Timothys finished the work with the cross-cut saw.

As soon as it had fallen the barkers attacked it like locusts, and in a short time not a particle of rind was left on the trunk and larger limbs. Marty South was an adept at peeling the upper parts; and there she stood encaged amid the mass of twigs and buds like a great bird, running her ripping-tool into the smallest branches, beyond the furthest points to which the skill and patience of the men enabled them to proceed – branches which, in their lifetime, had swayed high above the bulk of the wood, and caught the earliest rays of the sun and moon while the lower part of the forest was still in darkness.

'You seem to have a better instrument than they, Marty,' said Fitzpiers.

'No, sir,' she said, holding up the tool, a horse's leg-bone fitted into a handle and filed to an edge; ' 'tis only that they've less patience with the twigs, because their time is worth more than mine.'

A little shed had been constructed on the spot, of thatched hurdles and boughs, and in front of it was a fire, over which a kettle sang. Fitzpiers sat down inside the shelter and went on with his reading, except when he looked up to observe the scene and the actors.

The thought that he might settle here and become welded in with this sylvan life by marrying Grace Melbury crossed his mind for a moment. Why should he go further into the world than where he was? The secret of happiness lay in limiting the aspirations; these men's thoughts were conterminous with the margin of the Hintock woodlands, and why should not his be likewise limited – a small practice among the people around him being the bound of his desires?

Presently Marty South discontinued her operations upon the quivering boughs, came out from the reclining oak, and prepared tea. When it was ready the men were called; and Fitzpiers, being in a mood to join, sat down with them.

The latent reason of his lingering here so long revealed itself when the faint creaking of the joints of a vehicle became audible, and one of the men said, 'Here's he.' Turning their heads they saw Melbury's gig approaching, the wheels muffled by the yielding moss.

The timber-merchant was leading the horse past the tree-stumps, looking back at every few steps to warn his daughter, who kept her seat, where and how to duck her head so as to avoid overhanging branches. They stopped at the spot where the bark-ripping had been temporarily suspended; Melbury cursorily examined the heaps of bark, and drawing near to where the workmen were sitting down accepted their shouted invitation to have a dish of tea, for which purpose he hitched the horse to a bough.

Grace declined to take any of their beverage, and remained in her place in the vehicle, looking dreamily at the sunlight that came in thin threads through the hollies with which the oaks were interspersed.

When Melbury stepped up close to the shelter he for the first time perceived that the doctor was present, and warmly appreciated Fitzpiers's invitation to sit down on the log beside him.

'Bless my heart, who would have thought of finding you here,' he said, obviously much pleased at the circumstance. 'I wonder now if my daughter knows you are so nigh at hand? I don't expect she do.'

He looked out towards the gig wherein Grace sat, her face still turned sunward in the opposite direction.

'She doesn't see us,' said Melbury. 'Well, never mind; let her be.'

Grace was indeed quite unconscious of Fitzpiers's propinquity. She was thinking of something which had little connection with the scene before her – thinking of her friend, lost as soon as found, Mrs Charmond; of her capricious conduct, and of the contrasting scenes she was possibly enjoying at that very moment in other climes, to which Grace herself had hoped to be introduced by her friend's means. She wondered if this patronizing lady would return to Hintock during the summer, and whether the acquaintance which had been nipped on the last occasion of her residence there would develop on the next.

Melbury told ancient timber-stories as he sat, relating them directly to Fitzpiers and obliquely to the men, who had heard them often before. Marty, who poured out tea, was just saying, 'I think I'll take out a cup to Miss Grace,' when they heard a clashing of the gig-harness and turning round Melbury saw that the horse had become restless, and was jerking about the vehicle in a way which alarmed its occupant, though she refrained from screaming. Melbury jumped up immediately, but not more quickly than Fitzpiers; and while her father ran to the horse's head and speedily began to control him, Fitzpiers was alongside the gig assisting Grace to descend.

Her surprise at his appearance was so great that, far from making a calm and independent descent, she was very nearly lifted down in his arms. He relinquished her when she touched ground, and hoped she was not frightened.

'O no, not much,' she managed to say. 'There was no danger – unless the horse had run under the trees where the boughs are low enough to hit my head.'

'Which was by no means impossible, and justifies any amount of alarm.'

He referred to what he thought he saw written in her face, and she could not tell him that this had little to do with the horse, but much with himself. His contiguity had, in fact, the same effect upon her as on those former occasions when he had come closer to her than usual – that of producing in her an unaccountable tendency to tearfulness. Melbury soon put the horse to rights, and seeing that Grace was safe turned again to the work-people.

His daughter's nervous distress had passed off in a few moments, and she said quite gaily to Fitzpiers as she walked with him towards the group, 'There's destiny in it, you see. I was doomed to join in your picnic, although I did not intend to do so.'

Marty prepared her a comfortable place and she sat down in the circle, and listened to Fitzpiers while he drew from her father and the bark-rippers sundry narratives of their fathers', their grandfathers', and their own adventures in these woods; of the mysterious sights they had seen – only to be accounted for by supernatural agency; of white witches and black witches: and the standard story of the spirits of the Two Brothers who had fought and fallen, and had haunted King's Hintock Court a few miles off till they were exorcised by the priest, and compelled to retreat to a swamp, whence they were returning to their old quarters at the Court at the rate of a cock's stride every New Year's Day, Old Style; hence the local saying, 'On new-year's tide, a cock's stride.'

It was a pleasant time. The smoke from the little fire of peeled sticks rose between the sitters and the sunlight, and behind its blue films stretched the naked arms of the prostrate trees. The smell of the uncovered sap mingled with the smell of the burning wood, and the sticky inner surface of the scattered bark glistened as it revealed its pale madder hues to the eye. Melbury was so highly satisfied at having Fitzpiers as a sort of guest that he would have sat on for any length of time, but Grace, on whom Fitzpiers's eyes only too frequently alighted, seemed to think it incumbent upon her to make a show of going; and her father thereupon accompanied her to the gig.

As the doctor had helped her out of it he appeared to think that he had excellent reasons for helping her in, and performed the attention lingeringly enough.

'What were you almost in tears about just now?' he asked softly.

'I don't know,' she said; and the words were strictly true.

Melbury mounted on the other side, and they drove on out of the grove, their wheels silently crushing delicate-patterned mosses, hyacinths, primroses, lords-and-ladies, and other strange and common plants, and cracking up little sticks that lay across the track. Their way homeward ran along the western flank of the Vale, whence afar they beheld a wide district differing somewhat in feature and atmosphere from the Hintock precincts. It was the cider country more especially, which met the woodland district some way off. There the air was blue as sapphire – such a blue as outside that apple-region was never seen. Under the blue the orchards were in a blaze of pink bloom, some of the richly flowered trees running almost up to where they drove along. At a gate, which opened down an incline, a man leant on his arms regarding this fair promise so intently that he did not observe their passing.

'That was Giles,' said Melbury, when they had gone by.

'Was it? Poor Giles,' said she.

'All that apple-blooth means heavy autumn work for him and his hands. If no blight happens before the setting the cider yield will be such as we have not had for years.'

Meanwhile, in the wood they had come from, the men had sat on so long that they were indisposed to begin work again that evening; they were paid by the ton, and their time for labour was as they chose. They placed the last gatherings of bark in rows for the curers, which led them further and further away from the shed; and thus they gradually withdrew homeward as the sun went down.

Fitzpiers lingered yet. He had opened his book again, though he could hardly see a word in it, and sat before the dying fire scarcely knowing of the men's departure. He dreamed and mused till his consciousness seemed to occupy the whole space of the woodland round, so little was there of jarring sight or sound to hinder perfect mental unity with the sentiment of the place. The idea returned upon him of sacrificing all practical aims to live in calm contentment here, and instead of going on elaborating new conceptions with infinite pains, to accept quiet domesticity according to oldest and homeliest notions. These reflections detained him till the wood was embrowned with the coming night, and the shy little bird of this dusky time had begun to pour out all the intensity of his eloquence from a bush not very far off.

Fitzpiers's eyes commanded as much of the ground in front as was open. Entering upon this he saw a figure whose direction of movement was towards the spot where he sat. The surgeon was quite shrouded from observation by the recessed shadow of the hurdle-screen, and there was no reason why he should move till the stranger had passed by.

The shape resolved itself into a woman's; she was looking on the ground and walking slowly, as if searching for something that had been lost, her course being precisely that of Mr Melbury's gig. Fitzpiers, by a sort of divination, jumped to the idea that the figure was Grace's; her nearer approach made the guess a certainty.

Yes, she was looking for something; and she came round by the prostrate trees that would have been invisible but for their white nakedness, which enabled her to avoid them easily. Thus she approached the heap of ashes, and acting upon what was suggested by a still shining ember or two she took a stick and stirred the heap, which thereupon burst into a flame. On looking around by the light thus obtained she for the first time saw the illumined face of Fitzpiers precisely in the spot where she had left him.

Grace gave a start and a scream; she had not the least expected to find him there still. Fitzpiers lost not a moment in rising and going to her side.

'I frightened you dreadfully, I know,' he said. 'I ought to have spoken; but I did not at first expect it to be you. I have been sitting here ever since.'

He was actually supporting her with his arm as though under the impression that she was quite overcome and in danger of falling. As soon as she could collect her ideas she gently withdrew from his grasp and explained what she had returned for: in getting up or down from the gig, or when sitting by the hut fire, she had dropped her purse.

'Now we will find it,' said Fitzpiers.

He threw an armful of last year's leaves on to the fire, which made the flame leap higher, and the encompassing shades to weave themselves into a blacker contrast, turning eve into night in a moment. By this radiance they groped about on their hands and knees, till Fitzpiers rested on his elbow, and looked at Grace.

'We almost always meet in odd circumstances,' he said; 'and this is one of the oddest. I wonder if it means anything?'

'O no, I'm sure it doesn't,' said Grace in haste, quickly assuming an erect posture. 'Pray don't say it any more.'

'I hope there was not much money in the purse,' said Fitzpiers, rising to his feet more slowly, and brushing the leaves from his trousers.

'Scarcely any. I cared most about the purse itself, because it was given me. Indeed, money is of little more use at Hintock than on Crusoe's island: there's hardly any way of spending it.'

They had given up the search when Fitzpiers discerned something by his foot. 'Here it is!' he said. 'So that your father, mother, friend, or *admirer* will not have his or her feelings hurt by a sense of your negligence after all.'

'O, he knows nothing of what I do now.'

'The admirer?' said Fitzpiers slyly.

'I don't know if you would call him that,' said Grace with simplicity. 'The admirer is a superficial, conditional creature, and this person is quite different.'

'He has all the cardinal virtues?'

'Perhaps – though I don't know them precisely.'

'You unconsciously practise them, Miss Melbury, which is better. According to Schleiermacher they are Self-control, Perseverance, Wisdom, and Love; and his is the best list that I know.'

'I am afraid poor—'. She was going to say that she feared Winterborne, the giver of the purse years before, had not much perseverance, though he had all the other three; but she determined to go no further in this direction, and was silent.

These half-revelations made a perceptible difference in Fitzpiers. His sense of personal superiority wasted away, and Grace assumed in his eyes the true aspect of a mistress in her lover's regard.

'Miss Melbury,' he said suddenly; 'I divine that this virtuous man you mention has been refused by you?'

She could do no otherwise than admit it.

'I did not inquire without good reason. God forbid that I should kneel in another's place at any shrine unfairly. But, my dear Miss Melbury, now that he is gone from the temple, may I draw near?'

'I – I can't say anything about that!' she cried quickly. 'Because when a man has been refused you feel pity for him, and like him more than you did before.'

This increasing complication added still more value to Grace in the surgeon's eyes: it rendered her adorable. 'But cannot you say?' he pleaded distractedly.

'I'd rather not – I think I must go home at once.'

'O yes,' said Fitzpiers.

But as he did not move she felt it awkward to walk straight away from him; and so they stood silently together. A diversion was created by the accident of two large birds, that had either been roosting above their heads or nesting there, tumbling one over the other into the hot ashes at their feet, apparently engrossed in a desperate quarrel that prevented the use of their wings. They speedily parted, however, and flew up with a singed smell, and were seen no more.

'That's the end of what is called love,' said some one.

The speaker was neither Grace nor Fitzpiers, but Marty South, who approached with her face turned up to the sky in her endeavour to trace the birds. Suddenly perceiving Grace she exclaimed, 'O – Miss Melbury! – I have been looking at they pigeons, and didn't see you. And here's Mr Winterborne!' she continued shyly, as she looked towards Fitzpiers, who stood in the background.

'Marty,' Grace interrupted; 'I want you to walk home with me – will you? Come along.' And without lingering longer she took hold of Marty's arm and led her away.

They went between the spectral arms of the peeled trees as they lay, and onward among the growing ones by a path where there were no oaks, and no barking, and no Fitzpiers – nothing but copse-wood, between which the primroses could be discerned in pale bunches.

'I – didn't know Mr Winterborne was there,' said Marty, breaking the silence when they had nearly reached Grace's door.

'Nor was he,' said Grace.

'But, Miss Melbury – I saw him.'

'No,' said Grace. 'It was somebody else. Giles Winterborne is nothing to me.'

CHAPTER 20

THE leaves over Hintock unrolled their creased tissues, and the woodland seemed to change from an open filigree to a solid opaque body of infinitely larger shape and importance. The boughs cast green shades, which disagreed with the complexion of the girls who walked there; and a fringe of the same boughs which overhung Mr Melbury's garden dripped on his seed-plots when it rained, pitting their surface all over as with pock-marks, till Melbury declared that gardens in such a place were no good at all. The two trees that had creaked all the winter left off creaking, the whirr of the night-hawk, however, forming a very satisfactory continuation of uncanny music from that quarter. Except at midday the sun was not seen complete by the Hintock people, but rather in the form of numerous little stars staring through the leaves.

Such an appearance it had on Midsummer Eve of this year, and as the hour grew later, and nine o'clock drew on, the irradiation of the daytime became broken up by the weird shadows and ghostly nooks of indistinctness. Imagination could trace amid the trunks and boughs swarthy faces and funereal figures. This was before the moon rose. Later on, when that planet was getting command of the upper heaven, and consequently shining with an unbroken face into such open glades as there were in the neighbourhood of the hamlet, it became apparent that the margin of the wood which approached the timber-merchant's premises was not to be left to the customary stillness of that reposeful time.

Fitzpiers having heard a voice or voices was looking over his garden gate (where he now looked more frequently than into his books) fancying that Grace might be abroad with some friends. He was irretrievably committed in heart to Grace Melbury, though he was by no means sure that she was so far committed to him. That the Idea had for once completely fulfilled itself in the objective substance (which he had hitherto deemed an impossibility) he was enchanted enough to fancy must be the case at last.

It was not Grace who had passed, however, but several of the ordinary village girls in a group; some steadily walking, some in a mood of wild gaiety. He quietly asked his landlady, who was also in the garden, what these girls were intending, and she informed him that it being old Midsummer Eve they were about to attempt some spell or enchantment which would afford them a glimpse of their future partners for life. She declared it to be an ungodly performance, and one that she for her part would never countenance; saying which she entered her house and retired to bed.

The young man lit a cigar, and followed the bevy of maidens slowly up the road. They had turned into the wood at an opening between Melbury's and Marty South's; but Fitzpiers could easily track them by their voices, low as they endeavoured to keep their tones.

In the meantime other inhabitants of Little Hintock had become aware of the nocturnal experiment about to be tried, and were also sauntering stealthily after the frisky maidens. Miss Melbury had been informed by Marty South during the day of the proposed peep into futurity, and, being only a girl like the rest, she was sufficiently interested to wish to see the issue. The moon was so bright and the night so calm that she had no difficulty in persuading Mrs Melbury to accompany her; and thus, joined by Marty, these went onward in the same direction.

Passing Winterborne's house they heard a noise of hammering. Marty explained it. This was the last night on which his paternal roof would shelter him, the days of grace since it fell into hand having expired; and late as it was Giles was taking down his cupboards and bedsteads with a view to an early exit next morning. His encounter with Mrs Charmond had cost him dearly.

When they had proceeded a little further Marty was joined by Grammer Oliver (who was as young as the youngest in such matters), and Grace and Mrs Melbury went on by themselves till they had arrived at the spot chosen by the village daughters, whose primary intention of keeping their expedition a secret had been quite defeated. Grace and her stepmother paused by a holly tree; and at a little distance stood Fitzpiers under the shade of a young oak, intently observing Grace, who was in the full rays of the moon.

He watched her without speaking, and unperceived by any but Marty and Grammer, who had drawn up on the dark side of the same holly which sheltered Mrs and Miss Melbury on its bright side. The two former conversed in low tones.

'If they two come up in wood *next* Midsummer night they'll come as one,' said Grammer, signifying Fitzpiers and Grace. 'Instead of my skellinton he'll carry home her living carcase before long. But though she's a lady in herself, and worthy of any such as he, it do seem to me that he ought to marry somebody more of the sort of Mrs Charmond, and that Miss Grace should make the best of Winterborne.'

Marty returned no comment; and at that minute the girls, some of whom were from Great Hintock, were seen advancing to work the incantation, it being now about midnight.

'Directly we see anything we'll run home as fast as we can,' said one, whose courage had begun to fail her. To this the rest assented, not knowing that a dozen neighbours lurked in the bushes around.

'I wish we had not thought of trying this,' said another, 'but had contented ourselves with the hole-digging to-morrow at twelve, and hearing our husbands' trades. It is too much like having dealings with the evil one to try to raise their forms.'

However, they had gone too far to recede, and slowly began to march forward in a skirmishing line through the trees, each intending to plunge alone into a deep recess of the wood. As far as the listeners could gather, the particular form of black art to be practised on this occasion was one connected with the sowing of hempseed, a handful of which was carried by each girl.

At the moment of their advance they looked back, and discerned the figure of Miss Melbury who, alone of all the observers, stood in the full face of the moonlight, deeply engrossed in the proceedings. By contrast with her life of late years they made her feel as if she had receded a couple of centuries in the world's history. She was rendered doubly conspicuous by her light dress, and after a few whispered words one of the girls (a bouncing maiden called Suke, plighted to young Timothy Tangs) asked her if she would join in. Grace with some excitement said that she would, and moved on a little in the rear of the rest.

Soon the listeners could hear nothing of their proceedings beyond the faintest occasional rustle of leaves. Grammer whispered again to Marty: 'Why didn't ye go and try your luck with the rest of the maids?'

'I don't believe in it!' said Marty shortly. 'And they've spoilt it by letting people know.'

'Yes, half the parish is here; the silly hussies should have kept it quiet. I see Mr Winterborne through the leaves, just come up with Robert Creedle. Marty, we ought to act the part o' Providence sometimes. Do go and tell him that if he stands just behind the bush at the bottom of the slope, Miss Grace must pass down it when she comes back, and she will most likely rush into his arms; for as soon as the clock strikes they'll bundle back home-along like hares. I've seen such larries before.'

'Do you think I'd better?' said Marty reluctantly.

'O yes, he'll bless ye for it.'

'I don't want that kind of blessing!'

But after a moment's thought she went and delivered the information; and Grammer had the satisfaction of seeing Giles walk slowly to the bend in the leafy defile along which Grace would have to return.

Meanwhile Mrs Melbury, deserted by Grace, had perceived Fitzpiers and Winterborne, and also the move of the latter. An improvement on Grammer's idea entered the mind of Mrs Melbury, for she had lately discerned what her husband had not, that Grace was rapidly fascinating the surgeon. She therefore drew near to Fitzpiers.

'You should be where Mr Winterborne is standing,' she said to him significantly. 'She will run down through that opening much faster than she went up it, if she is like the rest of the girls.'

Fitzpiers did not require to be told twice. He went across to Winterborne, and stood beside him. Each knew the probable purpose of the other in standing there, and neither spoke, Fitzpiers scorning to look upon Winterborne as a rival, and Winterborne adhering to the off-hand manner of indifference which had grown upon him since his dismissal.

Neither Grammer nor Marty South had seen the surgeon's manoeuvre, and still to help Winterborne, as she supposed, the old woman suggested to the wood-girl that she should walk forward at the heels of Grace, and 'tole' her down the required way if she showed a tendency to run in another direction. Poor Marty, always doomed to sacrifice desire to obligation, walked forward accordingly, and waited as a beacon, still and silent, for the retreat of Grace and her giddy companions, now quite out of hearing.

The first sound to break the silence was the distant note of Great Hintock clock striking the significant hour. About a minute later that quarter of the wood to which the girls had wandered resounded with the flapping of disturbed birds; then two or three hares and rabbits bounded down the glade from the same direction, and after these the rustling and crackling of leaves and dead twigs denoted the hurried approach of the adventurers, whose fluttering gowns soon became visible.

Miss Melbury having gone forward quite in the rear of the rest was one of the first to return, and the excitement being contagious she ran laughing towards Marty, who still stood as a hand-post to guide her; then, passing on, she flew round the fatal bush where the undergrowth narrowed to a gorge. Marty arrived at her heels just in time to see the result. Fitzpiers had quickly stepped forward in front of Winterborne, who disdaining to shift his position had turned on his heel, and then the surgeon did what he would not have thought of doing but for Mrs Melbury's encouragement and the sentiment of an eve which effaced conventionality. Stretching out his arms as the white figure burst upon him he captured her in a moment, as if she had been a bird.

'O!' cried Grace in her fright.

'You are in my arms, dearest,' said Fitzpiers; 'and I am going to claim you, and keep you there all our two lives!'

She rested on him like one utterly mastered; and it was several seconds before she recovered from this helplessness. Subdued screams and struggles audible from neighbouring brakes revealed that there had been other lurkers thereabout for a similar purpose. Grace, unlike most of these companions of hers, instead of giggling and writhing, said in a trembling voice, 'Mr Fitzpiers, will you let me go?'

'Certainly,' he said, laughing; 'as soon as you have recovered.'

She waited another few moments, then quietly and firmly pushed him aside and glided on her path, the moon whitening her hot blush away. But it had been enough: new relations between them had begun.

The case of the other girls was different, as has been said. They wrestled and tittered, only escaping after a desperate struggle. Fitzpiers could hear these enactments still going on after Grace had left him, and he remained on the spot where he had caught her, Winterborne having gone away. On a sudden another girl came bounding down the same descent that had been followed by Grace; a fine-framed young woman, with bare arms. Seeing Fitzpiers standing there she said with playful effrontery: 'May'st kiss me if 'canst catch me, Tim!'

Fitzpiers recognized her as Suke Damson, a hoydenish maiden of the hamlet – the girl whom he had heard swear to herself when she got soiled by the newly painted gate. She was plainly mistaking him for her lover. He was impulsively disposed to profit by her error, and as soon as she began racing away he started in pursuit.

On she went under the boughs, now in light, now in shade, looking over her shoulder at him every few moments and kissing her hand; but so cunningly dodging about among the trees and moon-shades that she never allowed him to get dangerously near her. Thus they ran and doubled, Fitzpiers warming with the chase, till the sound of their companions had quite died away.

He began to lose hope of ever overtaking her, when all at once, by way of encouragement, she turned to a fence in which there was a stile, and leapt over it. Outside, the scene was a changed one; a meadow, where the half-made hay lay about in heaps, in the uninterrupted shine of the now high moon.

Fitzpiers saw in a moment that having taken to open ground she had placed herself at his mercy, and he promptly vaulted over after her. She flitted a little way down the mead, when all at once her elusive form disappeared, as if it had sunk into the earth. She had buried herself in one of the hay-cocks.

Fitzpiers, now thoroughly excited, was not going to let her escape him thus. He approached, and set about turning over the heaps one by one. As soon as he paused, tantalized and puzzled, he was directed anew by an imitative kiss which came from her hiding-place under the hay, and by snatches of a local ballad, in the smallest voice she could assume: –

'O come in from the foggy, foggy dew.'

In a minute or two he uncovered her.

'O – 'tis not Tim!' said she with a laugh, and burying her face.

Fitzpiers, however, disregarded her resistance by reason of its mildness, stooped, and imprinted the purposed kiss; then sank down on the same hay-cock, panting with his race.

'Whom do you mean by Tim?' he asked presently.

'My young man, Tim Tangs,' said she.

'Now honour bright, did you really think it was he?'

'I did at first.'

'But you didn't at last.'

'No. I didn't at last.'

'Do you much mind that it is not?'

'No,' she answered slyly.

Fitzpiers kissed her again, and pressed her close to him.

He did not pursue his questioning. In the moonlight Suke looked very beautiful, the scratches and blemishes incidental to her outdoor occupation being invisible under these pale rays. While they remained silent on the hay the coarse whirr of the eternal night-hawk burst sarcastically from the top of a tree at the nearest corner of the wood. Besides this not a sound of any kind reached their ears, the time of nightingales being now past, and Hintock lying at a distance of two miles at least. In the opposite direction the hay-field stretched away into remoteness till it was lost to the eye in a soft mist.

It was daybreak before Fitzpiers and Suke Damson re-entered Little Hintock.

CHAPTER 21

WHEN the general stampede occurred Winterborne had also been looking on, and encountering one of the girls had asked her what caused them all to fly.

She said with solemn breathlessness that they had seen something very different from what they had hoped to see, and that she for one would never attempt such unholy ceremonies again. 'We saw Satan pursuing us with his hour-glass. It was terrible!'

This account being a little mixed Giles went forward towards the spot whence the girls had retreated. After listening there a few minutes he heard slow footsteps rustling over the leaves, and, looking through a tangled screen of honeysuckle which hung from a bough, he saw in the open space beyond a short stout man in evening dress, carrying on one arm a light overcoat and also his hat, so awkwardly arranged as possibly to have suggested the 'hour-glass' to his timid observers – if this were the person whom the girls had seen. With the other hand he silently gesticulated, and the moonlight falling upon his bare brow showed him to have dark hair and a high forehead of the shape seen oftener in old prints and paintings than in real life. His curious and altogether alien aspect, his strange gestures, like those of one who is rehearsing a scene to himself, and the unusual place and hour, were sufficient to account for any trepidation among the Hintock daughters at encountering him.

He paused and looked round, as if he had forgotten where he was; not observing Giles, who was of the colour of his environment. The latter advanced into the light. The gentleman held up his hand and came towards Giles, the two meeting half way.

'I have lost my track,' said the stranger. 'Perhaps you can put me in the path again.' He wiped his forehead with the air of one suffering under an agitation more than that of simple fatigue.

'The turnpike-road is over there,' said Giles.

'I don't want the turnpike-road,' said the gentleman impatiently. 'I came from that. I want Hintock House. Is there not a path to it across here?'

'Well, yes, a sort of path. But it is hard to find from this point. I'll show you the way, sir, with pleasure.'

'Thanks, my good friend. The truth is that I decided to walk across the country after dinner from the hotel at Sherton, where I am staying for a day or two. But I did not know it was so far.'

'It is about a mile to the house from here.'

They walked on together. As there was no path Giles occasionally stepped in front and bent aside the under-boughs of the trees to give his companion a passage, saying every now and then when the twigs, on being released, flew back like whips, 'Mind your eyes, sir.' To which the stranger replied, 'Yes, yes,' in a preoccupied tone.

So they went on, the leaf-shadows running in their usual quick succession over the forms of the pedestrians, till the stranger said –

'Is it far?'

'Not much further,' said Winterborne. 'The plantation runs up into a corner here, close behind the house.' He added with hesitation, 'You know, I suppose, sir, that Mrs Charmond is not at home?'

'You mistake,' said the other shortly. 'Mrs Charmond has been away for some time, but she's at home now.'

Giles did not contradict him, though he felt sure that the gentleman was wrong.

'You are a native of this place?' the stranger said.

'Yes.'

'You are happy in having a home.'

'I hope you are too, sir.'

'It is what I don't possess.'

'You came from far, seemingly?'

'I come now from the south of Europe.'

'O indeed, sir. You are an Italian, or Spanish, or French gentleman, perhaps?'

'I am not either.'

Giles did not fill the pause which ensued, and the gentleman, who seemed of an emotional nature, unable to resist friendship, at length answered the question.

'I am an Italianized American; a South Carolinian by birth,' he said. 'I left my native country on the failure of the Southern cause, and have never returned to it since.'

He spoke no more about himself, and they came to the verge of the wood. Here, striding over the fence out upon the upland sward, they could at once see the chimneys of the house in the gorge immediately beneath their position, silent, still, and pale.

'Can you tell me the time?' the gentleman asked. 'My watch has stopped.'

'It is between twelve and one,' said Giles.

His companion expressed his astonishment. 'I thought it between nine and ten at latest! My! My!'

He now begged Giles to return and offered him a gold coin, which looked like a sovereign, for the assistance rendered. Giles declined to accept anything, to the surprise of the stranger, who on putting the money back into his pocket said awkwardly, 'I thought it was the custom here. I offered it because I want you to utter no word about this meeting with me. Will you promise?'

Winterborne promised readily. He stood still whilst the other descended the slope. At the bottom the stranger looked back mistrustfully. Giles would no longer remain when he was so evidently desired to leave, and returned through the boughs to Little Hintock.

He suspected that this man, who seemed so distressed and melancholy, might be that lover and persistent wooer of Mrs Charmond whom he had heard so frequently spoken of, and whom it was said she had treated cavalierly. But he received no confirmation of his suspicion beyond a report which reached him a few days later that a gentleman had called up the servants who were taking care of Hintock House at an hour past midnight; and on learning that Mrs Charmond, though returned from abroad, was as yet in London, he had sworn bitterly, and gone away without leaving a card or any trace of himself.

The girls who related the story added that he sighed three times before he swore, and seemed wandering in his mind, but this part of the narrative was not corroborated. Anyhow such a gentleman drove away from Sherton next day in a carriage hired at the inn.

CHAPTER 22

The sunny, leafy week which followed the tender doings of Midsummer Eve brought a visitor to Fitzpiers's door; a voice that he knew sounded in the passage. Mr Melbury had called.

At first he had a particular objection to enter the parlour because his boots were dusty, but as the surgeon insisted he waived the point and came in.

Looking neither to the right nor to the left, hardly at Fitzpiers himself, he put his hat under his chair and with a preoccupied gaze at the floor said, 'I have called to ask you, doctor, quite privately, a question that troubles me. I've a daughter, Grace, an only daughter as you may have heard. Well, she's been out in the dew; on Midsummer Eve in particular she went out in thin slippers to watch some vagary of the Hintock maids; and she's got a cough, a distinct hemming and hacking, that makes me uneasy. Now I have decided to send her away to some seaside place for a change—'

'Send her away!' Fitzpiers's countenance had fallen.

'Yes. And the question is, where would you advise me to send her?'

The timber-merchant had happened to call at a moment when Fitzpiers was at the spring-tide of a sentiment that Grace was a necessity of his existence. The sudden pressure of her form upon his breast as she came headlong round the bush had never ceased to linger with him since he adopted the manoeuvre for which the hour and the moonlight and the occasion had been the only excuse. Now she was to be sent away.

Ambition? – it could be postponed. Family? – a common culture and reciprocity of tastes had taken the place of family considerations nowadays. He allowed himself to be carried forward on the wave of his desire.

'How strange, how very strange it is,' he said, 'that you should have come to me about her just now. I have been thinking every day of coming to you on the very same errand.'

'Ah? You have noticed, too, that her health—'

'I have noticed nothing the matter with her health, because there is nothing. But, Mr Melbury, I have seen your daughter several times by accident. I have admired her infinitely, and I was coming to ask you if I may become better acquainted with her – pay my addresses to her?'

Melbury was looking down as he listened, and did not see the air of half-misgiving at his own rashness that spread over Fitzpiers's face as he made this declaration.

'You have – got to know her?' said Melbury, a spell of dead silence having preceded his utterance, during which his emotion rose with almost visible effect.

'Yes,' said Fitzpiers.

'And you wish to become better acquainted with her? You mean with a view to marrying o' her – is that what you mean?'

'Yes,' said the young man. 'I mean, get acquainted with her, with a view to being her accepted lover; and if we suited each other, what would naturally follow.'

The timber-dealer was much surprised, and fairly agitated; his hand trembled as he laid by his walking-stick.

'This takes me unawares,' said he, his voice well-nigh breaking down. 'I don't mean that there is anything unexpected in a gentleman being attracted by her; but it did not occur to me that it would be you. I always said,' continued he, with a lump in his throat, 'that my Grace would make a mark at her own level some day. That was why I educated her. I said to myself, "I'll do it, cost what it may"; though her stepmother was pretty frightened at my paying out so much money year after year. I knew it would tell in the end. "Where you've not good material to work on, such doings would be waste and vanity," I said. "But where you have that material, it is sure to be worth while."'

'I am glad you don't object,' said Fitzpiers, almost wishing that Grace had not been quite so cheap for him.

'If she is willing I don't object, certainly. Indeed,' added the honest man, 'it would be deceit if I were to pretend to feel anything else than highly honoured by your wish; and it is a great credit to her to have drawn to her a man of such good professional station and venerable old family. That huntsman-fellow little thought how wrong he was about her! Take her and welcome, sir.'

'I'll endeavour to ascertain her mind.'

'Yes, yes. But she will be agreeable, I think. She ought to be.'

'I hope she may. Well, now you'll expect to see me frequently?'

'O yes. But, name it all – about her cough, and her going away? I had quite forgot that that was what I came about.'

'I assure you,' said the surgeon, 'that her cough can only be the result of a slight cold, and it is not necessary to banish her to any seaside place at all.'

Melbury looked unconvinced, doubting whether he ought to take Fitzpiers's professional opinion in circumstances which naturally led him to wish to keep her by him. The doctor saw this, and honestly dreading to lose sight of her he said eagerly, 'Between ourselves, if I am successful with her I will take her away myself for a month or two, as soon as we are married, which I hope will be before the chilly weather comes on. This will be so very much better than letting her go now.'

The proposal pleased Melbury much. There could be hardly any danger in postponing desirable change of air as long as the warm weather lasted, and for such a reason.

Suddenly recollecting himself he said, 'Your time must be precious, doctor. I'll get home-along. I am much obliged to 'ee. As you will see her often you'll discover for yourself if anything serious is the matter.'

'I can assure you it is nothing,' said Fitzpiers, who had seen Grace much oftener already than her father knew of.

When he was gone Fitzpiers paused, silent, registering his sensations like a man who has made a plunge for a pearl into a medium of which he knows neither the density nor temperature. But he had done it, and Grace was the sweetest girl alive.

As for the departed visitor, his own last words lingered in Melbury's ears as he walked homeward; he felt that what he had said in the emotion of the moment was very stupid, ungenteel, and unsuited to a duologue with an educated gentleman, the smallness of whose practice was more than compensated by the former greatness of his family. He had uttered thoughts before they were weighed, and almost before they were shaped. They had expressed in a certain sense his feeling at Fitzpiers's news, but yet they were not right. Looking on the ground, and planting his stick at each tread as if it were a flagstaff, he reached his own precincts where, as he passed through the court, he automatically stopped to look at the men working in the shed and around. One of them asked him a question about waggon-spokes.

'Hey?' said Melbury, looking hard at him. The man repeated the words.

Melbury stood; then turning suddenly away without answering he went up the court and entered the house.

As time was no concern with the journeymen, except as a thing to get passed, they leisurely surveyed the door through which he had disappeared.

'What maggot has the gaffer got in his head now?' said Tangs the elder. 'Sommit to do with that chiel of his! When you've got a maid of yer own, John Upjohn, that costs 'ee what she costs him, that will take the squeak out of your Sunday shoes, John! But you'll never be man enough to accomplish such as she; and 'tis a lucky thing for 'ee, John, as things be. Well, he ought to have a dozen – that would bring him to reason. I see 'em walking together last Sunday, and when they came to a puddle he lifted her over like a waxen figure. He ought to have a dozen; he'd let 'em walk through puddles for themselves then.'

Meanwhile Melbury had entered the house with the eye of a man who sees a vision before him. His wife was in the room. Without taking off his hat he sat down at random.

'Luce – we've done it!' he said. 'Yes – the thing is as I expected. The spell, that I foresaw might be worked, has worked. She's done it, and done it well. Where is she – Grace, I mean?'

'Up in her room: what has happened?'

Mr Melbury explained the circumstances as coherently as he could. 'I told you so,' he said. 'A maid like her couldn't stay hid long, even in a place like this. But where is Grace? Let's have her down. Here – Gra-a-ce!'

She appeared after a reasonable interval, for she was sufficiently spoilt by this father of hers not to put herself in a hurry, however impatient his tones. 'What is it, father?' said she, with a smile.

'Why, you scamp, what's this you've been doing? Not home here more than six months, yet instead of confining yourself to your father's rank making havoc in the upper classes!'

Though accustomed to show herself instantly appreciative of her father's meanings Grace was fairly unable to look anyhow but at a loss now.

'No, no; of course you don't know what I mean, or you pretend you don't. Though for my part I believe women can see these things through a double hedge. But I suppose I must tell 'ee. Why, you've flung your grapnel over the doctor, and he's coming courting forthwith.'

'Only think of that, my dear! Don't you feel it a triumph?' said Mrs Melbury.

'Coming courting – I've done nothing to make him!' Grace exclaimed.

''Twasn't necessary that you should; 'tis voluntary that rules in these things. Well, he has behaved very honourably, and asked my consent. You'll know what to do when he gets here, I dare say. I needn't tell you to make it all smooth for him.'

'You mean, to lead him on to marry me?'

'I do. Haven't I educated you for it?'

Grace looked out of the window, and at the fireplace, with no animation in her face. 'Why is it settled off-hand in this way?' said she pettishly. 'You'll wait till you hear what I think of him, I suppose?'

'O yes, of course. But you see what a good thing it will be.'

She weighed the statement without speaking.

'You will be restored to the society you've been taken away from,' continued her father; 'for I don't suppose he'll stay here long.'

She shyly admitted the advantage; but it was plain that though Fitzpiers when he was present exercised a certain fascination over her – or even more, an almost psychic influence, as it is called – and though his impulsive act in the wood had stirred her feelings indescribably, she had never regarded him in the light of a destined husband. 'I don't know what to answer,' she said. 'I have learnt that he is very clever.'

'He's all right, and he's coming here to see you.'

A premonition that she could not resist him if he came strangely moved her. 'Of course, father, you remember that it is only lately that Giles—'

'You know that you can't think of him. He has given up all claim to you.'

She could not explain the subtleties of her feeling as clearly as he could state his opinion, even though she had skill in speech, and her father had none. That Fitzpiers acted upon her like a dram, exciting her, throwing her into a novel atmosphere which biassed her doings until the influence was over, when she felt something of the nature of regret for the mood she had experienced – could not be told to this worthy couple in words.

It so happened that on this very day Fitzpiers was called away from Hintock by an engagement to attend some medical meetings, and his visits therefore did not begin at once. A note, however, arrived from him addressed to Grace, deploring his enforced absence. As a material object this note was pretty and superfine, a note of a sort that she had been unaccustomed to see since her return to Hintock, except when a school friend wrote to her – a rare instance, for the girls were respecters of persons, and many cooled down towards the timber-dealer's daughter when she was out of sight. Thus the receipt of it pleased her, and she afterwards walked about with a reflective air.

In the evening her father, who knew that the note had come, said, 'Why be ye not sitting down to answer your letter? That's what young folks did in my time.'

She replied that it did not require an answer.

'O, you know best,' he said. Nevertheless he went about his business doubting if she were right in not replying; possibly she might be so mismanaging matters as to risk the loss of an alliance which would bring her much happiness.

Melbury's respect for Fitzpiers was based less on his professional position, which was not much, than on the standing of his family in the country in bygone days. That touching faith in members of long-established families as such, irrespective of their personal condition or character, which is still found among old-fashioned people in the rural districts, reached its full perfection in Melbury. His daughter's suitor was descended from a line he had heard of in his grandfather's time as being once among the greatest, a family which had conferred its name upon a neighbouring village; how then could anything be amiss in this betrothal?

'I must keep her up to this,' he said to his wife. 'She sees it is for her happiness; but still she's young, and may want a little prompting from an older tongue.'

CHAPTER 23

WITH this in view Melbury took her out for a walk, a custom of his when he wished to say anything specially impressive. Their way was towards that lofty ridge bordering their woodland and the western extremity of the Vale of Blackmoor, the ridge culminating further on in High-Stoy Hill. They could look back over the outskirts of the cider district where they had in the spring beheld the miles of apple-trees in bloom. All was now deep green.

The spot recalled to Grace's mind the last occasion of her sight of it, and she said, 'The promise of an enormous apple-crop is fulfilling itself, is it not? I suppose Giles is getting his mills and presses ready.'

This was just what her father had not come there to talk about. Without replying he raised his arm and moved his finger till he fixed it at a point round to the right.

'There,' he said. 'You see that hill rising out of the level like a great whale, and just behind the hill a particularly green sheltered bottom? That's where Mr Fitzpiers's family were lords of the manor for I don't know how many hundred years, and there stands the village of Oakbury Fitzpiers. A wonderful property 'twas – wonderful!'

'But they are not lords of the manor there now.'

'Why, no. But good and great folk fall as well as humble and foolish. The only ones representing the family now, I believe, are our doctor and a maiden lady living I don't know where. You can't help being happy, Grace, in allying yourself with such a romantical family. Why, on the mother's side he's connected with the long line of the Lords Baxby of Sherton. You'll feel as if you've stepped into history.'

'We've been at Hintock as long as they were at Oakbury; is it not so? You say our name occurs in old deeds continually.'

'O yes – as yeomen, copyholders, and such like. But think how much better this will be for 'ee. You'll be living a high, perusing life such as has now become natural to you; and though the doctor's practice is small here he'll no doubt go to a dashing town when he's got his hand in, and keep a stylish carriage, and you'll be brought to know a good many ladies of excellent society. If you should ever meet me then, Grace, you can drive past me, looking the other way. I shouldn't expect you to speak to me, or wish such a thing – unless it happened to be in some lonely private place where 'twouldn't lower 'ee at all. Don't think such men as neighbour Giles your equal. He and I shall be good friends enough, but he's not for the like of you. He's lived our rough and homely life here, and his wife's life must be rough and homely likewise.'

So much pressure could not but produce some displacement. As Grace was left very much to herself she took advantage of one fine day before Fitzpiers's return to drive into the aforesaid vale where stood the village of Oakbury Fitzpiers. On another day she drove to the ruins of Sherton Castle, the original stronghold of the Lords Baxby, Fitzpiers's maternal ancestors.

The remains were few, and consisted mostly of remnants of the lower vaulting, supported on low stout columns surmounted by the *crochet* capital of the period. The two or three arches of these vaults that were still in position had been utilized by the adjoining farmer as shelter for his calves, the floor being spread with straw, amid which the young creatures rustled, cooling their thirsty tongues by licking the quaint Norman carving, which glistened with the moisture. It was a degradation of even such a rude form of art as this to be treated so grossly, she thought, and for the first time the aspect of

Fitzpiers assumed in her imagination the hues of a melancholy romanticism.

She traversed the distance home with a preoccupied mind. The idea of so modern a man in science and aesthetics as the young surgeon springing out of relics so ancient was a kind of novelty she had never before experienced. The combination lent him a social and intellectual interest which she dreaded, so much weight did it add to the strange influence he exercised upon her whenever he came near her.

In an excitement which was not love, not ambition, rather a fearful consciousness of hazard in the air, she awaited his return.

Meanwhile her father was awaiting him also. In his house there was an old work on medicine, published towards the end of the eighteenth century, and to put himself in harmony with events Melbury spread this work on his knees when he had done his day's business, and read about Galen, Hippocrates, and Herophilus; of the dogmatic, the empiric, the hermetical, and other sects of practitioners that have arisen in history; and thence proceeded to study the classification of maladies and the rules for their treatment by copious bleeding, as laid down in this valuable book with absolute precision. Melbury regretted that the treatise was so old, fearing that he might in consequence be unable to hold as complete a conversation as he could wish with Mr Fitzpiers, primed, no doubt, with more recent discoveries.

The day of Fitzpiers's return arrived, and he sent to say that he would call immediately. In the little time that was afforded for putting the house in order the sweeping of Melbury's parlour was as the sweeping of the parlour at the Interpreter's which well-nigh choked the Pilgrim. Motes stood in the sunbeams, which sloped visibly into the room. At the end of it Mrs Melbury sat down, folded her hands and lips, and waited. Her husband restlessly walked in and out from the timber-yard, stared at the interior of the room, jerked out 'Ay, ay,' and retreated again.

Between four and five Fitzpiers arrived, hitching his horse to the hook under the uppingstock outside the door.

As soon as he had walked in and perceived that Grace was not in the parlour he seemed to have a misgiving. Nothing less than her actual presence could long keep him to the level of this impassioned enterprise; that lacking he appeared as one who wished to retrace his steps.

He mechanically talked at what he considered a woodland matron's level of thought till a rustling was heard on the stairs, and Grace came in. Fitzpiers was for once as agitated as she. Over and above the genuine emotion which she raised in his heart there hung the sense that he was casting a die by impulse which he might not have thrown by judgment.

Mr Melbury was not in the room at the moment. Having to attend to matters in the yard he had delayed putting on his afternoon coat and waistcoat till the doctor's appearance, when, not wishing to be backward in receiving him, he entered the parlour hastily buttoning up those garments. Grace's fastidiousness was a little distressed that Fitzpiers should see by this action the strain his visit was putting upon her father; and to make matters worse for her just then, old Grammer seemed to have a passion for incessantly pumping in the back kitchen, leaving the doors open so that the banging and splashing were distinct above the parlour conversation.

Whenever the chat over the tea sank into pleasant desultoriness Mr Melbury broke in with speeches of laboured precision on very remote topics, as if he feared to let Fitzpiers's mind dwell critically on the subject nearest the hearts of all. In truth a constrained manner was natural enough in Melbury just now, for the greatest interest of his life was reaching its crisis. Could the real have been beheld instead of the corporeal merely, the corner of the room in which he sat would have been filled with a form typical of anxious suspense, large-eyed, tight-lipped, awaiting the issue. That paternal hopes and fears so intense should be bound up in the person of one child so peculiarly circumstanced, and not have dispersed themselves over the larger field of a whole family, involved dangerous risks to his own future happiness.

Fitzpiers did not stay more than an hour, but that time had apparently advanced his sentiments towards Grace, once and for all, from a vaguely liquescent to an organic shape. She would not have accompanied him to the door, in response to his whispered 'Come!' if her mother had not said in a matter-of-fact way, 'Of course, Grace; go to the door with Mr Fitzpiers.' Accordingly Grace went, both her parents remaining in the room.

When the young pair were in the great brick-floored hall the lover took the girl's hand in his, drew it under his arm, and thus led her on to the front door, where he stealthily put his lips to her own.

She broke from him trembling, blushed, and turned aside, hardly knowing how things had advanced to this. Fitzpiers drove off kissing his hand to her, and waving it to Melbury, who was visible through the window. Her father returned the surgeon's action with a great flourish of his own hand, and a satisfied smile.

The intoxication that Fitzpiers had, as usual, produced in Grace's brain during the visit passed off somewhat with his withdrawal. She felt like a woman who did not know what she had been doing for the previous hour; but supposed with trepidation that the afternoon's proceedings, though vague, had amounted to an engagement between herself and the handsome, coercive, irresistible Fitzpiers.

This visit was a type of many which followed it during the long summer days of that year. Grace was borne along upon a stream of reasonings, arguments, and persuasions, supplemented, it must be added, by inclinations of her own at times. No woman is without aspirations, which may be innocent enough within limits; and Grace had been so trained socially, and educated intellectually, as to see clearly enough a pleasure in the position of wife to such a man as Fitzpiers. His material standing of itself, either present or future, had little in it to feed her ambition, but the possibilities of a refined and cultivated inner life, of subtle psychological intercourse, had their charm. It was this rather than any vulgar idea of marrying well which caused her to float with the current, and to yield to the immense influence which Fitzpiers exercised over her whenever she shared his society.

Any observer would shrewdly have prophesied that whether or not she loved him as yet in the ordinary sense, she was pretty sure to do so in time.

One evening just before dusk they had taken a rather long walk together, and for a short cut homeward passed through the shrubberies of Hintock House – still deserted, and still blankly confronting with its sightless shuttered windows the surrounding foliage and slopes.

Grace was tired, and they approached the wall, and sat together on one of the stone sills – still warm with the sun that had been pouring its rays upon them all the afternoon.

'This place would just do for us, would it not, dearest?' said her betrothed, as they sat, turning and looking idly at the old façade.

'O yes,' said Grace, plainly showing that no such fancy had ever crossed her mind. 'She is away from home still,' Grace added in a minute rather sadly, for she could not forget that she had somehow lost the valuable friendship of the lady of this bower.

'Who is? – O, you mean Mrs Charmond. Do you know, dear, that at one time I thought *you* lived here?'

'Indeed,' said Grace. 'How was that?'

He explained, as far as he could do so without mentioning his disappointment at finding it was otherwise; and then went on: 'Well, never mind that. Now I want to ask you something. There is one detail of our wedding which I am sure you will leave to me. My inclination is not to be married at the horrid little church here, with all the yokels staring round at us, and a droning parson reading.'

'Where then can it be? At a church in town?'

'No. Not at a church at all. At a registry office. It is a quieter, snugger, and more convenient place in every way.'

'O,' said she with real distress. 'How can I be married except at church, and with all my dear friends round me!'

'Yeoman Winterborne among them.'

'Yes – why not? You know there was nothing serious between him and me.'

'You see, dear, a noisy, bell-ringing marriage at church has this objection in our case: it would be a thing of report a long way round. Now I would gently, as gently as possible, indicate to you how inadvisable such publicity would be if we leave Hintock, and I purchase the practice that I contemplate purchasing at Budmouth – barely twenty miles off. Forgive my saying that it will be far better if nobody there knows much of where you come from, nor anything about your parents. Your beauty and knowledge and manners will carry you anywhere if you are not hampered by such retrospective criticism.'

'But could it not be a quiet ceremony, even at church?' she pleaded.

'I don't see the necessity of going there!' he said, a trifle impatiently. 'Marriage is a civil contract, and the shorter and simpler it is made the better. People don't go to church when they take a house, or even when they make a will.'

'O Edred – I don't like to hear you speak like that.'

'Well, well – I didn't mean to. But I have mentioned as much to your father, who has made no objection; and why should you?'

She deemed the point one on which she ought to allow sentiment to give way to policy – if there were indeed policy in his plan. But she was indefinably depressed as they walked homeward.

CHAPTER 24

He left her at the door of her father's house. As he receded and was clasped out of sight by the filmy shades he impressed Grace as a man who hardly appertained to her existence at all. Cleverer, greater than herself, one outside her mental orbit, as she considered him, he seemed to be her ruler rather than her equal, protector, and dear familiar friend.

The disappointment she had experienced at his wish, the shock given to her girlish sensibilities by his irreverent views of marriage, together with the sure and near approach of the day fixed for committing her future to his keeping, made her so restless that she could scarcely sleep at all that night. She rose when the sparrows began to creep out of the roof-holes, sat on the floor of her room in the dim light, and by and by peeped out behind the window curtains.

It was even now day out of doors, though the tones of morning were feeble and wan, and it was long before the sun would be perceptible in this overshadowed vale. Not a sound came from any of the outhouses as yet. The tree-trunks, the road, the out-buildings, the garden, every object, wore that aspect of mesmeric passivity which the quietude of daybreak lends to such scenes. Helpless immobility seemed to be combined with intense consciousness; a meditative inertness possessed all things, oppressively contrasting with her own active emotions. Beyond the road were some cottage roofs and orchards; over these roofs and over the apple-trees behind, high up the slope, and backed by the plantation on the crest, was the house yet occupied by her future husband, the rough-cast front showing whitely through its creepers. The window-shutters were closed, the bedroom curtains closely drawn, and not the thinnest coil of smoke rose from the rugged chimneys.

Something broke the stillness. The front-door of the house she was gazing at opened softly, and there came out into the porch a female figure, wrapped in a large cloak, beneath which was visible the white skirt of a long loose garment like a night-dress. A grey arm, stretching from within the porch, adjusted the cloak over the woman's shoulders; it was withdrawn and disappeared, the door closing behind her.

The woman went quickly down the box-edged path between the raspberries and currants, and as she walked her well-developed form and gait betrayed her individuality. It was Suke Damson, the affianced one of simple young Tim Tangs. At the bottom of the garden she entered the shelter of the tall hedge, and only the top of her head could be seen hastening in the direction of her own dwelling.

Grace had recognized, or thought she recognized, in the grey arm stretching from the porch, the sleeve of a dressing-gown which Mr Fitzpiers had been wearing on her own memorable visit to him. Her face fired red. She had just before thought of dressing herself and taking a lonely walk under the trees, so coolly green this early morning; but she now sat down on her bed and fell into reverie.

It seemed as if hardly any time had passed when she heard the household moving briskly about, and breakfast preparing downstairs; though, on rousing herself to robe and descend, she found that the sun was throwing his rays completely over the tree-tops, a progress in the world's diurnal turn denoting that at least three hours had elapsed since she last looked out of the window.

When attired she searched about the house for her father; she found him at last in the garden, stooping to examine the potatoes for signs of disease. Hearing her rustle he stood up and stretched his back and arms, saying, 'Morning t'ye, Gracie. I congratulate 'ee. It is only a month to-day to the time!'

She did not answer, but, without lifting her dress, waded between the dewy rows of tall potato-green into the middle of the plot where he was.

'I have been thinking very much about my position this morning – ever since it was light,' she began excitedly, and trembling so that she could hardly stand. 'And I feel it is a false one. I wish not to marry Mr Fitzpiers. I wish not to marry anybody; but I'll marry Giles Winterborne if you say I must as an alternative.'

Her father's face settled into rigidity, he turned pale, and came deliberately out of the plot before he answered her. She had never seen him look so incensed before.

'Now, hearken to me,' he said. 'There's a time for a woman to alter her mind; and there's a time when she can no longer alter it, if she has any right eye to her parents' honour and the seemliness of things. That time has come. I won't say to 'ee, you *shall* marry him. But I will say, that if you refuse, I shall for ever be ashamed and aweary of 'ee as a daughter, and shall look upon you as the hope of my life no more. What do you know about life and what it can bring forth, and how you ought to act to lead up to best ends? O, you are an ungrateful maid, Grace; you've seen that fellow Giles, and he has got over 'ee; that's where the secret lies, I'll warrant me!'

'No, father, no! It is not Giles – it is something I cannot tell you of—'

'Well, make fools of us all; make us laughing-stocks; break it off; have your own way!'

'But who knows of the engagement as yet; how can breaking it disgrace you?'

Melbury then by degrees admitted that he had mentioned the engagement to this acquaintance and to that, till she perceived that in his restlessness and pride he had published it everywhere. She went dismally away to a bower of laurel at the top of the garden. Her father followed her.

'It is that Giles Winterborne!' he said with an upbraiding gaze at her.

'No, it is not; though for that matter you encouraged him once!' she said, troubled to the verge of despair. 'It is not Giles, it is Mr Fitzpiers.'

'You've had a tiff – a lovers' tiff – that's all, I suppose?'

'It is some woman—'

'Ay, ay; you are jealous. The old story. Don't tell me. Now do you bide here. I'll send Fitzpiers to you. I saw him smoking in front of his house but a minute bygone.'

He went off hastily out of the garden-gate and up the lane. But she would not stay where she was; and edging through a slit in the garden fence walked away into the wood.

Just about here the trees were large and wide apart, and there was no undergrowth, so that she could be seen to some distance; a sylph-like greenish-white creature, as toned by the sunlight and leafage. She heard a footfall crushing dead leaves behind her, and turning hastily found herself reconnoitred by Fitzpiers himself, approaching gay and fresh as the morning around them.

His remote gaze at her had been one of mild interest rather than of rapture. But she looked so lovely in the green world about her; her pink cheeks, her simple white dress, and the delicate flexibility of her movements acquired such rarity from their wild-wood setting that his eyes kindled as he drew near.

'My darling, what is it? Your father says you are in the pouts, and jealous, and I don't know what. Ha! ha! ha! as if there were any rival to you except vegetable nature, in this home of recluses. We know better.'

'Jealous; O no, it is not so,' said she gravely. 'That's a mistake of his and yours, sir. I spoke to him so closely about the question of marriage with you that he did not apprehend my state of mind.'

'But there's something wrong – eh?' he asked, eyeing her narrowly, and bending to kiss her.

She shrank away, and his purposed kiss miscarried.

'What is it?' he said, more seriously for this little defeat.

She made no answer beyond, 'Mr Fitzpiers, I have had no breakfast, I must go in.'

'Come,' he insisted, fixing his eyes upon her. 'Tell me at once, I say.'

It was the greater strength against the smaller, but she was mastered less by his manner than by her own sense of the unfairness of silence.

'I looked out of the window,' she said with hesitation. 'I'll tell you by and by. I must go indoors. I have had no breakfast.'

By a sort of divination his conjecture went straight to the fact. 'Nor I,' said he lightly. 'Indeed, I rose late to-day. I have had a broken night, or rather morning. A girl of the village – I don't know her name – came and rang at my bell as soon as it was light – between four and five I should think it was – perfectly maddened with an aching tooth. As nobody heard her ring she threw some gravel at my window, till at last I heard her and slipped on my dressing-gown and went down. The poor thing had come half-dressed to beg me, with tears in her eyes, to take out her tormentor if I dragged her head off. Down she sat and out it came; a lovely molar, not a speck upon it; and off she went with it in her handkerchief, much contented, though it would have done good work for her for fifty years to come.'

It was all so plausible – so completely explained. Knowing nothing of the intimacy established in the hay-field on old Midsummer Eve, Grace felt that her suspicions were unworthy and absurd, and with the readiness of an honest heart she jumped at the opportunity of honouring his word. At the moment of her mental libration the bushes about the garden had moved, and her father emerged into the shady glade.

'Well, I hope it is made up?' he said cheerily.

'O yes,' said Fitzpiers, with his eyes fixed on Grace, whose eyes were shyly bent downwards.

'Now,' said her father, 'tell me, the pair of ye, that you still mean to take one another for good and all; and on the strength o't you shall have another couple of hundred paid down. I swear it by the Name.'

Fitzpiers took her hand. 'We declare it, do we not, my dear Grace?' said he.

Relieved of her doubt, somewhat overawed, and ever anxious to please, she was disposed to settle the matter. Yet, woman-like, she would not relinquish her opportunity of asking a concession of some sort. 'If our wedding can be at church, I say yes,' she answered in a measured voice. 'If not, I say no.'

Fitzpiers was generous in his turn. 'It shall be so,' he rejoined gracefully. 'To holy church we'll go – and much good may it do us.'

They returned through the bushes indoors, Grace walking full of thought between the other two, somewhat comforted both by Fitzpiers's ingenious explanation and by the sense that she was not to be deprived of a religious ceremony. 'So let it be,' she said to herself. 'Pray God it is for the best.'

From this hour there was no serious recalcitration on her part. Fitzpiers kept himself continually near her, dominating any rebellious impulse, and shaping her will into passive concurrence with all his desires. Apart from his lover-like anxiety to possess her the few golden hundreds of the timber-dealer, ready to hand, formed a warm background to Grace's lovely face, and went some way to remove his uneasiness at the prospect of endangering his professional and social chances by an alliance with the family of a simple countryman.

The interim closed up its perspective surely and silently. Whenever Grace had any doubts of her position the sense of contracting time was like a shortening chamber: at other moments she was comparatively blithe.

Day after day waxed and waned; the one or two woodmen who sawed, shaped, or spokeshaved on her father's premises at this inactive season of the year, regularly came and unlocked the doors in the morning, locked them in the evening, supped, leant over their garden-gates for a whiff of evening air, and to catch any last and furthest throb of news from the outer world, which entered and expired at Little Hintock like the exhausted swell of a wave in some innermost cavern of some innermost creek of an embayed sea; yet no news interfered with the nuptial purpose at their neighbour's house.

The sappy green twig-tips of the season's growth would not, she thought, be appreciably woodier on the day she became a wife, so near was the time; the tints of the foliage would hardly have changed. Everything was so much as usual that no itinerant stranger would have supposed a woman's fate to be hanging in the balance at that summer's decline.

But there were preparations, imaginable enough by those who had special knowledge. In the remote and fashionable city of Exonbury something was growing up under the hands of several persons who had never seen Grace Melbury, never would see her, or care anything about her at all; though their creation had such interesting relation to her life that it would enclose her very heart at a moment when that heart would beat, if not with more emotional ardour, at least with more emotional turbulence than at any previous time.

Why did Mrs Dollery's van on its return from Sherton, instead of passing along the highway to Abbot's Cernel direct, turn one Saturday night into Little Hintock Lane, and never pull up till it reached Mr Melbury's gates? The gilding sheen of evening fell upon a large flat box, not less than a yard square and safely tied with cord, as it was handed out from under the tilt with a great deal of care. But it was not heavy for its size; Mrs Dollery herself carried it into the house. Tim Tangs, the hollow-turner, Cawtree, Suke Damson, and others, looked knowing and made remarks to each other as they watched its entrance. Melbury stood at the door of the timber-shed in the attitude of a man to whom such an arrival was a trifling domestic detail with which he did not condescend to be concerned. Yet he well divined the contents of that box, and was in truth all the while in a pleasant exaltation at the proof that thus far, at any rate, no disappointment had supervened. While Mrs

Dollery remained – which was rather long, from her sense of the importance of her errand – he went into the outhouse; but as soon as she had had her say, been paid, and had rumbled away, he entered the dwelling, to find there what he knew he should find – his wife and daughter in a flutter of excitement over the wedding-gown, just arrived from the leading dress-maker of Exonbury city aforesaid.

During these weeks Giles Winterborne was nowhere to be seen or heard of. At the close of his tenure in Hintock he had sold some of his furniture, packed up the rest – a few pieces endeared by associations, or necessary to his occupation – in the house of a friendly neighbour, and gone away. People said that a certain laxity had crept into his life; that he had never gone near a church latterly, and had been sometimes seen on Sundays with unblacked boots, lying on his elbow under a tree, with a cynical gaze at surrounding objects. He was likely to return to Hintock when the cider-making season came round, his apparatus being stored there, and travel with his mill and press from village to village.

The narrow interval that stood before the day diminished yet. There was in Grace's mind sometimes a certain anticip-ative satisfaction, the satisfaction of feeling that she would be the heroine of an hour; moreover, she was proud, as a cultiv-ated woman, to be the wife of a cultivated man. It was an opportunity denied very frequently to young women in her position, nowadays not a few; those in whom parental discovery of the value of education has implanted tastes which parental circles fail to gratify. But what an attenuation this cold pride was of the dream of her youth, in which she had pictured herself walking in state towards the altar, flushed by the purple light and bloom of her own passion, without a single misgiving as to the sealing of the bond, and fervently receiving as her due

'The homage of a thousand hearts; the fond deep love of one.'

Everything had been clear then, in imagination; now some-thing was undefined. She had little carking anxieties; a curious fatefulness seemed to rule her, and she experienced a mournful want of some one to confide in.

The day loomed so big and nigh that her prophetic ear could in fancy catch the noise of it, hear the murmur of the villagers as she came out of church, imagine the jangle of the three thin-toned Hintock bells. The dialogues seemed to grow louder, and the ding-ding-dong of those three crazed bells more persistent. She awoke: the morning had come.

Five hours later she was the wife of Fitzpiers.

CHAPTER 25

THE chief hotel at Sherton Abbas was the 'Earl of Wessex' – a substantial inn of Ham-hill stone with a yawning back yard into which vehicles were driven by coachmen to stabling of wonderful commodiousness. The windows to the street were mullioned into narrow lights, and only commanded a view of the opposite houses; hence, perhaps, it arose that the best and most luxurious private sitting-room that the inn could afford overlooked the lateral parts of the establishment, where beyond the yard were to be seen gardens and orchards now bossed, nay encrusted, with scarlet and gold fruit, stretching to infinite distance under a luminous lavender mist. The time was early autumn,

> 'When the fair apples, red as evening sky,
> Do bend the tree unto the fruitful ground,
> When juicy pears, and berries of black dye
> Do dance in air, and call the eyes around.'

The landscape confronting the window might indeed have been part of the identical stretch of country which the 'marvellous boy' had in his mind when he penned those lines.

In this room sat she who had been the maiden Grace Melbury till the finger of fate touched her and turned her to a wife. It was two months after the wedding, and she was alone. Fitzpiers had walked out to see the abbey by the light of sunset, but she had been too fatigued to accompany him. They had reached the last stage of a long eight-weeks' tour, and were going on to Little Hintock that night.

In the yard between Grace and the orchards there progressed a scene natural to the locality at this time of the year. An apple-mill and press had been erected on the spot, to which some men were bringing fruit from divers points in mawn-baskets, while others were grinding them, and others wringing down the pomace, whose sweet juice gushed forth into tubs and pails. The superintendent of these proceedings, to whom the others spoke as master, was a young yeoman of prepossessing manner and aspect, whose form she recognized in a moment. He had hung his coat to a nail of the outhouse wall, and wore his shirt-sleeves rolled up beyond his elbows, to keep them unstained while he rammed the pomace into the bags of horse-hair. Fragments of apple-rind had alighted upon the brim of his hat – probably from the bursting of a bag – while brown pips of the same fruit were sticking among the down upon his fine round arms, and in his beard.

She realized in a moment how he had come there. Down in the heart of the apple-country nearly every farmer kept a cider-making apparatus and wring-house for his own use, building up the pomace in great straw 'cheeses', as they were called; but here, on the margin of Pomona's plain, was a debatable land neither orchard nor sylvan exclusively, where the apple-produce was hardly sufficient to warrant each proprietor in keeping a mill of his own. This was the field of the travelling cider-maker. His press and mill were fixed to wheels instead of being set up in a cider-house; and with a couple of horses, buckets, tubs, strainers, and an assistant or two, he wandered from place to place, deriving very satisfactory returns for his trouble in such a prolific season as the present.

The outskirts of the town were just now abounding with apple-gatherings. They stood in the yards in carts, baskets, and loose heaps; and the blue stagnant air of autumn which hung over everything was heavy with a sweet cidery smell. Cakes of pomace lay against the walls in the yellow sun, where they were drying to be used as fuel. Yet it was not the great make of the year as yet; before the standard crop came in there accumulated, in abundant times like this, a large superfluity of early apples, and windfalls from the trees of later harvest, which would not keep long. Thus in the baskets, and quivering in the hopper of the mill, she saw specimens of mixed dates, including the mellow countenances of streaked jacks, codlins, costards, stubbards, ratheripes, and other well-known friends of her ravenous youth.

Grace watched the head man with interest. The slightest sigh escaped her. Perhaps she thought of the day – not so far distant – when that friend of her childhood had met her by her father's arrangement in this same town, warm with hope, though diffident and trusting in a promise rather implied than given. Or she might have thought of days earlier yet – days of childhood – when her mouth was somewhat more ready to receive a kiss from his than was his to bestow one. However, all that was over. She had felt superior to him then, and she felt superior to him now.

She wondered why he never looked towards her open window. She did not know that in the slight commotion caused by their arrival at the inn that afternoon Winterborne had caught sight of her through the archway, had turned red, and was continuing his work with more concentrated attention on the very account of his discovery. Robert Creedle, too, who travelled with Giles, had been incidentally informed by the ostler that Dr Fitzpiers and his young wife were in the hotel; after which news Creedle kept shaking his head and saying to himself, 'Ah!' very audibly, between his thrusts at the screw of the cider-press.

'Why the deuce do you sigh like that, Robert?' asked Winterborne at last.

'Ah, maister, – 'tis my thoughts – 'tis my thoughts!... Yes, ye've lost a hundred load o' timber well seasoned; ye've lost five hundred pound in good money; ye've lost the stone-windered house that's big enough to hold a dozen families; ye've lost your share of half-a-dozen good waggons and their horses; – all lost! – through your letting slip she that was once yer own!'

'Good God, Creedle! you'll drive me mad!' said Giles sternly. 'Don't speak of that any more!'

Thus the subject had ended in the yard. Meanwhile the passive cause of all this loss still regarded the scene. She was beautifully dressed; she was seated in the most comfortable room that the inn afforded; her long journey had been full of variety, and almost luxuriously performed, for Fitzpiers did not study economy where pleasure was in question. Hence it perhaps arose that Giles and all his belongings seemed sorry and common to her for the moment – moving in a groove so far removed from her own of late that she could scarcely believe she had ever found congruity therein.

'No – I could never have married him!' she said, gently shaking her head. 'Dear father was right. It would have been too rough a life for me.' And she looked at the rings of sapphire and opal upon her white and slender fingers that had been gifts from Fitzpiers.

Seeing that Giles still kept his back turned, and with a little of the above-described pride of life – easily to be understood, possibly excused, in a young inexperienced woman who thought she had married well – she opened the window wider and cried with a smile on her lips, 'Mr Winterborne!'

He appeared to take no heed, and she said a second time, 'Mr Winterborne!'

Even now he seemed not to hear, though a person close enough to him to see the expression of his face might have doubted it; and she said a third time, with a timid loudness, 'Mr Winterborne! What, have you forgotten my voice?' She remained with her lips parted in a welcoming smile.

He turned without surprise and came deliberately towards the window.

'Why do you call me?' he said, with a sternness that took her completely unawares, his face being now pale. 'Is it not enough that you see me here moiling and muddling for my daily bread while you are sitting there in your success, that you can't refrain from opening old wounds by calling out my name?'

She flushed, and was struck dumb for some moments; but she forgave his unreasoning anger, knowing so well in what it had its root.

'I am sorry I offended you by speaking, Giles,' she replied. 'Believe me, I did not intend to do that. I could hardly sit here so near you without a word of recognition.'

Winterborne's heart had swollen big and his eyes grown moist by this time, so much had the gentle answer of that familiar voice moved him. He assured her hurriedly, and without looking at her, that he was not angry. He then managed to ask her, in a clumsy constrained way, if she had had a pleasant journey, and seen many interesting sights. She spoke of a few places that she had visited, and so the time passed till he withdrew to take his place at one of the levers which pulled round the screw.

Forgotten her voice! Indeed, he had not forgotten her voice, as his bitterness showed. But though in the heat of the moment he had reproached her keenly, his second mood was a far more tender one – that which could regard her renunciation of such as he as her glory and her privilege, his own fidelity notwithstanding. He could have declared with a contemporary poet –

> 'If I forget,
> The salt creek may forget the ocean;
> If I forget
> The heart whence flowed my heart's bright motion,
> May I sink meanlier than the worst,
> Abandoned, outcast, crushed, accurst, –
> If I forget.
>
> Though you forget,
> No word of mine shall mar your pleasure;
> Though you forget, –
> You filled my barren life with treasure;
> You may withdraw the gift you gave,
> You still are queen, I still am slave,
> Though you forget.'

She had tears in her eyes at the thought that she could not remind him of what he ought to have remembered; that not herself but the pressure of events had dissipated the dreams of their early youth.

Grace was thus unexpectedly worsted in her encounter with her old friend. She had opened the window with a faint sense of triumph, but he had turned it into sadness; she did not quite comprehend the reason why. In truth it was because she was not cruel enough in her cruelty. If you have to use the knife, use it, say the great surgeons; and for her own peace Grace should have handled Winterborne thoroughly or not at all. As it was, on closing the window an indescribable – some might have said dangerous – pity quavered in her bosom for him.

Presently her husband entered the room and told her what a wonderful sunset there was to be seen.

'I have not noticed it. But I have seen somebody out there that we know,' she replied, looking into the court.

Fitzpiers followed the direction of her eyes and said he did not recognize anybody.

'Why, Mr Winterborne – there he is cider-making. He combines that with his other business, you know.'

'O – that fellow,' said Fitzpiers, his curiosity becoming extinct.

She, reproachfully: 'What, call Mr Winterborne a fellow, Edred! It is true I was just saying to myself that I never could have married him; but I have much regard for him, and always shall.'

'Well, do by all means, my dear one. I dare say I am inhuman, and supercilious, and contemptibly proud of my poor old ramshackle family; but I do honestly confess to you that I feel as if I belonged to a different species from the people who are working in that yard.'

'And from me, too, then. For my blood is no better than theirs.'

He looked at her with a droll sort of awakening. It was, indeed, a startling anomaly that this woman of the tribe without should be standing there beside him as his wife, if his sentiments were as he had said. In their travels together she had ranged so unerringly at his level in ideas, tastes, and habits, that he had almost forgotten how his heart had played havoc with his ambition in taking her to him.

'Ah, *you* – you are refined and educated into something quite different,' he said self-assuringly.

'I don't quite like to think that,' she murmured with regret. 'And I think you under-estimate Giles Winterborne. Remember I was brought up with him till I was sent away to school, so I cannot be radically different. At any rate I don't feel so. That is no doubt my fault, and a great blemish in me. But I hope you will put up with it, Edred.'

Fitzpiers said that he would endeavour to do so, and as it was now getting on for dusk they prepared to perform the last stage of their journey, so as to arrive at Hintock before it grew very late.

In less than half-an-hour they started, the cider-makers in the yard having ceased their labours and gone away, so that the only sounds audible there now were the trickling of the juice from the tightly screwed press, and the buzz of a single wasp, which had drunk itself so tipsy that it was unconscious of nightfall.

Grace was very cheerful at the thought of being soon in her sylvan home; but Fitzpiers sat beside her almost silent. An indescribable oppressiveness had overtaken him with the near approach of the journey's end and the realities of life that lay there. It was two months since he married her.

'You don't say a word, Edred,' she observed. 'Aren't you glad to get back? I am.'

'You have friends here. I have none.'

'But my friends are yours.'

'O yes – in that sense.'

The conversation languished, and they drew near the end of Hintock Lane. It had been decided that they should, at least for a time, take up their abode in her father's roomy house, one wing of which was quite at their service, being almost disused by the Melburys. Workmen had been painting, papering, and whitewashing this set of rooms in the wedded pair's absence; and so scrupulous had been the timber-dealer that there should occur no hitch or disappointment on their arrival that not the smallest detail remained undone. To make it all complete a ground-floor room had been fitted up as a surgery, with an independent outer door, to which Fitzpiers's brass plate was screwed – for mere ornament, such a sign being quite superfluous where everybody knew the latitude and longitude of his neighbours for miles round.

Melbury and his wife welcomed the twain with affection, and all the house showed them deference. They went up to explore their rooms, that opened from a passage on the left hand of the staircase, the entrance to which could be shut off on the landing by a door that Melbury had hung for the purpose. A friendly fire was burning in the grate although it was not cold. Fitzpiers said it was too soon for any sort of meal, they having dined but shortly before leaving Sherton Abbas; he would walk across to his old lodging to learn how his deputy had got on in his absence.

In leaving Melbury's door he looked back at the house. There was economy in living under that roof – and economy was desirable; but in some way he was dissatisfied with the arrangement; it immersed him so deeply in son-in-lawship to Melbury. He went on to his former residence; his *locum tenens* was out, and Fitzpiers fell into conversation with his old landlady.

'Well, Mrs Cox, what's the best news?' he asked of her with cheery weariness.

She was a little soured at losing by his marriage so profitable a tenant as the surgeon had proved to be during his residence under her roof; and the more so in there being hardly the remotest chance of her getting such another settler in the Hintock solitudes. ' 'Tis what I don't wish to repeat, sir; least of all to you,' she mumbled.

'Never mind me, Mrs Cox; go ahead.'

'It is what people say about your hasty marrying, Dr Fitzpiers. Whereas they won't believe you know such clever doctrines in physic as they once supposed of 'ee, seeing as you could marry into Mr Melbury's family, which is only Hintock-born such as I be meself.'

'They are kindly welcome to their opinion,' said Fitzpiers, not allowing himself to recognize that he winced. 'Anything else?'

'Yes; *she's* come home at last.'

'Who's she?'

'Mrs Charmond.'

'O indeed,' said Fitzpiers, with but slight interest. 'I've never seen her.'

'She has seen you, sir, whether or no.'

'Never.'

'Yes. She saw you in some hotel or street for a minute or two whilst you were away travelling, and accidentally heard your name; and when she made some remark about you, Miss Ellis – that's her maid – told her you was on your wedding-tour with Mr Melbury's daughter; and she said, "He ought to have done better than that. I fear he has spoilt his chances," she says.'

Fitzpiers did not talk much longer to this cheering housewife, and walked home with no very brisk step. He entered the door quietly, and went straight upstairs to the drawing-room extemporized for their use by Melbury in his and his bride's absence, expecting to find her there as he had left her.

The fire was burning still but there were no lights; he looked into the next apartment fitted up as a dining-room, but no supper was laid. He went to the top of the stairs and heard a chorus of voices in the timber-merchant's parlour below, Grace's being occasionally intermingled.

Descending, and looking into the room from the doorway, he found quite a large gathering of neighbours and other acquaintances, praising and congratulating Mrs Fitzpiers on her return, among them being the dairyman, Farmer Cawtree, and the relieving officer from Great Hintock; also the road-contractor, the master-tanner, the exciseman, and some others with their wives. Grace – girl that she was – had quite forgotten her new dignity and her husband's; she was in the midst of them, blushing and receiving their compliments with all the pleasures of old comradeship.

Fitzpiers experienced a profound distaste for the situation. Melbury was nowhere in the room, but Melbury's wife, perceiving the doctor, came to him.

'We thought, Grace and I,' she said, 'that as they have called, hearing you were come, we could do no less than ask them to supper; and then Grace proposed that we should all sup together as it is the first night of your return.'

By this time Grace had come round to him. 'Is it not good of them to welcome me so warmly?' she exclaimed with tears of friendship in her eyes. 'After so much good feeling I could not think of our shutting ourselves up away from them in our own dining-room.'

'Certainly not – certainly not,' said Fitzpiers. And he entered the room with the heroic smile of a martyr.

As soon as they sat down to table Melbury came in, and seemed to see at once that Fitzpiers would much rather have received no such demonstrative reception. He thereupon privately chid his wife for her forwardness in the matter. Mrs Melbury declared that it was as much Grace's doing as hers, after which there was no more to be said by that young woman's tender father.

By this time Fitzpiers was making the best of his position among the wide-elbowed and genial company who sat eating and drinking, laughing and joking around him; and, getting warmed himself by the good cheer, he was obliged to admit that, after all, the supper was not the least enjoyable he had ever known.

At times, however, the words about his having spoiled his opportunities, repeated to him as coming from Mrs Charmond, haunted him like a handwriting on the wall. Then his manner would become suddenly abstracted. At one moment he would mentally put an indignant query why Mrs Charmond or any other woman should make it her business to have opinions about his opportunities: at another he thought that he could hardly be angry with her for taking an interest in the doctor of her own parish. Then he would drink a glass of grog and so get rid of the misgiving.

These hitches and quaffings were soon perceived by Grace as well as by her father; and hence both of them were much relieved when the first of the guests to discover that the hour was growing late rose and declared that he must think of moving homewards. At the words Melbury rose as alertly as if lifted by a spring; and in ten minutes they were gone.

'Now, Grace,' said her husband as soon as he found himself alone with her in their private apartments, 'we've had a very pleasant evening, and everybody has been very kind. But we must come to an understanding about our way of living here. If we continue in these rooms there must be no mixing in with your people below. I can't stand it, and that's the truth.'

She had been sadly surprised at the suddenness of his distaste for those old-fashioned woodland forms of life which in his courtship he had professed to regard with so much interest. But she assented in a moment.

'We must be simply your father's tenants,' he continued, 'and our goings and comings must be as independent as if we lived elsewhere.'

'Certainly, Edred – I quite see that it must be so.'

'But you joined in with all those people in my absence, without knowing whether I should approve or disapprove. When I came I couldn't help myself at all.'

She, sighing: 'Yes – I see I ought to have waited; though they came unexpectedly, and I thought I had acted for the best.'

Thus the discussion ended, and the next day Fitzpiers went on his old rounds as usual. But it was easy for so supersubtle an eye as his to discern, or to think he discerned, that he was no longer regarded as an extrinsic, unfathomed gentleman of limitless potentiality, scientific and social; but as Mr Melbury's compeer, and therefore in a degree only one of themselves. The

Hintock woodlanders held with all the strength of inherited conviction to the aristocratic principle, and as soon as they had discovered that Fitzpiers was one of the old Oakbury Fitzpierses they had accorded to him for nothing a touching of hat-brims, promptness of service, and deference of approach, which Melbury had to do without though he paid for it over and over. But now, having proved a traitor to his own cause by this marriage, Fitzpiers was believed in no more as a superior hedged by his own divinity; while as doctor he began to be rated no higher than old Jones, whom they had so long despised.

His few patients seemed in his two months' absence to have dwindled considerably in number, and no sooner had he returned than there came to him from the Board of Guardians a complaint that a pauper had been neglected by his substitute. In a fit of pride Fitzpiers resigned his appointment as one of the surgeons to the Union, which had been the nucleus of his practice here.

At the end of a fortnight he came indoors one evening to Grace more briskly than usual. 'They have written to me again about that practice in Budmouth that I once negotiated for,' he said to her. 'The premium asked is eight hundred pounds, and I think that between your father and myself it ought to be raised. Then we can get away from this place for ever.'

The question had been mooted between them before, and she was not unprepared to consider it. They had not proceeded far with the discussion when a knock came to the door, and in a minute Grammer ran up to say that a message had arrived from Hintock House requesting Dr Fitzpiers to attend there at once. Mrs Charmond had met with a slight accident through the overturning of her carriage.

'This is something, anyhow,' said Fitzpiers, rising with an interest which he could not have defined. 'I have had a presentiment that this mysterious woman and I were to be better acquainted.'

The latter words were murmured to himself alone.

'Good-night,' said Grace as soon as he was ready. 'I shall be asleep probably when you return.'

'Good-night,' he replied inattentively, and went downstairs. It was the first time since their marriage that he had left her without a kiss.

CHAPTER 26

WINTERBORNE had given up his house. On this account his face was seen but fitfully in Hintock; and he would probably have disappeared from the place altogether but for his slight business connection with Melbury, on whose premises Giles kept his cider-making apparatus now that he had no place of his own to stow it in.

Coming here one afternoon on his way to a hut beyond the wood, where he now slept, he noticed that the familiar brown-thatched pinion of his paternal roof had vanished from its site, and that the walls were levelled, according to the landlords' principle at this date of getting rid of cottages whenever possible. In present circumstances he had a feeling for the spot that might have been called morbid, and when he had supped in the hut aforesaid he made use of the spare hour before bedtime to return to Little Hintock in the twilight, and ramble over the patch of ground on which he had first seen the day.

He repeated this evening visit on several like occasions. Even in the gloom he could trace where the different rooms had stood; could mark the shape of the kitchen chimney-corner in which he had roasted apples and potatoes in his boyhood, cast his bullets, and burnt his initials on articles that did and did not belong to him. The apple-trees still remained to show where the garden had been, the oldest of them even now retaining the crippled slant to north-east given them by the great November gale of 1824, which carried a brig bodily over the Chesil Bank. They were at present bent to still greater obliquity by the heaviness of their produce. Apples bobbed against his head, and in the grass beneath he crunched scores of them as he walked. There was nobody to gather them now.

It was on the evening under notice that, half-sitting, half-leaning against one of these inclined trunks, Winterborne became lost in his thoughts as usual, till one little star after another had taken up a position in the piece of sky which now confronted him where his walls and chimneys had formerly raised their outlines. The house had jutted awkwardly into the road and the opening caused by its absence was very distinct.

In the silence the trot of horses and the spin of carriage wheels became audible; the vehicle soon shaped itself against the blank sky, bearing down upon him with the bend in the lane which here occurred, and of which the house had been the cause. He could discern the figure of a woman high up on the driving-seat of a phaeton, a groom being just visible behind.

Presently there was a slight scrape, then a scream. Winterborne went across to the spot, and found the phaeton half overturned, its driver sitting on the heap of rubbish which had once been his dwelling, and the man seizing the horses' heads. The equipage was Mrs Charmond's and the unseated charioteer that lady herself.

To his inquiry if she were hurt she made some incoherent reply to the effect that she did not know. The damage in other respects was little or none; the phaeton was righted, Mrs Charmond placed in it and the reins given to the servant. It appeared that she had been deceived by the removal of the house, imagining the gap caused by the demolition to be the opening of the road, so that she turned in upon the ruins instead of at the bend, a few yards further on.

'Drive home – drive home!' she cried impatiently; and they started on their way.

They had not however gone many paces when, the air being still, Winterborne heard her say, 'Stop; tell that man to call the doctor – Mr Fitzpiers – and send him on to the House. I find I am hurt more seriously than I thought.'

The seriousness seemed ludicrous to Winterborne; but he took the message from the groom, and proceeded to the doctor's at once. Having delivered it he stepped back into the darkness, and waited till he had seen Fitzpiers leave the door. He stood for a few minutes looking at the window which, by its light, revealed the room where Grace was sitting; and went away under the gloomy trees.

Fitzpiers duly arrived at Hintock House, whose doors he now saw open for the first time. Contrary to his expectation there was visible no sign of that confusion or alarm which a grave accident to the mistress of the abode would have occasioned. He was shown into a room at the top of the staircase, cosily and femininely draped, where by the light of the shaded lamp he saw a woman of elegant figure reclining upon a couch in such a position as not to disturb a pile of magnificent hair on the crown of her head. A deep purple dressing-gown formed an admirable foil to the peculiarly rich brown of her hair-plaits; her left arm, which was naked nearly up to the shoulder, was thrown upwards, and between the fingers of her right hand she held a cigarette, while she idly breathed from her delicately curled lips a thin stream of smoke towards the ceiling.

The doctor's first feeling was a sense of his exaggerated prevision in having brought appliances for a serious case; the next, something more curious. While the scene and the moment were new to him and unanticipated, the sentiment and essence of the moment were indescribably familiar. What could be the cause of it? Probably a dream.

Mrs Charmond did not move more than to raise her eyes to him, and he came and stood by her. She glanced up at his face across her brows and forehead, and then he observed a blush creep slowly over her decidedly handsome cheeks. Her eyes, which had lingered upon him with an inquiring, conscious expression, were hastily withdrawn, and she mechanically applied the cigarette again to her lips.

For a moment he forgot his errand, till suddenly arousing himself he addressed her, formally condoled with her, and made the usual professional inquiries about what had happened to her, and where she was hurt.

'That's what I want you to tell me,' she murmured in tones of indefinable reserve. 'I quite believe in you, for I know you are very accomplished, because you study so hard.'

'I'll do my best to justify your good opinion,' said the young man, bowing. 'And none the less that I am happy to find the accident has not been serious.'

'I am very much shaken,' she said.

'O yes,' he replied; and completed his examination, which convinced him that there was really nothing the matter with her, and more than ever puzzled him as to why he had been summoned, since she did not appear to be a timid woman. 'You must rest a while; and I'll send something,' he said.

'O, I forgot,' she returned. 'Look here.' And she showed him a little scrape on her arm – the full round arm that was exposed. 'Put some court-plaster on that, please.'

He obeyed. 'And now, doctor,' she said, 'before you go I want to put a question to you. Sit round there in front of me, on that low chair, and bring the candles, or one, to the little table. Do you smoke? Yes? That's right – I am learning. Take one of these; and here's a light.' She threw a match-box across.

Fitzpiers caught it, and having lit up regarded her from his new position, which, with the shifting of the candles, for the first time afforded him a full view of her face.

'How many years have passed since first we met?' she resumed, in a voice which she endeavoured to maintain at its former pitch of composure, and eyeing him with daring bashfulness.

'*We* met, do you say?'

She nodded. 'I saw you recently at an hotel in London, when you were passing through, I suppose, with your bride, and I recognized you as one I had met in my girlhood. Do you remember, when you were studying at Heidelberg, an English family that was staying there, who used to walk—'

'And the young lady who wore a long tail of rare-coloured hair – ah, I see it before my eyes! – who lost her handkerchief on the Great Terrace – who was going back in the dusk to find it – to whom I said, "I'll go for it," and who answered, "O, it is not worth coming all the way up again for." I *do* remember, and how very long we stayed talking there: I went next morning, whilst the dew was on the grass: there it lay – a little morsel of damp lacework, with "Felice" marked in one corner. I see it now! I picked it up, and then....'

'Well?'

'I kissed it,' he rejoined, rather shamefacedly.

'But you had hardly ever seen me except in the dusk?'

'Never mind. I was young then, and I kissed it. I wondered how I could make the most of my *trouvaille*, and decided that I would call at your hotel with it that afternoon. It rained, and I waited till next day. I called, and you were gone.'

'Yes,' answered she with dry melancholy. 'My mother, knowing my face was my only fortune, said she had no wish for such a chit as me to go falling in love with an impecunious student, and spirited me away to Baden. As it is all over and past I'll tell you one thing; I should have sent you a line had I known your name. That name I never knew till my maid said as you passed up the hotel stairs a month ago, "There's Dr Fitzpiers."'

'Good God,' said Fitzpiers musingly. 'How the time comes back to me! The evening, the morning, the dew, the spot. When I found that you really were gone it was as if a cold iron had been passed down my back. I went up to where you had stood when I last saw you – I flung myself on the grass, and – being not much more than a boy – my eyes were literally blinded with tears. Nameless, unknown to me as you were, I couldn't forget your voice!'

'For how long?'

'O – ever so long. Days and days.'

'Days and days! *Only* days and days? O, the heart of a man! Days and days!'

'But, my dear madam, I had not known you more than a day or two. It was not a full-blown love – it was the merest bud – red, fresh, vivid, but small. It was a colossal passion in embryo. It never matured.'

'So much the better perhaps.'

'Perhaps. But see how powerless is the human will against predestination! We were prevented meeting; we have met. One feature of the case remains the same amid many changes. While you have grown rich, I am still poor. Better than that, you have (judging by your last remark) outgrown the foolish impulsive passions of your early girlhood. I have not outgrown mine.'

'I beg your pardon,' said she with vibrations of feeling in her words. 'I have been placed in a position which hinders such outgrowings. Besides, I don't believe that the genuine subjects of emotion do outgrow them; I believe that the older such people get the worse they are. Possibly at ninety or a hundred they may feel they are cured: but a mere threescore and ten won't do it – at least for me, if I live so long.'

He gazed at her in undisguised admiration. Here was a soul of souls!

'You speak truly,' he exclaimed. 'But you speak sadly as well. Why is that?'

'I always am sad when I come here,' she said, dropping to a low tone with a sense of having been too demonstrative.

'Then may I inquire why you came?'

'A man brought me. Women are always carried about like corks upon the waves of masculine desires. . . . I hope I have not alarmed you; but Hintock has the curious effect of bottling up the emotions till one can no longer hold them; I am often obliged to fly away and discharge my sentiments somewhere, or I should die outright.'

'There is very good society in the country, I suppose, for those who have the privilege of entering it.'

'Perhaps so. But the misery of remote country life is that your neighbours have no toleration for difference of opinion and habit. My neighbours think I am an atheist, except those who think I am a Roman Catholic; and when I speak disrespectfully of the weather or the crops they think I am a blasphemer.'

'You don't wish me to stay any longer?' he inquired, when he found that she remained musing.

'No – I think not.'

'Then tell me that I am to be gone.'

'Why? cannot you go without?'

'I may consult my own feelings only, if left to myself.'

'Well, if you do, what then? Do you suppose you'll be in my way?'

'I feared it might be so.'

'Then fear no more. But good-night. Come to-morrow and see if I am going on right. This renewal of acquaintance touches me. I have already a friendship for you.'

'If it depends upon myself it shall last for ever.'

'My best hopes that it may!'

Fitzpiers went down the stairs absolutely unable to decide whether she had sent for him in the natural alarm which might have followed her mishap, or with the single view of making herself known to him as she had done, for which the capsize had afforded excellent opportunity.

Outside the house he mused over the spot under the light of the stars. It seemed very strange that he should have come there more than once when its inhabitant was absent, and observed the house with a nameless interest; that he should have assumed off-hand before he knew Grace that it was here she lived; that, in short, at sundry times and seasons the individuality of Hintock House should have forced itself upon him as appertaining to some existence with which he was concerned.

The intersection of his temporal orbit with Mrs Charmond's for a day or two in the past had created a sentimental interest in her at the time, but it had been so evanescent that in the ordinary onward roll of affairs he would scarce ever have recalled it again. To find her here, however, in these somewhat romantic circumstances, magnified that bygone and transitory tenderness to indescribable proportions.

On entering Little Hintock he found himself regarding that hamlet in a new way – from the Hintock House point of view rather than from his own and the Melburys'. The household had all gone to bed. As he went upstairs he heard the snore of the timber-merchant from his quarter of the building, and turned into the passage communicating with his own rooms in a strange access of sadness.

A light was burning for him in the chamber; but Grace, though in bed, was not asleep. In a moment her sympathetic voice came from behind the curtains.

'Edred, is she very seriously hurt?'

Fitzpiers had so entirely lost sight of Mrs Charmond as a patient that he was not on the instant ready with a reply.

'O no,' he said. 'There are no bones broken, but she is shaken. I am going again to-morrow.'

Another inquiry or two, and Grace said –

'Did she ask for me?'

'Well, I think she did – I don't quite remember; but I am under the impression that she spoke of you.'

'Cannot you recollect at all what she said?'

'I cannot, just this minute.'

'At any rate, she did not talk much about me?' said Grace with disappointment.

'O no.'

'But you did, perhaps,' she added, innocently fishing for a compliment.

'O yes – you may depend upon that!' replied he warmly, though scarcely thinking of what he was saying, so vividly was there present to his mind the personality of Mrs Charmond.

CHAPTER 27

THE doctor's professional visit to Hintock House was promptly repeated the next day and the next. He always found Mrs Charmond reclining on a sofa, and behaving generally as became a patient who was in no great hurry to lose that title. On each occasion he looked gravely at the little scratch on her arm, as if it had been a serious wound.

He had also, to his further satisfaction, found a slight scar on her temple, and it was very convenient to put a piece of black plaster on this conspicuous part of her person in preference to gold-beater's skin, so that it might catch the eyes of the servants and make his presence appear decidedly necessary, in case there should be any doubt of the fact.

'O – you hurt me!' she exclaimed one day.

He was peeling off the bit of plaster on her arm, under which the scrape had turned the colour of an unripe blackberry previous to vanishing altogether.

'Wait a moment then – I'll damp it,' said Fitzpiers. He put his lips to the place and kept them there, without any objecting on her part, till the plaster came off easily. 'It was at your request I put it on,' said he.

'I know it,' she replied. 'Is that blue vein still in my temple that used to show there? The scar must be just upon it. If the cut had been a little deeper it would have spilt my hot blood indeed!'

Fitzpiers examined so closely that his breath touched her tenderly, at which their eyes rose to an encounter – hers showing themselves as deep and mysterious as interstellar space. She turned her face away.

'Ah! none of that! none of that – I cannot coquet with you!' she cried. 'Don't suppose I consent to for one moment. Our poor, brief, youthful hour of love-making was too long ago to bear continuing now. It is as well that we should understand each other on that point before we go further.'

'Coquet! Nor I with you. As it was when I found the historic handkerchief, so it is now. I might have been and may be foolish; but I am no trifler. I naturally cannot forget that little space in which I flitted across the field of your vision in those days of the past, and the recollection opens up all sorts of imaginings.'

'Suppose my mother had not taken me away?' she murmured, her dreamy eyes resting on the swaying tip of a distant tree.

'I should have seen you again.'

'And then?'

'Then the fire would have burnt higher and higher. What would have immediately followed I know not, but sorrow and sickness of heart at last.'

'Why?'

'Well – that's the end of all love, according to Nature's law. I can give no other reason.'

'O, don't speak like that!' she exclaimed. 'Since we are only picturing the possibilities of that time, don't for pity's sake spoil the picture.' Her voice sank almost to a whisper as she added with an incipient pout upon her lips, 'Let me think at least that if you had really loved me at all seriously you would have loved me for ever and ever!'

'You are right – think it with all your heart,' said he. 'It is a pleasant thought, and costs nothing.'

She weighed that remark in silence a while. 'Did you ever hear anything of me from then till now?' she inquired.

'Not a word.'

'So much the better. I had to fight the battle of life as well as you. I may tell you about it some day. But don't ever ask me to do it, and particularly do not press me to tell you now.'

Thus the two or three days that they had spent in tender acquaintance on the romantic slopes above the Neckar were stretched out in retrospect to the length and importance of years; made to form a canvas for infinite fancies, idle dreams, luxurious melancholies, and pretty, alluring assertions which could neither be proved nor disproved.

Grace was never mentioned between them, but a rumour of his contemplated removal from the neighbourhood somehow reached Mrs Charmond's ears.

'Doctor, you are going away!' she exclaimed, confronting him with accusatory reproach in her large dark eyes no less than in her cooing voice. 'O yes, you are,' she went on, springing to her feet with an air which might almost have been called passionate. 'It is no use denying it! You have bought a practice at Budmouth. I don't blame you. Nobody can live at Hintock – least of all a professional man who wants to keep abreast of recent discovery. And there is nobody here to induce such a one to stay for other reasons. That's right, that's right – go away!'

'But no – I have not actually bought the practice as yet, though I am indeed in treaty for it. And, my dear friend, if I continue to feel about the business as I feel at this moment – perhaps I may conclude never to go at all.'

'But you hate Hintock, and everything and everybody in it that you don't mean to take away with you!'

Fitzpiers contradicted this idea in his most vibratory tones, and she lapsed into the frivolous archness under which she hid passions of no mean strength – strange, smouldering, erratic passions, kept down like a stifled conflagration, but bursting out now here, now there – the only certain element in their direction being its unexpectedness.

If one word could have expressed Felice Charmond it would have been Inconsequence. She was a woman of perversities, delighting in piquant contrasts. She liked mystery, in her life, in her love, in her history. To be fair to her, there was nothing in these which she had any great reason to be ashamed of, and many things of which she might have been proud; but her past had never been fathomed by the honest minds of Hintock, and she rarely volunteered her experiences. As for her capricious nature the people on her estates grew accustomed to it, and with that marvellous subtlety of contrivance in steering round odd tempers that is found in sons of the soil and dependents generally, they managed to get along under her government rather better than they would have done beneath a more equable rule.

Now, with regard to the doctor's notion of leaving Hintock, he had advanced further towards completing the purchase of the Budmouth surgeon's goodwill than he had admitted to Mrs Charmond. The whole matter hung upon what he might do in the ensuing twenty-four hours. The evening after leaving her he went out into the lane, and walked and pondered between the high hedges, now greenish-white with wild clematis – here called 'old-man's-beard' from its aspect later in the year.

The letter of acceptance was to be written that night, after which his departure from Hintock would be irrevocable. But could he go away, remembering what had just passed? The trees, the hills, the leaves, the grass – each had been endowed and quickened with a subtle light since he had discovered the person and history, and above all, the mood of their owner. There was every temporal reason for leaving: it would be entering again into a world which he had only quitted in a passion for isolation, induced by a fit of Achillean moodiness after an imagined slight. His wife herself saw the awkwardness of their position here, and cheerfully welcomed the purposed change, towards which every step had been taken but the last. But could he find it in his heart – as he found it clearly enough in his conscience – to go away? No.

He drew a troubled breath and went indoors. Here he rapidly penned a letter, wherein he withdrew, once for all, from the treaty for the Budmouth practice. As the postman had already left Little Hintock for that night he sent one of Melbury's men to intercept a mail-cart on another turnpike-road, and so got the letter off.

The man returned, met Fitzpiers in the lane, and told him

the thing was done. Fitzpiers went back to his house musing. Why had he carried out this impulse – taken such wild trouble to effect a probable injury to his own and his young wife's prospects? His motive was fantastic, glowing, shapeless as the fiery scenery about the western sky. Mrs Charmond could overtly be nothing more to him than a patient, and to his wife, at the outside, a patron. Yet in the unattached bachelor days of his first sojourn here how highly proper an emotional reason for lingering on would have appeared to troublesome dubiousness. Matrimonial ambition is such an honourable thing!

'My father has told me that you have sent off one of the men with a late letter to Budmouth,' cried Grace, coming out vivaciously to meet him under the declining light of the sky, wherein hung, solitary, the folding star. 'I said at once that you had finally agreed to pay the premium they ask, and that the tedious question had been settled. When do we go, Edred?'

'I have changed my mind,' said he. 'They want too much – seven hundred and fifty is too large a sum, – and in short I had declined to go further. We must wait for another opportunity. I fear I am not a good business man.'

He spoke the last words with a momentary faltering at the great foolishness of his act; and as he looked in her fair and honourable face his heart reproached him for what he had done.

Her manner that evening showed her disappointment. Personally she liked the home of her childhood much, and she was not ambitious. But her husband had seemed so dissatisfied with the circumstances hereabout since their marriage that she had sincerely hoped to go for his sake.

It was two or three days before he visited Mrs Charmond again. The morning had been windy, and little showers had scattered themselves like grain against the walls and window-panes of the Hintock cottages. He went on foot across the wilder recesses of the park, where slimy streams of fresh moisture, exuding from decayed holes caused by old amputations, ran down the bark of the oaks and elms, the rind below being coated with a lichenous wash as green as emerald. They were stout-trunked trees, that never rocked their stems in the fiercest gale, responding to it only by crooking their limbs. Wrinkled like an old crone's face, and antlered with dead branches that rose above the foliage of their summits, they were nevertheless still green – though yellow had invaded the leaves of other trees.

She was in a little boudoir or writing-room on the first floor, and Fitzpiers was much surprised to find that the window curtains were closed and a red-shaded lamp and candles burning, though out of doors it was broad daylight. Moreover a large fire was burning in the grate, though it was not cold.

'What does it all mean?' he asked.

She sat in an easy-chair, her face being turned away.

'O,' she murmured, 'it is because the world is so dreary outside! Sorrow and bitterness in the sky, and floods of agonized tears beating against the panes. I lay awake last night, and I could hear the scrape of snails creeping up the window glass; it was so sad! My eyes were so heavy this morning that I could have wept my life away. I cannot bear you to see my face; I keep it away from you purposely. O! why were we given hungry hearts and wild desires if we have to live in a world like this? Why should Death alone lend what Life is compelled to borrow – rest? Answer that, Dr Fitzpiers.'

'You must eat of a second tree of knowledge before *you* can do it, Felice Charmond.'

'Then, when my emotions have exhausted themselves, I become full of fears, till I think I shall die for very fear. The terrible insistencies of society – how severe they are, and cold, and inexorable – ghastly towards those who are made of wax and not of stone. O, I am afraid of them; a stab for this error, and a stab for that – correctives and regulations pretendedly framed that society may tend to perfection – an end which I don't care for in the least. Yet for this all I do care for has to be stunted and starved.'

Fitzpiers had seated himself near her. 'What sets you in this mournful mood?' he asked gently. In reality he thought that it was the result of a loss of tone from staying indoors so much, but he did not say so.

'My reflections. Doctor, you must not come here any more. They begin to think it a farce already. I say you must come no more. There – don't be angry with me!' – and she jumped up, pressed his hand, and looked anxiously at him. 'It is necessary. It is best for both you and me.'

'But,' said Fitzpiers gloomily, 'what have we done?'

'Done – we have done nothing. Perhaps we have thought the more. However, it is all vexation. I am going away to Middleton Abbey, near Shottsford, where a relative of my late husband lives, who is confined to her bed. The engagement was made in London, and I can't get out of it. Perhaps it is for the best that I go there till all this is past. When are you going to enter on your new practice, and leave Hintock behind for ever, with your pretty wife on your arm?'

'I have refused the opportunity. I love this place too well to depart.'

'You *have*?' she said, regarding him with wild uncertainty. 'Why do you ruin yourself in that way? Great heaven, what have I done!'

'Nothing. Besides, you are going away.'

'O yes; but only to Middleton Abbey for a month or two. Yet perhaps I shall gain strength there – particularly strength of mind – I require it. And when I come back I shall be a new woman; and you can come and see me safely then, and bring your wife with you, and we'll be friends – she and I. O, how this shutting up of one's self does lead to indulgence in idle sentiments! I shall not wish you to give your attendance to me after to-day. But I am glad that you are not going away – if your remaining does not injure your prospects at all.'

As soon as he had left the room the mild friendliness she had preserved in her tone at parting, the playful sadness with which she had conversed with him, equally departed from her. She became as heavy as lead – just as she had been before he arrived. Her whole being seemed to dissolve in a sad powerlessness to do anything, and the sense of it made her lips tremulous and her closed eyes wet.

His footsteps again startled her, and she turned round.

'I return for a moment to tell you that the evening is going to be fine. The sun is shining, so do open your curtains and put out those lights. Shall I do it for you?'

'Please – if you don't mind.'

He drew back the window curtains, whereupon the red glow of the lamp and the two candle-flames became almost invisible under the flood of late autumn sunlight that poured in.

'Shall I come round to you?' he asked, her back being towards him.

'No,' she replied.

'Why not?'

'Because I am going, and I don't want you to see my face in the full sun's rays.'

He stood a moment irresolute, and regretted that he had killed the rosy passionate lamplight by opening the curtains and letting in garish day.

'Then I am going,' he said.

'Very well,' she answered, stretching one hand round to him, and patting her eyes with a handkerchief held in the other.

'Shall I write a line to you at—?'

'No, no.' A gentle reasonableness came into her tone as she added, 'It must not be, you know. It won't do.'

'Very well. Good-bye.' The next moment he was gone.

In the evening with listless adroitness she encouraged the maid who dressed her for dinner to speak of Dr Fitzpiers's marriage.

'Mrs Fitzpiers was once supposed to favour Mr Winterborne,' said the young woman.

'But why didn't she marry him?' said Mrs Charmond.

'Because you see, ma'am, he lost his houses.'

'Lost his houses? How came he to do that?'

'The houses were held on lives, and the lives dropped, and your agent wouldn't renew them, though it is said that Mr

Winterborne had a very good claim. That's as I've heard it, ma'am, and it was through it that the match was broke off.'

Being just then distracted by a dozen emotions, Mrs Charmond sank into a mood of dismal self-reproach. 'In refusing that poor man his reasonable request,' she said to herself, 'my agent foredoomed my revived girlhood's romance. Who would have thought such a business matter could have nettled my own heart like this! Now for a winter of regrets and agonies and useless wishes, till I forget him in the spring. O! I am glad I am going away!'

She left her chamber, and went down to dine with a sigh. On the stairs she stood opposite the large window for a moment, and looked out upon the lawn. It was not yet quite dark. Half-way up the steep green slope confronting her stood old Timothy Tangs, who was shortening his way homeward by clambering here where there was no road; and in opposition to express orders that no path was to be made there. Tangs had momentarily stopped to take a pinch of snuff, but observing Mrs Charmond gazing at him he hastened to get over the top out of hail. His precipitancy made him miss his footing, and he rolled like a barrel to the bottom, his snuff-box rolling in front of him.

Her indefinite idle impossible passion for Fitzpiers, her constitutional cloud of misery, the sorrowful drops that still hung upon her eyelashes, all made way for the impulse started by the spectacle. She burst into an immoderate fit of laughter; her very gloom of the previous hour seeming to render it the more uncontrollable. It had not died out of her when she reached the dining-room; and even here, before the servants, her shoulders suddenly shook as the scene returned upon her; and the tears of her risibility mingled with the remnants of those engendered by her grief.

She resolved to be sad no more. She drank two glasses of champagne, and a little more still after those; and amused herself in the evening with singing pretty amatory songs.

'I must do something for that poor man Winterborne, however,' she said.

CHAPTER 28

A WEEK had passed, and Mrs Charmond had left Hintock House. Middleton Abbey, the place of her sojourn, was about a dozen miles distant by road, a little less by bridle-paths and footways.

Grace observed, for the first time, that her husband was restless, that at moments he even was disposed to avoid her. The scrupulous civility of mere acquaintanceship crept into his manner; yet when sitting at meals he seemed hardly to hear her remarks. Her little doings interested him no longer, whilst towards her father his bearing was not far from supercilious. It was plain that his mind was entirely outside her life, whereabouts outside it she could not tell; in some region of science possibly, or of psychological literature. But her hope that he was again immersing himself in those lucubrations which before her marriage had made his light a landmark in Hintock, was founded simply on the slender fact that he often sat up late.

One day she discovered him leaning over a gate on High-Stoy Hill, some way from Little Hintock, which opened on the brink of a declivity, slanting down directly into White-Hart or Blackmoor Vale, extending beneath the eye at this point to a distance of many miles. His attention was fixed on the landscape far away eastward, and Grace's approach was so noiseless that he did not hear her. When she came close she could see his lips moving unconsciously, as on some impassioned visionary theme.

She spoke, and Fitzpiers started. 'What are you looking at?' she asked.

'O! I was contemplating my mother's people's old place of Sherton Abbas, in my idle way,' he said.

It had seemed to her that he was looking much to the right of that cradle and tomb of his ancestral dignity; but she made no further observation, and taking his arm walked home beside him almost in silence. She did not know that Middleton Abbey lay in the direction of his gaze.

'Are you going to have out Darling this afternoon?' she asked presently.

Darling, the aged light-grey mare which Winterborne had bought for Grace, Fitzpiers now constantly used, the animal having turned out a wonderful bargain in combining a perfect docility with an almost human intelligence; moreover, she was not too young. Fitzpiers was unfamiliar with horses, and he valued these qualities.

'Yes,' he replied, 'but not to drive. I am riding her. I practise crossing a horse as often as I can now, for I find that I can take much shorter cuts on horseback.'

He had, in fact, taken these riding exercises for about a week, only since Mrs Charmond's absence; his universal practice hitherto having been to drive.

Some few days later Fitzpiers started on the back of this horse to see a patient in the aforesaid Vale. It was about five o'clock in the evening when he went away, and at bedtime he had not reached home. There was nothing very singular in this, though she was not aware that he had any patient more than five or six miles distant in that direction. The clock had struck one before Fitzpiers entered the house, and he came to his room softly, as if anxious not to disturb her.

The next morning she was stirring considerably earlier than he. In the yard there was a conversation going on about the mare; the man who attended to the horses, Darling included, insisted that the latter was 'hag-rid'; for when he had arrived at the stable that morning she was in such a state as no horse could be in by honest riding. It was true that the doctor had stabled her himself when he got home, so that she was not looked after as she would have been if the speaker had groomed and fed her; but that did not account for the appearance she presented, if Mr Fitzpiers's journey had been only where he had stated. The unprecedented exhaustion of Darling, as thus related, was sufficient to develop a whole series of tales about equestrian witches and demons, the narration of which occupied a considerable time.

Grace returned indoors. In passing through the outer room she picked up her husband's overcoat which he had carelessly flung down across a chair. A turnpike ticket fell out of the breast-pocket, and she saw that it had been issued at Middleton Gate. He had therefore visited Middleton the previous night, a distance of at least four-and-twenty miles on horseback, there and back.

During the day she made some inquiries, and learnt for the first time that Mrs Charmond was staying at Middleton Abbey. She could not resist an inference – strange as that inference was.

A few days later he prepared to start again, at the same time and in the same direction. She knew that the state of the cottager who lived that way was a mere pretext; she was quite sure he was going to Mrs Charmond.

Grace was amazed at the mildness of the anger which the suspicion engendered in her. She was but little excited, and her jealousy was languid even to death. It told tales of the nature of her affection for him. In truth, her ante-nuptial regard for Fitzpiers had been rather of the quality of awe towards a superior being than of tender solicitude for a lover. It had been based upon mystery and strangeness – the mystery of his past, of his knowledge, of his professional skill, of his beliefs. When this structure of ideals was demolished by the intimacy of common life, and she found him as merely human as the Hintock people themselves, a new foundation was in demand for an enduring and staunch affection – a sympathetic interdependence, wherein mutual weaknesses are made the grounds of a defensive alliance. Fitzpiers had furnished nothing of that single-minded confidence and truth out of which alone such a second union could spring; hence it was with a controllable emotion that she now watched the mare brought round.

'I'll walk with you to the hill if you are not in a great hurry,' she said, rather loth, after all, to let him go.

'Do; there's plenty of time,' replied her husband.

Accordingly he led along the horse, and walked beside her, impatient enough nevertheless. Thus they proceeded to the turnpike road, and ascended towards the base of High-Stoy and Dogbury Hill, till they were just beneath the gate he had been leaning over when she surprised him ten days before. This was the end of her excursion. Fitzpiers bade her adieu with affection, even with tenderness, and she observed that he looked weary-eyed.

'Why do you go to-night?' she said. 'You have been called up two nights in succession already.'

'I must go,' he answered, almost gloomily. 'Don't wait up for me.' With these words he mounted his horse, turned into a branch road by the turnpike; and ambled down the incline to the valley.

She ascended the slope of High-Stoy and watched his descent, and then his journey onward. His way was east, the evening sun which stood behind her back beaming full upon him as soon as he got out from the shade of the hill. Notwithstanding this untoward proceeding she was determined to be loyal if he proved true; and the determination to love one's best will carry a heart a long way towards making that best an ever-growing thing.

The conspicuous coat of the active though blanching mare made horse and rider easy objects for the vision. Though Darling had been chosen with such pains by Winterborne for Grace, she had never ridden the sleek creature; but her husband had found the animal exceedingly convenient, particularly now that he had taken to the saddle, plenty of staying power being left in Darling yet for journeys of moderate length. Fitzpiers, like others of his character, while despising Melbury and his station, did not at all disdain to spend Melbury's money, or appropriate to his own use the horse which belonged to Melbury's daughter.

And so the infatuated surgeon went along through the gorgeous autumn landscape of White-Hart Vale, surrounded by orchards lustrous with the reds of apple-crops, berries, and foliage, the whole intensified by the gilding of the declining sun. The earth this year had been prodigally bountiful, and now was the supreme moment of her bounty. In the poorest spots the hedges were bowed with haws and blackberries; acorns cracked underfoot, and the burst husks of chestnuts lay exposing their auburn contents as if arranged by anxious sellers in a fruit-market. In all this proud show some kernels were unsound as her own situation, and she wondered if there were one world in the universe where the fruit had no worm, and marriage no sorrow.

Her Tannhäuser still moved on, his plodding steed rendering him distinctly visible yet. Could she have heard Fitzpiers's voice at that moment she would have found it murmuring –

> '– Towards the loadstar of my one desire
> I flitted, like a dizzy moth, whose flight
> Is as a dead leaf's in the owlet light.'

But he was a silent spectacle to her. Soon he rose out of the valley, and skirted a high plateau of the chalk formation on his right, which rested abruptly upon the fruity district of deep loam, the character and herbage of the two formations being so distinct that the calcareous upland appeared but as a deposit of a few years' antiquity upon the level vale.

He kept along the edge of this high, uninclosed country, and the sky behind him being deep violet she could still see white Darling in relief upon it – a mere speck now – a Wouvermans eccentricity reduced to microscopic dimensions. Upon this high ground he gradually disappeared.

Thus she had beheld the pet animal purchased for her own use, in pure love of her, by one who had always been true, impressed to convey her husband away from her to the side of a new-found idol. While she was musing on the vicissitudes of horses and wives she discerned shapes moving up the valley towards her, quite near at hand, though till now hidden by the hedges. Surely they were Giles Winterborne, with two horses and a cider-apparatus, conducted by Robert Creedle. Up, upward they crept, a stray beam of the sun alighting every now and then like a star on the blades of the pomace-shovels, which had been converted to steel mirrors by the action of the malic acid. She descended to the road when he came close, and the panting horses rested as they achieved the ascent.

'How do you do, Giles?' said she, under a sudden impulse to be familiar with him.

He replied with much more reserve. 'You are going for a walk, Mrs Fitzpiers?' he added. 'It is pleasant just now.'

'No, I am returning,' said she.

The vehicles passed on, and Creedle with them, and Winterborne walked by her side in the rear of the apple-mill.

He looked and smelt like Autumn's very brother, his face being sunburnt to wheat-colour, his eyes blue as corn-flowers, his sleeves and leggings dyed with fruit-stains, his hands clammy with the sweet juice of apples, his hat sprinkled with pips, and everywhere about him that atmosphere of cider which at its first return each season has such an indescribable fascination for those who have been born and bred among the orchards. Her heart rose from its late sadness like a released bough; her senses revelled in the sudden lapse back to Nature unadorned. The consciousness of having to be genteel because of her husband's profession, the veneer of artificiality which she had acquired at the fashionable schools, were thrown off, and she became the crude country girl of her latent early instincts.

Nature was bountiful, she thought. No sooner had she been cast aside by Edred Fitzpiers than another being, impersonating chivalrous and undiluted manliness, had arisen out of the earth ready to her hand. This, however, was an excursion of the imagination which she did not wish to encourage, and she said suddenly, to disguise the confused regard which had followed her thoughts, 'Did you meet my husband?'

Winterborne with some hesitation: 'Yes.'

'Where did you meet him?'

'Near Reveller's Inn. I come from Middleton Abbey; I have been making there for the last week.'

'Haven't they a mill of their own?'

'Yes, but it's out of repair.'

'I think – I heard that Mrs Charmond had gone there to stay?'

'Yes, I have seen her at the windows once or twice.'

Grace waited an interval before she went on; 'Did Mr Fitzpiers take the way to Middleton?'

'Yes. . . . I met him on Darling.' As she did not reply, he added with a gentler inflection, 'You know why the mare was called that?'

'O yes – of course,' she answered quickly.

With their minds on these things they passed so far round the hill that the whole west sky was revealed. Between the broken clouds they could see far into the recesses of heaven as they mused and walked, the eye journeying on under a species of golden arcades, and past fiery obstructions, fancied cairns, logan-stones, stalactites and stalagmites of topaz. Deeper than this their gaze passed thin flakes of incandescence, till it plunged into a bottomless medium of soft green fire.

Her abandonment to the seductive hour and scene after her sense of ill-usage, her revolt for the nonce against social law, her passionate desire for primitive life may have showed in her face. Winterborne was looking at her, his eyes lingering on a flower that she wore in her bosom. Almost with the abstraction of a somnambulist he stretched out his hand and gently caressed the flower.

She drew back. 'What are you doing, Giles Winterborne?' she exclaimed, with severe surprise.

The evident absence of all premeditation from the act, however, speedily led her to think that it was not necessary to stand upon her dignity here and now. 'You must bear in mind, Giles,' she said kindly, 'that we are not as we were; and some people might have said that what you did was taking a liberty.'

It was more than she need have told him; his action of forgetfulness had made him so angry with himself that he flushed through his tan.

'I don't know what I am coming to!' he exclaimed savagely. 'Ah – I was not once like this!' Tears of vexation were in his eyes.

'No, now – it was nothing! I was too reproachful.'

'It would not have occurred to me if I had not seen something like it done elsewhere – at Middleton lately,' he said thoughtfully after a while.

'By whom?'

'Don't ask it.'

She scanned him narrowly. 'I know quite well enough,' she returned indifferently. 'It was by my husband, and the woman was Mrs Charmond. Association of ideas reminded you when you saw me. . . . Giles – tell me all you know about that – please do, Giles! But no – I won't hear it. Let the subject cease. And as you are my friend say nothing to my father.'

They had descended into the vale again to a place where their ways divided. Winterborne continued along the highway which kept outside the copse, and Grace opened a gate that entered it.

CHAPTER 29

SHE walked up the soft grassy ride, screened on either hand by nut-bushes just now heavy with clusters of twos and threes and fours. A little way on the track she pursued was crossed by a similar one at right angles. Here Grace stopped; some few yards up the transverse ride the buxom Suke Damson was visible – her gown tucked up high through her pocket-hole, and no bonnet on her head – in the act of pulling down boughs from which she was gathering and eating nuts with great rapidity, her lover Tim Tangs standing near her engaged in the same pleasant meal.

Crack, crack, went Suke's jaws every second or two. By an automatic leap of thought Grace's mind reverted to the tooth-drawing scene described by her husband; and for the first time she wondered if that narrative were really true, Susan's jaws being so obviously sound and strong. Grace turned up towards the nut-gatherers, and conquered her reluctance to speak to the girl, who was a little in advance of Tim. 'Good evening, Susan,' she said.

'Good evening, Miss Melbury' – (crack).

'Mrs Fitzpiers.'

'O yes, ma'am – Mrs Fitzpiers,' said Suke with a peculiar sniff and curtsey.

Grace, not to be daunted, continued, 'Take care of your teeth, Suke. That accounts for your toothache.'

'O, I don't know what an ache is, either in tooth, ear, or head, thank the Lord' – (crack).

'Nor the loss of one, either?'

'See for yourself, ma'am.' She parted her red lips and exhibited the whole double row, full up and unimpaired.

'You have never had one drawn?'

'Never.'

'So much the better for your stomach,' said Mrs Fitzpiers in an altered voice. And turning away quickly she went on thinking what gall she could drop into poor Tim Tangs's honey if she chose.

As her husband's character thus shaped itself under the touch of time, Grace was almost startled to find how little she suffered from that jealous excitement which is conventionally attributed to all wives in such circumstances. But though possessed by none of the feline wildness which it was her moral duty to experience, she did not fail to suspect that she had made a frightful mistake in her marriage. Acquiescence in her father's wishes had been degradation to herself. People are not given premonitions for nothing; she should have obeyed her impulse on that early morning when she peeped and saw the figure come from Fitzpiers's door, and have steadfastly refused her hand.

O that plausible tale which her then betrothed had told her about Suke – the dramatic account of her entreaties to him to draw the aching enemy, and the fine artistic finish he had given to the story by explaining that it was a lovely molar without a flaw!

She traced the remainder of the woodland track, dazed by the complications of her position. If his protestations to her before their marriage could be believed, her husband had felt affection of some sort for herself and this woman simultaneously; and was now again spreading the same conjoint emotion over Mrs Charmond and herself, his manner being still kind and fond at times. But surely, rather than that, he must have played the hypocrite towards her in each case with elaborate completeness; and the thought of this sickened her, for it involved the conjecture that if he had not loved her his only motive for making her his wife must have been her little fortune.

Yet here Grace made a mistake, for the love of men like Fitzpiers is unquestionably of such quality as to bear division and transference. He had indeed once declared, though not to her, that on one occasion he had noticed himself to be possessed by five distinct infatuations at the same time. If this were true, his differed from the highest affection as the lower orders of the animal world differ from advanced organisms, partition causing not death but a multiplied existence. He had loved her sincerely in his selfish way, and had by no means ceased to love her now. But such double and treble-barrelled hearts were naturally beyond her conception.

Of poor Suke Damson Grace thought no more. She had had her day.

'If he does not love me I will not love him!' said Grace proudly.

And though these were mere words it was a somewhat formidable thing for Fitzpiers that her heart was approximating to a state in which it might be possible to carry them out. That very absence of hot jealousy in her which made his courses so easy, and on which, indeed, he congratulated himself, meant, unknown to either wife or husband, more mischief than the inconvenient watchfulness of a jaundiced eye.

Her sleep that night was nervous. The wing allotted to her and her husband had never seemed so lonely. At last she got up, put on her dressing-gown, and went downstairs. Her father, who slept lightly, heard her descend, and came to the stair-head.

'Is that you, Grace? What's the matter?' he said.

'Nothing more than that I am restless. Edred is detained by a case in White-Hart Vale.'

'But how's that? I met the woman's husband going to Great Hintock just afore bedtime; and she was going on well, and the doctor gone then.'

'Then he's detained somewhere else,' said Grace. 'Never mind me; he will soon be home. I expect him about one.'

She went back to her room, and dozed and woke several times. One o'clock had been the hour of his return on the last occasion; but it had passed now by a long way, and still Fitzpiers did not come. Just before dawn she heard the men stirring in the yard, and the flashes of their lanterns spread every now and then through her window-blind. She remembered that her father had told her not to be disturbed if she noticed them, as they would be rising early to send off four loads of hurdles to a distant sheep-fair. Peeping out she saw them bustling about, the hollow-turner among the rest; he was loading his wares – wooden bowls, dishes, spigots, spoons, cheese-vats, funnels and so on – upon one of her father's waggons, who carried them to the fair for him every year out of neighbourly kindness.

The scene and the occasion would have enlivened her but that her husband was still absent, though it was now five o'clock. She could hardly suppose him, whatever his infatuation, to have prolonged to a later hour than ten an ostensibly professional call on Mrs Charmond at Middleton; and he could have ridden home in two hours. What then had become of him? That he had been out the greater part of the two preceding nights added to her uneasiness.

She dressed herself, descended, and went out, the weird twilight of advancing day chilling the rays from the lanterns, and making the men's faces wan. As soon as Melbury saw her he came round, showing his alarm.

'Edred is not come,' she said. 'And I have reason to know that he's not attending anybody. He has had no rest for two nights before this. I was going to the top of the hill to look for him.'

'I'll come with you,' said Melbury.

She begged him not to hinder himself; but he insisted, for he saw a peculiar and rigid gloom in her face over and above her uneasiness, and did not like the look of it. Telling the men he would be with them again soon he walked beside her into the turnpike-road, and partly up the way whence she had watched Fitzpiers the night before as he skirted the Great Blackmoor or White-Hart Valley.

They halted beneath a half-dead oak, hollow and disfigured with white tumours, its roots spreading out like claws grasping the ground. A chilly wind circled round them, upon whose currents the seeds of a neighbouring lime-tree, supported parachute-wise by the wing attached, flew out of the boughs downward like fledglings from their nest. The vale was wrapped in a dim atmosphere of unnaturalness, and the east was like a livid curtain edged with pink. There was no sign nor sound of Fitzpiers.

'It is no use standing here,' said her father. 'He may come home fifty ways.... Why, look here – here be Darling's tracks – turned homeward and nearly blown dry and hard! He must have come in hours ago without your seeing him.'

'He has not done that,' said she.

They went back hastily. On entering their own gates they perceived that the men had left the waggons, and were standing round the door of the stable which had been appropriated to the doctor's use.

'Is there anything the matter?' cried Grace.

'O no, ma'am. All's well that ends well,' said old Timothy Tangs. 'I've heard of such things before – amongst workfolk, though not amongst your gentle-people – that's true.'

They entered the stable, and saw the pale shape of Darling standing in the middle of her stall, with Fitzpiers on her back, sound asleep. Darling was munching hay as well as she could with the bit in her mouth, and the reins, which had fallen from Fitzpiers's hand, hung upon her neck.

Grace went and touched his hand; shook it, before she could arouse him. He moved, started, opened his eyes, and exclaimed, 'Ah, Felice. ... O, it's Grace. I could not see in the gloom. What – am I in the saddle!'

'Yes,' said she. 'How do you come here?'

He collected his thoughts, and in a few minutes stammered as he began dismounting: 'I was riding along homeward through the Vale, very, very sleepy, having been up so much of late. When I came opposite Lydden Spring the mare turned her head that way as if she wanted to drink. I let her go in, and she drank; I thought she would never finish. While she was drinking the clock of Newland Buckton church struck twelve. I distinctly remember counting the strokes. From that moment I positively recollect nothing till I saw you here by my side.'

'The Name! If it had been any other horse you'd have had a broken neck!' murmured Melbury.

' 'Tis wonderful, sure, how a quiet hoss will bring a man home at such times!' said John Upjohn. 'And – what's more wonderful than keeping your seat in a deep slumbering sleep – I've knowed men drowze off walking home from randies where the beer and other liquors have gone round well, and keep walking for more than a mile on end without waking. Well, doctor, 'tis a mercy you wasn't a-drownded, or a-splintered, or a-hanged up to a tree like Absalont – also a handsome gentleman like yerself, as the prophets say!'

'True,' murmured old Timothy piously, 'from the sole of his boots to the crown of his hat there was no blemish in him!'

'Or leastwise you might ha' been a-wounded into tatters a'most and no brother-tradesman to jine your few limbs together within seven mile!'

Whilst this impressive address was proceeding Fitzpiers had dismounted, and taking Grace's arm walked stiffly indoors with her. Melbury stood staring at the horse, which, in addition to being very weary, was spattered with mud. Whilst they were rubbing down the mare Melbury's mind coupled with the mud, which was not local, the name he had heard unconsciously muttered by the surgeon when Grace took his hand – 'Felice'. Who was Felice? Why, Mrs Charmond; and she, as he knew, was staying at Middleton.

Melbury had indeed pounced upon the image that filled Fitzpiers's half-awakened soul – wherein there had been a retrospect of a recent interview on a starlit lawn with a capriciously passionate woman, who had begged him not to come there again in tones whose modulation incited him to disobey, 'What are you doing here? Why do you pursue me? Another belongs to you. If they were to see you getting over the fence they would seize you as a thief!' And she had turbulently admitted to his wringing questions that her visit to Middleton had been undertaken less because of the invalid relative than in shamefaced fear of her own weakness if she remained near his home. A triumph then it was to Fitzpiers, poor and hampered as he had become, to recognize his real conquest of this beauty, delayed so many years. His was the passion of Congreve's Millamant, whose delight lay in seeing 'the heart which others bled for, bleed for me'.

When the horse had been attended to Melbury stood uneasily here and there about his premises; he was rudely disturbed in the comfortable views which had lately possessed him on his domestic concerns. It is true that he had for some days discerned that Grace more and more sought his company, preferred supervising his kitchen and bakehouse with her stepmother to occupying herself with the lighter details of her own apartments. She seemed no longer able to find in her own hearth an adequate focus for her life, and hence, like a weak queen-bee after leading off to an independent home, had hovered again into the parent hive. But he had not construed these and other incidents of the kind till now.

Something was wrong in the homestead. A ghastly sense beset him that he alone would be responsible for whatever unhappiness should be brought upon her for whom he almost solely lived; whom to retain under his roof he had faced the numerous inconveniences involved in giving up the best part of his house to Fitzpiers. There was no room for doubt that, had he allowed events to take their natural course she would have accepted Winterborne, and realized his old dream of restitution to that young man's family.

That Fitzpiers would allow himself to look for a moment on any other creature than Grace filled Melbury with grief and astonishment. In the simple life he had led it had scarcely occurred to him that after marriage a man might be faithless. That he could sweep to the heights of Mrs Charmond's position, lift the veil of Isis, so to speak, would have amazed Melbury by its audacity if he had not suspected encouragement from that quarter. What could he and his simple Grace do to countervail the passions of those two sophisticated beings – versed in the world's ways, armed with every apparatus for victory? In such an encounter the homely timber-dealer felt as inferior as a savage with his bow and arrows to the precise weapons of modern warfare.

Grace came out of the house as the morning drew on. The village was silent, most of the folk having gone to the fair. Fitzpiers had retired to bed, and was sleeping off his fatigue. She went to the stable and looked at poor Darling: in all probability Giles Winterborne, by obtaining for her a horse of such intelligence and docility, had been the means of saving her husband's life. She paused over the strange thought; and then there appeared her father behind her.

She saw that he knew things were not as they ought to be, from the troubled dulness of his eye, and from his face, different points of which had motions, twitchings, and tremblings, unknown to himself and involuntary.

'He was detained, I suppose, last night?' said Melbury.

'O yes; a bad case in the Vale,' she replied calmly.

'Nevertheless he should have stayed at home.'

'But he couldn't, father.'

Her father turned away. He could hardly bear to see his whilom truthful girl brought to the humiliation of having to talk like that.

That night carking care sat beside Melbury's pillow, and his stiff limbs tossed at its presence.

'I can't lie here any longer,' he muttered. Striking a light he wandered about the room. 'What have I done, what have I done for her!' he said to his wife. 'I had long planned that she should marry the son of the man I wanted to make amends to; do ye mind how I told you all about it, Lucy, the night before she came home? Ah! but I was not content with doing right, I wanted to do more!'

'Don't raft yourself without good need, George,' she replied. 'I won't quite believe that things are so much amiss. I won't believe that Mrs Charmond has encouraged him. Even supposing she has encouraged a great many, she can have no motive to do it now. What so likely as that she is not yet quite well, and doesn't care to let another doctor come near her?'

He did not heed. 'Grace used to be so busy every day with fixing a curtain here and driving a tin-tack there; but she cares for no employment now!'

'Do you know anything of Mrs Charmond's past history? Perhaps that would throw some light upon things. Before she came here as the wife of old Charmond four or five years ago, not a soul seems to have heard aught of her. Why not make inquiries? And then do ye wait and see more; there'll be plenty of opportunity. Time enough to cry when you know 'tis a crying matter; 'tis bad to meet troubles half way.'

There was some good sense in the notion of seeing further. Melbury resolved to inquire and wait, hoping still, but oppressed between whiles with much fear.

CHAPTER 30

EXAMINE Grace as her father might, she would admit nothing. For the present, therefore, he simply watched.

The suspicion that his darling child was slighted wrought almost a miraculous change in Melbury's nature. No man so furtive for the time as the ingenuous countryman who finds that his ingenuousness has been abused. Melbury's heretofore confidential candour towards his gentlemanly son-in-law was displaced by a feline stealth that did injury to his every action, thought, and mood.

He knew that a woman once given to a man for life took, as a rule, her lot as it came, and made the best of it, without external interference; but for the first time he asked himself why this so generally should be done. Besides, this case was not, he argued, like ordinary cases. Leaving out the question of Grace being anything but an ordinary woman, her peculiar situation, as it were in mid-air between two storeys of society, together with the loneliness of Hintock, made a husband's neglect a far more tragical matter to her than it would be to one who had a large circle of friends to fall back upon. Wisely or unwisely, and whatever other fathers did, he resolved to fight his daughter's battle still.

Mrs Charmond had returned. But Hintock House scarcely gave forth signs of life, so quietly had she re-entered it. Autumn drew shiveringly to its end. One day something seemed to be gone from the gardens; the tenderer leaves of vegetables had shrunk under the first smart frost, and hung like faded linen rags; the forest leaves, which had been descending at leisure, descended in haste and in multitudes, and all the golden colours that had hung overhead were now crowded together in a degraded mass underfoot, where the fallen myriads got redder and hornier, and curled themselves up to rot. The only suspicious features in Mrs Charmond's existence at this season were two; the first, that she lived with no companion or relative about her, which considering her age and attractions was somewhat unusual conduct for a young widow in a lonely country house; the other, that she did not, as in previous years, start from Hintock to winter abroad. In Fitzpiers, the only change from his last autumn's habits lay in his abandonment of night study; his lamp never shone from his new dwelling as from his old.

If the suspected ones met it was by such adroit contrivances that even Melbury's vigilance could not encounter them together. A simple call at her house by the doctor had nothing irregular about it, and that he had paid two or three such calls was certain. What had passed at those interviews was known only to the parties themselves; but that Felice Charmond was under some one's influence Melbury soon had opportunity of perceiving.

Winter had come on. Owls began to be noisy in the mornings and evenings, and flocks of wood-pigeons made themselves prominent again. On a day in February, about six months after the marriage of Fitzpiers, Melbury was returning from Great Hintock on foot down to Little Hintock, when he saw before him the surgeon also walking. Melbury would have overtaken him, but at that moment Fitzpiers turned in through a gate to one of the rambling drives among the trees at this side of the wood, which led to nowhere in particular, and the beauty of whose serpentine curves was the only justification of their existence. Felice almost simultaneously trotted into the road ahead of the timber-dealer, in a little basket-carriage which she sometimes drove about the estate, unaccompanied by a servant. She turned in at the same gate without having seen either Melbury or, apparently, Fitzpiers.

Melbury was soon at the spot, despite his aches and his sixty years. Mrs Charmond had come up with the doctor, inside the gate, who was standing immediately behind the carriage. She had turned to him, her arm being thrown carelessly over the back of the seat.

They looked in each other's faces without uttering a word, an arch yet gloomy smile wreathing her lips. Fitzpiers clasped her hanging hand, and, while she still remained in the same listless attitude, looking volumes into his eyes, he stealthily unbuttoned her glove, and stripped her hand of it by rolling back the gauntlet over the fingers, so that it came off inside out. He then raised her hand to his mouth, she still reclining passively, watching him as she might have watched a fly upon her dress. At last she said, 'Well, sir, what excuse for this disobedience?'

'I make none.'

'Then go your way, and let me go mine.' She snatched away her hand, touched the pony with the whip, and left him standing there, holding the reversed glove.

Melbury had not been seen, and his first impulse was to reveal his presence to Fitzpiers, and upbraid him bitterly. But a moment's thought was sufficient to show him the futility of any such simple proceeding. There was not, after all, so much in what he had witnessed as in what that scene might be the surface and froth of – probably a state of mind which censure aggravates rather than cures. Moreover, he said to himself that the point of attack should be the woman, if either. He therefore kept out of sight, and musing sadly, even tearfully – for he was meek as a child in matters concerning his daughter – continued his way towards Hintock.

The insight which is bred of deep sympathy was never more finely exemplified than in this instance. Through her guarded manner, her dignified speech, her placid countenance, he discerned the interior of Grace's life only too truly, hidden as were its incidents from every outer eye.

These incidents had become painful enough. Fitzpiers had latterly developed an irritable discontent which vented itself in monologues when Grace was present to hear them. The early morning of this day had been dull, after a night of wind, and on looking out of the window in the grey grim dawn Fitzpiers had observed some of Melbury's men dragging away a large limb which had been snapped off a beech-tree. Everything was cold and colourless.

'My good God!' he said, as he stood in his dressing-gown. 'This is life!'

He did not know whether Grace was awake or not, and he would not turn his head to ascertain. 'Ah, Edred,' he went on to himself, 'to clip your own wings when you were free to soar!... But I could not rest till I had done it. Why do I never recognize an opportunity till I have missed it, nor the good or ill of a step till it is irrevocable?... I fell in love!'

Grace moved. He thought she had heard some part of his soliloquy. He was sorry – though he had not taken any precaution to prevent her.

He expected a scene at breakfast, but she only exhibited an extreme reserve. It was enough, however, to make him repent that he should have done anything to produce discomfort; for he attributed her manner entirely to what he had said. But Grace's manner had not its cause either in his sayings or in his doings. She had not heard a single word of his regrets. Something even nearer home than her husband's blighted prospects – if blighted they were – was the origin of her mood.

She had made a discovery – one which to a girl of her nature was almost appalling. She had looked into her heart, and found that her early interest in Giles Winterborne had become revitalized into growth by her widening perceptions of what was great and little in life. His homeliness no longer offended her acquired tastes; his comparative want of so-called culture did not now jar on her intellect; his country dress even pleased her eye; his exterior roughness fascinated her. Having discovered by marriage how much that was humanly not great could co-exist with attainments of an exceptional order, there was a revulsion in her sentiments from all that she had formerly clung to in this kind. Honesty, goodness, manliness, tenderness, devotion, for her only existed in their purity now in the breasts of unvarnished men; and here was one who had manifested such towards her from his youth up.

There was, further, that never-ceasing pity in her soul for Giles as a man whom she had wronged – a man who had been unfortunate in his worldly transactions; who notwithstanding these things, had, like Hamlet's friend, borne himself throughout his scathing

'As one, in suffering all, that suffers nothing,'

investing himself thereby with a real touch of sublimity. It was these perceptions, and no subtle catching of her husband's murmurs, that had bred the abstraction visible in her.

When her father approached the house after witnessing the interview between Fitzpiers and Mrs Charmond, Grace was looking out of her sitting-room window, as if she had nothing to do, or think of, or care for. He stood still.

'Ah, Grace,' he said, regarding her fixedly.

'Yes, father,' she murmured.

'Waiting for your dear husband?' he inquired, speaking with the sarcasm of pitiful affection.

'O no – not especially. He has a great many patients to see this afternoon.'

Melbury came quite close. 'Grace, what's the use of talking like that when you know—? Here, come down and walk with me out in the garden, child.'

He unfastened the door in the ivy-laced wall, and waited. This apparent indifference alarmed him. He would far rather that she had rushed in all the fire of jealousy to Hintock House regardless of conventionality, confronted and attacked Felice Charmond *unguibus et rostro*, and accused her even in exaggerated shape of stealing away her husband. Such a storm might have cleared the air.

She emerged in a minute or two, and they went into the garden together. 'You know as well as I do,' he resumed, 'that there is something threatening mischief to your life, and yet you pretend you do not. Do you suppose I don't see the trouble in your face every day? I am very sure that this quietude is wrong conduct in you. You should look more into matters.'

'I am quiet because my sadness is not of a nature to stir me to action.'

Melbury wanted to ask her a dozen questions – did she not feel jealous? was she not indignant? – but a natural delicacy restrained him. 'You are very tame and let-alone, I am bound to say,' he remarked pointedly.

'I am what I feel, father,' she repeated.

He glanced at her, and there returned upon his mind the scene of her offering to wed Winterborne instead of Fitzpiers in the last days before her marriage; and he asked himself if it could be the fact that she loved Winterborne now that she had lost him more than she had ever done when she was comparatively free to choose him.

'What would you have me do?' she asked in a low voice.

He recalled his mind from the retrospective pain to the practical matter before them. 'I would have you go to Mrs Charmond,' he said.

'Go to Mrs Charmond – what for?' said she.

'Well – if I must speak plain, dear Grace – to ask her, appeal to her in the name of your common womanhood, and your many like sentiments on things, not to make unhappiness between you and your husband. It lies with her entirely to do one or the other – that I can see.'

Grace's face had heated at her father's words, and the very rustle of her skirts upon the box-edging bespoke disdain. 'I shall not *think* of going to her, father – of course, I could not!' she answered.

'Why – don't 'ee want to be happier than you be at present?' said Melbury, more moved on her account than she was herself.

'I don't wish to be more humiliated. If I have anything to bear I can bear it in silence.'

'But, my dear maid, you are too young – you don't know what the present state of things may lead to. Just see the harm done a'ready! Your husband would have gone away to Budmouth to a bigger practice if it had not been for this. Although it has gone such a little way it is poisoning your future even now. Mrs Charmond is thoughtlessly bad, not bad by calculation; and just a word to her now might save 'ee a peck of woes.'

'Ah, I loved her once,' said Grace with a broken articulation, 'and she would not care for me then! Now I no longer love her. Let her do her worst; I don't care.'

'You ought to care. You have got into a very good position to start with. You have been well educated, well tended, and you have become the wife of a professional man of unusually good family. Surely you ought to make the best of your position.'

'I don't see that I ought. I wish I had never got into it. I wish you had never, never thought of educating me. I wish I worked in the woods like Marty South! I hate genteel life, and I want to be no better than she!'

'Why?' said her amazed father.

'Because cultivation has only brought me inconveniences and troubles. I say again, I wish you had never sent me to those fashionable schools you set your mind on. It all arose out of that, father. If I had stayed at home I should have married—'

She closed up her mouth suddenly and was silent; and he saw that she was not far from crying.

Melbury was much grieved. 'What, and would you like to have grown up as we be here in Hintock – knowing no more, and with no more chance of seeing good life than we have here?'

'Yes. I have never got any happiness outside Hintock that I know of, and I have suffered many a heartache at being sent away. O, the misery of those January days when I got back to school, and left you all here in the wood so happy! I used to wonder why I had to bear it. And I was always a little despised by the other girls at school, because they knew where I came from, and that my parents were not in so good a station as theirs.'

Her poor father was much hurt at what he thought her ingratitude and intractability. He had admitted to himself bitterly enough that he should have let young hearts have their way, or rather should have helped on her affection for Winterborne, and given her to him according to his original plan; but he was not prepared for her deprecating those attainments whose completion had been a labour of years and a severe tax upon his purse.

'Very well,' he said with much heaviness of spirit. 'If you don't like to go to her I don't wish to force you.'

And so the question remained for him still: How should he remedy this perilous state of things? For days he sat in a moody attitude over the fire, a pitcher of cider standing on the hearth beside him, and his drinking-horn inverted upon the top of it. He spent a week and more thus, composing a letter to the chief offender, which he would every now and then attempt to complete and suddenly crumple up in his hand.

CHAPTER 31

As February merged in March, and lighter evenings broke the gloom of the woodmen's homeward journey, the Hintocks Great and Little began to have ears for a rumour of the events out of which had grown the timber-dealer's troubles.

It took the form of a wide sprinkling of conjecture, wherein no man knew the exact truth. Tantalizing phenomena, at once showing and concealing the real relationship of the persons concerned, caused a diffusion of excited surprise. Honest people as the woodlanders were, it was hardly to be expected that they could remain immersed in the study of their trees and gardens amid such circumstances, or sit with their backs turned like the good burghers of Coventry at the passage of the lady.

Rumour, for a wonder, exaggerated little. There threatened, in fact, in Grace's case as in thousands, the domestic disaster, old as the hills, which, with more or less variation, made a mourner of Ariadne, a byword of Vashti, and a corpse of Amy Dudley. The incidents were rencounters accidental and contrived, stealthy correspondence, sudden misgivings on one side, sudden self-reproaches on the other. The inner state of the twain was one as of confused noise that would not allow the accents of politic reason to be heard. Determination to go in this direction, and headlong plunges in that; dignified safeguards, undignified collapses; not a single rash step by deliberate intention, and all against judgment.

It was all that Melbury had expected and feared. It was more, for he had overlooked the publicity that would be likely to result, as it now had done. What should he do? Appeal to

Mrs Charmond himself, since Grace would not? He bethought himself of Winterborne, and resolved to consult him, feeling the strong need of some friend of his own sex to whom he might unburden his mind.

He had entirely lost faith in his own judgment. That judgment on which he had relied for so many years seemed recently, like a false companion unmasked, to have disclosed unexpected depths of hypocrisy and speciousness where all had seemed solidity. He felt almost afraid to form a conjecture on the weather, or the time, or the fruit-promise, so great was his self-mistrust.

He set out to look for Giles on a rimy evening when the woods seemed to be in a cold sweat; beads of perspiration hung from every bare twig; the sky had no colour, and the trees rose before him as haggard, grey phantoms whose days of substantiality were passed. Melbury seldom saw Winterborne now, but he believed him to be occupying a lonely hut just beyond the boundary of Mrs Charmond's estate, though still within the circuit of the woodland. The timber-merchant's thin legs stalked on through the pale damp scenery, his eyes declining on the dead leaves of last year; while every now and then a hasty 'ay!' escaped his lips in reply to some bitter mental proposition.

His notice was attracted by a thin blue haze of smoke, behind which arose sounds of voices and chopping; bending his steps that way he saw Winterborne just in front of him.

Though few knew of it, Giles had had a serious illness during the winter; but it just now happened that after being for a long time apathetic and unemployed on that account he had become one of the busiest men in the neighbourhood. It is often thus; fallen friends lost sight of we expect to find starving; we discover them going on fairly well. Without any solicitation or desire to profit on his part, he had been asked to execute a very large order for hurdles and other copse-ware, for which purpose he had been obliged to buy several acres of hazel brushwood standing. He was now engaged in the cutting and manufacture of the same, proceeding with the work daily like an automaton.

The hazel-tree did not belie its name to-day. The whole of the copsewood where the mist had cleared returned purest tints of that hue, amid which Winterborne himself was in the act of making a hurdle, the stakes being driven firmly into the ground in a row, over which he bent and wove the twigs. Beside him was a square, compact pile like the altar of Cain, formed of hurdles already finished, which bristled on all sides with the sharp points of their stakes. At a little distance the men in his employ were assisting him to carry out his contract. Rows of brushwood lay on the ground as it had fallen under the axe; and a shelter had been constructed near at hand, in front of which burnt the fire whose smoke had attracted Melbury. The air was so dank that the smoke hung heavily, and crept away amid the bushes without rising from the ground.

After wistfully regarding the scene awhile Melbury drew nearer, and briefly inquired of Giles how he came to be so busily engaged, with an undertone of slight surprise that Winterborne could recommence thriving, even to this degree, after being deprived of Grace. Melbury was not without emotion at the meeting, for Grace's affairs had divided them, and ended their intimacy of old times.

Winterborne explained just as briefly, without raising his eyes from his occupation of chopping a bough that he held in front of him.

' 'Twill be up in April before you get it all cleared,' said Melbury.

'Yes, there or thereabouts,' said Winterborne, a chop of the bill-hook jerking the last word into two pieces.

There was another interval; Melbury still looked on, a chip from Winterborne's hook occasionally flying against the waistcoat or legs of his visitor, who took no heed.

'Ah, Giles, you should have been my partner. You should have been my son-in-law,' the old man said at last. 'It would have been far better for her and for me!'

Winterborne saw that something had gone wrong with his former friend, and throwing down the switch he was about to interweave he responded only too readily to the mood of the timber-dealer. 'Is she ill?' he said hurriedly.

'No, no.' Melbury stood without speaking for some minutes, and then, as though he could not bring himself to proceed, turned to go away.

Winterborne told one of his men to pack up the tools for the night and walked after Melbury.

'Heaven forbid that I should seem too inquisitive, sir,' he said, 'especially since we don't stand as we used to stand to one another; but I hope it is well with them all over your way?'

'No,' said Melbury, 'no.'

He stopped, and struck the smooth trunk of a young ash-tree with the flat of his hand. 'I would that his ear had been where that rind is!' he exclaimed; 'I should have treated him to little compared wi' what he deserves.'

'Now,' said Winterborne, 'don't be in a hurry to go home. I've put some ale down to warm in my shelter here, and we'll sit and drink it and talk this over.'

Melbury turned unresistingly as Giles took his arm, and they went back to where the fire was, and sat down under the screen, the other woodmen having gone. He drew out the ale-cup from the ashes, and they drank together.

'Giles, you ought to have had her, as I said just now,' repeated Melbury. 'I'll tell you why for the first time.'

He thereupon told Winterborne, as with great relief, the story of how he won away Giles's father's chosen one – by nothing worse than a lover's cajoleries, it is true; but by means which, except in love, would certainly have been pronounced cruel and unfair. He explained how he had always intended to make reparation to Winterborne the father, by giving Grace to Winterborne the son; till the devil tempted him in the person of Fitzpiers, and he broke his virtuous vow.

'How highly I thought of that man to be sure! Who'd have supposed he'd have been so weak and wrong-headed as this! You ought to have had her, Giles, and there's an end on't.'

Winterborne knew how to preserve his calm under this unconsciously cruel tearing of a healing wound, to which Melbury's concentration on the more vital subject had blinded him. The young man endeavoured to make the best of the case for Grace's sake.

'She would hardly have been happy with me,' he said, in the dry, unimpassioned voice under which he hid his feelings. 'I was not well enough educated: too rough in short. I couldn't have surrounded her with the refinements she looked for, anyhow at all.'

'Nonsense – you are quite wrong there,' said the unwise old man doggedly. 'She told me only this day that she hates refinements and such like. All that my trouble and money bought for her in that way is thrown away upon her quite. She'd fain be like Marty South – think o' that! That's the top of her ambition! Perhaps she's right. Giles, she loved you – under the rind: and what's more she loves 'ee still – worse luck for the poor maid!'

If Melbury only had known what fires he was recklessly stirring up he might have held his peace. Winterborne was silent a long time. The darkness had closed in round them, and the monotonous drip of the fog from the branches quickened as it turned to fine rain.

'O, she never cared much for me,' Giles managed to say as he stirred the embers with a brand.

'She did, and does, I tell ye,' said the other obstinately. 'However, all that's vain talking now. What I come to ask you about is a more practical matter – how to make the best of things as they are. I am thinking of a desperate step – of calling on the woman Charmond. I am going to appeal to her since Grace will not. 'Tis she who holds the balance in her hands – not he. While she's got the will to lead him astray he will follow – poor unpractical lofty-notioned dreamer – and how long she'll do it depends upon her whim. Did ye ever hear anything about her character before she came to Hintock?'

'She's been a bit of a charmer in her time, I believe,' replied Giles, with the same level quietude, as he regarded the red coals. 'A body who has smiled where she has not loved, and loved where she has not married. Before Mr Charmond made her his wife she was a play-actress a short while.'

'Hey? But how close you have kept all this, Giles! What besides?'

'Mr Charmond was a rich man engaged in the iron trade in the north – twenty or thirty years older than she. He married her, and retired, and came down here and bought this property.'

'Yes, yes – I know all about that. But the other I did not know. I fear it bodes no good. For how can I go and appeal to the forbearance of a woman who made cross-loves and crooked passions her study for years? I thank ye, Giles, for finding it out; but it makes my plan the harder that she should have belonged to that unstable tribe!'

Another pause ensued, and they looked gloomily at the smoke that beat about the roof of hurdles through whose weavings a large drop of rain fell at intervals and spat smartly into the fire. Mrs Charmond had been no friend to Winterborne, but he was manly, and it was not in his heart to let her be condemned without a trial.

'She is said to be generous,' he answered. 'You might not appeal to her in vain.'

'It shall be done,' said Melbury, rising. 'For good, or for evil, to Mrs Charmond I'll go.'

CHAPTER 32

At nine o'clock the next morning Melbury dressed himself up in shining broadcloth, creased with folding and smelling of camphor, and started for Hintock House. He was the more impelled to go at once by the absence of his son-in-law in London for a few days, to attend really or ostensibly some professional meetings.

He said nothing of his destination either to his wife or to Grace, fearing that they might entreat him to abandon so risky a project; and went out unobserved. He had chosen his time with a view, he supposed, of conveniently catching Mrs Charmond when she had just finished her breakfast, before any other business people should be about, if any came. Plodding thoughtfully onward he crossed a glade lying between Little Hintock woods and the plantation which abutted on the park. The spot being open he was discerned there by Winterborne from the copse on the next hill, where he and his men were working. Knowing his mission the younger man hastened down from the copse and managed to intercept the timber-merchant.

'I have been thinking of this, sir,' he said, 'and I am of opinion that it would be best to put off your visit for the present.'

But Melbury would not even stop to hear him. His mind was fixed, the appeal was to be made; and Winterborne stood and watched him sadly till he entered the second plantation and disappeared.

Melbury rang at the tradesmen's door of the manor-house, and was at once informed that the lady was not yet visible, as indeed he might have guessed had he been anybody but the man he was. Melbury said he would wait, whereupon the young page informed him in a neighbourly way that, between themselves, she was in bed and asleep.

'Never mind,' said Melbury, retreating into the court, 'I'll stand about here.' Charged so fully with his mission he shrank from contact with anybody.

But he walked about the paved court till he was tired, and nobody came to him. He entered the house and sat down in a small waiting-room, from which he got glimpses of the kitchen-corridor, and of the white-capped maids flitting jauntily hither and thither. They had heard of his arrival, but had not seen him enter, and imagining him still in the court discussed freely the possible reason of his calling. They marvelled at his temerity; for though most of the tongues which had been let loose attributed the chief blame to Fitzpiers, these of her household preferred to regard their mistress as the deeper sinner.

Melbury sat with his hands resting on the familiar knobbed thorn walking-stick, whose growing he had seen before he enjoyed its use. The scene to him was not the material environment of his person, but a tragic vision that travelled with him like an envelope. Through this vision the incidents of the moment but gleamed confusedly here and there, as an outer landscape through the high-coloured scenes of a stained window.

He waited thus an hour, an hour and a half, two hours. He began to look pale and ill, whereupon the butler, who came in, asked him to have a glass of wine.

Melbury roused himself, and said, 'No, no. Is she almost ready?'

'She is just finishing breakfast, Mr Melbury,' said the butler. 'She will soon see you now. I am just going up to tell her you are here.'

'What, haven't you told her before?' said Melbury.

'O no,' said the other. 'You see you came so very early.'

At last the bell rang; Mrs Charmond could see him. She was not in her private sitting-room when he reached it, but in a minute he heard her coming from the front staircase, and she entered where he stood.

At this time of the morning Mrs Charmond looked her full age and more. She might almost have been taken for the typical *femme de trente ans*, though she was really not more than seven or eight and twenty. But the *édition définitive* of her beauty had been reached, even if it were not a little worn.

There being no fire in the room she came in with a shawl thrown loosely round her shoulders, and obviously without the least suspicion that Melbury had called upon any other errand than timber. Felice was, indeed, the only woman in the parish who had not heard the rumour of her own weaknesses; she was at this moment living in a fool's paradise in respect of that rumour though not in respect of the weaknesses themselves, which, if the truth be told, caused her grave misgivings.

'Do sit down, Mr Melbury. You have felled all the trees that were to be purchased by you this season, except the oaks, I believe?'

'Yes, yes,' said Melbury, in a reverie.

He did not take a chair, and she also remained standing. Resting upon his stick he began: 'Mrs Charmond, I have called upon a more serious matter – at least to me – than tree-throwing. And whatever mistakes I make in my manner of speaking upon it to you, madam, do me the justice to set 'em down to my want of practice, and not to my want of care.'

Mrs Charmond looked ill at ease. She might have begun to guess his meaning; but apart from that she had such dread of contact with anything painful, harsh, or even earnest, that his preliminaries alone were enough to distress her.

'Yes, what is it?' she said quickly.

'I am an old man,' said Melbury, 'that, somewhat late in life, God thought fit to bless with one child, and she a daughter. Her mother was a very dear wife to me; but she was taken away from us when the child was young; and the child became precious as the apple of my eye to me, for she was all I had left to love. For her sake entirely I married as second wife a homespun woman who had been kind as a mother to her. In due time the question of her education came on; and I said, "I will educate the maid well if I live upon bread to do it." Of her possible marriage I could not bear to think, for it seemed like a death that she should cleave to another man, and grow to think his house her home rather than mine. But I saw it was the law of nature that this should be, and that it was for the maid's happiness that she should have a home when I was gone; and I made up my mind without a murmur to help it on for her sake. In my youth I had wronged my dead friend, and to make amends I determined to give her, my most precious prize, to my friend's son, seeing that they liked each other well. Things came about which made me doubt if it would be for my daughter's happiness to do this, inasmuch as the young man was poor, and she was delicately reared. Another man came and paid court to her – one her equal in breeding and accomplishments; in every way it seemed to me that he only could give her the home which her training had made a necessity a'most. I urged her on, and she married him. But, ma'am, a fatal mistake was at the root of my reckoning; I found that this well-born gentleman I had calculated on so surely was not staunch of heart, and that therein lay a danger of great sorrow for my daughter. Madam, he saw you, and you know the rest. . . . I have come to make no demands – to utter no threats; I have come simply as a father in great grief about his only child, and I beseech you to deal kindly with my daughter and to do nothing which can turn her husband's heart away from her for ever! Forbid him your presence, ma'am, and speak to him on his duty, as one with your power over him well can do: and I am hopeful that the rent between them may be patched up. For it is not as if you would lose by so doing; your course is far higher than the courses of a professional man; and the gratitude you would win from me and mine by your kindness is more than I can say!'

Mrs Charmond had first rushed into a mood of indignation, on comprehending Melbury's story: hot and cold by turns she had murmured, 'Leave me, leave me!' But, as he seemed to take no notice of this, his words began to influence her, and when he ceased speaking she said with hurried breath, 'What has led you to think this of me? Who says I have won your daughter's husband away from her? Some monstrous calumnies are afloat – of which I have known nothing until now!'

Melbury started, and looked at her simply: 'But surely, ma'am, you know the truth better than I?'

Her features became a little pinched, and the touches of powder on her handsome face for the first time showed themselves as an extrinsic film.

'Will you leave me to myself?' she said with a faintness which suggested a guilty conscience. 'This is so utterly unexpected – you obtain admission to by presence by misrepresentation—'

'As God's in heaven, ma'am, that's not true. I made no pretence; and I thought in reason you would know why I had come. This gossip—'

'I have heard nothing of it. Tell me the gist of it, pray!'

'Tell you, ma'am – not I. What the gossip is, no matter. What really is, you know. Set facts right, and the scandal will right itself. But pardon me – I speak rough; and I came to speak gentle, to coax you, beg you to be my daughter's friend. She loved you once, ma'am; you began by loving her. Then you dropped her without a reason, and it hurt her warm heart more than I can tell ye. But you were within your right as the superior, no doubt. But if you would consider her position now – surely, surely, you would do her no harm!'

'Certainly I would do her no harm – I—'

Melbury's eye met hers. It was curious, but the allusion to Grace's former love for her seemed to touch her more than all Melbury's other arguments. 'O, Melbury,' she burst out, 'you have made me so unhappy! How could you come to me like this! It is too dreadful! Now go away – go, go!'

'I will, and leave you to think,' he said, in a husky tone.

As soon as he was out of the room she went to a corner and there burst into tears, and writhed, under an emotion in which hurt pride and vexation mingled with better sentiments.

Mrs Charmond's mobile spirit was subject to these fierce periods of high tide and storm. She had never so clearly perceived till now that her soul was being slowly invaded by a delirium which had brought about all this; that she was losing judgment and dignity under it, becoming an animated impulse only, a passion incarnate. A fascination had led her on; it was as if she had been seized by a hand of velvet; and this was where she found herself – overshadowed with sudden night, as if a tornado had passed.

While she sat, or rather crouched, unhinged by the interview, lunch-time came, and then the early afternoon, almost without her consciousness. Then 'a strange gentleman, who says it is not necessary to give his name,' was suddenly announced.

Felice knew who the strange gentleman was – that Continental follower on whom she had once smiled, among others too numerous to name. But to meet this lover now – the thought made her sick.

'I cannot see him, whoever he may be! I am not at home to anybody.'

She heard no more of her visitor: and shortly after, in an attempt to recover some mental serenity by violent physical exercise, she put on her hat and cloak and went out of doors, taking a path which led her up the slopes to the nearest spur of the wood. She disliked the woods, but they had the advantage of being a place in which she could walk comparatively unobserved.

CHAPTER 33

THERE was agitation that day in the lives of all whom these matters concerned. It was not till the Hintock dinner-time – one o'clock – that Grace discovered her father's absence from the house after a departure in the morning under somewhat unusual conditions. By a little reasoning and inquiry she was able to divine his errand.

Her husband, too, was away, and her father did not return. He had, in truth, gone on to Sherton after the interview, in the hope of calming himself by business; but this Grace did not know. In an indefinite dread that something serious would arise out of Melbury's visit by reason of the inequalities of temper and nervous irritation to which he was subject, something possibly that would bring her much more misery than accompanied her present negative state of mind, she left the house about three o'clock, and took a loitering walk in the woodland track by which she imagined he would come home. This track under the bare trees and over the cracking sticks, screened and roofed in from the outer world of wind by a network of boughs, led her slowly on till in time she had left the larger trees behind her and swept round into the coppice where Winterborne and his men were clearing the undergrowth.

Had Giles's attention been concentrated on his hurdles he would not have seen her, but ever since Melbury's passage across the opposite glade in the morning he had been as uneasy and unsettled as Grace herself; and her advent now was the one appearance which, since her father's avowal, could arrest him more than Melbury's return with his tidings.

Fearing that something might be the matter he hastened up to her.

She had not seen her old lover for a long time, and too conscious of the late pranks of her heart she could not behold him calmly. 'I am only looking for my father,' she said in an unnecessary tone of apology.

'I was looking for him too,' said Giles. 'I think he may perhaps have gone on further.'

'Then you knew he was going to the House, Giles?' she said, turning her large tender eyes anxiously upon him. 'Did he tell you what for?'

Winterborne glanced doubtingly at her, and softly hinted that her father had visited him the evening before, and that their old friendship was quite restored; on which she guessed the rest.

'O, I am glad indeed that you two are friends again!' she cried.

And then they stood facing each other, fearing each other, troubling each other's souls. Grace experienced acute regret at the sight of these wood-cutting scenes, because she had estranged herself from them; craving, even to its defects and inconveniences, that homely sylvan life of her father which in the best probable succession of events would shortly be denied her.

At a little distance, on the edge of the clearing, Marty South was shaping spar-gads to take home for manufacture during the evenings. Winterborne and Mrs Fitzpiers stood looking at her in their mutual embarrassment at each other's presence, and while doing so they beheld, approaching the girl, a lady in a dark fur mantle and black hat, having a white veil tied picturesquely round it. She spoke to Marty, who turned and curtsied, and the lady fell into conversation with her. It was Mrs Charmond.

After leaving her house Mrs Charmond had walked on, under the fret and fever of her mind, with more vigour than she was accustomed to show in her normal moods – a fever which the solace of a cigarette did not entirely allay. Reaching the coppice she had listlessly observed Marty at work, when she threw away her cigarette and drew near. Chop, chop, chop, went Marty's little bill-hook with never more assiduity, till Mrs Charmond spoke.

'Who is that young lady I see talking to the woodman yonder?' she asked.

'Mrs Fitzpiers, ma'am,' said Marty.

'O,' said Mrs Charmond, with something like a start; for she had not recognized Grace at that distance. 'And the man she is talking to?'

'That's Mr Winterborne.'

A redness stole into Marty's face as she mentioned Giles's name, which Mrs Charmond did not fail to notice. 'Are you engaged to him?' she asked softly.

'No, ma'am,' said Marty. '*She* was once; and I think— '

But Marty could not possibly explain the complications of her thought on this matter – a thought nothing less than one of extraordinary acuteness for a girl so young and inexperienced – namely, that she saw danger to two hearts, naturally honest, in Grace being thrown back into Winterborne's society by the neglect of her husband. Mrs Charmond, however, with the almost supersensory means to knowledge which women have on such occasions, quite understood what Marty had intended to convey; and the picture thus exhibited to her of lives drifting awry, involving the wreck of poor Marty's hopes, prompted her yet further in those generous resolves which Melbury's remonstrances had stimulated.

Full of such feelings she bade the girl good-afternoon, and went on over the stumps of hazel to where Grace and Winterborne were standing. They saw her approach, and Winterborne said, 'She is coming to you; it is a good omen. She dislikes me, so I'll go away.'

He accordingly retreated to where he had been working before Grace came, and Grace's formidable rival approached her, each woman taking the other's measure as she drew near.

'Dear – Mrs Fitzpiers!' said Felice Charmond, with some inward turmoil which stopped her speech. 'I have not seen you for a long time.'

She held out her hand tentatively, while Grace stood like a wild animal on first confronting a mirror or other puzzling product of civilization. Was it really Mrs Charmond speaking to her thus? If it was she could not longer form any guess as to what life signified.

'I want to talk to you,' said Mrs Charmond sensitively, for the gaze of the young woman had chilled her through. 'Can you walk on with me till we are quite alone?'

Sick with distaste Grace nevertheless complied as by clock-work, and they moved evenly side by side into the deeper recesses of the woods. They went further, much further than Mrs Charmond had meant to go; but mental indiscipline hindered her from beginning her conversation, and in default of it she kept walking.

'I have seen your father,' she at length observed. 'And – I am much troubled by what he told me.'

'What did he tell you? I have not been admitted to his confidence on anything he may have said to you.'

'Nevertheless, why should I repeat to you what you can easily divine?'

'True – true,' returned Grace mournfully. 'Why should you repeat what we both have in our minds already?'

'Mrs Fitzpiers, your husband— '

The moment that the speaker's tongue touched the dangerous subject a vivid look of self-consciousness flashed over her; in which her heart revealed, as by a lightning-gleam, what filled it to over-flowing. So transitory was the expression that none but a quick-sensed woman, and she in Grace's position, would have had the power to catch its meaning. Upon her the phase was not lost.

'Then you *do* love him!' she exclaimed in a tone of much surprise.

'What do you mean, my young friend?'

'Why,' cried Grace, 'I thought till now that you had only been cruelly flirting with my husband to amuse your idle moments – a rich lady with a poor professional gentleman whom in her heart she despised not much less than her who belongs to him. But I guess from your manner that you love him desperately; and I don't hate you as I did before. . . . Yes, indeed,' continued Mrs Fitzpiers, with a trembling tongue, 'since it is not sport in your case at all but *real* – O, I do pity you, more than I despise you! For *you* will suffer most!'

Mrs Charmond was now as much agitated as Grace. 'I ought not to allow myself to argue about this!' she exclaimed. 'I demean myself by doing it. But I liked you once, and for the sake of that time I try to tell you how mistaken you are!'

Much of her confusion resulted from her wonder and alarm at finding herself, in a sense, dominated mentally and emotionally by this simple school-girl. 'I do not love him!' she went on with insistent untruth. 'It was a kindness – my making somewhat more of him than one usually does of one's doctor. I was lonely; I talked – well, I trifled with him. I am very sorry if such child's play, out of pure friendship, has been a serious matter to you. Who could have expected it? But the world is so simple here!'

'O, that's affectation,' said Grace, shaking her head. 'It is no use – you *love* him! I can see in your face that in this matter of my husband you have not let your acts belie your feelings. During these last four or six months you have been terribly indiscreet, but you have not been insincere; and that almost disarms me.'

'I *have* been insincere – if you will have the word – I mean I *have* coquetted, and do not love him!'

But Grace clung to her position like a limpet. 'You may have trifled with others; but him you love as you never loved another man!'

'O, well – I won't argue,' said Mrs Charmond, laughing faintly. 'And you come to reproach me for it, child?'

'No,' said Grace magnanimously. 'You may go on loving him if you like – I don't mind at all. You'll find it, let me tell you, a bitterer business for yourself than for me in the end. He'll get tired of you soon, as tired as can be – you don't know him so well as I! – and then you may wish you had never seen him!'

Mrs Charmond had grown quite pale and weak under this prophecy. It was extraordinary that Grace, whom almost every one would have characterized as a gentle girl, should be of tougher fibre than her interlocutor.

'You exaggerate – cruel, silly young woman,' she reiterated, writhing with little agonies. 'It is nothing but playful friendship – nothing! It will be proved by my future conduct. I shall at once refuse to see him more – since it will make no difference to my heart, and much to my name.'

'I question if you will refuse to see him again,' said Grace dryly, as she bent a sapling back. 'But I am not incensed against you as you are against me,' she added, abandoning the tree to its natural perpendicular. 'Before I came I had been despising you for wanton cruelty; now I only pity your weakness for its misplaced affection. When Edred has gone out of the house in hope of seeing you, at seasonable hours and unseasonable; when I have found him riding miles and miles across the country at midnight, and risking his life, and getting covered with mud, to get a glimpse of you, I have called him a foolish man – the plaything of a finished coquette. I thought that what was getting to be a tragedy to me was a comedy to you. But now I see that tragedy lies on your side of the situation no less than on mine, and more; that if I have felt trouble at my position you have felt anguish at yours; that if I have had disappointments you have had despairs. Philosophy may fortify *me* – God help *you!*'

'I cannot attempt to reply to your ravings,' returned the other, struggling to restore a dignity which had completely collapsed. 'My acts will be my proofs. In the world which you have seen nothing of, friendships between men and women are not unknown; and it would have been better both for you and your father if you had each judged me more respectfully, and left me alone. As it is, I wish never, never to see or speak to you, madam, any more!'

Grace bowed, and Mrs Charmond haughtily turned away. The two went apart in directly opposite courses, and were soon hidden from each other by their umbrageous surroundings and by the shadows of eve.

In the excitement of their long argument they had walked onward and zigzagged about without regarding direction or distance. All sound of the woodcutters had long since faded into remoteness, and even had not the interval been too great for hearing them they would have been silent and homeward bound at this twilight hour.

But Grace went on her course without any misgiving, though there was much underwood here with only the narrowest passages for walking, across which brambles hung. She had not, however, traversed this, the wildest, part of the wood since her childhood, and the transformation of outlines had been great; old trees which once were landmarks had been felled or blown down, and the bushes which then had been small and scrubby were now large and overhanging. She soon found that her ideas as to direction were vague – that she had indeed no ideas as to direction at all. If the evening had not been growing so dark, and the wind had not put on its night-moan so distinctly, Grace would not have minded; but she was rather frightened now, and began to strike across hither and thither in random courses.

Denser grew the darkness, more developed the wind-voices, and still no recognizable spot or outlet of any kind appeared, nor any sound of the Hintocks floated near, though she had wandered probably between one and two hours, and began to be weary. She was vexed at her foolishness, since the ground she had covered, if in a straight line, must inevitably have taken her out of the wood to some remote village or other; but she had wasted her forces in countermarches; and now, in much alarm, wondered if she would have to pass the night here.

She stood still to meditate, and fancied that between the soughing of the wind she heard shuffling footsteps on the leaves heavier than those of rabbits or other startled 'beasts of beating heart' who lived there. Though fearing at first to meet anybody on the chance of his being a friend, she decided that her fellow-noctambulist, even if a poacher, would not injure her, and that he might possibly be some one sent to search for her. She accordingly shouted a rather timid 'Hoi!'

The cry was immediately returned by the other person; and Grace running at once in the direction whence it came beheld an indistinct figure hastening up to her as rapidly. They were almost in each other's arms before she recognized the outline and white veil of her whom she had parted from hours before – Mrs Charmond.

'I have lost my way, I have lost my way!' cried the latter. 'O – is it indeed you? I am so glad to meet you or anybody. I have been wandering up and down ever since we parted, and am nearly dead with terror and misery and fatigue!'

'So am I,' said Grace. 'What *shall* we – *shall* we do!'

'You won't go away from me?' asked her companion anxiously.

'No, indeed. Are you very tired?'

'I can scarcely move, and I am scratched dreadfully about the ankles.'

Grace reflected. 'Perhaps, as it is dry underfoot, the best thing for us to do would be to sit down for half-an-hour, and then start again when we have thoroughly rested. By walking straight we must come to a track leading somewhere, before the morning.'

They found a clump of bushy hollies which afforded a shelter from the wind, and sat down under it, some tufts of dead fern, crisp and dry, that remained from the previous season, forming a sort of nest for them. But it was cold, nevertheless, on this March night, particularly for Grace, who, with the sanguine prematureness of youth in matters of dress, had considered it spring-time, and hence was not so warmly clad as Mrs Charmond, who still wore her winter furs.

But after sitting awhile the latter lady shivered no less than Grace as the warmth imparted by her hasty walking began to go off; and they felt the cold air drawing through the holly leaves which scratched their backs and shoulders. Moreover they could hear some drops of rain falling on the trees, though none reached the nook in which they had ensconced themselves.

'If we were to cling close together,' said Mrs Charmond, 'we should keep each other warm.... But,' she added in an uneven voice, 'I suppose you won't come near me for the world!'

'Why not?'

'Because – well, you know.'

'Yes, I will – I don't hate you at all.'

They consequently crept up to one another, and being in the dark, lonely, and weary, did what neither had dreamed of doing beforehand – clasped each other closely. Mrs Charmond's furs consoled Grace's cold face; and each one's body, as she breathed, alternately heaved against that of her companion; while the funereal trees rocked and chanted dirges unceasingly.

When a few minutes had been spent thus Mrs Charmond said, 'I am so wretched!' in a heavy emotional whisper.

'You are frightened,' said Grace. 'But there is nothing to fear; I know these woods well.'

'I am not at all frightened at the wood; but I am at other things.'

Mrs Charmond embraced Grace more and more tightly, and put her face against that of her companion. The younger woman could feel her neighbour's breathings grow deeper and more spasmodic, as though uncontrollable feelings were germinating.

'After I had left you,' Felice went on, 'I regretted something I had said. I have to make a confession – I must make it!' she whispered brokenly, the instinct to indulge in warmth of sentiment which had led this woman of passions to respond to Fitzpiers in the first place, leading her now to find luxurious comfort in opening her heart to his wife. 'I said to you I could give him up without pain or deprivation – that he had only been my pastime. That was absolutely untrue – it was said to deceive you! I could not do it without much pain; and what is more dreadful I cannot give him up – even if I would – of myself alone.'

'Why? Because you love him, you mean.'

Felice Charmond denoted assent by a movement.

'I knew I was right!' said Grace exaltedly. 'But that should not deter you,' she presently added in a moral tone. 'O, do struggle against it, and you will conquer!'

'You are so simple, so simple!' cried Felice. 'You think, because you guessed my assumed indifference to him to be a sham, that you know the extremes that people are capable of going to! But a good deal more may have been going on than you have fathomed with all your insight. I *cannot* give him up until he chooses to give up me!'

'But surely you are the superior in station and in every way, and the cut must come from you.'

'Tchut! Must I tell verbatim, you simple child? O, I suppose I must! It will eat away my heart if I do not let out all, after meeting you like this and finding how guileless you are!'

She thereupon whispered a few words in the girl's ear, and burst into a violent fit of sobbing.

Grace started roughly away from the shelter of the furs, and sprang to her feet.

'O, my great God!' she exclaimed, thunderstruck at a revelation transcending her utmost suspicion. 'He's had you! Can it be – can it be!'

She turned as if to hasten away. But Felice Charmond's sobs came to her ear: deep darkness circled her about, the cold lips of the wind kissed her where Mrs Charmond's warm fur had been, and she did not know which way to go. After the moment of energy she felt mild again, and turned to the motionless woman at her feet.

'Are you rested?' she asked, in what seemed her own voice grown ten years older.

Without an answer Mrs Charmond slowly rose. 'You mean to betray me!' she asked out of the bitterest depths of her soul. 'O, fool, fool I!'

'No,' said Grace shortly. 'I mean no such thing. But let us be quick now. We have a serious undertaking before us. Think of nothing but going straight on.'

They walked on in profound silence, pulling back boughs now growing wet, and treading down woodbine, but still keeping a pretty straight course. Grace began to be thoroughly worn out, and her companion too, when, on a sudden, they broke into the deserted highway where the Sherton man had waited for Mrs Dollery's van. Grace recognized the spot as soon as she looked around her.

'How we have got here I cannot tell,' she said with cold civility. 'We have made a complete circuit of Little Hintock. The hazel copse is quite on the other side. Now we have only to follow the road.'

They dragged themselves onward, turned into the lane, passed the track to Little Hintock, and so reached the park.

'Here I turn back,' said Grace in the same passionless voice. 'You are quite near home.'

Mrs Charmond stood inert, seeming appalled by her late admission.

'I have told you something in a moment of irresistible desire to unburden my soul, which all but a fool would have kept silent as the grave,' she said. 'I cannot help it now. Is it to be a secret, or do you mean war?'

'A secret certainly,' said Grace mournfully. 'How can you expect war from such a helpless, wretched being as me?'

'And I'll do my best not to see him. I am his slave; but I'll try.'

Grace was naturally kind, but she could not help using a small dagger now.

'Pray don't distress yourself,' she said with fine scorn. 'You may see him as much as you like – for me.' Had she been wounded instead of mortified she could not have used the words; but Fitzpiers's hold upon her heart just now was slight.

They parted thus and there, kissing each other almost unintentionally, and Grace went moodily homeward. Passing Marty's cottage she observed through the window that the girl was writing instead of chopping as usual, and wondered what her correspondence could be. Directly afterwards she met people in search of her, and reached the house to find all in serious alarm. She soon explained that she had lost her way, and her general depression was attributed to exhaustion on that account.

Could she have known what Marty was writing she would have been surprised.

The rumour which agitated the other folk of Hintock had reached the young girl, and she was penning a letter to Fitzpiers to tell him that Mrs Charmond's magnificent pile of hair was made up of the writer's more largely than of her own. It was poor Marty's only card, and she played it, knowing nothing of fashion, and thinking her revelation a fatal one for a lover.

CHAPTER 34

It was at the beginning of April, a few days after the meeting between Grace and Mrs Charmond in the wood, that Fitzpiers, just returned from London, was travelling from Sherton Abbas to Hintock in a hired carriage. In his eye there was a doubtful light, and the lines of his fastidious face showed a vague disquietude. He appeared like one of those whose aspect seems to say to a beholder that they have suffered a certain wrong in being born.

His position was in truth gloomy, and to his impressible mind it looked even gloomier than it was. His practice had been slowly dwindling of late, and now threatened to die out altogether, the undaunted old Dr Jones capturing patients up to Fitzpiers's very door. Fitzpiers knew only too well the latest and greatest cause of his unpopularity; and yet, so illogical is man, the second branch of his sadness grew out of a remedial measure proposed for the first – a letter from Felice Charmond imploring him not to see her again. To bring about their severance still more effectually, she added, she had decided upon almost immediate departure for the Continent.

The time was that dull interval in a woodlander's life which coincides with great activity in the life of the woodland itself – a period following the close of the winter tree-cutting and preceding the barking season, when the saps are just beginning to heave with the force of hydraulic lifts inside all the trunks of the forest.

Winterborne's contract was completed, and the plantations were deserted. It was dusk: there were no leaves as yet; the nightingales would not begin to sing for a fortnight; and the Mother of the Months was in her most attenuated phase – starved and bent to a mere bowed skeleton, which glided along behind the bare twigs in Fitzpiers's company.

When he reached home he went straight up to his wife's sitting-room. He found it deserted and without a fire. He had mentioned no day for his return; nevertheless he wondered why she was not there waiting to receive him.

On descending to the other wing of the house and inquiring of Mrs Melbury he learnt with much surprise that Grace had gone on a visit to an acquaintance at Shottsford-Forum three days earlier: that tidings had on this morning reached her father of her being very unwell there, in consequence of which he had ridden over to see her.

Fitzpiers went upstairs again, and the little drawing-room, now lighted by a solitary candle, was not rendered more cheerful by the entrance of Grammer Oliver with an apronful of wood which she threw on the hearth while she raked out the grate and rattled about the fire-irons with a view to making things comfortable. Fitzpiers, guessing nothing of the revelations in the wood, considered that Grace ought to have let him know her plans more accurately before leaving home in a freak like this. He went desultorily to the window, the blind of which had not been pulled down, and looked out at the thin, fast-sinking moon, and at the stalk of smoke rising from the top of Suke Damson's chimney, signifying that the young woman had just lit her fire to prepare supper.

He became conscious of a discussion in progress on the opposite side of the court. Somebody had looked over the wall to talk to the sawyers, and was telling them in a loud voice news in which the name of Mrs Charmond soon arrested his ears.

'Grammer, don't make so much noise with that grate,' said the surgeon; at which Grammer reared herself upon her knees and held the fuel suspended in her hand, while Fitzpiers half opened the window.

'She is off to foreign lands again at last – have made up her mind quite sudden-like – and it is thoughted she'll leave in a day or two. She's been all as if her mind were low for some days past – with a sort of fret in her face, as if she chid her own soul. She's the wrong sort of woman for Hintock – hardly knowing a beech from a woak. But I don't care who the man is, she's been a very kind friend to me.'

'Well – the day after to-morrow is the Sabbath day, and without charity we be but tinkling simples; but this I do say, that her going will be a blessed thing for a certain married couple who remain.'

The fire was lighted, and Fitzpiers sat down in front of it, restless as the last leaf upon a tree. 'A sort of fret in her face, as if she chid her own soul. Poor, poor Felice!'

How her frame must be pulsing under the conditions of which he had just heard the caricature; how her fair temples must ache; what a mood of wretchedness she must be in! But for this mixing up of his name with hers, and her determination to sunder their too close acquaintance on that account, she would probably have sent for him professionally. She was now sitting alone, suffering, perhaps wishing she had not forbidden him to come again.

Unable to remain in this lonely room any longer, or to wait for the meal which was in course of preparation, he made himself ready for riding, descended to the yard, stood by the stable-door while Darling was saddled, and rode off down the lane. He would have preferred walking, but was weary with his day's travel.

As he approached the door of Marty South's cottage, which it was necessary to pass on his way, she came from the porch as if she had been awaiting him, and met him in the middle of the road, holding up a letter. Fitzpiers took it without stopping, and asked over his shoulder from whom it came.

Marty hesitated. 'From me,' she said with noticeable firmness.

This letter contained, in fact, Marty's declaration that she was the original owner of Mrs Charmond's supplementary locks, and inclosed a sample from the native stock, which had grown considerably by this time. It was her long contemplated apple of discord, and much her hand trembled as she handed the document up to him.

But it was impossible, on account of the gloom, for Fitzpiers to read it then, while he had the curiosity to do so, and he put it in his pocket. His imagination having already centred itself on Hintock House, in his pocket the letter remained unopened and forgotten, all the while that Marty was hopefully picturing its excellent weaning effect upon him.

He was not long in reaching the precincts of the manor-house. He drew rein under a group of oaks commanding a view of the front, and reflected awhile. His entry would not be altogether unnatural in the circumstances of her possible indisposition; but upon the whole he thought it best to avoid riding up to the door. By silently approaching he could retreat unobserved in the event of her not being alone. He dismounted, hitched Darling to a stray bough hanging a little below the general browsing line of the trees, and proceeded to the door on foot.

In the meantime Melbury had returned from Shottsford-Forum. The great court or quadrangle of the timber-merchant's house, divided from the shady lane by an ivy-covered wall, was entered by two white gates, one standing near each extremity of the wall. It had so happened that at the moment when Fitzpiers was riding out at the lower gate on his way to the manor-house, Melbury was approaching the upper gate to enter it. Fitzpiers, being in front of Melbury, was seen by the latter, but the surgeon, never turning his head, did not observe his father-in-law ambling up slowly and silently under the trees, though his horse, too, was a grey one.

'How is Grace?' said his wife, as soon as he entered.

Melbury looked gloomy. 'She is not at all well,' he said. 'I don't like the looks of her at all. I couldn't bear the notion of her staying away in a strange place any longer, and I begged her to let me get her home. At last she agreed to it, but not till after much persuading. I was then sorry that I rode over instead of driving; but I have hired a nice comfortable carriage – the easiest-going I could get – and she'll be here in a couple of hours or less. I rode on ahead to tell you to get her room ready; but I see her husband has come back.'

'Yes,' said Mrs Melbury. She expressed her concern that her husband had hired a carriage all the way from Shottsford. 'What it will cost!' she said.

'I don't care what it costs!' he exclaimed testily. 'I was determined to get her home. Why she went away, I can't think! She acts in a way that is not at all likely to mend matters as far as I can see.'

Grace had not told her father of her interview with Mrs Charmond and the disclosure that had been whispered in her startled ear.

'Since Edred is come,' he continued, 'he might have waited in till I got back, to ask me how she was, if it was only for a compliment. I saw him go out; where is he gone?'

Mrs Melbury reminded her husband that there was not much doubt about the place of his first visit after an absence. She had, in fact, seen Fitzpiers take the direction of the manor-house.

Melbury said no more. It was exasperating to him that just at this moment, when there was every reason for Fitzpiers to stay indoors, or, at any rate, to ride along the Shottsford road to meet his ailing wife, he should be doing despite to her by going elsewhere. The old man went out of doors again; and, his horse being hardly unsaddled as yet, he told Upjohn to re-tighten the girths; again mounting he rode off at the heels of the surgeon.

By the time that Melbury reached the park he was prepared to go any lengths in combating this rank and reckless errantry of his daughter's husband. He would fetch home Edred Fitzpiers to-night by some means, rough or fair; in his view there could come of his interference nothing worse than what existed at present. And yet to every bad there is a worse.

He had entered by the bridle-gate which admitted to the park on this side, and cantered over the soft turf almost in the tracks of Fitzpiers's horse, till he reached the clump of trees under which his precursor had halted. The whitish object that was indistinctly visible here in the gloom of the boughs he found to be Darling, as left by Fitzpiers.

'Damn him! why did he not ride up to the house in an honest way?' said Melbury.

He profited by Fitzpiers's example; dismounting, he tied his horse under an adjoining tree, and went on to the house on foot, as the other had done. He was no longer disposed to stick at trifles in his investigation, and did not hesitate to gently open the front door without ringing.

The large square hall, with its oak floor, staircase, and wainscot, was lighted by a dim lamp hanging from a beam. Not a soul was visible. He went into the corridor and listened at a door which he knew to be that of the drawing-room; there was no sound, and on turning the handle he found the room empty. A fire burning low in the grate was the sole light of the apartment; its beams flashed mockingly on the somewhat showy Versaillese furniture and gilding here, in style as unlike that of the structural parts of the building as it was possible to be, and probably introduced by Felice to counteract the fine old English gloom of the place. Disappointed in his hope of confronting his son-in-law at once, he went on to the dining-room, which was without light or fire, and pervaded by a cold atmosphere signifying that she had not dined there that day.

By this time Melbury's mood had a little mollified. Everything here was so pacific, so unaggressive in its repose, that he was no longer incited to provoke a collision with Fitzpiers or with anybody. The comparative stateliness of the apartments influenced him to an emotion, rather than to a belief, that where all was outwardly so good and proper there could not be quite that delinquency within which he had suspected. It occurred to him, too, that even if his suspicion were justified his abrupt, if not unwarrantable, entry into the house might end in confounding its inhabitant at the expense of his daughter's dignity and his own. Any ill result would be pretty sure to hit Grace hardest in the long run. He would, after all, adopt the more rational course and plead with Fitzpiers privately, as he had pleaded with Mrs Charmond.

He accordingly retreated as silently as he had come. Passing the door of the drawing-room anew he fancied that he heard a noise within which was not the crackling of the fire. Melbury gently reopened the door to a distance of a few inches and saw at the opposite window two figures in the act of stepping out – a man and a woman – in whom he recognized the lady of the house and his son-in-law. In a moment they had disappeared amid the gloom of the lawn.

He drew back into the hall and let himself out by the carriage-entrance door, coming round to the lawn-front in time to see the two figures parting at the railing which divided the precincts of the house from the open park.

Mrs Charmond turned to hasten back immediately that her lover had left her side; and Fitzpiers going onward was speedily absorbed into the duskiness of the trees.

Melbury waited till Mrs Charmond had re-entered the drawing-room window, and then followed after Fitzpiers. He would give that precious young man a piece of his mind to-night, even if he were not tempted to give him more.

On plunging however into the thick shade of the clump of oaks he could not discover Fitzpiers; neither could he perceive his horse Blossom anywhere; but feeling his way carefully along he by and by discerned Fitzpiers's mare Darling still standing as before under the tree adjoining that to which he had hitched Blossom. For a moment Melbury thought that his own horse, being young and strong, had broken away from her fastening; but on listening intently he could hear her ambling comfortably along a little way ahead, and a creaking of the saddle which showed that she had a rider. Walking on as far as the small gate in the corner of the park he met a labourer, who, in reply to

Melbury's inquiry if he had seen any person on a grey horse, said that he had only met Dr Fitzpiers.

It was just what Melbury had begun to suspect; Fitzpiers had mounted the mare which did not belong to him in mistake for his own – an oversight easily explicable, in a man ever unwitting in horseflesh, by the gloom of the spot and the near similarity of the animals in appearance, though Melbury's was readily enough seen to be the darker horse by day.

He hastened back, and did what seemed best in the circumstances – got upon old Darling, and rode rapidly after Fitzpiers.

Melbury had just entered the wood, and was winding along the cart-way which led through it, channelled deep in the leaf-mould with large ruts that were formed by the timber-waggons in fetching the spoil of the plantations, when all at once he descried in front, at a point where the road took a turning round a large chestnut tree, the form of his own horse Blossom. Melbury quickened Darling's pace, thinking to come up with Fitzpiers.

Nearer view revealed that the horse had no rider. At Melbury's approach it galloped friskily away under the trees in a homeward direction. Thinking something was wrong the timber-merchant dismounted as soon as he reached the chestnut, and after feeling about for a minute or two discovered Fitzpiers lying on the ground.

'Here – help!' cried the latter as soon as he felt Melbury's touch: 'I have been thrown off. . . . But there's not much harm done, I think.'

Since Melbury could not now very well read the younger man the lecture he had intended, and as friendliness would be hypocrisy, his instinct was to speak not a single word to his son-in-law. He raised Fitzpiers into a sitting posture, and found that he was a little stunned and stupefied, but, as he had said, not otherwise hurt. How this fall had come about was readily conjecturable: Fitzpiers, imagining there was only old Darling under him, had been taken unawares by the younger horse, anxious for the stable.

Melbury was a traveller of the old-fashioned sort: having just come from Shottsford-Forum he still had in his pocket the pilgrim's flask of rum which he always carried on journeys exceeding a dozen miles, though he seldom drank much of it. He poured it down the surgeon's throat with such effect that he quickly revived. Melbury got him on his legs; but the question was what to do with him. He could not walk more than a few steps, and the other horse had gone away.

With great exertion Melbury contrived to get him astride Darling, mounting himself behind and holding Fitzpiers round his waist with one arm. Darling being broad, straight-backed, and high in the withers, was well able to carry double, at any rate the short distance to Hintock and at a gentle pace.

CHAPTER 35

THE mare paced along with firm and cautious tread through the copse where Winterborne had worked, and into the heavier soil where the oaks grew: thence towards Marshcombe Bottom, intensely dark now with overgrowth, and popularly supposed to be haunted by spirits.

By this time Fitzpiers had quite recovered his physical strength. But he had eaten nothing since making a hasty breakfast in London that morning, his anxiety about Felice having hurried him away from home before dining; as a consequence the old rum administered by his father-in-law flew to the young man's head and loosened his tongue without his ever having recognized who it was that had lent him a kindly hand. He began to speak in desultory sentences, Melbury still supporting him.

'I've come all the way from London to-day,' said Fitzpiers. 'Ah, that's the place to meet your equals. I live at Hintock – worse, at Little Hintock! – and I am quite wasted there. There's not a man within ten miles of Hintock who can comprehend me.... I tell you, Farmer What's-your-name, that I'm a man of education. I know several languages: the poets and I are familiar friends: I used to read more in metaphysics than anybody within fifty miles; and since I gave that up there's nobody can match me in the whole county of South Wessex as a scientist.... Yet I am doomed to live with tradespeople in a miserable little hole like Hintock!'

'Indeed!' muttered Melbury.

Here Fitzpiers, with alcoholic energy, reared himself up suddenly from the bowed posture he had hitherto held, thrusting his shoulders so violently against Melbury's breast as to make it difficult for the old man to keep a hold on the reins.

'People don't appreciate me here!' the surgeon exclaimed; then, lowering his voice, he added softly and slowly, 'except one – except one! . . . A passionate soul, as warm as she is clever, as beautiful as she is warm, and as rich as she is beautiful. I say, old fellow, those claws of yours clutch me rather tight – rather like the eagle's, you know, that ate out the liver of Pro – Pre –, the man on Mount Caucasus. . . . People don't appreciate me, I say, except *her!* . . . Ah, God, I am an unlucky man! She would have been mine, she would have taken my name; but unfortunately it cannot be so! I stooped to mate beneath me; and now I rue it.'

The position was becoming a very trying one for Melbury, corporeally and mentally. He was obliged to steady Fitzpiers with his left arm, and he began to hate the contact. He hardly knew what to do. It was useless to remonstrate with Fitzpiers in his intellectual confusion from the rum and from the fall. He remained silent, his hold upon his companion, however, being stern rather than compassionate.

'You hurt me a little, farmer! – though I am much obliged to you for your kindness. . . . People don't appreciate me, I say. Between ourselves, I am losing my practice here; and why? Because I see matchless attraction where matchless attraction is, both in person and position. – I mention no names, so nobody will be the wiser. . . . But I have lost her, – in a legitimate sense, that is. If I were a free man now, things have come to such a pass between us that she could not refuse me; while with her fortune (which I don't covet for itself) I should have a chance of satisfying an honourable ambition – a chance I have not had yet! . . . and now never, never shall have probably!'

Melbury, his heart throbbing against the other's backbone, and his brain on fire with indignation, ventured to mutter huskily, 'Why?'

The horse ambled on some steps before Fitzpiers replied. 'Because I am tied and bound to another by law, as tightly as

I am to you by your arm – not that I complain of your arm – I thank you for helping me. Well, where are we? Not nearly home yet? . . . Home, say I. It *is* a home! When I might have been at the other house over there.' In a stupefied way he flung his hand in the direction of the park. 'I was just two months too early in committing myself. Had I only seen the other first—'

Here the old man's arm gave Fitzpiers a convulsive shake.

'What are you doing?' continued the latter. 'Keep still, please, or put me down. . . . I was saying that I lost her by a mere little two months! There is no chance for me now in this world, and it makes me reckless – reckless! Unless, indeed, anything should happen to the other one. She is amiable enough; but if anything should happen to her – and I hear she is ill at this moment – well, if it *should*, I should be free – and my fame, my happiness, would be insured!'

These were the last words that Fitzpiers uttered in his seat in front of the timber-merchant. Unable longer to master himself Melbury whipped away his spare arm from Fitzpiers's waist, and seized him by the collar.

'You heartless villain – after all that we have done for 'ee!' he cried with a quivering lip. 'And the money of hers that you've had, and the roof we've provided to shelter 'ee! – It is to me, George Melbury, that you dare to talk like that!' The exclamation was accompanied by a powerful swing from the shoulder, which flung the young man headlong into the road.

Fitzpiers fell with a heavy thud upon the stumps of some brushwood which had been cut during the winter preceding. Darling continued her walk for a few paces further and stopped.

'God forgive me!' Melbury murmured, repenting of what he had done. 'He tried me too sorely, and now perhaps I've murdered him!'

He turned round in the saddle and looked towards the spot on which Fitzpiers had fallen. To his great surprise he beheld the surgeon rise to his feet as if scarcely hurt, and walk away rapidly under the trees.

Melbury listened till the rustle of Fitzpiers's footsteps died away. 'It might have been a crime, but for the mercy of Providence in providing leaves for his fall,' he said to himself. And then his mind reverted to the words of Fitzpiers, and his indignation so mounted within him that he almost wished the fall had put an end to the surgeon there and then.

He had not ridden far when he discerned his own grey mare standing under some bushes. Leaving Darling for a moment, Melbury went forward and easily caught the younger animal, now disheartened at its freak. He made the pair of them fast to a tree, and turning back endeavoured to find some trace of Fitzpiers, feeling pitifully that, after all, he had gone further than he intended with the offender. But though he threaded the wood hither and thither, his toes ploughing layer after layer of the little horny scrolls that had once been leaves, he could not find him. He stood still, listening and looking round. The breeze was oozing through the network of boughs as through a strainer; the trunks and larger branches stood against the light of the sky in the forms of sentinels, gigantic candelabra, pikes, halberds, lances, and whatever else the fancy chose to make of them. Giving up the search Melbury came back to the horses, and walked slowly homeward leading one in each hand.

It happened that on the selfsame evening a boy had been returning through Hintock Park to Little Hintock about the time of Fitzpiers's passage home along that route. A horse-collar that had been left at the harness-mender's to be repaired was required for use at five o'clock next morning, and in consequence the boy had to fetch it overnight. He put his head through the collar, and the way of the park being a short cut he took it, whistling the one tune he knew as an antidote to fear.

The boy suddenly became aware of a horse brushing rather friskily along the track behind him. Not knowing whether to expect friend or foe, prudence suggested that he should cease his whistling and retreat among the trees till the horse and his rider had gone by, a course to which he was still more inclined when he found how noiselessly they approached, and saw that the horse looked pale, and remembered what he had read about Death in the Revelation. He therefore deposited the collar by a tree and hid himself behind it. The horseman came on, and the youth, whose eyes were as keen as telescopes, to his great relief recognized the doctor.

As Melbury surmised, Fitzpiers had in the darkness taken Blossom for Darling, and he had not discovered his mistake when he came up opposite the boy, though he was somewhat surprised at the liveliness of his usually placid mare. The only other pair of eyes on the spot whose vision was keen as the young carter's were those of the horse; and, with that strongly conservative objection to the unusual which animals show, Blossom, on eyeing the collar under the tree – quite invisible to Fitzpiers – exercised none of the patience of the older horse, but shied sufficiently to unseat so second-rate an equestrian as the surgeon.

He fell and did not move, lying as Melbury afterwards found him. The boy ran away, salving his conscience for the desertion by thinking how vigorously he would spread the alarm of the accident when he got to Hintock – which he uncompromisingly did, incrusting the skeleton event with a load of dramatic horrors.

Grace had returned, and the fly hired on her account, though not by her husband, at the Crown Hotel, Shottsford-Forum, had been paid for and dismissed. The long drive had somewhat revived her, her illness being a feverish intermittent nervousness which had more to do with mind than body, and she walked about her sitting-room in something of a hopeful mood. Mrs Melbury had told her as soon as she arrived that her husband had returned from London. He had gone out, she said, to see a patient as she supposed, and he must soon be back, since he had had no dinner or tea. Grace would not allow her mind to harbour any suspicion of his whereabouts, and her stepmother said nothing of Mrs Charmond's rumoured sorrows and plans of departure.

So the young wife sat by the fire, waiting silently. She had left Hintock in a turmoil of aversion from her husband, after the revelation of Mrs Charmond, and had intended not to be at home when he returned. But she had thought the matter over, and had allowed her father's influence to prevail and bring her back; and now somewhat regretted that Edred's arrival had preceded hers.

By and by Mrs Melbury came upstairs with a slight air of flurry and abruptness.

'I have something to tell – some bad news,' she said. 'But you must not be alarmed, as it is not so bad as it might have been. Edred has been thrown off his horse. We don't think he is hurt much. It happened in the wood the other side of Marshcombe Bottom.'

She went on to give a few of the particulars, but none of the invented horrors that had been communicated by the boy. 'I thought it better to tell you at once,' she added, 'in case he should not – be very well able to walk home, and somebody should bring him.'

Mrs Melbury really thought matters much worse than she represented, and Grace knew that she thought so. She sat down dazed for a few minutes, returning a negative to her stepmother's inquiry if she could do anything for her.

'Ah – yes – please go into the bedroom,' Grace said on second thoughts, 'and see if all is ready there – in case it is serious.' Mrs Melbury thereupon called Grammer, and they did as directed, supplying the room with everything they could think of for the accommodation of an injured man.

Nobody was left in the lower part of the house. Not many minutes had passed when Grace heard a knock at the door – a single knock, not loud enough to reach the ears of those in the bedroom.

She went to the top of the stairs and said faintly, 'Come up,' knowing that the door stood, as usual in such houses, wide open. Retreating into the gloom of the broad landing she saw rise up the stairs a woman whom at first she did not recognize, till her voice revealed her to be Suke Damson in great fright and sorrow. A streak of light from the partially closed door of Grace's room fell upon her face as she came forward, and it was drawn and pale.

'O, Miss Melbury – I would say Mrs Fitzpiers,' she said, wringing her hands. 'This terrible news – is he dead? Is he hurted very bad? Tell me; I couldn't help coming – please forgive me, Miss Melbury – Mrs Fitzpiers, I would say!'

Grace sank down on the oak chest which stood on the landing, and put her hands to her now flushed face and head. Ought she not to order Suke Damson downstairs and out of the house? Her husband might be brought in at any moment, and what would happen? But could she order this genuinely grieved woman away?

There was a dead silence of half a minute or so, till Suke said, 'Why don't ye speak? Is he here? Is he dead? If so, why can't I see him – would it be so very wrong?'

Before Grace had answered somebody else came to the door below – a footfall light as a roe's. There was a hurried tapping upon the panel, as if with the impatient tips of fingers whose owner thought not whether a knocker were there or no. Without a pause, and possibly guided by the stray beam of light on the landing, the newcomer ascended the staircase as the first had done. Grace started; it was a lady. Grace was sufficiently visible, and the lady came to her side.

'I could make nobody hear downstairs,' said Felice Charmond with lips whose dryness could almost be heard, and panting as she stood ready to sink on the floor with distress. 'What is – the matter – tell me the worst! Can he live?'

She looked at Grace imploringly, without perceiving poor Suke who, dismayed at such a presence, had shrunk away into the shade. Mrs Charmond's little feet were covered with mud: she was quite unconscious of her appearance now.

'I have heard such a dreadful report,' she went on: 'I came to ascertain the truth of it. Is he – killed?'

'She won't tell us – he's dying – he's in that room!' burst out Suke, regardless of consequences, as she heard the distant movements of Mrs Melbury and Grammer in the bedroom at the end of the passage.

'Where?' said Mrs Charmond; and on Suke pointing out the direction she made as if to go thither.

Grace barred the way.

'He is not there,' she said. 'I have not seen him any more than you. I have heard a report only – not so bad as you think. It must have been exaggerated to you.'

'Please do not conceal anything – let me know all!' said Felice doubtingly.

'You shall know all I know. Indeed, you have a perfect right to go into his bedroom; who can have a better than either of you?' said Grace with a delicate sting which was lost upon them now as, ceasing to obstruct the way, she led on to the chamber door, and flung it open. 'Wives all, let's enter together!... I repeat, I have only heard a less alarming account than you have heard; how much it means, and how little, I cannot say. I pray God that it means not much – in common humanity. You probably pray the same – *for other reasons*.'

Then she regarded them there in the dim light awhile, as, gathering with her round the empty bed of Fitzpiers, they stood dumb in their trouble, staring at it, and at his night-shirt lying on the pillow; not stinging back at her, not heeding her mood. A tenderness spread over Grace like a dew. It was well enough, conventionally, to address either one of them in the wife's regulation terms of virtuous sarcasm, as woman, creature, or thing. But life, what was it, after all? She had, like the singer of the Psalm of Asaph, been plagued and chastened all the day long; but could she, by retributive words, in order to please herself, the individual, 'offend against the generation', as that singer would not?

'He is dying, perhaps!' blubbered Suke Damson, putting her apron to her eyes.

In their gestures and faces there were anxieties, affection, agony of heart – all for a man who had wronged them – had never really behaved towards either of them anyhow but selfishly. Neither one but would have well-nigh sacrificed half her life to him, even now. The tears which his possible critical situation could not bring to her eyes surged over at the contemplation of these fellow-women whose relations with him were as close as her own without its conventionality. She went out to the balustrade, bent herself upon it, and wept.

Thereupon Felice following began to cry also, without using her handkerchief, letting the tears run down silently. While the three stood together thus, pitying another though most to be pitied themselves, the pacing of a horse or horses became audible in the court, and in a moment Melbury's voice was heard calling to his stableman.

Grace at once started up, ran down the stairs, and out into the quadrangle as her father crossed it towards the door. 'Father, what is the matter with him?' she cried.

'Who, Edred?' said Melbury abruptly. 'Matter? Nothing. What, my dear, and have you got home safe? Why, you are better already! But you ought not to be out in the air like this.'

'But he has been thrown off his horse!'

'I know; I know. I saw it. He got up again, and walked off as well as ever. A fall on the leaves didn't hurt a spry fellow like him. He did not come this way,' he added significantly. 'I suppose he went to look for his horse. I tried to find him, but could not. But after seeing him go away under the trees I found the horse, and have led it home for safety. So he must walk. Now, don't you stay out here in this night air.'

She returned to the house with her father. When she had again ascended to the landing and to her own rooms beyond, it was a great relief to her to find that both Petticoat the First and Petticoat the Second of her *Bien-aimé* had silently disappeared. They had in all probability heard the words of her father, and departed with their anxieties relieved.

Presently her parents came up to Grace, and busied themselves to see that she was comfortable. Perceiving soon that she would prefer to be left alone they went away.

Grace waited on. The clock raised its voice now and then, but her husband did not return. At her father's usual hour for retiring he again came in to see her. 'Do not stay up,' she said as soon as he entered. 'I am not at all tired. I will sit up for him.'

'I think it will be useless, Grace,' said Melbury slowly.

'Why?'

'I have had a bitter quarrel with him. And on that account I hardly think he will return to-night.'

'A quarrel? Was that after the fall seen by the boy?'

Melbury nodded an affirmative – without taking his eyes off the candle.

'Yes; it was as we were coming home together,' he said.

Something had been swelling up in Grace while her father was speaking. 'How could you want to quarrel with him?' she cried suddenly. 'Why could you not let him come home quietly, if he were inclined to? He is my husband; and now you have married me to him surely you need not provoke him unnecessarily? First you induce me to accept him, and then you do things that divide us more than we should naturally be divided!'

'How can you speak so unjustly to me, Grace?' said Melbury, with indignant sorrow. '*I* divide you from your husband, indeed! You little think—'

He was inclined to say more – to tell her the whole story of the encounter, and that the provocation he had received had lain entirely in hearing her despised. But it would have greatly distressed her, and he forbore.

'You had better lie down. You are tired,' he said soothingly. 'Good-night.'

The household went to bed, and a silence fell upon the dwelling, broken only by the occasional skirr of a halter in Melbury's stables. Despite her father's advice Grace still waited up. But nobody came.

It was a critical time in Grace's emotional life, that night. She thought of her husband a good deal, and for the nonce forgot Winterborne.

'How these unhappy women must have admired Edred!' she said to herself. 'How attractive he must be to everybody; and indeed, he is attractive.' The possibility is that, piqued by rivalry, these ideas might have been transmuted into their corresponding emotions by a show of the least reciprocity in Fitzpiers. There was, in truth, a lovebird yearning to fly from her heart; and it wanted a lodging badly.

But no husband came. The fact was that Melbury had been much mistaken about the condition of Fitzpiers. People do not fall headlong on stumps of underwood with impunity. Had the old man been able to watch Fitzpiers narrowly enough, he would have observed that, on rising and walking into the thicket, he dropped blood as he went; that he had not proceeded fifty yards before he showed signs of being dizzy, and, raising his hands to his head, reeled and fell.

CHAPTER 36

GRACE was not the only one who watched and meditated in Hintock that night. Felice Charmond was in no mood to retire to rest at a customary hour; and over her drawing-room fire at the manor-house she sat as motionless and in as deep a reverie as Grace in her little chamber at the homestead.

Having caught ear of Melbury's intelligence while she had stood on the landing at his house, and been eased of much of her mental distress, her sense of personal decorum had returned upon her with a rush. She descended the stairs and left the door like a ghost, keeping close to the walls of the building till she got round to the gate of the quadrangle, through which she noiselessly passed almost before Grace and her father had finished their discourse. Suke Damson had thought it well to imitate her superior in this respect, and, descending the back stairs as Felice descended the front, went out at the side door and home to her cottage.

Once outside Melbury's gates Mrs Charmond ran with all her speed to the manor-house without stopping or turning her head. She entered her own dwelling as she had emerged from it – by the drawing-room window. Everything was just as she had left it: she had been gone about three-quarters of an hour by the clock, and nobody seemed to have discovered her absence. Tired in body but tense in mind she sat down, palpitating, round-eyed, bewildered at what she had done.

She had been betrayed by affrighted love into a visit which, now that the emotion instigating it had calmed down under her belief that Fitzpiers was in no danger, was the saddest surprise to her. This was how she had set about doing her best to escape her passionate bondage to him! Somehow, in declaring to Grace and to herself the unseemliness of her infatuation, she had grown a convert to its irresistibility.

If Heaven would only give her strength; but Heaven never did! One thing was indispensable: she must go away from Hintock if she meant to withstand further temptation. The struggle was too wearying, too hopeless, while she remained. It was but a continual capitulation of conscience to what she dared not name.

By degrees, as she sat on and on, Felice's mind – helped perhaps by the anti-climax of supposing that her lover was unharmed after all her fright about him – grew wondrously strong in wise resolve. For the moment she was in a mood, in the words of Mrs Elizabeth Montagu, 'to run mad with discretion'; and was so persuaded that discretion lay in departure that she wished to set about going that very minute. Jumping up from her seat she began to gather together some small personal knick-knacks scattered about the room, to feel that preparations were really in train.

While moving here and there she fancied that she heard a slight noise out of doors, and stood still. Surely it was a tapping at the window. A thought entered her mind, and burnt her cheek. He had come to that window before; yet was it possible that he should dare to do so now! All the servants were in bed, and in the ordinary course of affairs she would have retired also. Then she remembered that on stepping in by the casement and closing it she had not fastened the window-shutter, so that a streak of light from the interior of the room might have revealed her vigil to an observer on the lawn. How all things conspired against her keeping faith with Grace!

The tapping recommenced, light as from the bill of a little bird: her illegitimate hope overcame her discretion: she went and pulled back the shutter, determining however to shake her head at him, and keep the casement securely closed.

What she saw outside might have struck terror into a heart

stouter than a helpless woman's at midnight. In the centre of the lowest pane of the window, close to the glass, was a human face which she barely recognized as the face of Fitzpiers. It was surrounded with the darkness of the night without, corpse-like in its pallor, and covered with blood. As disclosed in the square area of the pane it met her frightened eyes like a replica of the Sudarium of St Veronica.

He moved his lips and looked at her imploringly. Her rapid mind pieced together in an instant a possible concatenation of events which might have led to this tragical issue. She unlatched the casement with a terrified hand, and bending down to where he was crouching pressed her face to his with passionate solicitude. She assisted him into the room without a word, to do which it was almost necessary to lift him bodily.

Quickly closing the window and fastening the shutters she bent over him breathlessly.

'Are you hurt much, much?' she cried faintly. 'O, O, how is this!'

'Rather much – but don't be frightened,' he answered in a difficult whisper, and turning himself to obtain an easier position if possible. 'A little water, please.'

She ran across into the dining-room, and brought a bottle and glass, from which he eagerly drank. He could then speak much better, and with her help got upon the nearest couch.

'Are you dying, Edred?' she said. 'Do speak to me!'

'I am half dead,' gasped Fitzpiers. 'But perhaps I shall get over it. . . . It is chiefly loss of blood.'

'But I thought your fall did not hurt you?' said she. 'Who did this?'

'Felice – my father-in-law! . . . I have crawled to you more than a mile on my hands and knees – God, I thought I should never have got here! . . . I have come to you – because you are the only friend – I have in the world now. . . . I can never go back to Hintock – never – the roof of the Melburys! Not poppy nor mandragora will ever medicine this bitter feud. . . . If I were only well again—'

'Let me bind your head, now that you have rested.'

'Yes – but wait a moment – it stopped bleeding, fortunately, or I should be a dead man before now! While in the wood I managed to make a tourniquet of some halfpence and my handkerchief, as well as I could in the dark. . . . But listen, dear Felice! Can you hide me till I am well? Whatever comes, I can be seen in Hintock no more. My practice is nearly gone, you know – and after this I would not care to recover it if I could.'

By this time Felice's tears began to blind her. Where were now her discreet plans for sundering their lives for ever? To administer to him in his pain, and trouble, and poverty, was her single thought. The first step was to hide him, and she asked herself where. A place occurred to her mind.

She got him some wine from the dining-room, which strengthened him much. Then she managed to remove his boots, and, as he could now keep himself upright by leaning upon her on one side and a walking-stick on the other, they went thus in slow march out of the room and up the stairs. At the top she took him along a gallery, pausing whenever he required rest, and thence up a smaller staircase to the least used part of the house, where she unlocked a door. Within was a lumber-room, containing abandoned furniture of all descriptions, built up in piles which obscured the light of the windows, and formed between them nooks and lairs in which a person would not be discerned even should an eye gaze in at the door. The articles were mainly those that had belonged to the previous owner of the house, and had been bought in by the late Mr Charmond at the auction; but changing fashion, and the tastes of a young wife, had caused them to be relegated to this dungeon.

Here Fitzpiers sat on the floor against the wall till she had hauled out materials for a bed, which she spread on the floor in one of the aforesaid nooks. She obtained water and a basin, and washed the dried blood from his face and hands; and when he was comfortably reclining fetched food from the larder. While he ate her eyes lingered anxiously on his face, following its every movement with such loving-kindness as only a fond woman can show.

He was now in better condition, and discussed his position with her.

'What I fancy I said to Melbury must have been enough to enrage any man, if uttered in cold blood, and with knowledge of his presence. But I did not know him, and I was stupefied by what he had given me, so that I hardly was aware of what I said. Well – the veil of that temple is rent in twain! . . . As I am not going to be seen again in Hintock, my first efforts must be directed to allay any alarm that may be felt at my absence, before I am able to get clear away. Nobody must suspect that I have been hurt, or there will be a country talk about me. Felice, I must at once concoct a letter to check all search for me. I think if you can bring me a pen and paper I may be able to do it now. I could rest better if it were done. Poor thing! how I tire her with running up and down!'

She fetched writing materials and held up the blotting-book as a support to his hand, while he penned a brief note to his nominal wife.

'The animosity shown towards me by your father,' he wrote in this coldest of marital epistles, 'is such that I cannot return again to a roof which is his, even though it shelters you. A parting is unavoidable, as you are sure to be on his side in this division. I am starting on a journey which will take me a long way from Hintock, and you must not expect to see me there again for some time.'

He then gave Grace a few directions bearing upon his professional engagements and other practical matters, concluding without a hint of his destination, or a notion of when she would see him again. He offered to read the note to Felice before he closed it up; but she would not hear or see it: that side of his obligations distressed her beyond endurance. She turned away from Fitzpiers and sobbed bitterly.

'If you can get this posted at a place some miles away,' he whispered, exhausted by the effort of writing, 'at Sherton

Abbas, or Port-Bredy, or still better, Budmouth, it will divert all suspicion from this house as the place of my refuge.'

'I will drive to one or other of the places myself – anything to keep it unknown!' she murmured, her voice weighted with vague foreboding now that the excitement of helping him had passed away.

Fitzpiers told her that there was yet one thing more to be done. 'In creeping over the fence on to the lawn,' he said, 'I made the rail bloody, and it shows rather too plainly on the white paint – I could see it in the dark. At all hazards it should be washed off. Could you do that also, Felice?'

What will not women do on such devoted occasions? Weary as she was she went – all the way down the rambling staircases to the ground floor, then to search for a lantern, which she lighted and hid under her cloak; then for a wet sponge, and next forth into the night. The white railing stared out in the darkness at her approach, and a ray from the enshrouded lantern fell upon the blood – just where he had told her it would be found. She shuddered. It was almost too much to bear in one day; but with a shaking hand she sponged the rail clean, and returned to the house.

The time occupied by these several proceedings was not much less than two hours. When all was done, and she had smoothed his extemporized bed, and kissed him, and placed everything within his reach that she could think of, she took her leave of him and locked him in.

CHAPTER 37

When her husband's letter reached Grace's hands, bearing upon it the postmark of a distant town, it never once crossed her mind that Fitzpiers was lying wounded within a mile or two of her still. She felt relieved that he did not write more bitterly of the quarrel with her father, whatever its nature might have been; but the general frigidity of his communication quenched in her the incipient spark that events had kindled so shortly before.

From this centre of information it was made known in Hintock that the doctor had gone away, and as none but the Melbury household was aware that he did not return on the night of his accident, no excitement manifested itself in the village.

Thus the early days of May passed by. None but the nocturnal birds and animals observed that late one evening, towards the middle of the month, a closely wrapped figure, with a crutch under one arm and a stick in his hand, crept out from Hintock House across the lawn to the shelter of the trees, taking thence a slow and laborious walk to the nearest point of the turnpike-road.

The mysterious personage was so disguised that his own wife would hardly have known him. Felice Charmond was a practised hand at such work, as well she might be; and she had done her utmost in padding and painting Fitzpiers with the old materials of her art in recesses of that lumber-room.

In the highway he was met by a covered carriage which conveyed him to Sherton Abbas, whence he proceeded to the nearest port on the south coast, and immediately crossed the Channel.

But it was known to everybody that three days after this time Mrs Charmond executed her oft-deferred plan of setting out for a long term of travel and residence on the Continent. She went off one morning as unostentatiously as could be, and took no maid with her, having, she said, engaged one to meet her at a point further on in her route. After that, Hintock House, so frequently deserted, was to be let. Spring had not merged in summer when a clinching rumour, founded on the best of evidence, reached the parish and neighbourhood. Mrs Charmond and Fitzpiers had been seen together in Baden, in relations which set at rest the question that had agitated the little community ever since the winter.

Melbury had entered the Valley of Humiliation even further than Grace. His spirit seemed broken.

But once a week he mechanically went to market as usual, and here, as he was passing by the conduit one day, his mental condition expressed largely by his gait, he heard his name spoken by a voice formerly familiar. He turned and saw a certain Fred Beaucock – once a promising lawyer's clerk and local dandy, who had been called the cleverest fellow in Sherton, without whose brains the firm of solicitors employing him would be nowhere. But later on Beaucock had fallen into the mire. He was invited out a good deal, sang songs at agricultural meetings and burgesses' dinners: in sum, victualled himself with spirits more frequently than was good for the clever brains or body either. He lost his post, and after an absence spent in trying his powers elsewhere came back to his native town, where, at the time of the foregoing events in Hintock, he gave legal advice for astonishingly small fees – mostly carrying on his profession in public-house settles, in whose recesses he might often have been overheard making country-people's wills for half-a-crown, calling with a learned voice for pen and ink and a halfpenny sheet of paper, on which he drew up the testament while resting it in a little space wiped with his hand on the table amid the liquid circles formed by the cups and glasses. An idea implanted early in life is difficult to uproot, and many elderly tradespeople still clung to the notion that Fred Beaucock knew a great deal of law.

It was he who had called Melbury by name.

'You look very down, Mr Melbury – very, if I may say as much,' he observed, when the timber-merchant turned. 'But I know – I know. A very sad case – very. I was bred to the law, as you are aware, and am professionally no stranger to such matters. Well, Mrs Fitzpiers has her remedy.'

'How – what – a remedy?' said Melbury.

'Under the new law, sir. A new court was established last year, and under the new statute, twenty and twenty-one Vic., cap. eighty-five, unmarrying is as easy as marrying. No more Acts of Parliament necessary: no longer one law for the rich and another for the poor. But come inside – I was just going to have a nipperkin of rum-hot – I'll explain it all to you.'

The intelligence amazed Melbury, who saw little of newspapers. And though he was a severely correct man in his habits, and had no taste for entering a tavern with Fred Beaucock – nay, would have been quite uninfluenced by such a character on any other matter in the world – such fascination lay in the idea of delivering his poor girl from bondage that it deprived him of the critical faculty. He could not resist the ex-lawyer's clerk, and entered the inn.

Here they sat down to the rum, which Melbury paid for as a matter of course, Beaucock leaning back on the settle with a legal gravity, that would hardly allow him to be conscious of the spirits before him; which nevertheless disappeared with mysterious quickness.

How much of the exaggerated information on the then new divorce laws imparted by Beaucock to his listener was the result of ignorance, and how much of dupery, was never ascertained. But he related such a plausible story of the ease with which Grace could become a free woman that her father was irradiated with the project; and though he scarcely wetted his lips

Melbury never knew how he came out of the inn, or when or where he mounted his gig to pursue his way homeward.

But home he found himself, his brain having all the way seemed to ring sonorously as a gong in the intensity of its stir. Before he had seen Grace he was accidentally met by Winterborne, who found him as Stephen was beheld by the Council, with a face like the face of an angel.

He relinquished his horse and took Winterborne by the arm to a heap of rendlewood – as barked oak was here called – which lay under a privet hedge.

'Giles,' he said, when they had sat down upon the logs, 'there's a new law in the land! Grace can be free quite easily. I only knew it by the merest accident. I might not have found it out for the next ten years. She can get rid of him – d'ye hear – get rid of him. Think of that, my friend Giles!'

He related what he had learnt of the new legal remedy. A subdued tremulousness about the mouth was all the response that Winterborne made; and Melbury added, 'My boy, you shall have her yet – if you want her.' His feelings had gathered volume as he said this, and the articulate sound of the old idea drowned his sight in mist.

'Are you sure – about this new law?' asked Winterborne, so disquieted by a gigantic exultation which loomed alternately with fearful doubt that he evaded the full acceptance of Melbury's last statement.

Melbury said that he had no manner of doubt, for since his talk with Beaucock it had come into his mind that he had seen some time ago in the weekly paper an allusion to such a legal change; but, having no interest in those desperate remedies at the moment, he had passed it over.

'But I'm not going to let the matter rest doubtful for a single day,' he continued. 'I am going to London. Beaucock will go with me, and we shall get the best advice as soon as we possibly can. Beaucock is a thorough lawyer – nothing the matter with him but a fiery palate. I knew him as the stay and refuge of Sherton in knots of law at one time.'

Winterborne's replies were of the vaguest. The new possibility was almost unthinkable at the moment. He was what was called at Hintock 'a solid-going fellow'; he maintained his abeyant mood not from want of reciprocity, but from a taciturn hesitancy taught by life as he knew it.

'But,' continued the timber-merchant, a temporary crease or two of anxiety supplementing those already established in his forehead by time, 'Grace is not at all well. Nothing constitutional, you know; but she has been in a low nervous state ever since that night of fright. I don't doubt but that she will be all right soon.... I wonder how she is this evening?' He rose with the words as if he had too long forgotten her personality in the excitement of her previsioned career.

They had sat till evening was beginning to dye the garden brown, and now went towards Melbury's house, Giles a few steps in the rear of his old friend, who was stimulated by the enthusiasm of the moment to outstep the more ordinary pace of Winterborne. He felt shy of entering Grace's presence as her reconstituted lover – which was how her father's manner would be sure to present him – before definite information as to her future state was forthcoming: it seemed too nearly like the act of those who rush in where angels fear to tread.

A chill to counterbalance all the glowing promise of the day was prompt enough in coming. No sooner had he followed the timber-merchant in at the door than he heard Grammer inform him that Mrs Fitzpiers was still more unwell than she had been in the morning. Old Dr Jones being in the neighbourhood they had called him in, and he had instantly directed them to get her to bed. They were not, however, to consider her illness serious – a feverish, nervous attack, the result of recent events, was what she was suffering from – and she would doubtless be well in a few days.

Winterborne therefore did not remain, and his hope of seeing her that evening was disappointed.

Even this aggravation of her morning condition did not greatly depress Melbury. He knew, he said, that his daughter's constitution was sound enough. It was only these domestic troubles that were pulling her down. Once free she would be blooming again. Melbury diagnosed rightly, as parents usually do.

He set out for London the next morning, Jones having paid another visit and assured him that he might leave home without uneasiness, especially on an errand of that sort, which would the sooner put an end to her suspense.

The timber-merchant had been away only a day or two when it was told in Hintock that Mr Fitzpiers's hat had been found in the wood. Later on in the afternoon the hat was brought to Melbury's, and, by a piece of ill-fortune, into Grace's presence. It had doubtless lain in the wood ever since his fall from the horse; but it looked so clean and uninjured – the summer weather and leafy shelter having much favoured its preservation – that Grace could not believe it had remained so long concealed. A very little fact was enough to set her fevered fancy at work at this juncture – she thought him still in the neighbourhood, she feared his sudden appearance; and her nervous malady developed consequences so grave that Dr Jones began to look serious, and the household was alarmed.

It was the beginning of June, and the cuckoo at this time of the summer scarcely ceased his cry for more than a couple of hours during the night. The bird's note, so familiar to her ears from infancy, was now absolute torture to the poor girl. On the Friday following the Wednesday of Melbury's departure, and the day after the discovery of Fitzpiers's hat, the cuckoo began at two o'clock in the morning with a sudden cry from one of Melbury's apple-trees, not three yards from the window of Grace's room.

'O – he is coming!' she cried, and in her terror sprang clean out of the bed upon the floor.

These starts and frights continued till noon; and when the doctor had arrived and had seen her, and had talked with Mrs Melbury, he sat down and meditated. That ever-present terror it was indispensable to remove from her mind at all hazards; and he thought how this might be done.

Without saying a word to anybody in the house, or to the disquieted Winterborne waiting in the lane below, Dr Jones went home and wrote to Mr Melbury at the address in London he had obtained from his wife. The gist of his communication was that Mrs Fitzpiers should be assured as soon as possible that steps were taken to sever the bond which was becoming a torture to her; that she would soon be free; and was even then virtually so. 'If you can say it *at once* it may be the means of averting much harm,' he said. 'Write to herself; not to me.'

On Saturday he drove over to Hintock, and assured her with mysterious pacifications that in a day or two she might expect to receive some good news.

So it turned out. When Sunday morning came there was a letter for Grace from her father. It arrived at seven o'clock, the usual time at which the toddling postman passed by Hintock; at eight Grace awoke, having slept an hour or two for a wonder, and Mrs Melbury brought up the letter.

'Can you open it yourself?' said she.

'O yes, yes!' said Grace with feeble impatience. She tore the envelope, unfolded the sheet, and read; when a creeping blush tinctured her white neck and cheek.

Her father had exercised a bold discretion. He informed her that she need have no further concern about Fitzpiers's return; that she would shortly be a free woman; and therefore if she should desire to wed her old lover – which he trusted was the case, since it was his own deep wish – she would be in a position to do so. In this Melbury had not written beyond his belief. But he very much stretched the facts in adding that the legal formalities for dissolving her union were practically settled.

The truth was that on the arrival of the doctor's letter poor Melbury had been much agitated, and could with difficulty be prevented by Beaucock from returning to her bedside. What was the use of his rushing back to Hintock? Beaucock had asked him. The only thing that could do her any good was a breaking of the bond. Though he had not as yet had an interview with the eminent solicitor they were about to consult, he was on the point of seeing him; and the case was clear enough. Thus the simple Melbury, urged by his parental alarm at her danger, by the representations of his companion, and by the doctor's letter, had yielded, and sat down to tell her roundly that she was virtually free.

'And you'd better write also to the gentleman,' suggested Beaucock, who, scenting fame and the germ of a large practice in the case, wished to commit Melbury to it irretrievably: to effect which he knew that nothing would be so potent as awakening the passion of Grace for Winterborne, so that her father might not have the heart to withdraw from his attempt to make her love legitimate when he discovered that there were difficulties in the way.

The nervous, impatient Melbury was much pleased with the idea of 'starting them at once', as he called it. To put his long-delayed reparative scheme in train had become a passion with him now. He added to the letter addressed to his daughter a passage hinting that she ought to begin to encourage Winterborne, lest she should lose him altogether; and he wrote to Giles that the path was virtually open for him at last. Life was short, he declared; he, her father, was getting old; there were slips betwixt the cup and the lip; her interest in him should be reawakened at once, that all might be ready when the good time came for uniting them.

CHAPTER 38

At these warm words Winterborne was much moved. The novelty of the avowal rendered what it carried with it inapprehensible by him all at once. Only a few short months ago completely estranged from this family – beholding Grace going to and fro in the distance, clothed with the alienating radiance of obvious superiority, the wife of the then popular and fashionable Fitzpiers, hopelessly outside his social boundary down to so recent a time that flowers then folded were hardly faded yet – he was now asked by that jealously-guarding father of hers to take courage; to get himself ready for the day when he should be able to claim her.

The old times came back to him in dim procession. How he had been snubbed; how Melbury had despised his Christmas party: how that sweet, coy Grace herself had looked down upon him and his household arrangements, and poor Creedle's contrivances!

Well, he could not believe it. Surely the adamantine barrier of marriage with another could not be pierced like this! It did violence to custom. Yet a new law might do anything. But was it at all within the bounds of probability that a woman who, over and above her own attainments, had been accustomed to those of a cultivated professional man, could ever be the wife of such as he? – that the ceorl Giles Winterborne would be able to make such a dainty girl happy now that she stood in a position further removed from his own than at first? He was full of doubt.

Nevertheless, it was not in him to show backwardness. To act so promptly as Melbury desired him to act seemed, indeed, scarcely wise, because of the uncertainty of events. Giles knew nothing of legal procedure; but he did know that for him to step up to Grace as a lover before the bond which bound her was actually dissolved was simply an extravagant dream of her father's overstrained mind. He pitied Melbury for his almost childish enthusiasm and saw that the ageing man must have suffered acutely to be weakened to this unreasoning desire.

Winterborne was far too magnanimous to harbour any cynical conjecture that the timber-merchant, in his intense affection for Grace, was courting him now because that young lady, when disunited, would be left in an anomalous position, to escape which a bad husband was better than none. He felt quite sure that his old friend was simply on tenterhooks of anxiety to repair the almost irreparable error of dividing two whom nature had striven to join together in earlier days, and that in his ardour to do this he was oblivious of formalities. The cautious supervision of his past years had overleapt itself at last. Hence Winterborne perceived that, in this new beginning, the necessary care not to compromise Grace by too early advances must be exercised by himself.

There is no such thing as a stationary love: men are either loving more or loving less; but Giles recognized no decline in his sense of her dearness. He had been labouring ever since his rejection and her marriage to reduce his former passion to a docile friendship, out of pure regard to its expediency; but hitherto he had experienced no great success in his attempt.

A week and more passed and there was no further news of Melbury. But the effect of the intelligence he had already transmitted upon the elastic-nerved daughter of the woods had been much as the old surgeon Jones had surmised. It had soothed her perturbed spirit better than all the opiates in the pharmacopoeia. She had slept unbrokenly a whole night and a day. The 'new law' was to her a mysterious, beneficent, god-like entity, lately descended upon earth, that would make her as she once had been without trouble or annoyance. Her position fretted her, its abstract features rousing an aversion which was greater than her aversion to the personality of him who had caused it. It was mortifying, productive of slights, undignified. Him she could forget: her circumstances she had always with her.

She saw nothing of Winterborne during the days of her recovery; and perhaps on that account her fancy wove about him a more romantic tissue than it could have done if he had stood before her with all the specks and flaws inseparable from concrete humanity. He rose upon her memory as the fruit-god and the wood-god in alternation: sometimes leafy and smeared with green lichen, as she had seen him amongst the sappy boughs of the plantations: sometimes cider-stained and starred with apple-pips, as she had met him on his return from cider-making in Blackmoor Vale, with his vats and presses beside him. In her secret heart she approximated to her father's enthusiasm in wishing to show Giles once for all how she still regarded him.

The question whether the future would indeed bring them together for life was a standing wonder with her. She knew that it could not with any propriety do so just yet. But reverently believing in her father's sound judgment and knowledge, as good girls are wont to do, she remembered what he had written about her giving a hint to Winterborne lest there should be risk in delay, and her feelings were not averse to such a step, so far as it could be done without danger at this early stage of the proceedings.

From being but a frail phantom of her former self she returned in bounds to a condition of passable hopefulness. She bloomed again in the face in the course of a few days, and was well enough to go about as usual.

One day Mrs Melbury proposed that for a change she should be driven in the gig to Sherton market, whither Melbury's man was going on other errands. Grace had no business whatever in Sherton; but it crossed her mind that Winterborne would probably be there, and this made the thought of such a drive interesting.

On the way she saw nothing of him; but when the horse was walking slowly through the obstructions of Sheep Street she discerned the young man on the pavement. She thought of that time when he had been standing under his apple-tree on her return from school, and of the tender opportunity then missed through her fastidiousness. Her heart rose in her throat. She abjured all fastidiousness now. Nor did she forget the last occasion on which she had beheld him in that town, making cider in the courtyard of the Earl of Wessex Hotel, while she was figuring as a fine lady in the balcony above.

Grace directed the man to set her down there in the midst, and immediately went up to her lover. Giles had not before observed her, and his eyes now suppressedly looked his pleasure, without, perhaps, quite so much embarrassment as had formerly marked him at such meetings.

When a few words had been spoken she said invitingly, 'I have nothing to do. Perhaps you are deeply engaged?'

'I? Not a bit. My business now at the best of times is small, I am sorry to say.'

'Well, then – I am going into the Abbey. Come along with me.'

The proposition had suggested itself as a quick escape from publicity, for many eyes were regarding her. She had hoped that sufficient time had elapsed for the extinction of curiosity; but it was quite otherwise. The people looked at her with tender interest as the deserted girl-wife – without obtrusiveness, and without vulgarity; but she was ill prepared for scrutiny in any shape.

They walked about the Abbey aisles, and presently sat down. Not a soul was in the building save themselves. She regarded a high marble tomb to the last representative of an extinct Earldom, without a thought that it was the family with which Fitzpiers was maternally connected; and with her head sideways tentatively asked her companion if he remembered the last time they were in that town alone.

He remembered it perfectly, and remarked, 'You were a proud damsel then, and as dainty as you were high. Perhaps you are now?'

Grace slowly shook her head. 'Affliction has taken all that out of me,' she answered impressively. 'Perhaps I am too far the other way now.' As there was something lurking in this that she could not explain, she added so quickly as not to allow him time to think of it, 'Has my father written to you at all?'

'Yes,' said Winterborne.

She glanced ponderingly up at him. 'Not about me?'

'Yes.'

She saw that he had been bidden to take the hint as to the future which she had been bidden to give, and the discovery sent a scarlet pulsation through her for the moment. However it was only Giles who sat there, of whom she had no fear; and her self-possession returned.

'He said I was to sound you with a view to – what you will understand, if you care to,' continued Winterborne in a low voice. Having been put on this track by herself he was not disposed to abandon it in a hurry.

They had been children together, and there was between them that familiarity as to personal affairs which only such acquaintanceship can give. 'You know, Giles,' she answered, speaking in a very practical tone, 'that that is all very well; but I am in a very anomalous position at present, and I cannot say anything to the point about such things as those.'

'No?' he said, with a stray air as regarded the subject. He was looking at her with a curious consciousness of discovery.

He had not been imagining that their renewed intercourse would show her to him thus. For the first time he realized an unexpectedness in her, which after all should not have been unexpected. She before him was not the girl Grace Melbury, whom he had used to know. Of course, he might easily have prefigured as much; but it had never occurred to him. She was a woman who had been married; she had moved on; and without having lost her girlish modesty she had lost her girlish shyness. The inevitable change, though known to him, had not been heeded; and it struck him into a momentary fixity. The truth was that he had never come into close comradeship with her since her engagement to Fitzpiers, with the brief exception of the evening encounter under High-Stoy Hill, when she met him with his cider apparatus; and that interview had been of too cursory a kind for insight.

Winterborne had advanced, too. Shy though he was he could criticize her somewhat. Times had been when to criticize a single trait in Grace Melbury would have lain as far beyond his powers as to criticize a deity. And this thing was sure as the result of his criticism: it was a new woman in many ways whom he had come out to see: a creature of more ideas, more dignity, and, above all, more assurance, than the original Grace had been capable of. He could not at first decide whether he were pleased or displeased at this. But upon the whole the novelty attracted him.

She was so sweet and sensitive that she feared his silence betokened something in his brain of the nature of an enemy to her.

'What are you thinking of that makes those lines come in your forehead?' she asked. 'I did not mean to offend you by speaking of the time being premature.'

Touched by the genuine loving-kindness which had lain at the foundation of these words, and much moved, Winterborne turned his face aside as he took her by the hand. He was grieved that he had criticized her.

'You are very good, dear Grace,' he said in a low voice. 'You are better, much better, than you used to be.'

'How?'

He could not very well tell her how, and said with an evasive smile, 'You are prettier'; which was not what he really had meant. He then remained still holding her right hand in his own right, so that they faced in opposite ways; and, as he did not let go she ventured upon a tender remonstrance.

'I think we have gone as far as we ought to go at present – and far enough to satisfy my poor father that we are the same as ever. You see, Giles, my case is not settled yet, and if – O, suppose I *never* get free! – there should be any hitch or informality!'

She drew a catching breath and turned pale. The duologue had been affectionate comedy up to this point. The gloomy atmosphere of the past, and the still gloomy horizon of the present, had been for the interval forgotten. Now the whole environment came back; the due balance of shade among the light was restored.

'It is sure to be all right, I trust,' she resumed in uneasy accents. 'What did my father say the solicitor had told him?'

'O – that all is sure enough. The case is so clear – nothing can be clearer. But the legal part is not yet quite done and finished, as is natural.'

'O no, – of course not,' she said, sunk in meek thought. 'But father said it was *almost* – did he not? Do you know anything about the new law that makes these things so easy?'

'Nothing – except the general fact that it enables ill-assorted husbands and wives to part in a way they could not formerly do without an Act of Parliament.'

'Have you to sign a paper, or swear anything? Is it something like that?'

'Yes, I believe so.'

'How long has it been introduced?'

'About six months or a year, the lawyer said, I think.'

To hear these two Arcadian innocents talk of imperial law would have made a humane person weep who should have known what a dangerous structure they were building up on their supposed knowledge. They remained in thought, like children in the presence of the incomprehensible.

'Giles,' she said at last, 'it makes me quite weary when I think how serious my situation is, or has been. Shall we not go out from here now, as it may seem rather fast of me – our being so long together, I mean – if anybody were to see us? I am almost sure,' she added uncertainly, 'that I ought not to let you hold my hand yet, knowing that the documents – or whatever it may be – have not been signed; so that I am still as married as ever – or almost. My dear father has forgotten himself. Not that I feel morally bound to any one else after what has taken place – no woman of spirit could – now, too, that several months have passed. But I wish to keep the proprieties as well as I can.'

'Yes, yes. Still, your father reminds us that life is short. I myself feel that it is; that is why I wished to understand you in this that we have begun. At times, dear Grace, since receiving your father's letter, I am as uneasy and fearful as a child at what he said. If one of us were to die before the formal signing and sealing that is to release you have been done – if we should drop out of the world and never have made the most of this little, short, but real opportunity, I should think to myself as I sank down dying, "Would to my God that I had spoken out my whole heart – given her one poor little kiss when I had the chance to give it! But I never did, although she had promised to be mine some day; and now I never can." That's what I should think.'

She had begun by watching the words from his lips with a mournful regard, as though their passage were visible; but as he went on she dropped her glance.

'Yes,' she said, 'I have thought that, too. And, because I have thought it, I by no means meant, in speaking of the proprieties, to be reserved and cold to you who loved me so long ago, or to hurt your heart as I used to at that thoughtless time. O, not at all, indeed! But – ought I to allow you – O, it is too quick – surely!' Her eyes filled with tears of bewildered, alarmed emotion.

Winterborne was too straightforward to influence her further against her better judgment. 'Yes – I suppose it is,' he said repentantly. 'I'll wait till all is settled. What has your father said in his letters to you?'

He meant about his progress with the petition; but she, mistaking him, frankly spoke of the personal part. 'He says – what I have implied. Should I tell more plainly?'

'O no – don't, if it is a secret.'

'Not at all. I will tell every word, straight out, Giles, if you wish. He says I am to encourage you. There! But I cannot obey him further today. Come, let us go now.' She gently slid her hand from his and went in front of him out of the Abbey.

'I was thinking of getting some dinner,' said Winterborne, changing to the prosaic as they walked. 'And you, too, must require something. Do let me take you to a place I know.'

Grace was almost without a friend in the world outside her father's house; her life with Fitzpiers had brought her no society; had sometimes, indeed, brought her deeper solitude than any she had ever known before. Hence it was a treat to her to find herself again the object of thoughtful care. But she questioned if to go publicly to dine alone with Giles Winterborne were not a proposal due rather to his unsophistication than to his prudence. She said gently that she would much prefer his ordering her lunch at some place, and then coming to tell her it was ready, while she remained in the Abbey porch. Giles saw her secret reasoning, thought how hopelessly blind to propriety he was beside her, and went to do as she wished.

He was not absent more than ten minutes, and found Grace where he had left her.

'It will be quite ready by the time you get there,' he said, and told her the name of the inn at which the meal had been ordered, which was one that she had never heard of.

'I'll find it by inquiry,' said Grace, setting out.

'And shall I see you again?'

'O yes – come to me there. It will not be like going together. I shall want you to find my father's man and the gig for me.'

He waited on some ten minutes or a quarter of an hour, till he thought her lunch ended, and that he might fairly take advantage of her invitation to start her on her way home. He went straight to where he had sent her, an old commercial tavern, scrupulously clean, but humble and inexpensive. On his way he had an occasional misgiving as to whether the place had been elegant enough for her; and as soon as he entered it, and saw her ensconced there, he perceived that he had blundered.

Grace was seated in the only dining-room that the simple old hostelry could boast of, which was also a general parlour on market days: a long, low apartment, with a sanded floor herring-boned with a broom, a wide, red-curtained window to the street, and another to the garden. Grace had retreated to the end of the room looking out upon the latter, the front part being full of a mixed company of dairymen and butchers which had, to be just to him, dropped in since he was there.

She was in a mood of the greatest depression. On arriving and seeing what the tavern was like she had been taken by surprise; but having gone too far to retreat she had heroically entered and sat down on the well-scrubbed settle, opposite the narrow table with its knives and steel forks, tin pepper-boxes, blue salt-cellars, and posters advertising the sale of bullocks against the wall. The last time that she had taken any meal in a public place it had been with Fitzpiers at the dignified Earl of Wessex Hotel in that town, after a two months' roaming and sojourning at the gigantic hotels of the Continent.

How could she have expected any other kind of accommodation in present circumstances than such as Giles had provided? And yet how unprepared she was for this change! The tastes that she had acquired from Fitzpiers had been imbibed so subtly that she hardly knew she possessed them till confronted by this contrast. The elegant Fitzpiers, in fact, at that very moment owed a long bill at the above-mentioned hotel for the luxurious style in which he used to put her up there whenever they drove to Sherton. But such is social sentiment that she had been quite comfortable under those debt-impending conditions, whilst she felt humiliated by her present situation, which Winterborne had paid for honestly on the nail.

He had noticed in a moment that she shrank from her position, and all his pleasure was gone. It was the same susceptibility over again which had spoiled his Christmas party long ago.

But he did not know that this recrudescence was only the casual result of Grace's apprenticeship to what she was determined to learn in spite of it – a consequence of one of those sudden surprises which confront everybody bent upon turning over a new leaf. She had finished her lunch, which he saw had been a very mincing performance; and he brought her out of the house as soon as he could.

'Now,' he said, with great sad eyes, 'you have not finished at all well, I know! Come round to the Earl of Wessex. I'll order a tea there. I did not remember that what was good enough for me was not good enough for you.'

Her face faded into an aspect of deep distress when she saw what had happened. 'O no, Giles!' she said with extreme earnestness; 'certainly not. Why do you – say that, when you know better? You *ever* will misunderstand me.'

'Indeed, that's not so, Mrs Fitzpiers. Can you deny that you felt out of place at that tavern?'

'I don't know! . . . Well, since you make me speak, I do not deny it.'

'And yet I have felt at home there these twenty years. Your husband used always to take you to the Earl of Wessex, did he not?'

'Yes,' she reluctantly admitted. How could she explain in the street of a market-town that it was her superficial and transitory taste which had been offended, and not her nature or her affection?

Fortunately, or unfortunately, at that moment they saw Melbury's man driving vacantly along the street in search of her, the hour having passed at which he had been told to take her up. Winterborne hailed him, and she was powerless then to prolong the discourse. She entered the vehicle sadly, and the horse trotted away.

CHAPTER 39

All night did Winterborne think over that unsatisfactory ending of a pleasant time, forgetting the pleasant time itself. He feared anew that they could never be happy together, even should she be free to choose him. She was accomplished: he was unrefined. It was the original difficulty, which he was too thoughtful to recklessly ignore as some men would have done in his place.

He was one of those silent, unobtrusive beings who want little from others in the way of favour or condescension, and perhaps on that very account scrutinize those others' behaviour too closely. He was not versatile, but one in whom a hope or belief which had once had its rise, meridian, and decline, seldom again exactly recurred as in the breasts of more sanguine mortals. He had once worshipped her, laid out his life to suit her, wooed her, and lost her. Though it was with almost the same zest it was with not quite the same hope that he had begun to tread the old tracks again, and had allowed himself to be so charmed with her that day.

Move another step towards her he would not. He would even repulse her – as a tribute to conscience. It would be sheer sin to let her prepare a pitfall for her happiness not much smaller than the first by inveigling her into a union with such as he. Her poor father was now blind to these subtleties, which he had formerly beheld as in noontide light. It was his own duty to declare them – for her dear sake.

Grace, too, had a very uncomfortable night, and her solicitous embarrassment was not lessened the next morning when another letter from her father was put into her hands. Its tenor was an intenser strain of the one that had preceded it.

After stating how extremely glad he was to hear that she was better, and able to get out of doors, he went on:

'This is a wearisome business, the solicitor we have come to see being out of town. I do not know when I shall get home. My great anxiety in this delay is still lest you should lose Giles Winterborne. I cannot rest at night for thinking that while our business is hanging fire he may become estranged, or in his shyness go away from the neighbourhood. I have set my heart upon seeing him your husband if you ever have another. Do then, Grace, give him some temporary encouragement, even though it is over-early. For when I consider the past I do think God will forgive me and you for being a little forward. I have another reason for this, my dear. I feel myself going rapidly down hill, and late affairs have still further helped me that way. And until this thing is done I cannot rest in peace.'

He added a postscript:

'I have just heard that the solicitor is to be seen to-morrow. Possibly, therefore, I shall return in the evening after you get this.'

The paternal longing ran on all-fours with her own desire; and yet in forwarding it yesterday she had been on the brink of giving offence. While craving to be a country girl again, just as her father requested; to put off the old Eve, the fastidious miss – or rather madam – completely, her first attempt had been beaten by the unexpected vitality of that fastidiousness. Her father on returning and seeing the trifling coolness of Giles would be sure to say that the same perversity which had led her to make difficulties about marrying Fitzpiers was now prompting her to blow hot and cold with poor Winterborne.

If the latter had been the most subtle hand at touching the stops of her delicate soul instead of one who had just bound himself to let her be mute on all that appertained to his personality, he could not have acted more seductively than he did that day. He chanced to be superintending some temporary work in a field opposite her windows. She could not discover what he was doing, but she read his mood keenly and truly: she could see in his coming and going an air of determined abandonment of the whole prospect that lay in her direction.

O, how she longed to make it up with him! Her father coming in the evening – which meant, she supposed, that all formalities would be in train, her marriage virtually annulled, and she be free to be won again – how could she look him in the face if he should see them estranged thus?

It being a fair green afternoon in June she seated herself in the garden, in the rustic chair which stood under the laurel-bushes, made of peeled oak branches that came to Melbury's premises as refuse after barking-time. The mass of full-juiced leafage on the heights around her was just swayed into faint gestures by a nearly spent wind which, even in its enfeebled state, did not reach her shelter. She had expected Giles to call – to inquire how she had got home, or something or other; but he did not come. And he still tantalized her by going athwart and across that orchard opposite. She could see him as she sat.

A slight diversion was presently created by Creedle bringing him a letter. She knew from this that Creedle had just come from Sherton, and had called as usual at the post-office for anything that had arrived by the afternoon post, of which there was no delivery at Hintock. She pondered on what the letter might contain – particularly whether it were a second refresher for Winterborne from her father, like her own of the morning.

But it appeared to have no bearing upon herself whatever. Giles read its contents and almost immediately turned away to a gap in the hedge of the orchard – if that could be called a hedge which, owing to the drippings of the trees, was little more than a bank with a bush upon it here and there. He entered the plantation, and was no doubt going that way homeward to the mysterious hut he occupied on the other side of the woodland.

The sad sands were running swiftly through Time's glass; she had often felt it in these latter days; and, like Giles, she felt it doubly now after the solemn and pathetic reminder in her father's communication. Her freshness would pass, the long-suffering devotion of Giles might suddenly end – might end that very hour. Men were so strange. The thought took away from her all her former reticence and made her action bold. She started from her seat. If the little breach, quarrel, or whatever it might be called, of yesterday, was to be healed up it must be done by her on the instant. She crossed into the orchard and clambered through the gap after Giles, just as he was diminishing to a faun-like figure under the green canopy and over the brown floor.

Grace had been wrong – very far wrong – in assuming that the letter had no reference to herself because Giles had turned away into the wood after its perusal. It was, sad to say, because the missive had so much reference to herself that he had thus turned away. He feared that his grieved discomfiture might be observed.

The letter was from Beaucock, written a few hours later than Melbury's to his daughter. It announced failure.

Giles had once done that thriftless man a good turn, and now was the moment when Beaucock had chosen to remember it, in his own way. During his absence in town with Melbury the lawyer's clerk had naturally heard a great deal of the timber-merchant's family scheme of justice to Giles, and his communication was to inform Winterborne at the earliest possible moment that their attempt had failed, in order that the young man should not place himself in a false position towards Grace in the belief of its coming success. The news was, in sum, that Fitzpiers's conduct had not been sufficiently cruel to Grace to enable her to snap the bond. She was apparently doomed to be his wife till the end of the chapter.

Winterborne quite forgot his superficial differences with the poor girl under the warm rush of deep and distracting love for her which the almost tragical information engendered.

To renounce her for ever – that was then the end of it for him, after all. There was no longer any question about suitability, or room for tiffs on petty tastes. The curtain had fallen again between them. She could not be his. The cruelty of their late revived hope was now terrible. How could they all have been so simple as to suppose this thing could be done?

It was at this moment that, hearing some one coming behind him, he turned and saw her hastening on between the thickets. He perceived in an instant that she did not know the blighting news.

'Giles, why didn't you come across to me?' she asked with arch reproach. 'Didn't you see me sitting there ever so long?'

'O yes,' he said in unprepared, provisional tones, for her unexpected presence caught him without the slightest plan of behaviour in the conjuncture. His manner made her think that she had been too chiding in her speech; and a mild scarlet wave passed over her as she resolved to soften it.

'I have had another letter from my father,' she hastened to continue. 'He thinks he may come home this evening. And – in view of his hopes – it will grieve him if there is any little difference between us, Giles.'

'There is none,' he said, sadly regarding her from the face downwards as he pondered how to lay the cruel truth bare.

'Still – I fear you have not quite forgiven me about my being uncomfortable at the inn.'

'I have, I'm sure.'

'But you speak in quite an unhappy way,' she returned, coming up quite close to him with the most winning of the many pretty airs that appertained to her. 'Don't you think you will ever be happy, Giles?'

He did not reply for some instants. 'When the sun shines flat on the north front of Sherton Abbey – that's when my happiness will come to me!' said he, staring as it were into the earth.

'But – then that means there is something more than my offending you in not liking the Sherton tavern? If it is because I – did not like to let you kiss me in the Abbey – well, you know, Giles, that it was not on account of my cold feelings, but because I did certainly, just then, think it was rather premature, in spite of my poor father. That was the true reason – the sole one. But I do not want to be hard – God knows I do not!' she said, her voice fluctuating. 'And perhaps – as I am on the verge of freedom – I am not right, after all, in thinking there is any harm in your kissing me.'

'O Heaven!' groaned Winterborne to himself. His head was turned askance as he still resolutely regarded the ground. For the last several minutes he had seen this great temptation approaching him in regular siege; and now it had come. The wrong, the social sin, of now taking advantage of the offer of her lips, had a magnitude in the eyes of one whose life had been so primitive, so ruled by household laws as Giles's, which can hardly be explained.

'Did you say anything?' she asked timidly.

'O no – only that—'

'You mean that it must *be already* settled, since my father is coming home?' she said gladly.

'Ah – yes.'

'Then why don't you do what you want to?' She was almost pouting at his hesitation.

Winterborne, though fighting valiantly against himself all this while – though he would have protected Grace's good repute as the apple of his eye, was a man; and, as Desdemona said, men are not gods. In face of the agonizing seductiveness shown by her, in her unenlightened school-girl simplicity about the laws and ordinances, he betrayed a man's weakness. Since it was so – since it had come to this, that Grace, deeming herself free to do it, was virtually asking him to demonstrate that he loved her – since he could demonstrate it only too truly – since life was short and love was strong – he gave way to the temptation, notwithstanding that he perfectly well knew her to be wedded irrevocably to Fitzpiers. Indeed, he cared for nothing past or future, simply accepting the present and what it brought, deciding once in his life to clasp in his arms her he had watched over and loved so long.

She looked up suddenly from his long embrace and passionate kiss, influenced by a sort of inspiration. 'O, I suppose,' she stammered, 'that I am really free? – that this is right? Is there *really* a new law? Father cannot have been too sanguine in saying—'

He did not answer, and a moment afterwards Grace burst into tears in spite of herself. 'O, why does not my father come home and explain!' she sobbed upon his breast, 'and let me know clearly what I am! It is too trying, this, to ask me to – and then to leave me so long in so vague a state that I do not know what to do, and perhaps do wrong!'

Winterborne felt like a very Cain, over and above his previous sorrow. How he had sinned against her in not telling her himself only knew. He lifted her up and turned aside: the feeling of his cruelty mounted higher and higher. How could he have dreamt of kissing her? He could hardly refrain from tears. Surely nothing more pitiable had ever been known than the condition of this poor young thing, now as heretofore the victim of her father's well-meant but blundering policy.

Even in the hour of Melbury's greatest assurance Winterborne had harboured a suspicion that no law, new or old, could undo Grace's marriage without her appearance in public; though he was not sufficiently sure of what might have been enacted to destroy by his own words her pleasing idea that a mere dash of the pen, on her father's testimony, was going to be sufficient. But he had never suspected the sad fact that the position was irremediable.

Poor Grace, perhaps feeling that she had indulged in too much fluster for a mere embrace, even though it had been prolonged an unconscionable time, calmed herself at finding how grave he was.

'I am glad we are friends again anyhow,' she said, smiling through her tears. 'Giles, if you had only shown half the boldness before I married that you show now, you would have carried me off for your own, first instead of second. If we do marry I hope you will never think badly of me for encouraging you a little, but my father is *so* impatient, you know, as his years and infirmities increase, that he will wish to see us a little advanced when he comes. That is my only excuse.'

To Winterborne all this was sadder than it was sweet. How could she so trust her father's conjectures! He did not know how to tell her the truth and shame himself. And yet he felt that it must be done.

To hasten the revelation, however, was beyond even him. The endearments that had been begun between them were repeated as they walked, and the afternoon was far advanced before he could actually set about opening her eyes.

'We may have been wrong,' he began almost fearfully, 'in supposing that it can all be carried out whilst we stay here at Hintock. I am not sure but that people may have to appear in a public court even under the new Act; and if there should be any difficulty and we cannot marry after all—'

Her cheeks became slowly bloodless. 'O Giles,' she said, grasping his arm, 'you have heard something! What – cannot my father conclude it there and now? Surely, he has done it? O Giles, Giles, don't deceive me! After letting you go on like this – what terrible position am I in?'

He could not tell her, try as he would. The sense of her implicit trust in his honour disabled him. 'I cannot inform you,' he murmured, his voice as husky as that of the leaves under foot. 'Your father will soon be here. Then we shall know. I will take you home.'

Inexpressibly dear as she was to him he offered her his arm with the most reserved air as he added correctingly, 'I will take you at any rate into the drive.'

Thus they walked on together, Grace vibrating between happiness and misgiving. It was only a few minutes' walk to where the drive ran, and they had hardly descended into it when they heard a voice behind them cry, 'Take out that arm!'

For a moment they did not heed, and the voice repeated more loudly and hoarsely:

'Take out that arm!'

It was Melbury's. He had returned sooner than they expected, and now came up to them. Grace's hand had been withdrawn like lightning on her hearing the second command.

'I don't blame you, I don't blame you,' he said, in the weary cadence of one broken down with scourgings. 'But you two must walk together no more – I have been surprised – I have been cruelly deceived – Giles, don't say anything to me, but go away!'

He was evidently not aware that Winterborne had known the truth before he brought it; and Giles would not stay to discuss it with him then. When the younger man had gone Melbury took his daughter indoors to the room he used as his office. There he sat down and bent over the slope of the bureau, her bewildered gaze fixed upon him.

When Melbury had recovered a little he said, 'You are now as ever Fitzpiers's wife. I was deluded. He has not done you *enough* harm! You are still subject to his beck and call.'

'Then let it be, and never mind, father,' she said with dignified sorrow. 'I can bear it. It is your trouble that grieves me most!' She stooped over him and put her arm round his neck, which distressed Melbury still more.

'I don't mind at all what comes to me,' Grace continued; 'whose wife I am, or whose I am not! I do love Giles: I cannot help that; and I have gone further with him than I should have done if I had known exactly how things were. But I do not reproach you.'

'Then Giles did not tell you?' said Melbury.

'No,' said she. 'He could not have known it. His behaviour to me proved that he did not know.'

Her father said nothing more, and Grace went away to the solitude of her chamber.

Her heavy disquietude had many shapes; and for a time she put aside the dominant fact to think of her too free conduct towards Giles. His love-making had been brief as it was sweet; but would he on reflection contemn her for forwardness? How could she have been so simple as to suppose she was in a position to behave as she had done! Thus she mentally blamed her ignorance; and yet in the centre of her heart she blessed it a little for what it had momentarily brought her.

CHAPTER 40

LIFE among the people involved in these events seemed to be suppressed and hide-bound for a while. Grace seldom showed herself outside the house, never outside the garden; for she feared she might encounter Giles Winterborne; and that she could not bear.

This pensive intramural existence of the self-constituted nun appeared likely to continue for an indefinite time. She had learnt that there was one possibility in which her formerly imagined position might become real, and only one; that her husband's absence should continue long enough to amount to positive desertion. But she never allowed her mind to dwell much upon the thought; still less did she deliberately hope for such a result. Her regard for Winterborne had been rarefied by the shock which followed its avowal into an ethereal emotion that had little to do with living and doing.

As for Giles he was lying – or rather sitting – ill at his distant hut. A feverish indisposition which had been hanging about him for some time, the result of a chill caught the previous winter, seemed to acquire virulence with the prostration of his hopes. But not a soul knew of his languor, and he did not think the case serious enough to send for a medical man. After a few days he was better again, and crept about his home in a great-coat, attending to his simple wants as usual with his own hands.

So matters stood when the inertion of Grace's pool-like existence was disturbed as by a geyser. She received a letter from Fitzpiers.

A startling letter it was in its import, though couched in the gentlest language. In his absence Grace had grown to regard him with toleration, and her relation to him with equanimity, till she had almost forgotten how trying his presence would be. He wrote briefly and unaffectedly: he made no excuses, but informed her that he was living quite alone, and had been led to think that they ought to be together, if she would make up her mind to forgive him. He therefore purported to cross the Channel to Budmouth by the steamer on a day he named, which she found to be three days after the time of her present reading.

He said that he could not come to Hintock for obvious reasons, which her father would understand even better than herself. As the only alternative she was to be on the quay to meet the steamer when it arrived from the opposite coast, probably about half-an-hour before midnight, bringing with her any luggage she might require; join him there, and pass with him into the twin vessel, which left immediately the other entered the harbour: returning thus with him to his continental dwelling-place, which he did not name. He had no intention of showing himself on land at all.

The troubled Grace took the letter to her father, who now continued for long hours by the fireless summer chimney-corner as if he thought it were winter, the pitcher of cider standing beside him mostly untasted, and coated with a film of dust. After reading it he looked up.

'You sha'n't go,' said he.

'I had felt I would not,' she answered. 'But I did not know what you would say.'

'If he comes and lives in England, not too near here, and in a respectable way, and wants you to come to him, I am not sure that I'll oppose him in wishing it,' muttered Melbury. 'I'd stint myself to keep you both in a genteel and seemly style. But go abroad you never shall with my consent.'

There the question rested that day. Grace was unable to reply to her husband in the absence of an address, and the morrow came, and next day, and the evening on which he had requested her to meet him. Throughout the whole of it she remained within the four walls of her room.

The sense of her harassment, carking doubt of what might be impending, hung like a cowl of blackness over the Melbury household. They spoke almost in whispers, and wondered what Fitzpiers would do next. It was the hope of everyone that, finding she did not arrive, he would return again to France; and as for Grace, she was willing to write to him on the most kindly terms if he would only keep away.

The night passed, Grace lying tense and wide awake, and her relatives in great part likewise. When they met the next morning they were pale and anxious, though neither speaking of the subject which occupied all their thoughts. The day passed as quietly as the previous ones, and she began to think that in the rank caprice of his moods he had abandoned the idea of getting her to join him as quickly as it was formed.

All on a sudden some person who had just come from Casterbridge entered the house with the news that Mr Fitzpiers was on his way home to Hintock. He had been seen hiring a carriage at the King's Arms Hotel.

Her father and Grace were both present when the intelligence was announced.

'Now,' said Melbury, 'we must make the best of what has been a very bad matter. The man is repenting: the partner of his folly, I hear, is gone away from him to Switzerland, so that chapter of his life is probably over. If he chooses to make a home for 'ee I think you should not say him nay, Grace. Certainly he cannot very well live at Hintock without a blow to his pride; but if he can bear that, and likes Hintock best, why, there's the empty wing of the house as it was before.'

'O father!' said Grace, turning white with dismay.

'Why not?' said he, a little of his former doggedness returning. He was, in truth, disposed to somewhat more leniency towards her husband just now than he had shown formerly, from a conviction that he had treated him over roughly in his anger.

'Surely it is the most respectable thing to do?' he continued. 'I don't like this state that you are in – neither married nor single. It hurts me, and it hurts you, and it will always be remembered against us in Hintock. There has never been any scandal like it in the Melbury family before.'

'He will be here in less than an hour,' murmured Grace.

The twilight of the room prevented her father seeing the despondent misery of her face. The one intolerable condition, the condition she had deprecated above all others, was that of Fitzpiers's reinstatement there. 'O, I won't, I won't see him!' she said, sinking down. She was almost hysterical.

'Try if you cannot,' he returned moodily.

'O yes, I will, I will!' she went on inconsequently: 'I'll try'; and jumping up suddenly she left the room.

In the darkness of the apartment to which she flew nothing could have been seen during the next half-hour; but from a corner a quick breathing was audible from this impressionable creature, who combined modern nerves with primitive feelings, and was doomed by such co-existence to be numbered among the distressed, and to take her scourgings to their exquisite extremity.

The window was open. On this quiet, late summer evening whatever sound arose in so secluded a district – the chirp of a bird, a call from a voice, the turning of a wheel – extended over bush and tree to unwonted distances. Very few sounds did arise. But as Grace invisibly breathed in the brown glooms of the chamber the small remote noise of light wheels came to her, accompanied by the trot of a horse on the turnpike road. There seemed to be a sudden hitch or pause in the progress of the vehicle, which was what first drew her attention to it. She knew the point whence the sound proceeded – the upper ground down which travellers came on their way hitherward from the south – the place at which she had emerged from the wood with Mrs Charmond. Grace slid along the floor and bent her head over the window-sill, listening with open lips. The carriage had stopped, and she heard a man use exclamatory words. Then another said, 'What the devil is the matter with the horse?' She recognized the voice as her husband's.

The accident, such as it had been, was soon remedied, and the carriage could be heard resuming its descent, soon to turn into the lane leading out of the highway and then into the 'drong' which led to the house where she was.

A spasm passed through Grace. A Daphnean instinct, exceptionally strong in her as a girl, had been revived by her widowed seclusion; and it was not lessened by her affronted sentiments towards the comer, and her regard for another man. She opened some little ivory tablets that lay on the dressing-table, scribbled in pencil on one of them, 'I am gone to visit one of my school-friends,' gathered a few toilet necessaries into a hand-bag, and, not three minutes after that voice had been heard, her slim form, hastily wrapped up from observation, might have been seen passing out of the back door of Melbury's house. Thence she skimmed up the garden-path, through the gap in the hedge, and into the mossy cart-track under the trees which led into the depths of the woods.

The leaves overhead were now in their latter green – so opaque, that it was darker at some of the densest spots than in winter time, scarce a crevice existing by which a ray could get down to the ground. But in open places she could see well enough. Summer was ending: in the daytime singing insects hung in every sunbeam: vegetation was heavy nightly with globes of dew; and after showers creeping damps and twilight chills came up from the hollows.

The plantations were always weird at this hour of eve – more spectral far than in the leafless season, when there were fewer masses and more minute lineality. The smooth surfaces of glossy plants came out like weak, lidless eyes: there were strange faces and figures from expiring lights that had somehow wandered into the canopied obscurity; while now and then low peeps of the sky between the trunks were like sheeted shapes, and on the tips of boughs sat faint cloven tongues.

But Grace's fear just now was not imaginative or spiritual; and she heeded these impressions but little. She went on as silently as she could, avoiding the hollows wherein leaves had accumulated, and stepping upon soundless moss and grass-tufts. She paused breathlessly once or twice, and fancied that she could hear, above the sound of her strumming pulse, the vehicle containing Fitzpiers turning in at the gate of her father's premises. She hastened on again.

The Hintock woods owned by Mrs Charmond were presently left behind, and those into which she next plunged were divided from the latter by a highway. It was with some caution that Grace now walked, though she was quite free from any of the commonplace timidities of her ordinary pilgrimages to such spots. She feared no lurking harms, but that her effort would be all in vain, and her return to the house rendered imperative.

She had walked three or four miles westward when that prescriptive comfort and relief to wanderers in woods – a distant light – broke at last upon her searching eyes. It was so very small as to be almost sinister to a stranger, but to her it was what she sought. She pushed forward, and the dim outline of a dwelling was disclosed. It was the place she sought.

The house was a square cot of one story only, sloping up on all sides to a chimney in the midst. It had formerly been the home of a charcoal-burner, in times when that fuel was still used in the county houses. Its only appurtenance was a paled inclosure, there being no garden, the shade of the trees preventing the growth of vegetables. She advanced to the window whence the rays of light proceeded, and the shutters being as yet unclosed she could survey the whole interior through the panes.

The room within was kitchen, parlour, and bed-chamber all in one: the natural sandstone floor was worn into hills and dales by long treading, so that none of the furniture stood level, and the table slanted like a desk. A fire burnt on the hearth, in front of which revolved the skinned carcase of a very small rabbit, suspended by a string from a nail. Leaning with one arm on the mantel-shelf stood Winterborne, his eyes on the roasting animal, his face so rapt that speculation could build nothing on it concerning his thoughts, more than that they were not with the scene before him. She thought his features had changed a little since she saw them last. The firelight did not enable her to perceive that they were positively haggard.

Grace's throat emitted a gasp of relief at finding the result so nearly as she had hoped. She went to the door and tapped lightly.

He seemed to be accustomed to the noises of woodpeckers, squirrels and such small creatures, for he took no notice of her tiny signal, and she knocked again. This time he came and opened the door.

When the light of the room fell upon her face he started; and, hardly knowing what he did, crossed the threshold to her, placing his hands upon her two arms, while surprise, joy, alarm, sadness, chased through him by turns. With Grace it was the same; even in this stress there was the fond fact that they had met again.

Thus they stood,

> 'Long tears upon their faces, waxen white
> With extreme sad delight,'

till he broke the silence by saying in a whisper, 'Come in.'

'No, no, Giles!' she answered hurriedly, stepping yet further back from the door. 'I am passing by – and I have called on you, I won't enter. Will you help me? I am afraid. I want to get by a roundabout way to Ivell, and so to Exonbury. I have a school-fellow there – but I cannot get to Ivell alone. O, if you will only accompany me a little way! Don't condemn me, Giles, and be offended! I was obliged to come to you, because I have no other help here. Three months ago you were my lover; now you are only my friend. The law has stepped in and forbidden what we thought of. It must not be. But we can act honestly, and yet you can be my friend for one little hour! I have no other—'

She could get no further. Covering her eyes with one hand, by an effort of repression she wept silent tears without a sigh or sob. Winterborne took her other hand in both his.

'What has happened?' he said.

'He has come.'

There was a stillness as of death till Winterborne asked, 'You mean this, Grace – that I am to help you get away?'

'Yes,' said she. 'Appearance is no matter, when the reality is right. I have said to myself, I can trust you.'

Giles knew from this that she did not suspect his treachery – if it could be called such – earlier in the summer, when they met for the last time as lovers; and in the intensity of his contrition for that tender wrong he determined to deserve her faith now at least, and so wipe out that reproach from his conscience.

'I'll come at once,' he said. 'I'll light a lantern.'

He unhooked a dark lantern from a nail under the eaves, and she did not notice how his hand shook with the slight strain, or dream that in making this offer he was taxing a convalescence which could ill afford such self-sacrifice. The lantern was lit and they started.

CHAPTER 41

THE first hundred yards of their course lay under motionless trees, whose upper foliage began to hiss with falling drops of rain. By the time that they emerged upon a glade it rained heavily.

'This is awkward!' said Grace, with a forced little laugh to hide her concern.

Winterborne stopped. 'Gracie,' he said, preserving a strictly business manner which belied him; 'you cannot go to Ivell to-night.'

'But I must.'

'Why? It is seven or eight miles from here. It is almost an impossibility in this rain.'

'True – *why*,' she replied mournfully at the end of a silence. 'What is reputation to me?'

'Now hearken,' said Giles. 'You won't – go back to your—'

'No, no, no! Don't make me!' she cried piteously.

'Then let us turn.' They slowly retraced their steps, and again stood before his door. 'Now this house from this moment is yours, and not mine,' he said deliberately. 'I have a place near by where I can stay very well.'

Her face had dropped. 'O,' she murmured as she saw the dilemma. 'What have I done!'

There was a smell of something burning within, and he looked through the window. The young rabbit that he had been cooking to coax a weak appetite was beginning to char. 'Please go in and attend to it,' he said. 'Do what you like. Now I leave. You will find everything about the hut that is necessary.'

'But, Giles – your supper!' she exclaimed. 'An outhouse would do for me – anything – till to-morrow at daybreak!'

He signified a negative. 'I tell you to go in – you may catch agues out here in your weakly state. You can give me my supper through the window, if you feel well enough. I'll wait awhile.'

He gently urged her to pass the doorway, and was relieved when he saw her within sitting down on his bed. Without so much as crossing the threshold himself he closed the door upon her, and turned the key in the lock. Tapping at the window he signified that she should open the casement, and when she had done this he handed in the key to her.

'You are locked in,' he said; 'and your own mistress.'

Even in her trouble she could not refrain from a faint smile at his scrupulousness, as she took the door-key.

'Do you feel better?' he went on. 'If so, and you wish to give me some of your supper, please do. If not it is of no importance. I can get some elsewhere.'

The grateful sense of his kindness stirred her to action, though she only knew half what that kindness really was. At the end of some ten minutes she again came to the window, pushed it open, and said in a whisper 'Giles!' He at once emerged from the shade, and saw that she was preparing to hand him his share of the meal upon a plate.

'I don't like to treat you so hardly,' she murmured with deep regret in her words as she heard the rain pattering on the leaves. 'But – I suppose it is best to arrange like this?'

'O yes,' he said quickly.

'I feel that I could never have reached Ivell.'

'It was impossible.'

'Are you sure you have a snug place out there?' (With renewed misgiving.)

'Quite. Have you found everything you want? I am afraid it is rather rough accommodation.'

'Can I notice defects? I have long passed that stage, and you know it, Giles, or you ought to.'

His eyes contemplated her face as its responsiveness modulated through a crowd of expressions that showed only too clearly to what a pitch she was strung. If ever Winterborne's heart chafed his bosom it was at this sight of a perfectly defenceless creature conditioned by such harsh circumstances. He forgot his own agony in the satisfaction of having at least found her a shelter. He took his plate and cup from her hands, saying, 'Now I'll push the shutter to, and you will find an iron pin on the inside, which you must fix into the bolt. Do not stir in the morning till I come and call you.'

She expressed an alarmed hope that he would not go very far away.

'O no – I shall be quite within hail,' said Winterborne.

She bolted the window as directed, and he retreated. His 'snug place' without the hut proved to be a wretched little shelter of the roughest kind, formed of four hurdles thatched with brake-fern. Underneath were dry sacks, hay, and other litter of the sort, upon which he sat down; and there in the dark tried to eat his meal. But his appetite was quite gone. He pushed the plate aside, and shook up the hay and sacks, so as to form a rude couch, on which he flung himself down to sleep, for it was getting late.

But sleep he could not for many reasons, of which not the least was thought of his charge. He sat up, and looked towards the cot through the damp obscurity. With all its external features the same as usual, he could scarcely believe that it contained the dear friend – he would not use a warmer name – who had come to him so unexpectedly and, he could not help admitting, so rashly.

He had not ventured to ask her any particulars; but the position was pretty clear without them. Though social law had negatived for ever their opening paradise of the previous June, it was not without stoical pride that he accepted the present trying conjuncture. There was one man on earth in whom she believed absolutely, and he was that man. That this crisis could end in nothing but sorrow was a view for a moment effaced by his triumphant thought of her trust in him; and the purity of the affection with which he responded to that trust rendered him more than proof against any frailty that besieged him in relation to her.

The rain, which had never ceased, now drew his attention by beginning to drop through the meagre screen that covered him. He rose to attempt some remedy for this discomfort, but the trembling of his knees and the throbbing of his pulse told him that in his weakness he was unable to fence against the storm, and he lay down to bear it as best he might. He was angry with himself for his feebleness – he who had been so strong. It was imperative that she should know nothing of his present state, and to do that she must not see his face by daylight, for its thinness would inevitably betray him.

The next morning, accordingly, when it was hardly light, he rose and dragged his stiff limbs about the precincts, preparing for her everything she could require for getting breakfast within. On the bench outside the window-sill he placed water, wood, and other necessaries, writing with a piece of chalk beside them, 'It is best that I should not see you. Put my breakfast on the bench.'

At seven o'clock he tapped at her window as he had promised, retreating at once that she might not catch sight of him. But from his shelter under the boughs he could see her very well, when, in response to his signal, she opened the window and the light fell upon her face. The languid largeness of her eyes showed that her sleep had been little more than his own, and the pinkness of their lids that her waking hours had not been free from tears.

She read the writing, seemed, he thought, disappointed, but took up the materials he had provided, evidently thinking him some way off. Giles waited on, assured that a girl who, in spite of her culture, knew what country life was, would find no difficulty in the simple preparation of their food.

Within the cot it was all very much as he conjectured, though Grace had slept much longer than he. After the loneliness of the night she would have been glad to see him; but appreciating his feeling when she read the request she made no attempt to recall him. She found abundance of provisions laid in, his plan being to replenish his buttery weekly, and this being the day after the victualling-van had called from Ivell. When the meal was ready she put what he required outside, as she had done with the supper; and, notwithstanding her longing to see him, withdrew from the window promptly, and left him to himself.

It had been a leaden dawn, and the rain now steadily renewed its fall. As she heard no more of Winterborne she concluded that he had gone away to his daily work, and forgotten that he had promised to accompany her to Ivell; an erroneous conclusion, for he remained all day, by force of his condition, within fifty yards of where she was.

The morning wore on; and in her doubt when to start, and how to travel, she lingered yet; keeping the door carefully bolted lest an intruder should discover her. Locked in this place she was comparatively safe, at any rate, and doubted if she would be safe elsewhere.

The humid gloom of an ordinary wet day was doubled by the shade and drip of the leafage. Autumn, this year, was coming in with rains. Gazing in her enforced idleness from the one window of the single room, she could see various small members of the animal community that lived unmolested there – creatures of hair, fluff, and scale; the toothed kind and the billed kind; underground creatures jointed and ringed – circumambulating the hut under the impression that, Giles having gone away, nobody was there; and eyeing it inquisitively with a view to winter quarters. Watching these neighbours who knew neither law nor sin distracted her a little from her trouble; and she managed to while away some portion of the afternoon by putting Giles's home in order, and making little improvements which she deemed that he would value when she was gone.

Once or twice she fancied that she heard a faint noise amid the trees resembling a cough; but as it never came any nearer she concluded that it was a squirrel or a bird.

At last the daylight lessened and she made up a larger fire, for the evenings were chilly. As soon as it was too dark – which was comparatively early – to discern the human countenance in this place of shadows, there came to the window, to her great delight, a tapping which she knew from its method to be Giles's.

She opened the casement instantly, and put out her hand to him, though she could only just perceive his outline. He clasped her fingers, and she noticed the heat of his palm, and its shakiness.

'He has been walking fast in order to get here quickly,' she thought. How could she know that he had just crawled out from the straw of the shelter hard by: and that the heat of his hand was feverishness?

'My dear, good Giles!' she burst out impulsively.

'Anybody would have done it for you,' replied Winterborne, with as much matter-of-fact as he could summon.

'About my getting to Ivell and Exonbury?'

'I have been thinking,' responded Giles, with tender deference, 'that you had better stay where you are for the present, if you wish not to be caught. I need not tell you that the place is yours as long as you like; and perhaps in a day or two, finding you absent, he will go away. At any rate in two or three days I could do anything to assist – such as make inquiries, or go a great way towards Ivell with you; for the cider season will soon be coming on, and I want to run down that way to see how the crops are. But for a day or two I am busy here.' He was hoping that by the time mentioned he would be strong enough to engage himself actively on her behalf. 'I hope you do not feel over-much melancholy in being a prisoner?'

She declared that she did not mind it; but she sighed.

From long acquaintance they could read each other's heart-symptoms like books of large type. 'I fear you are sorry you came,' said Giles, 'and that you think I should have advised you more firmly than I did not to stay.'

'O no! dear, dear friend,' answered Grace with a heaving bosom. 'Don't think that that is what I regret. What I regret is my enforced treatment of you – dislodging you, excluding you from your own house. Why should I not speak out? You know what I feel for you – what I have felt for no other living man, what I shall never feel for a man again. But as I have vowed myself to somebody else than you, and cannot be released, I must behave as I do behave, and keep that vow. I am not bound to him by any divine law, after what he has done; but I have promised, and I will pay.'

The rest of the evening was passed in his handing her such things as she would require the next day, and casual remarks thereupon, an occupation which diverted her mind to some degree from pathetic views of her attitude towards him and of her life in general. The only infringement – if infringement it could be called – of his predetermined bearing towards her was an involuntary pressing of her hand to his lips when she put it through the casement to bid him good-night. He knew she was weeping, though he could not see her tears.

She again entreated his forgiveness for so selfishly appropriating the cottage. But it would only be for a day or two more, she thought, since go she must.

He yearningly replied: 'I – I don't like you to go away!'

'O Giles,' said she, 'I know – I know! But – I am a woman, and you are a man. I cannot speak more plainly. I yearn to let you in, but – you know what is in my mind, because you know me so well.'

'Yes, Gracie, yes. I do not at all mean that the question between us has not been settled by your marriage turning out hopelessly unalterable. I merely meant – well, a feeling – no more.'

'In a week, at the outside, I should be discovered if I stayed here; and I think that by law he could compel me to return to him.'

'Yes; perhaps you are right. Go when you wish, dear Grace.'

His last words that evening were a hopeful remark that all might be well with her yet: that Mr Fitzpiers would not intrude upon her life, if he found that his presence cost her so much pain. Then the window was closed, the shutters folded, and the rustle of his footsteps died away.

No sooner had she retired to rest that night than the wind began to rise, and after a few prefatory blasts to be accompanied by rain. The wind grew more violent, and as the storm went on it was difficult to believe that no opaque body, but only an invisible colourless thing, was trampling and climbing over the roof, making branches creak, springing out of the trees upon the chimney, popping its head into the flue, and shrieking and blaspheming at every corner of the walls. As in the grisly story, the assailant was a spectre which could be felt but not seen. She had never before been so struck with the devilry of a gusty night in a wood, because she had never been so entirely alone in spirit as she was now. She seemed almost to be apart from herself – a vacuous duplicate only. The recent self of physical animation and clear intentions was not there.

Sometimes a bough from an adjoining tree was swayed so low as to smite the roof in the manner of a gigantic hand smiting the mouth of an adversary, to be followed by a trickle of rain, as blood from the wound. To all this weather Giles must be more or less exposed; how much, she did not know.

At last Grace could hardly endure the idea of such a hardship in relation to him. Whatever he was suffering it was she who had caused it; he had vacated his single-roomed hut on account of her. She was not worth such self-sacrifice; she should not have accepted it of him. And then, as her anxiety increased with increasing thought, there returned upon her mind some incidents of her late intercourse with him, which she had heeded but little at the time. The look of his face – what had there been about his face which seemed different from its appearance of yore? Was it not thinner, less rich in hue, less like that of ripe Autumn's brother to whom she had formerly compared him? And his voice; she had distinctly noticed a change in tone. And his gait; surely it had been feebler, stiffer, more like the gait of a weary man. That slight occasional noise she had heard in the day, and attributed to squirrels; it might have been his cough after all.

Thus conviction took root in her perturbed mind that Winterborne was unwell, or had been so, and that he had carefully concealed his condition from her that she might have no scruples about accepting a hospitality which by the nature of the case expelled her entertainer.

'My own, own, true love – my dear kind friend!' she cried to herself. 'O, it shall not be – it shall not be!'

She hastily got out of bed, obtained a light, and partially dressed herself; and taking the key went at once to the door, which was close at hand, the cot possessing only one floor. Before turning the key in the lock she paused, her fingers still clutching it; and pressing her other hand to her forehead, she fell into agitating thought.

A tattoo on the window, caused by the tree-droppings blowing against it, brought her indecision to a close. She turned the key, and opened the door.

The darkness was intense, seeming to touch her pupils like a substance. She only now became aware how heavy the rainfall had been and was: the dripping of the eaves splashed like a fountain. She stood listening with parted lips, and holding the door in one hand, till her eyes growing accustomed to the obscurity she discerned the wild brandishing of their arms by the adjoining trees. At last she cried loudly with an effort: 'Giles! you must come in!'

There was no answer to her cry, and overpowered by her own temerity Grace retreated quickly, shut the door, and stood looking on the floor with flushed cheeks. Perhaps he was very well after all. But this mood was not for long. She again lifted the latch, and with far more determination than at first.

'Giles, Giles!' she cried, with the full strength of her voice, and without any of the shamefacedness that had characterized her first cry. 'O, come in – come in! Where are you? I have been wicked – I have thought too much of myself! Do you hear? I don't want to keep you out any longer. I cannot bear that you should suffer so. I want you here! Gi-i-iles!'

A reply? It was a reply! Through the darkness and wind a feeble voice reached her, floating upon the weather as though a part of it.

'Here I am – all right! Don't trouble about me.'

'Don't you want to come in? Are you not wet? *Come to me, dearest! I don't mind what they say or what they think of us any more.*'

'I am all right,' he repeated. 'It is not necessary for me to come. Good-night! good-night!'

Grace sighed, turned, and shut the door slowly. Could she have shocked him by her impulsive words? Perhaps, after all, she had perceived a change in him because she had not seen him for so long. Time sometimes did his ageing work in jerks, as she knew. Well, she had done all she could. He would not come in. She retired to rest again.

CHAPTER 42

THE next morning Grace was at the window early. She felt determined to see him somehow that day, and prepared his breakfast eagerly. Eight o'clock struck, and she then remembered that he had not come to arouse her by a knocking as usual, her own anxiety having caused her to stir.

His breakfast was set in its place without. But he did not appear to take it; and she waited on. Nine o'clock arrived, and the breakfast was cold; and still there was no Giles. A thrush who had been repeating himself a good deal on an opposite bush for some time, came and took a morsel from the plate, bolted it, waited, looked around, and took another. At ten o'clock she drew in the tray and sat down to her own solitary meal. He must have been called away on business early, the rain having cleared off.

Yet she would have liked to assure herself, by thoroughly exploring the precincts of the hut, that he was nowhere in its vicinity; but as the day was comparatively fine the dread lest some stray passenger or woodman should encounter her in such a reconnoitre paralyzed her wish. The solitude was further accentuated to-day by the stopping of the clock for want of winding, and the fall into the chimney-corner of flakes of soot loosened by the rains. At noon she heard a slight rustling outside the window, and found that it was caused by an eft which had crept out of the leaves to bask in the last sun-rays that would be worth having till the following May.

She continually peeped out through the lattice, but could see little. In front lay the brown leaves of last year, and upon them some yellowish green ones of this season that had been prematurely blown down by the gale. Above stretched an old beech, with vast arm-pits, and great pocket-holes in its sides where branches had been removed in past times; a black slug was trying to climb it. Dead boughs were scattered about like ichthyosauri in a museum, and beyond them were perishing woodbine stems resembling old ropes.

From the other window all she could see were more trees, in jackets of lichen and stockings of moss. At their roots were stemless yellow fungi like lemons and apricots, and tall fungi with more stem than stool. Next were more trees close together, wrestling for existence, their branches disfigured with wounds resulting from their mutual rubbings and blows. It was the struggle between these neighbours that she had heard in the night. Beneath them were the rotting stumps of those of the group that had been vanquished long ago, rising from their mossy setting like black teeth from green gums. Further on were other tufts of moss in islands divided by the shed leaves – variety upon variety, dark green and pale green; moss like little fir-trees, like plush, like malachite stars; like nothing on earth except moss.

The strain upon Grace's mind in various ways was so great on this the most desolate day she had passed there that she felt it would be well-nigh impossible to spend another in such circumstances. The evening came at last; the sun, when its chin was on the earth, found an opening through which to pierce the shade, and stretched irradiated gauzes across the damp atmosphere, making the wet trunks shine, and throwing splotches of such ruddiness on the leaves beneath the beech that they were turned to gory hues. When night at last arrived, and with it the time for his return, she was nearly broken down with suspense.

The simple evening meal, partly tea, partly supper, which Grace had prepared, stood waiting upon the hearth; and yet Giles did not come. It was now nearly twenty-four hours since she had seen him. As the room grew darker, and only the firelight broke against the gloom of the walls, she was convinced that it would be beyond her staying power to pass the night without hearing from him or from somebody. Yet eight o'clock drew on, and his form at the window did not appear.

The meal remained untasted. Suddenly rising from before the hearth of smouldering embers, where she had been crouching with her hands clasped over her knees, she crossed the room, unlocked the door, and listened. Every breath of wind had ceased with the decline of day, but the rain had resumed the steady dripping of the night before. Grace might have stood there five minutes when she fancied she heard that old sound, a cough, at no great distance; and it was presently repeated. If it were Winterborne's he must be near her; why, then, had he not visited her?

A horrid misgiving that he could not visit her took possession of Grace, and she looked up anxiously for the lantern, which was hanging above her head. To light it and go in the direction of the sound would be the obvious way to solve the dread problem; but the conditions made her hesitate, and in a moment a cold sweat pervaded her at further sounds from the same quarter.

They were low mutterings; at first like persons in conversation, but gradually resolving themselves into varieties of one voice. It was an endless monologue, like that we sometimes hear from inanimate nature in deep secret places where water flows, or where ivy leaves flap against stones; but by degrees she was convinced that the voice was Winterborne's. Yet who could be his listener, so mute, and so patient? for though he argued rapidly and persistently nobody replied.

A dreadful enlightenment spread through the mind of Grace. 'O,' she cried in her anguish as she hastily prepared herself to go out; 'how selfishly correct I am always – too, too correct! Can it be that cruel propriety is killing the dearest heart that ever woman clasped to her own!'

While speaking thus to herself she had lit the lantern, and hastening out without further thought took the direction whence the mutterings had proceeded. The course was marked by a little path, which ended at a distance of about forty yards in a small erection of hurdles, not much larger than a shock of corn, such as were frequent in the woods and copses when the cutting season was going on. It was too slight even to be called a hovel, and was not high enough to stand upright in; appearing, in short, to be erected for the temporary shelter of fuel. The side towards Grace was open, and turning the light upon the interior she beheld what her prescient fear had pictured in snatches all the way thither.

Upon the hay within her lover lay in his clothes, just as she had seen him during the whole of her stay here except that his hat was off, and his hair matted and wild.

Both his clothes and the hay were saturated with rain. His arms were flung over his head; his face was flushed to an unnatural crimson. His eyes had a burning brightness, and, though they met her own, she perceived that he did not recognize her.

'O, my Giles,' she cried, 'what have I done to you!'

But she stopped no longer even to reproach herself. She saw that the first thing to be thought of was to get him indoors.

How Grace performed that labour she never could have exactly explained. But by dint of clasping her arms around him, rearing him into a sitting posture and straining her strength to the uttermost, she put him on one of the hurdles that was loose alongside, and taking the end of it in both her hands, dragged him along the path to the entrance of the hut, and, after a pause for breath, in at the doorway.

It was somewhat singular that Giles in his semi-conscious state acquiesced unresistingly in all that she did. But he never for a moment recognized her, continuing his rapid conversation to himself and seeming to look upon her as some angel or other supernatural creature of the visionary world in which he was mentally living. The undertaking occupied her more than ten minutes; but by that time, to her great thankfulness, he was in the hut lying in her bed, his damp clothing removed.

Then the unhappy Grace regarded him by the light of the candle. There was something in his look which agonized her, in the rush of his thoughts, accelerating their speed from minute to minute. His soul seemed to be passing through the universe of ideas like a comet; erratic, inapprehensible, untraceable.

Grace's distraction was almost as great as his. In a few moments she firmly believed he was dying. Unable to withstand her impulse she knelt down beside him, kissed his hands, and his face, and his hair, moaning in a low voice: 'How could I! How could I!'

Her timid morality had, indeed, underrated his chivalry till now, though she knew him so well. The purity of his nature, his freedom from the grosser passions, his scrupulous delicacy, had never been fully understood by Grace till this strange self-sacrifice in lonely juxtaposition to her own person was revealed. The perception of it added something that was little short of reverence to the deep affection for him of a woman who, herself, had more of Artemis than of Aphrodite in her constitution.

All that a tender nurse could do Grace did; and the power to express her solicitude in action, unconscious though the sufferer was, brought her mournful satisfaction. She bathed his hot head, clasped his twitching hands, moistened his lips, cooled his fiery eyelids, sponged his heated skin, and administered whatever she could find in the house that the imagination could conceive as likely to be in any way alleviating. That she might have been the cause, or partially the cause, of all this, interfused misery with her sorrow.

Six months before this date a scene, almost similar in its mechanical parts, had been enacted at Hintock House. It was between a pair of persons most intimately connected in their lives with these. Outwardly like as it had been, it was yet infinite in spiritual difference; though a woman's devotion had been common to both.

Grace rose from her attitude of affection and, bracing her energies, saw that something practical must immediately be done. Much as she would have liked, in the emotion of the moment, to keep him entirely to herself, medical assistance was necessary whilst there remained a possibility of preserving him alive. Such assistance was fatal to her own concealment; but even had the chance of benefiting him been less than it was she would have run the hazard for his sake. The question was, where should she get a medical man, competent and near?

There was one such man, and only one, within accessible distance: a man who, if it were possible to save Winterborne's life, had the brain most likely to do it. If human pressure could bring him that man ought to be brought to the sick Giles's side. Though completely stultifying her flight the attempt should be made.

Yet she dreaded to leave her patient, and the minutes raced past, and still she postponed her departure. At last, when it was after eleven o'clock, Winterborne fell into a fitful sleep, and it seemed to afford her an opportunity.

She hastily made him as comfortable as she could, put on her things, cut a new candle from the bunch hanging in the cupboard, and having set it up, and placed it so that the light did not fall upon his eyes, she closed the door and started, there being now no rain.

The spirit of Winterborne seemed to keep her company and banish all sense of darkness from her mind. The rains had imparted a phosphorescence to the pieces of touchwood and rotting leaves that lay about her path, which, as scattered by her feet, spread abroad like luminous milk. She would not run the hazard of losing her way by plunging into any short, unfrequented track through the woodland, but followed a more open course round by the highway. She went along with great speed, animated by a devoted purpose which had much about it that was stoical; and it was with scarcely any faltering of spirit that, after an hour's progress, she saw High-Stoy Hill, and drew onwards towards that same Hintock and that same house out of which she had fled a few days before in irresistible alarm. But that had happened which, above all other things of chance and change, could make her deliberately frustrate her plan of flight, and sink all regard of personal consequences.

One speciality of Fitzpiers was respected by Grace as much as ever: his professional skill. In this she was right. Had his persistence equalled his insight instead of being the spasmodic and fitful thing it was, fame and fortune need never have remained a wish with him. His freedom from conventional errors and crusted prejudices had indeed been such as to retard rather than accelerate his advance in Hintock and its neighbourhood, where people could not believe that Nature herself effected cures, and that the doctor's business was only to smooth the way.

It was past midnight when Grace arrived opposite her father's house, now again temporarily occupied by her husband, unless he had already gone away. Ever since her emergence from the denser plantations about Winterborne's residence a pervasive lightness had hung in the damp autumn sky in spite of the vault of cloud, signifying that a moon of some age was shining above its arch. The two white gates were distinct, and the white balls on the pillars: and the puddles and damp ruts left by the recent rain had a cold corpse-eyed luminousness. She entered by the lower gate and crossed the quadrangle to the wing wherein the apartments that had been hers since her marriage were situate, till she stood under a window, which, if her husband were in the house, gave light to his bed-chamber.

She faltered, and paused with her hand on her heart, in spite of herself. Could she call to her presence the very cause of all her foregoing troubles? Alas! – old Jones was many miles off; Giles was possibly dying – what else could she do?

It was in a perspiration, wrought even more by consciousness than by exercise, that she picked up some gravel, threw it at the panes, and waited to see the result. The night-bell which had been fixed when Fitzpiers first took up his residence there still remained; but as it had fallen into disuse with the collapse of his practice, and his elopement, she did not venture to pull it now.

Whoever slept in the room had heard her signal, slight as it was. In half a minute the window was opened, and a voice said 'Yes?' inquiringly. Grace recognized her husband in the speaker at once. Her effort was now to disguise her own accents.

'Doctor,' she said, in as unusual a tone as she could command, 'a man is dangerously ill in One-Chimney Hut, by Delborough, and you must go to him at once – in all mercy!'

'I will, readily.'

The alacrity, surprise, and even pleasure, expressed in his reply, amazed her for a moment. But, in truth, they denoted the sudden relief of a man who, having got back in a mood of contrition from erratic abandonment to doubtful joys, found the soothing routine of professional practice unexpectedly opening anew to him. The highest desire of his soul just now was for a respectable life of painstaking. If this, his first summons since his return, had been to attend upon a cat or dog, he would scarcely have refused it in the circumstances.

'Do you know the way?' she asked.

'Yes, I think,' said he.

'One-Chimney Hut – in King's-Hintock Wood, by Delborough,' she repeated. 'And – immediately!'

'Yes, yes,' said Fitzpiers.

Grace remained no longer. She passed through the white gate without slamming it, and hastened on her way back. Her husband, then, had re-entered her father's house. How he had been able to effect a reconciliation with the old man, what were the terms of the treaty between them, she could not so much as conjecture. Some sort of truce must have been entered into, that was all she could say. But close as the question lay to her own life there was a more urgent one which banished it; and she traced her steps quickly along the meandering trackways.

Meanwhile Fitzpiers was preparing to leave the house. The state of his mind, over and above his professional zeal, was peculiar. At Grace's first remark he had not recognized or suspected her presence; but as she went on he was awakened to the great resemblance of the speaker's voice to his wife's. He had taken in such good faith the statement of the household on his arrival, that she had gone on a visit for a time because she could not at once bring her mind to be reconciled to him, that he could not quite believe this neighbour to be she. It was one of the features of Fitzpiers's repentant humour at this date that, on receiving the explanation of her absence, he had made no attempt to outrage her feelings by following her; though nobody had informed him how very shortly her departure had preceded his entry, and of all that might have been inferred from her precipitancy.

Melbury, after much alarm and consideration, had decided not to follow her either. He sympathized with her flight, much as he deplored it; moreover, the tragic colour of the antecedent events that he had been a great means of creating checked his instinct to interfere. He prayed and trusted that she had got into no danger on her way (as he supposed) to Ivell, and thence to Exonbury, if that were the place she had gone to, forbearing all inquiry which the strangeness of her departure would have made natural. A few months before this time a performance by Grace of one-tenth the magnitude of this would have aroused him to unwonted investigation.

It was in the same spirit that he had tacitly assented to Fitzpiers's domiciliation there. The two men had not met face to face, but Mrs Melbury had proposed herself as an intermediary who made the surgeon's re-entrance comparatively easy to him. Everything was provisional, and nobody asked questions. Fitzpiers had come in the performance of a plan of penitence which had originated in circumstances hereafter to be explained; his self-humiliation to the very bass-string was deliberate; and as soon as a voice reached him from the bedside of a dying man his desire was to set to work and do as much good as he could with the least possible fuss or show. He therefore refrained from calling up a stableman to get ready any horse or gig, and set out for One-Chimney Hut on foot as Grace had done.

CHAPTER 43

She re-entered the hut, flung off her bonnet and cloak, and approached the sufferer. He had begun anew those terrible mutterings, and his hands were cold. As soon as she saw him there returned to her that agony of mind which the stimulus of her journey had thrown off for a time.

Could he really be dying? She bathed him, kissed him, forgot all things but the fact that lying there before her was he who had loved her more than the mere lover would have loved; had immolated himself for her comfort, cared more for her self-respect than she had thought of caring. This mood continued till she heard quick, smart footsteps without; she knew whose footsteps they were.

Grace sat on the inside of the bed against the wall, holding her lover's hand, so that when her husband entered the patient lay between herself and him. He stood transfixed at first, noticing Grace only. Slowly he dropped his glance and discerned who the prostrate man was. Strangely enough, though Grace's distaste for her husband's company had amounted almost to dread, and culminated in actual flight, at this moment her last and least feeling was personal. Sensitive femininity was eclipsed by devoted purpose; and that it was a husband who stood there was forgotten. The first look that possessed her face was relief; satisfaction at the presence of the physician obliterated the thought of the man, which only returned in the form of a subconsciousness that did not interfere with her words.

'Is he dying – is there any hope?' she asked.

'Grace!' said Fitzpiers in an indescribable whisper – more than invocating – if not quite deprecatory.

He was arrested by the spectacle, not so much in its intrinsic character – though that was striking enough to a man who called himself the husband of the sufferer's friend and nurse – but in its character as the counterpart of one that had had its run many months before, in which he had figured as the patient, and the woman had been Felice Charmond.

'Is he in great danger – can you save him?' she asked again.

Fitzpiers aroused himself, came a little nearer, and examined Winterborne as he stood. His inspection was concluded in a mere glance. Before he spoke he looked at her contemplatively as to the effect of his coming words.

'He is dying,' he said with dry precision.

'What?' said she.

'Nothing can be done by me or any other man. It will soon be all over. The extremities are dead already.' His eyes still remained fixed on her, the conclusion to which he had come seeming to end his interest, professional and otherwise, in Winterborne for ever.

'But it cannot be! He was well a week ago.'

'Not well, I suspect. This seems like what we call a sequel, which has followed some previous disorder – possibly typhoid – it may have been months ago, or recently.'

'Ah – he was ill last year – you are right. And he must have been ill when I came!'

There was nothing more to do or say. She crouched down at the side of the bed, and Fitzpiers took a seat. Thus they remained in silence, and long as it lasted she never turned her eyes, or apparently her thoughts, at all to her husband. He occasionally murmured, with automatic authority, some slight directions for alleviating the pain of the dying man, which she mechanically obeyed, bending over him during the intervals in silent tears.

Winterborne never recovered consciousness of what was passing; and that he was going became soon perceptible also to her. In less than an hour the delirium ceased; then there was an interval of somnolent painlessness and soft breathing, at the end of which Winterborne passed quietly away.

Then Fitzpiers broke the silence. 'Have you lived here long?' he said.

Grace was wild with sorrow – bitter with all that had befallen her – with the cruelties that had attacked her – with life – with Heaven. She answered at random. 'Yes. By what right do you ask?'

'Don't think I claim any right,' said Fitzpiers. 'It is for you to do and say what you choose. I admit, quite as much as you feel, that I am a vagabond – a brute – not worthy to possess the smallest fragment of you. But here I am, and I have happened to take sufficient interest in you to make that inquiry.'

'He is everything to me!' said Grace, hardly heeding her husband, and laying her hand reverently on the dead man's eyelids, where she kept it a long time, pressing down their lashes with gentle touches, as if she were stroking a little bird.

He watched her awhile, and then glanced round the chamber, where his eyes fell upon a few dressing necessaries that she had brought.

'Grace – if I may call you so,' he said, 'I have been already humiliated almost to the depths. I have come back – since you refused to join me elsewhere – I have entered your father's house – and borne all which that cost me without flinching, because I have felt I deserved humiliation. But is there a yet greater humiliation in store for me? You say you have been living here with him – that he was everything to you. Am I to draw from that the obvious, the extremest inference?'

Triumph at any price is sweet to men and women – especially the latter. It was her first and last opportunity of repaying him for the slights which she had borne at his hands so docilely.

'Yes,' she answered; 'the extremest inference'; and there was that in her subtly compounded nature which made her feel a thrill of pride as she did so.

Yet the moment after she had so mightily belied her conduct she half repented. Her husband had turned as white as the wall behind him. It seemed as if all that remained to him of hope and spirit had been abstracted at a stroke. Yet he did not move, and in his efforts at self-control closed his mouth together as a vice. His determination was fairly successful, though she saw how very much greater than she had expected her triumph had been. Presently he looked across at Winterborne.

'Would it startle you to hear,' he said, as if he hardly had breath to utter words, 'that she who was to me what he was to you is dead also?'

'Dead – *she* dead?' exclaimed Grace.

'Yes. Felice Charmond is where this young man is.'

'Never!' said Grace vehemently.

He went on without heeding the insinuation: 'And I came back to try to make it up with you; but—'

Fitzpiers rose and moved across the room to go away, looking downwards with the droop of a man whose hope was turned to apathy, if not despair. In going round the door his eye fell upon her once more. She was still bending over the body of Winterborne, her face close to his.

'Have you been kissing him during his illness?' asked her husband.

'Yes.'

'Since his fevered state set in?'

'Yes.'

'On his lips?'

'Yes, a hundred times!'

'Then you will do well to take a few drops of this in water as soon as possible.'

He drew a small phial from his pocket, and returned to offer it to her.

Grace shook her head.

'If you don't do as I tell you, you may soon be like him.'

'I don't care! I wish to die.'

'I'll put it here,' said Fitzpiers, placing the bottle on a ledge beside him. 'The sin of not having warned you will not be upon my head at any rate, amongst my other sins. I am now going, and I will send somebody to you. Your father does not know that you are here, so I suppose I shall be bound to tell him?'

'Certainly.'

Fitzpiers left the cot, and the stroke of his feet was soon immersed in the silence that pervaded the spot. Grace remained kneeling and weeping, she hardly knew how long, and then she sat up, covered Giles's fixed statuesque features, and went towards the door where her husband had stood. No sign of any other comer greeted her ear, the only perceptible sounds being the tiny cracklings of the dead leaves which, like a feather bed, had not yet done rising to their normal level where indented by the pressure of her husband's receding footsteps. It reminded her that she had been struck with the change in his aspect; the extremely intellectual look that had always been in his face was wrought to a finer phase by thinness, and a care-worn dignity had been superadded. She returned to Winterborne's side, and during her meditations another tread drew near the door, entered the room, and halted at the foot of the bed.

'What – Marty!' said Grace.

'Yes. I have heard,' said Marty, whose demeanour had lost all its girlishness under the stroke that seemed almost literally to have bruised her.

'He died for me!' murmured Grace heavily.

Marty did not fully comprehend and she answered, 'He belongs to neither of us now, and your beauty is no more powerful with him than my plainness. I have come to help you, ma'am. He never cared for me, and he cared much for you; but he cares for us both alike now.'

'O don't, don't, Marty!'

Marty said no more, but knelt over Winterborne from the other side.

'Did you meet my hus— Mr Fitzpiers?'

'No.'

'Then what brought you here?'

'I come this way sometimes. I have got to go to the further side of the wood at this time o' year, and am obliged to get there before four o'clock in the morning, to begin heating the oven for the early baking. I have passed by here often at this time.'

Grace looked at her quickly. 'Then did you know I was here?'

'Yes, ma'am.'

'Did you tell anybody?'

'No. I knew you lived in the hut, that he had gi'ed it up to 'ee, and lodged out himself.'

'Did you know where he lodged?'

'No. That I couldn't find out. Was it at Delborough?'

'No. It was not there, Marty. Would it had been! It would have saved – saved—' To check her tears she turned, and seeing a book in the window-bench, took it up. 'Look, Marty, this is a Psalter. He was not an outwardly religious man; but he was pure and perfect in his heart. Shall we read a psalm over him?'

'O yes, we will; with all my heart!'

Grace opened the thin brown book, which poor Giles had kept at hand mainly for the convenience of whetting his pen-knife upon its leather covers. She began to read in that rich, devotional voice peculiar to women on such occasions. When it was over Marty said, 'I should like to pray for his soul.'

'So should I,' said her companion. 'But we must not.'

'Why? Nobody would know.'

Grace could not resist the argument, influenced as she was by the sense of making amends for having neglected him in the body; and their tender voices united and filled the narrow room with supplicatory murmurs that a Calvinist might have countenanced. They had hardly ended when new and more numerous footfalls were audible; also persons in conversation, one of whom Grace recognized as her father.

She rose and went to the outside of the hut, where there was only such light as beamed from the doorway. Melbury and Mrs Melbury were standing there.

'I don't reproach you, Grace,' said her father, with an estranged manner and in a voice not at all like his old voice. 'What has come upon you and us through you giving up yourself to him is beyond reproach, beyond weeping and beyond wailing. Perhaps I drove you to it. But I am hurt; I am scourged; I am astonished! In the face of this there is nothing to be said.'

Without replying Grace turned and glided back to the chamber. 'Marty,' she said quickly, 'I cannot look my father in the face until he knows the true circumstances of my life here. Go and tell him – what you have told me – what you saw – that he gave up his house to me.'

She sat down, her face buried in her hands, and Marty went, and after a short absence returned. Then Grace rose, and going out, asked her father if he had talked to Marty.

'Yes,' said Melbury.

'And you know all that has happened? I will let my husband think the utmost, but not you.'

'I do. Forgive me, Grace, for suspecting 'ee of worse than rashness – I ought to know 'ee better. Are you coming with me to what was once your home?'

'No. I stay here with him. Take no account of me any more.'

The tender, perplexing, agitating relations in which she had stood to Winterborne quite lately – brought about by Melbury's own contrivance – could not fail to soften the natural anger of a parent at her more recent doings. 'My daughter, things are bad,' he rejoined. 'But why do you persevere to make 'em worse? What good can you do to Giles by staying here with him? Mind, I ask no questions. I don't inquire why you decided to come here, or anything as to what your course would have been if he had not died, though I know there's no deliberate harm in 'ee. As for me, I have lost all claim upon you; and I make no complaint. But I do say that by coming back with me now you will show no less kindness to him, and escape any sound of shame.'

'But I don't wish to escape it.'

'If you don't on your own account, cannot you wish to on mine and hers? Nobody except our household knows that you have left home. Then why should you by a piece of perverseness bring down my hairs with sorrow to the grave?'

'If it were not for my husband—' she began, moved by his words. 'But how can I meet him there? How can any woman who is not a mere man's creature live with him after what has taken place?'

'He would go away again rather than keep you out of my house.'

'How do you know that, father?'

'We met him on our way here, and he told us so,' said Mrs Melbury. 'He had said something like it before. He seems very much upset altogether.'

'He declared to her when he came to our house that he would wait for time and devotion to bring about his forgiveness,' said Melbury. 'That was it, wasn't it, Lucy?'

'Yes. That he would not intrude upon you, Grace, till you gave him absolute permission,' Mrs Melbury added.

This antecedent considerateness in Fitzpiers was as welcome to Grace as it was unexpected; and though she did not desire his presence, she was sorry that by her retaliatory fiction she had given him a different reason for avoiding her. She made no further objections to accompanying her parents, taking them into the hut to give Winterborne a last look, and gathering up the two or three things that belonged to her. While she was doing this the two women came who had been called by Melbury, and at their heels poor Creedle.

'Forgive me, but I can't rule my mourning nohow as a man should, Mr Melbury,' he said. 'I ha'n't seen him since Thursday se'night, and have wondered for days and days where he's been keeping. There was I expecting him to come and tell me to wash out the cider-barrels against the making, and here was he. . . . Well, I've knowed him from table-high; I knowed his father – used to bide about upon two sticks in the sun afore he died! – and now I've seen the end of the family, which we can ill afford to lose, wi' such a scanty lot of good folk in Hintock as we've got. And now Robert Creedle will be nailed up in parish boards 'a b'lieve; and nobody will glutch down a sigh for he!'

They started for home, Marty and Creedle remaining behind. For a time Grace and her father walked side by side without speaking. It was just in the blue of the dawn, and the chilling tone of the sky was reflected in her cold, wet face. The whole wood seemed to be a house of death, pervaded by loss to its uttermost length and breadth. Winterborne was gone, and the copses seemed to show the want of him; those young trees, so many of which he had planted, and of which he had spoken so truly when he said that he should fall before they fell, were at that very moment sending out their roots in the direction that he had given them with his subtle hand.

'One thing made it tolerable to us that your husband should come back to the house,' said Melbury at last. 'The death of Mrs Charmond.'

'Ah, yes,' said Grace, arousing slightly to the recollection; 'he told me so.'

'Did he tell you how she died? It was no such death as Giles's. She was shot – by a disappointed lover. It occurred in Germany. The unfortunate man shot himself afterwards. He was that South Carolina gentleman of very passionate nature, who used to haunt this place to force her to favour him, and followed her about everywhere. So ends the brilliant Felice Charmond – once a good friend to me – but no friend to you.'

'I can forgive her,' said Grace absently. 'Did Edred tell you this?'

'No; but he put a London newspaper, giving an account of it, on the hall-table, folded in such a way that we should see it. It will be in the Sherton paper this week, no doubt. To make the event more solemn still to him he had just before had sharp words with her, and left her. He told Lucy this, as nothing about him appears in the newspaper. And the cause of the quarrel was, of all people, she we've left behind us.'

'Do you mean Marty?' Grace spoke the words but perfunctorily. For, pertinent and pointed as Melbury's story was, she had no care for it now.

'Yes. Marty South.' Melbury persisted in his narrative to divert her from her present grief if possible. 'Before he went away she wrote him a letter, which he kept in his pocket a long while before reading. He chanced to pull it out in Mrs Charmond's presence, and read it out loud. It contained something which teased her very much, and that led to the rupture. She was following him to make it up when she met with her terrible death.'

Melbury did not know enough to give the gist of the incident, which was that Marty South's letter had been concerning a certain personal adornment common to herself and Mrs Charmond. Her bullet reached its billet at last. The scene between Fitzpiers and Felice had been sharp, as only a scene can be which arises out of the mortification of one woman by another in the presence of a lover. True, Marty had not effected it by word of mouth; the charge about the locks of hair was made simply by Fitzpiers reading her letter to him aloud to Felice in the playfully ironical tones of one who had become a little weary of his situation, and was finding his friend, in the phrase of George Herbert, a 'flat delight'. He had stroked those false tresses with his hand many a time without knowing them to be transplanted, and it was impossible when the discovery was so abruptly made to avoid being finely satirical, despite his generous disposition.

That was how it had begun, and tragedy had been its end. On his abrupt departure she had followed him to the station, but the train was gone; and in travelling to Homburg in search of him she had met his rival, whose reproaches led to an altercation, and the death of both. Of that precipitate scene of passion and crime Fitzpiers had known nothing till he saw an account of it in the papers, where, fortunately for himself, no mention was made of his prior acquaintance with the unhappy lady; nor was there any allusion to him in the subsequent inquiry, the double death being attributed to some gambling losses, though in point of fact neither one of them had visited the tables.

Melbury and his daughter drew near their house, having seen but one living thing on their way, a squirrel, which did not run up its tree, but, dropping the sweet chestnut which it carried, cried chut-chut-chut and stamped with its hind-legs on the ground. When the roofs and chimneys of the homestead began to emerge from the screen of boughs Grace started, and checked herself in her abstracted advance.

'You clearly understand,' she said to her stepmother, some of her old misgiving returning, 'that I am coming back only on condition of his leaving as he promised? Will you let him know this, that there may be no mistake?'

Mrs Melbury, who had had some long private talks with Fitzpiers, assured Grace that she need have no doubts on that point, and that he would probably be gone by the evening. Grace then entered with them into Melbury's wing of the house, and sat down listlessly in the parlour while her stepmother went to Fitzpiers.

The prompt obedience to her wishes which the doctor showed did honour to him, if anything could. Before Mrs Melbury had returned to the room Grace, who was sitting on the parlour window-bench, saw her husband go from the door under the increasing light of morning, with a bag in his hand. While passing through the gate he turned his head. The fire-light of the room she sat in threw her figure into dark relief against the window as she looked through the panes, and he must have seen her distinctly. In a moment he went on, the gate fell to, and he disappeared. At the hut she had declared that another had usurped his rights; now she had banished him.

CHAPTER 44

FITZPIERS had hardly been gone an hour when Grace began to sicken. The next day she kept her room. Old Jones was called in: he murmured some statements in which the words 'feverish symptoms' occurred. Grace heard them, and guessed the means by which she had brought this visitation upon herself.

One day while she still lay there with her head throbbing, wondering if she were really going to join him who had gone before, Grammer Oliver came to her bedside. 'I don't know whe'r this is meant for you to take, ma'am,' she said. 'But I have found it on the table. It was left by Marty, I think, when she came this morning.'

Grace turned her hot eyes upon what Grammer held up. It was the phial left at the hut by her husband when he had begged her to take some drops of its contents, if she wished to preserve herself from falling a victim to the malady which had pulled down Winterborne. She examined it as well as she could. The liquid was of a brownish hue, and bore a label with an inscription in Italian. He had probably got it in his wanderings abroad. She knew but little Italian, but could understand that the cordial was a febrifuge of some sort. Her father, her mother, and all the household were anxious for her recovery, and she resolved to obey her husband's directions. Whatever the risk, if any, she was prepared to run it. A glass of water was brought, and the drops dropped in.

The effect, though not miraculous, was remarkable. In less than an hour she felt calmer, cooler, better able to reflect, less inclined to fret and chafe and wear herself away. She took a few drops more. From that time the fever retreated, and went out like a damped conflagration.

'How clever he is!' she said regretfully. 'Why could he not have had more principle, so as to turn his great talents to good account! Perhaps he has saved my useless life. But he doesn't know it, and doesn't care whether he has saved it or not; and on that account will never be told by me. Probably he only gave it to me in the arrogance of his skill, to show the greatness of his resources beside mine, as Elijah drew down fire from Heaven!'

As soon as she had quite recovered from this foiled attack upon her life Grace went to Marty South's cottage. The current of her being had again set towards the lost Giles Winterborne.

'Marty,' she said, 'we both loved him. We will go to his grave together.'

The church stood somewhat outside the village, and could be reached without passing through the street. In the dusk of the late September day they went thither by secret ways, walking mostly in silence side by side, each busied with her own thoughts. Grace had a trouble exceeding Marty's, that haunting sense of having put out the light of his life by her own hasty doings. She had tried to persuade herself that he might have died of his illness, even if she had not taken possession of his house. Sometimes she succeeded in her attempt; sometimes she did not.

They stood by the grave together, and though the sun had gone down they could get glimpses over the woodland for miles, and along the vale in which he had been accustomed to descend every year with his portable mill and press to make cider about this time.

Perhaps Grace's first grief, the discovery that if he had lived he could never have claimed her, had some power in softening this, the second. On Marty's part there was the same consideration; never would she have been his. As no anticipation of gratified affection had been in existence while he was with them there was none to be disappointed now that he had gone.

Grace was abased when, by degrees, she found that she had never understood Giles as Marty had done. Marty South alone, of all the women in Hintock and the world, had approximated to Winterborne's level of intelligent intercourse with Nature. In that respect she had formed his true complement in the other sex, had lived as his counterpart, had subjoined her thoughts to his as a corollary.

The casual glimpses which the ordinary population bestowed upon that wondrous world of sap and leaves called the Hintock woods had been with these two, Giles and Marty, a clear gaze. They had been possessed of its finer mysteries as of commonplace knowledge; had been able to read its hieroglyphs as ordinary writing; to them the sights and sounds of night, winter, wind, storm, amid those dense boughs, which had to Grace a touch of the uncanny, and even of the supernatural, were simple occurrences whose origin, continuance, and laws they foreknew. They had planted together, and together they had felled; together they had, with the run of the years, mentally collected those remoter signs and symbols which seen in few were of runic obscurity, but all together made an alphabet. From the light lashing of the twigs upon their faces when brushing through them in the dark either could pronounce upon the species of the tree whence they stretched; from the quality of the wind's murmur through a bough either could in like manner name its sort afar off. They knew by a glance at a trunk if its heart were sound, or tainted with incipient decay; and by the state of its upper twigs the stratum that had been reached by its roots. The artifices of the seasons were seen by them from the conjuror's own point of view, and not from that of the spectator.

'He ought to have married *you*, Marty, and nobody else in the world!' said Grace with conviction, after thinking in the above strain.

Marty shook her head. 'In all our outdoor days and years together, ma'am,' she replied, 'the one thing he never spoke of to me was love; nor I to him.'

'Yet you and he could speak in a tongue that nobody else knew – not even my father, though he came nearest knowing – the tongue of the trees and fruits and flowers themselves.'

She could indulge in mournful fancies like this to Marty; but the hard core to her grief – which Marty's had not – remained. Had she been sure that Giles's death resulted entirely from his exposure, it would have driven her well-nigh to insanity; but there was always the bare possibility that his exposure had only precipitated what was inevitable. She longed to believe that it had not done even this.

There was only one man whose opinion on the circumstances she would be at all disposed to trust. Her husband was that man. Yet to ask him it would be necessary to detail the true conditions in which she and Winterborne had lived during these three or four critical days that followed her flight; and in withdrawing her original defiant announcement on that point there seemed a weakness she did not care to show. She never doubted that Fitzpiers would believe her if she made a clean confession of the actual situation; but to volunteer the correction would seem like signalling for a truce, and that in her present frame of mind was what she did not feel the need of.

It will probably not appear a surprising statement, after what has been already declared of Fitzpiers, that the man whom Grace's matrimonial fidelity could not keep faithful was stung into passionate throbs of interest concerning her by her avowal of the contrary.

He declared to himself that he had never known her dangerously full compass if she were capable of such a reprisal; and, melancholy as it may be to admit the fact, his own humiliation and regret engendered a smouldering admiration of her.

He passed a month or two of nervous misery at some midland town – the place to which he had retired – quite as much misery indeed as Grace, could she have known of it, would have been inclined to inflict upon any living creature, how much soever he might have wronged her. Then a sudden hope dawned upon him; he wondered if her affirmation were true. He asked himself whether it were not the act of an innocent woman whose pique had for the moment blinded her to the contingencies of such an announcement. His wide experience of the sex had taught him that, in many cases, women who ventured on hazardous phrases did so because they lacked an imagination gross enough to feel their full force. In this light Grace's bold avowal might merely have denoted the desperation of one who was a child to the realities of faithlessness.

Fitzpiers's mental sufferings and suspense led him at last to take a melancholy journey to the neighbourhood of Little Hintock; and here he hovered for hours around the scene of the purest emotional experiences that he had ever known in his life. He walked about the woods that surrounded Melbury's house, keeping out of sight like a criminal. It was a fine evening, and on his way homeward he passed near Marty South's cottage. As usual she had lighted her candle without closing her shutters; he saw her within as he had seen her many times before.

She was polishing tools, and though he had not wished to show himself he could not resist speaking to her through the half-open door. 'What are you doing that for, Marty?'

'Because I want to clean them. They are not mine.' He could see indeed that they were not hers, for one was a spade, large and heavy, and another was a bill-hook which she could only have used with both hands. The spade, though not a new one, had been so completely burnished that it was bright as silver.

Fitzpiers somehow divined that they were Giles Winterborne's, and he put the question to her.

She replied in the affirmative. 'I am going to keep 'em,' she said, 'but I can't get his apple-mill and press. I wish I could; it is going to be sold, they say.'

'Then I will buy it for you,' said Fitzpiers. 'That will be making you a return for a kindness you did me.' His glance fell upon the girl's rare-coloured hair, which had grown again. 'O Marty, those locks of yours – and that letter! . . . But it was a kindness to send it, nevertheless,' he added musingly.

After this there was confidence between them – such confidence as there had never been before. Marty was shy, indeed, of speaking about the letter and her motives in writing it; but she thanked him warmly for his promise of the cider-press. She would travel with it in the autumn season as poor Giles had done, she said. She would be quite strong enough with old Creedle as an assistant.

'Ah! – there was one nearer to him than you,' said Fitzpiers, referring to Grace. 'One who lived where he lived, and was with him when he died.'

Then Marty, suspecting that he did not know the true circumstances, from the fact that Mrs Fitzpiers and himself were living apart, told him of Giles's generosity to Grace in giving up his house to her at the risk, and possibly the sacrifice, of his own life. When the surgeon heard it he almost envied Giles his chivalrous character. He expressed a wish to Marty that his visit to her should be kept secret, and went home thoughtful, feeling that in more than one sense his journey to Hintock had not been in vain.

He would have given much to win Grace's forgiveness then. But whatever he dared hope for in that kind from the future there was nothing to be done yet, while Giles Winterborne's memory was green. To wait was imperative. A little time might melt her frozen thoughts, and lead her to look on him with toleration, if not with love.

CHAPTER 45

WEEKS and months of mourning for Winterborne had been passed by Grace in the soothing monotony of the memorial act to which she and Marty had devoted themselves. Twice a week the pair went in the dusk to Hintock Churchyard, and, like the two mourners in *Cymbeline*, sweetened his sad grave with their flowers and their tears.

Nothing ever had brought home to her with such force as this death how little acquirements and culture weigh beside sterling personal character. While her simple sorrow for his loss took a softer edge with the lapse of the autumn and winter seasons, her self-reproach at having had a possible hand in causing it knew slight abatement.

Little occurred at Hintock during these months of the fall and decay of the leaf. Discussion of the almost contemporaneous death of Mrs Charmond abroad had waxed and waned. There was a rumour that her death had resulted less from the shot than from the effect of fright upon her personal condition at the time; but this was never verified. Fitzpiers had had a fortunate escape from being dragged into the inquiry which followed the catastrophe, through the accident of having parted from his mistress just before it, under the influence of Marty South's letter – the tiny instrument of a cause deep in nature.

Her body was not brought home. It seemed to accord well with the fitful fever of that impassioned woman's life that she should not have found an English grave. She had enjoyed but a life-interest in the estate, which after her death passed to a relative of her husband's – one who knew not Felice, one whose purpose seemed to be to blot out every vestige of her.

On a certain day in February – the cheerful day of St Valentine – a letter reached Mrs Fitzpiers, which had been mentally promised her for that particular day a long time before.

Her husband announced that he was living at some midland town, where he had obtained a temporary practice as assistant to a local medical man, whose curative principles were all wrong, though he dared not set them right. He had thought fit to communicate with her on that day of tender traditions to inquire if, in the event of his obtaining a substantial practice that he had in view elsewhere, she could forget the past and bring herself to join him.

There the practical part ended: he then went on: –

My last year of experience has added ten years to my age, dear Grace, and dearest wife that ever erring man undervalued. You may be absolutely indifferent to what I say, but let me say it; I have never loved any woman alive or dead as I love, respect, and honour you at this present moment. What you told me in the pride and naughtiness of your heart I never believed [this, by the way, was not strictly true]; but even if I had believed it, it could never have estranged me from you. Is there any use in telling you – no, there is not – that I dream of your fresh lips more frequently than I say my prayers: that the old familiar rustle of your dress often returns upon my mind till it distracts me? If you could condescend even only to see me again you would be breathing life into a corpse. My pure, pure Grace, modest as a turtledove, how came I ever to possess you? For the sake of being present in your mind on this lovers' day, I think I would almost rather have you hate me a little than not think of me at all. You may call my fancies whimsical; but remember, sweet, lost one, that 'nature is fine in love, and where 'tis fine it sends some instance of itself'. – I will not intrude upon you further now. Make me a little bit happy by sending back one line to say that you will consent, at any rate, to a short interview. I will meet you and leave you as a mere acquaintance, if you will only afford me this slight means of making a few explanations, and of putting my position before you. Believe me, in spite of all you may do or feel, your lover always (once your husband),

E.F.

It was, oddly enough, the first occasion, or nearly the first, on which Grace had ever received a love-letter from him, his courtship having taken place under conditions which rendered letter-writing unnecessary. Its perusal, therefore, had a certain novelty for her. She thought that, upon the whole, he wrote love-letters very well. But the chief rational interest of the letter to the reflective Grace lay in the chance that such a meeting as he proposed would afford her of setting her doubts at rest one way or the other on her actual share in Winterborne's death. The relief of consulting a skilled mind, the one professional man who had seen Giles at that time, would be immense. As for that statement that she had uttered in her disdainful grief, which at the time she had regarded as her triumph, she was quite prepared to admit to him that his belief was the true one; for in wronging herself as she did when she made it she had done what to her was a far more serious thing, wronged Winterborne's memory.

Without consulting her father, or any one in the house or out of it, Grace replied to the letter. She agreed to meet Fitzpiers on two conditions, of which the first was that the place of meeting should be the top of High-Stoy Hill, the second that he would not object to Marty South accompanying her.

Whatever art, much or little, there may have been in Fitzpiers's so-called valentine to his wife, he felt a delight as of the bursting of spring when her brief reply came. It was one of the few pleasures that he had experienced of late years at all resembling those of his early youth. He promptly replied that he accepted the conditions, and named the day and hour at which he would be on the spot she mentioned.

A few minutes before three on the appointed day found him climbing the well-known hill, which had been the axis of so many critical movements in their lives during his residence at Hintock.

The sight of each homely and well-remembered object swelled the regret that seldom left him now. Whatever paths might lie open to his future the soothing shades of Hintock were forbidden him for ever as a permanent dwelling-place.

He longed for the society of Grace. But to lay offerings on her slighted altar was his first aim, and until her propitiation was complete he would constrain her in no way to return to him. The least reparation that he could make, in a case where he would gladly have made much, would be to let her feel herself absolutely free to choose between living with him and without him.

Moreover, a subtlist in emotions, he cultivated as under glasses strange and mournful pleasures that he would not willingly let die just at present. To show any forwardness in suggesting a *modus vivendi* to Grace would be to put an end to these exotics. To be the vassal of her sweet will for a time – he demanded no more, and found solace in the contemplation of the soft miseries she caused him.

Approaching the hill with a mind strung to these notions Fitzpiers discerned a gay procession of people coming down the way, and was not long in perceiving it to be a wedding-party. Though the wind was keen the women were in light attire, and the flowered waistcoats of the men had a pleasing vividness of pattern. Each of the gentler ones clung to the arm of her partner so tightly as to have with him one step, rise, swing, gait, almost one centre of gravity. In the buxom bride Fitzpiers recognized no other than Suke Damson, who in her light gown looked a giantess; the small husband beside her he saw to be Tim Tangs.

Fitzpiers could not escape, for they had seen him; though of all the beauties of the world whom he did not wish to meet Suke was the chief. But he put the best face on the matter that he could and came on, the approaching company evidently discussing him and his separation from Mrs Fitzpiers. As the couples closed upon him he expressed his congratulations.

'We be just walking round the parishes to show ourselves a bit,' said Tim. 'First we het across to Great Hintock, then back to here, and from here we go to Revellers Inn and Marshwood, and then round by the cross roads home. Home, says I, but it won't be that long. We be off in a couple of months.'

'Indeed. Where to?'

Tim informed him that they were going to New Zealand. Not but that he would have been contented with Hintock, but his wife was ambitious and wanted to leave; so he had given way.

'Then good-bye,' said Fitzpiers; 'I may not see you again.' He shook hands with Tim and turned to the bride. 'Good-bye, Suke,' he said, taking her hand also. 'I wish you and your husband prosperity in the country you have chosen.' With this he left them, and hastened on to his appointment.

The wedding-party re-formed and resumed march likewise. But in restoring his arm to Suke, Tim noticed that her full and blooming countenance had undergone a change. 'Hullo! me dear – what's the matter?' said Tim.

'Nothing to speak o',' said she. But to give the lie to her assertion she was seized with lachrymose twitches, that soon produced a dribbling face.

'How – what the devil's this about?' exclaimed the bridegroom.

'She's a little wee bit overcome, poor dear!' said the first bridesmaid, unfolding her handkerchief and wiping Suke's eyes.

'I never did like parting from people!' said Suke as soon as she could speak.

'Why him in particular?'

'Well – he's such a clever doctor, that 'tis a thousand pities we sha'n't see him any more! There'll be no such clever doctor as he in New Zealand, if I should be wanting one in a few months; and the thought o't got the better of my feelings!'

They walked on, but Tim's face had grown rigid and pale, for he recalled slight circumstances disregarded at the time of their occurrence. The former boisterous laughter of the wedding-party at the groomsman's jokes was heard rising between the hedges no more.

By this time Fitzpiers had advanced on his way to the hill, where he saw two figures emerging from the bank on the right hand. These were the expected ones, Grace and Marty South, who had evidently come there by a short and secret path through the wood. Grace was muffled up in her winter dress, and he thought that she had never looked so seductive as at this moment, in the noontide, bright, but heatless sun, and the keen wind, and the purplish-grey masses of brushwood around. Fitzpiers continued to regard the nearing picture, till at length their glances met for a moment, when she demurely sent off hers at a tangent and gave him the benefit of her three-quarter face, while with courteous completeness of conduct he lifted his hat in a large arc. Marty dropped behind; and when Fitzpiers held out his hand Grace touched it with her fingers.

'I have agreed to be here mostly because I wanted to ask you something important,' said Mrs Fitzpiers, her intonation modulating in a direction that she had not quite wished it to take.

'I am most attentive,' said her husband. 'Shall we take to the trees for privacy?'

Grace demurred, and Fitzpiers gave in, and they kept outside by the gate.

At any rate, she would take his arm? This also was gravely negatived, the refusal being audible to Marty.

'Why not?' he inquired.

'O, Mr Fitzpiers – how can you ask?'

'Right, right,' said he, his effusiveness shrivelled up.

As they walked on she returned to her inquiry. 'It is about a matter that may perhaps be unpleasant to you. But I think I need not consider that too carefully.'

'Not at all,' said Fitzpiers heroically.

She then took him back to the time of poor Winterborne's death, and related the precise circumstances amid which his fatal illness had come upon him, particularizing the dampness of the shelter to which he had betaken himself, his concealment from her of the hardships that he was undergoing, all that he had put up with, all that he had done for her in his scrupulous considerateness. The retrospect brought her to tears as she asked him if he thought that the sin of having driven him to his death was upon her.

Fitzpiers could hardly help showing his satisfaction at what her narrative indirectly revealed, the actual harmlessness of an escapade with her lover which had at first, by her own showing, looked so grave, and he did not care to inquire whether that harmlessness had been the result of aim or of accident. With regard to her question he declared that in his judgment no human being could answer it. He thought that upon the whole the balance of probabilities turned in her favour. Winterborne's apparent strength, during the last months of his life, must have been delusive. It had often occurred that after a first attack of that insidious disease a person's apparent recovery was a physiological mendacity.

The relief which came to Grace lay almost as much in sharing her knowledge of the particulars with an intelligent mind as in the assurance Fitzpiers gave her. 'Well, then, to put this case before you and obtain your professional opinion was chiefly why I consented to come here to-day,' said she, when he had reached the aforesaid conclusion.

'For no other reason at all?' he asked ruefully.

'It was nearly the whole.'

They stood and looked over a gate at twenty or thirty starlings feeding in the grass, and he started the talk again by saying in a low voice, 'And yet I love you more than ever I loved you in my life.'

Grace did not move her eyes from the birds, and folded her delicate lips as if to keep them in subjection.

'It is a different kind of love altogether,' said he. 'Less passionate; more profound. It has nothing to do with the material conditions of the object at all; much to do with her character and goodness, as revealed by closer observation. "Love talks with better knowledge, and knowledge with dearer love."'

'That's out of *Measure for Measure*,' said she slily.

'O yes – I meant it as a citation,' blandly replied Fitzpiers. 'Well then, why not give me a very little bit of your heart again?'

The crash of a felled tree in the depths of the nearest wood recalled the past at that moment, and all the homely faithfulness of Winterborne. 'Don't ask it! My heart is in the grave with Giles,' she replied staunchly.

'Mine is with you – in no less deep a grave, I fear, according to that.'

'I am very sorry; but it cannot be helped.'

'How can you be sorry for me, when you wilfully keep open the grave?'

'O no – that's not so,' returned Grace quickly; and moved to go away from him.

'But dearest Grace!' said he. 'You have condescended to come; and I thought from it that perhaps when I had passed through a long state of probation you would be generous. But if there can be no hope of our getting completely reconciled, treat me gently – wretch though I am.'

'I did not say you were a wretch, nor have I ever said so.'

'But you have such a contemptuous way of looking at me that I fear you think so.'

Grace's heart struggled between the wish not to be harsh and the fear that she might mislead him. 'I cannot look contemptuous unless I feel contempt,' she said evasively, 'and all I feel is lovelessness.'

'I have been very bad I know,' he returned. 'But unless you can really love me again, Grace, I would rather go away from you for ever. I don't want you to receive me again for duty's sake, or anything of that sort. If I had not cared more for your affection and forgiveness than my own personal comfort I should never have come back here. I could have obtained a practice at a distance, and have lived my own life without coldness or reproach. But I have chosen to return to the one spot on earth where my name is tarnished – to enter the house of a man from whom I have had worse treatment than from any other man alive – all for you!'

This was undeniably true, and it had its weight with Grace, who began to look as if she thought she had been shockingly severe.

'Before you go,' he continued, 'I want to know your pleasure about me: what you wish me to do, or not to do.'

'You are independent of me, and it seems a mockery to ask that. Far be it from me to advise. But I will think it over. I rather need advice myself than stand in a position to give it.'

'*You* don't need advice, wisest, dearest woman that ever lived. If you did. . . .'

'Would you give it to me?'

'Would you act upon what I gave?'

'That's not a fair inquiry,' said she, smiling despite her gravity. 'I don't mind hearing it – what you do really think the most correct and proper course for me.'

'It is so easy for me to say, and yet I dare not, for it would be provoking you to remonstrances.'

Knowing, of course, what the advice would be, she did not press him further, and was about to beckon Marty forward and leave him, when he interrupted her with, 'O! one moment, dear Grace – you will meet me again?'

She eventually agreed to see him that day fortnight. Fitzpiers expostulated at the interval, but the half-alarmed earnestness with which she entreated him not to come sooner made him say hastily that he submitted to her will – that he would regard her as a friend only, anxious for his reform and well-being, till such time as she might allow him to exceed that privilege.

All this was to assure her; it was only too clear that he had not won her confidence yet. It amazed Fitzpiers, and overthrew all his deductions from previous experience, to find that this girl, though she had been married to him, could yet be so coy. Notwithstanding a certain fascination that it carried with it his reflections were sombre as he went homeward; he saw how deep had been his offence to produce so great a wariness in a gentle and once unsuspicious soul.

He was himself too fastidious to care to coerce her. To be an object of misgiving or dislike to a woman who shared his home was what he could not endure the thought of. Life as it stood was more tolerable.

When he was gone Marty joined Mrs Fitzpiers. She would fain have consulted Marty on the question of Platonic relations with her former husband, as she preferred to regard him. But Marty showed no great interest in their affairs, so Grace said nothing. They came onward and saw Melbury standing at the scene of the felling which had been audible to them, when, telling Marty that she wished her meeting with Mr Fitzpiers to be kept private, she left the girl to join her father. At any rate she would consult him on the expediency of occasionally seeing her husband.

Her father was cheerful, and walked by her side as he had done in earlier days. 'I was thinking of you when you came up,' he said. 'I have considered that what has happened is for the best. Since your husband is gone away, and seems not to wish to trouble you, why, let him go, and drop out of your life. Many women are worse off. You can live here comfortably enough, and he can emigrate, or do what he likes for his good. I wouldn't mind sending him the further sum of money he might naturally expect to come to him, so that you may not be bothered with him any more. He could hardly have gone on living here without speaking to me, or meeting me; and that would have been very unpleasant on both sides.'

These remarks checked her intentions. There was a sense of weakness in following them by saying that she had just met her husband by appointment. 'Then you would advise me not to communicate with him?' she observed.

'I shall never advise 'ee again. You are your own mistress – do as you like. But my opinion is that if you don't live with him you had better live without him, and not go shilly-shallying and playing bo-peep. You sent him away; and now he's gone. Very well; trouble him no more.'

Grace felt a guiltiness – she hardly knew why – and made no confession.

CHAPTER 46

THE woods were uninteresting, and Grace stayed indoors a great deal. She became quite a student, reading more than she had done since her marriage. But her seclusion was always broken for the periodical visit to Winterborne's grave with Marty, which was kept up with pious strictness for the purpose of putting snowdrops, primroses, and other vernal flowers thereon as they came.

One afternoon at sunset she was standing under the trees just at the back of her father's garden which, like the rest of the Hintock inclosures, abutted into the wood. A slight footpath led along here, forming a secret way to either of the houses by getting through its boundary hedge. Grace was about to adopt this mode of entry when a figure approached along the path, and held up his hand to detain her. It was her husband.

'I am delighted,' he said, coming up out of breath; and there seemed no reason to doubt his words. 'I saw you some way off – I was afraid you would go in before I could reach you.'

'It is a week before the time,' said she reproachfully. 'I said a fortnight from the last meeting.'

'My dear, you don't suppose I could wait a fortnight without trying to get a glimpse of you, even though you had declined to meet me! Would it make you angry to know that I have been along this path at dusk three or four times since our last meeting? Well, how are you?'

She did not refuse her hand, but when he showed a wish to retain it a moment longer than mere formality required she made it smaller, so that it slipped away from him, with again that same alarmed look which always followed his attempts in this direction. He saw that she was not yet out of the elusive mood; not yet to be treated presumingly; and he was correspondingly careful to tranquillize her.

His assertion had seemed to impress her somewhat. 'I had no idea you came so often,' she said. 'How far do you come from?'

'From Sherton Abbas where I am temporarily staying. I always walk the distance here, for if I hire people will know that I come; and my success with you so far has not been great enough to justify such overtness. Now, my dear one – as I *must* call you – I put it to you: will you see me a little oftener as the spring advances?'

Grace lapsed into unwonted sedateness and avoiding the question, said: 'I wish you would concentrate on your profession, and give up those strange studies that used to distract you so much. I am sure you would get on.'

'It is the very thing I am doing. I was going to ask you to burn – or, at least, get rid of – all my philosophical literature. It is in the book-cases in your rooms. The fact is I never cared much for abstruse studies.'

'I am so glad to hear you say that. And those other books – those piles of old plays – what good are they to a medical man?'

'None whatever!' he replied cheerfully. 'Sell them at Sherton for what they will fetch.'

'And those dreadful old French romances with their horrid spellings of "filz" and "ung" and "ilz" and "mary" and "ma foy"?'

'You haven't been reading them, Grace?'

'O no – I just looked into them, that was all.'

'Make a bonfire of 'em directly you get home. I meant to do it myself. I can't think what possessed me ever to collect them. I have only a few professional hand-books now, and am quite a practical man. I am in hopes of having some good news to tell you soon, and then do you think that you could – come to me again?'

'I would rather you did not press me on that just now,' she replied with some feeling. 'You have said you mean to lead a new, useful, effectual life; but I should like to see you put it in practice for a little while before you address that query to me. Besides – I could not live with you!'

'Why not?'

Grace was silent a few instants. 'I go with Marty to Giles's grave. I almost worship him. We swore we would show him that devotion. And I mean to keep it up.'

'Well, I wouldn't mind that at all. I have no right to expect anything else, and I will not wish you to keep away. I liked the man as well as any I ever knew. In short, I would accompany you a part of the way to the grave, and smoke a cigar on the stile while I waited till you came back.'

'Then you haven't given up smoking?'

'Well – ahem – no. I have thought of doing so, but—'

His extreme complaisance had rather disconcerted Grace, and the question about smoking had been to effect a diversion. Presently she said firmly, and with a moisture in her eye that he could not see, as her mind returned to poor Giles's 'frustrate ghost': 'I don't like you – to speak lightly on that subject, if you did speak lightly. To be frank with you – quite frank – I think of him as my betrothed lover still. I cannot help it. So that it would be wrong for me to join you.'

Fitzpiers was now uneasy. 'You say your betrothed lover still,' he rejoined. 'When, then, were you betrothed to him, or engaged, as we common people say?'

'When you were away.'

'How could that be?'

Grace would have avoided this; but her natural candour led her on. 'It was when I was under the impression that my marriage with you was about to be dissolved, and that he could then marry me. So I encouraged him to love me.'

Fitzpiers winced visibly; and yet, upon the whole, she was right in telling it. Indeed, his perception that she was right in her absolute sincerity kept up his affectionate admiration for her under the pain of the rebuff. Time had been when the avowal that Grace had deliberately taken steps to replace him would have brought him no sorrow. But she so far dominated him now that he could not bear to hear her words, although the object of her high regard was no more.

'It is rough upon me – that!' he said bitterly. 'O, Grace – I did not know you – tried to get rid of me! I suppose it is of no use, but I ask, cannot you hope to – find a little love in your heart for me again?'

'If I could I would oblige you; but I fear I cannot!' she replied, with illogical ruefulness. 'And I don't see why you should mind my having had one lover besides yourself in my life, when you have had so many.'

'But I can tell you honestly that I love you better than all of them put together, and that's what you will not tell me!'

'I am sorry, but I fear I cannot,' she said, sighing again.

'I wonder if you ever will?' He looked musingly into her indistinct face as if he would read the future there. 'Now have pity, and tell me: will you try?'

'To love you again?'

'Yes; if you can.'

'I don't know how to reply,' she answered, her embarrassment proving her truth. 'Will you promise to leave me quite free as to seeing you or not seeing you?'

'Certainly. Have I given any ground for you to doubt my first promise in that respect?'

She was obliged to admit that he had not.

'Then I think you might get your heart out of that grave,' said he with playful sadness. 'It has been there a long time.'

She faintly shook her head, but said: 'I'll try to think of you more – if I can.'

With this Fitzpiers was compelled to be satisfied, and he asked her when she would meet him again.

'As we arranged – in a fortnight.'

'If it must be a fortnight it must!'

'This time at least. I'll consider by the day I see you again if I can shorten the interval.'

'Well, be that as it may, I shall come at least twice a week to look at your window.'

'You must do as you like about that. Good-night.'

'Say "husband".'

She seemed almost inclined to give him the word; but exclaiming, 'No, no; I cannot,' slipped through the garden hedge and disappeared.

Fitzpiers did not exaggerate when he told her that he should haunt the precincts of the dwelling. But his persistence in this course did not result in his seeing her much oftener than at the fortnightly interval which she had herself marked out as proper. At these times, however, she punctually appeared, and as the spring wore on the meetings were kept up, though their character changed but little with the increase in their number.

The small garden of the cottage occupied by the Tangs family – father, son, and now son's wife – aligned with the larger one of the timber-dealer at its upper end; and when young Tim, after leaving work at Melbury's, stood at dusk in the little bower at the corner of his inclosure to smoke a pipe, he frequently observed the surgeon pass along the outside track before-mentioned. Fitzpiers always walked loiteringly, pensively, looking with a sharp eye into the gardens one after another as he proceeded; for Fitzpiers did not wish to leave the now absorbing spot too quickly after travelling so far to reach it; hoping always for a glimpse of her whom he passionately desired to take to his arms anew.

Now Tim began to be struck with these loitering progresses along the garden boundaries in the gloaming, and wondered what they boded. It was naturally quite out of his power to divine the singular sentimental revival in Fitzpiers's heart: the fineness of tissue which could take a deep, emotional – almost also an artistic – pleasure in being the yearning *innamorato* of a woman he once had deserted would have seemed an absurdity to the young sawyer. Mr and Mrs Fitzpiers were separated; therefore the question of affection as between them was settled. But his Suke had, since that meeting on their marriage day, repentantly admitted, to the urgency of his questioning, a good deal concerning her past levities. Putting all things together he could hardly avoid connecting Fitzpiers's mysterious visits to this spot with Suke's residence under his roof. But he made himself fairly easy; the vessel in which they were about to emigrate sailed that month; and then Suke would be out of Fitzpiers's way for ever.

The interval at last expired, and the eve of their departure arrived. They were pausing in the room of the cottage allotted to them by Tim's father, after a busy day of preparation which left them weary. In a corner stood their boxes, crammed and corded, their large case for the hold having already been sent away. The firelight shone upon Suke's plump face and form as she stood looking into it, and upon the face of Tim seated in a corner, and upon the walls of his father's house, which he was beholding that night almost for the last time.

Tim Tangs was not happy. This scheme of emigration was dividing him from his father – for old Tangs would on no account leave Hintock – and had it not been for Suke's reputation and his own dignity Tim would at the last moment have abandoned the project. As he sat in the back part of the room he regarded her moodily, and the fire, and the boxes. One thing he had particularly noticed this evening – she was very restless, fitful in her actions, unable to remain seated, and in a marked degree depressed.

'Sorry that you be going, after all, Suke?' he said.

She sighed involuntarily. 'I don't know but that I be,' she answered. ' 'Tis natural, isn't it, when one is going away?'

'But you wasn't born here as I was.'

'No.'

'There's folk left behind that you'd fain have with 'ee, I reckon?'

'Why do you think that?'

'I've seen things, and I've heard things; and Suke, I say 'twill be a good move for me to get 'ee away. I don't mind his leavings abroad, but I do mind 'em at home.'

Suke's face was not changed from its aspect of listless indifference by the words. She answered nothing; and shortly after he went out for his customary pipe of tobacco at the top of the garden.

The restlessness of Suke had indeed owed its presence to the gentleman of Tim's suspicions, but in a different and – it must be added in justice to her – more innocent sense than he supposed, judging from former doings. She had accidentally discovered that Fitzpiers was in the habit of coming secretly once or twice a week to Hintock, and knew that this evening was a favourite one of the seven for his journey. As she was going next day to leave the country Suke thought there could be no great harm in giving way to a little sentimentality by obtaining a glimpse of him quite unknown to himself or to anybody, and thus taking a silent last farewell. Aware that Fitzpiers's time for passing was at hand she thus betrayed her feeling. No sooner, therefore, had Tim left the room than she let herself noiselessly out of the house and hastened to the corner of the garden, whence she could witness the surgeon's transit across the scene, if he had not already gone by.

Her light cotton dress was visible to Tim lounging in the arbour of the opposite corner, though he was hidden from her. He saw her stealthily climb into the hedge, and so ensconce herself there that nobody could have the least doubt her purpose was to watch unseen for a passer-by.

He went across to the spot and stood behind her. Suke started, having in her blundering way forgotten that he might be near. She at once descended from the hedge.

'So he's coming to-night,' said Tim laconically. 'And we be always anxious to see our dears.'

'He is coming to-night,' she replied with defiance. 'And we *be* anxious for our dears!'

'Then will you step indoors, where your dear will soon jine 'ee? We've to mouster by half-past three to-morrow, and if we don't get to bed by eight at latest our faces will be as long as clock-cases all day.'

She hesitated for a minute but ultimately obeyed, going slowly down the garden to the house, where he heard the door-latch click behind her.

Tim was incensed beyond measure. His marriage had so far been a total failure, a source of bitter regret; and the only course for improving his case, that of leaving the country, was a sorry, and possibly might not be a very effectual one. Do what he would his domestic sky was likely to be overcast to the end of the day. Thus he brooded, and his resentment gathered force. He craved a means of striking one blow back at the cause of his cheerless plight while he was still on the scene of his discomfiture. For some minutes no method suggested itself, and then he had an idea.

Coming to a sudden resolution he hastened along the garden, and entered the one attached to the next cottage, which had formerly been the dwelling of a gamekeeper. Tim descended the path to the back of the house, where only an old woman lived at present, and reaching the wall he stopped. Owing to the slope of the ground the roof-eaves of the linhay were here within touch, and he thrust his arm up under them, feeling about in the space on the top of the wall plate.

'Ah, I thought my memory didn't deceive me!' he lipped silently.

With some exertion he drew down a cobwebbed object curiously framed in iron, which clanked as he moved it. It was about three feet in length and half as wide. Tim contemplated it as well as he could in the dying light of day, and raked off the cobwebs with his hand.

'That will spoil his pretty shins for'n, I reckon!' he said.

It was a man-trap.

CHAPTER 47

WERE the inventors of automatic machines to be ranged according to the excellence of their devices for producing sound artistic torture, the creator of the man-trap would occupy a very respectable, if not a very high, place.

It should rather, however, be said, the inventor of the particular form of man-trap of which this found in the keeper's outhouse was a specimen. For there were other shapes and other sizes, instruments which, if placed in a row beside one of the type disinterred by Tim, would have worn the subordinate aspect of the bears, wild boars, or wolves in a travelling menagerie as compared with the leading lion or tiger. In short, though many varieties had been in use during those centuries which we are accustomed to look back upon as the true and only period of merry England – in the rural districts more especially – and onward down to the third decade of the nineteenth century, this model had borne the palm, and had been most usually followed when the orchards and estates required new ones.

There had been the toothless variety used by the softer-hearted landlords – quite contemptible in their clemency. The jaws of these resembled the jaws of an old woman to whom time has left nothing but gums. There were also the intermediate or half-toothed sorts, probably devised by the middle-natured squires, or those under the influence of their wives: two inches of mercy, two inches of cruelty, two inches of mere nip, two inches of probe, and so on, through the whole extent of the jaws. There were also, as a class apart, the bruisers, which did not lacerate the flesh, but only crushed the bone.

The sight of one of these gins, when set, produced a vivid impression that it was endowed with life. It exhibited the combined aspects of a shark, a crocodile, and a scorpion. Each tooth was in the form of a tapering spine two and a quarter inches long, which, when the jaws were closed, stood in alternation from this side and from that. When they were open the two halves formed a complete circle between two and three feet in diameter, the plate or treading-place in the midst being about a foot square, while from beneath extended in opposite directions the soul of the apparatus, the pair of springs, each one having been in its prime of a stiffness to render necessary a lever or the whole weight of the body when forcing it down, though rust had weakened it somewhat now.

There were men at this time still living at Hintock who remembered when the gin and others like it were in use. Tim Tangs's great-uncle had endured a night of six hours in this very trap, which lamed him for life. Once a keeper of Hintock woods set it on the track of a poacher, and afterwards coming back that way forgetful of what he had done walked into it himself. The wound brought on lockjaw, of which he died. This event occurred during the thirties, and by the year 1840 the use of such implements was well-nigh discontinued in the neighbourhood. But being made entirely of iron they by no means disappeared, and in almost every village one could be found in some nook or corner as readily as this was found by Tim. It had indeed been a fearful amusement of Tim and other Hintock lads – especially those who had a dim sense of becoming renowned poachers when they reached their prime – to drag out this trap from its hiding, set it, and throw it with billets of wood, which were penetrated by the teeth to the depth of near an inch.

As soon as he had examined the trap and found that the hinges and springs were fairly perfect, he shouldered it without more ado and returned with his burden to his own garden, passing on through the hedge to the path immediately outside the boundary. Here by the help of a stout stake he set the trap, and laid it carefully behind a bush while he went forward to reconnoitre. As has been stated, nobody passed this way for days together sometimes; but there was just a possibility that some other pedestrian than the one in request might arrive, and it behoved Tim to be careful as to the identity of his victim.

Going about a hundred yards along the rising ground to the right he reached a ridge whereon a large and thick holly grew. Beyond this for some distance the wood was more open, and the course which Fitzpiers must pursue to reach the point, if he came to-night, was visible a long way forward.

For some time there was no sign of him or of anybody. Then there shaped itself a spot out of the dim mid-distance, between the masses of brushwood on each hand. It enlarged, and Tim could hear the brushing of feet over the tufts of sour grass. The airy gait revealed Fitzpiers even before his exact outline could be seen.

Tim Tangs turned about and ran down the opposite side of the hill till he was again at the head of his own garden. It was the work of a few moments to drag out the man-trap very gently – that the plate might not be disturbed sufficiently to throw it – to a space between a pair of young oaks which, rooted in contiguity, grew apart upward, forming a V-shaped opening between; and, being backed up by bushes, left this as the only course for a foot-passenger. In it he laid the trap with the same gentleness of handling, locked the chain round one of the trees, and finally slid back the guard which was placed to keep the gin from accidentally catching the arms of him who set it, or, to use the local and better word, 'toiled' it. Having completed these arrangements Tim sprang through the adjoining hedge of his father's garden, ran down the path, and softly entered the house.

Obedient to his order Suke had gone to bed; and as soon as he had bolted the door Tim unlaced and kicked off his boots at the foot of the stairs and retired likewise, without lighting a candle. His object seemed to be to undress as soon as possible. Before, however, he had completed the operation a long cry resounded without – penetrating, but indescribable.

'What's that?' said Suke, starting up in bed.

'Sounds as if somebody had caught a hare in his gin.'

'O no,' said she. 'It was not a hare, 'twas louder. Hark!'

'Do 'ee get to sleep,' said Tim. 'How be you going to wake at half-past three else?'

She lay down and was silent. Tim stealthily opened the window and listened. Above the low harmonies produced by the instrumentation of the various species of tree around the premises he could hear the twitching of a chain from the spot whereon he had set the man-trap. But further human sound there was none.

Tim was puzzled. In the haste of his project he had not calculated upon a cry; but if one, why not more? He soon ceased to essay an answer, for Hintock was dead to him already. In half-a-dozen hours he would be out of its precincts for life, on his way to the antipodes. He closed the window and lay down.

The hour which had brought these movements of Tim to birth had been operating actively elsewhere. Awaiting in her father's house the minute of her appointment with her husband, Grace Fitzpiers deliberated on many things. Should she inform her father before going out that the estrangement of herself and Edred was not so complete as he had imagined and deemed desirable for her happiness? If she did so she must in some measure become the apologist of her husband, and she was not prepared to go so far.

As for him, he kept her in a mood of considerate gravity. He certainly had changed. He had at his worst times always been gentle in his manner towards her. Could it be that she might make of him a true and worthy husband yet? She had married him; there was no getting over that; and ought she any longer to keep him at a distance? His suave deference to her lightest whim on the question of his comings and goings, when as her lawful husband he might show a little insistence, was a trait in his character as unexpected as it was engaging. If she had been his empress, and he her thrall, he could not have exhibited a more sensitive care to avoid intruding upon her against her will.

Impelled by a remembrance she took down a prayer-book and turned to the marriage-service. Reading it slowly through she became quite appalled at her recent off-handedness, when she re-discovered what awfully solemn promises she had made him at Hintock chancel steps not so very long ago. She became lost in long ponderings on how far a person's conscience might be bound by vows made without at the time a full recognition of their force. That particular sentence, beginning, 'Whom God hath joined together,' was a staggerer for a gentle woman of strong devotional sentiment. She wondered whether God really did join them together. Before she had done deliberating the time of her engagement drew near, and she went out of the house almost at the moment that Tim Tangs retired to his own.

The position of things at that critical juncture was as follows. Two hundred yards to the right of the upper end of Tangs's garden Fitzpiers was still advancing, having now nearly reached the summit of the wood-clothed ridge, the path being the actual one which further on passed between the two young oaks. Thus far it was according to Tim's conjecture. But about two hundred yards to the left, or rather less, was arising a condition which he had not divined, the emergence of Grace as aforesaid from the upper corner of her father's garden with the view of meeting Tim's intended victim. Midway between husband and wife was the diabolical trap, silent, open, ready.

Fitzpiers's walk that night had been cheerful, for he was convinced that the slow and gentle method he had adopted was promising success. The very restraint that he was obliged to exercise upon himself, so as not to kill the delicate bud of returning confidence, fed his flame. He walked so much more rapidly than Grace that if they continued advancing as they had begun, he would reach the trap a good half minute before she could reach the same spot. But here a new circumstance came in: to escape the unpleasantness of being watched or listened to by lurkers – naturally curious by reason of their strained relations – they had arranged that their meeting for to-night should be at the holm-tree on the ridge above-named. So soon, accordingly, as Fitzpiers reached the tree he stood still to await her.

He had not paused under the prickly foliage more than two minutes when he thought he heard a scream from the other side of the ridge. Fitzpiers wondered what it could mean; but such wind as there was just now blew in an adverse direction, and his mood was light. He set down the origin of the sound to one of the superstitious freaks or frolicsome scrimmages between sweethearts that still survived in Hintock from old-English times; and waited on where he stood till ten minutes had passed. Feeling then a little uneasy his mind reverted to the scream; and he went forward over the summit and down the embowered incline till he reached the pair of sister oaks with the narrow opening between them.

Fitzpiers stumbled and all but fell. Stretching down his hand to ascertain the obstruction it came in contact with a confused mass of silken drapery and ironwork that conveyed absolutely no explanatory idea to his mind at all. It was but the work of a moment to strike a match; and then he saw a sight which congealed his blood.

The man-trap was thrown; and between its jaws was part of a woman's clothing – a patterned silk skirt – gripped with such violence that the iron teeth had passed through it, skewering its tissue in a score of places. He immediately recognized the skirt as that of one of his wife's gowns – the gown that she had worn when she met him on the very last occasion.

Fitzpiers had often studied the effect of these instruments when examining the collection at Hintock House, and the conception instantly flashed through him that Grace had been caught, taken out mangled by some chance passer, and carried home, some of her clothes being left behind in the difficulty of getting her free. The shock of this conviction, striking into the very current of high hope, was so great that he cried out like one in corporal agony, and in his misery bowed himself down to the ground.

Of all the degrees and qualities of punishment that Fitzpiers had undergone since his sins against Grace first began, not any even approximated in intensity to this. 'O, my own – my darling! O, cruel Heaven – it is too much this!' he cried, writhing and rocking himself over the sorry accessories of her he deplored.

The voice of his distress was sufficiently loud to be audible to any one who might have been there to hear it; and one there was. Right and left of the narrow pass between the oaks were dense bushes; and now from behind these a female figure glided, whose appearance even in the gloom was, though graceful in outline, noticeably strange.

She was white up to the waist, and figured above. She was, in short, Grace, his wife, lacking the portion of her dress which the gin retained.

'Don't be grieved about me – don't, dear Edred!' she exclaimed, rushing up and bending over him. 'I am not hurt a bit! I was coming on to find you after I had released myself, but I heard footsteps; and I hid away because I was without some of my clothing, and I did not know who the person might be.'

Fitzpiers had sprung to his feet, and his next act was no less unpremeditated by him than it was irresistible by her, and would have been so by any woman not of Amazonian strength. He clasped his arms completely round her, pressed her to his breast and kissed her passionately.

'You are not dead! – you are not hurt! Thank God – thank God!' he said, almost sobbing in his delight and relief from the horror of his apprehension. 'Grace, my wife, my love, how is this – what has happened?'

'I was coming on to you,' she said as distinctly as she could in the half-smothered state of her face against his. 'I was trying to be as punctual as possible, and as I had started a minute late I ran along the path very swiftly – fortunately for myself. Just when I had passed between these trees I felt something clutch at my dress from behind with a noise, and the next moment I was pulled backwards by it, and fell to the ground. I screamed with terror, thinking it was a man lying down there to murder me, but the next moment I discovered it was iron, and that my clothes were caught in a trap. I pulled this way and that, but the thing would not let go, drag it as I would, and I did not know what to do. I did not want to alarm my father or anybody, as I wished nobody to know of these meetings with you, so I could think of no other plan than slipping off my skirt, meaning to run on and tell you what a strange accident had happened to me. But when I had just freed myself by leaving the dress behind I heard steps, and not being sure it was you I did not like to be seen in such a pickle, so I hid away.'

'It was only your speed that saved you! One or both of your legs would have been broken if you had come at ordinary walking pace.'

'Or yours, if you had got here first,' said she, beginning to realize the whole ghastliness of the possibility, or what seemed a possibility to them, though whether the old springs would have done quite so much mischief may be doubted. 'O, Edred, there has been an Eye watching over us to-night, and we should be thankful indeed!'

He continued to press his face to hers. 'You are mine – mine again now!'

She owned that she supposed she was. 'I heard what you said when you thought I was injured,' she went on shyly, 'and I know that a man who could suffer as you were suffering must have a tender regard for me. But how does this awful thing come here?'

'I suppose it has something to do with poachers.' Fitzpiers was still so shaken by the sense of her danger that he was obliged to sit awhile, and it was not until Grace said, 'If I could only get my skirt out nobody would know anything about it,' that he bestirred himself.

By their united efforts, each standing on one of the springs of the trap, they pressed them down sufficiently to insert across the jaws a billet which they dragged from a faggot near at hand, and it was then possible to extract the silk mouthful from the monster's bite, creased and pierced with small holes, but not torn. Fitzpiers assisted her to put it on again; and when her customary contours were thus restored they walked on together, Grace taking his arm till he effected an improvement by passing it round her waist.

The ice having been broken in this unexpected manner, she made no further attempt at reserve. 'I would ask you to come into the house,' she said, 'but my meetings with you have been kept secret from my father, and I should like to prepare him.'

'Never mind, dearest. I could not very well have accepted the invitation. I shall never live here again – as much for your sake as for mine. I have news to tell you on this very point, but my alarm had put it out of my head. I have bought a practice, or rather a partnership, in the Midlands, and I must go there in a week to take up permanent residence. My poor old great-aunt died about eight months ago, and left me enough to do this. I have taken a little furnished house for a time, till we can get one of our own.'

He described the place, and the surroundings, and the view from the windows; and Grace became much interested. 'But why are you not there now?' she said.

'Because I cannot tear myself away from here till I have your promise. Now, darling, you will accompany me there soon – will you not? Tonight has settled that?'

Grace's tremblings had gone off, and she did not say nay. They went on together.

The adventure, and the emotions consequent upon the reunion which that event had forced on, combined to render Grace oblivious of the direction of their desultory ramble, till she noticed they were in an encircled glade in the densest part of the wood. The moon, that had imperceptibly added her rays to the scene, shone almost vertically. It was an exceptionally soft, balmy evening for the time of year, which was just that transient period in the May month when beech trees have suddenly unfolded large limp young leaves of the softness of butterflies' wings. Boughs bearing such leaves hung low around and completely inclosed them, so that it was as if they were in a great green vase, which had moss for its bottom and leaf sides. Here they sat down.

The clouds having been packed in the west that evening so as to retain the departing glare a long while, the hour had seemed much earlier than it was. But suddenly the question of time occurred to her.

'I must go back,' she said, springing up; and without further delay they set their faces towards Hintock. As they walked he examined his watch by the aid of the now strong moonlight.

'By the gods, I think I have lost my train!' said Fitzpiers.

'Dear me – whereabouts are we?' said she.

'Two miles in the direction of Sherton.'

'Then do you hasten on, Edred. I am not in the least afraid. I recognize now the part of the wood we are in, and I can find my way back quite easily. I'll tell my father that we have made it up. I wish I had not kept our meetings so private, for it may vex him a little to know I have been seeing you. He is getting old and irritable, that was why I did not. Good-bye.'

'But, as I must stay at the Earl of Wessex to-night, for I cannot possibly catch the train, I think it would be safer for you to let me take care of you.'

'But what will my father think has become of me! He does not know in the least where I am – he thinks I only went into the garden for a few minutes.'

'He will surely guess – somebody has seen me for certain. I'll go all the way back with you to-morrow.'

'But that newly-done-up place – the Earl of Wessex!'

'If you are so very particular about the publicity I will stay at a little quiet one.'

'O no – it is not that I am particular – but I haven't a brush or comb or anything!'

CHAPTER 48

ALL the evening Melbury had been coming to his door saying, 'I wonder where in the world that girl is! Never in all my born days did I know her bide out like this! She surely said she was going into the garden to get some parsley.'

Melbury searched the garden, the outbuildings, and the orchard, but could find no trace of her, and then he made inquiries at the cottages of such of his workmen as had not gone to bed, avoiding Tangs's because he knew the young people were to rise early to leave. In these inquiries one of the men's wives somewhat incautiously let out the fact that she had heard a scream in the wood, though from which direction she could not say.

This set Melbury's fears on end. He told the men to light lanterns, and headed by himself they started, Creedle following at the last moment with a bundle of grapnels and ropes which he could not be persuaded to leave behind, and the company being joined by the hollow-turner and Cawtree as they went along.

They explored the precincts of the village, and in a short time lighted upon the man-trap. Its discovery simply added an item of fact without helping their conjectures; but Melbury's indefinite alarm was greatly increased when, holding a candle to the ground, he saw in the teeth of the instrument some frayings from Grace's clothing. No intelligence of any kind was gained till they met a woodman of Delborough, who said that he had seen a lady answering to the description her father gave of Grace, walking through the wood on a gentleman's arm in the direction of Sherton.

'Was he supporting her?' said Melbury.

'Well – rather,' said the man.

'Did she walk lame?'

'Well, 'tis true her head hung over towards him a bit.'

Creedle groaned tragically.

Melbury, not suspecting the presence of Fitzpiers, coupled this account with the man-trap and the scream; he could not understand what it all meant, but the sinister event of the trap made him follow on. Accordingly, they bore away towards the town shouting as they went, and in due course emerged upon the highway.

Nearing Sherton Abbas the previous information was confirmed by other strollers, though the gentleman's supporting arm had disappeared from these later accounts. At last they were so near Sherton that Melbury informed his faithful followers that he did not wish to drag them further at so late an hour, since he could go on by himself and inquire if the woman who had been seen were really Grace. But they would not leave him alone in his anxiety, and trudged onward till the lamplight from the town began to illuminate their faces. At the entrance to the borough they got fresh scent of the pursued, but coupled with the new condition that the lady in the costume described had been going up the street alone.

'Faith – I believe she's mesmerized, or walking in her sleep!' said Melbury.

However, the identity of this woman with Grace was by no means certain; but they plodded along the street. Percomb the hairdresser, who had despoiled Marty of her tresses, was standing at his door, and they duly put inquiries to him.

'Ah – how's Little Hintock folk by now!' he cried before replying. 'Never have I been over there since one winter night some three year ago – and then I lost myself finding it. How can ye live in such a one-eyed place? Great Hintock is bad enough – but Little Hintock – the bats and owls would drive me melancholy-mad! It took two days to raise my sperrits to their true pitch again after that night I went there.

Mr Melbury, sir, as a man that's put by money, why not retire and live here, and see something of the world?'

The responses at last given by him to their queries guided them to the building that offered the best accommodation in Sherton – having been rebuilt contemporaneously with the construction of the railway – namely, the Earl of Wessex Hotel.

Leaving the others without, Melbury made prompt inquiry here. His alarm was lessened, though his perplexity was increased, when he received a brief reply that such a lady was in the house.

'Do you know if it is my daughter?' asked Melbury.

The waiter did not.

'Do you know the lady's name?'

Of this, too, the household was ignorant, the hotel having been taken by brand-new people from a distance. They knew the gentleman very well by sight, and had not thought it necessary to ask him to enter his name.

'Oh, the gentleman appears again now,' said Melbury to himself. 'Well, I want to see the lady,' he declared.

A message was taken up, and after some delay the shape of Grace appeared descending round the bend of the staircase, looking as if she lived there, but in other respects rather guilty and frightened.

'Why – what the name—' began her father. 'I thought you went out to get parsley!'

'O yes – I did – but it is all right,' said Grace in a flurried whisper. 'I am not alone here. I am here with Edred. It is entirely owing to an accident, father.'

'Edred? An accident? How does he come here? I thought he was two hundred mile off.'

'Yes – so he is – I mean he has got a beautiful practice two hundred miles off: he has bought it with his own money, some that came to him. But he travelled here, and I was nearly caught in a man-trap, and that's how it is I am here. We were just thinking of sending a messenger to let you know.'

Melbury did not seem to be particularly enlightened by this explanation.

'You were caught in a man-trap?'

'Yes; my dress was. That's how it arose. Edred is upstairs in the sitting-room,' she went on. 'He would not mind seeing you, I am sure.'

'O faith, I don't want to see him! I have seen him too often a'ready. I'll see him another time, perhaps, if 'tis to oblige 'ee.'

'He came to see me; he wanted to consult me about this large partnership I speak of, as it is very promising.'

'Oh; I am glad to hear it,' said Melbury drily.

A pause ensued, during which the inquiring faces and whity-brown clothes of Melbury's companions appeared in the doorway.

'Then bain't you coming home with us?' he asked.

'I – I think not,' said Grace, blushing.

'H'm – very well – you are your own mistress,' he returned, in tones which seemed to assert otherwise. 'Good-night'; and Melbury retreated towards the door.

'Don't be angry, father,' she said, following him a few steps. 'I have done it for the best!'

'I am not angry, though it is true I have been a little misled in this! However, good-night. I must get home-along.'

He left the hotel, not without relief, for to be under the eyes of strangers while he conversed with his lost child had embarrassed him much. His search-party, too, had looked awkward there, having rushed to the task of investigation some in their shirt-sleeves, others in their leather aprons, and all much stained – just as they had come from their work of barking, and not in their Sherton marketing attire; while Creedle, with his ropes and grapnels and air of impending tragedy had added melancholy to gawkiness.

'Now, neighbours,' said Melbury, on joining them, 'as it is getting late we'll leg it home again as fast as we can. I ought to tell you that there has been some mistake – some arrangement entered into between Mr and Mrs Fitzpiers which I didn't quite understand – an important practice in the Midland counties has come to him, which made it necessary for her to join him to-night – so she says. That's all it was – and I'm sorry I dragged you out.'

'Well,' said the hollow-turner, 'here be we seven mile from home, and night-time, and not a hoss or four-footed creeping thing to our name. I say, we'll have a mossel and a drop o' summat to strengthen our nerves afore we vamp all the way back again! My throat's as dry as a kex. What d'ye say, so's?'

They all concurred on the need for sustenance, and proceeded to the antique back street in which the red curtain of the tavern to which Winterborne had taken Grace was the only radiant object. As soon as they had stumbled down into the room Melbury ordered them to be served, when they made themselves comfortable by the long table, and stretched out their legs upon the herring-boned sand of the floor. Melbury himself, restless as usual, walked to the door while he waited for them, and looked up and down the street.

'Well – he's her husband,' Melbury said to himself, 'and let her take him back to her bed if she will!... But let her bear in mind that the woman walks and laughs somewhere at this very moment whose neck he'll be coling next year as he does hers to-night; and as he did Felice Charmond's last year; and Suke Damson's the year afore!... It's a forlorn hope for her; and God knows how it will end!'

Inside the inn the talk was also of the reunited pair.

'I'd gie her a good shaking if she were my maid; pretending to go out in garden, and leading folk a dozen-mile traipse that have got to get up at five o'clock to-morrow,' said a bark-ripper; who, not working regularly for Melbury, could afford to indulge in strong opinions.

'I don't speak so warm as that,' said the hollow-turner, 'but if 'tis right for couples to make a country talk about their parting for ever, and excite the neighbours, and then make fools of 'em like this, why, I haven't stood upon one leg for five-and-twenty year.'

All his listeners knew that when he alluded to his foot-lathe in these enigmatic terms the speaker meant to be impressive; and Creedle chimed in with, 'Ah, young women do wax wanton in these days! Why couldn't she ha' bode with her father, and been faithful!' Poor Creedle was thinking of his old employer.

'But this deceiving of folks is nothing unusual in matrimony,' said Farmer Cawtree. 'I know'd a man and wife – faith, I don't mind owning, as there's no strangers here, that the pair were my own relations – they'd be at it that hot one hour that you'd hear the poker, and the tongs, and the bellows, and the warming-pan, flee across the house with the movements of their vengeance; and the next hour you'd hear 'em singing "The Spotted Cow" together, as peaceable as two holy twins; yes – and very good voices they had, and would strike in like street ballet-singers to one another's support in the high notes.'

' 'Tis so with couples: they do make up differences in all manner of queer ways,' said the bark-ripper. 'I knowed a woman; and the husband o' her went away for four-and-twenty year. And one night he came home when she was sitting by the fire, and thereupon he sat down himself on the other side of the chimney-corner. "Well," says she, "have ye got any news?" "Don't know as I have," says he; "have you?" "No," says she, "except that my daughter by the husband that succeeded 'ee was married last month, which was a year after I was made a widow by him." "Oh! Anything else?" he says. "No," says she. And there they sat, one on each side of that chimney-corner, and were found by the neighbours sound asleep in their chairs, not having known what to talk about at all.'

'Well, I don't care who the man is,' said Creedle, 'it took a good deal to interest 'em, and that's true. It won't be the same with these.'

'No. He is such a projick, you see. And she is a wonderful scholar too!'

'What women do know nowadays!' observed the hollow-turner. 'You can't deceive 'em as you could in my time.'

'What they knowed then was not small,' said John Upjohn. 'Always a good deal more than the men! Why, when I went courting my wife that is now, the skilfulness that she would show in keeping me on her pretty side as she walked was beyond all belief. Perhaps you've noticed that she's got a pretty side to her face as well as a plain one?'

'I can't say I've noticed it particular much,' said the hollow-turner blandly.

'Well,' continued Upjohn, not disconcerted, 'she has. All women under the sun be prettier one side than t'other. And, as I was saying, the pains she would take to make me walk on the pretty side were unending! I warrant that whether we were going with the sun or against the sun, uphill or downhill, in wind or in lewth, that wart of hers was always towards the hedge, and that dimple towards me. There was I, too simple to see her wheelings and turnings; and she so artful, though two years younger, that she could lead me with a cotton thread, like a blind ram; for that was in the third climate of our courtship.... No: I don't think the women have got cleverer, for they was never otherwise.'

'How many climates may there be in courtship, Mr Upjohn?' inquired a youth – the same who had assisted at Winterborne's Christmas party.

'Five – from the coolest to the hottest – leastwise there was five in mine.'

'Can ye give us the chronicle of 'em, Mr Upjohn?'

'Yes – I could. I could certainly. But 'tis quite unnecessary. They'll come to ye by nater, young man, too soon for your good.'

'At present Mrs Fitzpiers can lead the doctor as your mis'ess could lead you,' the hollow-turner remarked. 'She's got him quite tame. But how long 'twill last I can't say. I happened to be setting a wire on the top of my garden one night when he met her on the other side of the hedge; and the way she queened it, and fenced, and kept that poor feller at a distance was enough to freeze yer blood. I should never have supposed it of such a girl.'

Melbury now returned to the room, and the men having declared themselves refreshed they all started on the homeward journey, which was by no means cheerless under the rays of the high moon. Having to walk the whole distance they came by a footpath rather shorter than the highway, though difficult except to those who knew the country well. This brought them by way of the church: and passing the graveyard they observed as they talked a motionless figure standing by the gate.

'I think it was Marty South,' said the hollow-turner parenthetically.

'I think 'twas; 'a was always a lonely maid,' said Upjohn. And they passed on homeward, and thought of the matter no more.

It was Marty, as they had supposed. That evening had been the particular one of the week upon which Grace and herself had been accustomed to privately deposit flowers on Giles's grave, and this was the first occasion since his death eight months earlier on which Grace had failed to keep her appointment. Marty had waited in the road just outside Melbury's, where her fellow-pilgrim had been wont to join her, till she was weary; and at last, thinking that Grace had missed her, and gone on alone, she followed the way to the church, but saw no Grace in front of her. It got later, and Marty continued her walk till she reached the churchyard gate; but still no Grace. Yet her sense of comradeship would not allow her to go on to the grave alone, and still thinking the delay had been unavoidable she stood there with her little basket of flowers in her clasped hands, and her feet chilled by the damp ground, till more than two hours had passed. She then heard the footsteps of Melbury's men, who presently passed on their return from the search. In the silence of the night Marty could not help hearing fragments of their conversation, from which she acquired a general idea of what had occurred, and that Mrs Fitzpiers was by that time in the arms of another man than Giles.

Immediately they had dropped down the hill she entered the churchyard, going to a secluded corner behind the bushes where rose the unadorned stone that marked the last bed of Giles Winterborne. As this solitary and silent girl stood there in the moonlight, a straight slim figure, clothed in a plaitless gown, the contours of womanhood so undeveloped as to be scarcely perceptible in her, the marks of poverty and toil effaced by the misty hour, she touched sublimity at points, and looked almost like a being who had rejected with indifference the attribute of sex for the loftier quality of abstract humanism. She stooped down and cleared away the withered flowers that Grace and herself had laid there the previous week, and put her fresh ones in their place.

'Now, my own, own love,' she whispered, 'you are mine, and only mine; for she has forgot 'ee at last, although for her you died! But I – whenever I get up I'll think of 'ee, and whenever I lie down I'll think of 'ee again. Whenever I plant the young larches I'll think that none can plant as you planted; and whenever I split a gad, and whenever I turn the cider wring, I'll say none could do it like you. If ever I forget your name let me forget home and heaven!... But no, no, my love, I never can forget 'ee; for you was a good man, and did good things!'

APPENDIX

GENERAL PREFACE TO THE WESSEX EDITION OF 1912

In accepting a proposal for a definite edition of these productions in prose and verse I have found an opportunity of classifying the novels under heads that show approximately the author's aim, if not his achievement, in each book of the series at the date of its composition. Sometimes the aim was lower than at other times; sometimes, where the intention was primarily high, force of circumstances (among which the chief were the necessities of magazine publication) compelled a modification, great or slight, of the original plan. Of a few, however, of the longer novels, and of many of the shorter tales, it may be assumed that they stand to-day much as they would have stood if no accidents had obstructed the channel between the writer and the public. That many of them, if any, stand as they would stand if written *now* is not to be supposed.

In the classification of these fictitious chronicles – for which the name of 'The Wessex Novels' was adopted, and is still retained – the first group is called 'Novels of Character and Environment', and contains those which approach most nearly to uninfluenced works; also one or two which, whatever their quality in some few of their episodes, may claim a verisimilitude in general treatment and detail.

The second group is distinguished as 'Romances and Fantasies', a sufficiently descriptive definition. The third class – 'Novels of Ingenuity' – show a not infrequent disregard of the probable in the chain of events, and depend for their interest mainly on the incidents themselves. They might also be characterized as 'Experiments', and were written for the nonce simply; though despite the artificiality of their fable some of their scenes are not without fidelity to life.[1]

It will not be supposed that these differences are distinctly perceptible in every page of every volume. It was inevitable that blendings and alternations should occur in all. Moreover, as it was not thought desirable in every instance to change the arrangement of the shorter stories to which readers have grown accustomed, certain of these may be found under headings to which an acute judgment might deny appropriateness.

It has sometimes been conceived of novels that evolve their action on a circumscribed scene – as do many (though not all) of these that they cannot be so inclusive in their exhibition of human nature as novels wherein the scenes cover large extents of country, in which events figure amid towns and cities, even wander over the four quarters of the globe. I am not concerned to argue this point further than to suggest that the conception is an untrue one in respect of the elementary passions. But I would state that the geographical limits of the stage here trodden were not absolutely forced upon the writer by circumstances; he forced them upon himself from judgment. I considered that our magnificent heritage from the Greeks in dramatic literature found sufficient room for a large proportion of its action in an extent of their country not much larger than the half-dozen counties here reunited under the old name of Wessex, that the domestic emotions have throbbed in Wessex nooks with as much intensity as in the palaces of Europe, and that, anyhow, there was quite enough human nature in Wessex for one man's literary purpose. So far was I possessed by this idea that I kept within the frontiers when it would have been easier to overleap them and give more cosmopolitan features to the narrative.

[1]Novels of Character and Environment: *Tess of the d'Urbervilles*, *Far From the Madding Crowd*, *Jude the Obscure*, *The Return of the Native*, *The Mayor of Casterbridge*, *The Woodlanders*, *Under the Greenwood Tree*, *Life's Little Ironies and A Few-Crusted Characters*, *Wessex Tales*.

Romances and Fantasies: *A Pair of Blue Eyes*, *The Trumpet-Major*, *Two on a Tower*, *The Well-beloved*, *A Group of Noble Dames*.

Novels of Ingenuity: *Desperate Remedies*, *The Hand of Ethelberta*, *A Laodicean*.

Thus, though the people in most of the novels (and in much of the shorter verse) are dwellers in a province bounded on the north by the Thames, on the south by the English Channel, on the east by a line running from Hayling Island to Windsor Forest, and on the west by the Cornish coast, they were meant to be typically and essentially those of any and every place where

> Thought's the slave of life, and life time's fool

– beings in whose hearts and minds that which is apparently local should be really universal.

But whatever the success of this intention, and the value of these novels as delineations of humanity, they have at least a humble supplementary quality of which I may be justified in reminding the reader, though it is one that was quite unintentional and unforeseen. At the dates represented in the various narrations things were like that in Wessex; the inhabitants lived in certain ways, engaged in certain occupations, kept alive certain customs, just as they are shown doing in these pages. And in particularizing such I have often been reminded of Boswell's remarks on the trouble to which he was put and the pilgrimages he was obliged to make to authenticate some detail, though the labour was one which would bring him no praise. Unlike his achievement, however, on which an error would as he says have brought discredit, if these country customs and vocations, obsolete and obsolescent, had been detailed wrongly, nobody would have discovered such errors to the end of Time. Yet I have instituted inquiries to correct tricks of memory, and striven against temptations to exaggerate, in order to preserve for my own satisfaction a fairly true record of a vanishing life.

It is advisable also to state here, in response to inquiries from readers interested in landscape, prehistoric antiquities, and especially old English architecture, that the description of these backgrounds has been done from the real – that is to say, has something real for its basis, however illusively treated. Many features of the first two kinds have been given under their existing names; for instance, the Vale of Blackmoor or Blakemore, Hambledon Hill, Bulbarrow, Nettlecombe Tout,

Dogbury Hill, High-Stoy, Bubb-Down Hill, The Devil's Kitchen, Cross-in-Hand, Long-Ash Lane, Benvill Lane, Giant's Hill, Crimmercrock Lane, and Stonehenge. The rivers Froom, or Frome, and Stour, are, of course, well known as such. And the further idea was that large towns and points tending to mark the outline of Wessex – such as Bath, Plymouth, The Start, Portland Bill, Southampton, etc. – should be named clearly. The scheme was not greatly elaborated, but whatever its value, the names remain still.

In respect of places described under fictitious or ancient names in the novels – for reasons that seemed good at the time of writing them – and kept up in the poems – discerning people have affirmed in print that they clearly recognize the originals: such as Shaftesbury in 'Shaston', Sturminster Newton in 'Stourcastle', Dorchester in 'Casterbridge', Salisbury Plain in 'The Great Plain', Cranborne Chase in 'The Chase', Beaminster in 'Emminster', Bere Regis in 'Kingsbere', Woodbury Hill in 'Greenhill', Wool Bridge in 'Wellbridge', Harfoot or Harput Lane in 'Stagfoot Lane', Hazlebury in 'Nuttlebury', Bridport in 'Port Bredy', Maiden Newton in 'Chalk Newton', a farm near Nettlecombe Tout in 'Flintcomb Ash', Sherborne in 'Sherton Abbas', Milton Abbey in 'Middleton Abbey', Cerne Abbas in 'Abbot's Cernel', Evershot in 'Evershed', Taunton in 'Toneborough', Bournemouth in 'Sandbourne', Winchester in 'Wintoncester', Oxford in 'Christminster', Reading in 'Aldbrickham', Newbury in 'Kennetbridge', Wantage in 'Alfredston', Basingstoke in 'Stoke Barehills', and so on. Subject to the qualifications above given, that no detail is guaranteed – that the portraiture of fictitiously named towns and villages was only suggested by certain real places, and wantonly wanders from inventorial descriptions of them – I do not contradict these keen hunters for the real; I am satisfied with their statements as at least an indication of their interest in the scenes.

Thus much for the novels. Turning now to the verse – to myself the more individual part of my literary fruitage – I would say that, unlike some of the fiction, nothing interfered with the writer's freedom in respect of its form or content.

Several of the poems – indeed many – were produced before novel-writing had been thought of as a pursuit; but few saw the light till all the novels had been published. The limited stage to which the majority of the latter confine their exhibitions has not been adhered to here in the same proportion, the dramatic part especially having a very broad theatre of action. It may thus relieve the circumscribed areas treated in the prose, if such relief be needed. To be sure, one might argue that by surveying Europe from a celestial point of vision – as in *The Dynasts* – that continent becomes virtually a province – a Wessex, an Attica, even a mere garden – and hence is made to conform to the principle of the novels, however far it outmeasures their region. But that may be as it will.

The few volumes filled by the verse cover a producing period of some eighteen years first and last, while the seventeen or more volumes of novels represent correspondingly about four-and-twenty years. One is reminded by this disproportion in time and result how much more concise and quintessential expression becomes when given in rhythmic form than when shaped in the language of prose.

One word on what has been called the present writer's philosophy of life, as exhibited more particularly in this metrical section of his compositions. Positive views on the Whence and the Wherefore of things have never been advanced by this pen as a consistent philosophy. Nor is it likely, indeed, that imaginative writings extending over more than forty years would exhibit a coherent scientific theory of the universe even if it had been attempted – of that universe concerning which Spencer owns to the 'paralyzing thought' that possibly there exists no comprehension of it anywhere. But such objectless consistency never has been attempted, and the sentiments in the following pages have been stated truly to be mere impressions of the moment, and not convictions or arguments.

That these impressions have been condemned as 'pessimistic' – as if that were a very wicked adjective – shows a curious muddle-mindedness. It must be obvious that there is a higher characteristic of philosophy than pessimism, or than meliorism, or even than the optimism of these critics – which is truth. Existence is either ordered in a certain way, or it is not so ordered, and conjectures which harmonize best with experience are removed above all comparison with other conjectures which do not so harmonize. So that to say one view is worse than other views without proving it erroneous implies the possibility of a false view being better or more expedient than a true view; and no pragmatic proppings can make that *idolum specus* stand on its feet, for it postulates a prescience denied to humanity.

And there is another consideration. Differing natures find their tongue in the presence of differing spectacles. Some natures become vocal at tragedy, some are made vocal by comedy, and it seems to me that to whichever of these aspects of life a writer's instinct for expression the more readily responds, to that he should allow it to respond. That before a contrasting side of things he remains undemonstrative need not be assumed to mean that he remains unperceiving.

It was my hope to add to these volumes of verse as many more as would make a fairly comprehensive cycle of the whole. I had wished that those in dramatic, ballad, and narrative form should include most of the cardinal situations which occur in social and public life, and those in lyric form a round of emotional experiences of some completeness. But

The petty done, the undone vast!

The more written the more seems to remain to be written; and the night cometh. I realize that these hopes and plans, except possibly to the extent of a volume or two, must remain unfulfilled.

October 1911 T.H.

Map of the
WESSEX
of the
Novels and Poems
Scale of Miles
Fictitious names as
Exonbury
Real names as
Portsmouth
Isles of Lyonnesse
St. Launce's
Plymouth
Bristol Channel
Bristol
Bath
Christminster
NORTH WESSEX
Alfredston
Marygreen
Castle Royal
Aldbrickham
Kennetbridge
Gaymead
MID WESSEX
Marlbury Downs
Inkpen Beacon
Stoke Barehills
Quartershot
UPPER WESSEX
The Great Plain
Stonehenge
Stour Head
Melchester
Wintoncester
Southampton
Portsmouth
Solentsea
The Island
The Great Forest
Sandbourne
Shaston
Sherton Abbas
Vale of Blackmore
Shottsford Forum
Casterbridge
Budmouth
Isle of Slingers
Deadmans Bay
Port Bredy
Pilsdon
Emminster
Ivell
Glaston
Fountall
Mendip Hills
Toneborough
Dunkery Beacon
Exon Moor
Downstaple
Tiverworthy
Silverthorn
Exonbury
Idmouth
Tor-upon-Sea
LOWER WESSEX
OUTER WESSEX
SOUTH WESSEX
The Channel
Emery Walker sc.

Everyman's Library, founded in 1906 and relaunched in 1991, aims to offer the most scholarly and permanent library in the English language of the world's classics. This volume is set in the classic typeface *Baskerville* and printed on acid-free, cream-wove paper with a sewn full cloth binding.

Finalist for the 1962 National Book Award for Fiction

Named to "Best Novels" lists by *Time*, *Newsweek*, the Modern Library, the New York Public Library, the American Library Association, *The Observer* (UK), and *The Guardian* (UK)

"A monumental artifact of contemporary American literature, almost as assured of longevity as the statues on Easter Island. . . . *Catch-22* is a novel that reminds us once again of all that we have taken for granted in our world and should not, the madness we try not to bother to notice, the deceptions and falsehoods we lack the will to try to distinguish from truth."

—JOHN W. ALDRIDGE, *THE NEW YORK TIMES BOOK REVIEW* (1986)

"*Catch-22* I still think is one of the most phenomenal novels in the English language because of Heller's ability to make you laugh literally on every page while writing about the darkest of all human conditions, wartime. I'm still blown away by that book."

—CARL HIAASEN, *ENTERTAINMENT WEEKLY* (2010)

"Wildly original, brilliantly comic, brutally gruesome, it is a dazzling performance that will probably outrage nearly as many readers as it delights. . . . *Catch-22* is a funny book—vulgarly, bitterly, savagely funny."

—ORVILLE PRESCOTT, *THE NEW YORK TIMES BOOK REVIEW* (1961)

"*Catch-22* is a bitter, anguished joke of a novel that embraces the existential absurdity of war without ever quite succumbing to it."

—LEV GROSSMAN, *TIME* MAGAZINE'S "ALL TIME 100 NOVELS" (2005)

"You will meet in this astonishing novel, certainly one of the most original in years, madmen of every rank. Page after page, you will howl, you will roar. You may even fall off your chair as I did. Suddenly you will sit up and mumble: 'What's so funny?' To call it the finest comic novel of our day is faulting it. If Joseph Heller writes no other book, he will be well remembered for this apocalyptic masterpiece."

—STUDS TERKEL, *CHICAGO SUN-TIMES* (1961)

"A novel of great power and commanding skill. One of the very best to come out of the second world war."

—*NEWSWEEK* (1961)

BY JOSEPH HELLER

Catch as Catch Can

Portrait of an Artist, as an Old Man

Closing Time

Picture This

No Laughing Matter (with Speed Vogel)

God Knows

Good as Gold

Something Happened

Catch-22

JERRY BAUR

Joseph Heller was born in Brooklyn, New York, in 1923. In 1961, he published *Catch-22*, which became a bestseller and, in 1970, a film. He went on to write such novels as *Something Happened*, *God Knows*, *Picture This*, *Closing Time* (the sequel to *Catch-22*), and *Portrait of an Artist, as an Old Man.* Heller died in December 1999.

CATCH-22

50TH ANNIVERSARY EDITION

Joseph Heller

Introduction by Christopher Buckley

Simon & Schuster Paperbacks

NEW YORK · LONDON · TORONTO · SYDNEY

Simon & Schuster Paperbacks
A Division of Simon & Schuster, Inc.
1230 Avenue of the Americas
New York, NY 10020

This book is a work of fiction. Names, characters, places, and incidents either are products of the author's imagination or are used fictitiously. Any resemblance to actual events or locales or persons, living or dead, is entirely coincidental.

This Simon & Schuster trade paperback edition April 2011

SIMON & SCHUSTER PAPERBACKS and colophon are registered trademarks of Simon & Schuster, Inc.

Manufactured in the United States of America

15 17 19 20 18 16

Library of Congress Cataloging-in-Publication Data

Heller, Joseph.
Catch-22 / Joseph Heller
p. cm.
I. World War II, 1939–1945—Fiction. I. Title
PS3558.E476C3 1994
813'.54—dc20 94-13984

ISBN 978-1-4516-2117-4
ISBN 978-1-4516-2665-0 (pbk)
ISBN 978-1-4516-3296-5 (ebook)

Page 522 represents an extension of this copyright page.

To my mother
and to my wife, Shirley,
and my children, Erica and Ted
(1961)

To Candida Donadio, literary agent,
and Robert Gottlieb, editor.
Colleagues.
(1994)

INTRODUCTION

There was only one catch and that was Catch-22, which specified that a concern for one's own safety in the face of dangers that were real and immediate was the process of a rational mind. Orr was crazy and he could be grounded. All he had to do was ask; and as soon as he did, he would no longer be crazy and would have to fly more missions. Orr would be crazy to fly more missions and sane if he didn't, but if he was sane he had to fly them. If he flew them he was crazy and didn't have to; but if he didn't want to he was sane and had to. Yossarian was moved very deeply by the absolute simplicity of this clause of Catch-22 and let out a respectful whistle.

"That's some catch, that Catch-22," he observed.

"It's the best there is," Doc Daneeka agreed.

The phrase "Catch-22" has so permeated American language—or embedded itself, to put it in Desert Storm terminology—that we deploy it almost every day, usually to describe an encounter with the Department of Motor Vehicles. Its usage is so common that it's right there in the dictionary. Not many book titles end up being (sorry; unavoidable) catchphrases. My own *American Heritage Dictionary* defines it as: "1.a A situation in which a desired outcome or solution is impossible to attain because of a set of inherently illogical rules or conditions. *In the Catch-22 of a close repertoire, only music that is already familiar is thought to deserve familiarity. (Joseph McLennan).*"

Joseph . . . who? But it's possible, even likely in fact, that the other Joseph would be amused at not being mentioned until the very bottom of the entry. I can hear him chuckling and asking, "And how many copies of the *American Heritage Dictionary* have they sold so far?" I don't know, but my guess is, not as many as *Catch-22*, which, in the fifty years since it first appeared in October 1961, has sold over ten million.

In his memoir *Now and Then*, published the year he died, Heller tells us that he wrote the first chapter of his masterpiece in longhand on a yellow legal pad in 1953. It was published two years later in the quarterly *New American Writing #7*, under the title "Catch-18." Also in that number were stories by A. A. Alvarez, Dylan Thomas, Heinrich Böll, and one by someone calling himself "Jean-Louis"—Jack Kerouac, a piece from a book he was writing called *On The Road*. *Catch-22* and *On The Road*? Not a bad issue of *New American Writing*, that.

The full story of how *Catch-22* came about is told in Tracy Daugherty's fascinating new biography, *Just One Catch*. Briefly: the novel grew out of Heller's experiences as a bombardier in World War II, flying missions out of Corsica over Italy. It was seven years in the writing, while its author worked in the promotional departments of *McCall's* and *Time* magazines. Just before being published, the novel had to be retitled, when it was learned that Leon Uris was about to bring out a World War II novel called *Mila 18*. Which is why you didn't have a Catch-18 experience today at the Department of Motor Vehicles.

The novel got some good reviews, some mixed reviews, and some pretty nasty reviews. *The New Yorker*'s was literary waterboarding: ". . . doesn't even seem to have been written; instead it gives the impression of having been shouted onto paper . . . what remains is a debris of sour jokes." Heller dwells on that particular review in his memoir: "I am tempted to drown in my own gloating laughter even as I set this down. What restrains me is the knowledge that the lashings still smart, even after so many years, and if I ever pretend to be a jolly good sport about them, as I am doing now, I am only pretending." (That was Joe Heller. Whatever flaws he may have had as a writer and human being, he absolutely possessed what Hemingway called the writer's most essential tool: a first-class bullshit detector.) Evelyn Waugh, one of Heller's literary heroes, pointedly declined to provide a blurb for the jacket. *Catch* never won a literary prize and never made the *New York Times* hardcover bestseller list.

But a number of people fell for it—hard. To quote the novel's first line, "It was love at first sight." They took it up as a cause, not just a book, with evangelical ardor. Among these were S. J. Perelman, Art Buchwald, and TV newsman John Chancellor, who printed up YOSSARIAN LIVES bumper stickers. (The phrase eventually became an antiwar slogan, the "Kilroy Was Here" of the Vietnam era.) Word spread: *you have to read this book*. In England, it went straight to the top of the bestseller lists. A reviewer there called it, "*The Naked and the Dead* scripted for the Marx Brothers, a kind of *From Here to Insanity*."

Back on native soil, the novel took off after it was published in paperback. By April 1963, it had sold over a million copies, and by the end of the decade had gone through thirty printings. Daugherty concludes his *Catch-22* chapter with an arresting quote from a letter Heller received a few months after the hardcover came out: "For sixteen years, I have been waiting for the great anti-war book which I knew WWII must produce. I rather doubted, however, that it would come out of America; I would have guessed Germany. I am happy to have been wrong . . . thank you." The writer was historian Stephen Ambrose.

Joe Heller began work on his World War II novel around the time the Korean War was winding down and published it just as another American war, in Vietnam, was getting under way. He was not the first twentieth-century author to find dark humor in war. Jaroslav Hašek's unfinished classic *The Good Soldier Šchweik*—a book Heller knew well—got there first. But *Catch*'s tone of outraged bewilderment in the face of carnage and a deranged military mentality set the tone for the satires against the arms race and Vietnam. *Dr. Strangelove* appeared in 1964. Robert Altman's 1970 film *M*A*S*H,* with its Osterizer blend of black humor and stark horror, is a direct descendant of *Catch-22.* Ironically, that movie appeared the same year as Mike Nichols's film version of *Catch*. *M*A*S*H* is the better movie by far, but in a nice bit of irony, it propelled the novel—finally!—onto American bestseller lists.

When Heller died in December 1999, James Webb, the highly decorated Marine platoon leader, novelist (*Fields of Fire*), journalist, moviemaker, and now United States senator for Virginia, wrote an appreciation in *The Wall Street Journal*. Webb, a self-described Air Force brat, had first read and liked the novel as a teenager growing up on a Nebraska air base. He reread it in a foxhole in Vietnam in 1969, during a lull in fierce combat that took the lives of many of his men. One day, as he lay there feverish, insides crawling with hookworm from bad water, one of Webb's men began laughing "uncontrollably, waving a book in the air. He crawled underneath my poncho hooch and held the book in front of me, open at a favorite page.

"'Read this!' he said, unable to stop laughing. 'Read it!'"

Webb wrote, "In the next few days I devoured the book again. It mattered not to me that Joseph Heller was then protesting the war in which I was fighting, and it matters not a whit to me today. In his book, from that lonely place of blood and misery and disease, I found a soul mate who helped me face the next day and all the days and months that followed."

Soul mate. *Catch-22*'s admirers cross boundaries—ideological, generational, geographical. Daugherty relates a very funny anecdote about Bertrand Russell, the pacifist and philosopher. He had praised the book in print and invited Heller to visit him while in England. (Russell was then in his nineties.) When Heller presented himself at the door, Russell flew into a rage, screaming, "Go away, damn you! Never come back here again!" A perplexed Heller fled, only to be intercepted by Russell's manservant, who explained, "Mr. Russell thought you said 'Edward Teller.'" The ideological distance between Jim Webb and Bertrand Russell can be measured in light years. An author who reaches both of them exerts something like universal appeal.

Returning to a favorite book, one approaches with trepidation. Will it be as good as one remembers it? Has it dated? As Heller's friend and fan Christopher Hitchens would say, "Has it time-traveled?" Any answer is subjective, but a fifty-year-old book that continues to sell 85,000 copies a year must be doing something right, time travel–wise—even discounting the number assigned in the classroom.

I asked Salman Rushdie, another friend and admirer of Heller's, what he thought about the book all these years later.

"I think *Catch-22* stands the test of time pretty well," he replied, "because Heller's language-comedy, the twisted-sane logic of his twisted-insane world, is as funny now as it was when the book came out. The bits of *Catch-22* that survive best are the craziest bits: Milo Minderbinder's chocolate-coated cotton-wool, Major Major Major Major's name, and of course the immortal Catch itself ('it's the best there is'). The only storyline that now seems sentimental, even mawkish, is the one about 'Nately's whore.' Oh well. As Joe E. Brown said to Jack Lemmon, 'Nobody's perfect.'"

A book resonates along different bandwidths as it ages. *Catch-22*'s first readers were largely of the generation that went through World War II. For them, it provided a startlingly fresh take, a much-needed, much-delayed laugh at the terror and madness they endured. To the Vietnam generation, enduring its own terror and madness, crawling through malarial rice paddies while pacifying hamlets with napalm and Zippo lighters, the book amounted to existential comfort and the knowledge that they were not alone. (Note, too, that *Catch* ends with Yossarian setting off AWOL for Sweden, which, before becoming famous for IKEA and girls with dragon tattoos, was a haven for Vietnam-era draft evaders.)

As for *Catch*'s current readers, it's not hard to imagine a brave but frustrated American marine huddling in his Afghan foxhole, drawing sustenance and companionship from these pages in the midst of fighting an unwinnable war against stone-age fanatics.

Daugherty tells how Heller was required to take a barrage of psychological tests for a magazine job. (Fodder, surely, for an episode of *Mad Men*.) The color cards he was shown conjured in his mind terrible images of gore and amputated limbs. He mentioned to one of his examiners that he was working on a novel. One of them asked, *Oh, what's it about*? Joe wrote in his memoir forty years later, "That question still makes me squirm."

There's a certain numerology about *Catch-22*: Yossarian, helpless and furious as the brass keep raising the number of missions he has to fly before he can go home. He's Sisyphus, with attitude. Then there's the title itself, a sort of algorithm expressing the predicament of the soldier up against an implacable, martial bureaucracy. For us civilians, the algorithm describes a more prosaic conundrum, that of standing before the soft-faced functionary telling us that the car cannot be registered until we produce a document that *does not exist*. Bureaucracy, as Hannah Arendt defined it: the rule of nobody.

Roll credits. *Catch-22* is Joe Heller's book, but it did not arrive on the shelves all by itself. His literary agent, Candida Donadio, got the first chapter into the hands of Arabel Porter, editor of *New American Writing*, and then into the all-important hands of Robert Gottlieb at Simon and Schuster. Gottlieb, one of the great book editors of his day—he later became head of Alfred A. Knopf—played a critical role in shaping the text. Daugherty describes how the two of them pieced together a jigsaw puzzle from a total of nine separate manuscripts; *Catch-22* seems to have been stitched together with no less care and effort than the Bayeux Tapestry. Their collaboration was astonishingly devoid of friction. Gottlieb was a genius, but Heller was an editor's dream, that rare thing—an author without proprietary sensitivity, willing to make any change, to (in Scott Fitzgerald's wonderful phrase) murder any darling. As the work proceeded, it took on within the offices of Simon and Schuster "the aura of a Manhattan Project."

Nina Bourne, advertising manager at S&S, was passionate about the book and promoted it relentlessly after it initially faltered, with a zeal that would induce a sigh of envy in any author's breast. The jacket design with the red soldier dangling like a marionette against a blue background became iconic. It was the work of Paul Bacon, himself another World War II veteran, who also designed the original covers for *Slaughterhouse-Five*, *Rosemary's Baby*, *One Flew Over the Cuckoo's Nest*, *Ragtime*, and *Shogun*.

It was a fertile time for letters. While Heller was conjuring Yossarian and Major Major Major Major and Milo Minderbinder and Chaplain Tappman and the other members of the 488 Bomb Squadron, J. P. Donleavy was writing *The Ginger Man*, Ken Kesey was at work on *Cuckoo's Nest*, Thomas Pynchon on *V*. Heller's good friend Kurt Vonnegut was typing away at *Cat's Cradle*.

Joseph Heller will forever be known as the author of *Catch-22*—and who wouldn't be happy to wear that laurel? But in the opinion of some, including Bob Gottlieb, it is not his best novel. According to this view, that honor belongs to *Something Happened*, Heller's dark and brilliant 1974 novel about tragic office worker and family man Bob Slocum. The reviewer for *The New York Times* wryly observed that to film *Catch-22*, Mike Nichols assembled a fleet of eighteen B-25 bombers—in effect the world's twelfth largest air force. To turn *Something Happened* into a movie, the reviewer ventured, would cost roughly nothing.

I put it to Joe once, after a martini or two: So, did he think *Something Happened* was a better book?

He smiled and shrugged, "Who can choose?"

American literature is deplorably replete with books that secured fame for their authors, but little fortune. Think of poor old Melville schlepping about the streets of Manhattan as a customs inspector, having earned a lifetime profit of about $500 for *his* hyphenated masterpiece, *Moby-Dick*.

Joe made out rather better. Simon and Schuster paid him an advance of $1,500 (about $11,000 today). If the paperback royalties didn't make him rich, they certainly made him comfortable. The movie rights went for a tidy price, and larger paychecks lay ahead. Not bad for a kid who grew up poor in Coney Island. In fact, one might ask, *What's the catch?*

We became friends in his final years. I loved him. For someone who had flown sixty missions in a world war, who had endured a devastating, near-fatal illness (Guillain-Barré), who had gone through a rough and somewhat public divorce, Joe seemed to me a surprisingly *joyous* person. He sought joy, and seemed to find it often enough—in his myriad and devoted friends; in good food and dry martinis; in his wife Valerie, his son, Ted, and his daughter, Erica, who has written a touching and frank account of growing up as an Eloise of the Apthorp apartment building in Manhattan.

In that book, *Yossarian Slept Here*, she writes, "When *Catch* was finally beginning to make a real name for itself . . . my parents would often jump into a cab at night and ride around to all of the city's leading bookstores in order to see that jaunty riot of red, white and blue and the crooked little man, the covers of 'the book,' piled up in towers and pyramids, stacked in all the nighttime store windows. Was anything ever again as much fun for either of them, I wonder?"

A few months before Joe died, I wrote him in the midst of a too-long book tour, in somewhat low spirits. His tough love and sharp-elbowed humor always yanked me back from the brink of acedia. This time there were no jokes; instead something like resignation.

"The life of a novelist," he wrote me, "is almost inevitably destined for anguish, humiliations, and disappointment—when you get to read the two chapters in my new novel I've just finished you will recognize why."

That book, *Portrait of the Artist, as an Old Man*, is a sad one, about a novelist who has had great success early on, only to have less in later years. It was published after Joe died.

So perhaps in the end, there always *is* a catch. But the one Joe Heller left us remains, even after all these years, the best catch of all.

—Christopher Buckley
December 2010

THERE WAS ONLY ONE CATCH . . .
AND THAT WAS CATCH-22.

The island of Pianosa lies in the Mediterranean Sea eight miles south of Elba. It is very small and obviously could not accommodate all of the actions described. Like the setting of this novel, the characters, too, are fictitious.

CATCH-22

1

The Texan

It was love at first sight.

The first time Yossarian saw the chaplain he fell madly in love with him.

Yossarian was in the hospital with a pain in his liver that fell just short of being jaundice. The doctors were puzzled by the fact that it wasn't quite jaundice. If it became jaundice they could treat it. If it didn't become jaundice and went away they could discharge him. But this just being short of jaundice all the time confused them.

Each morning they came around, three brisk and serious men with efficient mouths and inefficient eyes, accompanied by brisk and serious Nurse Duckett, one of the ward nurses who didn't like Yossarian. They read the chart at the foot of the bed and asked impatiently about the pain. They seemed irritated when he told them it was exactly the same.

"Still no movement?" the full colonel demanded.

The doctors exchanged a look when he shook his head.

"Give him another pill."

Nurse Duckett made a note to give Yossarian another pill, and the four of them moved along to the next bed. None of the nurses liked Yossarian. Actually, the pain in his liver had gone away, but Yossarian didn't say anything and the doctors never suspected. They just suspected that he had been moving his bowels and not telling anyone.

Yossarian had everything he wanted in the hospital. The food wasn't too bad, and his meals were brought to him in bed. There were extra rations of fresh meat, and during the hot part of the afternoon he and the others were served chilled fruit juice or chilled chocolate milk. Apart from the doctors and the nurses, no one ever disturbed him. For a little while in the morning he had to censor letters, but he was free after that to spend the rest of each day lying around idly with a clear conscience. He was comfortable in the hospital, and it was easy to stay on because he always ran a temperature of 101. He was even more comfortable than Dunbar, who had to keep falling down on his face in order to get *his* meals brought to him in bed.

After he made up his mind to spend the rest of the war in the hospital, Yossarian wrote letters to everyone he knew saying that he was in the hospital but never mentioning why. One day he had a better idea. To everyone he knew he wrote that he was going on a very dangerous mission. "They asked for volunteers. It's very dangerous, but someone has to do it. I'll write you the instant I get back." And he had not written anyone since.

All the officer patients in the ward were forced to censor letters written by all the enlisted-men patients, who were kept in residence in wards of their own. It was a monotonous job, and Yossarian was disappointed to learn that the lives of enlisted men were only slightly more interesting than the lives of officers. After the first day he had no curiosity at all. To break the monotony he invented games. Death to all modifiers, he declared one day, and out of every letter that passed through his hands went every adverb and every adjective. The next day he made war on articles. He reached a much higher plane of creativity the following day when he blacked out everything in the letters but *a*, *an* and *the*. That erected more dynamic intralinear tensions, he felt, and in just about every case left a message far more universal. Soon he was proscribing parts of salutations and signatures and leaving the text untouched. One time he blacked out all but the salutation "Dear Mary" from a letter, and at the bottom he wrote, "I yearn for you tragically. A. T. Tappman, Chaplain, U.S. Army." A. T. Tappman was the group chaplain's name.

When he had exhausted all possibilities in the letters, he began attacking the names and addresses on the envelopes, obliterating whole homes and streets, annihilating entire metropolises with careless flicks of his wrist as though he were God. Catch-22 required that each censored letter bear the censoring officer's name. Most letters he didn't read at all. On those he didn't read at all he wrote his own name. On those he did read he wrote, "Washington Irving." When that grew monotonous he wrote, "Irving Washington." Censoring the envelopes had serious repercussions, produced a ripple of anxiety on some ethereal military echelon that floated a C.I.D. man back into the ward posing as a patient. They all knew he was a C.I.D. man because he kept inquiring about an officer named Irving or Washington and because after his first day there he wouldn't censor letters. He found them too monotonous.

It was a good ward this time, one of the best he and Dunbar had ever enjoyed. With them this time was the twenty-four-year-old fighter-pilot captain with the sparse golden mustache who had been shot into the Adriatic Sea in midwinter and had not even caught cold. Now the summer was upon them, the captain had not been shot down, and he said he had the grippe. In the bed on Yossarian's right, still lying amorously on his belly, was the startled captain with malaria in his blood and a mosquito bite on his ass. Across the aisle from Yossarian was Dunbar, and next to Dunbar was the artillery captain with whom Yossarian had stopped playing chess. The captain was a good chess player, and the games were always interesting. Yossarian had stopped playing chess with him because the games were so interesting they were foolish. Then there was the educated Texan from Texas who looked like someone in Technicolor and felt, patriotically, that people of means—decent folk—should be given more votes than drifters, whores, criminals, degenerates, atheists and indecent folk—people without means.

Yossarian was unspringing rhythms in the letters the day they brought the Texan in. It was another quiet, hot, untroubled day. The heat pressed heavily on the roof, stifling sound. Dunbar was lying motionless on his back again with his eyes staring up at the ceiling like a doll's. He was working hard at increasing his life span. He did it by cultivating boredom. Dunbar was working so hard at increasing his life span that Yossarian thought he was dead. They put the Texan in a bed in the middle of the ward, and it wasn't long before he donated his views.

Dunbar sat up like a shot. "That's it," he cried excitedly. "There was something missing—all the time I knew there was something missing—and now I know what it is." He banged his fist down into his palm. "No patriotism," he declared.

"You're right," Yossarian shouted back. "You're right, you're right, you're right. The hot dog, the Brooklyn Dodgers. Mom's apple pie. That's what everyone's fighting for. But who's fighting for the decent folk? Who's fighting for more votes for the decent folk? There's no patriotism, that's what it is. And no matriotism, either."

The warrant officer on Yossarian's left was unimpressed. "Who gives a shit?" he asked tiredly, and turned over on his side to go to sleep.

The Texan turned out to be good-natured, generous and likable. In three days no one could stand him.

He sent shudders of annoyance scampering up ticklish spines, and everybody fled from him—everybody but the soldier in white, who had no choice. The soldier in white was encased from head to toe in plaster and gauze. He had two useless legs and two useless arms. He had been smuggled into the ward during the night, and the men had no idea he was among them until they awoke in the morning and saw the two strange legs hoisted from the hips, the two strange arms anchored up perpendicularly, all four limbs pinioned strangely in air by lead weights suspended darkly above him that never moved. Sewn into the bandages over the insides of both elbows were zippered lips through which he was fed clear fluid from a clear jar. A silent zinc pipe rose from the cement on his groin and was coupled to a slim rubber hose that carried waste from his kidneys and dripped it efficiently into a clear, stoppered jar on the floor. When the jar on the floor was full, the jar feeding his elbow was empty, and the two were simply switched quickly so that stuff could drip back into him. All they ever really saw of the soldier in white was a frayed black hole over his mouth.

The soldier in white had been filed next to the Texan, and the Texan sat sideways on his own bed and talked to him throughout the morning, afternoon and evening in a pleasant, sympathetic drawl. The Texan never minded that he got no reply.

Temperatures were taken twice a day in the ward. Early each morning and late each afternoon Nurse Cramer entered with a jar full of thermometers and worked her way up one side of the ward and down the other, distributing a thermometer to each patient. She managed the soldier in white by inserting a thermometer into the hole over his mouth and leaving it balanced there on the lower rim. When she returned to the man in the first bed, she took his thermometer and recorded his temperature, and then moved on to the next bed and continued around the ward again. One afternoon when she had completed her first circuit of the ward and came a second time to the soldier in white, she read his temperature and discovered that he was dead.

"Murderer," Dunbar said quietly.

The Texan looked up at him with an uncertain grin.

"Killer," Yossarian said.

"What are you talkin' about?" the Texan asked nervously.

"You murdered him," said Dunbar.

"You killed him," said Yossarian.

The Texan shrank back. "You fellas are crazy. I didn't even touch him."

"You murdered him," said Dunbar.

"I heard you kill him," said Yossarian.

"You killed him because he was a nigger," Dunbar said.

"You fellas are crazy," the Texan cried. "They don't allow niggers in here. They got a special place for niggers."

"The sergeant smuggled him in," Dunbar said.

"The Communist sergeant," said Yossarian.

"And you knew it."

The warrant officer on Yossarian's left was unimpressed by the entire incident of the soldier in white. The warrant officer was unimpressed by everything and never spoke at all unless it was to show irritation.

The day before Yossarian met the chaplain, a stove exploded in the mess hall and set fire to one side of the kitchen. An intense heat flashed through the area. Even in Yossarian's ward, almost three hundred feet away, they could hear the roar of the blaze and the sharp cracks of flaming timber. Smoke sped past the orange-tinted windows. In about fifteen minutes the crash trucks from the airfield arrived to fight the fire. For a frantic half hour it was touch and go. Then the firemen began to get the upper hand. Suddenly there was the monotonous old drone of bombers returning from a mission, and the firemen had to roll up their hoses and speed back to the field in case one of the planes crashed and caught fire. The planes landed safely. As soon as the last one was down, the firemen wheeled their trucks around and raced back up the hill to resume their fight with the fire at the hospital. When they got there, the blaze was out. It had died of its own accord, expired completely without even an ember to be watered down, and there was nothing for the disappointed firemen to do but drink tepid coffee and hang around trying to screw the nurses.

The chaplain arrived the day after the fire. Yossarian was busy expurgating all but romance words from the letters when the chaplain sat down in a chair between the beds and asked him how he was feeling. He had placed himself a bit to one side, and the captain's bars on the tab of his shirt collar were all the insignia Yossarian could see. Yossarian had no idea who he was and just took it for granted that he was either another doctor or another madman.

"Oh, pretty good," he answered. "I've got a slight pain in my liver and I haven't been the most regular of fellows, I guess, but all in all I must admit that I feel pretty good."

"That's good," said the chaplain.

"Yes," Yossarian said. "Yes, that is good."

"I meant to come around sooner," the chaplain said, "but I really haven't been well."

"That's too bad," Yossarian said.

"Just a head cold," the chaplain added quickly.

"I've got a fever of a hundred and one," Yossarian added just as quickly.

"That's too bad," said the chaplain.

"Yes," Yossarian agreed. "Yes, that is too bad."

The chaplain fidgeted. "Is there anything I can do for you?" he asked after a while.

"No, no." Yossarian sighed. "The doctors are doing all that's humanly possible, I suppose."

"No, no." The chaplain colored faintly. "I didn't mean anything like that. I meant cigarettes . . . or books . . . or . . . toys."

"No, no," Yossarian said. "Thank you. I have everything I need, I suppose—everything but good health."

"That's too bad."

"Yes," Yossarian said. "Yes, that is too bad."

The chaplain stirred again. He looked from side to side a few times, then gazed up at the ceiling, then down at the floor. He drew a deep breath.

"Lieutenant Nately sends his regards," he said.

Yossarian was sorry to hear they had a mutual friend. It seemed there was a basis to their conversation after all. "You know Lieutenant Nately?" he asked regretfully.

"Yes, I know Lieutenant Nately quite well."

"He's a bit loony, isn't he?"

The chaplain's smile was embarrassed. "I'm afraid I couldn't say. I don't think I know him that well."

"You can take my word for it," Yossarian said. "He's as goofy as they come."

The chaplain weighed the next silence heavily and then shattered it with an abrupt question. "You are Captain Yossarian, aren't you?"

"Nately had a bad start. He came from a good family."

"Please excuse me," the chaplain persisted timorously. "I may be committing a very grave error. Are you Captain Yossarian?"

"Yes," Captain Yossarian confessed. "I am Captain Yossarian."

"Of the 256th Squadron?"

"Of the fighting 256th Squadron," Yossarian replied. "I didn't know there were any other Captain Yossarians. As far as I know, I'm the only Captain Yossarian I know, but that's only as far as I know."

"I see," the chaplain said unhappily.

"That's two to the fighting eighth power," Yossarian pointed out, "if you're thinking of writing a symbolic poem about our squadron."

"No," mumbled the chaplain. "I'm not thinking of writing a symbolic poem about your squadron."

Yossarian straightened sharply when he spied the tiny silver cross on the other side of the chaplain's collar. He was thoroughly astonished, for he had never really talked with a chaplain before.

"You're a chaplain," he exclaimed ecstatically. "I didn't know you were a chaplain."

"Why, yes," the chaplain answered. "Didn't you know I was a chaplain?"

"Why, no. I didn't know you were a chaplain." Yossarian stared at him with a big, fascinated grin. "I've never really seen a chaplain before."

The chaplain flushed again and gazed down at his hands. He was a slight man of about thirty-two with tan hair and brown diffident eyes. His face was narrow and rather pale. An innocent nest of ancient pimple pricks lay in the basin of each cheek. Yossarian wanted to help him.

"Can I do anything at all to help you?" the chaplain asked.

Yossarian shook his head, still grinning. "No, I'm sorry. I have everything I need and I'm quite comfortable. In fact, I'm not even sick."

"That's good." As soon as the chaplain said the words, he was sorry and shoved his knuckles into his mouth with a giggle of alarm, but Yossarian remained silent and disappointed him. "There are other men in the group I must visit," he apologized finally. "I'll come to see you again, probably tomorrow."

"Please do that," Yossarian said.

"I'll come only if you want me to," the chaplain said, lowering his head shyly. "I've noticed that I make many of the men uncomfortable."

Yossarian glowed with affection. "I want you to," he said. "You won't make me uncomfortable."

The chaplain beamed gratefully and then peered down at a slip of paper he had been concealing in his hand all the while. He counted along the beds in the ward, moving his lips, and then centered his attention dubiously on Dunbar.

"May I inquire," he whispered softly, "if that is Lieutenant Dunbar?"

"Yes," Yossarian answered loudly, "that is Lieutenant Dunbar."

"Thank you," the chaplain whispered. "Thank you very much. I must visit with him. I must visit with every member of the group who is in the hospital."

"Even those in the other wards?" Yossarian asked.

"Even those in the other wards."

"Be careful in those other wards, Father," Yossarian warned. "That's where they keep the mental cases. They're filled with lunatics."

"It isn't necessary to call me Father," the chaplain explained. "I'm an Anabaptist."

"I'm dead serious about those other wards," Yossarian continued grimly. "M.P.s won't protect you, because they're craziest of all. I'd go with you myself, but I'm scared stiff. Insanity is contagious. This is the only sane ward in the whole hospital. Everybody is crazy but us. This is probably the only sane ward in the whole world, for that matter."

The chaplain rose quickly and edged away from Yossarian's bed, and then nodded with a conciliating smile and promised to conduct himself with appropriate caution. "And now I must visit with Lieutenant Dunbar," he said. Still he lingered, remorsefully. "How is Lieutenant Dunbar?" he asked at last.

"As good as they go," Yossarian assured him. "A true prince. One of the finest, least dedicated men in the whole world."

"I didn't mean that," the chaplain answered, whispering again. "Is he very sick?"

"No, he isn't very sick. In fact, he isn't sick at all."

"That's good." The chaplain sighed with relief.

"Yes," Yossarian said. "Yes, that is good."

"A chaplain," Dunbar said when the chaplain had visited him and gone. "Did you see that? A chaplain."

"Wasn't he sweet?" said Yossarian. "Maybe they should give him three votes."

"Who's they?" Dunbar demanded suspiciously.

In a bed in the small private section at the end of the ward, always working ceaselessly behind the green plyboard partition, was the solemn middle-aged colonel who was visited every day by a gentle, sweet-faced woman with curly ash-blond hair who was not a nurse and not a Wac and not a Red Cross girl but who nevertheless appeared faithfully at the hospital in Pianosa each afternoon wearing pretty pastel summer dresses that were very smart and white leather pumps with heels half high at the base of nylon seams that were inevitably straight. The colonel was in Communications, and he was kept busy day and night transmitting glutinous messages from the interior into square pads of gauze which he sealed meticulously and delivered to a covered white pail that stood on the night table beside his bed. The colonel was gorgeous. He had a cavernous mouth, cavernous cheeks, cavernous, sad, mildewed eyes. His face was the color of clouded silver. He coughed quietly, gingerly, and dabbed the pads slowly at his lips with a distaste that had become automatic.

The colonel dwelt in a vortex of specialists who were still specializing in trying to determine what was troubling him. They hurled lights in his eyes to see if he could see, rammed needles into nerves to hear if he could feel. There was a urologist for his urine, a lymphologist for his lymph, an endocrinologist for his endocrines, a psychologist for his psyche, a dermatologist for his derma; there was a pathologist for his pathos, a cystologist for his cysts, and a bald and pedantic cetologist from the zoology department at Harvard who had been shanghaied ruthlessly into the Medical Corps by a faulty anode in an I.B.M. machine and spent his sessions with the dying colonel trying to discuss *Moby Dick* with him.

The colonel had really been investigated. There was not an organ of his body that had not been drugged and derogated, dusted and dredged, fingered and photographed, removed, plundered and replaced. Neat, slender and erect, the woman touched him often as she sat by his bedside and was the epitome of stately sorrow each time she smiled. The colonel was tall, thin and stooped. When he rose to walk, he bent forward even more, making a deep cavity of his body, and placed his feet down very carefully, moving ahead by inches from the knees down. There were violet pools under his eyes. The woman spoke softly, softer even than the colonel coughed, and none of the men in the ward ever heard her voice.

In less than ten days the Texan cleared the ward. The artillery captain broke first, and after that the exodus started. Dunbar, Yossarian and the fighter captain all bolted the same morning. Dunbar stopped having dizzy spells, and the fighter captain blew his nose. Yossarian told the doctors that the pain in his liver had gone away. It was as easy as that. Even the warrant officer fled. In less than ten days, the Texan drove everybody in the ward back to duty—everybody but the C.I.D. man, who had caught cold from the fighter captain and come down with pneumonia.

2

Clevinger

In a way the C.I.D. man was pretty lucky, because outside the hospital the war was still going on. Men went mad and were rewarded with medals. All over the world, boys on every side of the bomb line were laying down their lives for what they had been told was their country, and no one seemed to mind, least of all the boys who were laying down their young lives. There was no end in sight. The only end in sight was Yossarian's own, and he might have remained in the hospital until doomsday had it not been for that patriotic Texan with his infundibuliform jowls and his lumpy, rumpleheaded, indestructible smile cracked forever across the front of his face like the brim of a black ten-gallon hat. The Texan wanted everybody in the ward to be happy but Yossarian and Dunbar. He was really very sick.

But Yossarian couldn't be happy, even though the Texan didn't want him to be, because outside the hospital there was still nothing funny going on. The only thing going on was a war, and no one seemed to notice but Yossarian and Dunbar. And when Yossarian tried to remind people, they drew away from him and thought he was crazy. Even Clevinger, who should have known better but didn't, had told him he was crazy the last time they had seen each other, which was just before Yossarian had fled into the hospital.

Clevinger had stared at him with apoplectic rage and indignation and, clawing the table with both hands, had shouted, "You're crazy!"

"Clevinger, what do you want from people?" Dunbar had replied wearily above the noises of the officers' club.

"I'm not joking," Clevinger persisted.

"They're trying to kill me," Yossarian told him calmly.

"No one's trying to kill you," Clevinger cried.

"Then why are they shooting at me?" Yossarian asked.

"They're shooting at *everyone*," Clevinger answered. "They're trying to kill everyone."

"And what difference does that make?"

Clevinger was already on the way, half out of his chair with emotion, his eyes moist and his lips quivering and pale. As always occurred when he quarreled over principles in which he believed passionately, he would end up gasping furiously for air and blinking back bitter tears of conviction. There were many principles in which Clevinger believed passionately. He was crazy.

"Who's they?" he wanted to know. "Who, specifically, do you think is trying to murder you?"

"Every one of them," Yossarian told him.

"Every one of whom?"

"Every one of whom do you think?"

"I haven't any idea."

"Then how do you know they aren't?"

"Because . . ." Clevinger sputtered, and turned speechless with frustration.

Clevinger really thought he was right, but Yossarian had proof, because strangers he didn't know shot at him with cannons every time he flew up into the air to drop bombs on them, and it wasn't funny at all. And if that wasn't funny, there were lots of things that weren't even funnier. There was nothing funny about living like a bum in a tent in Pianosa between fat mountains behind him and a placid blue sea in front that could gulp down a person with a cramp in the twinkling of an eye and ship him back to shore three days later, all charges paid, bloated, blue and putrescent, water draining out through both cold nostrils.

The tent he lived in stood right smack up against the wall of the shallow, dull-colored forest separating his own squadron from Dunbar's. Immediately alongside was the abandoned railroad ditch that carried the pipe that carried the aviation gasoline down to the fuel trucks at the airfield. Thanks to Orr, his roommate, it was the most luxurious tent in the squadron. Each time Yossarian returned from one of his holidays in the hospital or rest leaves in Rome, he was surprised by some new comfort Orr had installed in his absence—running water, wood-burning fireplace, cement floor. Yossarian had chosen the site, and he and Orr had raised the tent together. Orr, who was a grinning pygmy with pilot's wings and thick, wavy brown hair parted in the middle, furnished all the knowledge, while Yossarian, who was taller, stronger, broader and faster, did most of the work. Just the two of them lived there, although the tent was big enough for six. When summer came, Orr rolled up the side flaps to allow a breeze that never blew to flush away the air baking inside.

Immediately next door to Yossarian was Havermeyer, who liked peanut brittle and lived all by himself in the two-man tent in which he shot tiny field mice every night with huge bullets from the .45 he had stolen from the dead man in Yossarian's tent. On the other side of Havermeyer stood the tent McWatt no longer shared with Clevinger, who had still not returned when Yossarian came out of the hospital. McWatt shared his tent now with Nately who was away in Rome courting the sleepy whore he had fallen so deeply in love with there who was bored with her work and bored with him too. McWatt was crazy. He was a pilot and flew his plane as low as he dared over Yossarian's tent as often as he could, just to see how much he could frighten him, and loved to go buzzing with a wild, close roar over the wooden raft floating on empty oil drums out past the sand bar at the immaculate white beach where the men went swimming naked. Sharing a tent with a man who was crazy wasn't easy, but Nately didn't care. He was crazy, too, and had gone every free day to work on the officers' club that Yossarian had not helped build.

Actually, there were many officers' clubs that Yossarian had not helped build, but he was proudest of the one on Pianosa. It was a sturdy and complex monument to his powers of determination. Yossarian never went there to help until it was finished; then he went there often, so pleased was he with the large, fine, rambling shingled building. It was truly a splendid structure, and Yossarian throbbed with a mighty sense of accomplishment each time he gazed at it and reflected that none of the work that had gone into it was his.

There were four of them seated together at a table in the officers' club the last time he and Clevinger had called each other crazy. They were seated in back near the crap table on which Appleby always managed to win. Appleby was as good at shooting crap as he was at playing Ping-Pong, and he was as good at playing Ping-Pong as he was at everything else. Everything Appleby did, he did well. Appleby was a fair-haired boy from Iowa who believed in God, Motherhood and the American Way of Life, without ever thinking about any of them, and everybody who knew him liked him.

"I hate that son of a bitch," Yossarian growled.

The argument with Clevinger had begun a few minutes earlier when Yossarian had been unable to find a machine gun. It was a busy night. The bar was busy, the crap table was busy, the Ping-Pong table was busy. The people Yossarian wanted to machine-gun were busy at the bar singing sentimental old favorites that nobody else ever tired of.

Instead of machine-gunning them, he brought his heel down hard on the Ping-Pong ball that came rolling toward him off the paddle of one of the two officers playing.

"That Yossarian," the two officers laughed, shaking their heads, and got another ball from the box on the shelf.

"That Yossarian," Yossarian answered them.

"Yossarian," Nately whispered cautioningly.

"You see what I mean?" asked Clevinger.

The officers laughed again when they heard Yossarian mimicking them. "That Yossarian," they said more loudly.

"That Yossarian," Yossarian echoed.

"Yossarian, please," Nately pleaded.

"You see what I mean?" asked Clevinger. "He has antisocial aggressions."

"Oh, shut up," Dunbar told Clevinger. Dunbar liked Clevinger because Clevinger annoyed him and made the time go slow.

"Appleby isn't even here," Clevinger pointed out triumphantly to Yossarian.

"Who said anything about Appleby?" Yossarian wanted to know.

"Colonel Cathcart isn't here, either."

"Who said anything about Colonel Cathcart?"

"What son of a bitch *do* you hate, then?"

"What son of a bitch *is* here?"

"I'm not going to argue with you," Clevinger decided. "You don't know who you hate."

"Whoever's trying to poison me," Yossarian told him.

"Nobody's trying to poison you."

"They poisoned my food twice, didn't they? Didn't they put poison in my food during Ferrara and during the Great Big Siege of Bologna?"

"They put poison in *everybody's* food," Clevinger explained.

"And what difference does *that* make?"

"And it wasn't even poison!" Clevinger cried heatedly, growing more emphatic as he grew more confused.

As far back as Yossarian could recall, he explained to Clevinger with a patient smile, somebody was always hatching a plot to kill him. There were people who cared for him and people who didn't, and those who didn't hated him and were out to get him. They hated him because he was Assyrian. But they couldn't touch him, he told Clevinger, because he had a sound mind in a pure body and was as strong as an ox. They couldn't touch him because he was Tarzan, Mandrake, Flash Gordon. He was Bill Shakespeare. He was Cain, Ulysses, the Flying Dutchman; he was Lot in Sodom, Deirdre of the Sorrows, Sweeney in the nightingales among trees. He was miracle ingredient Z-247. He was—

"Crazy!" Clevinger interrupted, shrieking. "That's what you are! Crazy!"

"—immense. I'm a real, slam-bang, honest-to-goodness, three-fisted humdinger. I'm a bona fide supraman."

"Superman?" Clevinger cried. "Superman?"

"Sup*ra*man," Yossarian corrected.

"Hey, fellas, cut it out," Nately begged with embarrassment. "Everybody's looking at us."

"You're crazy," Clevinger shouted vehemently, his eyes filling with tears. "You've got a Jehovah complex."

"I think everyone is Nathaniel."

Clevinger arrested himself in mid-declamation, suspiciously. "Who's Nathaniel?"

"Nathaniel who?" inquired Yossarian innocently.

Clevinger skirted the trap neatly. "You think everybody is Jehovah. You're no better than Raskolnikov—"

"Who?"

"—yes, Raskolnikov, who—"

"Raskolnikov!"

"—who—I mean it—who felt he could justify killing an old woman—"

"No better than?"

"—yes, justify, that's right—with an ax! And I can prove it to you!" Gasping furiously for air, Clevinger enumerated Yossarian's symptoms: an unreasonable belief that everybody around him was crazy, a homicidal impulse to machine-gun strangers, retrospective falsification, an unfounded suspicion that people hated him and were conspiring to kill him.

But Yossarian knew he was right, because, as he explained to Clevinger, to the best of his knowledge he had never been wrong. Everywhere he looked was a nut, and it was all a sensible young gentleman like himself could do to maintain his perspective amid so much madness. And it was urgent that he did, for he knew his life was in peril.

Yossarian eyed everyone he saw warily when he returned to the squadron from the hospital. Milo was away, too, in Smyrna for the fig harvest. The mess hall ran smoothly in Milo's absence. Yossarian had responded ravenously to the pungent aroma of spicy lamb while he was still in the cab of the ambulance bouncing down along the knotted road that lay like a broken suspender between the hospital and the squadron. There was shish-kabob for lunch, huge, savory hunks of spitted meat sizzling like the devil over charcoal after marinating seventy-two hours in a secret mixture Milo had stolen from a crooked trader in the Levant, served with Iranian rice and asparagus tips Parmesan, followed by cherries jubilee for dessert and then steaming cups of fresh coffee with Benedictine and brandy. The meal was served in enormous helpings on damask tablecloths by the skilled Italian waiters Major —— de Coverley had kidnapped from the mainland and given to Milo.

Yossarian gorged himself in the mess hall until he thought he would explode and then sagged back in a contented stupor, his mouth filmy with a succulent residue. None of the officers in the squadron had ever eaten so well as they ate regularly in Milo's mess hall, and Yossarian wondered awhile if it wasn't perhaps all worth it. But then he burped and remembered that they were trying to kill him, and he sprinted out of the mess hall wildly and ran looking for Doc Daneeka to have himself taken off combat duty and sent home. He found Doc Daneeka in sunlight, sitting on a high stool outside his tent.

"Fifty missions," Doc Daneeka told him, shaking his head. "The colonel wants fifty missions."

"But I've only got forty-four!"

Doc Daneeka was unmoved. He was a sad, birdlike man with the spatulate face and scrubbed, tapering features of a well-groomed rat.

"Fifty missions," he repeated, still shaking his head. "The colonel wants fifty missions."

3

Havermeyer

Actually, no one was around when Yossarian returned from the hospital but Orr and the dead man in Yossarian's tent. The dead man in Yossarian's tent was a pest, and Yossarian didn't like him, even though he had never seen him. Having him lying around all day annoyed Yossarian so much that he had gone to the orderly room several times to complain to Sergeant Towser, who refused to admit that the dead man even existed, which, of course, he no longer did. It was still more frustrating to try to appeal directly to Major Major, the long and bony squadron commander, who looked a little bit like Henry Fonda in distress and went jumping out the window of his office each time Yossarian bullied his way past Sergeant Towser to speak to him about it. The dead man in Yossarian's tent was simply not easy to live with. He even disturbed Orr, who was not easy to live with, either, and who, on the day Yossarian came back, was tinkering with the faucet that fed gasoline into the stove he had started building while Yossarian was in the hospital.

"What are you doing?" Yossarian asked guardedly when he entered the tent, although he saw at once.

"There's a leak here," Orr said. "I'm trying to fix it."

"Please stop it," said Yossarian. "You're making me nervous."

"When I was a kid," Orr replied, "I used to walk around all day with crab apples in my cheeks. One in each cheek."

Yossarian put aside the musette bag from which he had begun removing his toilet articles and braced himself suspiciously. A minute passed. "Why?" he found himself forced to ask finally.

Orr tittered triumphantly. "Because they're better than horse chestnuts," he answered.

Orr was kneeling on the floor of the tent. He worked without pause, taking the faucet apart, spreading all the tiny pieces out carefully, counting and then studying each one interminably as though he had never seen anything remotely similar before, and then reassembling the whole small apparatus, over and over and over and over again, with no loss of patience or interest, no sign of fatigue, no indication of ever concluding. Yossarian watched him tinkering and felt certain he would be compelled to murder him in cold blood if he did not stop. His eyes moved toward the hunting knife that had been slung over the mosquito-net bar by the dead man the day he arrived. The knife hung beside the dead man's empty leather gun holster, from which Havermeyer had stolen the gun.

"When I couldn't get crab apples," Orr continued, "I used horse chestnuts. Horse chestnuts are about the same size as crab apples and actually have a better shape, although the shape doesn't matter a bit."

"Why did you walk around with crab apples in your cheeks?" Yossarian asked again. "That's what I asked."

"Because they've got a better shape than horse chestnuts," Orr answered. "I just told you that."

"Why," swore Yossarian at him approvingly, "you evil-eyed, mechanically-aptituded, disaffiliated son of a bitch, did you walk around with *anything* in your cheeks?"

"I didn't," Orr said, "walk around with *anything* in my cheeks. I walked around with crab apples in my cheeks. When I couldn't get crab apples I walked around with horse chestnuts. In my cheeks."

Orr giggled. Yossarian made up his mind to keep his mouth shut and did. Orr waited. Yossarian waited longer.

"One in each cheek," Orr said.

"Why?"

Orr pounced. "Why what?"

Yossarian shook his head, smiling, and refused to say.

"It's a funny thing about this valve," Orr mused aloud.

"What is?" Yossarian asked.

"Because I wanted—"

Yossarian knew. "Jesus Christ! Why did you want—"

"—apple cheeks."

"—apple cheeks?" Yossarian demanded.

"I wanted apple cheeks," Orr repeated. "Even when I was a kid I wanted apple cheeks someday, and I decided to work at it until I got them, and by God, I did work at it until I got them, and that's how I did it, with crab apples in my cheeks all day long." He giggled again. "One in each cheek."

"Why did you want apple cheeks?"

"I didn't want apple cheeks," Orr said. "I wanted *big* cheeks. I didn't care about the color so much, but I wanted them big. I worked at it just like one of those crazy guys you read about who go around squeezing rubber balls all day long just to strengthen their hands. In fact, I *was* one of those crazy guys. I used to walk around all day with rubber balls in my hands, too."

"Why?"

"Why what?"

"Why did you walk around all day with rubber balls in your hands?"

"Because rubber balls—" said Orr.

"—are better than crab apples?"

Orr sniggered as he shook his head. "I did it to protect my good reputation in case anyone ever caught me walking around with crab apples in my cheeks. With rubber balls in my hands I could deny there were crab apples in my cheeks. Every time someone asked me why I was walking around with crab apples in my cheeks, I'd just open my hands and show them it was rubber balls I was walking around with, not crab apples, and that they were in my hands, not my cheeks. It was a good story. But I never knew if it got across or not, since it's pretty tough to make people understand you when you're talking to them with two crab apples in your cheeks."

Yossarian found it pretty tough to understand him then, and he wondered once again if Orr wasn't talking to him with the tip of his tongue in one of his apple cheeks.

Yossarian decided not to utter another word. It would be futile. He knew Orr, and he knew there was not a chance in hell of finding out from him then why he had wanted big cheeks. It would do no more good to ask than it had done to ask him why that whore had kept beating him over the head with her shoe that morning in Rome in the cramped vestibule outside the open door of Nately's whore's kid sister's room. She was a tall, strapping girl with long hair and incandescent blue veins converging populously beneath her cocoa-colored skin where the flesh was most tender, and she kept cursing and shrieking and jumping high up into the air on her bare feet to keep right on hitting him on the top of his head with the spiked heel of her shoe. They were both naked, and raising a rumpus that brought everyone in the apartment into the hall to watch, each couple in a bedroom doorway, all of them naked except the aproned and sweatered old woman, who clucked reprovingly, and the lecherous, dissipated old man, who cackled aloud hilariously through the whole episode with a kind of avid and superior glee. The girl shrieked and Orr giggled. Each time she landed with the heel of her shoe, Orr giggled louder, infuriating her still further so that she flew up still higher into the air for another shot at his noodle, her wondrously full breasts soaring all over the place like billowing pennants in a strong wind and her buttocks and strong thighs shim-sham-shimmying this way and that way like some horrifying bonanza. She shrieked and Orr giggled right up to the time she shrieked and knocked him cold with a good solid crack on the temple that made him stop giggling and sent him off to the hospital in a stretcher with a hole in his head that wasn't very deep and a very mild concussion that kept him out of combat only twelve days.

Nobody could find out what had happened, not even the cackling old man and clucking old woman, who were in a position to find out everything that happened in that vast and endless brothel with its multitudinous bedrooms on facing sides of the narrow hallways going off in opposite directions from the spacious sitting room with its shaded windows and single lamp. Every time she met Orr after that, she'd hoist her skirts up over her tight white elastic panties and, jeering coarsely, bulge her firm, round belly out at him, cursing him contemptuously and then roaring with husky laughter as she saw him giggle fearfully and take refuge behind Yossarian. Whatever he had done or tried to do or failed to do behind the closed door of Nately's whore's kid sister's room was still a secret. The girl wouldn't tell Nately's whore or any of the other whores or Nately or Yossarian. Orr might tell, but Yossarian had decided not to utter another word.

"Do you want to know why I wanted big cheeks?" Orr asked.

Yossarian kept his mouth shut.

"Do you remember," Orr said, "that time in Rome when that girl who can't stand you kept hitting me over the head with the heel of her shoe? Do you want to know why she was hitting me?"

It was still impossible to imagine what he could have done to make her angry enough to hammer him over the head for fifteen or twenty minutes, yet not angry enough to pick him up by the ankles and dash his brains out. She was certainly tall enough, and Orr was certainly short enough. Orr had buck teeth and bulging eyes to go with his big cheeks and was even smaller than young Huple, who lived on the wrong side of the railroad tracks in the tent in the administration area in which Hungry Joe lay screaming in his sleep every night.

The administration area in which Hungry Joe had pitched his tent by mistake lay in the center of the squadron between the ditch, with its rusted railroad tracks, and the tilted black bituminous road. The men could pick up girls along that road if they promised to take them where they wanted to go, buxom, young, homely, grinning girls with missing teeth whom they could drive off the road and lie down in the wild grass with, and Yossarian did whenever he could, which was not nearly as often as Hungry Joe, who could get a jeep but couldn't drive, begged him to try. The tents of the enlisted men in the squadron stood on the other side of the road alongside the open-air movie theater in which, for the daily amusement of the dying, ignorant armies clashed by night on a collapsible screen, and to which another U.S.O. troupe came that same afternoon.

The U.S.O. troupes were sent by General P. P. Peckem, who had moved his headquarters up to Rome and had nothing better to do while he schemed against General Dreedle. General Peckem was a general with whom neatness definitely counted. He was a spry, suave and very precise general who knew the circumference of the equator and always wrote "enhanced" when he meant "increased." He was a prick, and no one knew this better than General Dreedle, who was incensed by General Peckem's recent directive requiring all tents in the Mediterranean theater of operations to be pitched along parallel lines with entrances facing back proudly toward the Washington Monument. To General Dreedle, who ran a fighting outfit, it seemed a lot of crap. Furthermore, it was none of General Peckem's goddam business how the tents in General Dreedle's wing were pitched. There then followed a hectic jurisdictional dispute between these overlords that was decided in General Dreedle's favor by ex-P.F.C. Wintergreen, mail clerk at Twenty-seventh Air Force Headquarters. Wintergreen determined the outcome by throwing all communications from General Peckem into the wastebasket. He found them too prolix. General Dreedle's views, expressed in less pretentious literary style, pleased ex-P.F.C. Wintergreen and were sped along by him in zealous observance of regulations. General Dreedle was victorious by default.

To regain whatever status he had lost, General Peckem began sending out more U.S.O. troupes than he had ever sent out before and assigned to Colonel Cargill himself the responsibility of generating enough enthusiasm for them.

But there was no enthusiasm in Yossarian's group. In Yossarian's group there was only a mounting number of enlisted men and officers who found their way solemnly to Sergeant Towser several times a day to ask if the orders sending them home had come in. They were men who had finished their fifty missions. There were more of them now than when Yossarian had gone into the hospital, and they were still waiting. They worried and bit their nails. They were grotesque, like useless young men in a depression. They moved sideways, like crabs. They were waiting for the orders sending them home to safety to return from Twenty-seventh Air Force Headquarters in Italy, and while they waited they had nothing to do but worry and bite their nails and find their way solemnly to Sergeant Towser several times a day to ask if the orders sending them home to safety had come.

They were in a race and knew it, because they knew from bitter experience that Colonel Cathcart might raise the number of missions again at any time. They had nothing better to do than wait. Only Hungry Joe had something better to do each time he finished his missions. He had screaming nightmares and won fist fights with Huple's cat. He took his camera to the front row of every U.S.O. show and tried to shoot pictures up the skirt of the yellow-headed singer with two big ones in a sequined dress that always seemed ready to burst. The pictures never came out.

Colonel Cargill, General Peckem's troubleshooter, was a forceful, ruddy man. Before the war he had been an alert, hard-hitting, aggressive marketing executive. He was a very bad marketing executive. Colonel Cargill was so awful a marketing executive that his services were much sought after by firms eager to establish losses for tax purposes. Throughout the civilized world, from Battery Park to Fulton Street, he was known as a dependable man for a fast tax write-off. His prices were high, for failure often did not come easily. He had to start at the top and work his way down, and with sympathetic friends in Washington, losing money was no simple matter. It took months of hard work and careful misplanning. A person misplaced, disorganized, miscalculated, overlooked everything and opened every loophole, and just when he thought he had it made, the government gave him a lake or a forest or an oilfield and spoiled everything. Even with such handicaps, Colonel Cargill could be relied on to run the most prosperous enterprise into the ground. He was a self-made man who owed his lack of success to nobody.

"Men," Colonel Cargill began in Yossarian's squadron, measuring his pauses carefully. "You're American officers. The officers of no other army in the world can make that statement. Think about it."

Sergeant Knight thought about it and then politely informed Colonel Cargill that he was addressing the enlisted men and that the officers were to be found waiting for him on the other side of the squadron. Colonel Cargill thanked him crisply and glowed with self-satisfaction as he strode across the area. It made him proud to observe that twenty-nine months in the service had not blunted his genius for ineptitude.

"Men," he began his address to the officers, measuring his pauses carefully. "You're American officers. The officers of no other army in the world can make that statement. Think about it." He waited a moment to permit them to think about it. "These people are your guests!" he shouted suddenly. "They've traveled over three thousand miles to entertain you. How are they going to feel if nobody wants to go out and watch them? What's going to happen to their morale? Now, men, it's no skin off my behind. But that girl that wants to play the accordion for you today is old enough to be a mother. How would *you* feel if your own mother traveled over three thousand miles to play the accordion for some troops that didn't want to watch her? How is that kid whose mother that accordion player is old enough to be going to feel when he grows up and learns about it? We all know the answer to that one. Now, men, don't misunderstand me. This is all voluntary, of course. I'd be the last colonel in the world to order you to go to that U.S.O. show and have a good time, but I want every one of you who isn't sick enough to be in a hospital to go to that U.S.O. show right now and have a good time, and *that's an order!*"

Yossarian did feel almost sick enough to go back into the hospital, and he felt even sicker three combat missions later when Doc Daneeka still shook his melancholy head and refused to ground him.

"You think you've got troubles?" Doc Daneeka rebuked him grievingly. "What about me? I lived on peanuts for eight years while I learned how to be a doctor. After the peanuts, I lived on chicken feed in my own office until I could build up a practice decent enough to even pay expenses. Then, just as the shop was finally starting to show a profit, they drafted me. I don't know what you're complaining about."

Doc Daneeka was Yossarian's friend and would do just about nothing in his power to help him. Yossarian listened very carefully as Doc Daneeka told him about Colonel Cathcart at Group, who wanted to be a general, about General Dreedle at Wing and General Dreedle's nurse, and about all the other generals at Twenty-seventh Air Force Headquarters, who insisted on only forty missions as a completed tour of duty.

"Why don't you just smile and make the best of it?" he advised Yossarian glumly. "Be like Havermeyer."

Yossarian shuddered at the suggestion. Havermeyer was a lead bombardier who never took evasive action going in to the target and thereby increased the danger of all the men who flew in the same formation with him.

"Havermeyer, why the hell don't you ever take evasive action?" they would demand in a rage after the mission.

"Hey, you men leave Captain Havermeyer alone," Colonel Cathcart would order. "He's the best damned bombardier we've got."

Havermeyer grinned and nodded and tried to explain how he dum-dummed the bullets with a hunting knife before he fired them at the field mice in his tent every night. Havermeyer *was* the best damned bombardier they had, but he flew straight and level all the way from the I.P. to the target, and even far beyond the target until he saw the falling bombs strike ground and explode in a darting spurt of abrupt orange that flashed beneath the swirling pall of smoke and pulverized debris geysering up wildly in huge, rolling waves of gray and black. Havermeyer held mortal men rigid in six planes as steady and still as sitting ducks while he followed the bombs all the way down through the Plexiglas nose with deep interest and gave the German gunners below all the time they needed to set their sights and take their aim and pull their triggers or lanyards or switches or whatever the hell they did pull when *they* wanted to kill people they didn't know.

Havermeyer was a lead bombardier who never missed. Yossarian was a lead bombardier who had been demoted because he no longer gave a damn whether he missed or not. He had decided to live forever or die in the attempt, and his only mission each time he went up was to come down alive.

The men had loved flying behind Yossarian, who used to come barreling in over the target from all directions and every height, climbing and diving and twisting and turning so steeply and sharply that it was all the pilots of the other five planes could do to stay in formation with him, leveling out only for the two or three seconds it took for the bombs to drop and then zooming off again with an aching howl of engines, and wrenching his flight through the air so violently as he wove his way through the filthy barrages of flak that the six planes were soon flung out all over the sky like prayers, each one a pushover for the German fighters, which was just fine with Yossarian, for there were no German fighters any more and he did not want any exploding planes near his when they exploded. Only when all the *Sturm und Drang* had been left far behind would he tip his flak helmet back wearily on his sweating head and stop barking directions to McWatt at the controls, who had nothing better to wonder about at a time like that than where the bombs had fallen.

"Bomb bay clear," Sergeant Knight in the back would announce.

"Did we hit the bridge?" McWatt would ask.

"I couldn't see, sir, I kept getting bounced around back here pretty hard and I couldn't see. Everything's covered with smoke now and I can't see."

"Hey, Aarfy, did the bombs hit the target?"

"What target?" Captain Aardvaark, Yossarian's plump, pipe-smoking navigator would say from the confusion of maps he had created at Yossarian's side in the nose of the ship. "I don't think we're at the target yet. Are we?"

"Yossarian, did the bombs hit the target?"

"What bombs?" answered Yossarian, whose only concern had been the flak.

"Oh, well," McWatt would sing, "what the hell."

Yossarian did not give a damn whether he hit the target or not, just as long as Havermeyer or one of the other lead bombardiers did and they never had to go back. Every now and then someone grew angry enough at Havermeyer to throw a punch at him.

"I said you men leave Captain Havermeyer alone," Colonel Cathcart warned them all angrily. "I said he's the best damned bombardier we've got, didn't I?"

Havermeyer grinned at the colonel's intervention and shoved another piece of peanut brittle inside his face.

Havermeyer had grown very proficient at shooting field mice at night with the gun he had stolen from the dead man in Yossarian's tent. His bait was a bar of candy and he would presight in the darkness as he sat waiting for the nibble with a finger of his other hand inside a loop of the line he had run from the frame of his mosquito net to the chain of the unfrosted light bulb overhead. The line was taut as a banjo string, and the merest tug would snap it on and blind the shivering quarry in a blaze of light. Havermeyer would chortle exultantly as he watched the tiny mammal freeze and roll its terrified eyes about in frantic search of the intruder. Havermeyer would wait until the eyes fell upon his own and then he laughed aloud and pulled the trigger at the same time, showering the rank, furry body all over the tent with a reverberating crash and dispatching its timid soul back to his or her Creator.

Late one night, Havermeyer fired a shot at a mouse that brought Hungry Joe bolting out at him barefoot, ranting at the top of his screechy voice and emptying his own .45 into Havermeyer's tent as he came charging down one side of the ditch and up the other and vanished all at once inside one of the slit trenches that had appeared like magic beside every tent the morning after Milo Minderbinder had bombed the squadron. It was just before dawn during the Great Big Siege of Bologna, when tongueless dead men peopled the night hours like living ghosts and Hungry Joe was half out of his mind with anxiety because he had finished his missions again and was not scheduled to fly. Hungry Joe was babbling incoherently when they fished him out from the dank bottom of the slit trench, babbling of snakes, rats and spiders. The others flashed their searchlights down just to make sure. There was nothing inside but a few inches of stagnant rain water.

"You see?" cried Havermeyer. "I told you. I told you he was crazy, didn't I?"

4

Doc Daneeka

Hungry Joe *was* crazy and no one knew it better than Yossarian, who did everything he could to help him. Hungry Joe just wouldn't listen to Yossarian. Hungry Joe just wouldn't listen because he thought Yossarian was crazy.

"Why should he listen to you?" Doc Daneeka inquired of Yossarian without looking up.

"Because he's got troubles."

Doc Daneeka snorted scornfully. "He thinks he's got troubles? What about me?" Doc Daneeka continued slowly with a gloomy sneer. "Oh, I'm not complaining. I know there's a war on. I know a lot of people are going to have to suffer for us to win it. But why must I be one of them? Why don't they draft some of these old doctors who keep shooting their kissers off in public about what big sacrifices the medical game stands ready to make? I don't want to make sacrifices. I want to make dough."

Doc Daneeka was a very neat, clean man whose idea of a good time was to sulk. He had a dark complexion and a small, wise, saturnine face with mournful pouches under both eyes. He brooded over his health continually and went almost daily to the medical tent to have his temperature taken by one of the two enlisted men there who ran things for him practically on their own, and ran it so efficiently that he was left with little else to do but sit in the sunlight with his stuffed nose and wonder what other people were so worried about. Their names were Gus and Wes and they had succeeded in elevating medicine to an exact science. All men reporting on sick call with temperatures above 102 were rushed to the hospital. All those except Yossarian reporting on sick call with temperatures below 102 had their gums and toes painted with gentian violet solution and were given a laxative to throw away into the bushes. All those reporting on sick call with temperatures of exactly 102 were asked to return in an hour to have their temperatures taken again. Yossarian, with his temperature of 101, could go to the hospital whenever he wanted to because he was not afraid of them.

The system worked just fine for everybody, especially for Doc

Daneeka, who found himself with all the time he needed to watch old Major —— de Coverley pitching horseshoes in his private horseshoe-pitching pit, still wearing the transparent eye patch Doc Daneeka had fashioned for him from the strip of celluloid stolen from Major Major's orderly room window months before when Major —— de Coverley had returned from Rome with an injured cornea after renting two apartments there for the officers and enlisted men to use on their rest leaves. The only time Doc Daneeka ever went to the medical tent was the time he began to feel he was a very sick man each day and stopped in just to have Gus and Wes look him over. They could never find anything wrong with him. His temperature was always 96.8, which was perfectly all right with them, as long as he didn't mind. Doc Daneeka did mind. He was beginning to lose confidence in Gus and Wes and was thinking of having them both transferred back to the motor pool and replaced by someone who *could* find something wrong.

Doc Daneeka was personally familiar with a number of things that were drastically wrong. In addition to his health, he worried about the Pacific Ocean and flight time. Health was something no one ever could be sure of for a long enough time. The Pacific Ocean was a body of water surrounded on all sides by elephantiasis and other dread diseases to which, if he ever displeased Colonel Cathcart by grounding Yossarian, he might suddenly find himself transferred. And flight time was the time he had to spend in airplane flight each month in order to get his flight pay. Doc Daneeka hated to fly. He felt imprisoned in an airplane. In an airplane there was absolutely no place in the world to go except to another part of the airplane. Doc Daneeka had been told that people who enjoyed climbing into an airplane were really giving vent to a subsconscious desire to climb back into the womb. He had been told this by Yossarian, who made it possible for Dan Daneeka to collect his flight pay each month without ever climbing back into the womb. Yossarian would persuade McWatt to enter Doc Daneeka's name on his flight log for training missions or trips to Rome.

"You know how it is," Doc Daneeka had wheedled, with a sly, conspiratorial wink. "Why take chances when I don't have to?"

"Sure," Yossarian agreed.

"What difference does it make to anyone if I'm in the plane or not?"

"No difference."

"Sure, that's what I mean," Doc Daneeka said. "A little grease is what makes this world go round. One hand washes the other. Know what I mean? You scratch my back, I'll scratch yours."

Yossarian knew what he meant.

"That's not what I meant," Doc Daneeka said as Yossarian began scratching his back. "I'm talking about cooperation. Favors. You do a favor for me, I'll do one for you. Get it?"

"Do one for me," Yossarian requested.

"Not a chance," Doc Daneeka answered.

There was something fearful and minute about Doc Daneeka as he sat despondently outside his tent in the sunlight as often as he could, dressed in khaki summer trousers and a short-sleeved summer shirt that was bleached almost to an antiseptic gray by the daily laundering to which he had it subjected. He was like a man who had grown frozen with horror once and had never come completely unthawed. He sat all tucked up into himself, his slender shoulders huddled halfway around his head, his suntanned hands with their luminous silver fingernails massaging the backs of his bare, folded arms gently as though he were cold. Actually, he was a very warm, compassionate man who never stopped feeling sorry for himself.

"Why me?" was his constant lament, and the question was a good one.

Yossarian knew it was a good one because Yossarian was a collector of good questions and had used them to disrupt the educational sessions Clevinger had once conducted two nights a week in Captain Black's intelligence tent with the corporal in eyeglasses who everybody knew was probably a subversive. Captain Black knew he was a subversive because he wore eyeglasses and used words like *panacea* and *utopia*, and because he disapproved of Adolf Hitler, who had done such a great job of combating un-American activities in Germany. Yossarian attended the education sessions because he wanted to find out why so many people were working so hard to kill him. A handful of other men were also interested, and the questions were many and good when Clevinger and the subversive corporal finished and made the mistake of asking if there were any.

"Who is Spain?"

"Why is Hitler?"

"When is right?"

"Where was that stooped and mealy-colored old man I used to call Poppa when the merry-go-round broke down?"

"How was trump at Munich?"

"Ho-ho beriberi."

and

"Balls!"

all rang out in rapid succession, and then there was Yossarian with the question that had no answer:

"Where are the Snowdens of yesteryear?"

The question upset them, because Snowden had been killed over Avignon when Dobbs went crazy in mid-air and seized the controls away from Huple.

The corporal played it dumb. "What?" he asked.

"Where are the Snowdens of yesteryear?"

"I'm afraid I don't understand."

"*Où sont les Neigedens d'antan?*" Yossarian said to make it easier for him.

"*Parlez en anglais*, for Christ's sake," said the corporal. "*Je ne parle pas français*."

"Neither do I," answered Yossarian, who was ready to pursue him through all the words in the world to wring the knowledge from him if he could, but Clevinger intervened, pale, thin, and laboring for breath, a humid coating of tears already glistening in his undernourished eyes.

Group Headquarters was alarmed, for there was no telling what people might find out once they felt free to ask whatever questions they wanted to. Colonel Cathcart sent Colonel Korn to stop it, and Colonel Korn succeeded with a rule governing the asking of questions. Colonel Korn's rule was a stroke of genius, Colonel Korn explained in his report to Colonel Cathcart. Under Colonel Korn's rule, the only people permitted to ask questions were those who never did. Soon the only people attending were those who never asked questions, and the sessions were discontinued altogether, since Clevinger, the corporal and Colonel Korn agreed that it was neither possible nor necessary to educate people who never questioned anything.

Colonel Cathcart and Lieutenant Colonel Korn lived and worked in the Group Headquarters building, as did all the members of the headquarters staff, with the exception of the chaplain. The Group Headquarters building was an enormous, windy, antiquated structure built of powdery red stone and banging plumbing. Behind the building was the modern skeet-shooting range that had been constructed by Colonel Cathcart for the exclusive recreation of the officers at Group and at which every officer and enlisted man on combat status now, thanks to General Dreedle, had to spend a minimum of eight hours a month.

Yossarian shot skeet, but never hit any. Appleby shot skeet and never missed. Yossarian was as bad at shooting skeet as he was at gambling. He could never win money gambling either. Even when he cheated he couldn't win, because the people he cheated against were always better at cheating too. These were two disappointments to which he had resigned himself: he would never be a skeet shooter, and he would never make money.

"It takes brains *not* to make money," Colonel Cargill wrote in one of the homiletic memoranda he regularly prepared for circulation over General Peckem's signature. "Any fool can make money these days and most of them do. But what about people with talent and brains? Name, for example, one poet who makes money."

"T. S. Eliot," ex-P.F.C. Wintergreen said in his mail-sorting cubicle at Twenty-seventh Air Force Headquarters, and slammed down the telephone without identifying himself.

Colonel Cargill, in Rome, was perplexed.

"Who was it?" asked General Peckem.

"I don't know," Colonel Cargill replied.

"What did he want?"

"I don't know."

"Well, what did he say?"

"'T. S. Eliot,'" Colonel Cargill informed him.

"What's that?"

"'T. S. Eliot,'" Colonel Cargill repeated.

"Just 'T. S.—'"

"Yes, sir. That's all he said. Just 'T. S. Eliot.—'"

"I wonder what it means," General Peckem reflected.

Colonel Cargill wondered, too.

"T. S. Eliot," General Peckem mused.

"T. S. Eliot," Colonel Cargill echoed with the same funereal puzzlement.

General Peckem roused himself after a moment with an unctuous and benignant smile. His expression was shrewd and sophisticated. His eyes gleamed maliciously. "Have someone get me General Dreedle," he requested Colonel Cargill. "Don't let him know who's calling."

Colonel Cargill handed him the phone.

"T. S. Eliot," General Peckem said, and hung up.

"Who was it?" asked Colonel Moodus.

General Dreedle, in Corsica, did not reply. Colonel Moodus was General Dreedle's son-in-law, and General Dreedle, at the insistence of his wife and against his own better judgment, had taken him into the military business. General Dreedle gazed at Colonel Moodus with level hatred. He detested the very sight of his son-in-law, who was his aide and therefore in constant attendance upon him. He had opposed his daughter's marriage to Colonel Moodus because he disliked attending weddings. Wearing a menacing and preoccupied scowl, General Dreedle moved to the full-length mirror in his office and stared at his stocky reflection. He had a grizzled, broad-browed head with iron-gray tufts over his eyes and a blunt and belligerent jaw. He brooded in ponderous speculation over the cryptic message he had just received. Slowly his face softened with an idea, and he curled his lips with wicked pleasure.

"Get Peckem," he told Colonel Moodus. "Don't let the bastard know who's calling."

"Who was it?" asked Colonel Cargill, back in Rome.

"That same person," General Peckem replied with a definite trace of alarm. "Now he's after me."

"What did he want?"

"I don't know."

"What did he say?"

"The same thing."

"'T. S. Eliot'?"

"Yes, 'T. S. Eliot.' That's all he said." General Peckem had a hopeful thought. "Perhaps it's a new code or something, like the colors of the day. Why don't you have someone check with Communications and see if it's a new code or something or the colors of the day?"

Communications answered that T. S. Eliot was not a new code or the colors of the day.

Colonel Cargill had the next idea. "Maybe I ought to phone Twenty-seventh Air Force Headquarters and see if they know anything about it. They have a clerk up there named Wintergreen I'm pretty close to. He's the one who tipped me off that our prose was too prolix."

Ex-P.F.C. Wintergreen told Colonel Cargill that there was no record at Twenty-seventh Air Force Headquarters of a T. S. Eliot.

"How's our prose these days?" Colonel Cargill decided to inquire while he had ex-P.F.C. Wintergreen on the phone. "It's much better now, isn't it?"

"It's still too prolix," ex-P.F.C. Wintergreen replied.

"It wouldn't surprise me if General Dreedle were behind the whole thing," General Peckem confessed at last. "Remember what he did to that skeet-shooting range?"

General Dreedle had thrown open Colonel Cathcart's private skeet-shooting range to every officer and enlisted man in the group on combat duty. General Dreedle wanted his men to spend as much time out on the skeet-shooting range as the facilities and their flight schedule would allow. Shooting skeet eight hours a month was excellent training for them. It trained them to shoot skeet.

Dunbar loved shooting skeet because he hated every minute of it and the time passed so slowly. He had figured out that a single hour on the skeet-shooting range with people like Havermeyer and Appleby could be worth as much as eleven-times-seventeen years.

"I think you're crazy," was the way Clevinger had responded to Dunbar's discovery.

"Who wants to know?" Dunbar answered.

"I mean it," Clevinger insisted.

"Who cares?" Dunbar answered.

"I really do. I'll even go so far as to concede that life seems longer i—"

"—*is* longer i—"

"—*is* longer—*Is* longer? All right, *is* longer if it's filled with periods of boredom and discomfort, b—"

"Guess how fast?" Dunbar said suddenly.

"Huh?"

"They go," Dunbar explained.

"Who?"

"Years."

"Years?"

"Years," said Dunbar. "Years, years, years."

"Clevinger, why don't you let Dunbar alone?" Yossarian broke in. "Don't you realize the toll this is taking?"

"It's all right," said Dunbar magnanimously. "I have some decades to spare. Do you know how long a year takes when it's going away?"

"And you shut up also," Yossarian told Orr, who had begun to snigger.

"I was just thinking about that girl," Orr said. "That girl in Sicily. That girl in Sicily with the bald head."

"You'd *better* shut up also," Yossarian warned him.

"It's your fault," Dunbar said to Yossarian. "Why don't you let him snigger if he wants to? It's better than having him talking."

"All right. Go ahead and snigger if you want to."

"Do you know how long a year takes when it's going away?" Dunbar repeated to Clevinger. "This long." He snapped his fingers. "A second ago you were stepping into college with your lungs full of fresh air. Today you're an old man."

"Old?" asked Clevinger with surprise. "What are you talking about?"

"Old."

"I'm not old."

"You're inches away from death every time you go on a mission. How much older can you be at your age? A half minute before that you were stepping into high school, and an unhooked brassiere was as close as you ever hoped to get to Paradise. Only a fifth of a second before that you were a small kid with a ten-week summer vacation that lasted a hundred thousand years and still ended too soon. Zip! They go rocketing by so fast. How the hell else are you ever going to slow time down?" Dunbar was almost angry when he finished.

"Well, maybe it is true," Clevinger conceded unwillingly in a subdued tone. "Maybe a long life does have to be filled with many unpleasant conditions if it's to seem long. But in that event, who wants one?"

"I do," Dunbar told him.

"Why?" Clevinger asked.

"What else is there?"

5

Chief White Halfoat

Doc Daneeka lived in a splotched gray tent with Chief White Halfoat, whom he feared and despised.

"I can just picture his liver," Doc Daneeka grumbled.

"Picture my liver," Yossarian advised him.

"There's nothing wrong with your liver."

"That shows how much you don't know," Yossarian bluffed, and told Doc Daneeka about the troublesome pain in his liver that had troubled Nurse Duckett and Nurse Cramer and all the doctors in the hospital because it wouldn't become jaundice and wouldn't go away.

Doc Daneeka wasn't interested. "You think you've got troubles?" he wanted to know. "What about me? You should've been in my office the day those newlyweds walked in."

"What newlyweds?"

"Those newlyweds that walked into my office one day. Didn't I ever tell you about them? She was lovely."

So was Doc Daneeka's office. He had decorated his waiting room with goldfish and one of the finest suites of cheap furniture. Whatever he could he bought on credit, even the goldfish. For the rest, he obtained money from greedy relatives in exchange for shares of the profits. His office was in Staten Island in a two-family firetrap just four blocks away from the ferry stop and only one block south of a supermarket, three beauty parlors, and two corrupt druggists. It was a corner location, but nothing helped. Population turnover was small, and people clung through habit to the same physicians they had been doing business with for years. Bills piled up rapidly, and he was soon faced with the loss of his most precious medical instruments: his adding machine was repossessed, and then his typewriter. The goldfish died. Fortunately, just when things were blackest, the war broke out.

"It was a godsend," Doc Daneeka confessed solemnly. "Most of the other doctors were soon in the service, and things picked up overnight. The corner location really started paying off, and I soon found myself handling more patients than I could handle competently. I upped my kickback fee with those two drugstores. The beauty parlors were good for two, three abortions a week. Things couldn't have been better, and then look what happened. They had to send a guy from the draft board around to look me over. I was Four-F. I had examined myself pretty thoroughly and discovered that I was unfit for military service. You'd think my word would be enough, wouldn't you, since I was a doctor in good standing with my county medical society and with my local Better Business Bureau. But no, it wasn't, and they sent this guy around just to make sure I really did have one leg amputated at the hip and was helplessly bedridden with incurable rheumatoid arthritis. Yossarian, we live in an age of distrust and deteriorating spiritual values. It's a terrible thing," Doc Daneeka protested in a voice quavering with strong emotion. "It's a terrible thing when even the word of a licensed physician is suspected by the country he loves."

Doc Daneeka had been drafted and shipped to Pianosa as a flight surgeon, even though he was terrified of flying.

"I don't have to go looking for trouble in an airplane," he noted, blinking his beady, brown, offended eyes myopically. "It comes looking for me. Like that virgin I'm telling you about that couldn't have a baby."

"What virgin?" Yossarian asked. "I thought you were telling me about some newlyweds."

"That's the virgin I'm telling you about. They were just a couple of young kids, and they'd been married, oh, a little over a year when they came walking into my office without an appointment. You should have seen her. She was so sweet and young and pretty. She even blushed when I asked about her periods. I don't think I'll ever stop loving that girl. She was built like a dream and wore a chain around her neck with a medal of Saint Anthony hanging down inside the most beautiful bosom I never saw. 'It must be a terrible temptation for Saint Anthony,' I joked—just to put her at ease, you know. 'Saint Anthony?' her husband said. 'Who's Saint Anthony?' 'Ask your wife,' I told him. 'She can tell you who Saint Anthony is.' 'Who is Saint Anthony?' he asked her. 'Who?' she wanted to know. 'Saint Anthony,' he told her. 'Saint Anthony?' she said. 'Who's Saint Anthony?' When I got a good look at her inside my examination room I found she was still a virgin. I spoke to her husband alone while she was pulling her girdle back on and hooking it onto her stockings. 'Every night,' he boasted. A real wise guy, you know. 'I never miss a night,' he boasted. He meant it, too. 'I even been puttin' it to her mornings before the breakfasts she makes me before we go to work,' he boasted. There was only one explanation. When I had them both together again I gave them a demonstration of intercourse with the rubber models I've got in my office. I've got these rubber models in my office with all the reproductive organs of both sexes that I keep locked up in separate cabinets to avoid a scandal. I mean I used to have them. I don't have anything any more, not even a practice. The only thing I have now is this low temperature that I'm really starting to worry about. Those two kids I've got working for me in the medical tent aren't worth a damn as diagnosticians. All they know how to do is complain. They think they've got troubles? What about me? They should have been in my office that day with those two newlyweds looking at me as though I were telling them something nobody'd ever heard of before. You never saw anybody so interested. 'You mean like this?' he asked me, and worked the models for himself awhile. You know, I can see where a certain type of person might get a big kick out of doing just that. 'That's it,' I told him. 'Now, you go home and try it my way for a few months and see what happens. Okay?' 'Okay,' they said, and paid me in cash without any argument. 'Have a good time,' I told them, and they thanked me and walked out together. He had his arm around her waist as though he couldn't wait to get her home and put it to her again. A few days later he came back all by himself and told my nurse he had to see me right away. As soon as we were alone, he punched me in the nose."

"He did what?"

"He called me a wise guy and punched me in the nose. 'What are you, a wise guy?' he said, and knocked me flat on my ass. Pow! Just like that. I'm not kidding."

"I know you're not kidding," Yossarian said. "But why did he do it?"

"How should I know why he did it?" Doc Daneeka retorted with annoyance.

"Maybe it had something to do with Saint Anthony?"

Doc Daneeka looked at Yossarian blankly. "Saint Anthony?" he asked with astonishment. "Who's Saint Anthony?"

"How should I know?" answered Chief White Halfoat, staggering inside the tent just then with a bottle of whiskey cradled in his arm and sitting himself down pugnaciously between the two of them.

Doc Daneeka rose without a word and moved his chair outside the tent, his back bowed by the compact kit of injustices that was his perpetual burden. He could not bear the company of his roommate.

Chief White Halfoat thought he was crazy. "I don't know what's the matter with that guy," he observed reproachfully. "He's got no brains, that's what's the matter with him. If he had any brains he'd grab a shovel and start digging. Right here in the tent, he'd start digging, right under my cot. He'd strike oil in no time. Don't he know how that enlisted man struck oil with a shovel back in the States? Didn't he ever hear what happened to that kid—what was the name of that rotten rat bastard pimp of a snotnose back in Colorado?"

"Wintergreen."

"Wintergreen."

"He's afraid," Yossarian explained.

"Oh, no. Not Wintergreen." Chief White Halfoat shook his head with undisguised admiration. "That stinking little punk wise-guy son of a bitch ain't afraid of nobody."

"Doc Daneeka's afraid. That's what's the matter with him."

"What's he afraid of?"

"He's afraid of you," Yossarian said. "He's afraid you're going to die of pneumonia."

"He'd *better* be afraid," Chief White Halfoat said. A deep, low laugh tumbled through his massive chest. "I will, too, the first chance I get. You just wait and see."

Chief White Halfoat was a handsome, swarthy Indian from Oklahoma with a heavy, hard-boned face and tousled black hair, a half-blooded Creek from Enid who, for occult reasons of his own, had made up his mind to die of pneumonia. He was a glowering, vengeful, disillusioned Indian who hated foreigners with names like Cathcart, Korn, Black and Havermeyer and wished they'd all go back to where their lousy ancestors had come from.

"You wouldn't believe it, Yossarian," he ruminated, raising his voice deliberately to bait Doc Daneeka, "but this used to be a pretty good country to live in before they loused it up with their goddam piety."

Chief White Halfoat was out to revenge himself upon the white man. He could barely read or write and had been assigned to Captain Black as assistant intelligence officer.

"How could I learn to read or write?" Chief White Halfoat demanded with simulated belligerence, raising his voice again so that Doc Daneeka would hear. "Every place we pitched our tent, they sank an oil well. Every time they sank a well, they hit oil. And every time they hit oil, they made us pack up our tent and go someplace else. We were human divining rods. Our whole family had a natural affinity for petroleum deposits, and soon every oil company in the world had technicians chasing us around. We were always on the move. It was one hell of a way to bring a child up, I can tell you. I don't think I ever spent more than a week in one place."

His earliest memory was of a geologist.

"Every time another White Halfoat was born," he continued, "the stock market turned bullish. Soon whole drilling crews were following us around with all their equipment just to get the jump on each other. Companies began to merge just so they could cut down on the number of people they had to assign to us. But the crowd in back of us kept growing. We never got a good night's sleep. When we stopped, they stopped. When we moved, they moved, chuckwagons, bulldozers, derricks, generators. We were a walking business boom, and we began to receive invitations from some of the best hotels just for the amount of business we would drag into town with us. Some of those invitations were mighty generous, but we couldn't accept any because we were Indians and all the best hotels that were inviting us wouldn't accept Indians as guests. Racial prejudice is a terrible thing, Yossarian. It really is. It's a terrible thing to treat a decent, loyal Indian like a nigger, kike, wop or spic." Chief White Halfoat nodded slowly with conviction.

"Then, Yossarian, it finally happened—the beginning of the end. They began to follow us around from in front. They would try to guess where we were going to stop next and would begin drilling before we even got there, so we couldn't even stop. As soon as we'd begin to unroll our blankets, they would kick us off. They had confidence in us. They wouldn't even wait to strike oil before they kicked us off. We were so tired we almost didn't care the day our time ran out. One morning we found ourselves completely surrounded by oilmen waiting for us to come their way so they could kick us off. Everywhere you looked there was an oilman on a ridge, waiting there like Indians getting ready to attack. It was the end. We couldn't stay where we were because we had just been kicked off. And there was no place left for us to go. Only the Army saved me. Luckily, the war broke out just in the nick of time, and a draft board picked me right up out of the middle and put me down safely in Lowery Field, Colorado. I was the only survivor."

Yossarian knew he was lying, but did not interrupt as Chief White Halfoat went on to claim that he had never heard from his parents again. That didn't bother him too much, though, for he had only their word for it that they were his parents, and since they had lied to him about so many other things, they could just as well have been lying to him about that too. He was much better acquainted with the fate of a tribe of first cousins who had wandered away north in a diversionary movement and pushed inadvertently into Canada. When they tried to return, they were stopped at the border by American immigration authorities who would not let them back into the country. They could not come back in because they were red.

It was a horrible joke, but Doc Daneeka didn't laugh until Yossarian came to him one mission later and pleaded again, without any real expectation of success, to be grounded. Doc Daneeka snickered once and was soon immersed in problems of his own, which included Chief White Halfoat, who had been challenging him all that morning to Indian wrestle, and Yossarian, who decided right then and there to go crazy.

"You're wasting your time," Doc Daneeka was forced to tell him.

"Can't you ground someone who's crazy?"

"Oh, sure. I have to. There's a rule saying I have to ground anyone who's crazy."

"Then why don't you ground me? I'm crazy. Ask Clevinger."

"Clevinger? Where *is* Clevinger? You find Clevinger and I'll ask him."

"Then ask any of the others. They'll tell you how crazy I am."

"They're crazy."

"Then why don't you ground them?"

"Why don't they ask me to ground them?"

"Because they're crazy, that's why."

"Of course they're crazy," Doc Daneeka replied. "I just told you they're crazy, didn't I? And you can't let crazy people decide whether you're crazy or not, can you?"

Yossarian looked at him soberly and tried another approach. "Is Orr crazy?"

"He sure is," Doc Daneeka said.

"Can you ground him?"

"I sure can. But first he has to ask me to. That's part of the rule."

"Then why doesn't he ask you to?"

"Because he's crazy," Doc Daneeka said. "He has to be crazy to keep flying combat missions after all the close calls he's had. Sure, I can ground Orr. But first he has to ask me to."

"That's all he has to do to be grounded?"

"That's all. Let him ask me."

"And then you can ground him?" Yossarian asked.

"No. Then I can't ground him."

"You mean there's a catch?"

"Sure there's a catch," Doc Daneeka replied. "Catch-22. Anyone who wants to get out of combat duty isn't really crazy."

There was only one catch and that was Catch-22, which specified that a concern for one's own safety in the face of dangers that were real and immediate was the process of a rational mind. Orr was crazy and could be grounded. All he had to do was ask; and as soon as he did, he would no longer be crazy and would have to fly more missions. Orr would be crazy to fly more missions and sane if he didn't, but if he was sane he had to fly them. If he flew them he was crazy and didn't have to; but if he didn't want to he was sane and had to. Yossarian was moved very deeply by the absolute simplicity of this clause of Catch-22 and let out a respectful whistle.

"That's some catch, that Catch-22," he observed.

"It's the best there is," Doc Daneeka agreed.

Yossarian saw it clearly in all its spinning reasonableness. There was an elliptical precision about its perfect pairs of parts that was graceful and shocking, like good modern art, and at times Yossarian wasn't quite sure that he saw it all, just the way he was never quite sure about good modern art or about the flies Orr saw in Appleby's eyes. He had Orr's word to take for the flies in Appleby's eyes.

"Oh, they're there, all right," Orr had assured him about the flies in Appleby's eyes after Yossarian's fist fight with Appleby in the officers' club, "although he probably doesn't even know it. That's why he can't see things as they really are."

"How come he doesn't know it?" inquired Yossarian.

"Because he's got flies in his eyes," Orr explained with exaggerated patience. "How can he see he's got flies in his eyes if he's got flies in his eyes?"

It made as much sense as anything else, and Yossarian was willing to give Orr the benefit of the doubt because Orr was from the wilderness outside New York City and knew so much more about wildlife than Yossarian did, and because Orr, unlike Yossarian's mother, father, sister, brother, aunt, uncle, in-law, teacher, spiritual leader, legislator, neighbor and newspaper, had never lied to him about anything crucial before. Yossarian had mulled his newfound knowledge about Appleby over in private for a day or two and then decided, as a good deed, to pass the word along to Appleby himself.

"Appleby, you've got flies in your eyes," he whispered helpfully as they passed by each other in the doorway of the parachute tent on the day of the weekly milk run to Parma.

"What?" Appleby responded sharply, thrown into confusion by the fact that Yossarian had spoken to him at all.

"You've got flies in your eyes," Yossarian repeated. "That's probably why you can't see them."

Appleby retreated from Yossarian with a look of loathing bewilderment and sulked in silence until he was in the jeep with Havermeyer riding down the long, straight road to the briefing room, where Major Danby, the fidgeting group operations officer, was waiting to conduct the preliminary briefing with all the lead pilots, bombardiers and navigators. Appleby spoke in a soft voice so that he would not be heard by the driver or by Captain Black, who was stretched out with his eyes closed in the front seat of the jeep.

"Havermeyer," he asked hesitantly. "Have I got flies in my eyes?"

Havermeyer blinked quizzically. "Sties?" he asked.

"No, flies," he was told.

Havermeyer blinked again. "Flies?"

"In my eyes."

"You must be crazy," Havermeyer said.

"No, I'm not crazy. Yossarian's crazy. Just tell me if I've got flies in my eyes or not. Go ahead. I can take it."

Havermeyer popped another piece of peanut brittle into his mouth and peered very closely into Appleby's eyes.

"I don't see any," he announced.

Appleby heaved an immense sigh of relief. Havermeyer had tiny bits of peanut brittle adhering to his lips, chin and cheeks.

"You've got peanut brittle crumbs on your face," Appleby remarked to him.

"I'd rather have peanut brittle crumbs on my face than flies in my eyes," Havermeyer retorted.

The officers of the other five planes in each flight arrived in trucks for the general briefing that took place thirty minutes later. The three enlisted men in each crew were not briefed at all, but were carried directly out on the airfield to the separate planes in which they were scheduled to fly that day, where they waited around with the ground crew until the officers with whom they had been scheduled to fly swung off the rattling tailgates of the trucks delivering them and it was time to climb aboard and start up. Engines rolled over disgruntledly on lollipop-shaped hardstands, resisting first, then idling smoothly awhile, and then the planes lumbered around and nosed forward lamely over the pebbled ground like sightless, stupid, crippled things until they taxied into the line at the foot of the landing strip and took off swiftly, one behind the other, in a zooming, rising roar, banking slowly into formation over mottled treetops, and circling the field at even speed until all the flights of six had been formed and then setting course over cerulean water on the first leg of the journey to the target in northern Italy or France. The planes gained altitude steadily and were above nine thousand feet by the time they crossed into enemy territory. One of the surprising things always was the sense of calm and utter silence, broken only by the test rounds fired from the machine guns, by an occasional toneless, terse remark over the intercom, and, at last, by the sobering pronouncement of the bombardier in each plane that they were at the I.P. and about to turn toward the target. There was always sunshine, always a tiny sticking in the throat from the rarefied air.

The B-25s they flew in were stable, dependable, dull-green ships with twin rudders and engines and wide wings. Their single fault, from where Yossarian sat as a bombardier, was the tight crawlway separating the bombardier's compartment in the Plexiglas nose from the nearest escape hatch. The crawlway was a narrow, square, cold tunnel hollowed out beneath the flight controls, and a large man like Yossarian could squeeze through only with difficulty. A chubby, moon-faced navigator with little reptilian eyes and a pipe like Aarfy's had trouble, too, and Yossarian used to chase him back from the nose as they turned toward the target, now minutes away. There was a time of tension then, a time of waiting with nothing to hear and nothing to see and nothing to do but wait as the antiaircraft guns below took aim and made ready to knock them all sprawling into infinite sleep if they could.

The crawlway was Yossarian's lifeline to outside from a plane about to fall, but Yossarian swore at it with seething antagonism, reviled it as an obstacle put there by providence as part of the plot that would destroy him. There was room for an additional escape hatch right there in the nose of a B-25, but there was no escape hatch. Instead there was the crawlway, and since the mess on the mission over Avignon he had learned to detest every mammoth inch of it, for it slung him seconds and seconds away from his parachute, which was too bulky to be taken up front with him, and seconds and seconds more after that away from the escape hatch on the floor between the rear of the elevated flight deck and the feet of the faceless top turret gunner mounted high above. Yossarian longed to be where Aarfy could be once Yossarian had chased him back from the nose; Yossarian longed to sit on the floor in a huddled ball right on top of the escape hatch inside a sheltering igloo of extra flak suits that he would have been happy to carry along with him, his parachute already hooked to his harness where it belonged, one fist clenching the red-handled rip cord, one fist gripping the emergency hatch release that would spill him earthward into air at the first dreadful squeal of destruction. That was where he wanted to be if he had to be there at all, instead of hung out there in front like some goddam cantilevered goldfish in some goddam cantilevered goldfish bowl while the goddam foul black tiers of flak were bursting and booming and billowing all around and above and below him in a climbing, cracking, staggered, banging, phantasmagorical, cosmological wickedness that jarred and tossed and shivered, clattered and pierced, and threatened to annihilate them all in one splinter of a second in one vast flash of fire.

Aarfy had been no use to Yossarian as a navigator or as anything else, and Yossarian drove him back from the nose vehemently each time so that they would not clutter up each other's way if they had to scramble suddenly for safety. Once Yossarian had driven him back from the nose, Aarfy was free to cower on the floor where Yossarian longed to cower, but he stood bolt upright instead with his stumpy arms resting comfortably on the backs of the pilot's and co-pilot's seats, pipe in hand, making affable small talk to McWatt and whoever happened to be co-pilot and pointing out amusing trivia in the sky to the two men, who were too busy to be interested. McWatt was too busy responding at the controls to Yossarian's strident instructions as Yossarian slipped the plane in on the bomb run and then whipped them all away violently around the ravenous pillars of exploding shells with curt, shrill, obscene commands to McWatt that were much like the anguished, entreating nightmare yelpings of Hungry Joe in the dark. Aarfy would puff reflectively on his pipe throughout the whole chaotic clash, gazing with unruffled curiosity at the war through McWatt's window as though it were a remote disturbance that could not affect him. Aarfy was a dedicated fraternity man who loved cheerleading and class reunions and did not have brains enough to be afraid. Yossarian did have brains enough and was, and the only thing that stopped him from abandoning his post under fire and scurrying back through the crawlway like a yellow-bellied rat was his unwillingness to entrust the evasive action out of the target area to anybody else. There was nobody else in the world he would honor with so great a responsibility. There was nobody else he knew who was as big a coward. Yossarian was the best man in the group at evasive action, but had no idea why.

There was no established procedure for evasive action. All you needed was fear, and Yossarian had plenty of that, more fear than Orr or Hungry Joe, more fear even than Dunbar, who had resigned himself submissively to the idea that he must die someday. Yossarian had not resigned himself to that idea, and he bolted for his life wildly on each mission the instant his bombs were away, hollering, "*Hard, hard, hard, hard, you bastard, hard!*" at McWatt and hating McWatt viciously all the time as though McWatt were to blame for their being up there at all to be rubbed out by strangers, and everybody else in the plane kept off the intercom, except for the pitiful time of the mess on the mission to Avignon when Dobbs went crazy in mid-air and began weeping pathetically for help.

"Help him, help him," Dobbs sobbed. "Help him, help him."

"Help who? Help who?" called back Yossarian, once he had plugged his headset back into the intercom system, after it had been jerked out when Dobbs wrested the controls away from Huple and hurled them all down suddenly into the deafening, paralyzing, horrifying dive which had plastered Yossarian helplessly to the ceiling of the plane by the top of his head and from which Huple had rescued them just in time by seizing the controls back from Dobbs and leveling the ship out almost as suddenly right back in the middle of the buffeting layer of cacophonous flak from which they had escaped successfully only a moment before. *Oh, God! Oh, God, oh, God,* Yossarian had been pleading wordlessly as he dangled from the ceiling of the nose of the ship by the top of his head, unable to move.

"The bombardier, the bombardier," Dobbs answered in a cry when Yossarian spoke. "He doesn't answer, he doesn't answer. Help the bombardier, help the bombardier."

"I'm the bombardier," Yossarian cried back at him. "I'm the bombardier. I'm all right. I'm all right."

"Then help him, help him," Dobbs begged. "Help him, help him."

And Snowden lay dying in back.

6

Hungry Joe

Hungry Joe did have fifty missions, but they were no help. He had his bags packed and was waiting again to go home. At night he had eerie, ear-splitting nightmares that kept everyone in the squadron awake but Huple, the fifteen-year-old pilot who had lied about his age to get into the Army and lived with his pet cat in the same tent with Hungry Joe. Huple was a light sleeper, but claimed he never heard Hungry Joe scream. Hungry Joe was sick.

"So what?" Doc Daneeka snarled resentfully. "I had it made, I tell you. Fifty grand a year I was knocking down, and almost all of it tax-free, since I made my customers pay me in cash. I had the strongest trade association in the world backing me up. And look what happened. Just when I was all set to really start stashing it away, they had to manufacture fascism and start a war horrible enough to affect even me. I gotta laugh when I hear someone like Hungry Joe screaming his brains out every night. I really gotta laugh. *He's* sick? How does he think I feel?"

Hungry Joe was too firmly embedded in calamities of his own to care how Doc Daneeka felt. There were the noises, for instance. Small ones enraged him and he hollered himself hoarse at Aarfy for the wet, sucking sounds he made puffing on his pipe, at Orr for tinkering, at McWatt for the explosive snap he gave each card he turned over when he dealt at blackjack or poker, at Dobbs for letting his teeth chatter as he went blundering clumsily about bumping into things. Hungry Joe was a throbbing, ragged mass of motile irritability. The steady ticking of a watch in a quiet room crashed like torture against his unshielded brain.

"Listen, kid," he explained harshly to Huple very late one evening, "if you want to live in this tent, you've got to do like I do. You've got to roll your wrist watch up in a pair of wool socks every night and keep it on the bottom of your foot locker on the other side of the room."

Huple thrust his jaw out defiantly to let Hungry Joe know he couldn't be pushed around and then did exactly as he had been told.

Hungry Joe was a jumpy, emaciated wretch with a fleshless face of dingy skin and bone and twitching veins squirming subcutaneously in the blackened hollows behind his eyes like severed sections of snake. It was a desolate, cratered face, sooty with care like an abandoned mining town. Hungry Joe ate voraciously, gnawed incessantly at the tips of his fingers, stammered, choked, itched, sweated, salivated, and sprang from spot to spot fanatically with an intricate black camera with which he was always trying to take pictures of naked girls. They never came out. He was always forgetting to put film in the camera or turn on lights or remove the cover from the lens opening. It wasn't easy persuading naked girls to pose, but Hungry Joe had the knack.

"Me big man," he would shout. "Me big photographer from *Life* magazine. Big picture on heap big cover. *Si, si, si!* Hollywood star. Multi *dinero*. Multi divorces. Multi ficky-fick all day long."

Few women anywhere could resist such wily cajolery, and prostitutes would spring to their feet eagerly and hurl themselves into whatever fantastic poses he requested of them. Women killed Hungry Joe. His response to them as sexual beings was one of frenzied worship and idolatry. They were lovely, satisfying, maddening manifestations of the miraculous, instruments of pleasure too powerful to be measured, too keen to be endured, and too exquisite to be intended for employment by base, unworthy man. He could interpret their naked presence in his hands only as a cosmic oversight destined to be rectified speedily, and he was driven always to make what carnal use of them he could in the fleeting moment or two he felt he had before Someone caught wise and whisked them away. He could never decide whether to furgle them or photograph them, for he had found it impossible to do both simultaneously. In fact, he was finding it almost impossible to do either, so scrambled were his powers of performance by the compulsive need for haste that invariably possessed him. The pictures never came out, and Hungry Joe never got in. The odd thing was that in civilian life Hungry Joe really had been a photographer for *Life* magazine.

He was a hero now, the biggest hero the Air Force had, Yossarian felt, for he had flown more combat tours of duty than any other hero the Air Force had. He had flown six combat tours of duty. Hungry Joe had finished flying his first combat tour of duty when twenty-five missions were all that were necessary for him to pack his bags, write happy letters home and begin hounding Sergeant Towser humorously for the arrival of the orders rotating him back to the States. While he waited, he spent each day shuffling rhythmically around the entrance of the operations tent, making boisterous wisecracks to everybody who came by and jocosely calling Sergeant Towser a lousy son of a bitch every time Sergeant Towser popped out of the orderly room.

Hungry Joe had finished flying his first twenty-five missions during the week of the Salerno beachhead, when Yossarian was laid up in the hospital with a burst of clap he had caught on a low-level mission over a Wac in bushes on a supply flight to Marrakech. Yossarian did his best to catch up with Hungry Joe and almost did, flying six missions in six days, but his twenty-third mission was to Arezzo, where Colonel Nevers was killed, and that was as close as he had ever been able to come to going home. The next day Colonel Cathcart was there, brimming with tough pride in his new outfit and celebrating his assumption of command by raising the number of missions required from twenty-five to thirty. Hungry Joe unpacked his bags and rewrote the happy letters home. He stopped hounding Sergeant Towser humorously. He began hating Sergeant Towser, focusing all blame upon him venomously, even though he knew Sergeant Towser had nothing to do with the arrival of Colonel Cathcart or the delay in the processing of shipping orders that might have rescued him seven days earlier and five times since.

Hungry Joe could no longer stand the strain of waiting for shipping orders and crumbled promptly into ruin every time he finished another tour of duty. Each time he was taken off combat status, he gave a big party for the little circle of friends he had. He broke out the bottles of bourbon he had managed to buy on his four-day weekly circuits with the courier plane and laughed, sang, shuffled and shouted in a festival of inebriated ecstasy until he could no longer keep awake and receded peacefully into slumber. As soon as Yossarian, Nately and Dunbar put him to bed he began screaming in his sleep. In the morning he stepped from his tent looking haggard, fearful and guilt-ridden, an eaten shell of a human building rocking perilously on the brink of collapse.

The nightmares appeared to Hungry Joe with celestial punctuality every single night he spent in the squadron throughout the whole harrowing ordeal when he was not flying combat missions and was waiting once again for the orders sending him home that never came. Impressionable men in the squadron like Dobbs and Captain Flume were so deeply disturbed by Hungry Joe's shrieking nightmares that they would begin to have shrieking nightmares of their own, and the piercing obscenities they flung into the air every night from their separate places in the squadron rang against each other in the darkness romantically like the mating calls of songbirds with filthy minds. Colonel Korn acted decisively to arrest what seemed to him to be the beginning of an unwholesome trend in Major Major's squadron. The solution he provided was to have Hungry Joe fly the courier ship once a week, removing him from the squadron for four nights, and the remedy, like all Colonel Korn's remedies, was successful.

Every time Colonel Cathcart increased the number of missions and returned Hungry Joe to combat duty, the nightmares stopped and Hungry Joe settled down into a normal state of terror with a smile of relief. Yossarian read Hungry Joe's shrunken face like a headline. It was good when Hungry Joe looked bad and terrible when Hungry Joe looked good. Hungry Joe's inverted set of responses was a curious phenomenon to everyone but Hungry Joe, who denied the whole thing stubbornly.

"Who dreams?" he answered, when Yossarian asked him what he dreamed about.

"Joe, why don't you go see Doc Daneeka?" Yossarian advised.

"Why should I go see Doc Daneeka? I'm not sick."

"What about your nightmares?"

"I don't have nightmares," Hungry Joe lied.

"Maybe he can do something about them."

"There's nothing wrong with nightmares," Hungry Joe answered. "Everybody has nightmares."

Yossarian thought he had him. "Every night?" he asked.

"Why not every night?" Hungry Joe demanded.

And suddenly it all made sense. Why *not* every night, indeed? It made sense to cry out in pain every night. It made more sense than Appleby, who was a stickler for regulations and had ordered Kraft to order Yossarian to take his Atabrine tablets on the flight overseas after Yossarian and Appleby had stopped talking to each other. Hungry Joe made more sense than Kraft, too, who was dead, dumped unceremoniously into doom over Ferrara by an exploding engine after Yossarian took his flight of six planes in over the target a second time. The group had missed the bridge at Ferrara again for the seventh straight day with the bombsight that could put bombs into a pickle barrel at forty thousand feet, and one whole week had already passed since Colonel Cathcart had volunteered to have his men destroy the bridge in twenty-four hours. Kraft was a skinny, harmless kid from Pennsylvania who wanted only to be liked, and was destined to be disappointed in even so humble and degrading an ambition. Instead of being liked, he was dead, a bleeding cinder on the barbarous pile whom nobody had heard in those last precious moments while the plane with one wing plummeted. He had lived innocuously for a little while and then had gone down in flame over Ferrara on the seventh day, while God was resting, when McWatt turned and Yossarian guided him in over the target on a second bomb run because Aarfy was confused and Yossarian had been unable to drop his bombs the first time.

"I guess we do have to go back again, don't we?" McWatt had said somberly over the intercom.

"I guess we do," said Yossarian.

"Do we?" said McWatt.

"Yeah."

"Oh, well," sang McWatt, "what the hell."

And back they had gone while the planes in the other flights circled safely off in the distance and every crashing cannon in the Hermann Goering Division below was busy crashing shells this time only at them.

Colonel Cathcart had courage and never hesitated to volunteer his men for any target available. No target was too dangerous for his group to attack, just as no shot was too difficult for Appleby to handle on the Ping-Pong table. Appleby was a good pilot and a superhuman Ping-Pong player with flies in his eyes who never lost a point. Twenty-one serves were all it ever took for Appleby to disgrace another opponent. His prowess on the Ping-Pong table was legendary, and Appleby won every game he started until the night Orr got tipsy on gin and juice and smashed open Appleby's forehead with his paddle after Appleby has smashed back each of Orr's first five serves. Orr leaped on top of the table after hurling his paddle and came sailing off the other end in a running broad jump with both feet planted squarely in Appleby's face. Pandemonium broke loose. It took almost a full minute for Appleby to disentangle himself from Orr's flailing arms and legs and grope his way to his feet, with Orr held off the ground before him by the shirt front in one hand and his other arm drawn back in a fist to smite him dead, and at that moment Yossarian stepped forward and took Orr away from him. It was a night of surprises for Appleby, who was as large as Yossarian and as strong and who swung at Yossarian as hard as he could with a punch that flooded Chief White Halfoat with such joyous excitement that he turned and busted Colonel Moodus in the nose with a punch that filled General Dreedle with such mellow gratification that he had Colonel Cathcart throw the chaplain out of the officers' club and ordered Chief White Halfoat moved into Doc Daneeka's tent, where he could be under a doctor's care twenty-four hours a day and be kept in good enough physical condition to bust Colonel Moodus in the nose again whenever General Dreedle wanted him to. Sometimes General Dreedle made special trips down from Wing Headquarters with Colonel Moodus and his nurse just to have Chief White Halfoat bust his son-in-law in the nose.

Chief White Halfoat would much rather have remained in the trailer he shared with Captain Flume, the silent, haunted squadron public-relations officer who spent most of each evening developing the pictures he took during the day to be sent out with his publicity releases. Captain Flume spent as much of each evening as he could working in his darkroom and then lay down on his cot with his fingers crossed and a rabbit's foot around his neck and tried with all his might to stay awake. He lived in mortal fear of Chief White Halfoat. Captain Flume was obsessed with the idea that Chief White Halfoat would tiptoe up to his cot one night when he was sound asleep and slit his throat open for him from ear to ear. Captain Flume had obtained this idea from Chief White Halfoat himself, who did tiptoe up to his cot one night as he was dozing off, to hiss portentously that one night when he, Captain Flume, was sound asleep he, Chief White Halfoat, was going to slit his throat open for him from ear to ear. Captain Flume turned to ice, his eyes, flung open wide, staring directly up into Chief White Halfoat's, glinting drunkenly only inches away.

"Why?" Captain Flume managed to croak finally.

"Why not?" was Chief White Halfoat's answer.

Each night after that, Captain Flume forced himself to keep awake as long as possible. He was aided immeasurably by Hungry Joe's nightmares. Listening so intently to Hungry Joe's maniacal howling night after night, Captain Flume grew to hate him and began wishing that Chief White Halfoat would tiptoe up to *his* cot one night and slit *his* throat open for him from ear to ear. Actually, Captain Flume slept like a log most nights and merely *dreamed* he was awake. So convincing were these dreams of lying awake that he awoke from them each morning in complete exhaustion and fell right back to sleep.

Chief White Halfoat had grown almost fond of Captain Flume since his amazing metamorphosis. Captain Flume had entered his bed that night a buoyant extrovert and left it the next morning a brooding introvert, and Chief White Halfoat proudly regarded the new Captain Flume as his own creation. He had never intended to slit Captain

Flume's throat open for him from ear to ear. Threatening to do so was merely his idea of a joke, like dying of pneumonia, busting Colonel Moodus in the nose or challenging Doc Daneeka to Indian wrestle. All Chief White Halfoat wanted to do when he staggered in drunk each night was go right to sleep, and Hungry Joe often made that impossible. Hungry Joe's nightmares gave Chief White Halfoat the heebie-jeebies, and he often wished that someone would tiptoe into Hungry Joe's tent, lift Huple's cat off his face and slit his throat open for him from ear to ear, so that everybody in the squadron but Captain Flume could get a good night's sleep.

Even though Chief White Halfoat kept busting Colonel Moodus in the nose for General Dreedle's benefit, he was still outside the pale. Also outside the pale was Major Major, the squadron commander, who had found *that* out the same time he found out that he *was* squadron commander from Colonel Cathcart, who came blasting into the squadron in his hopped-up jeep the day after Major Duluth was killed over Perugia. Colonel Cathcart slammed to a screeching stop inches short of the railroad ditch separating the nose of his jeep from the lopsided basketball court on the other side, from which Major Major was eventually driven by the kicks and shoves and stones and punches of the men who had almost become his friends.

"You're the new squadron commander," Colonel Cathcart had bellowed across the ditch at him. "But don't think it means anything, because it doesn't. All it means is that you're the new squadron commander."

And Colonel Cathcart had roared away as abruptly as he'd come, whipping the jeep around with a vicious spinning of wheels that sent a spray of fine grit blowing into Major Major's face. Major Major was immobilized by the news. He stood speechless, lanky and gawking, with a scuffed basketball in his long hands as the seeds of rancor sown so swiftly by Colonel Cathcart took root in the soldiers around him who had been playing basketball with him and who had let him come as close to making friends with them as anyone had ever let him come before. The whites of his moony eyes grew large and misty as his mouth struggled yearningly and lost against the familiar, impregnable loneliness drifting in around him again like suffocating fog.

Like all the other officers at Group Headquarters except Major Danby, Colonel Cathcart was infused with the democratic spirit: he believed that all men were created equal, and he therefore spurned all men outside Group Headquarters with equal fervor. Nevertheless, he believed in his men. As he told them frequently in the briefing room, he believed they were at least ten missions better than any other outfit and felt that any who did not share this confidence he had placed in them could get the hell out. The only way they could get the hell out, though, as Yossarian learned when he flew to visit ex-P.F.C. Wintergreen, was by flying the extra ten missions.

"I still don't get it," Yossarian protested. "Is Doc Daneeka right or isn't he?"

"How many did he say?"

"Forty."

"Daneeka was telling the truth," ex-P.F.C. Wintergreen admitted. "Forty missions is all you have to fly as far as Twenty-seventh Air Force Headquarters is concerned."

Yossarian was jubilant. "Then I can go home, right? I've got forty-eight."

"No, you can't go home," ex-P.F.C. Wintergreen corrected him. "Are you crazy or something?"

"Why not?"

"Catch-22."

"Catch-22?" Yossarian was stunned. "What the hell has Catch-22 got to do with it?"

"Catch-22," Doc Daneeka answered patiently, when Hungry Joe had flown Yossarian back to Pianosa, "says you've always got to do what your commanding officer tells you to."

"But Twenty-seventh Air Force says I can go home with forty missions."

"But they don't say you have to go home. And regulations do say you have to obey every order. That's the catch. Even if the colonel were disobeying a Twenty-seventh Air Force order by making you fly more missions, you'd still have to fly them, or you'd be guilty of disobeying an order of his. And then Twenty-seventh Air Force Headquarters would really jump on you."

Yossarian slumped with disappointment. "Then I really do have to fly the fifty missions, don't I?" he grieved.

"The fifty-five," Doc Daneeka corrected him.

"What fifty-five?"

"The fifty-five missions the colonel now wants all of you to fly."

Hungry Joe heaved a huge sigh of relief when he heard Doc Daneeka and broke into a grin. Yossarian grabbed Hungry Joe by the neck and made him fly them both right back to ex-P.F.C. Wintergreen.

"What would they do to me," he asked in confidential tones, "if I refused to fly them?"

"We'd probably shoot you," ex-P.F.C. Wintergreen replied.

"We?" Yossarian cried in surprise. "What do you mean, *we?* Since when are you on their side?"

"If you're going to be shot, whose side do you expect me to be on?" ex-P.F.C. Wintergreen retorted.

Yossarian winced. Colonel Cathcart had raised him again.

7

McWatt

Ordinarily, Yossarian's pilot was McWatt, who, shaving in loud red, clean pajamas outside his tent each morning, was one of the odd, ironic, incomprehensible things surrounding Yossarian. McWatt was the craziest combat man of them all probably, because he was perfectly sane and still did not mind the war. He was a short-legged, wide-shouldered, smiling young soul who whistled bouncy show tunes continuously and turned over cards with sharp snaps when he dealt at blackjack or poker until Hungry Joe disintegrated into quaking despair finally beneath their cumulative impact and began ranting at him to stop snapping the cards.

"You son of a bitch, you only do it because it hurts me," Hungry Joe would yell furiously as Yossarian held him back soothingly with one hand. "That's the only reason he does it, because he likes to hear me scream—you goddam son of a bitch!"

McWatt crinkled his fine, freckled nose apologetically and vowed not to snap the cards any more, but always forgot. McWatt wore fleecy bedroom slippers with his red pajamas and slept between freshly pressed colored bedsheets like the one Milo had retrieved half of for him from the grinning thief with the sweet tooth in exchange for none of the pitted dates Milo had borrowed from Yossarian. McWatt was deeply impressed with Milo, who, to the amusement of Corporal Snark, his mess sergeant, was already buying eggs for seven cents apiece and selling them for five cents. But McWatt was never as impressed with Milo as Milo had been with the letter Yossarian had obtained for his liver from Doc Daneeka.

"What's this?" Milo had cried out in alarm when he came upon the enormous corrugated carton filled with packages of dried fruit and cans of fruit juices and desserts that two of the Italian laborers Major —— de Coverley had kidnapped for his kitchen were about to carry off to Yossarian's tent.

"This is Captain Yossarian, sir," said Corporal Snark with a superior smirk. Corporal Snark was an intellectual snob who felt he was twenty years ahead of his time and did not enjoy cooking down to the masses.

"He has a letter from Doc Daneeka entitling him to all the fruit and fruit juices he wants."

"What's this?" cried out Yossarian as Milo went white and began to sway.

"This is Lieutenant Milo Minderbinder, sir," said Corporal Snark with a derisive wink. "One of our new pilots. He became mess officer while you were in the hospital this last time."

"What's this?" cried out McWatt, late in the afternoon, as Milo handed him half his bedsheet.

"It's half of the bedsheet that was stolen from your tent this morning," Milo explained with nervous self-satisfaction, his rusty mustache twitching rapidly. "I'll bet you didn't even know it was stolen."

"Why should anyone want to steal a bedsheet?" Yossarian asked.

Milo grew flustered. "You don't understand," he protested.

And Yossarian also did not understand why Milo needed so desperately to invest in the letter from Doc Daneeka, which came right to the point. "Give Yossarian all the dried fruit and fruit juices he wants," Doc Daneeka had written. "He says he has a liver condition."

"A letter like this," Milo mumbled despondently, "could ruin any mess officer in the world." Milo had come to Yossarian's tent just to read the letter again, following his carton of lost provisions across the squadron like a mourner. "I have to give you as much as you ask for. Why, the letter doesn't even say you have to eat all of it yourself."

"And it's a good thing it doesn't," Yossarian told him, "because I never eat any of it. I have a liver condition."

"Oh, yes, I forgot," said Milo, in a voice lowered deferentially. "Is it bad?

"Just bad enough," Yossarian answered cheerfully.

"I see," said Milo. "What does that mean?"

"It means that it couldn't be better . . ."

"I don't think I understand."

". . . without being worse. Now do you see?"

"Yes, now I see. But I still don't think I understand."

"Well, don't let it trouble you. Let it trouble me. You see, I don't really have a liver condition. I've just got the symptoms. I have a Garnett-Fleischaker syndrome."

"I see," said Milo. "And what is a Garnett-Fleischaker syndrome?"

"A liver condition."

"I see," said Milo, and began massaging his black eyebrows together wearily with an expression of interior pain, as though waiting for some stinging discomfort he was experiencing to go away. "In that case," he continued finally, "I suppose you do have to be very careful about what you eat, don't you?"

"Very careful indeed," Yossarian told him. "A good Garnett-Fleischaker syndrome isn't easy to come by, and I don't want to ruin mine. That's why I never eat any fruit."

"Now I do see," said Milo. "Fruit is bad for your liver?"

"No, fruit is good for my liver. That's why I never eat any."

"Then what do you do with it?" demanded Milo, plodding along doggedly through his mounting confusion to fling out the question burning on his lips. "Do you sell it?"

"I give it away."

"To who?" cried Milo, in a voice cracking with dismay.

"To anyone who wants it," Yossarian shouted back.

Milo let out a long, melancholy wail and staggered back, beads of perspiration popping out suddenly all over his ashen face. He tugged on his unfortunate mustache absently, his whole body trembling.

"I give a great deal of it to Dunbar," Yossarian went on.

"Dunbar?" Milo echoed numbly.

"Yes. Dunbar can eat all the fruit he wants and it won't do him a damned bit of good. I just leave the carton right out there in the open for anyone who wants any to come and help himself. Aarfy comes here to get prunes because he says he never gets enough prunes in the mess hall. You might look into that when you've got some time because it's no fun having Aarfy hanging around here. Whenever the supply runs low I just have Corporal Snark fill me up again. Nately always takes a whole load of fruit along with him whenever he goes to Rome. He's in love with a whore there who hates me and isn't at all interested in him. She's got a kid sister who never leaves them alone in bed together, and they live in an apartment with an old man and woman and a bunch of other girls with nice fat thighs who are always kidding around also. Nately brings them a whole cartonful every time he goes."

"Does he sell it to them?"

"No, he *gives* it to them."

Milo frowned. "Well, I suppose that's very generous of him," he remarked with no enthusiasm.

"Yes, very generous," Yossarian agreed.

"And I'm sure it's perfectly legal," said Milo, "since the food is yours once you get it from me. I suppose that with conditions as hard as they are, these people are very glad to get it."

"Yes, very glad," Yossarian assured him. "The two girls sell it all on the black market and use the money to buy flashy costume jewelry and cheap perfume."

Milo perked up. "Costume jewelry!" he exclaimed. "I didn't know that. How much are they paying for cheap perfume?"

"The old man uses his share to buy raw whiskey and dirty pictures. He's a lecher."

"A lecher?"

"You'd be surprised."

"Is there much of a market in Rome for dirty pictures?" Milo asked.

"You'd be surprised. Take Aarfy, for instance. Knowing him, you'd never suspect, would you?"

"That he's a lecher?"

"No, that he's a navigator. You know Captain Aardvaark, don't you? He's that nice guy who came up to you your first day in the squadron and said, 'Aardvaark's my name, and navigation is my game.' He wore a pipe in his face and probably asked you what college you went to. Do you know him?"

Milo was paying no attention. "Let me be your partner," he blurted out imploringly.

Yossarian turned him down, even though he had no doubt that the truckloads of fruit *would* be theirs to dispose of any way they saw fit once Yossarian had requisitioned them from the mess hall with Doc Daneeka's letter. Milo was crestfallen, but from that moment on he trusted Yossarian with every secret but one, reasoning shrewdly that anyone who would not steal from the country he loved would not steal from anybody. Milo trusted Yossarian with every secret but the location of the holes in the hills in which he began burying his money once he returned from Smyrna with his planeload of figs and learned from Yossarian that a C.I.D. man had come to the hospital. To Milo, who had been gullible enough to volunteer for it, the position of mess officer was a sacred trust.

"I didn't even realize we weren't serving enough prunes," he had admitted that first day. "I suppose it's because I'm still so new. I'll raise the question with my first chef."

Yossarian eyed him sharply. "What first chef?" he demanded. "You don't have a first chef."

"Corporal Snark," Milo explained, looking away a little guiltily. "He's the only chef I have, so he really is my first chef, although I hope to move him over to the administrative side. Corporal Snark tends to be a little too creative, I feel. He thinks being a mess sergeant is some sort of art form and is always complaining about having to prostitute his talents. Nobody is asking him to do any such thing! Incidentally, do you happen to know why he was busted to private and is only a corporal now?"

"Yes," said Yossarian. "He poisoned the squadron."

Milo went pale again. "He did *what?*"

"He mashed hundreds of cakes of GI soap into the sweet potatoes just to show that people have the taste of Philistines and don't know the difference between good and bad. Every man in the squadron was sick. Missions were canceled."

"Well!" Milo exclaimed, with thin-lipped disapproval. "He certainly found out how wrong *he* was, didn't he?"

"On the contrary," Yossarian corrected. "He found out how *right* he was. We packed it away by the plateful and clamored for more. We all knew we were sick, but we had no idea we'd been poisoned."

Milo sniffed in consternation twice, like a shaggy brown hare. "In that case, I certainly do want to get him over to the administrative side. I don't want anything like that happening while I'm in charge. You see," he confided earnestly, "what I hope to do is give the men in this squadron the best meals in the whole world. That's really something to shoot at, isn't it? If a mess officer aims at anything less, it seems to me, he has no right being mess officer. Don't you agree?"

Yossarian turned slowly to gaze at Milo with probing distrust. He saw a simple, sincere face that was incapable of subtlety or guile, an honest, frank face with disunited large eyes, rusty hair, black eyebrows and an unfortunate reddish-brown mustache. Milo had a long, thin nose with sniffing, damp nostrils heading sharply off to the right, always pointing away from where the rest of him was looking. It was the face of a man of hardened integrity who could no more consciously violate the moral principles on which his virtue rested than he could transform himself into a despicable toad. One of these moral principles was that it was never a sin to charge as much as the traffic would bear. He was capable of mighty paroxysms of righteous indignation, and he was indignant as could be when he learned that a C.I.D. man was in the area looking for him.

"He's not looking for you," Yossarian said, trying to placate him. "He's looking for someone up in the hospital who's been signing Washington Irving's name to the letters he's been censoring."

"I never signed Washington Irving's name to any letters," Milo declared.

"Of course not."

"But that's just a trick to get me to confess I've been making money in the black market." Milo hauled violently at a disheveled hunk of his off-colored mustache. "I don't like guys like that. Always snooping around people like us. Why doesn't the government get after ex-P.F.C. Wintergreen, if it wants to do some good? He's got no respect for rules and regulations and keeps cutting prices on me."

Milo's mustache was unfortunate because the separated halves never matched. They were like Milo's disunited eyes, which never looked at the same thing at the same time. Milo could see more things than most people, but he could see none of them too distinctly. In contrast to his reaction to news of the C.I.D. man, he learned with calm courage from Yossarian that Colonel Cathcart had raised the number of missions to fifty-five.

"We're at war," he said. "And there's no use complaining about the number of missions we have to fly. If the colonel says we have to fly fifty-five missions, we have to fly them."

"Well, I don't have to fly them," Yossarian vowed. "I'll go see Major Major."

"How can you? Major Major never sees anybody."

"Then I'll go back into the hospital."

"You just came out of the hospital ten days ago," Milo reminded him reprovingly. "You can't keep running into the hospital every time something happens you don't like. No, the best thing to do is fly the missions. It's our duty."

Milo had rigid scruples that would not even allow him to borrow a package of pitted dates from the mess hall that day of McWatt's stolen bedsheet, for the food at the mess hall was all still the property of the government.

"But I can borrow it from you," he explained to Yossarian, "since all this fruit is yours once you get it from me with Doctor Daneeka's letter. You can do whatever you want with it, even sell it at a high profit instead of giving it away free. Wouldn't you want to do that together?"

"No."

Milo gave up. "Then lend me one package of pitted dates," he requested. "I'll give it back to you. I swear I will, and there'll be a little something extra for you."

Milo proved good as his word and handed Yossarian a quarter of McWatt's yellow bedsheet when he returned with the unopened package of dates and with the grinning thief with the sweet tooth who had stolen the bedsheet from McWatt's tent. The piece of bedsheet now belonged to Yossarian. He had earned it while napping, although he did not understand how. Neither did McWatt.

"What's this?" cried McWatt, staring in mystification at the ripped half of his bedsheet.

"It's half of the bedsheet that was stolen from your tent this morning," Milo explained. "I'll bet you didn't even know it was stolen."

"Why should anyone want to steal half a bedsheet?" Yossarian asked.

Milo grew flustered. "You don't understand," he protested. "He stole the whole bedsheet, and I got it back with the package of pitted dates you invested. That's why the quarter of the bedsheet is yours. You made a very handsome return on your investment, particularly since you've gotten back every pitted date you gave me." Milo next addressed himself to McWatt. "Half the bedsheet is yours because it was all yours to begin with, and I really don't understand what you're complaining about, since you wouldn't have any of it if Captain Yossarian and I hadn't intervened in your behalf."

"Who's complaining?" McWatt exclaimed. "I'm just trying to figure out what I can do with half a bedsheet."

"There are lots of things you can do with half a bedsheet," Milo assured him. "The remaining quarter of the bedsheet I've set aside for myself as a reward for my enterprise, work and initiative. It's not for myself, you understand, but for the syndicate. That's something you might do with half the bedsheet. You can leave it in the syndicate and watch it grow."

"What syndicate?"

"The syndicate I'd like to form someday so that I can give you men the good food you deserve."

"You want to form a syndicate?"

"Yes, I do. No, a mart. Do you know what a mart is?"

"It's a place where you buy things, isn't it?"

"And sell things," corrected Milo.

"And sell things."

"All my life I've wanted a mart. You can do lots of things if you've got a mart. But you've got to have a mart."

"You want a mart?"

"And every man will have a share."

Yossarian was still puzzled, for it was a business matter, and there was much about business matters that always puzzled him.

"Let me try to explain it again," Milo offered with growing weariness and exasperation, jerking his thumb toward the thief with the sweet tooth, still grinning beside him. "I knew he wanted the dates more than the bedsheet. Since he doesn't understand a word of English, I made it a point to conduct the whole transaction in English."

"Why didn't you just hit him over the head and take the bedsheet away from him?" Yossarian asked.

Pressing his lips together with dignity, Milo shook his head. "That would have been most unjust," he scolded firmly. "Force is wrong, and two wrongs never make a right. It was much better my way. When I held the dates out to him and reached for the bedsheet, he probably thought I was offering to trade."

"What were you doing?"

"Actually, I *was* offering to trade, but since he doesn't understand English, I can always deny it."

"Suppose he gets angry and wants the dates?"

"Why, we'll just hit him over the head and take them away from him," Milo answered without hesitation. He looked from Yossarian to McWatt and back again. "I really can't see what everyone is complaining about. We're all much better off than before. Everybody is happy but this thief, and there's no sense worrying about him, since he doesn't even speak our language and deserves whatever he gets. Don't you understand?"

But Yossarian still didn't understand either how Milo could buy eggs in Malta for seven cents apiece and sell them at a profit in Pianosa for five cents.

8

Lieutenant Scheisskopf

Not even Clevinger understood how Milo could do that, and Clevinger knew everything. Clevinger knew everything about the war except why Yossarian had to die while Corporal Snark was allowed to live, or why Corporal Snark had to die while Yossarian was allowed to live. It was a vile and muddy war, and Yossarian could have lived without it—lived forever, perhaps. Only a fraction of his countrymen would give up their lives to win it, and it was not his ambition to be among them. To die or not to die, that was the question, and Clevinger grew limp trying to answer it. History did not demand Yossarian's premature demise, justice could be satisfied without it, progress did not hinge upon it, victory did not depend on it. That men would die was a matter of necessity; which men would die, though, was a matter of circumstance, and Yossarian was willing to be the victim of anything but circumstance. But that was war. Just about all he could find in its favor was that it paid well and liberated children from the pernicious influence of their parents.

Clevinger knew so much because Clevinger was a genius with a pounding heart and blanching face. He was a gangling, gawky, feverish, famish-eyed brain. As a Harvard undergraduate he had won prizes in scholarship for just about everything, and the only reason he had not won prizes in scholarship for everything else was that he was too busy signing petitions, circulating petitions and challenging petitions, joining discussion groups and resigning from discussion groups, attending youth congresses, picketing other youth congresses and organizing student committees in defense of dismissed faculty members. Everyone agreed that Clevinger was certain to go far in the academic world. In short, Clevinger was one of those people with lots of intelligence and no brains, and everyone knew it except those who soon found it out.

In short, he was a dope. He often looked to Yossarian like one of those people hanging around modern museums with both eyes together on one side of a face. It was an illusion, of course, generated by

Clevinger's predilection for staring fixedly at one side of a question and never seeing the other side at all. Politically, he was a humanitarian who did know right from left and was trapped uncomfortably between the two. He was constantly defending his Communist friends to his right-wing enemies and his right-wing friends to his Communist enemies, and he was thoroughly detested by both groups, who never defended him to anyone because they thought he was a dope.

He was a very serious, very earnest and very conscientious dope. It was impossible to go to a movie with him without getting involved afterward in a discussion on empathy, Aristotle, universals, messages and the obligations of the cinema as an art form in a materialistic society. Girls he took to the theater had to wait until the first intermission to find out from him whether or not they were seeing a good or a bad play, and then found out at once. He was a militant idealist who crusaded against racial bigotry by growing faint in its presence. He knew everything about literature except how to enjoy it.

Yossarian tried to help him. "Don't be a dope," he had counseled Clevinger when they were both at cadet school in Santa Ana, California.

"I'm going to tell him," Clevinger insisted, as the two of them sat high in the reviewing stands looking down on the auxiliary parade-ground at Lieutenant Scheisskopf raging back and forth like a beardless Lear.

"Why me?" Lieutenant Scheisskopf wailed.

"Keep still, idiot," Yossarian advised Clevinger avuncularly.

"You don't know what you're talking about," Clevinger objected.

"I know enough to keep still, idiot."

Lieutenant Scheisskopf tore his hair and gnashed his teeth. His rubbery cheeks shook with gusts of anguish. His problem was a squadron of aviation cadets with low morale who marched atrociously in the parade competition that took place every Sunday afternoon. Their morale was low because they did not want to march in parades every Sunday afternoon and because Lieutenant Scheisskopf had appointed cadet officers from their ranks instead of permitting them to elect their own.

"I *want* someone to tell me," Lieutenant Scheisskopf beseeched them all prayerfully. "If any of it is my fault, I *want* to be told."

"He wants someone to tell him," Clevinger said.

"He *wants* everyone to keep still, idiot," Yossarian answered.

"Didn't you hear him?" Clevinger argued.

"I heard him," Yossarian replied. "I heard him say very loudly and very distinctly that he wants every one of us to keep our mouths shut if we know what's good for us."

"I won't punish you," Lieutenant Scheisskopf swore.

"He says he won't punish me," said Clevinger.

"He'll castrate you," said Yossarian.

"I swear I won't punish you," said Lieutenant Scheisskopf. "I'll be grateful to the man who tells me the truth."

"He'll hate you," said Yossarian. "To his dying day he'll hate you."

Lieutenant Scheisskopf was an R.O.T.C. graduate who was rather glad that war had broken out, since it gave him an opportunity to wear an officer's uniform every day and say "Men" in a clipped, military voice to the bunches of kids who fell into his clutches every eight weeks on their way to the butcher's block. He was an ambitious and humorless Lieutenant Scheisskopf, who confronted his responsibilities soberly and smiled only when some rival officer at the Santa Ana Army Air Force Base came down with a lingering disease. He had poor eyesight and chronic sinus trouble, which made war especially exciting for him, since he was in no danger of going overseas. The best thing about him was his wife and the best thing about his wife was a girl friend named Dori Duz who did whenever she could and had a Wac uniform that Lieutenant Scheisskopf's wife put on every weekend and took off every weekend for every cadet in her husband's squadron who wanted to creep into her.

Dori Duz was a lively little tart of copper-green and gold who loved doing it best in toolsheds, phone booths, field houses and bus kiosks. There was little she hadn't tried and less she wouldn't. She was shameless, slim, nineteen and aggressive. She destroyed egos by the score and made men hate themselves in the morning for the way she found them, used them and tossed them aside. Yossarian loved her. She was a marvelous piece of ass who found him only fair. He loved the feel of springy muscle beneath her skin everywhere he touched her the only time she'd let him. Yossarian loved Dori Duz so much that he couldn't help flinging himself down passionately on top of Lieutenant Scheisskopf's wife every week to revenge himself upon Lieutenant Scheisskopf for the way Lieutenant Scheisskopf was revenging himself upon Clevinger.

Lieutenant Scheisskopf's wife was revenging herself upon Lieutenant Scheisskopf for some unforgettable crime of his she couldn't recall. She was a plump, pink, sluggish girl who read good books and kept urging

Yossarian not to be so bourgeois without the *r.* She was never without a good book close by, not even when she was lying in bed with nothing on her but Yossarian and Dori Duz's dog tags. She bored Yossarian, but he was in love with her, too. She was a crazy mathematics major from the Wharton School of Business who could not count to twenty-eight each month without getting into trouble.

"Darling, we're going to have a baby again," she would say to Yossarian every month.

"You're out of your goddam head," he would reply.

"I mean it, baby," she insisted.

"So do I."

"Darling, we're going to have a baby again," she would say to her husband.

"I haven't the time," Lieutenant Scheisskopf would grumble petulantly. "Don't you know there's a parade going on?"

Lieutenant Scheisskopf cared very deeply about winning parades and about bringing Clevinger up on charges before the Action Board for conspiring to advocate the overthrow of the cadet officers Lieutenant Scheisskopf had appointed. Clevinger was a troublemaker and a wise guy. Lieutenant Scheisskopf knew that Clevinger might cause even more trouble if he wasn't watched. Yesterday it was the cadet officers; tomorrow it might be the world. Clevinger had a mind, and Lieutenant Scheisskopf had noticed that people with minds tended to get pretty smart at times. Such men were dangerous, and even the new cadet officers whom Clevinger had helped into office were eager to give damning testimony against him. The case against Clevinger was open and shut. The only thing missing was something to charge him with.

It could not be anything to do with parades, for Clevinger took the parades almost as seriously as Lieutenant Scheisskopf himself. The men fell out for the parades early each Sunday afternoon and groped their way into ranks of twelve outside the barracks. Groaning with hangovers, they limped in step to their station on the main parade-ground, where they stood motionless in the heat for an hour or two with the men from the sixty or seventy other cadet squadrons until enough of them had collapsed to call it a day. On the edge of the field stood a row of ambulances and teams of trained stretcher bearers with walkie-talkies. On the roofs of the ambulances were spotters with binoculars. A tally clerk kept score. Supervising this entire phase of the operation was a medical officer with a flair for accounting who okayed pulses and checked the figures of the tally clerk. As soon as enough unconscious men had been collected in the ambulances, the medical officer signaled the bandmaster to strike up the band and end the parade. One behind the other, the squadrons marched up the field, executed a cumbersome turn around the reviewing stand and marched down the field and back to their barracks.

Each of the parading squadrons was graded as it marched past the reviewing stand, where a bloated colonel with a big fat mustache sat with the other officers. The best squadron in each wing won a yellow pennant on a pole that was utterly worthless. The best squadron on the base won a red pennant on a longer pole that was worth even less, since the pole was heavier and was that much more of a nuisance to lug around all week until some other squadron won it the following Sunday. To Yossarian, the idea of pennants as prizes was absurd. No money went with them, no class privileges. Like Olympic medals and tennis trophies, all they signified was that the owner had done something of no benefit to anyone more capably than everyone else.

The parades themselves seemed equally absurd. Yossarian hated a parade. Parades were so martial. He hated hearing them, hated seeing them, hated being tied up in traffic by them. He hated being made to take part in them. It was bad enough being an aviation cadet without having to act like a soldier in the blistering heat every Sunday afternoon. It was bad enough being an aviation cadet because it was obvious now that the war would not be over before he had finished his training. That was the only reason he had volunteered for cadet training in the first place. As a soldier who had qualified for aviation cadet training, he had weeks and weeks of waiting for assignment to a class, weeks and weeks more to become a bombardier-navigator, weeks and weeks more of operational training after that to prepare him for overseas duty. It seemed inconceivable then that the war could last that long, for God was on his side, he had been told, and God, he had also been told, could do whatever He wanted to. But the war was not nearly over, and his training was almost complete.

Lieutenant Scheisskopf longed desperately to win parades and sat up half the night working on it while his wife waited amorously for him in bed thumbing through Krafft-Ebing to her favorite passages. He read books on marching. He manipulated boxes of chocolate soldiers until they melted in his hands and then maneuvered in ranks of twelve a set of plastic cowboys he had bought from a mail-order house under an assumed name and kept locked away from everyone's eyes during the day. Leonardo's exercises in anatomy proved indispensable. One evening he felt the need for a live model and directed his wife to march around the room.

"Naked?" she asked hopefully.

Lieutenant Scheisskopf smacked his hands over his eyes in exasperation. It was the despair of Lieutenant Scheisskopf's life to be chained to a woman who was incapable of looking beyond her own dirty, sexual desires to the titanic struggles for the unattainable in which noble man could become heroically engaged.

"Why don't you ever whip me?" she pouted one night.

"Because I haven't the time," he snapped at her impatiently. "I haven't the time. Don't you know there's a parade going on?"

And he really did not have the time. There it was Sunday already, with only seven days left in the week to get ready for the next parade. He had no idea where the hours went. Finishing last in three successive parades had given Lieutenant Scheisskopf an unsavory reputation, and he considered every means of improvement, even nailing the twelve men in each rank to a long two-by-four beam of seasoned oak to keep them in line. The plan was not feasible, for making a ninety-degree turn would have been impossible without nickel-alloy swivels inserted in the small of every man's back, and Lieutenant Scheisskopf was not sanguine at all about obtaining that many nickel-alloy swivels from Quartermaster or enlisting the co-operation of the surgeons at the hospital.

The week after Lieutenant Scheisskopf followed Clevinger's recommendation and let the men elect their own cadet officers, the squadron won the yellow pennant. Lieutenant Scheisskopf was so elated by this unexpected achievement that he gave his wife a sharp crack over the head with the pole when she tried to drag him into bed to celebrate by showing their contempt for the sexual mores of the lower middle classes in Western civilization. The next week the squadron won the red flag, and Lieutenant Scheisskopf was beside himself with rapture. And the week after that his squadron made history by winning the red pennant two weeks in a row! Now Lieutenant Scheisskopf had confidence enough in his powers to spring his big surprise. Lieutenant Scheisskopf had discovered in his extensive research that the hands of marchers, instead of swinging freely, as was then the popular fashion, ought never to be moved more than three inches from the center of the thigh, which meant, in effect, that they were scarcely to be swung at all.

Lieutenant Scheisskopf's preparations were elaborate and clandestine. All the cadets in his squadron were sworn to secrecy and rehearsed in the dead of night on the auxiliary paradeground. They marched in darkness that was pitch and bumped into each other blindly, but they did not panic, and they were learning to march without swinging their hands. Lieutenant Scheisskopf's first thought had been to have a friend of his in the sheet metal shop sink pegs of nickel alloy into each man's thighbones and link them to the wrists by strands of copper wire with exactly three inches of play, but there wasn't time—there was never enough time—and good copper wire was hard to come by in wartime. He remembered also that the men, so hampered, would be unable to fall properly during the impressive fainting ceremony preceding the marching and that an inability to faint properly might affect the unit's rating as a whole.

And all week long he chortled with repressed delight at the officers' club. Speculation grew rampant among his closest friends.

"I wonder what that Shithead is up to," Lieutenant Engle said.

Lieutenant Scheisskopf responded with a knowing smile to the queries of his colleagues. "You'll find out Sunday," he promised. "You'll find out."

Lieutenant Scheisskopf unveiled his epochal surprise that Sunday with all the aplomb of an experienced impresario. He said nothing while the other squadrons ambled past the reviewing stand crookedly in their customary manner. He gave no sign even when the first ranks of his own squadron hove into sight with their swingless marching and the first stricken gasps of alarm were hissing from his startled fellow officers. He held back even then until the bloated colonel with the big fat mustache whirled upon him savagely with a purpling face, and then he offered the explanation that made him immortal.

"Look, Colonel," he announced. "No hands."

And to an audience stilled with awe, he distributed certified photostatic copies of the obscure regulation on which he had built his unforgettable triumph. This was Lieutenant Scheisskopf's finest hour. He won the parade, of course, hands down, obtaining permanent possession of the red pennant and ending the Sunday parades altogether, since good red pennants were as hard to come by in wartime as good copper wire. Lieutenant Scheisskopf was made First Lieutenant Scheisskopf on the spot and began his rapid rise through the ranks. There were few who did not hail him as a true military genius for his important discovery.

"That Lieutenant Scheisskopf," Lieutenant Travers remarked. "He's a military genius."

"Yes, he really is," Lieutenant Engle agreed. "It's a pity the schmuck won't whip his wife."

"I don't see what that has to do with it," Lieutenant Travers answered coolly. "Lieutenant Bemis whips Mrs. Bemis beautifully every time they have sexual intercourse, and he isn't worth a farthing at parades."

"I'm talking about flagellation," Lieutenant Engle retorted. "Who gives a damn about parades?"

Actually, no one but Lieutenant Scheisskopf really gave a damn about the parades, least of all the bloated colonel with the big fat mustache, who was chairman of the Action Board and began bellowing at Clevinger the moment Clevinger stepped gingerly into the room to plead innocent to the charges Lieutenant Scheisskopf had lodged against him. The colonel beat his fist down upon the table and hurt his hand and became so further enraged with Clevinger that he beat his fist down upon the table even harder and hurt his hand some more. Lieutenant Scheisskopf glared at Clevinger with tight lips, mortified by the poor impression Clevinger was making.

"In sixty days you'll be fighting Billy Petrolle," the colonel with the big fat mustache roared. "And you think it's a big fat joke."

"I don't think it's a joke, sir," Clevinger replied.

"Don't interrupt."

"Yes, sir."

"And say 'sir' when you do," ordered Major Metcalf.

"Yes, sir."

"Weren't you just ordered not to interrupt?" Major Metcalf inquired coldly.

"But I didn't interrupt, sir," Clevinger protested.

"No. And you didn't say 'sir,' either. Add that to the charges against him," Major Metcalf directed the corporal who could take shorthand. "Failure to say 'sir' to superior officers when not interrupting them."

"Metcalf," said the colonel, "you're a goddam fool. Do you know that?"

Major Metcalf swallowed with difficulty. "Yes, sir."

"Then keep your goddam mouth shut. You don't make sense."

There were three members of the Action Board, the bloated colonel with the big fat mustache, Lieutenant Scheisskopf and Major Metcalf, who was trying to develop a steely gaze. As a member of the Action Board, Lieutenant Scheisskopf was one of the judges who would weigh the merits of the case against Clevinger as presented by the prosecutor. Lieutenant Scheisskopf was also the prosecutor. Clevinger had an officer defending him. The officer defending him was Lieutenant Scheisskopf.

It was all very confusing to Clevinger, who began vibrating in terror as the colonel surged to his feet like a gigantic belch and threatened to rip his stinking, cowardly body apart limb from limb. One day he had stumbled while marching to class; the next day he was formally charged with "breaking ranks while in formation, felonious assault, indiscriminate behavior, mopery, high treason, provoking, being a smart guy, listening to classical music, and so on." In short, they threw the book at him, and there he was, standing in dread before the bloated colonel, who roared once more that in sixty days he would be fighting Billy Petrolle and demanded to know how the hell he would like being washed out and shipped to the Solomon Islands to bury bodies. Clevinger replied with courtesy that he would not like it; he was a dope who would rather be a corpse than bury one. The colonel sat down and settled back, calm and cagey suddenly, and ingratiatingly polite.

"What did you mean," he inquired slowly, "when you said we couldn't punish you?"

"When, sir?"

"I'm asking the questions. You're answering them."

"Yes, sir. I—"

"Did you think we brought you here to ask questions and for me to answer them?"

"No, sir. I—"

"What did we bring you here for?"

"To answer questions."

"You're goddam right," roared the colonel. "Now suppose you start answering some before I break your goddam head. Just what the hell did you mean, you bastard, when you said we couldn't punish you?"

"I don't think I ever made that statement, sir."

"Will you speak up, please? I couldn't hear you."

"Yes, sir. I—"

"Will you speak up, please? He couldn't hear you."

"Yes, sir. I—"

"Metcalf."

"Sir?"

"Didn't I tell you to keep your stupid mouth shut?"

"Yes, sir."

"Then keep your stupid mouth shut when I tell you to keep your stupid mouth shut. Do you understand? Will you speak up, please? I couldn't hear you."

"Yes, sir. I—"

"Metcalf, is that your foot I'm stepping on?"

"No, sir. It must be Lieutenant Scheisskopf's foot."

"It isn't my foot," said Lieutenant Scheisskopf.

"Then maybe it is my foot after all," said Major Metcalf.

"Move it."

"Yes, sir. You'll have to move your foot first, Colonel. It's on top of mine."

"Are you telling me to move my foot?"

"No, sir. Oh, no, sir."

"Then move your foot and keep your stupid mouth shut. Will you speak up, please? I still couldn't hear you."

"Yes, sir. I said that I didn't say that you couldn't punish me."

"Just what the hell are you talking about?"

"I'm answering your question, sir."

"What question?"

"'Just what the hell did you mean, you bastard, when you said we couldn't punish you?'" said the corporal who could take shorthand, reading from his steno pad.

"All right," said the colonel. "Just what the hell did you mean?"

"I didn't say you couldn't punish me, sir."

"When?" asked the colonel.

"When what, sir?"

"Now you're asking me questions again."

"I'm sorry, sir. I'm afraid I don't understand your question."

"When didn't you say we couldn't punish you? Don't you understand my question?"

"No, sir. I don't understand."

"You've just told us that. Now suppose you answer my question."

"But how can I answer it?"

"That's another question you're asking me."

"I'm sorry, sir. But I don't know how to answer it. I never said you couldn't punish me."

"Now you're telling us when you did say it. I'm asking you to tell us when you didn't say it."

Clevinger took a deep breath. "I always didn't say you couldn't punish me, sir."

"That's much better, Mr. Clevinger, even though it is a barefaced lie. Last night in the latrine. Didn't you whisper that we couldn't punish you to that other dirty son of a bitch we don't like? What's his name?"

"Yossarian, sir," Lieutenant Scheisskopf said.

"Yes, Yossarian. That's right. Yossarian. Yossarian? Is that his name? Yossarian? What the hell kind of a name is Yossarian?"

Lieutenant Scheisskopf had the facts at his finger tips. "It's Yossarian's name, sir," he explained.

"Yes, I suppose it is. Didn't you whisper to Yossarian that we couldn't punish you?"

"Oh, no, sir. I whispered to him that you couldn't find me guilty—"

"I may be stupid," interrupted the colonel, "but the distinction escapes me. I guess I am pretty stupid, because the distinction escapes me."

"W—"

"You're a windy son of a bitch, aren't you? Nobody asked you for clarification and you're giving me clarification. I was making a statement, not asking for clarification. You are a windy son of a bitch, aren't you?"

"No, sir."

"No, sir? Are you calling me a goddam liar?"

"Oh, no, sir."

"Then you're a windy son of a bitch, aren't you?"

"No, sir."

"Are you trying to pick a fight with me?"

"No, sir."

"Are you a windy son of a bitch?"

"No, sir."

"Goddammit, you *are* trying to pick a fight with me. For two stinking cents I'd jump over this big fat table and rip your stinking, cowardly body apart limb from limb."

"Do it! Do it!" cried Major Metcalf.

"Metcalf, you stinking son of a bitch. Didn't I tell you to keep your stinking, cowardly, stupid mouth shut?"

"Yes, sir. I'm sorry, sir."

"Then suppose you do it."

"I was only trying to learn, sir. The only way a person can learn is by trying."

"Who says so?"

"Everybody says so, sir. Even Lieutenant Scheisskopf says so."

"Do you say so?"

"Yes, sir," said Lieutenant Scheisskopf. "But everybody says so."

"Well, Metcalf, suppose you try keeping that stupid mouth of yours shut, and maybe that's the way you'll learn how. Now, where were we? Read me back the last line."

"'Read me back the last line,'" read back the corporal who could take shorthand.

"Not *my* last line, stupid!" the colonel shouted. "Somebody else's."

"'Read me back the last line,'" read back the corporal.

"That's *my* last line again!" shrieked the colonel, turning purple with anger.

"Oh, no, sir," corrected the corporal. "That's *my* last line. I read it to you just a moment ago. Don't you remember, sir? It was only a moment ago."

"Oh, my God! Read me back *his* last line, stupid. Say, what the hell's your name, anyway?"

"Popinjay, sir."

"Well, you're next, Popinjay. As soon as this trial ends, your trial begins. Get it?"

"Yes, sir. What will I be charged with?"

"What the hell difference does that make? Did you hear what he asked me? You're going to learn, Popinjay—the minute we finish with Clevinger you're going to learn. Cadet Clevinger, what did—You are Cadet Clevinger, aren't you, and not Popinjay?"

"Yes, sir."

"Good. What did—"

"I'm Popinjay, sir."

"Popinjay, is your father a millionaire, or a member of the Senate?"

"No, sir."

"Then you're up shit creek, Popinjay, without a paddle. He's not a general or a high-ranking member of the Administration, is he?"

"No, sir."

"That's good. What does your father do?"

"He's dead, sir."

"That's very good. You really are up the creek, Popinjay. Is Popinjay really your name? Just what the hell kind of a name is Popinjay, anyway? I don't like it."

"It's Popinjay's name, sir," Lieutenant Scheisskopf explained.

"Well, I don't like it, Popinjay, and I just can't wait to rip your stinking, cowardly body apart limb from limb. Cadet Clevinger, will you please repeat what the hell it was you did or didn't whisper to Yossarian late last night in the latrine?"

"Yes, sir. I said that you couldn't find me guilty—"

"We'll take it from there. Precisely what did you mean, Cadet Clevinger, when you said we couldn't find you guilty?"

"I didn't say you couldn't find me guilty, sir."

"When?"

"When what, sir?"

"Goddammit, are you going to start pumping me again?"

"No, sir. I'm sorry, sir."

"Then answer the question. When didn't you say we couldn't find you guilty?"

"Late last night in the latrine, sir."

"Is that the only time you didn't say it?"

"No, sir. I always didn't say you couldn't find me guilty, sir. What I did say to Yossarian was—"

"Nobody asked you what you did say to Yossarian. We asked you what you didn't say to him. We're not at all interested in what you did say to Yossarian. Is that clear?"

"Yes, sir."

"Then we'll go on. What did you say to Yossarian?"

"I said to him, sir, that you couldn't find me guilty of the offense with which I am charged and still be faithful to the cause of . . ."

"Of what? You're mumbling."

"Stop mumbling."

"Yes, sir."

"And mumble 'sir' when you do."

"Metcalf, you bastard!"

"Yes, sir," mumbled Clevinger. "Of justice, sir. That you couldn't find—"

"Justice?" The colonel was astounded. "What is justice?"

"Justice, sir—"

"That's not what justice is," the colonel jeered, and began pounding the table again with his big fat hand. "That's what Karl Marx is. I'll tell you what justice is. Justice is a knee in the gut from the floor on the chin at night sneaky with a knife brought up down on the magazine of a battleship sandbagged underhanded in the dark without a word of warning. Garroting. That's what justice is when we've all got to be tough enough and rough enough to fight Billy Petrolle. From the hip. Get it?"

"No, sir."

"Don't sir me!"

"Yes, sir."

"And say 'sir' when you don't," ordered Major Metcalf.

Clevinger was guilty, of course, or he would not have been accused, and since the only way to prove it was to find him guilty, it was their patriotic duty to do so. He was sentenced to walk fifty-seven punishment tours. Popinjay was locked up to be taught a lesson, and Major Metcalf was shipped to the Solomon Islands to bury bodies. A punishment tour for Clevinger was fifty minutes of a weekend hour spent pacing back and forth before the provost marshal's building with a ton of an unloaded rifle on his shoulder.

It was all very confusing to Clevinger. There were many strange things taking place, but the strangest of all, to Clevinger, was the hatred, the brutal, uncloaked, inexorable hatred of the members of the Action Board, glazing their unforgiving expressions with a hard, vindictive surface, glowing in their narrowed eyes malignantly like inextinguishable coals. Clevinger was stunned to discover it. They would have lynched him if they could. They were three grown men and he was a boy, and they hated him and wished him dead. They had hated him before he came, hated him while he was there, hated him after he left, carried their hatred for him away malignantly like some pampered treasure after they separated from each other and went to their solitude.

Yossarian had done his best to warn him the night before. "You haven't got a chance, kid," he had told him glumly. "They hate Jews."

"But I'm not Jewish," answered Clevinger.

"It will make no difference," Yossarian promised, and Yossarian was right. "They're after everybody."

Clevinger recoiled from their hatred as though from a blinding light. These three men who hated him spoke his language and wore his uniform, but he saw their loveless faces set immutably into cramped, mean lines of hostility and understood instantly that nowhere in the world, not in all the fascist tanks or planes or submarines, not in the bunkers behind the machine guns or mortars or behind the blowing flame throwers, not even among all the expert gunners of the crack Hermann Goering Antiaircraft Division or among the grisly connivers in all the beer halls in Munich and everywhere else, were there men who hated him more.

9

Major Major Major Major

Major Major Major Major had had a difficult time from the start.

Like Miniver Cheevy, he had been born too late—exactly thirty-six hours too late for the physical well-being of his mother, a gentle, ailing woman who, after a full day and a half's agony in the rigors of childbirth, was depleted of all resolve to pursue further the argument over the new child's name. In the hospital corridor, her husband moved ahead with the unsmiling determination of someone who knew what he was about. Major Major's father was a towering, gaunt man in heavy shoes and a black woolen suit. He filled out the birth certificate without faltering, betraying no emotion at all as he handed the completed form to the floor nurse. The nurse took it from him without comment and padded out of sight. He watched her go, wondering what she had on underneath.

Back in the ward, he found his wife lying vanquished beneath the blankets like a desiccated old vegetable, wrinkled, dry and white, her enfeebled tissues absolutely still. Her bed was at the very end of the ward, near a cracked window thickened with grime. Rain splashed from a moiling sky and the day was dreary and cold. In other parts of the hospital chalky people with aged, blue lips were dying on time. The man stood erect beside the bed and gazed down at the woman a long time.

"I have named the boy Caleb," he announced to her finally in a soft voice. "In accordance with your wishes." The woman made no answer, and slowly the man smiled. He had planned it all perfectly, for his wife was asleep and would never know that he had lied to her as she lay on her sickbed in the poor ward of the county hospital.

From this meager beginning had sprung the ineffectual squadron commander who was now spending the better part of each working day in Pianosa forging Washington Irving's name to official documents. Major Major forged diligently with his left hand to elude identification, insulated against intrusion by his own undesired authority and camouflaged in his false mustache and dark glasses as an additional safeguard against detection by anyone chancing to peer in through the dowdy celluloid window from which some thief had carved out a slice. In between these two low points of his birth and his success lay thirty-one dismal years of loneliness and frustration.

Major Major had been born too late and too mediocre. Some men are born mediocre, some men achieve mediocrity, and some men have mediocrity thrust upon them. With Major Major it had been all three. Even among men lacking all distinction he inevitably stood out as a man lacking more distinction than all the rest, and people who met him were always impressed by how unimpressive he was.

Major Major had three strikes on him from the beginning—his mother, his father and Henry Fonda, to whom he bore a sickly resemblance almost from the moment of his birth. Long before he even suspected who Henry Fonda was, he found himself the subject of unflattering comparisons everywhere he went. Total strangers saw fit to deprecate him, with the result that he was stricken early with a guilty fear of people and an obsequious impulse to apologize to society for the fact that he was *not* Henry Fonda. It was not an easy task for him to go through life looking something like Henry Fonda, but he never once thought of quitting, having inherited his perseverance from his father, a lanky man with a good sense of humor.

Major Major's father was a sober God-fearing man whose idea of a good joke was to lie about his age. He was a long-limbed farmer, a God-fearing, freedom-loving, law-abiding rugged individualist who held that federal aid to anyone but farmers was creeping socialism. He advocated thrift and hard work and disapproved of loose women who turned him down. His specialty was alfalfa, and he made a good thing out of not growing any. The government paid him well for every bushel of alfalfa he did not grow. The more alfalfa he did not grow, the more money the government gave him, and he spent every penny he didn't earn on new land to increase the amount of alfalfa he did not produce. Major Major's father worked without rest at not growing alfalfa. On long winter evenings he remained indoors and did not mend harness, and he sprang out of bed at the crack of noon every day just to make certain that the chores would not be done. He invested in land wisely and soon was not growing more alfalfa than any other man in the county. Neighbors sought him out for advice on all subjects, for he had made much money and was therefore wise. "As ye sow, so shall ye reap," he counseled one and all, and everyone said, "Amen."

Major Major's father was an outspoken champion of economy in government, provided it did not interfere with the sacred duty of government to pay farmers as much as they could get for all the alfalfa they produced that no one else wanted or for not producing any alfalfa at all. He was a proud and independent man who was opposed to unemployment insurance and never hesitated to whine, whimper, wheedle, and extort for as much as he could get from whomever he could. He was a devout man whose pulpit was everywhere.

"The Lord gave us good farmers two strong hands so that we could take as much as we could grab with both of them," he preached with ardor on the courthouse steps or in the front of the A & P as he waited for the bad-tempered gum-chewing young cashier he was after to step outside and give him a nasty look. "If the Lord didn't want us to take as much as we could get," he preached, "He wouldn't have given us two good hands to take it with." And the others murmured, "Amen."

Major Major's father had a Calvinist's faith in predestination and could perceive distinctly how everyone's misfortunes but his own were expressions of God's will. He smoked cigarettes and drank whiskey, and he thrived on good wit and stimulating intellectual conversation, particularly his own when he was lying about his age or telling that good one about God and his wife's difficulties in delivering Major Major. The good one about God and his wife's difficulties had to do with the fact that it had taken God only six days to produce the whole world, whereas his wife had spent a full day and a half in labor just to produce Major Major. A lesser man might have wavered that day in the hospital corridor, a weaker man might have compromised on such excellent substitutes as Drum Major, Minor Major, Sergeant Major, or C Sharp Major, but Major Major's father had waited fourteen years for just such an opportunity, and he was not a person to waste it. Major Major's father had a good joke about opportunity. "Opportunity only knocks once in this world," he would say. Major Major's father repeated this good joke at every opportunity.

Being born with a sickly resemblance to Henry Fonda was the first of a long series of practical jokes of which destiny was to make Major Major the unhappy victim throughout his joyless life. Being born Major Major Major was the second. The fact that he *had* been born Major Major Major was a secret known only to his father. Not until Major Major was enrolling in kindergarten was the discovery of his real name made, and then the effects were disastrous. The news killed his mother, who just lost her will to live and wasted away and died, which was just fine with his father, who had decided to marry the bad-tempered girl at the A & P if he had to and who had not been optimistic about his chances of getting his wife off the land without paying her some money or flogging her.

On Major Major himself the consequences were only slightly less severe. It was a harsh and stunning realization that was forced upon him at so tender an age, the realization that he was not, as he had always been led to believe, Caleb Major, but instead was some total stranger named Major Major Major about whom he knew absolutely nothing and about whom nobody else had ever heard before. What playmates he had withdrew from him and never returned, disposed, as they were, to distrust all strangers, especially one who had already deceived them by pretending to be someone they had known for years. Nobody would have anything to do with him. He began to drop things and to trip. He had a shy and hopeful manner in each new contact, and he was always disappointed. Because he needed a friend so desperately, he never found one. He grew awkwardly into a tall, strange, dreamy boy with fragile eyes and a very delicate mouth whose tentative, groping smile collapsed instantly into hurt disorder at every fresh rebuff.

He was polite to his elders, who disliked him. Whatever his elders told him to do, he did. They told him to look before he leaped, and he always looked before he leaped. They told him never to put off until the next day what he could do the day before, and he never did. He was told to honor his father and his mother, and he honored his father and his mother. He was told that he should not kill, and he did not kill, until he got into the Army. Then he was told to kill, and he killed. He turned the other cheek on every occasion and always did unto others exactly as he would have had others do unto him. When he gave to charity, his left hand never knew what his right hand was doing. He never once took the name of the Lord his God in vain, committed adultery or coveted his neighbor's ass. In fact, he loved his neighbor and never even bore false witness against him. Major Major's elders disliked him because he was such a flagrant nonconformist.

Since he had nothing better to do well in, he did well in school. At the state university he took his studies so seriously that he was suspected by the homosexuals of being a Communist and suspected by the Communists of being a homosexual. He majored in English history, which was a mistake.

"*English* history!" roared the silver-maned senior Senator from his state indignantly. "What's the matter with American history? American history is as good as any history in the world!"

Major Major switched immediately to American literature, but not before the F.B.I. had opened a file on him. There were six people and a Scotch terrier inhabiting the remote farmhouse Major Major called home, and five of them and the Scotch terrier turned out to be agents for the F.B.I. Soon they had enough derogatory information on Major Major to do whatever they wanted to with him. The only thing they could find to do with him, however, was take him into the Army as a private and make him a major four days later so that Congressmen with nothing else on their minds could go trotting back and forth through the streets of Washington, D.C., chanting, "Who promoted Major Major? Who promoted Major Major?"

Actually, Major Major had been promoted by an I.B.M. machine with a sense of humor almost as keen as his father's. When war broke out, he was still docile and compliant. They told him to enlist, and he enlisted. They told him to apply for aviation cadet training, and he applied for aviation cadet training, and the very next night found himself standing barefoot in icy mud at three o'clock in the morning before a tough and belligerent sergeant from the Southwest who told them he could beat hell out of any man in his outfit and was ready to prove it. The recruits in his squadron had all been shaken roughly awake only minutes before by the sergeant's corporals and told to assemble in front of the administration tent. It was still raining on Major Major. They fell into ranks in the civilian clothes they had brought into the Army with them three days before. Those who had lingered to put shoes and socks on were sent back to their cold, wet, dark tents to remove them, and they were all barefoot in the mud as the sergeant ran his stony eyes over their faces and told them he could beat hell out of any man in his outfit. No one was inclined to dispute him.

Major Major's unexpected promotion to major the next day plunged the belligerent sergeant into a bottomless gloom, for he was no longer able to boast that he could beat hell out of any man in his outfit. He brooded for hours in his tent like Saul, receiving no visitors, while his elite guard of corporals stood discouraged watch outside. At three o'clock in the morning he found his solution, and Major Major and the other recruits were again shaken roughly awake and ordered to assemble barefoot in the drizzly glare at the administration tent, where the sergeant was already waiting, his fists clenched on his hips cockily, so eager to speak that he could hardly wait for them to arrive.

"Me and Major Major," he boasted, in the same tough, clipped tones of the night before, "can beat hell out of any man in my outfit."

The officers on the base took action on the Major Major problem later that same day. How could they cope with a major like Major Major? To demean him personally would be to demean all other officers of equal or lesser rank. To treat him with courtesy, on the other hand, was unthinkable. Fortunately, Major Major had applied for aviation cadet training. Orders transferring him away were sent to the mimeograph room late in the afternoon, and at three o'clock in the morning Major Major was again shaken roughly awake, bidden Godspeed by the sergeant and placed aboard a plane heading west.

Lieutenant Scheisskopf turned white as a sheet when Major Major reported to him in California with bare feet and mud-caked toes. Major Major had taken it for granted that he was being shaken roughly awake again to stand barefoot in the mud and had left his shoes and socks in the tent. The civilian clothing in which he reported for duty to Lieutenant Scheisskopf was rumpled and dirty. Lieutenant Scheisskopf, who had not yet made his reputation as a parader, shuddered violently at the picture Major Major would make marching barefoot in his squadron that coming Sunday.

"Go to the hospital quickly," he mumbled, when he had recovered sufficiently to speak, "and tell them you're sick. Stay there until your allowance for uniforms catches up with you and you have some money to buy some clothes. And some shoes. Buy some shoes."

"Yes, sir."

"I don't think you have to call me 'sir,' sir," Lieutenant Scheisskopf pointed out. "You outrank me."

"Yes, sir. I may outrank you, sir, but you're still my commanding officer."

"Yes, sir, that's right," Lieutenant Scheisskopf agreed. "You may outrank me, sir, but I'm still your commanding officer. So you better do what I tell you, sir, or you'll get into trouble. Go to the hospital and tell them you're sick, sir. Stay there until your uniform allowance catches up with you and you have some money to buy some uniforms."

"Yes, sir."

"And some shoes, sir. Buy some shoes the first chance you get, sir."

"Yes, sir. I will, sir."

"Thank you, sir."

Life in cadet school for Major Major was no different than life had been for him all along. Whoever he was with always wanted him to be with someone else. His instructors gave him preferred treatment at every stage in order to push him along quickly and be rid of him. In almost no time he had his pilot's wings and found himself overseas, where things began suddenly to improve. All his life, Major Major had longed for but one thing, to be absorbed, and in Pianosa, for a while, he finally was. Rank meant little to the men on combat duty, and relations between officers and enlisted men were relaxed and informal. Men whose names he didn't even know said "Hi" and invited him to go swimming or play basketball. His ripest hours were spent in the day-long basketball games no one gave a damn about winning. Score was never kept, and the number of players might vary from one to thirty-five. Major Major had never played basketball or any other game before, but his great, bobbing height and rapturous enthusiasm helped make up for his innate clumsiness and lack of experience. Major Major found true happiness there on the lopsided basketball court with the officers and enlisted men who were almost his friends. If there were no winners, there were no losers, and Major Major enjoyed every gamboling moment right up till the day Colonel Cathcart roared up in his jeep after Major Duluth was killed and made it impossible for him ever to enjoy playing basketball there again.

"You're the new squadron commander," Colonel Cathcart had shouted rudely across the railroad ditch to him. "But don't think it means anything, because it doesn't. All it means is that you're the new squadron commander."

Colonel Cathcart had nursed an implacable grudge against Major Major for a long time. A superfluous major on his rolls meant an untidy table of organization and gave ammunition to the men at Twenty-seventh Air Force Headquarters who Colonel Cathcart was positive were his enemies and rivals. Colonel Cathcart had been praying for just some stroke of good luck like Major Duluth's death. He had been plagued by one extra major; he now had an opening for one major. He appointed Major Major squadron commander and roared away in his jeep as abruptly as he had come.

For Major Major, it meant the end of the game. His face flushed with discomfort, and he was rooted to the spot in disbelief as the rain clouds gathered above him again. When he turned to his teammates, he encountered a reef of curious, reflective faces all gazing at him woodenly with morose and inscrutable animosity. He shivered with shame. When the game resumed, it was not good any longer. When he dribbled, no one tried to stop him; when he called for a pass, whoever had the ball passed it; and when he missed a basket, no one raced him for the rebound. The only voice was his own. The next day was the same, and the day after that he did not come back.

Almost on cue, everyone in the squadron stopped talking to him and started staring at him. He walked through life self-consciously with downcast eyes and burning cheeks, the object of contempt, envy, suspicion, resentment and malicious innuendo everywhere he went. People who had hardly noticed his resemblance to Henry Fonda before now never ceased discussing it, and there were even those who hinted sinisterly that Major Major had been elevated to squadron commander *because* he resembled Henry Fonda. Captain Black, who had aspired to the position himself, maintained that Major Major really *was* Henry Fonda but was too chickenshit to admit it.

Major Major floundered bewilderedly from one embarrassing catastrophe to another. Without consulting him, Sergeant Towser had his belongings moved into the roomy trailer Major Duluth had occupied alone, and when Major Major came rushing breathlessly into the orderly room to report the theft of his things, the young corporal there scared him half out of his wits by leaping to his feet and shouting "*Attention!*" the moment he appeared. Major Major snapped to attention with all the rest in the orderly room, wondering what important personage had entered behind him. Minutes passed in rigid silence, and the whole lot of them might have stood there at attention till doomsday if Major Danby had not dropped by from Group to congratulate Major Major twenty minutes later and put them all at ease.

Major Major fared even more lamentably at the mess hall, where Milo, his face fluttery with smiles, was waiting to usher him proudly to a small table he had set up in front and decorated with an embroided tablecloth and a nosegay of posies in a pink cut-glass vase. Major Major hung back with horror, but he was not bold enough to resist with all the others watching. Even Havermeyer had lifted his head from his plate to gape at him with his heavy, pendulous jaw. Major Major submitted meekly to Milo's tugging and cowered in disgrace at his private table throughout the whole meal. The food was ashes in his mouth, but he swallowed every mouthful rather than risk offending any of the men connected with its preparation. Alone with Milo later, Major Major felt protest stir for the first time and said he would prefer to continue eating with the other officers. Milo told him it wouldn't work.

"I don't see what there is to work," Major Major argued. "Nothing ever happened before."

"You were never the squadron commander before."

"Major Duluth was the squadron commander and he always ate at the same table with the rest of the men."

"It was different with Major Duluth, sir."

"In what way was it different with Major Duluth?"

"I wish you wouldn't ask me that, sir," said Milo.

"Is it because I look like Henry Fonda?" Major Major mustered the courage to demand.

"Some people say you *are* Henry Fonda," Milo answered.

"Well, I'm not Henry Fonda," Major Major exclaimed, in a voice quavering with exasperation. "And I don't look the least bit like him. And even if I do look like Henry Fonda, what difference does that make?"

"It doesn't make any difference. That's what I'm trying to tell you, sir. It's just not the same with you as it was with Major Duluth."

And it just wasn't the same, for when Major Major, at the next meal, stepped from the food counter to sit with the others at the regular tables, he was frozen in his tracks by the impenetrable wall of antagonism thrown up by their faces and stood petrified with his tray quivering in his hands until Milo glided forward wordlessly to rescue him, by leading him tamely to his private table. Major Major gave up after that and always ate at his table alone with his back to the others. He was certain they resented him because he seemed too good to eat with them now that he was squadron commander. There was never any conversation in the mess tent when Major Major was present. He was conscious that other officers tried to avoid eating at the same time, and everyone was greatly relieved when he stopped coming there altogether and began taking his meals in his trailer.

Major Major began forging Washington Irving's name to official documents the day after the first C.I.D. man showed up to interrogate him about somebody at the hospital who had been doing it and gave him the idea. He had been bored and dissatisfied in his new position. He had been made squadron commander but had no idea what he was supposed to *do* as squadron commander, unless all he was supposed to do was forge Washington Irving's name to official documents and listen to the isolated clinks and thumps of Major —— de Coverley's horseshoes falling to the ground outside the window of his small office in the rear of the orderly-room tent. He was hounded incessantly by an impression of vital duties left unfulfilled and waited in vain for his responsibilities to overtake him. He seldom went out unless it was absolutely necessary, for he could not get used to being stared at.

Occasionally, the monotony was broken by some officer or enlisted man Sergeant Towser referred to him on some matter that Major Major was unable to cope with and referred right back to Sergeant Towser for sensible disposition. Whatever he was supposed to get done as squadron commander apparently was getting done without any assistance from him. He grew moody and depressed. At times he thought seriously of going with all his sorrows to see the chaplain, but the chaplain seemed so overburdened with miseries of his own that Major Major shrank from adding to his troubles. Besides, he was not quite sure if chaplains were for squadron commanders.

He had never been quite sure about Major —— de Coverley, either, who, when he was not away renting apartments or kidnapping foreign laborers, had nothing more pressing to do than pitch horseshoes. Major Major often paid strict attention to the horseshoes falling softly against the earth or riding down around the small steel pegs in the ground. He peeked out at Major —— de Coverley for hours and marveled that someone so august had nothing more important to do. He was often tempted to join Major —— de Coverley, but pitching horseshoes all day long seemed almost as dull as signing "Major Major Major" to official documents, and Major —— de Coverley's countenance was so forbidding that Major Major was in awe of approaching him.

Major Major wondered about his relationship to Major —— de Coverley and about Major —— de Coverley's relationship to him. He knew that Major —— de Coverley was his executive officer, but he did not know what that meant, and he could not decide whether in Major —— de Coverley he was blessed with a lenient superior or cursed with a delinquent subordinate. He did not want to ask Sergeant Towser, of whom he was secretly afraid, and there was no one else he could ask, least of all Major —— de Coverley. Few people ever dared approach Major —— de Coverley about anything and the only officer foolish enough to pitch one of his horseshoes was stricken the very next day with the worst case of Pianosan crud that Gus or Wes or even Doc Daneeka had ever seen or even heard about. Everyone was positive the disease had been inflicted upon the poor officer in retribution by Major —— de Coverley, although no one was sure how.

Most of the official documents that came to Major Major's desk did not concern him at all. The vast majority consisted of allusions to prior communications which Major Major had never seen or heard of. There was never any need to look them up, for the instructions were invariably to disregard. In the space of a single productive minute, therefore, he might endorse twenty separate documents each advising him to pay absolutely no attention to any of the others. From General Peckem's office on the mainland came prolix bulletins each day headed by such cheery homilies as "Procrastination Is the Thief of Time" and "Cleanliness Is Next to Godliness."

General Peckem's communications about cleanliness and procrastination made Major Major feel like a filthy procrastinator, and he always got those out of the way as quickly as he could. The only official documents that interested him were those occasional ones pertaining to the unfortunate second lieutenant who had been killed on the mission over Orvieto less than two hours after he arrived on Pianosa and whose partly unpacked belongings were still in Yossarian's tent. Since the unfortunate lieutenant had reported to the operations tent instead of to the orderly room, Sergeant Towser had decided that it would be safest to report him as never having reported to the squadron at all, and the occasional documents relating to him dealt with the fact that he seemed to have vanished into thin air, which, in one way, was exactly what did happen to him. In the long run, Major Major was grateful for the official documents that came to his desk, for sitting in his office signing them all day long was a lot better than sitting in his office all day long not signing them. They gave him something to do.

Inevitably, every document he signed came back with a fresh page added for a new signature by him after intervals of from two to ten days. They were always much thicker than formerly, for in between the sheet bearing his last endorsement and the sheet added for his new endorsement were the sheets bearing the most recent endorsements of all the other officers in scattered locations who were also occupied in signing their names to that same official document. Major Major grew despondent as he watched simple communications swell prodigiously into huge manuscripts. No matter how many times he signed one, it always came back for still another signature, and he began to despair of ever being free of any of them. One day—it was the day after the C.I.D. man's first visit—Major Major signed Washington Irving's name to one of the documents instead of his own, just to see how it would feel. He liked it. He liked it so much that for the rest of that afternoon he did the same with all the official documents. It was an act of impulsive frivolity and rebellion for which he knew afterward he would be punished severely. The next morning he entered his office in trepidation and waited to see what would happen. Nothing happened.

He had sinned, and it was good, for none of the documents to which he had signed Washington Irving's name ever came back! Here, at last, was progress, and Major Major threw himself into his new career with uninhibited gusto. Signing Washington Irving's name to official documents was not much of a career, perhaps, but it was less monotonous than signing "Major Major Major." When Washington Irving did grow monotonous, he could reverse the order and sign Irving Washington until that grew monotonous. And he was getting something done, for none of the documents signed with either of these names ever came back to the squadron.

What did come back, eventually, was a *second* C.I.D. man, masquerading as a pilot. The men knew he was a C.I.D. man because he confided to them he was and urged each of them not to reveal his true identity to any of the other men to whom he had already confided that he was a C.I.D. man.

"You're the only one in the squadron who knows I'm a C.I.D. man," he confided to Major Major, "and it's absolutely essential that it remain a secret so that my efficiency won't be impaired. Do you understand?"

"Sergeant Towser knows."

"Yes, I know. I had to tell him in order to get in to see you. But I know he won't tell a soul under any circumstances."

"He told me," said Major Major. "He told me there was a C.I.D. man outside to see me."

"That bastard. I'll have to throw a security check on him. I wouldn't leave any top-secret documents lying around here if I were you. At least not until I make my report."

"I don't get any top-secret documents," said Major Major.

"That's the kind I mean. Lock them in your cabinet where Sergeant Towser can't get his hands on them."

"Sergeant Towser has the only key to the cabinet."

"I'm afraid we're wasting time," said the second C.I.D. man rather stiffly. He was a brisk, pudgy, high-strung person whose movements were swift and certain. He took a number of photostats out of a large red expansion envelope he had been hiding conspicuously beneath a leather flight jacket painted garishly with pictures of airplanes flying through orange bursts of flak and with orderly rows of little bombs signifying fifty-five combat missions flown. "Have you ever seen any of these?"

Major Major looked with a blank expression at copies of personal correspondence from the hospital on which the censoring officer had written "Washington Irving" or "Irving Washington."

"No."

"How about these?"

Major Major gazed next at copies of official documents addressed to him to which he had been signing the same signatures.

"No."

"Is the man who signed these names in your squadron?"

"Which one? There are two names here."

"Either one. We figure that Washington Irving and Irving Washington are one man and that he's using two names just to throw us off the track. That's done very often, you know."

"I don't think there's a man with either of those names in my squadron."

A look of disappointment crossed the second C.I.D. man's face. "He's a lot cleverer than we thought," he observed. "He's using a third name and posing as someone else. And I think . . . yes, I think I know what the third name is." With excitement and inspiration, he held another photostat out for Major Major to study. "How about this?"

Major Major bent forward slightly and saw a copy of the piece of V mail from which Yossarian had blacked out everything but the name Mary and on which he had written, "I yearn for you tragically. A. T. Tappman, Chaplain, U.S. Army." Major Major shook his head.

"I've never seen it before."

"Do you know who A. T. Tappman is?"

"He's the group chaplain."

"That locks it up," said the second C.I.D. man. "Washington Irving is the group chaplain."

Major Major felt a twinge of alarm. "A. T. Tappman is the group chaplain," he corrected.

"Are you sure?"

"Yes."

"Why should the group chaplain write this on a letter?"

"Perhaps somebody else wrote it and forged his name."

"Why would somebody want to forge the group chaplain's name?"

"To escape detection."

"You may be right," the second C.I.D. man decided after an instant's hesitation, and smacked his lips crisply. "Maybe we're confronted with a gang, with two men working together who just happen to have opposite names. Yes, I'm sure that's it. One of them here in the squadron, one of them up at the hospital and one of them with the chaplain. That makes three men, doesn't it? Are you absolutely sure you never saw any of these official documents before?"

"I would have signed them if I had."

"With whose name?" asked the second C.I.D. man cunningly. "Yours or Washington Irving's?"

"With my own name," Major Major told him. "I don't even know Washington Irving's name."

The second C.I.D. man broke into a smile.

"Major, I'm glad you're in the clear. It means we'll be able to work together, and I'm going to need every man I can get. Somewhere in the European theater of operations is a man who's getting his hands on communications addressed to you. Have you any idea who it can be?"

"No."

"Well, I have a pretty good idea," said the second C.I.D. man, and leaned forward to whisper confidentially. "That bastard Towser. Why else would he go around shooting his mouth off about me? Now, you keep your eyes open and let me know the minute you hear anyone even talking about Washington Irving. I'll throw a security check on the chaplain and everyone else around here."

The moment he was gone, the first C.I.D. man jumped into Major Major's office through the window and wanted to know who the second C.I.D. man was. Major Major barely recognized him.

"He was a C.I.D. man," Major Major told him.

"Like hell he was," said the first C.I.D. man. "I'm the C.I.D. man around here."

Major Major barely recognized him because he was wearing a faded maroon corduroy bathrobe with open seams under both arms, linty flannel pajamas, and worn house slippers with one flapping sole. This was regulation hospital dress, Major Major recalled. The man had added about twenty pounds and seemed bursting with good health.

"I'm really a very sick man," he whined. "I caught cold in the hospital from a fighter pilot and came down with a very serious case of pneumonia."

"I'm very sorry," Major Major said.

"A lot of good that does me," the C.I.D. man sniveled. "I don't want your sympathy. I just want you to know what I'm going through. I came down to warn you that Washington Irving seems to have shifted his base of operations from the hospital to your squadron. You haven't heard anyone around here talking about Washington Irving, have you?"

"As a matter of fact, I have," Major Major answered. "That man who was just in there. He was talking about Washington Irving."

"Was he really?" the first C.I.D. man cried with delight. "This might be just what we needed to crack the case wide open! You keep him under surveillance twenty-four hours a day while I rush back to the hospital and write my superiors for further instructions." The C.I.D. man jumped out of Major Major's office through the window and was gone.

A minute later, the flap separating Major Major's office from the orderly room flew open and the second C.I.D. man was back, puffing frantically in haste. Gasping for breath, he shouted, "I just saw a man in red pajamas come jumping out of your window and go running up the road! Didn't you see him?"

"He was here talking to me," Major Major answered.

"I thought that looked mighty suspicious, a man jumping out the window in red pajamas." The man paced about the small office in vigorous circles. "At first I thought it was you, hightailing it for Mexico. But now I see it wasn't you. He didn't say anything about Washington Irving, did he?"

"As a matter of fact," said Major Major, "he did."

"He did?" cried the second C.I.D. man. "That's fine! This might be just the break we needed to crack the case wide open. Do you know where we can find him?"

"At the hospital. He's really a very sick man."

"That's great!" exclaimed the second C.I.D. man. "I'll go right up there after him. It would be best if I went incognito. I'll go explain the situation at the medical tent and have them send me there as a patient."

"They won't send me to the hospital as a patient unless I'm sick," he reported back to Major Major. "Actually, I am pretty sick. I've been meaning to turn myself in for a checkup, and this will be a good opportunity. I'll go back to the medical tent and tell them I'm sick, and I'll get sent to the hospital that way."

"Look what they did to me," he reported back to Major Major with purple gums. His distress was inconsolable. He carried his shoes and socks in his hands, and his toes had been painted with gentian-violet solution, too. "Who ever heard of a C.I.D. man with purple gums?" he moaned.

He walked away from the orderly room with his head down and tumbled into a slit trench and broke his nose. His temperature was still normal, but Gus and Wes made an exception of him and sent him to the hospital in an ambulance.

Major Major had lied, and it was good. He was not really surprised that it was good, for he had observed that people who did lie were, on the whole, more resourceful and ambitious and successful than people who did not lie. Had he told the truth to the second C.I.D. man, he would have found himself in trouble. Instead he had lied, and he was free to continue his work.

He became more circumspect in his work as a result of the visit from the second C.I.D. man. He did all his signing with his left hand and only while wearing the dark glasses and false mustache he had used unsuccessfully to help him begin playing basketball again. As an additional precaution, he made a happy switch from Washington Irving to John Milton. John Milton was supple and concise. Like Washington Irving, he could be reversed with good effect whenever he grew monotonous. Furthermore, he enabled Major Major to double his output, for John Milton was so much shorter than either his own name or Washington Irving's and took so much less time to write. John Milton proved fruitful in still one more respect. He was versatile, and Major Major soon found himself incorporating the signature in fragments of imaginary dialogues. Thus, typical endorsements on the official documents might read, "John, Milton is a sadist" or "Have you seen Milton, John?" One signature of which he was especially proud read, "Is anybody in the John, Milton?" John Milton threw open whole new vistas filled with charming, inexhaustible possibilities that promised to ward off monotony forever. Major Major went back to Washington Irving when John Milton grew monotonous.

Major Major had bought the dark glasses and false mustache in Rome in a final, futile attempt to save himself from the swampy degradation into which he was steadily sinking. First there had been the awful humiliation of the Great Loyalty Oath Crusade, when not one of the thirty or forty people circulating competitive loyalty oaths would even allow him to sign. Then, just when that was blowing over, there was the matter of Clevinger's plane disappearing so mysteriously in thin air with every member of the crew, and blame for the strange mishap centering balefully on him because he had never signed any of the loyalty oaths.

The dark glasses had large magenta rims. The false black mustache was a flamboyant organ grinder's, and he wore them both to the basketball game one day when he felt he could endure his loneliness no longer. He affected an air of jaunty familiarity as he sauntered to the court and prayed silently that he would not be recognized. The others pretended not to recognize him, and he began to have fun. Just as he finished congratulating himself on his innocent ruse he was bumped hard by one of his opponents and knocked to his knees. Soon he was bumped hard again, and it dawned on him that they did recognize him and that they were using his disguise as a license to elbow, trip and maul him. They did not want him at all. And just as he did realize this, the players on his team fused instinctively with the players on the other team into a single, howling, bloodthirsty mob that descended upon him from all sides with foul curses and swinging fists. They knocked him to the ground, kicked him while he was on the ground, attacked him again after he had struggled blindly to his feet. He covered his face with his hands and could not see. They swarmed all over each other in their frenzied compulsion to bludgeon him, kick him, gouge him, trample him. He was pummeled spinning to the edge of the ditch and sent slithering down on his head and shoulders. At the bottom he found his footing, clambered up the other wall and staggered away beneath the hail of hoots and stones with which they pelted him until he lurched into shelter around a corner of the orderly-room tent. His paramount concern throughout the entire assault was to keep his dark glasses and false mustache in place so that he might continue pretending he was somebody else and be spared the dreaded necessity of having to confront them with his authority.

Back in his office, he wept; and when he finished weeping he washed the blood from his mouth and nose, scrubbed the dirt from the abrasions on his cheek and forehead, and summoned Sergeant Towser.

"From now on," he said, "I don't want anyone to come in to see me while I'm here. Is that clear?"

"Yes, sir," said Sergeant Towser. "Does that include me?"

"Yes."

"I see. Will that be all?"

"Yes."

"What shall I say to the people who do come to see you while you're here?"

"Tell them I'm in and ask them to wait."

"Yes, sir. For how long?"

"Until I've left."

"And then what shall I do with them?"

"I don't care."

"May I send them in to see you after you've left?"

"Yes."

"But you won't be here then, will you?"

"No."

"Yes, sir. Will that be all?"

"Yes."

"Yes, sir."

"From now on," Major Major said to the middle-aged enlisted man who took care of his trailer, "I don't want you to come here while I'm here to ask me if there's anything you can do for me. Is that clear?"

"Yes, sir," said the orderly. "When should I come here to find out if there's anything you want me to do for you?"

"When I'm not here."

"Yes, sir. And what should I do?"

"Whatever I tell you to."

"But you won't be here to tell me. Will you?"

"No."

"Then what should I do?"

"Whatever has to be done."

"Yes, sir."

"That will be all," said Major Major.

"Yes, sir," said the orderly. "Will that be all?"

"No," said Major Major. "Don't come in to clean, either. Don't come in for anything unless you're sure I'm not here."

"Yes, sir. But how can I always be sure?"

"If you're not sure, just assume that I am here and go away until you are sure. Is that clear?"

"Yes, sir."

"I'm sorry to have to talk to you in this way, but I have to. Goodbye."

"Goodbye, sir."

"And thank you. For everything."

"Yes, sir."

"From now on," Major Major said to Milo Minderbinder, "I'm not going to come to the mess hall any more. I'll have all my meals brought to me in my trailer."

"I think that's a good idea sir," Milo answered. "Now I'll be able to serve you special dishes that the others will never know about. I'm sure you'll enjoy them. Colonel Cathcart always does."

"I don't want any special dishes. I want exactly what you serve all the other officers. Just have whoever brings it knock once on my door and leave the tray on the step. Is that clear?"

"Yes, sir," said Milo. "That's very clear. I've got some live Maine lobsters hidden away that I can serve you tonight with an excellent Roquefort salad and two frozen eclairs that were smuggled out of Paris only yesterday together with an important member of the French underground. Will that do for a start?"

"No."

"Yes, sir. I understand."

For dinner that night Milo served him broiled Maine lobster with excellent Roquefort salad and two frozen eclairs. Major Major was annoyed. If he sent it back, though, it would only go to waste or to somebody else, and Major Major had a weakness for broiled lobster. He ate with a guilty conscience. The next day for lunch there was terrapin Maryland with a whole quart of Dom Pérignon 1937, and Major Major gulped it down without a thought.

After Milo, there remained only the men in the orderly room, and Major Major avoided them by entering and leaving every time through the dingy celluloid window of his office. The window unbuttoned and was low and large and easy to jump through from either side. He managed the distance between the orderly room and his trailer by darting around the corner of the tent when the coast was clear, leaping down into the railroad ditch and dashing along with his head bowed until he attained the sanctuary of the forest. Abreast of his trailer, he left the ditch and wove his way speedily toward home through the dense underbrush, in which the only person he ever encountered was Captain Flume, who, drawn and ghostly, frightened him half to death one twilight by materializing without warning out of a patch of dewberry bushes to complain that Chief White Halfoat had threatened to slit his throat open from ear to ear.

"If you ever frighten me like that again," Major Major told him, "*I'll* slit your throat open from ear to ear."

Captain Flume gasped and dissolved right back into the patch of dewberry bushes, and Major Major never set eyes on him again.

When Major Major looked back on what he had accomplished, he was pleased. In the midst of a few foreign acres teeming with more than two hundred people, he had succeeded in becoming a recluse. With a little ingenuity and vision, he had made it all but impossible for anyone in the squadron to talk to him, which was just fine with everyone, he noticed, since no one wanted to talk to him anyway. No one, it turned out, but that madman Yossarian, who brought him down with a flying tackle one day as he was scooting along the bottom of the ditch to his trailer for lunch.

The last person in the squadron Major Major wanted to be brought down with a flying tackle by was Yossarian. There was something inherently disreputable about Yossarian, always carrying on so disgracefully about that dead man in his tent who wasn't even there and then taking off all his clothes after the Avignon mission and going around without them right up to the day General Dreedle stepped up to pin a medal on him for his heroism over Ferrara and found him standing in formation stark naked. No one in the world had the power to remove the dead man's disorganized effects from Yossarian's tent. Major Major had forfeited the authority when he permitted Sergeant Towser to report the lieutenant who had been killed over Orvieto less than two hours after he arrived in the squadron as never having arrived in the squadron at all. The only one with any right to remove his belongings from Yossarian's tent, it seemed to Major Major, was Yossarian himself, and Yossarian, it seemed to Major Major, had no right.

Major Major groaned after Yossarian brought him down with a flying tackle, and tried to wiggle to his feet. Yossarian wouldn't let him.

"Captain Yossarian," Yossarian said, "requests permission to speak to the major at once about a matter of life or death."

"Let me up, please," Major Major bid him in cranky discomfort. "I can't return your salute while I'm lying on my arm."

Yossarian released him. They stood up slowly. Yossarian saluted again and repeated his request.

"Let's go to my office," Major Major said. "I don't think this is the best place to talk."

"Yes, sir," answered Yossarian.

They smacked the gravel from their clothing and walked in constrained silence to the entrance of the orderly room.

"Give me a minute or two to put some Mercurochrome on these cuts. Then have Sergeant Towser send you in."

"Yes, sir."

Major Major strode with dignity to the rear of the orderly room without glancing at any of the clerks and typists working at the desks and filing cabinets. He let the flap leading to his office fall closed behind him. As soon as he was alone in his office, he raced across the room to the window and jumped outside to dash away. He found Yossarian blocking his path. Yossarian was waiting at attention and saluted again.

"Captain Yossarian requests permission to speak to the major at once about a matter of life and death," he repeated determinedly.

"Permission denied," Major Major snapped.

"That won't do it."

Major Major gave in. "All right," he conceded wearily. "I'll talk to you. Please jump inside my office."

"After you."

They jumped inside the office. Major Major sat down, and Yossarian moved around in front of his desk and told him that he did not want to fly any more combat missions. *What could he do?* Major Major asked himself. All he could do was what he had been instructed to do by Colonel Korn and hope for the best.

"Why not?" he asked.

"I'm afraid."

"That's nothing to be ashamed of," Major Major counseled him kindly. "We're all afraid."

"I'm not ashamed," Yossarian said. "I'm just afraid."

"You wouldn't be normal if you were never afraid. Even the bravest men experience fear. One of the biggest jobs we all face in combat is to overcome fear."

"Oh, come on, Major. Can't we do without that horseshit?"

Major Major lowered his gaze sheepishly and fiddled with his fingers. "What do you want me to tell you?"

"That I've flown enough missions and can go home."

"How many have you flown?"

"Fifty-one."

"You've only got four more to fly."

"He'll raise them. Every time I get close he raises them."

"Perhaps he won't this time."

"He never sends anyone home, anyway. He just keeps them around waiting for rotation orders until he doesn't have enough men left for the crews, and then raises the number of missions and throws them all back on combat status. He's been doing that ever since he got here."

"You mustn't blame Colonel Cathcart for any delay with the orders," Major Major advised. "It's Twenty-seventh Air Force's responsibility to process the orders promptly once they get them from us."

"He could still ask for replacements and send us home when the orders did come back. Anyway, I've been told that Twenty-seventh Air Force wants only forty missions and that it's only his own idea to get us to fly fifty-five."

"I wouldn't know anything about that," Major Major answered. "Colonel Cathcart is our commanding officer and we must obey him. Why don't you fly the four more missions and see what happens?"

"I don't want to."

What could you do? Major Major asked himself again. What could you do with a man who looked you squarely in the eye and said he would rather die than be killed in combat, a man who was at least as mature and intelligent as you were and who you had to pretend was not? What could you say to him?

"Suppose we let you pick your missions and fly milk runs," Major Major said. "That way you can fly the four missions and not run any risks."

"I don't want to fly milk runs. I don't want to be in the war any more."

"Would you like to see our country lose?" Major Major asked.

"We won't lose. We've got more men, more money and more material. There are ten million men in uniform who could replace me. Some people are getting killed and a lot more are making money and having fun. Let somebody else get killed."

"But suppose everybody on our side felt that way."

"Then I'd certainly be a damned fool to feel any other way. Wouldn't I?"

What could you possibly say to him? Major Major wondered forlornly. One thing he could not say was that there was nothing he could do. To say there was nothing he could do would suggest he *would* do something if he could and imply the existence of an error or injustice in Colonel Korn's policy. Colonel Korn had been most explicit about that. He must never say there was nothing he could do.

"I'm sorry," he said. "But there's nothing I can do."

10

Wintergreen

Clevinger was dead. That was the basic flaw in his philosophy. Eighteen planes had let down through a beaming white cloud off the coast of Elba one afternoon on the way back from the weekly milk run to Parma; seventeen came out. No trace was ever found of the other, not in the air or on the smooth surface of the jade waters below. There was no debris. Helicopters circled the white cloud till sunset. During the night the cloud blew away, and in the morning there was no more Clevinger.

The disappearance was astounding, as astounding, certainly, as the Grand Conspiracy of Lowery Field, when all sixty-four men in a single barrack vanished one payday and were never heard of again. Until Clevinger was snatched from existence so adroitly, Yossarian had assumed that the men had simply decided unanimously to go AWOL the same day. In fact, he had been so encouraged by what appeared to be a mass desertion from sacred responsibility that he had gone running outside in elation to carry the exciting news to ex-P.F.C. Wintergreen.

"What's so exciting about it?" ex-P.F.C. Wintergreen sneered obnoxiously, resting his filthy GI shoe on his spade and lounging back in a surly slouch against the wall of one of the deep, square holes it was his military specialty to dig.

Ex-P.F.C. Wintergreen was a snide little punk who enjoyed working at cross-purposes. Each time he went AWOL, he was caught and sentenced to dig and fill up holes six feet deep, wide and long for a specified length of time. Each time he finished his sentence, he went AWOL again. ex-P.F.C. Wintergreen accepted his role of digging and filling up holes with all the uncomplaining dedication of a true patriot.

"It's not a bad life," he would observe philosophically. "And I guess somebody has to do it."

He had wisdom enough to understand that digging holes in Colorado was not such a bad assignment in wartime. Since the holes were in no great demand, he could dig them and fill them up at a leisurely pace, and he was seldom overworked. On the other hand, he was busted down to buck private each time he was court-martialed. He regretted this loss of rank keenly.

"It was kind of nice being a P.F.C.," he reminisced yearningly. "I had status—you know what I mean?—and I used to travel in the best circles." His face darkened with resignation. "But that's all behind me now," he guessed. "The next time I go over the hill it will be as a buck private, and I just know it won't be the same." There was no future in digging holes. "The job isn't even steady. I lose it each time I finish serving my sentence. Then I have to go over the hill again if I want it back. And I can't even keep doing that. There's a catch, Catch-22. The next time I go over the hill, it will mean the stockade. I don't know what's going to become of me. I might even wind up overseas if I'm not careful." He did not want to keep digging holes for the rest of his life, although he had no objection to doing it as long as there was a war going on and it was part of the war effort. "It's a matter of duty," he observed, "and we each have our own to perform. My duty is to keep digging these holes, and I've been doing such a good job of it that I've just been recommended for the Good Conduct Medal. Your duty is to screw around in cadet school and hope the war ends before you get out. The duty of the men in combat is to win the war, and I just wish they were doing their duty as well as I've been doing mine. It wouldn't be fair if I had to go overseas and do their job too, would it?"

One day ex-P.F.C. Wintergreen struck open a water pipe while digging in one of his holes and almost drowned to death before he was fished out nearly unconscious. Word spread that it was oil, and Chief White Halfoat was kicked off the base. Soon every man who could find a shovel was outside digging frenziedly for oil. Dirt flew everywhere; the scene was almost like the morning in Pianosa seven months later after the night Milo bombed the squadron with every plane he had accumulated in his M & M syndicate, and the airfield, bomb dump and repair hangars as well, and all the survivors were outside hacking cavernous shelters into the solid ground and roofing them over with sheets of armor plate stolen from the repair sheds at the field and with tattered squares of waterproof canvas stolen from the side flaps of each other's tents. Chief White Halfoat was transferred out of Colorado at the first rumor of oil and came to rest finally in Pianosa as a replacement for Lieutenant Coombs, who had gone out on a mission as a guest one day just to see what combat was like and had died over Ferrara in the plane with Kraft. Yossarian felt guilty each time he remembered Kraft, guilty because Kraft had been killed on Yossarian's second bomb run, and guilty because Kraft had got mixed up innocently also in the Splendid Atabrine Insurrection that had begun in Puerto Rico on the first leg of their flight overseas and ended in Pianosa ten days later with Appleby striding dutifully into the orderly room the moment he arrived to report Yossarian for refusing to take his Atabrine tablets. The sergeant there invited him to be seated.

"Thank you, Sergeant, I think I will," said Appleby. "About how long will I have to wait? I've still got a lot to get done today so that I can be fully prepared bright and early tomorrow morning to go into combat the minute they want me to."

"Sir?"

"What's that, Sergeant?"

"What was your question?"

"About how long will I have to wait before I can go in to see the major?"

"Just until he goes out to lunch," Sergeant Towser replied. "Then you can go right in."

"But he won't be there then. Will he?"

"No, sir. Major Major won't be back in his office until after lunch."

"I see," Appleby decided uncertainly. "I think I'd better come back after lunch, then."

Appleby turned from the orderly room in secret confusion. The moment he stepped outside, he thought he saw a tall, dark officer who looked a little like Henry Fonda come jumping out the window of the orderly-room tent and go scooting out of sight around the corner. Appleby halted and squeezed his eyes closed. An anxious doubt assailed him. He wondered if he were suffering from malaria, or, worse, from an overdose of Atabrine tablets. Appleby had been taking four times as many Atabrine tablets as the amount prescribed because he wanted to be four times as good a pilot as everyone else. His eyes were still shut when Sergeant Towser tapped him lightly on the shoulder and told him he could go in now if he wanted to, since Major Major had just gone out. Appleby's confidence returned.

"Thank you, Sergeant. Will he be back soon?"

"He'll be back right after lunch. Then you'll have to go right out and wait for him in front till he leaves for dinner. Major Major never sees anyone in his office while he's in his office."

"Sergeant, what did you just say?"

"I said that Major Major never sees anyone in his office while he's in his office."

Appleby stared at Sergeant Towser intently and attempted a firm tone. "Sergeant, are you trying to make a fool out of me just because I'm new in the squadron and you've been overseas a long time?"

"Oh, no, sir," answered the sergeant deferentially. "Those are my orders. You can ask Major Major when you see him."

"That's just what I intend to do, Sergeant. When *can* I see him?"

"Never."

Crimson with humiliation, Appleby wrote down his report about Yossarian and the Atabrine tablets on a pad the sergeant offered him and left quickly, wondering if perhaps Yossarian were not the only man privileged to wear an officer's uniform who was crazy.

By the time Colonel Cathcart had raised the number of missions to fifty-five, Sergeant Towser had begun to suspect that perhaps every man who wore a uniform was crazy. Sergeant Towser was lean and angular and had fine blond hair so light it was almost without color, sunken cheeks, and teeth like large white marshmallows. He ran the squadron and was not happy doing it. Men like Hungry Joe glowered at him with blameful hatred, and Appleby subjected him to vindictive discourtesy now that he had established himself as a hot pilot and a Ping-Pong player who never lost a point. Sergeant Towser ran the squadron because there was no one else in the squadron to run it. He had no interest in war or advancement. He was interested in shards and Hepplewhite furniture.

Almost without realizing it, Sergeant Towser had fallen into the habit of thinking of the dead man in Yossarian's tent in Yossarian's own terms—as a dead man in Yossarian's tent. In reality, he was no such thing. He was simply a replacement pilot who had been killed in combat before he had officially reported for duty. He had stopped at the operations tent to inquire the way to the orderly-room tent and had been sent right into action because so many men had completed the thirty-five missions required then that Captain Piltchard and Captain Wren were finding it difficult to assemble the number of crews specified by Group. Because he had never officially gotten into the squadron, he could never officially be gotten out, and Sergeant Towser sensed that the multiplying communications relating to the poor man would continue reverberating forever.

His name was Mudd. To Sergeant Towser, who deplored violence and waste with equal aversion, it seemed like such an abhorrent extravagance to fly Mudd all the way across the ocean just to have him blown into bits over Orvieto less than two hours after he arrived. No one could recall who he was or what he had looked like, least of all Captain Piltchard and Captain Wren, who remembered only that a new officer had shown up at the operations tent just in time to be killed and who colored uneasily every time the matter of the dead man in Yossarian's tent was mentioned. The only ones who might have seen Mudd, the men in the same plane, had all been blown to bits with him.

Yossarian, on the other hand, knew exactly who Mudd was. Mudd was the unknown soldier who had never had a chance, for that was the only thing anyone ever did know about all the unknown soldiers—they never had a chance. They had to be dead. And this dead one was really unknown, even though his belongings still lay in a tumble on the cot in Yossarian's tent almost exactly as he had left them three months earlier the day he never arrived—all contaminated with death less than two hours later, in the same way that all was contaminated with death the very next week during the Great Big Siege of Bologna when the moldy odor of mortality hung wet in the air with the sulphurous fog and every man scheduled to fly was already tainted.

There was no escaping the mission to Bologna once Colonel Cathcart had volunteered his group for the ammunition dumps there that the heavy bombers on the Italian mainland had been unable to destroy from their higher altitudes. Each day's delay deepened the awareness and deepened the gloom. The clinging, overpowering conviction of death spread steadily with the continuing rainfall, soaking mordantly into each man's ailing countenance like the corrosive blot of some crawling disease. Everyone smelled of formaldehyde. There was nowhere to turn for help, not even to the medical tent, which had been ordered closed by Colonel Korn so that no one could report for sick call, as the men had done on the one clear day with a mysterious epidemic of diarrhea that had forced still another postponement. With sick call suspended and the door to the medical tent nailed shut, Doc Daneeka spent the intervals between rain perched on a high stool, wordlessly absorbing the bleak outbreak of fear with a sorrowing neutrality, roosting like a melancholy buzzard below the ominous, hand-lettered sign tacked up on the closed door of the medical tent by Captain Black as a joke and left hanging there by Doc Daneeka because it was no joke. The sign was bordered in dark crayon and read: "CLOSED UNTIL FURTHER NOTICE. DEATH IN THE FAMILY."

The fear flowed everywhere, into Dunbar's squadron, where Dunbar poked his head inquiringly through the entrance of the medical tent there one twilight and spoke respectfully to the blurred outline of

Dr. Stubbs, who was sitting in the dense shadows inside before a bottle of whiskey and a bell jar filled with purified drinking water.

"Are you all right?" he asked solicitously.

"Terrible," Dr. Stubbs answered.

"What are you doing here?"

"Sitting."

"I thought there was no more sick call."

"There ain't."

"Then why are you sitting here?"

"Where else should I sit? At the goddam officers' club with Colonel Cathcart and Korn? Do you know what I'm doing here?"

"Sitting."

"In the squadron, I mean. Not in the tent. Don't be such a goddam wise guy. Can you figure out what a doctor is doing here in the squadron?"

"They've got the doors to the medical tents nailed shut in the other squadrons," Dunbar remarked.

"If anyone sick walks through my door I'm going to ground him," Dr. Stubbs vowed. "I don't give a damn what they say."

"You can't ground anyone," Dunbar reminded. "Don't you know the orders?"

"I'll knock him flat on his ass with an injection and really ground him." Dr. Stubbs laughed with sardonic amusement at the prospect. "They think they can order sick call out of existence. The bastards. Ooops, there it goes again." The rain began falling again, first in the trees, then in the mud puddles, then, faintly, like a soothing murmur, on the tent top. "Everything's wet," Dr. Stubbs observed with revulsion. "Even the latrines and urinals are backing up in protest. The whole goddam world smells like a charnel house."

The silence seemed bottomless when he stopped talking. Night fell. There was a sense of vast isolation.

"Turn on the light," Dunbar suggested.

"There is no light. I don't feel like starting my generator. I used to get a big kick out of saving people's lives. Now I wonder what the hell's the point, since they all have to die anyway."

"Oh, there's a point, all right," Dunbar assured him.

"Is there? What is the point?"

"The point is to keep them from dying for as long as you can."

"Yeah, but what's the point, since they all have to die anyway?"

"The trick is not to think about that."

"Never mind the trick. What the hell's the point?"

Dunbar pondered in silence for a few moments. "Who the hell knows?"

Dunbar didn't know. Bologna should have exulted Dunbar, because the minutes dawdled and the hours dragged like centuries. Instead it tortured him, because he knew he was going to be killed.

"Do you really want some more codeine?" Dr. Stubbs asked.

"It's for my friend Yossarian. He's sure he's going to be killed."

"Yossarian? Who the hell is Yossarian? What the hell kind of a name is Yossarian, anyway? Isn't he the one who got drunk and started that fight with Colonel Korn at the officers' club the other night?"

"That's right. He's Assyrian."

"That crazy bastard."

"He's not so crazy," Dunbar said. "He swears he's not going to fly to Bologna."

"That's just what I mean," Dr. Stubbs answered. "That crazy bastard may be the only sane one left."

11

Captain Black

Corporal Kolodny learned about it first in a phone call from Group and was so shaken by the news that he crossed the intelligence tent on tiptoe to Captain Black, who was resting drowsily with his bladed shins up on the desk, and relayed the information to him in a shocked whisper.

Captain Black brightened immediately. "Bologna?" he exclaimed with delight. "Well, I'll be damned." He broke into loud laughter. "Bologna, huh?" He laughed again and shook his head in pleasant amazement. "Oh, boy! I can't wait to see those bastards' faces when they find out they're going to Bologna. Ha, ha ha!"

It was the first really good laugh Captain Black had enjoyed since the day Major Major outsmarted him and was appointed squadron commander, and he rose with torpid enthusiasm and stationed himself behind the front counter in order to wring the most enjoyment from the occasion when the bombardiers arrived for their map kits.

"That's right, you bastards, Bologna," he kept repeating to all the bombardiers who inquired incredulously if they were really going to Bologna. "Ha! Ha! Ha! Eat your livers, you bastards. This time you're really in for it."

Captain Black followed the last of them outside to observe with relish the effect of the knowledge upon all of the other officers and enlisted men who were assembling with their helmets, parachutes and flak suits around the four trucks idling in the center of the squadron area. He was a tall, narrow, disconsolate man who moved with a crabby listlessness. He shaved his pinched, pale face every third or fourth day, and most of the time he appeared to be growing a reddish-gold mustache over his skinny upper lip. He was not disappointed in the scene outside. There was consternation darkening every expression, and Captain Black yawned deliciously, rubbed the last lethargy from his eyes and laughed gloatingly each time he told someone else to eat his liver.

Bologna turned out to be the most rewarding event in Captain

Black's life since the day Major Duluth was killed over Perugia and he was almost selected to replace him. When word of Major Duluth's death was radioed back to the field, Captain Black responded with a surge of joy. Although he had never really contemplated the possibility before, Captain Black understood at once that he was the logical man to succeed Major Duluth as squadron commander. To begin with, he was the squadron intelligence officer, which meant he was more intelligent than everyone else in the squadron. True, he was not on combat status, as Major Duluth had been and as all squadron commanders customarily were; but this was really another powerful argument in his favor, since his life was in no danger and he would be able to fill the post for as long as his country needed him. The more Captain Black thought about it, the more inevitable it seemed. It was merely a matter of dropping the right word in the right place quickly. He hurried back to his office to determine a course of action. Settling back in his swivel chair, his feet up on the desk and his eyes closed, he began imagining how beautiful everything would be once he was squadron commander.

While Captain Black was imagining, Colonel Cathcart was acting, and Captain Black was flabbergasted by the speed with which, he concluded, Major Major had outsmarted him. His great dismay at the announcement of Major Major's appointment as squadron commander was tinged with an embittered resentment he made no effort to conceal. When fellow administrative officers expressed astonishment at Colonel Cathcart's choice of Major Major, Captain Black muttered that there was something funny going on; when they speculated on the political value of Major Major's resemblance to Henry Fonda, Captain Black asserted that Major Major really was Henry Fonda; and when they remarked that Major Major was somewhat odd, Captain Black announced that he was a Communist.

"They're taking over everything," he declared rebelliously. "Well, you fellows can stand around and let them if you want to, but I'm not going to. I'm going to do something about it. From now on I'm going to make every son of a bitch who comes to my intelligence tent sign a loyalty oath. And I'm not going to let that bastard Major Major sign one even if he wants to."

Almost overnight the Glorious Loyalty Oath Crusade was in full flower, and Captain Black was enraptured to discover himself spearheading it. He had really hit on something. All the enlisted men and officers on combat duty had to sign a loyalty oath to get their map cases from the intelligence tent, a second loyalty oath to receive their flak suits and parachutes from the parachute tent, a third loyalty oath for Lieutenant Balkington, the motor vehicle officer, to be allowed to ride from the squadron to the airfield in one of the trucks. Every time they turned around there was another loyalty oath to be signed. They signed a loyalty oath to get their pay from the finance officer, to obtain their PX supplies, to have their hair cut by the Italian barbers. To Captain Black, every officer who supported his Glorious Loyalty Oath Crusade was a competitor, and he planned and plotted twenty-four hours a day to keep one step ahead. He would stand second to none in his devotion to country. When other officers had followed his urging and introduced loyalty oaths of their own, he went them one better by making every son of a bitch who came to his intelligence tent sign two loyalty oaths, then three, then four; then he introduced the pledge of allegiance, and after that "The Star-Spangled Banner," one chorus, two choruses, three choruses, four choruses. Each time Captain Black forged ahead of his competitors, he swung upon them scornfully for their failure to follow his example. Each time they followed his example, he retreated with concern and racked his brain for some new stratagem that would enable him to turn upon them scornfully again.

Without realizing how it had come about, the combat men in the squadron discovered themselves dominated by the administrators appointed to serve them. They were bullied, insulted, harassed and shoved about all day long by one after the other. When they voiced objection, Captain Black replied that people who were loyal would not mind signing all the loyalty oaths they had to. To anyone who questioned the effectiveness of the loyalty oaths, he replied that people who really did owe allegiance to their country would be proud to pledge it as often as he forced them to. And to anyone who questioned the morality, he replied that "The Star-Spangled Banner" was the greatest piece of music ever composed. The more loyalty oaths a person signed, the more loyal he was; to Captain Black it was as simple as that, and he had Corporal Kolodny sign hundreds with his name each day so that he could always prove he was more loyal than anyone else.

"The important thing is to keep them pledging," he explained to his cohorts. "It doesn't matter whether they mean it or not. That's why they make little kids pledge allegiance even before they know what 'pledge' and 'allegiance' mean."

To Captain Piltchard and Captain Wren, the Glorious Loyalty Oath Crusade was a glorious pain in the ass, since it complicated their task of organizing the crews for each combat mission. Men were tied up all over the squadron signing, pledging and singing, and the missions took hours longer to get under way. Effective emergency action became impossible, but Captain Piltchard and Captain Wren were both too timid to raise any outcry against Captain Black, who scrupulously enforced each day the doctrine of "Continual Reaffirmation" that he had originated, a doctrine designed to trap all those men who had become disloyal since the last time they had signed a loyalty oath the day before. It was Captain Black who came with advice to Captain Piltchard and Captain Wren as they pitched about in their bewildering predicament. He came with a delegation and advised them bluntly to make each man sign a loyalty oath before allowing him to fly on a combat mission.

"Of course, it's up to you," Captain Black pointed out. "Nobody's trying to pressure you. But everyone else is making them sign loyalty oaths, and it's going to look mighty funny to the F.B.I. if you two are the only ones who don't care enough about your country to make them sign loyalty oaths, too. If you want to get a bad reputation, that's nobody's business but your own. All we're trying to do is help."

Milo was not convinced and absolutely refused to deprive Major Major of food, even if Major Major was a Communist, which Milo secretly doubted. Milo was by nature opposed to any innovation that threatened to disrupt the normal course of affairs. Milo took a firm moral stand and absolutely refused to participate in the Glorious Loyalty Oath Crusade until Captain Black called upon him with his delegation and requested him to.

"National defense is *everybody's* job," Captain Black replied to Milo's objection. "And this whole program is voluntary, Milo—don't forget that. The men don't *have* to sign Piltchard and Wren's loyalty oath if they don't want to. But we need you to starve them to death if they don't. It's just like Catch-22. Don't you get it? You're not against Catch-22, are you?"

Doc Daneeka was adamant.

"What makes you so sure Major Major is a Communist?"

"You never heard him denying it until we began accusing him, did you? And you don't see him signing any of our loyalty oaths."

"You aren't letting him sign any."

"Of course not," Captain Black explained. "That would defeat the whole purpose of our crusade. Look, you don't have to play ball with us if you don't want to. But what's the point of the rest of us working so hard if you're going to give Major Major medical attention the minute Milo begins starving him to death? I just wonder what they're going to think up at Group about the man who's undermining our whole security program. They'll probably transfer you to the Pacific."

Doc Daneeka surrendered swiftly. "I'll go tell Gus and Wes to do whatever you want them to."

Up at Group, Colonel Cathcart had already begun wondering what was going on.

"It's that idiot Black off on a patriotism binge," Colonel Korn reported with a smile. "I think you'd better play ball with him for a while, since you're the one who promoted Major Major to squadron commander."

"That was your idea," Colonel Cathcart accused him petulantly. "I never should have let you talk me into it."

"And a very good idea it was, too," retorted Colonel Korn, "since it eliminated that superfluous major that's been giving you such an awful black eye as an administrator. Don't worry, this will probably run its course soon. The best thing to do now is send Captain Black a letter of total support and hope he drops dead before he does too much damage." Colonel Korn was struck with a whimsical thought. "I wonder! You don't suppose that imbecile will try to turn Major Major out of his trailer, do you?"

"The next thing we've got to do is turn that bastard Major Major out of his trailer," Captain Black decided. "I'd like to turn his wife and kids out into the woods, too. But we can't. He has no wife and kids. So we'll just have to make do with what we have and turn him out. Who's in charge of the tents?"

"He is."

"You see?" cried Captain Black. "They're taking over *everything!* Well, I'm not going to stand for it. I'll take this matter right to Major —— de Coverley himself if I have to. I'll have Milo speak to him about it the minute he gets back from Rome."

Captain Black had boundless faith in the wisdom, power and justice of Major —— de Coverley, even though he had never spoken to him before and still found himself without the courage to do so. He deputized Milo to speak to Major —— de Coverley for him and stormed out impatiently as he waited for the tall executive officer to return. Along with everyone else in the squadron, he lived in profound awe and reverence of the majestic, white-haired major with the craggy face and Jehovean bearing, who came back from Rome finally with an injured eye inside a new celluloid eye patch and smashed his whole Glorious Crusade to bits with a single stroke.

Milo carefully said nothing when Major —— de Coverley stepped into the mess hall with his fierce and austere dignity the day he returned and found his way blocked by a wall of officers waiting in line to sign loyalty oaths. At the far end of the food counter, a group of men who had arrived earlier were pledging allegiance to the flag, with trays of food balanced in one hand, in order to be allowed to take seats at the table. Already at the tables, a group that had arrived still earlier was singing "The Star-Spangled Banner" in order that they might use the salt and pepper and ketchup there. The hubbub began to subside slowly as Major —— de Coverley paused in the doorway with a frown of puzzled disapproval, as though viewing something bizarre. He started forward in a straight line, and the wall of officers before him parted like the Red Sea. Glancing neither left nor right, he strode indomitably up to the steam counter and, in a clear, full-bodied voice that was gruff with age and resonant with ancient eminence and authority, said:

"Gimme eat."

Instead of eat, Corporal Snark gave Major —— de Coverley a loyalty oath to sign. Major —— de Coverley swept it away with mighty displeasure the moment he recognized what it was, his good eye flaring up blindingly with fiery disdain and his enormous old corrugated face darkening in mountainous wrath.

"Gimme eat, I said," he ordered loudly in harsh tones that rumbled ominously through the silent tent like claps of distant thunder.

Corporal Snark turned pale and began to tremble. He glanced toward Milo pleadingly for guidance. For several terrible seconds there was not a sound. Then Milo nodded.

"Give him eat," he said.

Corporal Snark began giving Major —— de Coverley eat. Major —— de Coverley turned from the counter with his tray full and came to a stop. His eyes fell on the groups of other officers gazing at him in mute appeal, and, with righteous belligerence, he roared:

"Give *everybody* eat!"

"Give *everybody* eat!" Milo echoed with joyful relief, and the Glorious Loyalty Oath Crusade came to an end.

Captain Black was deeply disillusioned by this treacherous stab in the back from someone in high place upon whom he had relied so confidently for support. Major —— de Coverley had let him down.

"Oh, it doesn't bother me a bit," he responded cheerfully to everyone who came to him with sympathy. "We completed our task. Our purpose was to make everyone we don't like afraid and to alert people to the danger of Major Major, and we certainly succeeded at that. Since we weren't going to let him sign loyalty oaths anyway, it doesn't really matter whether we have them or not."

Seeing everyone in the squadron he didn't like afraid once again throughout the appalling, interminable Great Big Siege of Bologna reminded Captain Black nostalgically of the good old days of his Glorious Loyalty Oath Crusade when he had been a man of real consequence, and when even big shots like Milo Minderbinder, Doc Daneeka and Piltchard and Wren had trembled at his approach and groveled at his feet. To prove to newcomers that he really had been a man of consequence once, he still had the letter of commendation he had received from Colonel Cathcart.

12

Bologna

Actually, it was not Captain Black but Sergeant Knight who triggered the solemn panic of Bologna, slipping silently off the truck for two extra flak suits as soon as he learned the target and signaling the start of the grim procession back into the parachute tent that degenerated into a frantic stampede finally before all the extra flak suits were gone.

"Hey, what's going on?" Kid Sampson asked nervously. "Bologna can't be that rough, can it?"

Nately, sitting trancelike on the floor of the truck, held his grave young face in both hands and did not answer him.

It was Sergeant Knight and the cruel series of postponements, for just as they were climbing up into their planes that first morning, along came a jeep with the news that it was raining in Bologna and that the mission would be delayed. It was raining in Pianosa too by the time they returned to the squadron, and they had the rest of that day to stare woodenly at the bomb line on the map under the awning of the intelligence tent and ruminate hypnotically on the fact that there was no escape. The evidence was there vividly in the narrow red ribbon tacked across the mainland: the ground forces in Italy were pinned down forty-two insurmountable miles south of the target and could not possibly capture the city in time. Nothing could save the men in Pianosa from the mission to Bologna. They were trapped.

Their only hope was that it would never stop raining, and they had no hope because they all knew it would. When it did stop raining in Pianosa, it rained in Bologna. When it stopped raining in Bologna, it began again in Pianosa. If there was no rain at all, there were freakish, inexplicable phenomena like the epidemic of diarrhea or the bomb line that moved. Four times during the first six days they were assembled and briefed and then sent back. Once, they took off and were flying in formation when the control tower summoned them down. The more it rained, the worse they suffered. The worse they suffered, the more they prayed that it would continue raining. All through the night, men looked at the sky and were saddened by the stars. All through the day, they looked at the bomb line on the big, wobbling easel map of Italy that blew over in the wind and was dragged in under the awning of the intelligence tent every time the rain began. The bomb line was a scarlet band of narrow satin ribbon that delineated the forwardmost position of the Allied ground forces in every sector of the Italian mainland.

The morning after Hungry Joe's fist fight with Huple's cat, the rain stopped falling in both places. The landing strip began to dry. It would take a full twenty-four hours to harden; but the sky remained cloudless. The resentments incubating in each man hatched into hatred. First they hated the infantrymen on the mainland because they had failed to capture Bologna. Then they began to hate the bomb line itself. For hours they stared relentlessly at the scarlet ribbon on the map and hated it because it would not move up high enough to encompass the city. When night fell, they congregated in the darkness with flashlights, continuing their macabre vigil at the bomb line in brooding entreaty as though hoping to move the ribbon up by the collective weight of their sullen prayers.

"I really can't believe it," Clevinger exclaimed to Yossarian in a voice rising and falling in protest and wonder. "It's a complete reversion to primitive superstition. They're confusing cause and effect. It makes as much sense as knocking on wood or crossing your fingers. They really believe that we wouldn't have to fly that mission tomorrow if someone would only tiptoe up to the map in the middle of the night and move the bomb line over Bologna. Can you imagine? You and I must be the only rational ones left."

In the middle of the night Yossarian knocked on wood, crossed his fingers, and tiptoed out of his tent to move the bomb line up over Bologna.

Corporal Kolodny tiptoed steathily into Captain Black's tent early the next morning, reached inside the mosquito net and gently shook the moist shoulder blade he found there until Captain Black opened his eyes.

"What are you waking me up for?" whimpered Captain Black.

"They captured Bologna, sir," said Corporal Kolodny. "I thought you'd want to know. Is the mission canceled?"

Captain Black tugged himself erect and began scratching his scrawny long thighs methodically. In a little while he dressed and emerged from his tent, squinting, cross and unshaven. The sky was clear and warm. He peered without emotion at the map. Sure enough, they had captured Bologna. Inside the intelligence tent, Corporal Kolodny was already removing the maps of Bologna from the navigation kits. Captain Black seated himself with a loud yawn, lifted his feet to the top of his desk and phoned Colonel Korn.

"What are you waking me up for?" whimpered Colonel Korn.

"They captured Bologna during the night, sir. Is the mission canceled?"

"What are you talking about, Black?" Colonel Korn growled. "Why should the mission be canceled?"

"Because they captured Bologna, sir. Isn't the mission canceled?"

"Of course the mission is canceled. Do you think we're bombing our own troops now?"

"What are you waking me up for?" Colonel Cathcart whimpered to Colonel Korn.

"They captured Bologna," Colonel Korn told him. "I thought you'd want to know."

"Who captured Bologna?"

"We did."

Colonel Cathcart was overjoyed, for he was relieved of the embarrassing commitment to bomb Bologna without blemish to the reputation for valor he had earned by volunteering his men to do it. General Dreedle was pleased with the capture of Bologna, too, although he was angry with Colonel Moodus for waking him up to tell him about it. Headquarters was also pleased and decided to award a medal to the officer who had captured the city. There was no officer who had captured the city, so they gave the medal to General Peckem instead, because General Peckem was the only officer with sufficient initiative to ask for it.

As soon as General Peckem had received his medal, he began asking for increased responsibility. It was General Peckem's opinion that all combat units in the theater should be placed under the jurisdiction of the Special Service Corps, of which General Peckem himself was the commanding officer. If dropping bombs on the enemy was not a special service, he reflected aloud frequently with the martyred smile of sweet reasonableness that was his loyal confederate in every dispute, then he could not help wondering what in the world was. With amiable regret, he declined the offer of a combat post under General Dreedle.

"Flying combat missions *for* General Dreedle is not exactly what I had in mind," he explained indulgently with a smooth laugh. "I was thinking more in terms of *replacing* General Dreedle, or perhaps of something *above* General Dreedle where I could exercise supervision over a great many *other* generals too. You see, my most precious abilities are mainly administrative ones. I have a happy facility for getting different people to agree."

"He has a happy facility for getting different people to agree what a prick he is," Colonel Cargill confided invidiously to ex-P.F.C. Wintergreen in the hope that ex-P.F.C. Wintergreen would spread the unfavorable report along through Twenty-seventh Air Force Headquarters. "If anyone deserves that combat post, I do. It was even my idea that we ask for the medal."

"You really want to go into combat?" ex-P.F.C. Wintergreen inquired.

"Combat?" Colonel Cargill was aghast. "Oh, no—you misunderstand me. Of course, I wouldn't actually *mind* going into combat, but my best abilities are mainly administrative ones. I too have a happy facility for getting different people to agree."

"He too has a happy facility for getting different people to agree what a prick he is," ex-P.F.C. Wintergreen confided with a laugh to Yossarian, after he had come to Pianosa to learn if it was really true about Milo and the Egyptian cotton. "If anyone deserves a promotion, I do." Actually, he had risen already to ex-corporal, having shot through the ranks shortly after his transfer to Twenty-seventh Air Force Headquarters as a mail clerk and been busted right down to private for making odious audible comparisons about the commissioned officers for whom he worked. The heady taste of success had infused him further with morality and fired him with ambition for loftier attainments. "Do you want to buy some Zippo lighters?" he asked Yossarian. "They were stolen right from quartermaster."

"Does Milo know you're selling cigarette lighters?"

"What's it his business? Milo's not carrying cigarette lighters too now, is he?"

"He sure is," Yossarian told him. "And his aren't stolen."

"That's what you think," ex-P.F.C. Wintergreen answered with a laconic snort. "I'm selling mine for a buck apiece. What's he getting for his?"

"A dollar and a penny."

Ex-P.F.C. Wintergreen snickered triumphantly. "I beat him every time," he gloated. "Say, what about all that Egyptian cotton he's stuck with? How much did he buy?"

"All."

"In the whole world? Well, I'll be damned!" ex-P.F.C. Wintergreen crowed with malicious glee. "What a dope! You were in Cairo with him. Why'd you let him do it?"

"Me?" Yossarian answered with a shrug. "I have no influence on him. It was those Teletype machines they have in all the good restaurants there. Milo had never seen a stock ticker before, and the quotation for Egyptian cotton happened to be going in just as he asked the headwaiter to explain it to him. 'Egyptian cotton?' Milo said with that look of his. 'How much is Egyptian cotton selling for?' The next thing I knew he had bought the whole goddam harvest. And now he can't unload any of it."

"He has no imagination. I can unload plenty of it in the black market if he'll make a deal."

"Milo knows the black market. There's no demand for cotton."

"But there is a demand for medical supplies. I can roll the cotton up on wooden toothpicks and peddle them as sterile swabs. Will he sell to me at a good price?"

"He won't sell to you at any price," Yossarian answered. "He's pretty sore at you for going into competition with him. In fact, he's pretty sore at everybody for getting diarrhea last weekend and giving his mess hall a bad name. Say, you can help us." Yossarian suddenly seized his arm. "Couldn't you forge some official orders on that mimeograph machine of yours and get us out of flying to Bologna?"

Ex-P.F.C. Wintergreen pulled away slowly with a look of scorn. "Sure I could," he explained with pride. "But I would never dream of doing anything like that."

"Why not?"

"Because it's your job. We all have our jobs to do. My job is to unload these Zippo lighters at a profit if I can and pick up some cotton from Milo. Your job is to bomb the ammunition dumps at Bologna."

"But I'm going to be killed at Bologna," Yossarian pleaded. "We're all going to be killed."

"Then you'll just have to be killed," replied ex-P.F.C. Wintergreen. "Why can't you be a fatalist about it the way I am? If I'm destined to unload these lighters at a profit and pick up some Egyptian cotton cheap from Milo, then that's what I'm going to do. And if you're destined to be killed over Bologna, then you're going to be killed, so you might just as well go out and die like a man. I hate to say this, Yossarian, but you're turning into a chronic complainer."

Clevinger agreed with ex-P.F.C. Wintergreen that it was Yossarian's job to get killed over Bologna and was livid with condemnation when Yossarian confessed that it was he who had moved the bomb line and caused the mission to be canceled.

"Why the hell not?" Yossarian snarled, arguing all the more vehemently because he suspected he was wrong. "Am I supposed to get my ass shot off just because the colonel wants to be a general?"

"What about the men on the mainland?" Clevinger demanded with just as much emotion. "Are they supposed to get their asses shot off just because you don't want to go? Those men are entitled to air support!"

"But not necessarily by me. Look, they don't care who knocks out those ammunition dumps. The only reason we're going is because that bastard Cathcart volunteered us."

"Oh, I know all that," Clevinger assured him, his gaunt face pale and his agitated brown eyes swimming in sincerity. "But the fact remains that those ammunition dumps are still standing. You know very well that I don't approve of Colonel Cathcart any more than you do." Clevinger paused for emphasis, his mouth quivering, and then beat his fist down softly against his sleeping bag. "But it's not for us to determine what targets must be destroyed or who's to destroy them or—"

"Or who gets killed doing it? And why?"

"Yes, even that. We have no right to question—"

"You're insane!"

"—no right to question—"

"Do you really mean that it's not my business how or why I get killed and that it is Colonel Cathcart's? Do you really mean that?"

"Yes, I do," Clevinger insisted, seeming unsure. "There are men entrusted with winning the war who are in a much better position than we are to decide what targets have to be bombed."

"We are talking about two different things," Yossarian answered with exaggerated weariness. "You are talking about the relationship of the Air Corps to the infantry, and I am talking about the relationship of me to Colonel Cathcart. You are talking about winning the war, and I am talking about winning the war and keeping alive."

"Exactly," Clevinger snapped smugly. "And which do you think is more important?"

"To whom?" Yossarian shot back. "Open your eyes, Clevinger. It doesn't make a damned bit of difference *who* wins the war to someone who's dead."

Clevinger sat for a moment as though he'd been slapped. "Congratulations!" he exclaimed bitterly, the thinnest milk-white line enclosing his lips tightly in a bloodless, squeezing ring. "I can't think of another attitude that could be depended upon to give greater comfort to the enemy."

"The enemy," retorted Yossarian with weighted precision, "is anybody who's going to get you killed, no matter *which* side he's on, and that includes Colonel Cathcart. And don't you forget that, because the longer you remember it, the longer you might live."

But Clevinger did forget it, and now he was dead. At the time, Clevinger was so upset by the incident that Yossarian did not dare tell him he had also been responsible for the epidemic of diarrhea that had caused the other unnecessary postponement. Milo was even more upset by the possibility that someone had poisoned his squadron again, and he came bustling fretfully to Yossarian for assistance.

"Please find out from Corporal Snark if he put laundry soap in the sweet potatoes again," he requested furtively. "Corporal Snark trusts you and will tell you the truth if you give him your word you won't tell anyone else. As soon as he tells you, come and tell me."

"Of course I put laundry soap in the sweet potatoes," Corporal Snark admitted to Yossarian. "That's what you asked me to do, isn't it? Laundry soap is the best way."

"He swears to God he didn't have a thing to do with it," Yossarian reported back to Milo.

Milo pouted dubiously. "Dunbar says there is no God."

There was no hope left. By the middle of the second week, everyone in the squadron began to look like Hungry Joe, who was not scheduled to fly and screamed horribly in his sleep. He was the only one who could sleep. All night long, men moved through the darkness outside their tents like tongueless wraiths with cigarettes. In the daytime they stared at the bomb line in futile, drooping clusters or at the still figure of Doc Daneeka sitting in front of the closed door of the medical tent beneath the morbid hand-lettered sign. They began to invent humorless, glum jokes of their own and disastrous rumors about the destruction awaiting them at Bologna.

Yossarian sidled up drunkenly to Colonel Korn at the officers' club one night to kid with him about the new Lepage gun that the Germans had moved in.

"What Lepage gun?" Colonel Korn inquired with curiosity.

"The new three-hundred-and-forty-four-millimeter Lepage glue gun," Yossarian answered. "It glues a whole formation of planes together in mid-air."

Colonel Korn jerked his elbow free from Yossarian's clutching fingers in startled affront. "Let go of me, you idiot!" he cried out furiously, glaring with vindictive approval as Nately leaped upon Yossarian's back and pulled him away. "Who is that lunatic, anyway?"

Colonel Cathcart chortled merrily. "That's the man you made me give a medal to after Ferrara. You had me promote him to captain, too, remember? It serves you right."

Nately was lighter than Yossarian and had great difficulty maneuvering Yossarian's lurching bulk across the room to an unoccupied table. "Are you crazy?" Nately kept hissing with trepidation. "That was Colonel Korn. Are you crazy?"

Yossarian wanted another drink and promised to leave quietly if Nately brought him one. Then he made Nately bring him two more. When Nately finally coaxed him to the door, Captain Black came stomping in from outside, banging his sloshing shoes down hard on the wood floor and spilling water from his eaves like a high roof.

"Boy, are you bastards in for it!" he announced exuberantly, splashing away from the puddle forming at his feet. "I just got a call from Colonel Korn. Do you know what they've got waiting for you at Bologna? Ha! Ha! They've got the new Lepage glue gun. It glues a whole formation of planes together right in mid-air."

"My God, it's true!" Yossarian shrieked, and collapsed against Nately in terror.

"There is no God," answered Dunbar calmly, coming up with a slight stagger.

"Hey, give me a hand with him, will you? I've got to get him back in his tent."

"Says who?"

"Says me. Gee, look at the rain."

"We've got to get a car."

"Steal Captain Black's car," said Yossarian. "That's what I always do."

"We can't steal anybody's car. Since you began stealing the nearest car every time you wanted one, nobody leaves the ignition on."

"Hop in," said Chief White Halfoat, driving up drunk in a covered jeep. He waited until they had crowded inside and then spurred ahead with a suddenness that rolled them all over backward. He roared with laughter at their curses. He drove straight ahead when he left the parking lot and rammed the car into the embankment on the other side of the road. The others piled forward in a helpless heap and began cursing him again. "I forgot to turn," he explained.

"Be careful, will you?" Nately cautioned. "You'd better put your headlights on."

Chief White Halfoat pulled back in reverse, made his turn and shot away up the road at top speed. The wheels were sibilant on the whizzing black-top surface.

"Not so fast," urged Nately.

"You'd better take me to your squadron first so I can help you put him to bed. Then you can drive me back to my squadron."

"Who the hell are you?"

"Dunbar."

"Hey, put your headlights on," Nately shouted. "And watch the road!"

"They are on. Isn't Yossarian in this car? That's the only reason I let the rest of you bastards in." Chief White Halfoat turned completely around to stare into the back seat.

"Watch the road!"

"Yossarian? Is Yossarian in here?"

"I'm here, Chief. Let's go home. What makes you so sure? You never answered my question."

"You see? I *told* you he was here."

"What question?"

"Whatever it was we were talking about."

"Was it important?"

"I don't remember if it was important or not. I wish to God I knew what it was."

"There is no God."

"*That's* what we were talking about," Yossarian cried. "What makes you so sure?"

"Hey, are you sure your headlights are on?" Nately called out.

"They're on, they're on. What does he want from me? It's all this rain on the windshield that makes it look dark from back there."

"Beautiful, beautiful rain."

"I hope it never stops raining. Rain, rain, go a—"

"—way. Come a—"

"—gain some oth—"

"—er day. Little Yo-Yo wants—"

"—to play. In—"

"—the meadow, in—"

Chief White Halfoat missed the next turn in the road and ran the jeep all the way up to the crest of a steep embankment. Rolling back down, the jeep turned over on its side and settled softly in the mud. There was a frightened silence.

"Is everyone all right?" Chief White Halfoat inquired in a hushed voice. No one was injured, and he heaved a long sigh of relief. "You know, that's my trouble," he groaned. "I never listen to anybody. Somebody kept telling me to put my headlights on, but I just wouldn't listen."

"I kept telling you to put your headlights on."

"I know, I know. And I just wouldn't listen, would I? I wish I had a drink. I *do* have a drink. Look. It's not broken."

"It's raining in," Nately noticed. "I'm getting wet."

Chief White Halfoat got the bottle of rye open, drank and handed it off. Lying tangled up on top of each other, they all drank but Nately, who kept groping ineffectually for the door handle. The bottle fell against his head with a clunk, and whiskey poured down his neck. He began writhing convulsively.

"Hey, we've got to get out of here!" he cried. "We'll all drown."

"Is anybody in there?" asked Clevinger with concern, shining a flashlight down from the top.

"It's Clevinger!" they shouted, and tried to pull him in through the window as he reached down to aid them.

"Look at them!" Clevinger exclaimed indignantly to McWatt, who sat grinning at the wheel of the staff car. "Lying there like a bunch of drunken animals. You too, Nately? You ought to be ashamed! Come on—help me get them out of there before they all die of pneumonia."

"You know, that don't sound like such a bad idea," Chief White Halfoat reflected. "I think I will die of pneumonia."

"Why?"

"Why not?" answered Chief White Halfoat, and lay back in the mud contentedly with the bottle of rye cuddled in his arms.

"Oh, now look what he's doing!" Clevinger exclaimed with irritation. "Will you get up and get into the car so we can all go back to the squadron?"

"We can't all go back. Someone has to stay here and help the Chief with this car he signed out of the motor pool."

Chief White Halfoat settled back in the staff car with an ebullient, prideful chuckle. "That's Captain Black's car," he informed them jubilantly. "I stole it from him at the officers' club just now with an extra set of keys he thought he lost this morning."

"Well, I'll be damned! That calls for a drink."

"Haven't you had enough to drink?" Clevinger began scolding as soon as McWatt started the car. "Look at you. You don't care if you drink yourselves to death or drown yourselves to death, do you?"

"Just as long as we don't fly ourselves to death."

"Hey, open it up, open it up," Chief White Halfoat urged McWatt. "And turn off the headlights. That's the only way to do it."

"Doc Daneeka is right," Clevinger went on. "People don't know enough to take care of themselves. I really am disgusted with all of you."

"Okay, fatmouth, out of the car," Chief White Halfoat ordered. "Everybody get out of the car but Yossarian. Where's Yossarian?"

"Get the hell off me." Yossarian laughed, pushing him away. "You're all covered with mud."

Clevinger focused on Nately. "You're the one who really surprises me. Do you know what you smell like? Instead of trying to keep him out of trouble, you get just as drunk as he is. Suppose he got in another fight with Appleby?" Clevinger's eyes opened wide with alarm when he heard Yossarian chuckle. "He didn't get in another fight with Appleby, did he?"

"Not this time," said Dunbar.

"No, not this time. This time I did even better."

"This time he got in a fight with Colonel Korn."

"He didn't!" gasped Clevinger.

"He did?" exclaimed Chief White Halfoat with delight. "That calls for a drink."

"But that's terrible!" Clevinger declared with deep apprehension. "Why in the world did you have to pick on Colonel Korn? Say, what happened to the lights? Why is everything so dark?"

"I turned them off," answered McWatt. "You know, Chief White Halfoat is right. It's much better with the headlights off."

"Are you crazy?" Clevinger screamed, and lunged forward to snap the headlights on. He whirled around upon Yossarian in near hysteria. "You see what you're doing? You've got them all acting like you! Suppose it stops raining and we have to fly to Bologna tomorrow. You'll be in fine physical condition."

"It won't ever gonna stop raining. No, sir, a rain like this really might go on forever."

"It *has* stopped raining!" someone said, and the whole car fell silent.

"You poor bastards," Chief White Halfoat murmured compassionately after a few moments had passed.

"Did it really stop raining?" Yossarian asked meekly.

McWatt switched off the windshield wipers to make certain. The rain had stopped. The sky was starting to clear. The moon was sharp behind a gauzy brown mist.

"Oh, well," sang McWatt soberly. "What the hell."

"Don't worry, fellas," Chief White Halfoat said. "The landing strip is too soft to use tomorrow. Maybe it'll start raining again before the field dries out."

"You goddam stinking lousy son of a bitch," Hungry Joe screamed from his tent as they sped into the squadron.

"Jesus, is he back here tonight? I thought he was still in Rome with the courier ship."

"Oh! Ooooh! Oooooooh!" Hungry Joe screamed.

Chief White Halfoat shuddered. "That guy gives me the willies," he confessed in a grouchy whisper. "Hey, whatever happened to Captain Flume?"

"There's a guy that gives me the willies. I saw him in the woods last week eating wild berries. He never sleeps in his trailer any more. He looked like hell."

"Hungry Joe's afraid he'll have to replace somebody who goes on sick call, even though there is no sick call. Did you see him the other night when he tried to kill Havermeyer and fell into Yossarian's slit trench?"

"Ooooh!" screamed Hungry Joe. "Oh! Ooooh! Oooooooh!"

"It sure is a pleasure not having Flume around in the mess hall any more. No more of that 'Pass the salt, Walt.'"

"Or 'Pass the bread, Fred.'"

"Or 'Shoot me a beet, Pete.'"

"Keep away, keep away," Hungry Joe screamed. "I said keep away, keep away, you goddam stinking lousy son of a bitch."

"At least we found out what he dreams about," Dunbar observed wryly. "He dreams about goddam stinking lousy sons of bitches."

Late that night Hungry Joe dreamed that Huple's cat was sleeping on his face, suffocating him, and when he woke up, Huple's cat *was* sleeping on his face. His agony was terrifying, the piercing, unearthly howl with which he split the moonlit dark vibrating in its own impact for seconds afterward like a devastating shock. A numbing silence followed, and then a riotous din rose from inside his tent.

Yossarian was among the first ones there. When he burst through the entrance, Hungry Joe had his gun out and was struggling to wrench his arm free from Huple to shoot the cat, who kept spitting and feinting at him ferociously to distract him from shooting Huple. Both humans were in their GI underwear. The unfrosted light bulb overhead was swinging crazily on its loose wire, and the jumbled black shadows kept swirling and bobbing chaotically, so that the entire tent seemed to be reeling. Yossarian reached out instinctively for balance and then launched himself forward in a prodigious dive that crushed the three combatants to the ground beneath him. He emerged from the melee with the scruff of a neck in each hand—Hungry Joe's neck and the cat's. Hungry Joe and the cat glared at each other savagely. The cat spat viciously at Hungry Joe, and Hungry Joe tried to hit it with a haymaker.

"A fair fight," Yossarian decreed, and all the others who had come running to the uproar in horror began cheering ecstatically in a tremendous overflow of relief. "We'll have a fair fight," he explained officially to Hungry Joe and the cat after he had carried them both outside, still holding them apart by the scruffs of their necks. "Fists, fangs and claws. But no guns," he warned Hungry Joe. "And no spitting," he warned the cat sternly. "When I turn you both loose, go. Break clean in the clinches and come back fighting. Go!"

There was a huge, giddy crowd of men who were avid for any diversion, but the cat turned chicken the moment Yossarian released him and fled from Hungry Joe ignominiously like a yellow dog. Hungry Joe was declared the winner. He swaggered away happily with the proud smile of a champion, his shriveled head high and his emaciated chest out. He went back to bed victorious and dreamed again that Huple's cat was sleeping on his face, suffocating him.

13

Major —— de Coverley

Moving the bomb line did not fool the Germans, but it did fool Major —— de Coverley, who packed his musette bag, commandeered an airplane and, under the impression that Florence too had been captured by the allies, had himself flown to that city to rent two apartments for the officers and the enlisted men in the squadron to use on rest leaves. He had still not returned by the time Yossarian jumped back outside Major Major's office and wondered whom to appeal to next for help.

Major —— de Coverley was a splendid, awe-inspiring, grave old man with a massive leonine head and an angry shock of wild white hair that raged like a blizzard around his stern, patriarchal face. His duties as squadron executive officer did consist entirely, as both Doc Daneeka and Major Major had conjectured, of pitching horseshoes, kidnapping Italian laborers, and renting apartments for the enlisted men and officers to use on rest leaves, and he excelled at all three.

Each time the fall of a city like Naples, Rome or Florence seemed imminent, Major —— de Coverley would pack his musette bag, commandeer an airplane and a pilot, and have himself flown away, accomplishing all this without uttering a word, by the sheer force of his solemn, domineering visage and the peremptory gestures of his wrinkled finger. A day or two after the city fell, he would be back with leases on two large and luxurious apartments there, one for the officers and one for the enlisted men, both already staffed with competent, jolly cooks and maids. A few days after that, newspapers would appear throughout the world with photographs of the first American soldiers bludgeoning their way into the shattered city through rubble and smoke. Inevitably, Major —— de Coverley was among them, seated straight as a ramrod in a jeep he had obtained from somewhere, glancing neither right nor left as the artillery fire burst about his invincible head and lithe young infantrymen with carbines went loping up along the sidewalks in the shelter of burning buildings or fell dead in doorways. He seemed eternally indestructible as he sat there surrounded by danger, his features molded firmly into that same fierce, regal, just and forbidding countenance which was recognized and revered by every man in the squadron.

To German intelligence, Major —— de Coverley was a vexatious enigma; not one of the hundreds of American prisoners would ever supply any concrete information about the elderly white-haired officer with the gnarled and menacing brow and blazing, powerful eyes who seemed to spearhead every important advance so fearlessly and successfully. To American authorities his identity was equally perplexing; a whole regiment of crack C.I.D. men had been thrown into the front lines to find out who he was, while a battalion of combat-hardened public-relations officers stood on red alert twenty-four hours a day with orders to begin publicizing him the moment he was located.

In Rome, Major —— de Coverley had outdone himself with the apartments. For the officers, who arrived in groups of four or five, there was an immense double room for each in a new white stone building, with three spacious bathrooms with walls of shimmering aquamarine tile and one skinny maid named Michaela who tittered at everything and kept the apartment in spotless order. On the landing below lived the obsequious owners. On the landing above lived the beautiful rich black-haired countess and her beautiful rich black-haired daughter-in-law, both of whom would put out only for Nately, who was too shy to want them, and for Aarfy, who was too stuffy to take them and tried to dissuade them from ever putting out for anyone but their husbands, who had chosen to remain in the north with the family's business interests.

"They're really a couple of good kids," Aarfy confided earnestly to Yossarian, whose recurring dream it was to have the nude milk-white female bodies of both these beautiful rich black-haired good kids lying stretched out in bed erotically with him at the same time.

The enlisted men descended upon Rome in gangs of twelve or more with Gargantuan appetites and heavy crates filled with canned food for the women to cook and serve to them in the dining room of their own apartment on the sixth floor of a red brick building with a clinking elevator. There was always more activity at the enlisted men's place. There were always more enlisted men, to begin with, and more women to cook and serve and sweep and scrub, and then there were always the gay and silly sensual young girls that Yossarian had found and brought there and those that the sleepy enlisted men returning to Pianosa after their exhausting seven-day debauch had brought there on their own and were leaving behind for whoever wanted them next. The girls had shelter and food for as long as they wanted to stay. All they had to do in return was hump any of the men who asked them to, which seemed to make everything just about perfect for them.

Every fourth day or so Hungry Joe came crashing in like a man in torment, hoarse, wild, and frenetic, if he had been unlucky enough to finish his missions again and was flying the courier ship. Most times he slept at the enlisted men's apartment. Nobody was certain how many rooms Major —— de Coverley had rented, not even the stout black-bodiced woman in corsets on the first floor from whom he had rented them. They covered the whole top floor, and Yossarian knew they extended down to the fifth floor as well, for it was in Snowden's room on the fifth floor that he had finally found the maid in the lime-colored panties with a dust mop the day after Bologna, after Hungry Joe had discovered him in bed with Luciana at the officers' apartment that same morning and had gone running like a fiend for his camera.

The maid in the lime-colored panties was a cheerful, fat, obliging woman in her mid-thirties with squashy thighs and swaying hams in lime-colored panties that she was always rolling off for any man who wanted her. She had a plain broad face and was the most virtuous woman alive: she laid for *everybody*, regardless of race, creed, color or place of national origin, donating herself sociably as an act of hospitality, procrastinating not even for the moment it might take to discard the cloth or broom or dust mop she was clutching at the time she was grabbed. Her allure stemmed from her accessibility; like Mt. Everest, she was there, and the men climbed on top of her each time they felt the urge. Yossarian was in love with the maid in the lime-colored panties because she seemed to be the only woman left he could make love to without falling in love with. Even the bald-headed girl in Sicily still evoked in him strong sensations of pity, tenderness and regret.

Despite the multiple perils to which Major —— de Coverley exposed himself each time he rented apartments, his only injury had occurred, ironically enough, while he was leading the triumphal procession into the open city of Rome, where he was wounded in the eye by a flower fired at him from close range by a seedy, cackling, intoxicated old man, who, like Satan himself, had then bounded up on Major —— de Coverley's car with malicious glee, seized him roughly and contemptuously by his venerable white head and kissed him mockingly on each cheek with a mouth reeking with sour fumes of wine, cheese and garlic, before dropping back into the joyous celebrating throngs with a hollow, dry, excoriating laugh. Major —— de Coverley, a Spartan in adversity, did not flinch once throughout the whole hideous ordeal. And not until he had returned to Pianosa, his business in Rome completed, did he seek medical attention for his wound.

He resolved to remain binocular and specified to Doc Daneeka that his eye patch be transparent so that he could continue pitching horseshoes, kidnapping Italian laborers and renting apartments with unimpaired vision. To the men in the squadron, Major —— de Coverley was a colossus, although they never dared tell him so. The only one who ever did dare address him was Milo Minderbinder, who approached the horseshoe-pitching pit with a hard-boiled egg his second week in the squadron and held it aloft for Major —— de Coverley to see. Major —— de Coverley straightened with astonishment at Milo's effrontery and concentrated upon him the full fury of his storming countenance with its rugged overhang of gullied forehead and huge crag of a humpbacked nose that came charging out of his face wrathfully like a Big Ten fullback. Milo stood his ground, taking shelter behind the hard-boiled egg raised protectively before his face like a magic charm. In time the gale began to subside, and the danger passed.

"What is that?" Major —— de Coverley demanded at last.

"An egg," Milo answered.

"What kind of an egg?" Major —— de Coverley demanded.

"A hard-boiled egg," Milo answered.

"What kind of a hard-boiled egg?" Major —— de Coverley demanded.

"A fresh hard-boiled egg," Milo answered.

"Where did the fresh egg come from?" Major —— de Coverley demanded.

"From a chicken," Milo answered.

"Where is the chicken?" Major —— de Coverley demanded.

"The chicken is in Malta," Milo answered.

"How many chickens are there in Malta?"

"Enough chickens to lay fresh eggs for every officer in the squadron at five cents apiece from the mess fund," Milo answered.

"I have a weakness for fresh eggs," Major —— de Coverley confessed.

"If someone put a plane at my disposal, I could fly down there once a week in a squadron plane and bring back all the fresh eggs we need," Milo answered. "After all, Malta's not so far away."

"Malta's not so far away," Major —— de Coverley observed. "You could probably fly down there once a week in a squadron plane and bring back all the fresh eggs we need."

"Yes," Milo agreed. "I suppose I could do that, if someone wanted me to and put a plane at my disposal."

"I like my fresh eggs fried," Major —— de Coverley remembered. "In fresh butter."

"I can find all the fresh butter we need in Sicily for twenty-five cents a pound," Milo answered. "Twenty-five cents a pound for fresh butter is a good buy. There's enough money in the mess fund for butter too, and we could probably sell some to the other squadrons at a profit and get back most of what we pay for our own."

"What's your name, son?" asked Major —— de Coverley.

"My name is Milo Minderbinder, sir. I am twenty-seven years old."

"You're a good mess officer, Milo."

"I'm not the mess officer, sir."

"You're a good mess officer, Milo."

"Thank you, sir. I'll do everything in my power to be a good mess officer."

"Bless you, my boy. Have a horseshoe."

"Thank you, sir. What should I do with it?"

"Throw it."

"Away?"

"At that peg there. Then pick it up and throw it at this peg. It's a game, see? You get the horseshoe back."

"Yes, sir. I see. How much are horseshoes selling for?"

The smell of a fresh egg snapping exotically in a pool of fresh butter carried a long way on the Mediterranean trade winds and brought General Dreedle racing back with a voracious appetite, accompanied by his nurse, who accompanied him everywhere, and his son-in-law, Colonel Moodus. In the beginning General Dreedle devoured all his meals in Milo's mess hall. Then the other three squadrons in Colonel Cathcart's group turned their mess halls over to Milo and gave him an airplane and a pilot each so that he could buy fresh eggs and fresh butter for them too. Milo's planes shuttled back and forth seven days a week as every officer in the four squadrons began devouring fresh eggs in an insatiable orgy of fresh-egg eating. General Dreedle devoured fresh eggs for breakfast, lunch and dinner—between meals he devoured more fresh eggs—until Milo located abundant sources of fresh veal, beef, duck, baby lamb chops, mushroom caps, broccoli,

South African rock lobster tails, shrimp, hams, puddings, grapes, ice cream, strawberries and artichokes. There were three other bomb groups in General Dreedle's combat wing, and they each jealously dispatched their own planes to Malta for fresh eggs, but discovered that fresh eggs were selling there for seven cents apiece. Since they could buy them from Milo for five cents apiece, it made more sense to turn over *their* mess halls to his syndicate, too, and give him the planes and pilots needed to ferry in all the other good food he promised to supply as well.

Everyone was elated with this turn of events, most of all Colonel Cathcart, who was convinced he had won a feather in his cap. He greeted Milo jovially each time they met and, in an excess of contrite generosity, impulsively recommended Major Major for promotion. The recommendation was rejected at once at Twenty-seventh Air Force Headquarters by ex-P.F.C. Wintergreen, who scribbled a brusque, unsigned reminder that the Army had only one Major Major Major Major and did not intend to lose him by promotion just to please Colonel Cathcart. Colonel Cathcart was stung by the blunt rebuke and skulked guiltily about his room in smarting repudiation. He blamed Major Major for this black eye and decided to bust him down to lieutenant that very same day.

"They probably won't let you," Colonel Korn remarked with a condescending smile, savoring the situation. "For precisely the same reasons that they wouldn't let you promote him. Besides, you'd certainly look foolish trying to bust him down to lieutenant right after you tried to promote him to my rank."

Colonel Cathcart felt hemmed in on every side. He had been much more successful in obtaining a medal for Yossarian after the debacle of Ferrara, when the bridge spanning the Po was still standing undamaged seven days after Colonel Cathcart had volunteered to destroy it. Nine missions his men had flown there in six days, and the bridge was not demolished until the tenth mission on the seventh day, when Yossarian killed Kraft and his crew by taking his flight of six planes in over the target a second time. Yossarian came in carefully on his second bomb run because he was brave then. He buried his head in his bombsight until his bombs were away; when he looked up, everything inside the ship was suffused in a weird orange glow. At first he thought that his own plane was on fire. Then he spied the plane with the burning engine directly above him and screamed to McWatt through the intercom to turn left hard. A second later, the wing of Kraft's plane blew off. The flaming wreck dropped, first the fuselage, then the spinning wing, while a shower of tiny metal fragments began tap dancing on the roof of Yossarian's own plane and the incessant *cachung! cachung! cachung!* of the flak was still thumping all around him.

Back on the ground, every eye watched grimly as he walked in dull dejection up to Captain Black outside the green clapboard briefing room to make his intelligence report and learned that Colonel Cathcart and Colonel Korn were waiting to speak to him inside. Major Danby stood barring the door, waving everyone else away in ashen silence. Yossarian was leaden with fatigue and longed to remove his sticky clothing. He stepped into the briefing room with mixed emotions, uncertain how he was supposed to feel about Kraft and the others, for they had all died in the distance of a mute and secluded agony at a moment when he was up to his own ass in the same vile, excruciating dilemma of duty and damnation.

Colonel Cathcart, on the other hand, was all broken up by the event. "Twice?" he asked.

"I would have missed it the first time," Yossarian replied softly, his face lowered.

Their voices echoed slightly in the long, narrow bungalow.

"But *twice?*" Colonel Cathcart repeated, in vivid disbelief.

"I would have missed it the first time," Yossarian repeated.

"But Kraft would be alive."

"And the bridge would still be up."

"A trained bombardier is supposed to drop his bombs the first time," Colonel Cathcart reminded him. "The other five bombardiers dropped their bombs the first time."

"And missed the target," Yossarian said. "We'd have had to go back there again."

"And maybe you would have gotten it the first time then."

"And maybe I wouldn't have gotten it at all."

"But maybe there wouldn't have been any losses."

"And maybe there would have been more losses, with the bridge still left standing. I thought you wanted the bridge destroyed."

"Don't contradict me," Colonel Cathcart said. "We're all in enough trouble."

"I'm not contradicting you, sir."

"Yes you are. Even that's a contradiction."

"Yes, sir. I'm sorry."

Colonel Cathcart cracked his knuckles violently. Colonel Korn, a stocky, dark, flaccid man with a shapeless paunch, sat completely relaxed on one of the benches in the front row, his hands clasped comfortably over the top of his bald and swarthy head. His eyes were amused behind his glinting rimless spectacles.

"We're trying to be perfectly objective about this," he prompted Colonel Cathcart.

"We're trying to be perfectly objective about this," Colonel Cathcart said to Yossarian with the zeal of sudden inspiration. "It's not that I'm being sentimental or anything. I don't give a damn about the men or the airplane. It's just that it looks so lousy on the report. How am I going to cover up something like this in the report?"

"Why don't you give me a medal?" Yossarian suggested timidly.

"For going around twice?"

"You gave one to Hungry Joe when he cracked up that airplane by mistake."

Colonel Cathcart snickered ruefully. "You'll be lucky if we don't give you a court-martial."

"But I got the bridge the second time around," Yossarian protested. "I thought you wanted the bridge destroyed."

"Oh, I don't know what I wanted," Colonel Cathcart cried out in exasperation. "Look, of course I wanted the bridge destroyed. That bridge has been a source of trouble to me ever since I decided to send you men out to get it. But why couldn't you do it the first time?"

"I didn't have enough time. My navigator wasn't sure we had the right city."

"The right city?" Colonel Cathcart was baffled. "Are you trying to blame it all on Aarfy now?"

"No, sir. It was my mistake for letting him distract me. All I'm trying to say is that I'm not infallible."

"Nobody is infallible," Colonel Cathcart said sharply, and then continued vaguely, with an afterthought: "Nobody is indispensable, either."

There was no rebuttal. Colonel Korn stretched sluggishly. "We've got to reach a decision," he observed casually to Colonel Cathcart.

"We've got to reach a decision," Colonel Cathcart said to Yossarian. "And it's all your fault. Why did you have to go around twice? Why couldn't you drop your bombs the first time like all the others?"

"I would have missed the first time."

"It seems to me that *we're* going around twice," Colonel Korn interrupted with a chuckle.

"But what are we going to do?" Colonel Cathcart exclaimed with distress. "The others are all waiting outside."

"Why *don't* we give him a medal?" Colonel Korn proposed.

"For going around twice? What can we give him a medal for?"

"For going around twice," Colonel Korn answered with a reflective, self-satisfied smile. "After all, I suppose it did take a lot of courage to go over that target a second time with no other planes around to divert the antiaircraft fire. And he did hit the bridge. You know, that might be the answer—to act boastfully about something we ought to be ashamed of. That's a trick that never seems to fail."

"Do you think it will work?"

"I'm sure it will. And let's promote him to captain, too, just to make certain."

"Don't you think that's going a bit farther than we have to?"

"No, I don't think so. It's best to play safe. And a captain's not much difference."

"All right," Colonel Cathcart decided. "We'll give him a medal for being brave enough to go around over the target twice. And we'll make him a captain, too."

Colonel Korn reached for his hat.

"Exit smiling," he joked, and put his arm around Yossarian's shoulders as they stepped outside the door.

14

Kid Sampson

By the time of the mission to Bologna, Yossarian was brave enough not to go around over the target even once, and when he found himself aloft finally in the nose of Kid Sampson's plane, he pressed in the button of his throat mike and asked,

"Well? What's wrong with the plane?"

Kid Sampson let out a shriek. "Is something wrong with the plane? What's the matter?"

Kid Sampson's cry turned Yossarian to ice. "Is something the matter?" he yelled in horror. "Are we bailing out?"

"I don't know!" Kid Sampson shot back in anguish, wailing excitedly. "Someone said we're bailing out! Who is this, anyway? Who is this?"

"This is Yossarian in the nose! Yossarian in the nose. I heard you say there was something the matter. Didn't you say there was something the matter?"

"I thought you said there was something wrong. Everything seems okay. Everything is all right."

Yossarian's heart sank. Something was terribly wrong if everything was all right and they had no excuse for turning back. He hesitated gravely.

"I can't hear you," he said.

"I said everything is all right."

The sun was blinding white on the porcelain-blue water below and on the flashing edges of the other airplanes. Yossarian took hold of the colored wires leading into the jackbox of the intercom system and tore them loose.

"I still can't hear you," he said.

He heard nothing. Slowly he collected his map case and his three flak suits and crawled back to the main compartment. Nately, sitting stiffly in the co-pilot's seat, spied him through the corner of his eye as he stepped up on the flight deck behind Kid Sampson. He smiled at Yossarian wanly, looking frail and exceptionally young and bashful in the bulky dungeon of his earphones, hat, throat mike, flak suit and parachute. Yossarian bent close to Kid Sampson's ear.

"I still can't hear you," he shouted above the even drone of the engines.

Kid Sampson glanced back at him with surprise. Kid Sampson had an angular, comical face with arched eyebrows and a scrawny blond mustache.

"What?" he called out over his shoulder.

"I still can't hear you," Yossarian repeated.

"You'll have to talk louder," Kid Sampson said. "I still can't hear you."

"I said I still can't hear you!" Yossarian yelled.

"I can't help it," Kid Sampson yelled back at him. "I'm shouting as loud as I can."

"I couldn't hear you over my intercom," Yossarian bellowed in mounting helplessness. "You'll have to turn back."

"For an intercom?" asked Kid Sampson incredulously.

"Turn back," said Yossarian, "before I break your head."

Kid Sampson looked for moral support toward Nately, who stared away from him pointedly. Yossarian outranked them both. Kid Sampson resisted doubtfully for another moment and then capitulated eagerly with a triumphant whoop.

"That's just fine with me," he announced gladly, and blew out a shrill series of whistles up into his mustache. "Yes sirree, that's just fine with old Kid Sampson." He whistled again and shouted over the intercom. "Now hear this, my little chickadees. This is Admiral Kid Sampson talking. This is Admiral Kid Sampson squawking, the pride of the Queen's marines. Yessiree. We're turning back, boys, by crackee, *we're turning back!*"

Nately ripped off his hat and earphones in one jubilant sweep and began rocking back and forth happily like a handsome child in a high chair. Sergeant Knight came plummeting down from the top gun turret and began pounding them all on the back with delirious enthusiasm. Kid Sampson turned the plane away from the formation in a wide, graceful arc and headed toward the airfield. When Yossarian plugged his headset into one of the auxiliary jackboxes, the two gunners in the rear section of the plane were both singing "La Cucaracha."

Back at the field, the party fizzled out abruptly. An uneasy silence replaced it, and Yossarian was sober and self-conscious as he climbed down from the plane and took his place in the jeep that was already waiting for them. None of the men spoke at all on the drive back through the heavy, mesmerizing quiet blanketing mountains, sea and forests. The feeling of desolation persisted when they turned off the road at the squadron. Yossarian got out of the car last. After a minute, Yossarian and a gentle warm wind were the only things stirring in the haunting tranquillity that hung like a drug over the vacated tents. The squadron stood insensate, bereft of everything human but Doc Daneeka, who roosted dolorously like a shivering turkey buzzard beside the closed door of the medical tent, his stuffed nose jabbing away in thirsting futility at the hazy sunlight streaming down around him. Yossarian knew Doc Daneeka would not go swimming with him. Doc Daneeka would never go swimming again; a person could swoon or suffer a mild coronary occlusion in an inch or two of water and drown to death, be carried out to sea by an undertow, or made vulnerable to poliomyelitis or meningococcus infection through chilling or overexertion. The threat of Bologna to others had instilled in Doc Daneeka an even more poignant solicitude for his own safety. At night now, he heard burglars.

Through the lavender gloom clouding the entrance of the operations tent, Yossarian glimpsed Chief White Halfoat, diligently embezzling whiskey rations, forging the signatures of nondrinkers and pouring off the alcohol with which he was poisoning himself into separate bottles rapidly in order to steal as much as he could before Captain Black roused himself with recollection and came hurrying over indolently to steal the rest himself.

The jeep started up again softly. Kid Sampson, Nately and the others wandered apart in a noiseless eddy of motion and were sucked away into the cloying yellow stillness. The jeep vanished with a cough. Yossarian was alone in a ponderous, primeval lull in which everything green looked black and everything else was imbued with the color of pus. The breeze rustled leaves in a dry and diaphanous distance. He was restless, scared and sleepy. The sockets of his eyes felt grimy with exhaustion. Wearily he moved inside the parachute tent with its long table of smoothed wood, a nagging bitch of a doubt burrowing painlessly inside a conscience that felt perfectly clear. He left his flak suit and parachute there and crossed back past the water wagon to the intelligence tent to return his map case to Captain Black, who sat drowsing in his chair with his skinny long legs up on his desk and inquired with indifferent curiosity why Yossarian's plane had turned back. Yossarian ignored him. He set the map down on the counter and walked out.

Back in his own tent, he squirmed out of his parachute harness and then out of his clothes. Orr was in Rome, due back that same afternoon from the rest leave he had won by ditching his plane in the waters off Genoa. Nately would already be packing to replace him, entranced to find himself still alive and undoubtedly impatient to resume his wasted and heartbreaking courtship of his prostitute in Rome. When Yossarian was undressed, he sat down on his cot to rest. He felt much better as soon as he was naked. He never felt comfortable in clothes. In a little while he put fresh undershorts back on and set out for the beach in his moccasins, a khaki-colored bath towel draped over his shoulders.

The path from the squadron led him around a mysterious gun emplacement in the woods; two of the three enlisted men stationed there lay sleeping on the circle of sand bags and the third sat eating a purple pomegranate, biting off large mouthfuls between his churning jaws and spewing the ground roughage out away from him into the bushes. When he bit, red juice ran out of his mouth. Yossarian padded ahead into the forest again, caressing his bare, tingling belly adoringly from time to time as though to reassure himself it was all still there. He rolled a piece of lint out of his navel. Along the ground suddenly, on both sides of the path, he saw dozens of new mushrooms the rain had spawned poking their nodular fingers up through the clammy earth like lifeless stalks of flesh, sprouting in such necrotic profusion everywhere he looked that they seemed to be proliferating right before his eyes. There were thousands of them swarming as far back into the underbrush as he could see, and they appeared to swell in size and multiply in number as he spied them. He hurried away from them with a shiver of eerie alarm and did not slacken his pace until the soil crumbled to dry sand beneath his feet and they had been left behind. He glanced back apprehensively, half expecting to find the limp white things crawling after him in sightless pursuit or snaking up through the treetops in a writhing and ungovernable mutative mass.

The beach was deserted. The only sounds were hushed ones, the bloated gurgle of the stream, the respirating hum of the tall grass and shrubs behind him, the apathetic moaning of the dumb, translucent waves. The surf was always small, the water clear and cool. Yossarian left his things on the sand and moved through the knee-high waves until he was completely immersed. On the other side of the sea, a bumpy sliver of dark land lay wrapped in mist, almost invisible. He swam languorously out to the raft, held on a moment, and swam languorously back to where he could stand on the sand bar. He submerged himself head first into the green water several times until he felt clean and wide-awake and then stretched himself out face down in the sand and slept until the planes returning from Bologna were almost overhead and the great, cumulative rumble of their many engines came crashing in through his slumber in an earth-shattering roar.

He woke up blinking with a slight pain in his head and opened his eyes upon a world boiling in chaos in which everything was in proper order. He gasped in utter amazement at the fantastic sight of the twelve flights of planes organized calmly into exact formation. The scene was too unexpected to be true. There were no planes spurting ahead with wounded, none lagging behind with damage. No distress flares smoked in the sky. No ship was missing but his own. For an instant he was paralyzed with a sensation of madness. Then he understood, and almost wept at the irony. The explanation was simple: clouds had covered the target before the planes could bomb it, and the mission to Bologna was still to be flown.

He was wrong. There had been no clouds. Bologna had been bombed. Bologna was a milk run. There had been no flak there at all.

15

Piltchard & Wren

Captain Piltchard and Captain Wren, the inoffensive joint squadron operations officers, were both mild, soft-spoken men of less than middle height who enjoyed flying combat missions and begged nothing more of life and Colonel Cathcart than the opportunity to continue flying them. They had flown hundreds of combat missions and wanted to fly hundreds more. They assigned themselves to every one. Nothing so wonderful as war had ever happened to them before; and they were afraid it might never happen to them again. They conducted their duties humbly and reticently, with a minimum of fuss, and went to great lengths not to antagonize anyone. They smiled quickly at everyone they passed. When they spoke, they mumbled. They were shifty, cheerful, subservient men who were comfortable only with each other and never met anyone else's eye, not even Yossarian's eye at the open-air meeting they called to reprimand him publicly for making Kid Sampson turn back from the mission to Bologna.

"Fellas," said Captain Piltchard, who had thinning dark hair and smiled awkwardly. "When you turn back from a mission, try to make sure it's for something important, will you? Not for something unimportant . . . like a defective intercom . . . or something like that. Okay? Captain Wren has more he wants to say to you on that subject."

"Captain Piltchard's right, fellas," said Captain Wren. "And that's all I'm going to say to you on that subject. Well, we finally got to Bologna today, and we found out it's a milk run. We were all a little nervous, I guess, and didn't do too much damage. Well, listen to this. Colonel Cathcart got permission for us to go back. And tomorrow we're really going to paste those ammunition dumps. Now, what do you think about that?"

And to prove to Yossarian that they bore him no animosity, they even assigned him to fly lead bombardier with McWatt in the first formation when they went back to Bologna the next day. He came in on the target like a Havermeyer, confidently taking no evasive action at all, and suddenly they were shooting the living shit out of him!

Heavy flak was everywhere! He had been lulled, lured and trapped, and there was nothing he could do but sit there like an idiot and watch the ugly black puffs smashing up to kill him. There was nothing he could do until his bombs dropped but look back into the bombsight, where the fine cross-hairs in the lens were glued magnetically over the target exactly where he had placed them, intersecting perfectly deep inside the yard of his block of camouflaged warehouses before the base of the first building. He was trembling steadily as the plane crept ahead. He could hear the hollow *boom-boom-boom-boom* of the flak pounding all around him in overlapping measures of four, the sharp, piercing *crack!* of a single shell exploding suddenly very close by. His head was busting with a thousand dissonant impulses as he prayed for the bombs to drop. He wanted to sob. The engines droned on monotonously like a fat, lazy fly. At last the indices on the bombsight crossed, tripping away the eight 500-pounders one after the other. The plane lurched upward buoyantly with the lightened load. Yossarian bent away from the bombsight crookedly to watch the indicator on his left. When the pointer touched zero, he closed the bomb bay doors and, over the intercom, at the very top of his voice, shrieked:

"*Turn right hard!*"

McWatt responded instantly. With a grinding howl of engines, he flipped the plane over on one wing and wrung it around remorselessly in a screaming turn away from the twin spires of flak Yossarian had spied stabbing toward them. Then Yossarian had McWatt climb and keep climbing higher and higher until they tore free finally into a calm, diamond-blue sky that was sunny and pure everywhere and laced in the distance with long white veils of tenuous fluff. The wind strummed soothingly against the cylindrical panes of his windows, and he relaxed exultantly only until they picked up speed again and then turned McWatt left and plunged him right back down, noticing with a transitory spasm of elation the mushrooming clusters of flak leaping open high above him and back over his shoulder to the right, exactly where he could have been if he had not turned left and dived. He leveled McWatt out with another harsh cry and whipped him upward and around again into a ragged blue patch of unpolluted air just as the bombs he had dropped began to strike. The first one fell in the yard, exactly where he had aimed, and then the rest of the bombs from his own plane and from the other planes in his flight burst open on the ground in a charge of rapid orange flashes across the tops of the buildings, which collapsed instantly in a vast, churning wave of pink and gray and coal-black smoke that went rolling out turbulently in all directions and quaked convulsively in its bowels as though from great blasts of red and white and golden sheet lightning.

"Well, will you look at that," Aarfy marveled sonorously right beside Yossarian, his plump, orbicular face sparkling with a look of bright enchantment. "There must have been an ammunition dump down there."

Yossarian had forgotten about Aarfy. "Get out!" he shouted at him. "Get out of the nose!"

Aarfy smiled politely and pointed down toward the target in a generous invitation for Yossarian to look. Yossarian began slapping at him insistently and signaled wildly toward the entrance of the crawlway.

"Get back in the ship!" he cried frantically. "Get back in the ship!"

Aarfy shrugged amiably. "I can't hear you," he explained.

Yossarian seized him by the straps of his parachute harness and pushed him backward toward the crawlway just as the plane was hit with a jarring concussion that rattled his bones and made his heart stop. He knew at once they were all dead.

"Climb!" he screamed into the intercom at McWatt when he saw he was still alive. "*Climb, you bastard! Climb, climb, climb, climb!*"

The plane zoomed upward again in a climb that was swift and straining, until he leveled it out with another harsh shout at McWatt and wrenched it around once more in a roaring, merciless forty-five-degree turn that sucked his insides out in one enervating sniff and left him floating fleshless in mid-air until he leveled McWatt out again just long enough to hurl him back around toward the right and then down into a screeching dive. Through endless blobs of ghostly black smoke he sped, the hanging smut wafting against the smooth Plexiglas nose of the ship like an evil, damp, sooty vapor against his cheeks. His heart was hammering again in aching terror as he hurtled upward and downward through the blind gangs of flak charging murderously into the sky at him, then sagging inertly. Sweat gushed from his neck in torrents and poured down over his chest and waist with the feeling of warm slime. He was vaguely aware for an instant that the planes in his formation were no longer there, and then he was aware of only himself. His throat hurt like a raw slash from the strangling intensity with which he shrieked each command to McWatt. The engines rose to a deafening, agonized, ululating bellow each time McWatt changed direction. And far out in front the bursts of flak were still swarming into the sky from new batteries of guns poking around for accurate altitude as they waited sadistically for him to fly into range.

The plane was slammed again suddenly with another loud, jarring explosion that almost rocked it over on its back, and the nose filled immediately with sweet clouds of blue smoke. *Something was on fire!* Yossarian whirled to escape and smacked into Aarfy, who had struck a match and was placidly lighting his pipe. Yossarian gaped at his grinning, moon-faced navigator in utter shock and confusion. It occurred to him that one of them was mad.

"Jesus Christ!" he screamed at Aarfy in tortured amazement. "Get the hell out of the nose! Are you crazy? Get out!"

"What?" said Aarfy.

"Get out!" Yossarian yelled hysterically, and began clubbing Aarfy backhanded with both fists to drive him away. "Get out!"

"I still can't hear you," Aarfy called back innocently with an expression of mild and reproving perplexity. "You'll have to talk a little louder."

"Get out of the nose!" Yossarian shrieked in frustration. "They're trying to kill us! Don't you understand? They're trying to kill us!"

"Which way should I go, goddammit?" McWatt shouted furiously over the intercom in a suffering, high-pitched voice. "Which way should I go?"

"Turn left! *Left*, you goddam dirty son of a bitch! Turn left *hard!*"

Aarfy crept up close behind Yossarian and jabbed him sharply in the ribs with the stem of his pipe. Yossarian flew up toward the ceiling with a whinnying cry, then jumped completely around on his knees, white as a sheet and quivering with rage. Aarfy winked encouragingly and jerked his thumb back toward McWatt with a humorous *moue*.

"What's eating *him?*" he asked with a laugh.

Yossarian was struck with a weird sense of distortion. "Will you get out of here?" he yelped beseechingly, and shoved Aarfy over with all his strength. "Are you deaf or something? Get back in the plane!" And to McWatt he screamed, "Dive! *Dive!*"

Down they sank once more into the crunching, thudding, voluminous barrage of bursting antiaircraft shells as Aarfy came creeping back behind Yossarian and jabbed him sharply in the ribs again. Yossarian shied upward with another whinnying gasp.

"I still couldn't hear you," Aarfy said.

"I said get *out of here!*" Yossarian shouted, and broke into tears. He began punching Aarfy in the body with both hands as hard as he could. "Get *away* from me! Get *away!*"

Punching Aarfy was like sinking his fists into a limp sack of inflated rubber. There was no resistance, no response at all from the soft, insensitive mass, and after a while Yossarian's spirit died and his arms dropped helplessly with exhaustion. He was overcome with a humiliating feeling of impotence and was ready to weep in self-pity.

"What did you say?" Aarfy asked.

"Get *away* from me," Yossarian answered, pleading with him now. "Go back in the plane."

"I still can't hear you."

"Never mind," wailed Yossarian, "never mind. Just leave me alone."

"Never mind what?"

Yossarian began hitting himself in the forehead. He seized Aarfy by the shirt front and, struggling to his feet for traction, dragged him to the rear of the nose compartment and flung him down like a bloated and unwieldy bag in the entrance of the crawlway. A shell banged open with a stupendous clout right beside his ear as he was scrambling back toward the front, and some undestroyed recess of his intelligence wondered that it did not kill them all. They were climbing again. The engines were howling again as though in pain, and the air inside the plane was acrid with the smell of machinery and fetid with the stench of gasoline. The next thing he knew, *it was snowing!*

Thousands of tiny bits of white paper were falling like snowflakes inside the plane, milling around his head so thickly that they clung to his eyelashes when he blinked in astonishment and fluttered against his nostrils and lips each time he inhaled. When he spun around in bewilderment, Aarfy was grinning proudly from ear to ear like something inhuman as he held up a shattered paper map for Yossarian to see. A large chunk of flak had ripped up from the floor through Aarfy's colossal jumble of maps and had ripped out through the ceiling inches away from their heads. Aarfy's joy was sublime.

"Will you look at this?" he murmured, waggling two of his stubby fingers playfully into Yossarian's face through the hole in one of his maps. "Will you look at this?"

Yossarian was dumbfounded by his state of rapturous contentment. Aarfy was like an eerie ogre in a dream, incapable of being bruised or evaded, and Yossarian dreaded him for a complex of reasons he was too petrified to untangle. Wind whistling up through the jagged gash in the floor kept the myriad bits of paper circulating like alabaster particles in a paperweight and contributed to a sensation of lacquered, waterlogged unreality. Everything seemed strange, so tawdry and grotesque. His head was throbbing from a shrill clamor that drilled relentlessly into both ears. It was McWatt, begging for directions in an incoherent frenzy. Yossarian continued staring in tormented fascination at Aarfy's spherical countenance beaming at him so serenely and vacantly through the drifting whorls of white paper bits and concluded that he was a raving lunatic just as eight bursts of flak broke open successively at eye level off to the right, then eight more, and then eight more, the last group pulled over toward the left so that they were almost directly in front.

"Turn left hard!" he hollered to McWatt as Aarfy kept grinning, and McWatt did turn left hard, but the flak turned left hard with them, catching up fast, and Yossarian hollered, "I said *hard, hard, hard, hard, you bastard, hard!*"

And McWatt bent the plane around even harder still, and suddenly, miraculously, they were out of range. The flak ended. The guns stopped booming at them. And they were alive.

Behind him, men were dying. Strung out for miles in a stricken, tortuous, squirming line, the other flights of planes were making the same hazardous journey over the target, threading their swift way through the swollen masses of new and old bursts of flak like rats racing in a pack through their own droppings. One was on fire, and flapped lamely off by itself, billowing gigantically like a monstrous blood-red star. As Yossarian watched, the burning plane floated over on its side and began spiraling down slowly in wide, tremulous, narrowing circles, its huge flaming burden blazing orange and flaring out in back like a long, swirling cape of fire and smoke. There were parachutes, one, two, three . . . four, and then the plane gyrated into a spin and fell the rest of the way to the ground, fluttering insensibly inside its vivid pyre like a shred of colored tissue paper. One whole flight of planes from another squadron had been blasted apart.

Yossarian sighed barrenly, his day's work done. He was listless and sticky. The engines crooned mellifluously as McWatt throttled back to loiter and allow the rest of the planes in his flight to catch up. The abrupt stillness seemed alien and artificial, a little insidious. Yossarian unsnapped his flak suit and took off his helmet. He sighed again, restlessly, and closed his eyes and tried to relax.

"Where's Orr?" someone asked suddenly over his intercom.

Yossarian bounded up with a one-syllable cry that crackled with anxiety and provided the only rational explanation for the whole mysterious phenomenon of the flak at Bologna: *Orr!* He lunged forward over the bombsight to search downward through the Plexiglas for some reassuring sign of Orr, who drew flak like a magnet and who had undoubtedly attracted the crack batteries of the whole Hermann Goering Division to Bologna overnight from wherever the hell they had been stationed the day before when Orr was still in Rome. Aarfy launched himself forward an instant later and cracked Yossarian on the bridge of the nose with the sharp rim of his flak helmet. Yossarian cursed him as his eyes flooded with tears.

"There he is," Aarfy orated funereally, pointing down dramatically at a hay wagon and two horses standing before the barn of a gray stone farmhouse. "Smashed to bits. I guess their numbers were all up."

Yossarian swore at Aarfy again and continued searching intently, cold with a compassionate kind of fear now for the little bouncy and bizarre buck-toothed tentmate who had smashed Appleby's forehead open with a Ping-Pong racket and who was scaring the daylights out of Yossarian once again. At last Yossarian spotted the two-engined, twin-ruddered plane as it flew out of the green background of the forests over a field of yellow farmland. One of the propellers was feathered and perfectly still, but the plane was maintaining altitude and holding a proper course. Yossarian muttered an unconscious prayer of thankfulness and then flared up at Orr savagely in a ranting fusion of resentment and relief.

"That bastard!" he began. "That goddam stunted, red-faced, big-cheeked, curlyheaded, buck-toothed rat bastard son of a bitch!"

"What?" said Aarfy.

"That dirty goddam midget-assed, apple-cheeked, goggle-eyed, undersized, buck-toothed, grinning, crazy sonofabitchinbastard!" Yossarian sputtered.

"What?"

"*Never mind!*"

"I still can't hear you," Aarfy answered.

Yossarian swung himself around methodically to face Aarfy. "You prick," he began.

"Me?"

"You pompous, rotund, neighborly, vacuous, complacent . . ."

Aarfy was unperturbed. Calmly he struck a wooden match and sucked noisily at his pipe with an eloquent air of benign and magnanimous forgiveness. He smiled sociably and opened his mouth to speak. Yossarian put his hand over Aarfy's mouth and pushed him away wearily. He shut his eyes and pretended to sleep all the way back to the field so that he would not have to listen to Aarfy or see him.

At the briefing room Yossarian made his intelligence report to

Captain Black and then waited in muttering suspense with all the others until Orr chugged into sight overhead finally with his one good engine still keeping him aloft gamely. Nobody breathed. Orr's landing gear would not come down. Yossarian hung around only until Orr had crash-landed safely, and then stole the first jeep he could find with a key in the ignition and raced back to his tent to begin packing feverishly for the emergency rest leave he had decided to take in Rome, where he found Luciana and her invisible scar that same night.

16

Luciana

He found Luciana sitting alone at a table in the Allied officers' night club, where the drunken Anzac major who had brought her there had been stupid enough to desert her for the ribald company of some singing comrades at the bar.

"All right, I'll dance with you," she said, before Yossarian could even speak. "But I won't let you sleep with me."

"Who asked you?" Yossarian asked her.

"You don't want to sleep with me?" she exclaimed with surprise.

"I don't want to dance with you."

She seized Yossarian's hand and pulled him out on the dance floor. She was a worse dancer than even he was, but she threw herself about to the synthetic jitterbug music with more uninhibited pleasure than he had ever observed until he felt his legs falling asleep with boredom and yanked her off the dance floor toward the table at which the girl he should have been screwing was still sitting tipsily with one hand around Aarfy's neck, her orange satin blouse still hanging open slovenly below her full white lacy brassiere as she made dirty sex talk ostentatiously with Huple, Orr, Kid Sampson and Hungry Joe. Just as he reached them, Luciana gave him a forceful, unexpected shove that carried them both well beyond the table, so that they were still alone. She was a tall, earthy, exuberant girl with long hair and a pretty face, a buxom, delightful, flirtatious girl.

"All right," she said, "I will let you buy me dinner. But I won't let you sleep with me."

"Who asked you?" Yossarian asked with surprise.

"You don't want to sleep with me?"

"I don't want to buy you dinner."

She pulled him out of the night club into the street and down a flight of steps into a black-market restaurant filled with lively, chirping, attractive girls who all seemed to know each other and with the self-conscious military officers from different countries who had come there with them. The food was elegant and expensive, and the aisles were overflowing with great streams of flushed and merry proprietors, all stout and balding. The bustling interior radiated with enormous, engulfing waves of fun and warmth.

Yossarian got a tremendous kick out of the rude gusto with which Luciana ignored him completely while she shoveled away her whole meal with both hands. She ate like a horse until the last plate was clean, and then she placed her silverware down with an air of conclusion and settled back lazily in her chair with a dreamy and congested look of sated gluttony. She drew a deep, smiling, contented breath and regarded him amorously with a melting gaze.

"Okay, Joe," she putted, her glowing dark eyes drowsy and grateful. "Now I will let you sleep with me."

"My name is Yossarian."

"Okay, Yossarian," she answered with a soft repentant laugh. "Now I will let you sleep with me."

"Who asked you?" said Yossarian.

Luciana was stunned. "You don't want to sleep with me?"

Yossarian nodded emphatically, laughing, and shot his hand up under her dress. The girl came to life with a horrified start. She jerked her legs away from him instantly, whipping her bottom around. Blushing with alarm and embarrassment, she pushed her skirt back down with a number of prim, sidelong glances about the restaurant.

"Now I will let you sleep with me," she explained cautiously in a manner of apprehensive indulgence. "But not now."

"I know. When we get back to my room."

The girl shook her head, eyeing him mistrustfully and keeping her knees pressed together. "No, now I must go home to my mamma, because my mamma does not like me to dance with soldiers or let them take me to dinner, and she will be very angry with me if I do not come home now. But I will let you write down for me where you live. And tomorrow morning I will come to your room for ficky-fick before I go to my work at the French office. *Capisci?*"

"Bullshit!" Yossarian exclaimed with angry disappointment.

"*Cosa vuol dire* bullshit?" Luciana inquired with a blank look.

Yossarian broke into loud laughter. He answered her finally in a tone of sympathetic good humor. "It means that I want to escort you now to wherever the hell I have to take you next so that I can rush back to that night club before Aarfy leaves with that wonderful tomato he's got without giving me a chance to ask about an aunt or friend she must have who's just like her."

"*Come?*"

"*Subito, subito,*" he taunted her tenderly. "Mamma is waiting. Remember?"

"*Sì, sì,* Mamma."

Yossarian let the girl drag him through the lovely Roman spring night for almost a mile until they reached a chaotic bus depot honking with horns, blazing with red and yellow lights and echoing with the snarling vituperations of unshaven bus drivers pouring loathsome, hair-raising curses out at each other, at their passengers and at the strolling, unconcerned knots of pedestrians clogging their paths, who ignored them until they were bumped by the buses and began shouting curses back. Luciana vanished aboard one of the diminutive green vehicles, and Yossarian hurried as fast as he could all the way back to the cabaret and the bleary-eyed bleached blonde in the open orange satin blouse. She seemed infatuated with Aarfy, but he prayed intensely for her luscious aunt as he ran, or for a luscious girl friend, sister, cousin or mother who was just as libidinous and depraved. She would have been perfect for Yossarian, a debauched, coarse, vulgar, amoral, appetizing slattern whom he had longed for and idolized for months. She was a real find. She paid for her own drinks, and she had an automobile, an apartment and a salmon-colored cameo ring that drove Hungry Joe clean out of his senses with its exquisitely carved figures of a naked boy and girl on a rock. Hungry Joe snorted and pranced and pawed at the floor in salivating lust and groveling need, but the girl would not sell him the ring, even though he offered her all the money in all their pockets and his complicated black camera thrown in. She was not interested in money or cameras. She was interested in fornication.

She was gone when Yossarian got there. They were all gone, and he walked right out and moved in wistful dejection through the dark, emptying streets. Yossarian was not often lonely when he was by himself, but he was lonely now in his keen envy of Aarfy, who he knew was in bed that very moment with the girl who was just right for Yossarian, and who could also make out any time he wanted to, *if* he ever wanted to, with either or both of the two slender, stunning, aristocratic women who lived in the apartment upstairs and fructified Yossarian's sex fantasies whenever he had sex fantasies, the beautiful rich black-haired countess with the red, wet, nervous lips and her beautiful rich black-haired daughter-in-law. Yossarian was madly in love with all of them as he made his way back to the officers' apartment, in love with Luciana, with the prurient intoxicated girl in the unbuttoned satin blouse, and with the beautiful rich countess and her beautiful rich daughter-in-law, both of whom would never let him touch them or even flirt with them. They doted kittenishly on Nately and deferred passively to Aarfy, but they thought Yossarian was crazy and recoiled from him with distasteful contempt each time he made an indecent proposal or tried to fondle them when they passed on the stairs. They were both superb creatures with pulpy, bright, pointed tongues and mouths like round warm plums, a little sweet and sticky, a little rotten. They had class; Yossarian was not sure what class was, but he knew that they had it and he did not, and that they knew it, too. He could picture, as he walked, the kind of underclothing they wore against their svelte feminine parts, filmy, smooth, clinging garments of deepest black or of opalescent pastel radiance with flowering lace borders, fragrant with the tantalizing fumes of pampered flesh and scented bath salts rising in a germinating cloud from their blue-white breasts. He wished again that he was where Aarfy was, making obscene, brutal, cheerful love with a juicy drunken tart who didn't give a tinker's dam about him and would never think of him again.

But Aarfy was already back in the apartment when Yossarian arrived, and Yossarian gaped at him with that same sense of persecuted astonishment he had suffered that same morning over Bologna at his malign and cabalistic and irremovable presence in the nose of the plane.

"What are you doing here?" he asked.

"That's right, ask him!" Hungry Joe exclaimed in a rage. "Make him tell you what he's doing here!"

With a long, theatrical moan, Kid Sampson made a pistol of his thumb and forefinger and blew his own brains out. Huple, chewing away on a bulging wad of bubble gum, drank everything in with a callow, vacant expression on his fifteen-year-old face. Aarfy was tapping the bowl of his pipe against his palm leisurely as he paced back and forth in corpulent self-approval, obviously delighted by the stir he was causing.

"Didn't you go home with that girl?" Yossarian demanded.

"Oh, sure, I went home with her," Aarfy replied. "You didn't think I was going to let her try to find her way home alone, did you?"

"Wouldn't she let you stay with her?"

"Oh, she wanted me to stay with her, all right." Aarfy chuckled. "Don't you worry about good old Aarfy. But I wasn't going to take advantage of a sweet kid like that just because she'd had a little too much to drink. What kind of a guy do you think I am?"

"Who said anything about taking advantage of her?" Yossarian railed at him in amazement. "All she wanted to do was get into bed with someone. That's the only thing she kept talking about all night long."

"That's because she was a little mixed up," Aarfy explained. "But I gave her a little talking to and really put some sense into her."

"You bastard!" Yossarian exclaimed, and sank down tiredly on the divan beside Kid Sampson. "Why the hell didn't you give her to one of us if you didn't want her?"

"You see?" Hungry Joe asked. "There's something wrong with him."

Yossarian nodded and looked at Aarfy curiously. "Aarfy, tell me something. Don't you ever screw any of them?"

Aarfy chuckled again with conceited amusement. "Oh, sure, I prod them. Don't you worry about me. But never any nice girls. I know what kind of girls to prod and what kind of girls not to prod, and I never prod any nice girls. This one was a sweet kid. You could see her family had money. Why, I even got her to throw that ring of hers away right out the car window."

Hungry Joe flew into the air with a screech of intolerable pain. "You did *what?*" he screamed. "You did *what?*" He began whaling away at Aarfy's shoulders and arms with both fists, almost in tears. "I ought to *kill* you for what you did, you lousy bastard. He's *sinful*, that's what he is. He's got a dirty mind, ain't he? Ain't he got a dirty mind?"

"The dirtiest," Yossarian agreed.

"What are you fellows talking about?" Aarfy asked with genuine puzzlement, tucking his face away protectively inside the cushioning insulation of his oval shoulders. "Aw, come on, Joe," he pleaded with a smile of mild discomfort. "Quit punching me, will you?"

But Hungry Joe would not quit punching until Yossarian picked him up and pushed him away toward his bedroom. Yossarian moved listlessly into his own room, undressed and went to sleep. A second later it was morning, and someone was shaking him.

"What are you waking me up for?" he whimpered.

It was Michaela, the skinny maid with the merry disposition and homely sallow face, and she was waking him up because he had a visitor waiting just outside the door. *Luciana!* He could hardly believe it. And she was alone in the room with him after Michaela had departed, lovely, hale and statuesque, steaming and rippling with an irrepressible affectionate vitality even as she remained in one place and frowned at him irately. She stood like a youthful female colossus with her magnificent columnar legs apart on high white shoes with wedged heels, wearing a pretty green dress and swinging a large, flat white leather pocketbook, with which she cracked him hard across the face when he leaped out of bed to grab her. Yossarian staggered backward out of range in a daze, clutching his stinging cheek with bewilderment.

"Pig!" she spat out at him viciously, her nostrils flaring in a look of savage disdain. "*Vive com' un animale!*"

With a fierce, guttural, scornful, disgusted oath, she strode across the room and threw open the three tall casement windows, letting inside an effulgent flood of sunlight and crisp fresh air that washed through the stuffy room like an invigorating tonic. She placed her pocketbook on a chair and began tidying the room, picking his things up from the floor and off the tops of the furniture, throwing his socks, handkerchief and underwear into an empty drawer of the dresser and hanging his shirt and trousers up in the closet.

Yossarian ran out of the bedroom into the bathroom and brushed his teeth. He washed his hands and face and combed his hair. When he ran back, the room was in order and Luciana was almost undressed. Her expression was relaxed. She left her earrings on the dresser and padded barefoot to the bed wearing just a pink rayon chemise that came down to her hips. She glanced about the room prudently to make certain there was nothing she had overlooked in the way of neatness and then drew back the coverlet and stretched herself out luxuriously with an expression of feline expectation. She beckoned to him longingly, with a husky laugh.

"Now," she announced in a whisper, holding both arms out to him eagerly. "Now I will let you sleep with me."

She told him some lies about a single weekend in bed with a slaughtered fiancé in the Italian Army, and they all turned out to be true, for she cried "*finito!*" almost as soon as he started and wondered why he didn't stop, until he had *finito*ed too and explained to her.

He lit cigarettes for both of them. She was enchanted by the deep suntan covering his whole body. He wondered about the pink chemise that she would not remove. It was cut like a man's undershirt, with narrow shoulder straps, and concealed the invisible scar on her back that she refused to let him see after he had made her tell him it was there. She grew tense as fine steel when he traced the mutilated contours with his finger tip from a pit in her shoulder blade almost to the base of her spine. He winced at the many tortured nights she had spent in the hospital, drugged or in pain, with the ubiquitous, ineradicable odors of ether, fecal matter and disinfectant, of human flesh mortified and decaying amid the white uniforms, the rubber-soled shoes, and the eerie night lights glowing dimly until dawn in the corridors. She had been wounded in an air raid.

"Dove?" he asked, and he held his breath in suspense.

"Napoli."

"Germans?"

"Americani."

His heart cracked, and he fell in love. He wondered if she would marry him.

"Tu sei pazzo," she told him with a pleasant laugh.

"Why am I crazy?" he asked.

"Perchè non posso sposare."

"Why can't you get married?"

"Because I am not a virgin," she answered.

"What has that got to do with it?"

"Who will marry me? No one wants a girl who is not a virgin."

"I will. I'll marry you."

"Ma non posso sposarti."

"Why can't you marry me?"

"Perchè sei pazzo."

"Why am I crazy?"

"Perchè vuoi sposarmi."

Yossarian wrinkled his forehead with quizzical amusement. "You won't marry me because I'm crazy, and you say I'm crazy because I want to marry you? Is that right?"

"Sì."

"Tu sei pazz'!" he told her loudly.

"Perchè?" she shouted back at him indignantly, her unavoidable round breasts rising and falling in a saucy huff beneath the pink chemise as she sat up in bed indignantly. "Why am I crazy?"

"Because you won't marry me."

"Stupido!" she shouted back at him, and smacked him loudly and flamboyantly on the chest with the back of her hand. *"Non posso sposarti! Non capisci? Non posso sposarti."*

"Oh, sure, I understand. And why can't you marry me?"

"Perchè sei pazzo!"

"And why am I crazy?"

"Perchè vuoi sposarmi."

"Because I want to marry you. *Carina, ti amo,*" he explained, and he drew her gently back down to the pillow. "*Ti amo molto.*"

"*Tu sei pazzo,*" she murmured in reply, flattered.

"*Perchè?*"

"Because you say you love me. How can you love a girl who is not a virgin?"

"Because I can't marry you."

She bolted right up again in a threatening rage. "Why can't you marry me?" she demanded, ready to clout him again if he gave an uncomplimentary reply. "Just because I am not a virgin?"

"No, no, darling. Because *you're* crazy."

She stared at him in blank resentment for a moment and then tossed her head back and roared appreciatively with hearty laughter. She gazed at him with new approval when she stopped, the lush, responsive tissues of her dark face turning darker still and blooming somnolently with a swelling and beautifying infusion of blood. Her eyes grew dim. He crushed out both their cigarettes, and they turned into each other wordlessly in an engrossing kiss just as Hungry Joe came meandering into the room without knocking to ask if Yossarian wanted to go out with him to look for girls. Hungry Joe stopped on a dime when he saw them and shot out of the room. Yossarian shot out of bed even faster and began shouting at Luciana to get dressed. The girl was dumbfounded. He pulled her roughly out of bed by her arm and flung her away toward her clothing, then raced for the door in time to slam it shut as Hungry Joe was running back in with his camera. Hungry Joe had his leg wedged in the door and would not pull it out.

"Let me in!" he begged urgently, wriggling and squirming maniacally. "Let me in!" He stopped struggling for a moment to gaze up into Yossarian's face through the crack in the door with what he must have supposed was a beguiling smile. "Me no Hungry Joe," he explained earnestly. "Me heap big photographer from *Life* magazine. Heap big picture on heap big cover. I make you big Hollywood star, Yossarian. Multi *dinero*. Multi divorces. Multi ficky-fick all day long. *Sì, sì, sì!*"

Yossarian slammed the door shut when Hungry Joe stepped back a bit to try to shoot a picture of Luciana dressing. Hungry Joe attacked the stout wooden barrier fanatically, fell back to reorganize his energies and hurled himself forward fanatically again. Yossarian slithered into his own clothes between assaults. Luciana had her green-and-white summer dress on and was holding the skirt bunched up above her waist. A wave of misery broke over him as he saw her about to vanish inside her panties forever. He reached out to grasp her and drew her to him by the raised calf of her leg. She hopped forward and molded herself against him. Yossarian kissed her ears and her closed eyes romantically and rubbed the backs of her thighs. She began to hum sensually a moment before Hungry Joe hurled his frail body against the door in still one more desperate attack and almost knocked them both down. Yossarian pushed her away.

"*Vite! Vite!*" he scolded her. "Get your things on!"

"What the hell are you talking about?" she wanted to know.

"Fast! Fast! Can't you understand English? Get your clothes on fast!"

"*Stupido!*" she snarled back at him. "*Vite* is French, not Italian. *Subito, subito!* That's what you mean. *Subito!*"

"*Sì, sì.* That's what I mean. *Subito, subito!*"

"*Sì, sì,*" she responded cooperatively, and ran for her shoes and earrings.

Hungry Joe had paused in his attack to shoot pictures through the closed door. Yossarian could hear the camera shutter clicking. When both he and Luciana were ready, Yossarian waited for Hungry Joe's next charge and yanked the door open on him unexpectedly. Hungry Joe spilled forward into the room like a floundering frog. Yossarian skipped nimbly around him, guiding Luciana along behind him through the apartment and out into the hallway. They bounced down the stairs with a great roistering clatter, laughing out loud breathlessly and knocking their hilarious heads together each time they paused to rest. Near the bottom they met Nately coming up and stopped laughing. Nately was drawn, dirty and unhappy. His tie was twisted and his shirt was rumpled, and he walked with his hands in his pockets. He wore a hangdog, hopeless look.

"What's the matter, kid?" Yossarian inquired compassionately.

"I'm flat broke again," Nately replied with a lame and distracted smile. "What am I going to do?"

Yossarian didn't know. Nately had spent the last thirty-two hours at twenty dollars an hour with the apathetic whore he adored, and he had nothing left of his pay or of the lucrative allowance he received every month from his wealthy and generous father. That meant he could not spend time with her any more. She would not allow him to walk beside her as she strolled the pavements soliciting other servicemen, and she was infuriated when she spied him trailing her from a distance. He was free to hang around her apartment if he cared to, but there was no certainty that she would be there. And she would give him nothing unless he could pay. She found sex uninteresting. Nately wanted the assurance that she was not going to bed with anyone unsavory or with someone he knew. Captain Black always made it a point to buy her each time he came to Rome, just so he could torment Nately with the news that he had thrown his sweetheart another hump and watch Nately eat his liver as he related the atrocious indignities to which he had forced her to submit.

Luciana was touched by Nately's forlorn air, but broke loudly into robust laughter again the moment she stepped outside into the sunny street with Yossarian and heard Hungry Joe beseeching them from the window to come back and take their clothes off, because he really was a photographer from *Life* magazine. Luciana fled mirthfully along the sidewalk in her high white wedgies, pulling Yossarian along in tow with the same lusty and ingenuous zeal she had displayed in the dance hall the night before and at every moment since. Yossarian caught up and walked with his arm around her waist until they came to the corner and she stepped away from him. She straightened her hair in a mirror from her pocketbook and put lipstick on.

"Why don't you ask me to let you write my name and address on a piece of paper so that you will be able to find me again when you come to Rome?" she suggested.

"Why don't you let me write your name and address down on a piece of paper?" he agreed.

"Why?" she demanded belligerently, her mouth curling suddenly into a vehement sneer and her eyes flashing with anger. "So you can tear it up into little pieces as soon as I leave?"

"Who's going to tear it up?" Yossarian protested in confusion. "What the hell are you talking about?"

"You will," she insisted. "You'll tear it up into little pieces the minute I'm gone and go walking away like a big shot because a tall, young, beautiful girl like me, Luciana, let you sleep with her and did not ask you for money."

"How much money are you asking me for?" he asked her.

"*Stupido!*" she shouted with emotion. "I am not asking you for any money!" She stamped her foot and raised her arm in a turbulent gesture that made Yossarian fear she was going to crack him in the face again with her great pocketbook. Instead, she scribbled her name and address on a slip of paper and thrust it at him. "Here," she taunted him sardonically, biting on her lip to still a delicate tremor. "Don't forget. Don't forget to tear it into tiny pieces as soon as I am gone."

Then she smiled at him serenely, squeezed his hand and, with a whispered regretful "*Addio*," pressed herself against him for a moment and then straightened and walked away with unconscious dignity and grace.

The minute she was gone, Yossarian tore the slip of paper up and walked away in the other direction, feeling very much like a big shot because a beautiful young girl like Luciana had slept with him and did not ask for money. He was pretty pleased with himself until he looked up in the dining room of the Red Cross building and found himself eating breakfast with dozens and dozens of other servicemen in all kinds of fantastic uniforms, and then all at once he was surrounded by images of Luciana getting out of her clothes and into her clothes and caressing and haranguing him tempestuously in the pink rayon chemise she wore in bed with him and would not take off. Yossarian choked on his toast and eggs at the enormity of his error in tearing her long, lithe, nude, young vibrant limbs into tiny pieces of paper so impudently and dumping her down so smugly into the gutter from the curb. He missed her terribly already. There were so many strident faceless people in uniform in the dining room with him. He felt an urgent desire to be alone with her again soon and sprang up impetuously from his table and went running outside and back down the street toward the apartment in search of the tiny bits of paper in the gutter, but they had all been flushed away by a street cleaner's hose.

He couldn't find her again in the Allied officers' night club that evening or in the sweltering, burnished, hedonistic bedlam of the black-market restaurant with its vast bobbing wooden trays of elegant food and its chirping flock of bright and lovely girls. He couldn't even find the restaurant. When he went to bed alone, he dodged flak over Bologna again in a dream, with Aarfy hanging over his shoulder abominably in the plane with a bloated sordid leer. In the morning he ran looking for Luciana in all the French offices he could find, but nobody knew what he was talking about, and then he ran in terror, so jumpy, distraught and disorganized that he just had to keep running in terror somewhere, to the enlisted men's apartment for the squat maid in the lime-colored panties, whom he found dusting in Snowden's room on the fifth floor in her drab brown sweater and heavy dark skirt. Snowden was still alive then, and Yossarian could tell it was Snowden's room from the name stenciled in white on the blue duffel bag he tripped over as he plunged through the doorway at her in a frenzy of creative desperation. The woman caught him by the wrists before he could fall as he came stumbling toward her in need and pulled him along down on top of her as she flopped over backward onto the bed and enveloped him hospitably in her flaccid and consoling embrace, her dust mop aloft in her hand like a banner as her broad, brutish, congenial face gazed up at him fondly with a smile of unperjured friendship. There was a sharp elastic snap as she rolled the lime-colored panties off beneath them both without disturbing him.

He stuffed money into her hand when they were finished. She hugged him in gratitude. He hugged her. She hugged him back and then pulled him down on top of her on the bed again. He stuffed more money into her hand when they were finished this time and ran out of the room before she could begin hugging him in gratitude again. Back at his own apartment, he threw his things together as fast as he could, left for Nately what money he had, and ran back to Pianosa on a supply plane to apologize to Hungry Joe for shutting him out of the bedroom. The apology was unnecessary, for Hungry Joe was in high spirits when Yossarian found him. Hungry Joe was grinning from ear to ear, and Yossarian turned sick at the sight of him, for he understood instantly what the high spirits meant.

"Forty missions," Hungry Joe announced readily in a voice lyrical with relief and elation. "The colonel raised them again."

Yossarian was stunned. "But I've got thirty-two, goddammit! Three more and I would have been through."

Hungry Joe shrugged indifferently. "The colonel wants forty missions," he repeated.

Yossarian shoved him out of the way and ran right into the hospital.

17

The Soldier in White

Yossarian ran right into the hospital, determined to remain there forever rather than fly one mission more than the thirty-two missions he had. Ten days after he changed his mind and came out, the colonel raised the missions to forty-five and Yossarian ran right back in, determined to remain in the hospital forever rather than fly one mission more than the six missions more he had just flown.

Yossarian could run into the hospital whenever he wanted to because of his liver and because of his eyes; the doctors couldn't fix his liver condition and couldn't meet his eyes each time he told them he had a liver condition. He could enjoy himself in the hospital, just as long as there was no one really very sick in the same ward. His system was sturdy enough to survive a case of someone else's malaria or influenza with scarcely any discomfort at all. He could come through other people's tonsillectomies without suffering any postoperative distress, and even endure their hernias and hemorrhoids with only mild nausea and revulsion. But that was just about as much as he could go through without getting sick. After that he was ready to bolt. He could relax in the hospital, since no one there expected him to do anything. All he was expected to do in the hospital was die or get better, and since he was perfectly all right to begin with, getting better was easy.

Being in the hospital was better than being over Bologna or flying over Avignon with Huple and Dobbs at the controls and Snowden dying in back.

There were usually not nearly as many sick people inside the hospital as Yossarian saw outside the hospital, and there were generally fewer people inside the hospital who were seriously sick. There was a much lower death rate inside the hospital than outside the hospital, and a much healthier death rate. Few people died unnecessarily. People knew a lot more about dying inside the hospital and made a much neater, more orderly job of it. They couldn't dominate Death inside the hospital, but they certainly made her behave. They had taught her manners. They couldn't keep Death out, but while she was in she had to act like a lady. People gave up the ghost with delicacy and taste inside the hospital. There was none of that crude, ugly ostentation about dying that was so common outside the hospital. They did not blow up in mid-air like Kraft or the dead man in Yossarian's tent, or freeze to death in the blazing summertime the way Snowden had frozen to death after spilling his secret to Yossarian in the back of the plane.

"I'm cold," Snowden had whimpered. "I'm cold."

"There, there," Yossarian had tried to comfort him. "There, there."

They didn't take it on the lam weirdly inside a cloud the way Clevinger had done. They didn't explode into blood and clotted matter. They didn't drown or get struck by lightning, mangled by machinery or crushed in landslides. They didn't get shot to death in hold-ups, strangled to death in rapes, stabbed to death in saloons, bludgeoned to death with axes by parents or children, or die summarily by some other act of God. Nobody choked to death. People bled to death like gentlemen in an operating room or expired without comment in an oxygen tent. There was none of that tricky now-you-see-me-now-you-don't business so much in vogue outside the hospital, none of that now-I-am-and-now-I-ain't. There were no famines or floods. Children didn't suffocate in cradles or iceboxes or fall under trucks. No one was beaten to death. People didn't stick their heads into ovens with the gas on, jump in front of subway trains or come plummeting like dead weights out of hotel windows with a *whoosh!*, accelerating at the rate of thirty-two feet per second to land with a hideous *plop!* on the sidewalk and die disgustingly there in public like an alpaca sack full of hairy strawberry ice cream, bleeding, pink toes awry.

All things considered, Yossarian often preferred the hospital, even though it had its faults. The help tended to be officious, the rules, if heeded, restrictive, and the management meddlesome. Since sick people *were* apt to be present, he could not always depend on a lively young crowd in the same ward with him, and the entertainment was not always good. He was forced to admit that the hospitals had altered steadily for the worse as the war continued and one moved closer to the battlefront, the deterioration in the quality of the guests becoming most marked within the combat zone itself where the effects of booming wartime conditions were apt to make themselves conspicuous immediately. The people got sicker and sicker the deeper he moved into combat, until finally in the hospital that last time there had been the soldier in white, who could not have been any sicker without being dead, and he soon was.

The soldier in white was constructed entirely of gauze, plaster and a thermometer, and the thermometer was merely an adornment left balanced in the empty dark hole in the bandages over his mouth early each morning and late each afternoon by Nurse Cramer and Nurse Duckett right up to the afternoon Nurse Cramer read the thermometer and discovered he was dead. Now that Yossarian looked back, it seemed that Nurse Cramer, rather than the talkative Texan, had murdered the soldier in white; if she had not read the thermometer and reported what she had found, the soldier in white might still be lying there alive exactly as he had been lying there all along, encased from head to toe in plaster and gauze with both strange, rigid legs elevated from the hips and both strange arms strung up perpendicularly, all four bulky limbs in casts, all four strange, useless limbs hoisted up in the air by taut wire cables and fantastically long lead weights suspended darkly above him. Lying there that way might not have been much of a life, but it was all the life he had, and the decision to terminate it, Yossarian felt, should hardly have been Nurse Cramer's.

The soldier in white was like an unrolled bandage with a hole in it or like a broken block of stone in a harbor with a crooked zinc pipe jutting out. The other patients in the ward, all but the Texan, shrank from him with a tenderhearted aversion from the moment they set eyes on him the morning after the night he had been sneaked in. They gathered soberly in the farthest recess of the ward and gossiped about him in malicious, offended undertones, rebelling against his presence as a ghastly imposition and resenting him malevolently for the nauseating truth of which he was a bright reminder. They shared a common dread that he would begin moaning.

"I don't know what I'll do if he does begin moaning," the dashing young fighter pilot with the golden mustache had grieved forlornly. "It means he'll moan during the night, too, because he won't be able to tell time."

No sound at all came from the soldier in white all the time he was there. The ragged round hole over his mouth was deep and jet black and showed no sign of lip, teeth, palate or tongue. The only one who ever came close enough to look was the affable Texan, who came close enough several times a day to chat with him about more votes for the decent folk, opening each conversation with the same unvarying greeting: "What do you say, fella? How you coming along?" The rest of the men avoided them both in their regulation maroon corduroy bathrobes and unraveling flannel pajamas, wondering gloomily who the soldier in white was, why he was there and what he was really like inside.

"He's all right, I tell you," the Texan would report back to them encouragingly after each of his social visits. "Deep down inside he's really a regular guy. He's just feeling a little shy and insecure now because he doesn't know anybody here and can't talk. Why don't you all just step right up to him and introduce yourselves? He won't hurt you."

"What the goddam hell are you talking about?" Dunbar demanded. "Does he even know what you're talking about?"

"Sure he knows what I'm talking about. He's not stupid. There ain't nothing wrong with him."

"Can he hear you?"

"Well, I don't know if he can hear me or not, but I'm sure he knows what I'm talking about."

"Does that hole over his mouth ever move?"

"Now, what kind of a crazy question is that?" the Texan asked uneasily.

"How can you tell if he's breathing if it never moves?"

"How can you tell it's a he?"

"Does he have pads over his eyes underneath that bandage over his face?"

"Does he ever wiggle his toes or move the tips of his fingers?"

The Texan backed away in mounting confusion. "Now, what kind of a crazy question is that? You fellas must all be crazy or something. Why don't you just walk right up to him and get acquainted? He's a real nice guy, I tell you."

The soldier in white was more like a stuffed and sterilized mummy than a real nice guy. Nurse Duckett and Nurse Cramer kept him spick-and-span. They brushed his bandages often with a whiskbroom and scrubbed the plaster casts on his arms, legs, shoulders, chest and pelvis with soapy water. Working with a round tin of metal polish, they waxed a dim gloss on the dull zinc pipe rising from the cement on his groin. With damp dish towels they wiped the dust several times a day from the slim black rubber tubes leading in and out of him to the two large stoppered jars, one of them, hanging on a post beside his bed, dripping fluid into his arm constantly through a slit in the bandages while the other, almost out of sight on the floor, drained the fluid away through the zinc pipe rising from his groin. Both young nurses polished the glass jars unceasingly. They were proud of their housework.

The more solicitous of the two was Nurse Cramer, a shapely, pretty, sexless girl with a wholesome unattractive face. Nurse Cramer had a cute nose and a radiant, blooming complexion dotted with fetching sprays of adorable freckles that Yossarian detested. She was touched very deeply by the soldier in white. Her virtuous, pale-blue, saucerlike eyes flooded with leviathan tears on unexpected occasions and made Yossarian mad.

"How the hell do you know he's even in there?" he asked her.

"Don't you dare talk to me that way!" she replied indignantly.

"Well, how do you? You don't even know if it's really him."

"Who?"

"Whoever's supposed to be in all those bandages. You might really be weeping for somebody else. How do you know he's even alive?"

"What a terrible thing to say!" Nurse Cramer exclaimed. "Now, you get right into bed and stop making jokes about him."

"I'm not making jokes. Anybody might be in there. For all we know, it might even be Mudd."

"What are you talking about?" Nurse Cramer pleaded with him in a quavering voice.

"Maybe that's where the dead man is."

"What dead man?"

"I've got a dead man in my tent that nobody can throw out. His name is Mudd."

Nurse Cramer's face blanched and she turned to Dunbar desperately for aid. "Make him stop saying things like that," she begged.

"Maybe there's no one inside," Dunbar suggested helpfully. "Maybe they just sent the bandages here for a joke."

She stepped away from Dunbar in alarm. "You're crazy," she cried, glancing about imploring. "You're both crazy."

Nurse Duckett showed up then and chased them all back to their own beds while Nurse Cramer changed the stoppered jars for the soldier in white. Changing the jars for the soldier in white was no trouble at all, since the same clear fluid was dripped back inside him over and over again with no apparent loss. When the jar feeding the inside of his elbow was just about empty, the jar on the floor was just about full, and the two were simply uncoupled from their respective hoses and reversed quickly so that the liquid could be dripped right back into him. Changing the jars was no trouble to anyone but the men who watched them changed every hour or so and were baffled by the procedure.

"Why can't they hook the two jars up to each other and eliminate the middleman?" the artillery captain with whom Yossarian had stopped playing chess inquired. "What the hell do they need him for?"

"I wonder what he did to deserve it," the warrant officer with malaria and a mosquito bite on his ass lamented after Nurse Cramer had read her thermometer and discovered that the soldier in white was dead.

"He went to war," the fighter pilot with the golden mustache surmised.

"We all went to war," Dunbar countered.

"That's what I mean," the warrant officer with malaria continued. "Why him? There just doesn't seem to be any logic to this system of rewards and punishment. Look what happened to me. If I had gotten syphilis or a dose of clap for my five minutes of passion on the beach instead of this damned mosquito bite, I could see some justice. But malaria? *Malaria?* Who can explain malaria as a consequence of fornication?" The warrant officer shook his head in numb astonishment.

"What about me?" Yossarian said. "I stepped out of my tent in Marrakech one night to get a bar of candy and caught your dose of clap when that Wac I never even saw before hissed me into the bushes. All I really wanted was a bar of candy, but who could turn it down?"

"That sounds like my dose of clap, all right," the warrant officer agreed. "But I've still got somebody else's malaria. Just for once I'd like to see all these things sort of straightened out, with each person getting exactly what he deserves. It might give me some confidence in this universe."

"I've got somebody else's three hundred thousand dollars," the dashing young fighter captain with the golden mustache admitted. "I've been goofing off since the day I was born. I cheated my way through prep school and college, and just about all I've been doing ever since is shacking up with pretty girls who think I'd make a good husband. I've got no ambition at all. The only thing I want to do after the war is marry some girl who's got more money than I have and shack up with lots more pretty girls. The three hundred thousand bucks was left to me before I was born by a grandfather who made a fortune selling hogwash on an international scale. I know I don't deserve it, but I'll be damned if I give it back. I wonder who it really belongs to."

"Maybe it belongs to my father," Dunbar conjectured. "He spent a lifetime at hard work and never could make enough money to even send my sister and me through college. He's dead now, so you might as well keep it."

"Now, if we can just find out who my malaria belongs to, we'd be all set. It's not that I've got anything against malaria. I'd just as soon goldbrick with malaria as with anything else. It's only that I feel an injustice has been committed. Why should I have somebody else's malaria and you have my dose of clap?"

"I've got more than your dose of clap," Yossarian told him. "I've got to keep flying combat missions because of that dose of yours until they kill me."

"That makes it even worse. What's the justice in that?"

"I had a friend named Clevinger two and a half weeks ago who used to see plenty of justice in it."

"It's the highest kind of justice of all," Clevinger had gloated, clapping his hands with a merry laugh. "I can't help thinking of the *Hippolytus* of Euripides, where the early licentiousness of Theseus is probably responsible for the asceticism of the son that helps bring about the tragedy that ruins them all. If nothing else, that episode with the Wac should teach you the evil of sexual immorality."

"It teaches me the evil of candy."

"Can't you see that you're not exactly without blame for the predicament you're in?" Clevinger had continued with undisguised relish. "If you hadn't been laid up in the hospital with venereal disease for ten days back there in Africa, you might have finished your twenty-five missions in time to be sent home before Colonel Nevers was killed and Colonel Cathcart came to replace him."

"And what about you?" Yossarian had replied. "You never got clap in Marrakech and you're in the same predicament."

"I don't know," confessed Clevinger, with a trace of mock concern. "I guess I must have done something very bad in my time."

"Do you really believe that?"

Clevinger laughed. "No, of course not. I just like to kid you along a little."

There were too many dangers for Yossarian to keep track of. There was Hitler, Mussolini and Tojo, for example, and they were all out to kill him. There was Lieutenant Scheisskopf with his fanaticism for parades and there was the bloated colonel with his big fat mustache and his fanaticism for retribution, and they wanted to kill him, too. There was Appleby, Havermeyer, Black and Korn. There was Nurse Cramer and Nurse Duckett, who he was almost certain wanted him dead, and there was the Texan and the C.I.D. man, about whom he had no doubt. There were bartenders, bricklayers and bus conductors all over the world who wanted him dead, landlords and tenants, traitors and patriots, lynchers, leeches and lackeys, and they were all out to bump him off. That was the secret Snowden had spilled to him on the mission to Avignon—they were out to get him; and Snowden had spilled it all over the back of the plane.

There were lymph glands that might do him in. There were kidneys, nerve sheaths and corpuscles. There were tumors of the brain. There was Hodgkin's disease, leukemia, amyotrophic lateral sclerosis. There were fertile red meadows of epithelial tissue to catch and coddle a cancer cell. There were diseases of the skin, diseases of the bone, diseases of the lung, diseases of the stomach, diseases of the heart, blood and arteries. There were diseases of the head, diseases of the neck, diseases of the chest, diseases of the intestines, diseases of the crotch. There even were diseases of the feet. There were billions of conscientious body cells oxidating away day and night like dumb animals at their complicated job of keeping him alive and healthy, and every one was a potential traitor and foe. There were so many diseases that it took a truly diseased mind to even think about them as often as he and Hungry Joe did.

Hungry Joe collected lists of fatal diseases and arranged them in alphabetical order so that he could put his finger without delay on any one he wanted to worry about. He grew very upset whenever he misplaced some or when he could not add to his list, and he would go rushing in a cold sweat to Doc Daneeka for help.

"Give him Ewing's tumor," Yossarian advised Doc Daneeka, who would come to Yossarian for help in handling Hungry Joe, "and follow it up with melanoma. Hungry Joe likes lingering diseases, but he likes the fulminating ones even more."

Doc Daneeka had never heard of either. "How do you manage to keep up on so many diseases like that?" he inquired with high professional esteem.

"I learn about them at the hospital when I study the *Reader's Digest*."

Yossarian had so many ailments to be afraid of that he was sometimes tempted to turn himself in to the hospital for good and spend the rest of his life stretched out there inside an oxygen tent with a battery of specialists and nurses seated at one side of his bed twenty-four hours a day waiting for something to go wrong and at least one surgeon with a knife poised at the other, ready to jump forward and begin cutting away the moment it became necessary. Aneurisms, for instance; how else could they ever defend him in time against an aneurism of the aorta? Yossarian felt much safer inside the hospital than outside the hospital, even though he loathed the surgeon and his knife as much as he had ever loathed anyone. He could start screaming inside a hospital and people would at least come running to try to help; outside the hospital they would throw him in prison if he ever started screaming about all the things he felt everyone ought to start screaming about, or they would put him in the hospital. One of the things he wanted to start screaming about was the surgeon's knife that was almost certain to be waiting for him and everyone else who lived long enough to die. He wondered often how he would ever recognize the first chill, flush, twinge, ache, belch, sneeze, stain, lethargy, vocal slip, loss of balance or lapse of memory that would signal the inevitable beginning of the inevitable end.

He was afraid also that Doc Daneeka would still refuse to help him when he went to him again after jumping out of Major Major's office, and he was right.

"You think you've got something to be afraid about?" Doc Daneeka demanded, lifting his delicate immaculate dark head up from his chest to gaze at Yossarian irascibly for a moment with lachrymose eyes. "What about me? My precious medical skills are rusting away here on this lousy island while other doctors are cleaning up. Do you think I enjoy sitting here day after day refusing to help you? I wouldn't mind it so much if I could refuse to help you back in the States or in some place like Rome. But saying no to you here isn't easy for me, either."

"Then stop saying no. Ground me."

"I can't ground you," Doc Daneeka mumbled. "How many times do you have to be told?"

"Yes you can. Major Major told me you're the only one in the squadron who *can* ground me."

Doc Daneeka was stunned. "Major Major told you that? When?"

"When I tackled him in the ditch."

"Major Major told you that? In a ditch?"

"He told me in his office after we left the ditch and jumped inside. He told me not to tell anyone he told me, so don't start shooting your mouth off."

"Why that dirty, scheming liar!" Doc Daneeka cried. "He wasn't supposed to tell anyone. Did he tell you how I could ground you?"

"Just by filling out a little slip of paper saying I'm on the verge of a nervous collapse and sending it to Group. Dr. Stubbs grounds men in his squadron all the time, so why can't you?"

"And what happens to the men after Stubbs does ground them?" Doc Daneeka retorted with a sneer. "They go right back on combat status, don't they? And he finds himself right up the creek. Sure, I can ground you by filling out a slip saying you're unfit to fly. But there's a catch."

"Catch-22?"

"Sure. If I take you off combat duty, Group has to approve my action, and Group isn't going to. They'll put you right back on combat status, and then where will I be? On my way to the Pacific Ocean, probably. No, thank you. I'm not going to take any chances for you."

"Isn't it worth a try?" Yossarian argued. "What's so hot about Pianosa?"

"Pianosa is terrible. But it's better than the Pacific Ocean. I wouldn't mind being shipped someplace civilized where I might pick up a buck or two in abortion money every now and then. But all they've got in the Pacific is jungles and monsoons. I'd rot there."

"You're rotting here."

Doc Daneeka flared up angrily. "Yeah? Well, at least I'm going to come out of this war alive, which is a lot more than you're going to do."

"That's just what I'm trying to tell you, goddammit. I'm asking you to save my life."

"It's not my business to save lives," Doc Daneeka retorted sullenly.

"What is your business?"

"I don't know what my business is. All they ever told me was to uphold the ethics of my profession and never give testimony against another physician. Listen. You think you're the only one whose life is in danger? What about me? Those two quacks I've got working for me in the medical tent still can't find out what's wrong with me."

"Maybe it's Ewing's tumor," Yossarian muttered sarcastically.

"Do you really think so?" Doc Daneeka exclaimed with fright.

"Oh, I don't know," Yossarian answered impatiently. "I just know I'm not going to fly any more missions. They wouldn't really shoot me, would they? I've got fifty-one."

"Why don't you at least finish the fifty-five before you take a stand?" Doc Daneeka advised. "With all your bitching, you've never finished a tour of duty even once."

"How the hell can I? The colonel keeps raising them every time I get close."

"You never finish your missions because you keep running into the hospital or going off to Rome. You'd be in a much stronger position if you had your fifty-five finished and then refused to fly. Then maybe I'd see what I could do."

"Do you promise?"

"I promise."

"What do you promise?"

"I promise that maybe I'll think about doing something to help if you finish your fifty-five missions and if you get McWatt to put my name on his flight log again so that I can draw my flight pay without going up in a plane. I'm afraid of airplanes. Did you read about that airplane crash in Idaho three weeks ago? Six people killed. It was terrible. I don't know why they want me to put in four hours' flight time every month in order to get my flight pay. Don't I have enough to worry about without worrying about being killed in an airplane crash too?"

"I worry about airplane crashes also," Yossarian told him. "You're not the only one."

"Yeah, but I'm also pretty worried about that Ewing's tumor," Doc Daneeka boasted. "Do you think that's why my nose is stuffed all the time and why I always feel so chilly? Take my pulse."

Yossarian also worried about Ewing's tumor and melanoma. Catastrophes were lurking everywhere, too numerous to count. When he contemplated the many diseases and potential accidents threatening him, he was positively astounded that he had managed to survive in good health for as long as he had. It was miraculous. Each day he faced was another dangerous mission against mortality. And he had been surviving them for twenty-eight years.

18

The Soldier Who Saw Everything Twice

Yossarian owed his good health to exercise, fresh air, teamwork and good sportsmanship; it was to get away from them all that he had first discovered the hospital. When the physical-education officer at Lowery Field ordered everyone to fall out for calisthenics one afternoon, Yossarian, the private, reported instead at the dispensary with what he said was a pain in his right side.

"Beat it," said the doctor on duty there, who was doing a crossword puzzle.

"We can't tell him to beat it," said a corporal. "There's a new directive out about abdominal complaints. We have to keep them under observation five days because so many of them have been dying after we make them beat it."

"All right," grumbled the doctor. "Keep him under observation five days and *then* make him beat it."

They took Yossarian's clothes away and put him in a ward, where he was very happy when no one was snoring nearby. In the morning a helpful young English intern popped in to ask him about his liver.

"I think it's my appendix that's bothering me," Yossarian told him.

"Your appendix is no good," the Englishman declared with jaunty authority. "If your appendix goes wrong, we can take it out and have you back on active duty in almost no time at all. But come to us with a liver complaint and you can fool us for weeks. The liver, you see, is a large, ugly mystery to us. If you've ever eaten liver you know what I mean. We're pretty sure today that the liver exists, and we have a fairly good idea of what it does whenever it's doing what it's supposed to be doing. Beyond that, we're really in the dark. After all, what is a liver? My father, for example, died of cancer of the liver and was never sick a day of his life right up till the moment it killed him. Never felt a twinge of pain. In a way, that was too bad, since I hated my father. Lust for my mother, you know."

"What's an English medical officer doing on duty here?" Yossarian wanted to know.

The officer laughed. "I'll tell you all about that when I see you tomorrow morning. And throw that silly ice bag away before you die of pneumonia."

Yossarian never saw him again. That was one of the nice things about all the doctors at the hospital; he never saw any of them a second time. They came and went and simply disappeared. In place of the English intern the next day, there arrived a group of doctors he had never seen before to ask him about his appendix.

"There's nothing wrong with my appendix," Yossarian informed them. "The doctor yesterday said it was my liver."

"Maybe it is his liver," replied the white-haired officer in charge. "What does his blood count show?"

"He hasn't had a blood count."

"Have one taken right away. We can't afford to take chances with a patient in his condition. We've got to keep ourselves covered in case he dies." He made a notation on his clipboard and spoke to Yossarian. "In the meantime, keep that ice bag on. It's very important."

"I don't have an ice bag on."

"Well, get one. There must be an ice bag around here somewhere. And let someone know if the pain becomes unendurable."

At the end of ten days, a new group of doctors came to Yossarian with bad news: he was in perfect health and had to get out. He was rescued in the nick of time by a patient across the aisle who began to see everything twice. Without warning, the patient sat up in bed and shouted,

"I see everything twice!"

A nurse screamed and an orderly fainted. Doctors came running up from every direction with needles, lights, tubes, rubber mallets and oscillating metal tines. They rolled up complicated instruments on wheels. There was not enough of the patient to go around, and specialists pushed forward in line with raw tempers and snapped at their colleagues in front to hurry up and give somebody else a chance. A colonel with a large forehead and horn-rimmed glasses soon arrived at a diagnosis.

"It's meningitis," he called out emphatically, waving the others back. "Although Lord knows there's not the slightest reason for thinking so."

"Then why pick meningitis?" inquired a major with a suave chuckle. "Why not, let's say, acute nephritis?"

"Because I'm a meningitis man, that's why, and not an acute-nephritis man," retorted the colonel. "And I'm not going to give him up to any of your kidney birds without a struggle. I was here first."

In the end, the doctors were all in accord. They agreed they had no idea what was wrong with the soldier who saw everything twice, and they rolled him away into a room in the corridor and quarantined everyone else in the ward for fourteen days.

Thanksgiving Day came and went without any fuss while Yossarian was still in the hospital. The only bad thing about it was the turkey for dinner, and even that was pretty good. It was the most rational Thanksgiving he had ever spent, and he took a sacred oath to spend every future Thanksgiving Day in the cloistered shelter of a hospital. He broke his sacred oath the very next year, when he spent the holiday in a hotel room instead in intellectual conversation with Lieutenant Scheisskopf's wife, who had Dori Duz's dog tags on for the occasion and who henpecked Yossarian sententiously for being cynical and callous about Thanksgiving, even though she didn't believe in God just as much as he didn't.

"I'm probably just as good an atheist as you are," she speculated boastfully. "But even I feel that we all have a great deal to be thankful for and that we shouldn't be ashamed to show it."

"Name one thing I've got to be thankful for," Yossarian challenged her without interest.

"Well . . ." Lieutenant Scheisskopf's wife mused and paused a moment to ponder dubiously. "Me."

"Oh, come on," he scoffed.

She arched her eyebrows in surprise. "Aren't you thankful for me?" she asked. She frowned peevishly, her pride wounded. "I don't have to shack up with you, you know," she told him with cold dignity. "My husband has a whole squadron full of aviation cadets who would be only too happy to shack up with their commanding officer's wife just for the added fillip it would give them."

Yossarian decided to change the subject. "Now you're changing the subject," he pointed out diplomatically. "I'll bet I can name two things to be miserable about for every one you can name to be thankful for."

"Be thankful you've got me," she insisted.

"I am, honey. But I'm also goddam good and miserable that I can't have Dori Duz again, too. Or the hundreds of other girls and women I'll see and want in my short lifetime and won't be able to go to bed with even once."

"Be thankful you're healthy."

"Be bitter you're not going to stay that way."

"Be glad you're even alive."

"Be *furious* you're going to die."

"Things could be much worse," she cried.

"They could be one hell of a lot better," he answered heatedly.

"You're naming only one thing," she protested. "You said you could name two."

"And don't tell me God works in mysterious ways," Yossarian continued, hurtling on over her objection. "There's nothing so mysterious about it. He's not working at all. He's playing. Or else He's forgotten all about us. That's the kind of God you people talk about—a country bumpkin, a clumsy, bungling, brainless, conceited, uncouth hayseed. Good God, how much reverence can you have for a Supreme Being who finds it necessary to include such phenomena as phlegm and tooth decay in His divine system of creation? What in the world was running through that warped, evil, scatological mind of His when He robbed old people of the power to control their bowel movements? Why in the world did He ever create pain?"

"Pain?" Lieutenant Scheisskopf's wife pounced upon the word victoriously. "Pain is a useful symptom. Pain is a warning to us of bodily dangers."

"And who created the dangers?" Yossarian demanded. He laughed caustically. "Oh, He was really being charitable to us when He gave us pain! Why couldn't He have used a doorbell instead to notify us, or one of His celestial choirs? Or a system of blue-and-red neon tubes right in the middle of each person's forehead. Any jukebox manufacturer worth his salt could have done that. Why couldn't He?"

"People would certainly look silly walking around with red neon tubes in the middle of their foreheads."

"They certainly look beautiful now writhing in agony or stupefied with morphine, don't they? What a colossal, immortal blunderer! When you consider the opportunity and power He had to really do a job, and then look at the stupid, ugly little mess He made of it instead, His sheer incompetence is almost staggering. It's obvious He never met a payroll. Why, no self-respecting businessman would hire a bungler like Him as even a shipping clerk!"

Lieutenant Scheisskopf's wife had turned ashen in disbelief and was ogling him with alarm. "You'd better not talk that way about Him, honey," she warned him reprovingly in a low and hostile voice. "He might punish you."

"Isn't He punishing me enough?" Yossarian snorted resentfully. "You know, we mustn't let Him get away with it. Oh no, we certainly mustn't let Him get away scot-free for all the sorrow He's caused us. Someday I'm going to make Him pay. I know when. On the Judgment Day. Yes, that's the day I'll be close enough to reach out and grab that little yokel by His neck and—"

"Stop it! Stop it!" Lieutenant Scheisskopf's wife screamed suddenly, and began beating him ineffectually about the head with both fists. "Stop it!"

Yossarian ducked behind his arm for protection while she slammed away at him in feminine fury for a few seconds, and then he caught her determinedly by the wrists and forced her gently back down on the bed. "What the hell are you getting so upset about?" he asked her bewilderedly in a tone of contrite amusement. "I thought you didn't believe in God."

"I don't," she sobbed, bursting violently into tears. "But the God I don't believe in is a good God, a just God, a merciful God. He's not the mean and stupid God you make Him out to be."

Yossarian laughed and turned her arms loose. "Let's have a little more religious freedom between us," he proposed obligingly. "You don't believe in the God you want to, and I won't believe in the God I want to. Is that a deal?"

That was the most illogical Thanksgiving he could ever remember spending, and his thoughts returned wishfully to his halcyon fourteen-day quarantine in the hospital the year before; but even that idyll had ended on a tragic note: he was still in good health when the quarantine period was over, and they told him again that he had to get out and go to war. Yossarian sat up in bed when he heard the bad news and shouted,

"I see everything twice!"

Pandemonium broke loose in the ward again. The specialists came running up from all directions and ringed him in a circle of scrutiny so confining that he could feel the humid breath from their various noses blowing uncomfortably upon the different sectors of his body. They went snooping into his eyes and ears with tiny beams of light, assaulted his legs and feet with rubber hammers and vibrating forks, drew blood from his veins, held anything handy up for him to see on the periphery of his vision.

The leader of this team of doctors was a dignified, solicitous gentleman who held one finger up directly in front of Yossarian and demanded, "How many fingers do you see?"

"Two," said Yossarian.

"How many fingers do you see now?" asked the doctor, holding up two.

"Two," said Yossarian.

"And how many now?" asked the doctor, holding up none.

"Two," said Yossarian.

The doctor's face wreathed with a smile. "By Jove, he's right," he declared jubilantly. "He *does* see everything twice."

They rolled Yossarian away on a stretcher into the room with the other soldier who saw everything twice and quarantined everyone else in the ward for another fourteen days.

"I see everything twice!" the soldier who saw everything twice shouted when they rolled Yossarian in.

"I see everything twice!" Yossarian shouted back at him just as loudly, with a secret wink.

"The walls! The walls!" the other soldier cried. "Move back the walls!"

"The walls! The walls!" Yossarian cried. "Move back the walls!"

One of the doctors pretended to shove the wall back. "Is that far enough?"

The soldier who saw everything twice nodded weakly and sank back on his bed. Yossarian nodded weakly too, eyeing his talented roommate with great humility and admiration. He knew he was in the presence of a master. His talented roommate was obviously a person to be studied and emulated. During the night, his talented roommate died, and Yossarian decided that he had followed him far enough.

"I see everything once!" he cried quickly.

A new group of specialists came pounding up to his bedside with their instruments to find out if it was true.

"How many fingers do you see?" asked the leader, holding up one.

"One."

The doctor held up two fingers. "How many fingers do you see now?"

"One."

The doctor held up ten fingers. "And how many now?"

"One."

The doctor turned to the other doctors with amazement. "He does see everything once!" he exclaimed. "We made him all better."

"And just in time, too," announced the doctor with whom Yossarian next found himself alone, a tall, torpedo-shaped congenial man with an unshaven growth of brown beard and a pack of cigarettes in his shirt pocket that he chain-smoked insouciantly as he leaned against the wall. "There are some relatives here to see you. Oh, don't worry," he added with a laugh. "Not your relatives. It's the mother, father and brother of that chap who died. They've traveled all the way from New York to see a dying soldier, and you're the handiest one we've got."

"What are you talking about?" Yossarian asked suspiciously. "I'm not dying."

"Of course you're dying. We're all dying. Where the devil else do you think you're heading?"

"They didn't come to see me," Yossarian objected. "They came to see their son."

"They'll have to take what they can get. As far as we're concerned, one dying boy is just as good as any other, or just as bad. To a scientist, all dying boys are equal. I have a proposition for you. You let them come in and look you over for a few minutes and I won't tell anyone you've been lying about your liver symptoms."

Yossarian drew back from him farther. "You know about that?"

"Of course I do. Give us some credit." The doctor chuckled amiably and lit another cigarette. "How do you expect anyone to believe you have a liver condition if you keep squeezing the nurses' tits every time you get a chance? You're going to have to give up sex if you want to convince people you've got an ailing liver."

"That's a hell of a price to pay just to keep alive. Why didn't you turn me in if you knew I was faking?"

"Why the devil should I?" asked the doctor with a flicker of surprise. "We're all in this business of illusion together. I'm always willing to lend a helping hand to a fellow conspirator along the road to survival if he's willing to do the same for me. These people have come a long way, and I'd rather not disappoint them. I'm sentimental about old people."

"But they came to see their son."

"They came too late. Maybe they won't even notice the difference."

"Suppose they start crying."

"They probably will start crying. That's one of the reasons they came. I'll listen outside the door and break it up if it starts getting tacky."

"It all sounds a bit crazy," Yossarian reflected. "What do they want to watch their son die for, anyway?"

"I've never been able to figure that one out," the doctor admitted, "but they always do. Well, what do you say? All you've got to do is lie there a few minutes and die a little. Is that asking so much?"

"All right," Yossarian gave in. "If it's just for a few minutes and you promise to wait right outside." He warmed to his role. "Say, why don't you wrap a bandage around me for effect?"

"That sounds like a splendid idea," applauded the doctor.

They wrapped a batch of bandages around Yossarian. A team of medical orderlies installed tan shades on each of the two windows and lowered them to douse the room in depressing shadows. Yossarian suggested flowers, and the doctor sent an orderly out to find two small bunches of fading ones with a strong and sickening smell. When everything was in place, they made Yossarian get back into bed and lie down. Then they admitted the visitors.

The visitors entered uncertainly as though they felt they were intruding, tiptoeing in with stares of meek apology, first the grieving mother and father, then the brother, a glowering heavy-set sailor with a deep chest. The man and woman stepped into the room stiffly side by side as though right out of a familiar, though esoteric, anniversary daguerreotype on a wall. They were both short, sere and proud. They seemed made of iron and old, dark clothing. The woman had a long, brooding, oval face of burnt umber, with coarse graying black hair parted severely in the middle and combed back austerely behind her neck without curl, wave or ornamentation. Her mouth was sullen and sad, her lined lips compressed. The father stood very rigid and quaint in a double-breasted suit with padded shoulders that were much too tight for him. He was broad and muscular on a small scale and had a magnificently curled silver mustache on his crinkled face. His eyes were creased and rheumy, and he appeared tragically ill at ease as he stood awkwardly with the brim of his black felt fedora held in his two brawny laborer's hands out in front of his wide lapels. Poverty and hard work had inflicted iniquitous damage on both. The brother was looking for a fight. His round white cap was cocked at an insolent tilt, his hands were clenched, and he glared at everything in the room with a scowl of injured truculence.

The three creaked forward timidly, holding themselves close to each other in a stealthy, funereal group and inching forward almost in step, until they arrived at the side of the bed and stood staring down at Yossarian. There was a gruesome and excruciating silence that threatened to endure forever. Finally Yossarian was unable to bear it any longer and cleared his throat. The old man spoke at last.

"He looks terrible," he said.

"He's sick, Pa."

"Giuseppe," said the mother, who had seated herself in a chair with her veiny fingers clasped in her lap.

"My name is Yossarian," Yossarian said.

"His name is Yossarian, Ma. Yossarian, don't you recognize me? I'm your brother John. Don't you know who I am?"

"Sure I do. You're my brother John."

"He does recognize me! Pa, he knows who I am. Yossarian, here's Papa. Say hello to Papa."

"Hello, Papa," said Yossarian.

"Hello, Giuseppe."

"His name is Yossarian, Pa."

"I can't get over how terrible he looks," the father said.

"He's very sick, Pa. The doctor says he's going to die."

"I didn't know whether to believe the doctor or not," the father said. "You know how crooked those guys are."

"Giuseppe," the mother said again, in a soft, broken chord of muted anguish.

"His name is Yossarian, Ma. She don't remember things too good any more. How're they treating you in here, kid? They treating you pretty good?"

"Pretty good," Yossarian told him.

"That's good. Just don't let anybody in here push you around. You're just as good as anybody else in here even though you are Italian. You've got rights, too."

Yossarian winced and closed his eyes so that he would not have to look at his brother John. He began to feel sick.

"*Now* see how terrible he looks," the father observed.

"Giuseppe," the mother said.

"Ma, his name is Yossarian," the brother interrupted her impatiently. "Can't you remember?"

"It's all right," Yossarian interrupted him. "She can call me Giuseppe if she wants to."

"Giuseppe," she said to him.

"Don't worry, Yossarian," the brother said. "Everything is going to be all right."

"Don't worry, Ma," Yossarian said. "Everything is going to be all right."

"Did you have a priest?" the brother wanted to know.

"Yes," Yossarian lied, wincing again.

"That's good," the brother decided. "Just as long as you're getting everything you've got coming to you. We came all the way from New York. We were afraid we wouldn't get here in time."

"In time for what?"

"In time to see you before you died."

"What difference would it make?"

"We didn't want you to die by yourself."

"What difference would it make?"

"He must be getting delirious," the brother said. "He keeps saying the same thing over and over again."

"That's really very funny," the old man replied. "All the time I thought his name was Giuseppe, and now I find out his name is Yossarian. That's really very funny."

"Ma, make him feel good," the brother urged. "Say something to cheer him up."

"Giuseppe."

"It's not Giuseppe, Ma. It's Yossarian."

"What difference does it make?" the mother answered in the same mourning tone, without looking up. "He's dying."

Her tumid eyes filled with tears and she began to cry, rocking back and forth slowly in her chair with her hands lying in her lap like fallen moths. Yossarian was afraid she would start wailing. The father and brother began crying also. Yossarian remembered suddenly why they were all crying, and he began crying too. A doctor Yossarian had never seen before stepped inside the room and told the visitors courteously that they had to go. The father drew himself up formally to say goodbye.

"Giuseppe," he began.

"Yossarian," corrected the son.

"Yossarian," said the father.

"Giuseppe," corrected Yossarian.

"Soon you're going to die."

Yossarian began to cry again. The doctor threw him a dirty look from the rear of the room, and Yossarian made himself stop.

The father continued solemnly with his head lowered. "When you talk to the man upstairs," he said, "I want you to tell Him something for me. Tell Him it ain't right for people to die when they're young. I mean it. Tell Him if they got to die at all, they got to die when they're old. I want you to tell Him that. I don't think He knows it ain't right, because He's supposed to be good and it's been going on for a long, long time. Okay?"

"And don't let anybody up there push you around," the brother advised. "You'll be just as good as anybody else in heaven, even though you are Italian."

"Dress warm," said the mother, who seemed to know.

19

Colonel Cathcart

Colonel Cathcart was a slick, successful, slipshod, unhappy man of thirty-six who lumbered when he walked and wanted to be a general. He was dashing and dejected, poised and chagrined. He was complacent and insecure, daring in the administrative stratagems he employed to bring himself to the attention of his superiors and craven in his concern that his schemes might all backfire. He was handsome and unattractive, a swashbuckling, beefy, conceited man who was putting on fat and was tormented chronically by prolonged seizures of apprehension. Colonel Cathcart was conceited because he was a full colonel with a combat command at the age of only thirty-six; and Colonel Cathcart was dejected because although he was already thirty-six he was still only a full colonel.

Colonel Cathcart was impervious to absolutes. He could measure his own progress only in relationship to others, and his idea of excellence was to do something at least as well as all the men his own age who were doing the same thing even better. The fact that there were thousands of men his own age and older who had not even attained the rank of major enlivened him with foppish delight in his own remarkable worth; on the other hand, the fact that there were men of his own age and younger who were already generals contaminated him with an agonizing sense of failure and made him gnaw at his fingernails with an unappeasable anxiety that was even more intense than Hungry Joe's.

Colonel Cathcart was a very large, pouting, broad-shouldered man with close-cropped curly dark hair that was graying at the tips and an ornate cigarette holder that he purchased the day before he arrived in Pianosa to take command of his group. He displayed the cigarette holder grandly on every occasion and had learned to manipulate it adroitly. Unwittingly, he had discovered deep within himself a fertile aptitude for smoking with a cigarette holder. As far as he could tell, his was the only cigarette holder in the whole Mediterranean theater of operations, and the thought was both flattering and disquieting. He had no doubts at all that someone as debonair and intellectual as

General Peckem approved of his smoking with a cigarette holder, even though the two were in each other's presence rather seldom, which in a way was very lucky, Colonel Cathcart recognized with relief, since General Peckem might not have approved of his cigarette holder at all. When such misgivings assailed Colonel Cathcart, he choked back a sob and wanted to throw the damned thing away, but he was restrained by his unswerving conviction that the cigarette holder never failed to embellish his masculine, martial physique with a high gloss of sophisticated heroism that illuminated him to dazzling advantage among all the other full colonels in the American Army with whom he was in competition. Although how could he be sure?

Colonel Cathcart was indefatigable that way, an industrious, intense, dedicated military tactician who calculated day and night in the service of himself. He was his own sarcophagus, a bold and infallible diplomat who was always berating himself disgustedly for all the chances he had missed and kicking himself regretfully for all the errors he had made. He was tense, irritable, bitter and smug. He was a valorous opportunist who pounced hoggishly upon every opportunity Colonel Korn discovered for him and trembled in damp despair immediately afterward at the possible consequences he might suffer. He collected rumors greedily and treasured gossip. He believed all the news he heard and had faith in none. He was on the alert constantly for every signal, shrewdly sensitive to relationships and situations that did not exist. He was someone in the know who was always striving pathetically to find out what was going on. He was a blustering, intrepid bully who brooded inconsolably over the terrible ineradicable impressions he knew he kept making on people of prominence who were scarcely aware that he was even alive.

Everybody was persecuting him. Colonel Cathcart lived by his wits in an unstable, arithmetical world of black eyes and feathers in his cap, of overwhelming imaginary triumphs and catastrophic imaginary defeats. He oscillated hourly between anguish and exhilaration, multiplying fantastically the grandeur of his victories and exaggerating tragically the seriousness of his defeats. Nobody ever caught him napping. If word reached him that General Dreedle or General Peckem had been seen smiling, frowning, or doing neither, he could not make himself rest until he had found an acceptable interpretation and grumbled mulishly until Colonel Korn persuaded him to relax and take things easy.

Lieutenant Colonel Korn was a loyal, indispensable ally who got on Colonel Cathcart's nerves. Colonel Cathcart pledged eternal gratitude to Colonel Korn for the ingenious moves he devised and was furious with him afterward when he realized they might not work. Colonel Cathcart was greatly indebted to Colonel Korn and did not like him at all. The two were very close. Colonel Cathcart was jealous of Colonel Korn's intelligence and had to remind himself often that Colonel Korn was still only a lieutenant colonel, even though he was almost ten years older than Colonel Cathcart, and that Colonel Korn had obtained his education at a state university. Colonel Cathcart bewailed the miserable fate that had given him for an invaluable assistant someone as common as Colonel Korn. It was degrading to have to depend so thoroughly on a person who had been educated at a state university. If someone did have to become indispensable to him, Colonel Cathcart lamented, it could just as easily have been someone wealthy and well groomed, someone from a better family who was more mature than Colonel Korn and who did not treat Colonel Cathcart's desire to become a general as frivolously as Colonel Cathcart secretly suspected Colonel Korn secretly did.

Colonel Cathcart wanted to be a general so desperately he was willing to try anything, even religion, and he summoned the chaplain to his office late one morning the week after he had raised the number of missions to sixty and pointed abruptly down toward his desk to his copy of *The Saturday Evening Post.* The colonel wore his khaki shirt collar wide open, exposing a shadow of tough black bristles of beard on his egg-white neck, and had a spongy hanging underlip. He was a person who never tanned, and he kept out of the sun as much as possible to avoid burning. The colonel was more than a head taller than the chaplain and over twice as broad, and his swollen, overbearing authority made the chaplain feel frail and sickly by contrast.

"Take a look, Chaplain," Colonel Cathcart directed, screwing a cigarette into his holder and seating himself affluently in the swivel chair behind his desk. "Let me know what you think."

The chaplain looked down at the open magazine compliantly and saw an editorial spread dealing with an American bomber group in England whose chaplain said prayers in the briefing room before each mission. The chaplain almost wept with happiness when he realized the colonel was not going to holler at him. The two had hardly spoken since the tumultuous evening Colonel Cathcart had thrown him out of the officers' club at General Dreedle's bidding after Chief White Halfoat had punched Colonel Moodus in the nose. The chaplain's initial fear had been that the colonel intended reprimanding him for having gone back into the officers' club without permission the evening before. He had gone there with Yossarian and Dunbar after the two had come unexpectedly to his tent in the clearing in the woods to ask him to join them. Intimidated as he was by Colonel Cathcart, he nevertheless found it easier to brave his displeasure than to decline the thoughtful invitation of his two new friends, whom he had met on one of his hospital visits just a few weeks before and who had worked so effectively to insulate him against the myriad social vicissitudes involved in his official duty to live on closest terms of familiarity with more than nine hundred unfamiliar officers and enlisted men who thought him an odd duck.

The chaplain glued his eyes to the pages of the magazine. He studied each photograph twice and read the captions intently as he organized his response to the colonel's question into a grammatically complete sentence that he rehearsed and reorganized in his mind a considerable number of times before he was able finally to muster the courage to reply.

"I think that saying prayers before each mission is a very moral and highly laudatory procedure, sir," he offered timidly, and waited.

"Yeah," said the colonel. "But I want to know if you think they'll work here."

"Yes, sir," answered the chaplain after a few moments. "I should think they would."

"Then I'd like to give it a try." The colonel's ponderous, farinaceous cheeks were tinted suddenly with glowing patches of enthusiasm. He rose to his feet and began walking around excitedly. "Look how much good they've done for these people in England. Here's a picture of a colonel in *The Saturday Evening Post* whose chaplain conducts prayers before each mission. If the prayers work for him, they should work for us. Maybe if we say prayers, they'll put *my* picture in *The Saturday Evening Post.*"

The colonel sat down again and smiled distantly in lavish contemplation. The chaplain had no hint of what he was expected to say next. With a pensive expression on his oblong, rather pale face, he allowed his gaze to settle on several of the high bushels filled with red plum tomatoes that stood in rows against each of the walls. He pretended to concentrate on a reply. After a while he realized that he *was* staring at rows and rows of bushels of red plum tomatoes and grew so intrigued by the question of what bushels brimming with red plum tomatoes were doing in a group commander's office that he forgot completely about the discussion of prayer meetings until Colonel Cathcart, in a genial digression, inquired:

"Would you like to buy some, Chaplain? They come right off the farm Colonel Korn and I have up in the hills. I can let you have a bushel wholesale."

"Oh, no, sir. I don't think so."

"That's quite all right," the colonel assured him liberally. "You don't have to. Milo is glad to snap up all we can produce. These were picked only yesterday. Notice how firm and ripe they are, like a young girl's breasts."

The chaplain blushed, and the colonel understood at once that he had made a mistake. He lowered his head in shame, his cumbersome face burning. His fingers felt gross and unwieldy. He hated the chaplain venomously for being a chaplain and making a coarse blunder out of an observation that in any other circumstances, he knew, would have been considered witty and urbane. He tried miserably to recall some means of extricating them both from their devastating embarrassment. He recalled instead that the chaplain was only a captain, and he straightened at once with a shocked and outraged gasp. His cheeks grew tight with fury at the thought that he had just been duped into humiliation by a man who was almost the same age as he was and still only a captain, and he swung upon the chaplain avengingly with a look of such murderous antagonism that the chaplain began to tremble. The colonel punished him sadistically with a long, glowering, malignant, hateful, silent stare.

"We were speaking about something else," he reminded the chaplain cuttingly at last. "We were not speaking about the firm, ripe breasts of young girls but about something else entirely. We were speaking about conducting religious services in the briefing room before each mission. Is there any reason why we can't?"

"No, sir," the chaplain mumbled.

"Then we'll begin with this afternoon's mission." The colonel's hostility softened gradually as he applied himself to details. "Now, I want you to give a lot of thought to the kind of prayers we're going to say. I don't want anything heavy or sad. I'd like you to keep it light and snappy, something that will send the boys out feeling pretty good. Do you know what I mean? I don't want any of this Kingdom of God or Valley of Death stuff. That's all too negative. What are you making such a sour face for?"

"I'm sorry, sir," the chaplain stammered. "I happened to be thinking of the Twenty-third Psalm just as you said that."

"How does that one go?"

"That's the one you were just referring to, sir. 'The Lord is my shepherd; I—'"

"*That's* the one I was just referring to. It's out. What else have you got?"

"'Save me, O God; for the waters are come in unto—'"

"No waters," the colonel decided, blowing ruggedly into his cigarette holder after flipping the butt down into his combed-brass ash tray. "Why don't we try something musical? How about the harps on the willows?"

"That has the rivers of Babylon in it, sir," the chaplain replied. "'. . . there we sat down, yea, we wept, when we remembered Zion.'"

"Zion? Let's forget about *that* one right now. I'd like to know how that one even got in there. Haven't you got anything humorous that stays away from waters and valleys and God? I'd like to keep away from the subject of religion altogether if we can."

The chaplain was apologetic. "I'm sorry, sir, but just about all the prayers I know *are* rather somber in tone and make at least some passing reference to God."

"Then let's get some new ones. The men are already doing enough bitching about the missions I send them on without our rubbing it in with any sermons about God or death or Paradise. Why can't we take a more positive approach? Why can't we all pray for something good, like a tighter bomb pattern, for example? Couldn't we pray for a tighter bomb pattern?"

"Well, yes, sir, I suppose so," the chaplain answered hesitantly. "You wouldn't even need me if that's all you wanted to do. You could do that yourself."

"I know I could," the colonel responded tartly. "But what do you think you're here for? I could shop for my own food, too, but that's Milo's job, and that's why he's doing it for every group in the area. Your job is to lead us in prayer, and from now on you're going to lead us in a prayer for a tighter bomb pattern before every mission. Is that clear? I think a tighter bomb pattern is something really worth praying for. It will be a feather in all our caps with General Peckem. General Peckem feels it makes a much nicer aerial photograph when the bombs explode close together."

"General Peckem, sir?"

"That's right, Chaplain," the colonel replied, chuckling paternally at the chaplain's look of puzzlement. "I wouldn't want this to get around, but it looks like General Dreedle is finally on the way out and that

General Peckem is slated to replace him. Frankly, I'm not going to be sorry to see that happen. General Peckem is a very good man, and I think we'll be all much better off under him. On the other hand, it might never take place, and we'd still remain under General Dreedle. Frankly, I wouldn't be sorry to see that happen either, because General Dreedle is another very good man, and I think we'll all be much better off under him too. I hope you're going to keep all this under your hat, Chaplain. I wouldn't want either one to get the idea I was throwing my support on the side of the other."

"Yes, sir."

"That's good," the colonel exclaimed, and stood up jovially. "But all this gossip isn't getting us into *The Saturday Evening Post*, eh, Chaplain? Let's see what kind of procedure we can evolve. Incidentally, Chaplain, not a word about this beforehand to Colonel Korn. Understand?"

"Yes, sir."

Colonel Cathcart began tramping back and forth reflectively in the narrow corridors left between his bushels of plum tomatoes and the desk and wooden chairs in the center of the room. "I suppose we'll have to keep you waiting outside until the briefing is over, because all that information is classified. We can slip you in while Major Danby is synchronizing the watches. I don't think there's anything secret about the right time. We'll allocate about a minute and a half for you in the schedule. Will a minute and a half be enough?"

"Yes, sir. If it doesn't include the time necessary to excuse the atheists from the room and admit the enlisted men."

Colonel Cathcart stopped in his tracks. "What atheists?" he bellowed defensively, his whole manner changing in a flash to one of virtuous and belligerent denial. "There are no atheists in my outfit! Atheism is against the law, isn't it?"

"No, sir."

"It isn't?" The colonel was surprised. "Then it's un-American, isn't it?"

"I'm not sure, sir," answered the chaplain.

"Well, I am!" the colonel declared. "I'm not going to disrupt our religious services just to accommodate a bunch of lousy atheists. They're getting no special privileges from me. They can stay right where they are and pray with the rest of us. And what's all this about enlisted men? Just how the hell do they get into this act?"

The chaplain felt his face flush. "I'm sorry, sir. I just assumed you would want the enlisted men to be present, since they would be going along on the same mission."

"Well, I don't. They've got a God and a chaplain of their own, haven't they?"

"No, sir."

"What are you talking about? You mean they pray to the same God we do?"

"Yes, sir."

"And He *listens?*"

"I think so, sir."

"Well, I'll be damned," remarked the colonel, and he snorted to himself in quizzical amusement. His spirits drooped suddenly a moment later, and he ran his hand nervously over his short, black, graying curls. "Do you really think it's a good idea to let the enlisted men in?" he asked with concern.

"I should think it only proper, sir."

"I'd like to keep them out," confided the colonel, and began cracking his knuckles savagely as he wandered back and forth. "Oh, don't get me wrong, Chaplain. It isn't that I think the enlisted men are dirty, common and inferior. It's that we just don't have enough room. Frankly, though, I'd just as soon the officers and enlisted men didn't fraternize in the briefing room. They see enough of each other during the mission, it seems to me. Some of my very best friends are enlisted men, you understand, but that's about as close as I care to let them come. Honestly now, Chaplain, you wouldn't want your sister to marry an enlisted man, would you?"

"My sister is an enlisted man, sir," the chaplain replied.

The colonel stopped in his tracks again and eyed the chaplain sharply to make certain he was not being ridiculed. "Just what do you mean by that remark, Chaplain? Are you trying to be funny?"

"Oh, no, sir," the chaplain hastened to explain with a look of excruciating discomfort. "She's a master sergeant in the Marines."

The colonel had never liked the chaplain and now he loathed and distrusted him. He experienced a keen premonition of danger and wondered if the chaplain too was plotting against him, if the chaplain's reticent, unimpressive manner was really just a sinister disguise masking a fiery ambition that, way down deep, was crafty and unscrupulous. There was something funny about the chaplain, and the colonel soon detected what it was. The chaplain was standing stiffly at attention, for the colonel had forgotten to put him at ease. Let him stay that way, the colonel decided vindictively, just to show him who was boss and to safeguard himself against any loss of dignity that might devolve from his acknowledging the omission.

Colonel Cathcart was drawn hypnotically toward the window with a massive, dull stare of moody introspection. The enlisted men were always treacherous, he decided. He looked downward in mournful gloom at the skeet-shooting range he had ordered built for the officers on his headquarters staff, and he recalled the mortifying afternoon General Dreedle had tongue-lashed him ruthlessly in front of Colonel Korn and Major Danby and ordered him to throw open the range to all the enlisted men and officers on combat duty. The skeet-shooting range had been a real black eye for him, Colonel Cathcart was forced to conclude. He was positive that General Dreedle had never forgotten it, even though he was positive that General Dreedle didn't even remember it, which was really very unjust, Colonel Cathcart lamented, since the idea of a skeet-shooting range itself should have been a real feather in his cap, even though it had been such a real black eye. Colonel Cathcart was helpless to assess exactly how much ground he had gained or lost with his goddam skeet-shooting range and wished that Colonel Korn were in his office right then to evaluate the entire episode for him still one more time and assuage his fears.

It was all very perplexing, all very discouraging. Colonel Cathcart took the cigarette holder out of his mouth, stood it on end inside the pocket of his shirt, and began gnawing on the fingernails of both hands grievously. Everybody was against him, and he was sick to his soul that Colonel Korn was not with him in this moment of crisis to help him decide what to do about the prayer meetings. He had almost no faith at all in the chaplain, who was still only a captain. "Do you think," he asked, "that keeping the enlisted men out might interfere with our chances of getting results?"

The chaplain hesitated, feeling himself on unfamiliar ground again. "Yes, sir," he replied finally. "I think it's conceivable that such an action could interfere with your chances of having the prayers for a tighter bomb pattern answered."

"I wasn't even thinking about that!" cried the colonel, with his eyes blinking and splashing like puddles. "You mean that God might even decide to punish me by giving us a *looser* bomb pattern?"

"Yes, sir," said the chaplain. "It's conceivable He might."

"The hell with it, then," the colonel asserted in a huff of independence. "I'm not going to set these damned prayer meetings up just to make things *worse* than they are." With a scornful snicker, he settled himself behind his desk, replaced the empty cigarette holder in his mouth and lapsed into parturient silence for a few moments. "Now that I think about it," he confessed, as much to himself as to the chaplain, "having the men pray to God probably wasn't such a hot idea anyway. The editors of *The Saturday Evening Post* might not have cooperated."

The colonel abandoned his project with remorse, for he had conceived it entirely on his own and had hoped to unveil it as a striking demonstration to everyone that he had no real need for Colonel Korn. Once it was gone, he was glad to be rid of it, for he had been troubled from the start by the danger of instituting the plan without first checking it out with Colonel Korn. He heaved an immense sigh of contentment. He had a much higher opinion of himself now that his idea was abandoned, for he had made a very wise decision, he felt, and, most important, he had made this wise decision without consulting Colonel Korn.

"Will that be all, sir?" asked the chaplain.

"Yeah," said Colonel Cathcart. "Unless you've got something else to suggest."

"No, sir. Only . . ."

The colonel lifted his eyes as though affronted and studied the chaplain with aloof distrust. "Only what, Chaplain?"

"Sir," said the chaplain, "some of the men are very upset since you raised the number of missions to sixty. They've asked me to speak to you about it."

The colonel was silent. The chaplain's face reddened to the roots of his sandy hair as he waited. The colonel kept him squirming a long time with a fixed, uninterested look devoid of all emotion.

"Tell them there's a war going on," he advised finally in a flat voice.

"Thank you, sir, I will," the chaplain replied in a flood of gratitude because the colonel had finally said something. "They were wondering why you couldn't requisition some of the replacement crews that are waiting in Africa to take their places and then let them go home."

"That's an administrative matter," the colonel said. "It's none of their business." He pointed languidly toward the wall. "Help yourself to a plum tomato, Chaplain. Go ahead, it's on me."

"Thank you, sir. Sir—"

"Don't mention it. How do you like living out there in the woods, Chaplain? Is everything hunky-dory?"

"Yes, sir."

"That's good. You get in touch with us if you need anything."

"Yes, sir. Thank you, sir. Sir—"

"Thanks for dropping around, Chaplain. I've got some work to do now. You'll let me know if you can think of anything for getting our names into *The Saturday Evening Post*, won't you?"

"Yes, sir, I will." The chaplain braced himself with a prodigious effort of the will and plunged ahead brazenly. "I'm particularly concerned about the condition of one of the bombardiers, sir. Yossarian."

The colonel glanced up quickly with a start of vague recognition. "Who?" he asked in alarm.

"Yossarian, sir."

"Yossarian?"

"Yes, sir. Yossarian. He's in a very bad way, sir. I'm afraid he won't be able to suffer much longer without doing something desperate."

"Is that a fact, Chaplain?"

"Yes, sir. I'm afraid it is."

The colonel thought about it in heavy silence for a few moments. "Tell him to trust in God," he advised finally.

"Thank you, sir," said the chaplain. "I will."

20

Corporal Whitcomb

The late-August morning sun was hot and steamy, and there was no breeze on the balcony. The chaplain moved slowly. He was downcast and burdened with self-reproach when he stepped without noise from the colonel's office on his rubber-soled and rubber-heeled brown shoes. He hated himself for what he construed to be his own cowardice. He had intended to take a much stronger stand with Colonel Cathcart on the matter of the sixty missions, to speak out with courage, logic and eloquence on a subject about which he had begun to feel very deeply. Instead he had failed miserably, had choked up once again in the face of opposition from a stronger personality. It was a familiar, ignominious experience, and his opinion of himself was low.

He choked up even more a second later when he spied Colonel Korn's tubby monochrome figure trotting up the curved, wide, yellow stone staircase toward him in lackadaisical haste from the great dilapidated lobby below with its lofty walls of cracked dark marble and circular floor of cracked grimy tile. The chaplain was even more frightened of Colonel Korn than he was of Colonel Cathcart. The swarthy, middle-aged lieutenant colonel with the rimless, icy glasses and faceted, bald, domelike pate that he was always touching sensitively with the tips of his splayed fingers disliked the chaplain and was impolite to him frequently. He kept the chaplain in a constant state of terror with his curt, derisive tongue and his knowing, cynical eyes that the chaplain was never brave enough to meet for more than an accidental second. Inevitably, the chaplain's attention, as he cowered meekly before him, focused on Colonel Korn's midriff, where the shirttails bunching up from inside his sagging belt and ballooning down over his waist gave him an appearance of slovenly girth and made him seem inches shorter than his middle height. Colonel Korn was an untidy disdainful man with an oily skin and deep, hard lines running almost straight down from his nose between his crepuscular jowls and his square, clefted chin. His face was dour, and he glanced at the chaplain without recognition as the two drew close on the staircase and prepared to pass.

"Hiya, Father," he said tonelessly without looking at the chaplain. "How's it going?"

"Good morning, sir," the chaplain replied, discerning wisely that Colonel Korn expected nothing more in the way of a response.

Colonel Korn was proceeding up the stairs without slackening his pace, and the chaplain resisted the temptation to remind him again that he was not a Catholic but an Anabaptist, and that it was therefore neither necessary nor correct to address him as Father. He was almost certain now that Colonel Korn remembered and that calling him Father with a look of such bland innocence was just another one of Colonel Korn's methods of taunting him because he was only an Anabaptist.

Colonel Korn halted without warning when he was almost by and came whirling back down upon the chaplain with a glare of infuriated suspicion. The chaplain was petrified.

"What are you doing with that plum tomato, Chaplain?" Colonel Korn demanded roughly.

The chaplain looked down his arm with surprise at the plum tomato Colonel Cathcart had invited him to take. "I got it in Colonel Cathcart's office, sir," he managed to reply.

"Does the colonel know you took it?"

"Yes, sir. He gave it to me."

"Oh, in that case I guess it's okay," Colonel Korn said, mollified. He smiled without warmth, jabbing the crumpled folds of his shirt back down inside his trousers with his thumbs. His eyes glinted keenly with a private and satisfying mischief. "What did Colonel Cathcart want to see you about, Father?" he asked suddenly.

The chaplain was tongue-tied with indecision for a moment. "I don't think I ought—"

"Saying prayers to the editors of *The Saturday Evening Post?*"

The chaplain almost smiled. "Yes, sir."

Colonel Korn was enchanted with his own intuition. He laughed disparagingly. "You know, I was afraid he'd begin thinking about something so ridiculous as soon as he saw this week's *Saturday Evening Post.* I hope you succeeded in showing him what an atrocious idea it is."

"He has decided against it, sir."

"That's good. I'm glad you convinced him that the editors of *The Saturday Evening Post* were not likely to run that same story twice just to give some publicity to some obscure colonel. How are things in the wilderness, Father? Are you able to manage out there?"

"Yes, sir. Everything is working out."

"That's good. I'm happy to hear you have nothing to complain about. Let us know if you need anything to make you comfortable. We all want you to have a good time out there."

"Thank you, sir. I will."

Noise of a growing stir rose from the lobby below. It was almost lunchtime, and the earliest arrivals were drifting into the headquarters mess halls, the enlisted men and officers separating into different dining halls on facing sides of the archaic rotunda. Colonel Korn stopped smiling.

"You had lunch with us here just a day or so ago, didn't you, Father?" he asked meaningfully.

"Yes, sir. The day before yesterday."

"That's what I thought," Colonel Korn said, and paused to let his point sink in. "Well, take it easy, Father. I'll see you around when it's time for you to eat here again."

"Thank you, sir."

The chaplain was not certain at which of the five officers' and five enlisted men's mess halls he was scheduled to have lunch that day, for the system of rotation worked out for him by Colonel Korn was complicated, and he had forgotten his records back in his tent. The chaplain was the only officer attached to Group Headquarters who did not reside in the moldering red stone Group Headquarters building itself or in any of the smaller satellite structures that rose about the grounds in disjuncted relationship. The chaplain lived in a clearing in the woods about four miles away between the officers' club and the first of the four squadron areas that stretched away from Group Headquarters in a distant line. The chaplain lived alone in a spacious, square tent that was also his office. Sounds of revelry traveled to him at night from the officers' club and kept him awake often as he turned and tossed on his cot in passive, half-voluntary exile. He was not able to gauge the effect of the mild pills he took occasionally to help him sleep and felt guilty about for days afterward.

The only one who lived with the chaplain in his clearing in the woods was Corporal Whitcomb, his assistant. Corporal Whitcomb, an atheist, was a disgruntled subordinate who felt he could do the chaplain's job much better than the chaplain was doing it and viewed himself, therefore, as an underprivileged victim of social inequity. He lived in a tent of his own as spacious and square as the chaplain's. He was openly rude and contemptuous to the chaplain once he discovered that the chaplain would let him get away with it. The borders of the two tents in the clearing stood no more than four or five feet apart.

It was Colonel Korn who had mapped out this way of life for the chaplain. One good reason for making the chaplain live outside the Group Headquarters building was Colonel Korn's theory that dwelling in a tent as most of his parishioners did would bring him into closer communication with them. Another good reason was the fact that having the chaplain around Headquarters all the time made the other officers uncomfortable. It was one thing to maintain liaison with the Lord, and they were all in favor of that; it was something else, though, to have Him hanging around twenty-four hours a day. All in all, as Colonel Korn described it to Major Danby, the jittery and goggle-eyed group operations officer, the chaplain had it pretty soft; he had little more to do than listen to the troubles of others, bury the dead, visit the bedridden and conduct religious services. And there were not so many dead for him to bury any more, Colonel Korn pointed out, since opposition from German fighter planes had virtually ceased and since close to ninety per cent of what fatalities there still were, he estimated, perished behind the enemy lines or disappeared inside clouds, where the chaplain had nothing to do with disposing of the remains. The religious services were certainly no great strain, either, since they were conducted only once a week at the Group Headquarters building and were attended by very few of the men.

Actually, the chaplain was learning to love it in his clearing in the woods. Both he and Corporal Whitcomb had been provided with every convenience so that neither might ever plead discomfort as a basis for seeking permission to return to the Headquarters building. The chaplain rotated his breakfasts, lunches and dinners in separate sets among the eight squadron mess halls and ate every fifth meal in the enlisted men's mess at Group Headquarters and every tenth meal at the officers' mess there. Back home in Wisconsin the chaplain had been very fond of gardening, and his heart welled with a glorious impression of fertility and fruition each time he contemplated the low, prickly boughs of the stunted trees and the waist-high weeds and thickets by which he was almost walled in. In the spring he had longed to plant begonias and zinnias in a narrow bed around his tent but he had been deterred by his fear of Corporal Whitcomb's rancor. The chaplain relished the privacy and isolation of his verdant surroundings and the reveries and meditation that living there fostered. Fewer people came to him with their troubles than formerly, and he allowed himself a measure of gratitude for that too. The chaplain did not mix freely and was not comfortable in conversation. He missed his wife and his three small children, and she missed him.

What displeased Corporal Whitcomb most about the chaplain, apart from the fact that the chaplain believed in God, was his lack of initiative and aggressiveness. Corporal Whitcomb regarded the low attendance at religious services as a sad reflection of his own status. His mind germinated feverishly with challenging new ideas for sparking the great spiritual revival of which he dreamed himself the architect—box lunches, church socials, form letters to the families of men killed and injured in combat, censorship, Bingo. But the chaplain blocked him. Corporal Whitcomb bridled with vexation beneath the chaplain's restraint, for he spied room for improvement everywhere. It was people like the chaplain, he concluded, who were responsible for giving religion such a bad name and making pariahs out of them both. Unlike the chaplain, Corporal Whitcomb detested the seclusion of the clearing in the woods. One of the first things he intended to do after he deposed the chaplain was move back into the Group Headquarters building, where he could be right in the thick of things.

When the chaplain drove back into the clearing after leaving Colonel Korn, Corporal Whitcomb was outside in the muggy haze talking in conspiratorial tones to a strange chubby man in a maroon corduroy bathrobe and gray flannel pajamas. The chaplain recognized the bathrobe and pajamas as official hospital attire. Neither of the two men gave him any sign of recognition. The stranger's gums had been painted purple; his corduroy bathrobe was decorated in back with a picture of a B-25 nosing through orange bursts of flak and in front with six neat rows of tiny bombs signifying sixty combat missions flown. The chaplain was so struck by the sight that he stopped to stare. Both men broke off their conversation and waited in stony silence for him to go. The chaplain hurried inside his tent. He heard, or imagined he heard, them tittering.

Corporal Whitcomb walked in a moment later and demanded, "What's doing?"

"There isn't anything new," the chaplain replied with averted eyes. "Was anyone here to see me?"

"Just that crackpot Yossarian again. He's a real troublemaker, isn't he?"

"I'm not so sure he's a crackpot," the chaplain observed.

"That's right, take his part," said Corporal Whitcomb in an injured tone, and stamped out.

The chaplain could not believe that Corporal Whitcomb was offended again and had really walked out. As soon as he did realize it, Corporal Whitcomb walked back in.

"You always side with other people," Corporal Whitcomb accused. "You don't back up your men. That's one of the things that's wrong with you."

"I didn't intend to side with him," the chaplain apologized. "I was just making a statement."

"What did Colonel Cathcart want?"

"It wasn't anything important. He just wanted to discuss the possibility of saying prayers in the briefing room before each mission."

"All right, don't tell me," Corporal Whitcomb snapped and walked out again.

The chaplain felt terrible. No matter how considerate he tried to be, it seemed he always managed to hurt Corporal Whitcomb's feelings. He gazed down remorsefully and saw that the orderly forced upon him by Colonel Korn to keep his tent clean and attend to his belongings had neglected to shine his shoes again.

Corporal Whitcomb came back in. "You never trust me with information," he whined truculently. "You don't have confidence in your men. That's another one of the things that's wrong with you."

"Yes, I do," the chaplain assured him guiltily. "I have lots of confidence in you."

"Then how about those letters?"

"No, not now," the chaplain pleaded, cringing. "Not the letters. Please don't bring that up again. I'll let you know if I have a change of mind."

Corporal Whitcomb looked furious. "Is that so? Well, it's all right for you to just sit there and shake your head while I do all the work. Didn't you see that guy outside with all those pictures painted on his bathrobe?"

"Is he here to see me?"

"No," Corporal Whitcomb said, and walked out.

It was hot and humid inside the tent, and the chaplain felt himself turning damp. He listened like an unwilling eavesdropper to the muffled, indistinguishable drone of the lowered voices outside. As he sat inertly at the rickety bridge table that served as a desk, his lips were closed, his eyes were blank, and his face, with its pale ochre hue and ancient, confined clusters of minute acne pits, had the color and texture of an uncracked almond shell. He racked his memory for some clue to the origin of Corporal Whitcomb's bitterness toward him. In some way he was unable to fathom, he was convinced he had done him some unforgivable wrong. It seemed incredible that such lasting ire as Corporal Whitcomb's could have stemmed from his rejection of Bingo or the form letters home to the families of the men killed in combat. The chaplain was despondent with an acceptance of his own ineptitude. He had intended for some weeks to have a heart-to-heart talk with Corporal Whitcomb in order to find out what was bothering him, but was already ashamed of what he might find out.

Outside the tent, Corporal Whitcomb snickered. The other man chuckled. For a few precarious seconds, the chaplain tingled with a weird, occult sensation of having experienced the identical situation before in some prior time or existence. He endeavored to trap and nourish the impression in order to predict, and perhaps even control, what incident would occur next, but the afflatus melted away unproductively, as he had known beforehand it would. *Déjà vu.* The subtle, recurring confusion between illusion and reality that was characteristic of paramnesia fascinated the chaplain, and he knew a number of things about it. He knew, for example, that it was called paramnesia, and he was interested as well in such corollary optical phenomena as *jamais vu*, never seen, and *presque vu*, almost seen. There were terrifying, sudden moments when objects, concepts and even people that the chaplain had lived with almost all his life inexplicably took on an unfamiliar and irregular aspect that he had never seen before and which made them seem totally strange: *jamais vu.* And there were other moments when he almost saw absolute truth in brilliant flashes of clarity that almost came to him: *presque vu.* The episode of the naked man in the tree at Snowden's funeral mystified him thoroughly. It was not *déjà vu*, for at the time he had experienced no sensation of ever having seen a naked man in a tree at Snowden's funeral before. It was not *jamais vu*, since the apparition was not of someone, or something, familiar appearing to him in an unfamiliar guise. And it was certainly not *presque vu*, for the chaplain did see him.

A jeep started up with a backfire directly outside and roared away. Had the naked man in the tree at Snowden's funeral been merely a hallucination? Or had it been a true revelation? The chaplain trembled at the mere idea. He wanted desperately to confide in Yossarian, but each time he thought about the occurrence he decided not to think about it any further, although now that he did think about it he could not be sure that he ever really *had* thought about it.

Corporal Whitcomb sauntered back in wearing a shiny new smirk and leaned his elbow impertinently against the center pole of the chaplain's tent.

"Do you know who that guy in the red bathrobe was?" he asked boastfully. "That was a C.I.D. man with a fractured nose. He came down here from the hospital on official business. He's conducting an investigation."

The chaplain raised his eyes quickly in obsequious commiseration. "I hope you're not in any trouble. Is there anything I can do?"

"No, I'm not in any trouble," Corporal Whitcomb replied with a grin. "You are. They're going to crack down on you for signing Washington Irving's name to all those letters you've been signing Washington Irving's name to. How do you like that?"

"I haven't been signing Washington Irving's name to any letters," said the chaplain.

"You don't have to lie to me," Corporal Whitcomb answered. "I'm not the one you have to convince."

"But I'm not lying."

"I don't care whether you're lying or not. They're going to get you for intercepting Major Major's correspondence, too. A lot of that stuff is classified information."

"What correspondence?" asked the chaplain plaintively in rising exasperation. "I've never seen any of Major Major's correspondence."

"You don't have to lie to me," Corporal Whitcomb replied. "I'm not the one you have to convince."

"But I'm not lying!" protested the chaplain.

"I don't see why you have to shout at me," Corporal Whitcomb retorted with an injured look. He came away from the center pole and shook his finger at the chaplain for emphasis. "I just did you the biggest favor anybody ever did you in your whole life, and you don't even realize it. Every time he tries to report you to his superiors, somebody up at the hospital censors out the details. He's been going batty for weeks trying to turn you in. I just put a censor's okay on his letter without even reading it. That will make a very good impression for you up at C.I.D. headquarters. It will let them know that we're not the least bit afraid to have the whole truth about you come out."

The chaplain was reeling with confusion. "But you aren't authorized to censor letters, are you?"

"Of course not," Corporal Whitcomb answered. "Only officers are ever authorized to do that. I censored it in your name."

"But I'm not authorized to censor letters either. Am I?"

"I took care of that for you, too," Corporal Whitcomb assured him. "I signed somebody else's name for you."

"Isn't that forgery?"

"Oh, don't worry about that either. The only one who might complain in a case of forgery is the person whose name you forged, and I looked out for your interests by picking a dead man. I used Washington Irving's name." Corporal Whitcomb scrutinized the chaplain's face closely for some sign of rebellion and then breezed ahead confidently with concealed irony. "That was pretty quick thinking on my part, wasn't it?"

"I don't know," the chaplain wailed softly in a quavering voice, squinting with grotesque contortions of anguish and incomprehension. "I don't think I understand all you've been telling me. How will it make a good impression for me if you signed Washington Irving's name instead of my own?"

"Because they're convinced that you are Washington Irving. Don't you see? They'll know it was you."

"But isn't that the very belief we want to dispel? Won't this help them prove it?"

"If I thought you were going to be so stuffy about it, I wouldn't even have tried to help," Corporal Whitcomb declared indignantly, and walked out. A second later he walked back in. "I just did you the biggest favor anybody ever did you in your whole life and you don't even know it. You don't know how to show your appreciation. That's another one of the things that's wrong with you."

"I'm sorry," the chaplain apologized contritely. "I really am sorry. It's just that I'm so completely stunned by all you're telling me that I don't even realize what I'm saying. I'm really very grateful to you."

"Then how about letting me send out those form letters?" Corporal Whitcomb demanded immediately. "Can I begin working on the first drafts?"

The chaplain's jaw dropped in astonishment. "No, no," he groaned. "Not now."

Corporal Whitcomb was incensed. "I'm the best friend you've got and you don't even know it," he asserted belligerently, and walked out of the chaplain's tent. He walked back in. "I'm on your side and you don't even realize it. Don't you know what serious trouble you're in?

That C.I.D. man has gone rushing back to the hospital to write a brand-new report on you about that tomato."

"What tomato?" the chaplain asked, blinking.

"The plum tomato you were hiding in your hand when you first showed up here. There it is. The tomato you're still holding in your hand right this very minute!"

The chaplain unclenched his fingers with surprise and saw that he was still holding the plum tomato he had obtained in Colonel Cathcart's office. He set it down quickly on the bridge table. "I got this tomato from Colonel Cathcart," he said, and was struck by how ludicrous his explanation sounded. "He insisted I take it."

"You don't have to lie to me," Corporal Whitcomb answered. "I don't care whether you stole it from him or not."

"Stole it?" the chaplain exclaimed with amazement. "Why should I want to steal a plum tomato?"

"That's exactly what had us both stumped," said Corporal Whitcomb. "And then the C.I.D. man figured out you might have some important secret papers hidden away inside it."

The chaplain sagged limply beneath the mountainous weight of his despair. "I don't have any important secret papers hidden away inside it," he stated simply. "I didn't even want it to begin with. Here, you can have it. Take it and see for yourself."

"I don't want it."

"Please take it away," the chaplain pleaded in a voice that was barely audible. "I want to be rid of it."

"I don't want it," Corporal Whitcomb snapped again, and stalked out with an angry face, suppressing a smile of great jubilation at having forged a powerful new alliance with the C.I.D. man and at having succeeded again in convincing the chaplain that he was really displeased.

Poor Whitcomb, sighed the chaplain, and blamed himself for his assistant's malaise. He sat mutely in a ponderous, stultifying melancholy, waiting expectantly for Corporal Whitcomb to walk back in. He was disappointed as he heard the peremptory crunch of Corporal Whitcomb's footsteps recede into silence. There was nothing he wanted to do next. He decided to pass up lunch for a Milky Way and a Baby Ruth from his foot locker and a few swallows of lukewarm water from his canteen. He felt himself surrounded by dense, overwhelming fogs of possibilities in which he could perceive no glimmer of light. He dreaded what Colonel Cathcart would think when the news that he was suspected of being Washington Irving was brought to him, then fell to fretting over what Colonel Cathcart was already thinking about him for even having broached the subject of the sixty missions. There was so much unhappiness in the world, he reflected, bowing his head dismally beneath the tragic thought, and there was nothing he could do about anybody's, least of all his own.

21

General Dreedle

Colonel Cathcart was not thinking anything at all about the chaplain, but was tangled up in a brand-new, menacing problem of his own: *Yossarian!*

Yossarian! The mere sound of that execrable, ugly name made his blood run cold and his breath come in labored gasps. The chaplain's first mention of the name *Yossarian!* had tolled deep in his memory like a portentous gong. As soon as the latch of the door had clicked shut, the whole humiliating recollection of the naked man in formation came cascading down upon him in a mortifying, choking flood of stinging details. He began to perspire and tremble. There was a sinister and unlikely coincidence exposed that was too diabolical in implication to be anything less than the most hideous of omens. The name of the man who had stood naked in ranks that day to receive his Distinguished Flying Cross from General Dreedle had also been—*Yossarian!* And now it was a man named Yossarian who was threatening to make trouble over the sixty missions he had just ordered the men in his group to fly. Colonel Cathcart wondered gloomily if it was the same Yossarian.

He climbed to his feet with an air of intolerable woe and began moving about his office. He felt himself in the presence of the mysterious. The naked man in formation, he conceded cheerlessly, had been a real black eye for him. So had the tampering with the bomb line before the mission to Bologna and the seven-day delay in destroying the bridge at Ferrara, even though destroying the bridge at Ferrara finally, he remembered with glee, had been a real feather in his cap, although losing a plane there the second time around, he recalled in dejection, had been another black eye, even though he had won another real feather in his cap by getting a medal approved for the bombardier who had gotten him the real black eye in the first place by going around over the target twice. That bombardier's name, he remembered suddenly with another stupefying shock, had also been *Yossarian!* Now there were *three!* His viscous eyes bulged with astonishment and he whipped himself around in alarm to see what was taking place behind him. A moment ago there had been no Yossarians in his life; now they were multiplying like hobgoblins. He tried to make himself grow calm. Yossarian was not a common name; perhaps there were not really three Yossarians but only two Yossarians, or maybe even only one Yossarian—*but that really made no difference!* The colonel was still in grave peril. Intuition warned him that he was drawing close to some immense and inscrutable cosmic climax, and his broad, meaty, towering frame tingled from head to toe at the thought that Yossarian, whoever he would eventually turn out to be, was destined to serve as his nemesis.

Colonel Cathcart was not superstitious, but he did believe in omens and he sat right back down behind his desk and made a cryptic notation on his memorandum pad to look into the whole suspicious business of the Yossarians right away. He wrote his reminder to himself in a heavy and decisive hand, amplifying it sharply with a series of coded punctuation marks and underlining the whole message twice, so that it read:

Yossarian!!!(?)!

The colonel sat back when he had finished and was extremely pleased with himself for the prompt action he had just taken to meet this sinister crisis. *Yossarian*—the very sight of the name made him shudder. There were so many esses in it. It just had to be subversive. It was like the word *subversive* itself. It was like *seditious* and *insidious* too, and like *socialist*, *suspicious*, *fascist* and *Communist*. It was an odious, alien, distasteful name, a name that just did not inspire confidence. It was not at all like such clean, crisp, honest, American names as Cathcart, Peckem and Dreedle.

Colonel Cathcart rose slowly and began drifting about his office again. Almost unconsciously, he picked up a plum tomato from the top of one of the bushels and took a voracious bite. He made a wry face at once and threw the rest of the plum tomato into his wastebasket. The colonel did not like plum tomatoes, not even when they were his own, and these were not even his own. These had been purchased in different market places all over Pianosa by Colonel Korn under various identities, moved up to the colonel's farmhouse in the hills in the dead of night, and transported down to Group Headquarters the next morning for sale to Milo, who paid Colonel Cathcart and Colonel Korn premium prices for them. Colonel Cathcart often wondered if what they were doing with the plum tomatoes was legal, but Colonel Korn said it was, and he tried not to brood about it too often. He had no way of knowing whether or not the house in the hills was legal, either, since Colonel Korn had made all the arrangements. Colonel Cathcart did not know if he owned the house or rented it, from whom he had acquired it or how much, if anything, it was costing. Colonel Korn was the lawyer, and if Colonel Korn assured him that fraud, extortion, currency manipulation, embezzlement, income tax evasion and black-market speculations were legal, Colonel Cathcart was in no position to disagree with him.

All Colonel Cathcart knew about his house in the hills was that he had such a house and hated it. He was never so bored as when spending there the two or three days every other week necessary to sustain the illusion that his damp and drafty stone farmhouse in the hills was a golden palace of carnal delights. Officers' clubs everywhere pulsated with blurred but knowing accounts of lavish, hushed-up drinking and sex orgies there and of secret, intimate nights of ecstasy with the most beautiful, the most tantalizing, the most readily aroused and most easily satisfied Italian courtesans, film actresses, models and countesses. No such private nights of ecstasy or hushed-up drinking and sex orgies ever occurred. They might have occurred if either General Dreedle or General Peckem had once evinced an interest in taking part in orgies with him, but neither ever did, and the colonel was certainly not going to waste his time and energy making love to beautiful women unless there was something in it for him.

The colonel dreaded his dank lonely nights at his farmhouse and the dull, uneventful days. He had much more fun back at Group, browbeating everyone he wasn't afraid of. However, as Colonel Korn kept reminding him, there was not much glamour in having a farmhouse in the hills if he never used it. He drove off to his farmhouse each time in a mood of self-pity. He carried a shotgun in his jeep and spent the monotonous hours there shooting it at birds and at the plum tomatoes that did grow there in untended rows and were too much trouble to harvest.

Among those officers of inferior rank toward whom Colonel Cathcart still deemed it prudent to show respect, he included Major —— de Coverley, even though he did not want to and was not sure he even had to. Major —— de Coverley was as great a mystery to him as he was to Major Major and to everyone else who ever took notice of him. Colonel Cathcart had no idea whether to look up or look down in his attitude toward Major —— de Coverley. Major —— de Coverley was only a major, even though he was ages older than Colonel Cathcart; at the same time, so many other people treated Major —— de Coverley with such profound and fearful veneration that Colonel Cathcart had a hunch they might all know something. Major —— de Coverley was an ominous, incomprehensible presence who kept him constantly on edge and of whom even Colonel Korn tended to be wary. Everyone was afraid of him, and no one knew why. No one even knew Major —— de Coverley's first name, because no one had ever had the temerity to ask him. Colonel Cathcart knew that Major —— de Coverley was away and he rejoiced in his absence until it occurred to him that Major —— de Coverley might be away somewhere conspiring against him, and then he wished that Major —— de Coverley were back in his squadron where he belonged so that he could be watched.

In a little while Colonel Cathcart's arches began to ache from pacing back and forth so much. He sat down behind his desk again and resolved to embark upon a mature and systematic evaluation of the entire military situation. With the businesslike air of a man who knows how to get things done, he found a large white pad, drew a straight line down the middle and crossed it near the top, dividing the page into two blank columns of equal width. He rested a moment in critical rumination. Then he huddled over his desk, and at the head of the left column, in a cramped and finicky hand, he wrote, *"Black Eyes!!!"* At the top of the right column he wrote, *"Feathers in My Cap!!!!!"* He leaned back once more to inspect his chart admiringly from an objective perspective. After a few seconds of solemn deliberation, he licked the tip of his pencil carefully and wrote under *"Black Eyes!!!,"* after intent intervals:

Ferrara
Bologna (bomb line moved on map during)
Skeet range
Naked man in formation (after Avignon)

Then he added:

Food poisoning (during Bologna)

and

Moaning (epidemic of during Avignon briefing)

Then he added:

Chaplain (banging around officers' club every night)

He decided to be charitable about the chaplain, even though he did not like him, and under "*Feathers in My Cap!!!!!*" he wrote:

Chaplain (banging around officers' club every night)

The two chaplain entries, therefore, neutralized each other. Alongside "*Ferrara*" and "*Naked man in formation (after Avignon)*" he then wrote:

Yossarian!

Alongside "*Bologna (bomb line moved on map during)*" "*Food poisoning (during Bologna)*" and "*Moaning (epidemic of during Avignon briefing)*" he wrote in a bold, decisive hand:

?

Those entries labeled "*?*" were the ones he wanted to investigate immediately to determine if Yossarian had played any part in them.

Suddenly his arm began to shake, and he was unable to write any more. He rose to his feet in terror, feeling sticky and fat, and rushed to the open window to gulp in fresh air. His gaze fell on the skeet range, and he reeled away with a sharp cry of distress, his wild and feverish eyes scanning the walls of his office frantically as though they were swarming with Yossarians.

Nobody loved him. General Dreedle hated him, although General Peckem liked him, although he couldn't be sure, since Colonel Cargill, General Peckem's aide, undoubtedly had ambitions of his own and was probably sabotaging him with General Peckem at every opportunity. The only good colonel, he decided, was a dead colonel, except for himself. The only colonel he trusted was Colonel Moodus, and even *he* had an in with his father-in-law. Milo, of course, had been the big feather in his cap, although having his group bombed by Milo's planes had probably been a terrible black eye for him, even though Milo had ultimately stilled all protest in disclosing the huge net profit the syndicate had realized on the deal with the enemy and convincing everyone that bombing his own men and planes had therefore really been a commendable and very lucrative blow on the side of private enterprise. The colonel was insecure about Milo because other colonels were trying to lure him away, and Colonel Cathcart still had that lousy Big Chief White Halfoat in his group who that lousy, lazy Captain Black claimed was the one really responsible for the bomb line's being moved during the Big Siege of Bologna. Colonel Cathcart liked Big Chief White Halfoat because Big Chief White Halfoat kept punching that lousy Colonel Moodus in the nose every time he got drunk and Colonel Moodus was around. He wished that Big Chief White Halfoat would begin punching Colonel Korn in his fat face, too. Colonel Korn was a lousy smart aleck. Someone at Twenty-seventh Air Force Headquarters had it in for him and sent back every report he wrote with a blistering rebuke, and Colonel Korn had bribed a clever mail clerk there named Wintergreen to try to find out who it was. Losing that plane over Ferrara the second time around had not done him any good, he had to admit, and neither had having that other plane disappear inside that cloud—*that was one he hadn't even written down!* He tried to recall, longingly, if Yossarian had been lost in that plane in the cloud and realized that Yossarian could not possibly have been lost in that plane in the cloud if he was still around now raising such a big stink about having to fly a lousy five missions more.

Maybe sixty missions *were* too many for the men to fly, Colonel Cathcart reasoned, if Yossarian objected to flying them, but he then remembered that forcing his men to fly more missions than everyone else was the most tangible achievement he had going for him. As Colonel Korn often remarked, the war was crawling with group commanders who were merely doing their duty, and it required just some sort of dramatic gesture like making his group fly more combat missions than any other bomber group to spotlight his unique qualities of leadership. Certainly none of the generals seemed to object to what he was doing, although as far as he could detect they weren't particularly impressed either, which made him suspect that perhaps sixty combat missions were not nearly enough and that he ought to increase the number at once to seventy, eighty, a hundred, or even two hundred, three hundred, or six thousand!

Certainly he would be much better off under somebody suave like General Peckem than he was under somebody boorish and insensitive like General Dreedle, because General Peckem had the discernment, the intelligence and the Ivy League background to appreciate and enjoy him at his full value, although General Peckem had never given the slightest indication that he appreciated or enjoyed him at all. Colonel Cathcart felt perceptive enough to realize that visible signals of recognition were never necessary between sophisticated, self-assured people like himself and General Peckem who could warm to each other from a distance with innate mutual understanding. It was enough that they were of like kind, and he knew it was only a matter of waiting discreetly for preferment until the right time, although it rotted Colonel Cathcart's self-esteem to observe that General Peckem never deliberately sought him out and that he labored no harder to impress Colonel Cathcart with his epigrams and erudition than he did to impress anyone else in earshot, even enlisted men. Either Colonel Cathcart wasn't getting through to General Peckem or General Peckem was not the scintillating, discriminating, intellectual, forward-looking personality he pretended to be and it was really General Dreedle who was sensitive, charming, brilliant and sophisticated and under whom he would certainly be much better off, and suddenly Colonel Cathcart had absolutely no conception of how strongly he stood with anyone and began banging on his buzzer with his fist for Colonel Korn to come running into his office and assure him that everybody loved him, that Yossarian was a figment of his imagination, and that he was making wonderful progress in the splendid and valiant campaign he was waging to become a general.

Actually, Colonel Cathcart did not have a chance in hell of becoming a general. For one thing, there was ex-P.F.C. Wintergreen, who also wanted to be a general and who always distorted, destroyed, rejected or misdirected any correspondence by, for or about Colonel Cathcart that might do him credit. For another, there already was a general, General Dreedle, who knew that General Peckem was after his job but did not know how to stop him.

General Dreedle, the wing commander, was a blunt, chunky, barrel-chested man in his early fifties. His nose was squat and red, and he had lumpy white, bunched-up eyelids circling his small gray eyes like haloes of bacon fat. He had a nurse and a son-in-law, and he was prone to long, ponderous silences when he had not been drinking too much. General Dreedle had wasted too much of his time in the Army doing his job well, and now it was too late. New power alignments had coalesced without him and he was at a loss to cope with them. At unguarded moments his hard and sullen face slipped into a somber, preoccupied look of defeat and frustration. General Dreedle drank a great deal. His moods were arbitrary and unpredictable. "War is hell," he declared frequently, drunk or sober, and he really meant it, although that did not prevent him from making a good living out of it or from taking his son-in-law into the business with him, even though the two bickered constantly.

"That bastard," General Dreedle would complain about his son-in-law with a contemptuous grunt to anyone who happened to be standing beside him at the curve of the bar of the officers' club. "Everything he's got he owes to me. I made him, that lousy son of a bitch! He hasn't got brains enough to get ahead on his own."

"He thinks he knows everything," Colonel Moodus would retort in a sulking tone to his own audience at the other end of the bar. "He can't take criticism and he won't listen to advice."

"All he can do is give advice," General Dreedle would observe with a rasping snort. "If it wasn't for me, he'd still be a corporal."

General Dreedle was always accompanied by both Colonel Moodus and his nurse, who was as delectable a piece of ass as anyone who saw her had ever laid eyes on. General Dreedle's nurse was chubby, short and blond. She had plump dimpled checks, happy blue eyes, and neat curly turned-up hair. She smiled at everyone and never spoke at all unless she was spoken to. Her bosom was lush and her complexion clear. She was irresistible, and men edged away from her carefully. She was succulent, sweet, docile and dumb, and she drove everyone crazy but General Dreedle.

"You should see her naked," General Dreedle chortled with croupy relish, while his nurse stood smiling proudly right at his shoulder. "Back at Wing she's got a uniform in my room made of purple silk that's so tight her nipples stand out like bing cherries. Milo got me the fabric. There isn't even room enough for panties or a brassiere underneath. I make her wear it some nights when Moodus is around just to drive him crazy." General Dreedle laughed hoarsely. "You should see what goes on inside that blouse of hers every time she shifts her weight. She drives him out of his mind. The first time I catch him putting a hand on her or any other woman I'll bust the horny bastard right down to private and put him on K.P. for a year."

"He keeps her around just to drive me crazy," Colonel Moodus accused aggrievedly at the other end of the bar. "Back at Wing she's got a uniform made out of purple silk that's so tight her nipples stand out like bing cherries. There isn't even room for panties or a brassiere underneath. You should hear that silk rustle every time she shifts her weight. The first time I make a pass at her or any other girl he'll bust me right down to private and put me on K.P. for a year. She drives me out of my mind."

"He hasn't gotten laid since we shipped overseas," confided General Dreedle, and his square grizzled head bobbed with sadistic laughter at the fiendish idea. "That's one of the reasons I never let him out of my sight, just so he can't get to a woman. Can you imagine what that poor son of a bitch is going through?"

"I haven't been to bed with a woman since we shipped overseas," Colonel Moodus whimpered tearfully. "Can you imagine what I'm going through?"

General Dreedle could be as intransigent with anyone else when displeased as he was with Colonel Moodus. He had no taste for sham, tact or pretension, and his credo as a professional soldier was unified and concise: he believed that the young men who took orders from him should be willing to give up their lives for the ideals, aspirations and idiosyncrasies of the old men he took orders from. The officers and enlisted men in his command had identity for him only as military quantities. All he asked was that they do their work; beyond that, they were free to do whatever they pleased. They were free, as Colonel Cathcart was free, to force their men to fly sixty missions if they chose, and they were free, as Yossarian had been free, to stand in formation naked if they wanted to, although General Dreedle's granite jaw swung open at the sight and he went striding dictatorially right down the line to make certain that there really was a man wearing nothing but moccasins waiting at attention in ranks to receive a medal from him. General Dreedle was speechless. Colonel Cathcart began to faint when he spied Yossarian, and Colonel Korn stepped up behind him and squeezed his arm in a strong grip. The silence was grotesque. A steady warm wind flowed in from the beach, an old cart filled with dirty straw rumbled into view on the main road, drawn by a black donkey and driven by a farmer in a flopping hat and faded brown work clothes who paid no attention to the formal military ceremony taking place in the small field on his right.

At last General Dreedle spoke. "Get back in the car," he snapped over his shoulder to his nurse, who had followed him down the line. The nurse toddled away with a smile toward his brown staff car, parked about twenty yards away at the edge of the rectangular clearing. General Dreedle waited in austere silence until the car door slammed and then demanded, "Which one is this?"

Colonel Moodus checked his roster. "This one is Yossarian, Dad. He gets a Distinguished Flying Cross."

"Well, I'll be damned," mumbled General Dreedle, and his ruddy monolithic face softened with amusement. "Why aren't you wearing clothes, Yossarian?"

"I don't want to."

"What do you mean you don't want to? Why the hell don't you want to?"

"I just don't want to, sir."

"Why isn't he wearing clothes?" General Dreedle demanded over his shoulder of Colonel Cathcart.

"He's talking to you," Colonel Korn whispered over Colonel Cathcart's shoulder from behind, jabbing his elbow sharply into Colonel Cathcart's back.

"Why isn't he wearing clothes?" Colonel Cathcart demanded of Colonel Korn with a look of acute pain, tenderly nursing the spot where Colonel Korn had just jabbed him.

"Why isn't he wearing clothes?" Colonel Korn demanded of Captain Piltchard and Captain Wren.

"A man was killed in his plane over Avignon last week and bled all over him," Captain Wren replied. "He swears he's never going to wear a uniform again."

"A man was killed in his plane over Avignon last week and bled all over him," Captain Korn reported directly to General Dreedle. "His uniform hasn't come back from the laundry yet."

"Where are his other uniforms?"

"They're in the laundry, too."

"What about his underwear?" General Dreedle demanded.

"All his underwear's in the laundry, too," answered Colonel Korn.

"That sounds like a lot of crap to me," General Dreedle declared.

"It is a lot of crap, sir," Yossarian said.

"Don't you worry, sir," Colonel Cathcart promised General Dreedle with a threatening look at Yossarian. "You have my personal word for it that this man will be severely punished."

"What the hell do I care if he's punished or not?" General Dreedle replied with surprise and irritation. "He's just won a medal. If he wants to receive it without any clothes on, what the hell business is it of yours?"

"Those are my sentiments exactly, sir!" Colonel Cathcart echoed with resounding enthusiasm and mopped his brow with a damp white handkerchief. "But would you say that, sir, even in the light of General Peckem's recent memorandum on the subject of appropriate military attire in combat areas?"

"Peckem?" General Dreedle's face clouded.

"Yes, sir, sir," said Colonel Cathcart obsequiously. "General Peckem even recommends that we send our men into combat in full-dress uniform so they'll make a good impression on the enemy when they're shot down."

"Peckem?" repeated General Dreedle, still squinting with bewilderment. "Just what the hell does Peckem have to do with it?"

Colonel Korn jabbed Colonel Cathcart sharply again in the back with his elbow.

"Absolutely nothing, sir!" Colonel Cathcart responded sprucely, wincing in extreme pain and gingerly rubbing the spot where Colonel Korn had just jabbed him again. "And that's exactly why I decided to take absolutely no action at all until I first had an opportunity to discuss it with you. Shall we ignore it completely, sir?"

General Dreedle ignored him completely, turning away from him in baleful scorn to hand Yossarian his medal in its case.

"Get my girl back from the car," he commanded Colonel Moodus crabbily, and waited in one spot with his scowling face down until his nurse had rejoined him.

"Get word to the office right away to kill that directive I just issued ordering the men to wear neckties on the combat missions," Colonel Cathcart whispered to Colonel Korn urgently out of the corner of his mouth.

"I told you not to do it," Colonel Korn snickered. "But you just wouldn't listen to me."

"Shhhh!" Colonel Cathcart cautioned. "Goddammit, Korn, what did you do to my back?"

Colonel Korn snickered again.

General Dreedle's nurse always followed General Dreedle everywhere he went, even into the briefing room just before the mission to Avignon, where she stood with her asinine smile at the side of the platform and bloomed like a fertile oasis at General Dreedle's shoulder in her pink-and-green uniform. Yossarian looked at her and fell in love, desperately. His spirits sank, leaving him empty inside and numb. He sat gazing in clammy want at her full red lips and dimpled cheeks as he listened to Major Danby describe in a monotonous, didactic male drone the heavy concentrations of flak awaiting them at Avignon, and he moaned in deep despair suddenly at the thought that he might never see again this lovely woman to whom he had never spoken a word and whom he now loved so pathetically. He throbbed and ached with sorrow, fear and desire as he stared at her; she was so beautiful. He worshipped the ground she stood on. He licked his parched, thirsting lips with a sticky tongue and moaned in misery again, loudly enough this time to attract the startled, searching glances of the men sitting around him on the rows of crude wooden benches in their chocolate-colored coveralls and stitched white parachute harnesses.

Nately turned to him quickly with alarm. "What is it?" he whispered. "What's the matter?"

Yossarian did not hear him. He was sick with lust and mesmerized with regret. General Dreedle's nurse was only a little chubby, and his senses were stuffed to congestion with the yellow radiance of her hair and the unfelt pressure of her soft short fingers, with the rounded, untasted wealth of her nubile breasts in her Army-pink shirt that was opened wide at the throat and with the rolling, ripened, triangular confluences of her belly and thighs in her tight, slick forest-green gabardine officer's pants. He drank her in insatiably from head to painted toenail. He never wanted to lose her. "Oooooooooooooh," he moaned again, and this time the whole room rippled at his quavering, drawn-out cry. A wave of startled uneasiness broke over the officers on the dais, and even Major Danby, who had begun synchronizing the watches, was distracted momentarily as he counted out the seconds and almost had to begin again. Nately followed Yossarian's transfixed gaze down the long frame auditorium until he came to General Dreedle's nurse. He blanched with trepidation when he guessed what was troubling Yossarian.

"Cut it out, will you?" Nately warned in a fierce whisper.

"Ooooooooooooooooooooh," Yossarian moaned a fourth time, this time loudly enough for everyone to hear him distinctly.

"Are you crazy?" Nately hissed vehemently. "You'll get into trouble."

"Ooooooooooooooooooooh," Dunbar answered Yossarian from the opposite end of the room.

Nately recognized Dunbar's voice. The situation was now out of control, and he turned away with a small moan. "Ooh."

"Oooooooooooooooooooh," Dunbar moaned back at him.

"Oooooooooooooooooooh," Nately moaned out loud in exasperation when he realized that he had just moaned.

"Ooooooooooooooooooooh," Dunbar moaned back at him again.

"Oooooooooooooooooooooh," someone entirely new chimed in from another section of the room, and Nately's hair stood on end.

Yossarian and Dunbar both replied while Nately cringed and hunted about futilely for some hole in which to hide and take Yossarian with him. A sprinkling of people were smothering laughter. An elfin impulse possessed Nately and he moaned intentionally the next time there was a lull. Another new voice answered. The flavor of disobedience was titillating, and Nately moaned deliberately again, the next time he could squeeze one in edgewise. Still another new voice echoed him. The room was boiling irrepressibly into bedlam. An eerie hubbub of voices was rising. Feet were scuffled, and things began to drop from people's fingers—pencils, computers, map cases, clattering steel flak helmets. A number of men who were not moaning were now giggling openly, and there was no telling how far the unorganized insurrection of moaning might have gone if General Dreedle himself had not come forward to quell it, stepping out determinedly in the center of the platform directly in front of Major Danby, who, with his earnest, persevering head down, was still concentrating on his wrist watch and saying ". . . twenty-five seconds . . . twenty . . . fifteen . . ." General Dreedle's great, red domineering face was gnarled with perplexity and oaken with awesome resolution.

"That will be all, men," he ordered tersely, his eyes glaring with disapproval and his square jaw firm, and that's all there was. "I run a fighting outfit," he told them sternly, when the room had grown absolutely quiet and the men on the benches were all cowering sheepishly, "and there'll be no more moaning in this group as long as I'm in command. Is that clear?"

It was clear to everybody but Major Danby, who was still concentrating on his wrist watch and counting down the seconds aloud. ". . . four . . . three . . . two . . . one . . . time!" called out Major Danby, and raised his eyes triumphantly to discover that no one had been listening to him and that he would have to begin all over again. "Ooooh," he moaned in frustration.

"*What was that?*" roared General Dreedle incredulously, and whirled around in a murderous rage upon Major Danby, who staggered back in terrified confusion and began to quail and perspire. "*Who is this man?*"

"M-major Danby, sir," Colonel Cathcart stammered. "My group operations officer."

"Take him out and shoot him," ordered General Dreedle.

"S-sir?"

"I said take him out and shoot him. Can't you hear?"

"Yes, sir!" Colonel Cathcart responded smartly, swallowing hard, and turned in a brisk manner to his chauffeur and his meteorologist. "Take Major Danby out and shoot him."

"S-sir?" his chauffeur and his meteorologist stammered.

"I said take Major Danby out and shoot him," Colonel Cathcart snapped. "Can't you hear?"

The two young lieutenants nodded lumpishly and gaped at each other in stunned and flaccid reluctance, each waiting for the other to initiate the procedure of taking Major Danby outside and shooting him. Neither had ever taken Major Danby outside and shot him before. They inched their way dubiously toward Major Danby from opposite sides. Major Danby was white with fear. His legs collapsed suddenly and he began to fall, and the two young lieutenants sprang forward and seized him under both arms to save him from slumping to the floor. Now that they had Major Danby, the rest seemed easy, but there were no guns. Major Danby began to cry. Colonel Cathcart wanted to rush to his side and comfort him, but did not want to look like a sissy in front of General Dreedle. He remembered that Appleby and Havermeyer always brought their .45 automatics on the missions, and he began to scan the rows of men in search of them.

As soon as Major Danby began to cry, Colonel Moodus, who had been vacillating wretchedly on the sidelines, could restrain himself no longer and stepped out diffidently toward General Dreedle with a sickly air of self-sacrifice. "I think you'd better wait a minute, Dad," he suggested hesitantly. "I don't think you *can* shoot him."

General Dreedle was infuriated by his intervention. "Who the hell says I can't?" he thundered pugnaciously in a voice loud enough to rattle the whole building. Colonel Moodus, his face flushing with embarrassment, bent close to whisper into his ear. "Why the hell can't I?" General Dreedle bellowed. Colonel Moodus whispered some more. "You mean I can't shoot anyone I want to?" General Dreedle demanded with uncompromising indignation. He pricked up his ears with interest as Colonel Moodus continued whispering. "Is that a fact?" he inquired, his rage tamed by curiosity.

"Yes, Dad. I'm afraid it is."

"I guess you think you're pretty goddam smart, don't you?" General Dreedle lashed out at Colonel Moodus suddenly.

Colonel Moodus turned crimson again. "No, Dad, it isn't—"

"All right, let the insubordinate son of a bitch go," General Dreedle snarled, turning bitterly away from his son-in-law and barking peevishly at Colonel Cathcart's chauffeur and Colonel Cathcart's meteorologist. "But get him out of this building and keep him out. And let's continue this goddam briefing before the war ends. I've never seen so much incompetence."

Colonel Cathcart nodded lamely at General Dreedle and signaled his men hurriedly to push Major Danby outside the building. As soon as Major Danby had been pushed outside, though, there was no one to continue the briefing. Everyone gawked at everyone else in oafish surprise. General Dreedle turned purple with rage as nothing happened. Colonel Cathcart had no idea what to do. He was about to begin moaning aloud when Colonel Korn came to the rescue by stepping forward and taking control. Colonel Cathcart sighed with enormous, tearful relief, almost overwhelmed with gratitude.

"Now, men, we're going to synchronize our watches," Colonel Korn began promptly in a sharp, commanding manner, rolling his eyes flirtatiously in General Dreedle's direction. "We're going to synchronize our watches one time and one time only, and if it doesn't come off in that one time, General Dreedle and I are going to want to know why. Is that clear?" He fluttered his eyes toward General Dreedle again to make sure his plug had registered. "Now set your watches for nine-eighteen."

Colonel Korn synchronized their watches without a single hitch and moved ahead with confidence. He gave the men the colors of the day and reviewed the weather conditions with an agile, flashy versatility, casting sidelong, simpering looks at General Dreedle every few seconds to draw increased encouragement from the excellent impression he saw he was making. Preening and pruning himself effulgently and strutting vaingloriously about the platform as he picked up momentum, he gave the men the colors of the day again and shifted nimbly into a rousing pep talk on the importance of the bridge at Avignon to the war effort and the obligation of each man on the mission to place love of country above love of life. When his inspiring dissertation was finished, he gave the men the colors of the day still one more time, stressed the angle of approach and reviewed the weather conditions again. Colonel Korn felt himself at the full height of his powers. He *belonged* in the spotlight.

Comprehension dawned slowly on Colonel Cathcart; when it came, he was struck dumb. His face grew longer and longer as he enviously watched Colonel Korn's treachery continue, and he was almost afraid to listen when General Dreedle moved up beside him and, in a whisper blustery enough to be heard throughout the room, demanded,

"Who is that man?"

Colonel Cathcart answered with wan foreboding, and General Dreedle then cupped his hand over his mouth and whispered something that made Colonel Cathcart's face glow with immense joy. Colonel Korn saw and quivered with uncontainable rapture. Had he just been promoted in the field by General Dreedle to full colonel? He could not endure the suspense. With a masterful flourish, he brought the briefing to a close and turned expectantly to receive ardent congratulations from General Dreedle—who was already striding out of the building without a glance backward, trailing his nurse and Colonel Moodus behind him. Colonel Korn was stunned by this disappointing sight, but only for an instant. His eyes found Colonel Cathcart, who was still standing erect in a grinning trance, and he rushed over jubilantly and began pulling on his arm.

"What'd he say about me?" he demanded excitedly in a fervor of proud and blissful anticipation. "What did General Dreedle say?"

"He wanted to know who you were."

"I know that. I know that. But what'd he say about me? What'd he say?"

"You make him sick."

22

Milo the Mayor

That was the mission on which Yossarian lost his nerve. Yossarian lost his nerve on the mission to Avignon because Snowden lost his guts, and Snowden lost his guts because their pilot that day was Huple, who was only fifteen years old, and their co-pilot was Dobbs, who was even worse and who wanted Yossarian to join with him in a plot to murder Colonel Cathcart. Huple was a good pilot, Yossarian knew, but he was only a kid, and Dobbs had no confidence in him, either, and wrested the controls away without warning after they had dropped their bombs, going berserk in mid-air and tipping the plane over into that heart-stopping, ear-splitting, indescribably petrifying fatal dive that tore Yossarian's earphones free from their connection and hung him helplessly to the roof of the nose by the top of his head.

Oh, God! Yossarian had shrieked soundlessly as he felt them all falling. *Oh, God! Oh, God! Oh, God! Oh, God!* he had shrieked beseechingly through lips that could not open as the plane fell and he dangled without weight by the top of his head until Huple managed to seize the controls back and leveled the plane out down inside the crazy, craggy, patchwork canyon of crashing antiaircraft fire from which they had climbed away and from which they would now have to escape again. Almost at once there was a thud and a hole the size of a big fist in the Plexiglas. Yossarian's cheeks were stinging with shimmering splinters. There was no blood.

"What happened? What happened?" he cried, and trembled violently when he could not hear his own voice in his ears. He was cowed by the empty silence on the intercom and almost too horrified to move as he crouched like a trapped mouse on his hands and knees and waited without daring to breathe until he finally spied the gleaming cylindrical jack plug of his headset swinging back and forth in front of his eyes and jammed it back into its receptacle with fingers that rattled. *Oh, God!* he kept shrieking with no abatement of terror as the flak thumped and mushroomed all about him. *Oh, God!*

Dobbs was weeping when Yossarian jammed his jack plug back into the intercom system and was able to hear again.

"Help him, help him," Dobbs was sobbing. "Help him, help him."

"Help who? Help who?" Yossarian called back. "Help who?"

"The bombardier, the bombardier," Dobbs cried. "He doesn't answer. Help the bombardier, help the bombardier."

"I'm the bombardier," Yossarian cried back at him. "I'm the bombardier. I'm all right. I'm all right."

"Then help him, help him," Dobbs wept. "Help him, help him."

"Help who? Help who?"

"The radio-gunner," Dobbs begged. "Help the radio-gunner."

"I'm cold," Snowden whimpered feebly over the intercom system then in a bleat of plaintive agony. "Please help me. I'm cold."

And Yossarian crept out through the crawlway and climbed up over the bomb bay and down into the rear section of the plane where Snowden lay on the floor wounded and freezing to death in a yellow splash of sunlight near the new tail gunner lying stretched out on the floor beside him in a dead faint.

Dobbs was the worst pilot in the world and knew it, a shattered wreck of a virile young man who was continually striving to convince his superiors that he was no longer fit to pilot a plane. None of his superiors would listen, and it was the day the number of missions was raised to sixty that Dobbs stole into Yossarian's tent while Orr was out looking for gaskets and disclosed the plot he had formulated to murder Colonel Cathcart. He needed Yossarian's assistance.

"You want us to kill him in cold blood?" Yossarian objected.

"That's right," Dobbs agreed with an optimistic smile, encouraged by Yossarian's ready grasp of the situation. "We'll shoot him to death with the Luger I brought back from Sicily that nobody knows I've got."

"I don't think I could do it," Yossarian concluded, after weighing the idea in silence awhile.

Dobbs was astonished. "Why not?"

"Look. Nothing would please me more than to have the son of a bitch break his neck or get killed in a crash or to find out that someone else had shot him to death. But I don't think I could kill him."

"He'd do it to you," Dobbs argued. "In fact, you're the one who told me he *is* doing it to us by keeping us in combat so long."

"But I don't think I could do it to him. He's got a right to live, too, I guess."

"Not as long as he's trying to rob you and me of our right to live. What's the matter with you?" Dobbs was flabbergasted. "I used to listen to you arguing that same thing with Clevinger. And look what happened to him. Right inside that cloud."

"Stop shouting, will you?" Yossarian shushed him.

"I'm not shouting!" Dobbs shouted louder, his face red with revolutionary fervor. His eyes and nostrils were running, and his palpitating crimson lower lip was splattered with a foamy dew. "There must have been close to a hundred men in the group who had finished their fifty-five missions when he raised the number to sixty. There must have been at least another hundred like you with just a couple more to fly. He's going to kill us all if we let him go on forever. We've got to kill him first."

Yossarian nodded expressionlessly, without committing himself. "Do you think we could get away with it?"

"I've got it all worked out. I—"

"Stop shouting, for Christ's sake!"

"I'm not shouting. I've got it—"

"Will you stop shouting!"

"I've got it all worked out," Dobbs whispered, gripping the side of Orr's cot with white-knuckled hands to constrain them from waving. "Thursday morning when he's due back from that goddam farmhouse of his in the hills, I'll sneak up through the woods to that hairpin turn in the road and hide in the bushes. He has to slow down there, and I can watch the road in both directions to make sure there's no one else around. When I see him coming, I'll shove a big log out into the road to make him stop his jeep. Then I'll step out of the bushes with my Luger and shoot him in the head until he's dead. I'll bury the gun, come back down through the woods to the squadron, and go about my business just like everybody else. What could possibly go wrong?"

Yossarian had followed each step attentively. "Where do I come in?" he asked in puzzlement.

"I couldn't do it without you," Dobbs explained. "I need you to tell me to go ahead."

Yossarian found it hard to believe him. "Is that all you want me to do? Just tell you to go ahead?"

"That's all I need from you," Dobbs answered. "Just tell me to go ahead and I'll blow his brains out all by myself the day after tomorrow." His voice was accelerating with emotion and rising again. "I'd like to shoot Colonel Korn in the head, too, while we're at it, although I'd like to spare Major Danby, if that's all right with you. Then I'd like to murder Appleby and Havermeyer also, and after we finish murdering Appleby and Havermeyer I'd like to murder McWatt."

"McWatt?" cried Yossarian, almost jumping up in horror. "McWatt's a friend of mine. What do you want from McWatt?"

"I don't know," Dobbs confessed with an air of floundering embarrassment. "I just thought that as long as we were murdering Appleby and Havermeyer we might as well murder McWatt too. Don't you want to murder McWatt?"

Yossarian took a firm stand. "Look, I might keep interested in this if you stop shouting it all over the island and if you stick to killing Colonel Cathcart. But if you're going to turn this into a blood bath, you can forget about me."

"All right, all right." Dobbs sought to placate him. "Just Colonel Cathcart. Should I do it? Tell me to go ahead."

Yossarian shook his head. "I don't think I could tell you to go ahead."

Dobbs was frantic. "I'm willing to compromise," he pleaded vehemently. "You don't have to tell me to go ahead. Just tell me it's a good idea. Okay? Is it a good idea?"

Yossarian still shook his head. "It would have been a great idea if you had gone ahead and done it without even speaking to me. Now it's too late. I don't think I can tell you anything. Give me some more time. I might change my mind."

"Then it *will* be too late."

Yossarian kept shaking his head. Dobbs was disappointed. He sat for a moment with a hangdog look, then spurted to his feet suddenly and stamped away to have another impetuous crack at persuading Doc Daneeka to ground him, knocking over Yossarian's washstand with his hip when he lurched around and tripping over the fuel line of the stove Orr was still constructing. Doc Daneeka withstood Dobbs's blustering and gesticulating attack with a series of impatient nods and sent him to the medical tent to describe his symptoms to Gus and Wes, who painted his gums purple with gentian-violet solution the moment he started to talk. They painted his toes purple, too, and forced a laxative down his throat when he opened his mouth again to complain, and then they sent him away.

Dobbs was in even worse shape than Hungry Joe, who could at least fly missions when he was not having nightmares. Dobbs was almost as bad as Orr, who seemed happy as an undersized, grinning lark with his deranged and galvanic giggle and shivering warped buck teeth and who was sent along for a rest leave with Milo and Yossarian on the trip to Cairo for eggs when Milo bought cotton instead and took off at dawn for Istanbul with his plane packed to the gun turrets with exotic spiders and unripened red bananas. Orr was one of the homeliest freaks Yossarian had ever encountered, and one of the most attractive. He had a raw bulgy face, with hazel eyes squeezing from their sockets like matching brown halves of marbles and thick, wavy particolored hair sloping up to a peak on the top of his head like a pomaded pup tent. Orr was knocked down into the water or had an engine shot out almost every time he went up, and he began jerking on Yossarian's arm like a wild man after they had taken off for Naples and come down in Sicily to find the scheming, cigar-smoking, ten-year-old pimp with the two twelve-year-old virgin sisters waiting for them in town in front of the hotel in which there was room for only Milo. Yossarian pulled back from Orr adamantly, gazing with some concern and bewilderment at Mt. Etna instead of Mt. Vesuvius and wondering what they were doing in Sicily instead of Naples as Orr kept entreating him in a tittering, stuttering, concupiscent turmoil to go along with him behind the scheming ten-year-old pimp to his two twelve-year-old virgin sisters who were not really virgins and not really sisters and who were really only twenty-eight.

"Go with him," Milo instructed Yossarian laconically. "Remember your mission."

"All right," Yossarian yielded with a sigh, remembering his mission. "But at least let me try to find a hotel room first so I can get a good night's sleep afterward."

"You'll get a good night's sleep with the girls," Milo replied with the same air of intrigue. "Remember your mission."

But they got no sleep at all, for Yossarian and Orr found themselves jammed into the same double bed with the two twelve-year-old twenty-eight-year-old prostitutes, who turned out to be oily and obese and who kept waking them up all night long to ask them to switch partners. Yossarian's perceptions were soon so fuzzy that he paid no notice to the beige turban the fat one crowding into him kept wearing until late the next morning when the scheming ten-year-old pimp with the Cuban panatella snatched it off in public in a bestial caprice that exposed in the brilliant Sicilian daylight her shocking, misshapen and denudate skull. Vengeful neighbors had shaved her hair to the gleaming bone because she had slept with Germans. The girl screeched in feminine outrage and waddled comically after the scheming ten-year-old pimp, her grisly, bleak, violated scalp slithering up and down ludicrously around the queer darkened wart of her face like something bleached and obscene. Yossarian had never laid eyes on anything so bare before. The pimp spun the turban high on his finger like a trophy and kept himself skipping inches ahead of her finger tips as he led her in a tantalizing circle around the square congested with people who were howling with laughter and pointing to Yossarian with derision when Milo strode up with a grim look of haste and puckered his lips reprovingly at the unseemly spectacle of so much vice and frivolity. Milo insisted on leaving at once for Malta.

"We're sleepy," Orr whined.

"That's your own fault," Milo censured them both self-righteously. "If you had spent the night in your hotel room instead of with these immoral girls, you'd both feel as good as I do today."

"You told us to go with them," Yossarian retorted accusingly. "And we didn't have a hotel room. You were the only one who could get a hotel room."

"That wasn't my fault, either," Milo explained haughtily. "How was I supposed to know all the buyers would be in town for the chick-pea harvest?"

"You knew it," Yossarian charged. "That explains why we're here in Sicily instead of Naples. You've probably got the whole damned plane filled with chick-peas already."

"Shhhhhh!" Milo cautioned sternly, with a meaningful glance toward Orr. "Remember your mission."

The bomb bay, the rear and tail sections of the plane and most of the top turret gunner's section were all filled with bushels of chick-peas when they arrived at the airfield to take off for Malta.

Yossarian's mission on the trip was to distract Orr from observing where Milo bought his eggs, even though Orr was a member of Milo's syndicate and, like every other member of Milo's syndicate, owned a share. His mission was silly, Yossarian felt, since it was common knowledge that Milo bought his eggs in Malta for seven cents apiece and sold them to the mess halls in his syndicate for five cents apiece.

"I just don't trust him," Milo brooded in the plane, with a backward nod toward Orr, who was curled up like a tangled rope on the low bushels of chick-peas, trying torturedly to sleep. "And I'd just as soon buy my eggs when he's not around to learn my business secrets. What else don't you understand?"

Yossarian was riding beside him in the co-pilot's seat. "I don't understand why you buy eggs for seven cents apiece in Malta and sell them for five cents."

"I do it to make a profit."

"But how can you make a profit? You lose two cents an egg."

"But I make a profit of three and a quarter cents an egg by selling them for four and a quarter cents an egg to the people in Malta I buy them from for seven cents an egg. Of course, *I* don't make the profit. The syndicate makes the profit. And everybody has a share."

Yossarian felt he was beginning to understand. "And the people you sell the eggs to at four and a quarter cents apiece make a profit of two and three quarter cents apiece when they sell them back to you at seven cents apiece. Is that right? Why don't you sell the eggs directly to you and eliminate the people you buy them from?"

"Because I'm the people I buy them from," Milo explained. "I make a profit of three and a quarter cents apiece when I sell them to me and a profit of two and three quarter cents apiece when I buy them back from me. That's a total profit of six cents an egg. I lose only two cents an egg when I sell them to the mess halls at five cents apiece, and that's how I can make a profit buying eggs for seven cents apiece and selling them for five cents apiece. I pay only one cent apiece at the hen when I buy them in Sicily."

"In Malta," Yossarian corrected. "You buy your eggs in Malta, not Sicily."

Milo chortled proudly. "I don't buy eggs in Malta," he confessed, with an air of slight and clandestine amusement that was the only departure from industrious sobriety Yossarian had even seen him make. "I buy them in Sicily for one cent apiece and transfer them to Malta secretly at four and a half cents apiece in order to get the price of eggs up to seven cents apiece when people come to Malta looking for them."

"Why do people come to Malta for eggs when they're so expensive there?"

"Because they've always done it that way."

"Why don't they look for eggs in Sicily?"

"Because they've never done it that way."

"Now I really don't understand. Why don't you sell your mess halls the eggs for seven cents apiece instead of for five cents apiece?"

"Because my mess halls would have no need for me then. Anyone can buy seven-cents-apiece eggs for seven cents apiece."

"Why don't they bypass you and buy the eggs directly from you in Malta at four and a quarter cents apiece?"

"Because I wouldn't sell it to them."

"Why wouldn't you sell it to them?"

"Because then there wouldn't be as much room for a profit. At least this way I can make a bit for myself as a middleman."

"Then you do make a profit for yourself," Yossarian declared.

"Of course I do. But it all goes to the syndicate. And everybody has a share. Don't you understand? It's exactly what happens with those plum tomatoes I sell to Colonel Cathcart."

"*Buy*," Yossarian corrected him. "You don't *sell* plum tomatoes to Colonel Cathcart and Colonel Korn. You *buy* plum tomatoes from them."

"No, *sell*," Milo corrected Yossarian. "I distribute my plum tomatoes in markets all over Pianosa under an assumed name so that Colonel Cathcart and Colonel Korn can buy them up from me under their assumed names at four cents apiece and sell them back to me the next day for the syndicate at five cents apiece. They make a profit of one cent apiece, I make a profit of three and a half cents apiece, and everybody comes out ahead."

"Everybody but the syndicate," said Yossarian with a snort. "The syndicate is paying five cents apiece for plum tomatoes that cost you only half a cent apiece. How does the syndicate benefit?"

"The syndicate benefits when I benefit," Milo explained, "because everybody has a share. And the syndicate gets Colonel Cathcart's and Colonel Korn's support so that they'll let me go out on trips like this one. You'll see how much profit that can mean in about fifteen minutes when we land in Palermo."

"Malta," Yossarian corrected him. "We're flying to Malta now, not Palermo."

"No, we're flying to Palermo," Milo answered. "There's an endive exporter in Palermo I have to see for a minute about a shipment of mushrooms to Bern that were damaged by mold."

"Milo, how do you do it?" Yossarian inquired with laughing amazement and admiration. "You fill out a flight plan for one place and then you go to another. Don't the people in the control towers ever raise hell?"

"They all belong to the syndicate," Milo said. "And they know that what's good for the syndicate is good for the country, because that's what makes Sammy run. The men in the control towers have a share, too, and that's why they always have to do whatever they can to help the syndicate."

"Do I have a share?"

"Everybody has a share."

"Does Orr have a share?"

"Everybody has a share."

"And Hungry Joe? He has a share, too?"

"Everybody has a share."

"Well, I'll be damned," mused Yossarian, deeply impressed with the idea of a share for the very first time.

Milo turned toward him with a faint glimmer of mischief. "I have a sure-fire plan for cheating the federal government out of six thousand dollars. We can make three thousand dollars apiece without any risk to either of us. Are you interested?"

"No."

Milo looked at Yossarian with profound emotion. "That's what I like about you," he exclaimed. "You're honest! You're the only one I know that I can really trust. That's why I wish you'd try to be of more help to me. I really was disappointed when you ran off with those two tramps in Catania yesterday."

Yossarian stared at Milo in quizzical disbelief. "Milo, you told me to go with them. Don't you remember?"

"That wasn't my fault," Milo answered with dignity. "I had to get rid of Orr some way once we reached town. It will be a lot different in Palermo. When we land in Palermo, I want you and Orr to leave with the girls right from the airport."

"With what girls?"

"I radioed ahead and made arrangements with a four-year-old pimp to supply you and Orr with two eight-year-old virgins who are half Spanish. He'll be waiting at the airport in a limousine. Go right in as soon as you step out of the plane."

"Nothing doing," said Yossarian, shaking his head. "The only place I'm going is to sleep."

Milo turned livid with indignation, his slim long nose flickering spasmodically between his black eyebrows and his unbalanced orange-brown mustache like the pale, thin flame of a single candle. "Yossarian, remember your mission," he reminded reverently.

"To hell with my mission," Yossarian responded indifferently. "And to hell with the syndicate too, even though I do have a share. I don't want any eight-year-old virgins, even if they are half Spanish."

"I don't blame you. But these eight-year-old virgins are really only thirty-two. And they're not really half Spanish but only one-third Estonian."

"I don't care for any virgins."

"And they're not even virgins," Milo continued persuasively. "The one I picked out for you was married for a short time to an elderly schoolteacher who slept with her only on Sundays, so she's really almost as good as new."

But Orr was sleepy, too, and Yossarian and Orr were both at Milo's side when they rode into the city of Palermo from the airport and discovered that there was no room for the two of them at the hotel there either, and, more important, that Milo was mayor.

The weird, implausible reception for Milo began at the airfield, where civilian laborers who recognized him halted in their duties respectfully to gaze at him with full expressions of controlled exuberance and adulation. News of his arrival preceded him into the city, and the outskirts were already crowded with cheering citizens as they sped by in their small uncovered truck. Yossarian and Orr were mystified and mute and pressed close against Milo for security.

Inside the city, the welcome for Milo grew louder as the truck slowed and eased deeper toward the middle of town. Small boys and girls had been released from school and were lining the sidewalks in new clothes, waving tiny flags. Yossarian and Orr were absolutely speechless now. The streets were jammed with joyous throngs, and strung overhead were huge banners bearing Milo's picture. Milo had posed for these pictures in a drab peasant's blouse with a high round collar, and his scrupulous, paternal countenance was tolerant, wise, critical and strong as he stared out at the populace omnisciently with his undisciplined mustache and disunited eyes. Sinking invalids blew kisses to him from windows. Aproned shopkeepers cheered ecstatically from the narrow doorways of their shops. Tubas crumped. Here and there a person fell and was trampled to death. Sobbing old women swarmed through each other frantically around the slow-moving truck to touch Milo's shoulder or press his hand. Milo bore the tumultuous celebration with benevolent grace. He waved back to everyone in elegant reciprocation and showered generous handfuls of foil-covered Hershey kisses to the rejoicing multitudes. Lines of lusty young boys and girls skipped along behind him with their arms linked, chanting in hoarse and glassy-eyed adoration, "*Mi-lo! Mi-lo! Mi-lo!*"

Now that his secret was out, Milo relaxed with Yossarian and Orr and inflated opulently with a vast, shy pride. His cheeks turned flesh-colored. Milo had been elected mayor of Palermo—and of nearby Carini, Monreale, Bagheria, Termini Imerese, Cefalù, Mistretta and Nicosia as well—because he had brought Scotch to Sicily.

Yossarian was amazed. "The people here like to drink Scotch that much?"

"They don't drink any of the Scotch," Milo explained. "Scotch is very expensive, and these people here are very poor."

"Then why do you import it to Sicily if nobody drinks any?"

"To build up a price. I move the Scotch here from Malta to make more room for profit when I sell it back to me for somebody else. I created a whole new industry here. Today Sicily is the third-largest exporter of Scotch in the world, and *that's* why they elected me mayor."

"How about getting us a hotel room if you're such a hotshot?" Orr grumbled impertinently in a voice slurred with fatigue.

Milo responded contritely. "That's just what I'm going to do," he promised. "I'm really sorry about forgetting to radio ahead for hotel rooms for you two. Come along to my office and I'll speak to my deputy mayor about it right now."

Milo's office was a barbershop, and his deputy mayor was a pudgy barber from whose obsequious lips cordial greetings foamed as effusively as the lather he began whipping up in Milo's shaving cup.

"Well, Vittorio," said Milo, settling back lazily in one of Vittorio's barber chairs, "how were things in my absence this time?"

"Very sad, Signor Milo, very sad. But now that you are back, the people are all happy again."

"I was wondering about the size of the crowds. How come all the hotels are full?"

"Because so many people from other cities are here to see you, Signor Milo. And because we have all the buyers who have come into town for the artichoke auction."

Milo's hand soared up perpendicularly like an eagle and arrested Vittorio's shaving brush. "What's artichoke?" he inquired.

"Artichoke, Signor Milo? An artichoke is a very tasty vegetable that is popular everywhere. You must try some artichokes while you are here, Signor Milo. We grow the best in the world."

"Really?" said Milo. "How much are artichokes selling for this year?"

"It looks like a very good year for artichokes. The crops were very bad."

"Is that a fact?" mused Milo, and was gone, sliding from his chair so swiftly that his striped barber's apron retained his shape for a second or two after he had gone before it collapsed. Milo had vanished from sight by the time Yossarian and Orr rushed after him to the doorway.

"Next?" barked Milo's deputy mayor officiously. "Who's next?"

Yossarian and Orr walked from the barbershop in dejection. Deserted by Milo, they trudged homelessly through the reveling masses in futile search of a place to sleep. Yossarian was exhausted. His head throbbed with a dull, debilitating pain, and he was irritable with Orr, who had found two crab apples somewhere and walked with them in his cheeks until Yossarian spied them there and made him take them out. Then Orr found two horse chestnuts somewhere and slipped those in until Yossarian detected them and snapped at him again to take the crab apples out of his mouth. Orr grinned and replied that they were not crab apples but horse chestnuts and that they were not in his mouth but in his hands, but Yossarian was not able to understand a single word he said because of the horse chestnuts in his mouth and made him take them out anyway. A sly light twinkled in Orr's eyes. He rubbed his forehead harshly with his knuckles, like a man in an alcoholic stupor, and snickered lewdly.

"Do you remember that girl—" He broke off to snicker lewdly again. "Do you remember that girl who was hitting me over the head with that shoe in that apartment in Rome, when we were both naked?" he asked with a look of cunning expectation. He waited until Yossarian nodded cautiously. "If you let me put the chestnuts back in my mouth I'll tell you why she was hitting me. Is that a deal?"

Yossarian nodded, and Orr told him the whole fantastic story of why the naked girl in Nately's whore's apartment was hitting him over the head with her shoe, but Yossarian was not able to understand a single word because the horse chestnuts were back in his mouth. Yossarian roared with exasperated laughter at the trick, but in the end there was nothing for them to do when night fell but eat a damp dinner in a dirty restaurant and hitch a ride back to the airfield, where they slept on the chill metal floor of the plane and turned and tossed in groaning torment until the truck drivers blasted up less than two hours later with their crates of artichokes and chased them out onto the ground while they filled up the plane. A heavy rain began falling. Yossarian and Orr were dripping wet by the time the trucks drove away and had no choice but to squeeze themselves back into the plane and roll themselves up like shivering anchovies between the jolting corners of the crates of artichokes that Milo flew up to Naples at dawn and exchanged for the cinnamon sticks, cloves, vanilla beans and pepper pods that he rushed right back down south with that same day to Malta, where it turned out, he was Assistant Governor-General. There was no room for

Yossarian and Orr in Malta either. Milo was Major Sir Milo Minderbinder in Malta and had a gigantic office in the governor-general's building. His mahogany desk was immense. In a panel of the oak wall, between crossed British flags, hung a dramatic arresting photograph of Major Sir Milo Minderbinder in the dress uniform of the Royal Welsh Fusiliers. His mustache in the photograph was clipped and narrow, his chin was chiseled, and his eyes were sharp as thorns. Milo had been knighted, commissioned a major in the Royal Welsh Fusiliers and named Assistant Governor-General of Malta because he had brought the egg trade there. He gave Yossarian and Orr generous permission to spend the night on the thick carpet in his office, but shortly after he left a sentry in battle dress appeared and drove them from the building at the tip of his bayonet, and they rode out exhaustedly to the airport with a surly cab driver, who overcharged them, and went to sleep inside the plane again, which was filled now with leaking gunny sacks of cocoa and freshly ground coffee and reeking with an odor so rich that they were both outside retching violently against the landing gear when Milo was chauffeured up the first thing the next morning, looking fit as a fiddle, and took right off for Oran, where there was again no room at the hotel for Yossarian and Orr, and where Milo was Vice-Shah. Milo had at his disposal sumptuous quarters inside a salmon-pink palace, but Yossarian and Orr were not allowed to accompany him inside because they were Christian infidels. They were stopped at the gates by gargantuan Berber guards with scimitars and chased away. Orr was snuffling and sneezing with a crippling head cold. Yossarian's broad back was bent and aching. He was ready to break Milo's neck, but Milo was Vice-Shah of Oran and his person was sacred. Milo was not only the Vice-Shah of Oran, as it turned out, but also the Caliph of Baghdad, the Imam of Damascus, and the Sheik of Araby. Milo was the corn god, the rain god and the rice god in backward regions where such crude gods were still worshipped by ignorant and superstitious people, and deep inside the jungles of Africa, he intimated with becoming modesty, large graven images of his mustached face could be found overlooking primitive stone altars red with human blood. Everywhere they touched he was acclaimed with honor, and it was one triumphal ovation after another for him in city after city until they finally doubled back through the Middle East and reached Cairo, where Milo cornered the market on cotton that no one else in the world wanted and brought himself promptly to the brink of ruin. In Cairo there was at last room at the hotel for Yossarian and Orr. There were soft beds for them with fat fluffed-up pillows and clean, crisp sheets. There were closets with hangers for their clothes. There was water to wash with. Yossarian and Orr soaked their rancid, unfriendly bodies pink in a steaming-hot tub and then went from the hotel with Milo to eat shrimp cocktails and filet mignon in a very fine restaurant with a stock ticker in the lobby that happened to be clicking out the latest quotation for Egyptian cotton when Milo inquired of the captain of waiters what kind of machine it was. Milo had never imagined a machine so beautiful as a stock ticker before.

"Really?" he exclaimed when the captain of waiters had finished his explanation. "And how much is Egyptian cotton selling for?" The captain of waiters told him, and Milo bought the whole crop.

But Yossarian was not nearly so frightened by the Egyptian cotton Milo bought as he was by the bunches of green red bananas Milo had spotted in the native market place as they drove into the city, and his fears proved justified, for Milo shook him awake out of a deep sleep just after twelve and shoved a partly peeled banana toward him. Yossarian choked back a sob.

"Taste it," Milo urged, following Yossarian's writhing face around with the banana insistently.

"Milo, you bastard," moaned Yossarian. "I've got to get some sleep."

"Eat it and tell me if it's good," Milo persevered. "Don't tell Orr I gave it to you. I charged him two piasters for his."

Yossarian ate the banana submissively and closed his eyes after telling Milo it was good, but Milo shook him awake again and instructed him to get dressed as quickly as he could, because they were leaving at once for Pianosa.

"You and Orr have to load the bananas into the plane right away," he explained. "The man said to watch out for spiders while you're handling the bunches."

"Milo, can't we wait until morning?" Yossarian pleaded. "I've got to get some sleep."

"They're ripening very quickly," answered Milo, "and we don't have a minute to lose. Just think how happy the men back at the squadron will be when they get these bananas."

But the men back at the squadron never even saw any of the bananas, for it was a seller's market for bananas in Istanbul and a buyer's market in Beirut for the caraway seeds Milo rushed with to Bengasi after selling the bananas, and when they raced back into Pianosa breathlessly six days later at the conclusion of Orr's rest leave, it was with a load of best white eggs from Sicily that Milo said were from Egypt and sold to his mess halls for only *four* cents apiece so that all the commanding officers in his syndicate would implore him to speed right back to Cairo for more bunches of green red bananas to sell in Turkey for the caraway seeds in demand in Bengasi. And everybody had a share.

23

Nately's Old Man

The only one back in the squadron who did see any of Milo's red bananas was Aarfy, who picked up two from an influential fraternity brother of his in the Quartermaster Corps when the bananas ripened and began streaming into Italy through normal black-market channels and who was in the officers' apartment with Yossarian the evening Nately finally found his whore again after so many fruitless weeks of mournful searching and lured her back to the apartment with two girl friends by promising them thirty dollars each.

"Thirty dollars each?" remarked Aarfy slowly, poking and patting each of the three strapping girls skeptically with the air of a grudging connoisseur. "Thirty dollars is a lot of money for pieces like these. Besides, I never paid for it in my life."

"I'm not asking you to pay for it," Nately assured him quickly. "I'll pay for them all. I just want you guys to take the other two. Won't you help me out?"

Aarfy smirked complacently and shook his soft round head. "Nobody has to pay for it for good old Aarfy. I can get all I want any time I want it. I'm just not in the mood right now."

"Why don't you just pay all three and send the other two away?" Yossarian suggested.

"Because then mine will be angry with me for making her work for her money," Nately replied with an anxious look at his girl, who was glowering at him restlessly and starting to mutter. "She says that if I really liked her I'd send *her* away and go to bed with one of the others."

"I have a better idea," boasted Aarfy. "Why don't we keep the three of them here until after the curfew and then threaten to push them out into the street to be arrested unless they give us all their money. We can even threaten to push them out the window."

"Aarfy!" Nately was aghast.

"I was only trying to help," said Aarfy sheepishly. Aarfy was always trying to help Nately because Nately's father was rich and prominent and in an excellent position to help Aarfy after the war. "Gee whiz," he defended himself querulously. "Back in school we were always doing things like that. I remember one day we tricked these two dumb high-school girls from town into the fraternity house and made them put out for all the fellows there who wanted them by threatening to call up their parents and say they were putting out for us. We kept them trapped in bed there for more than ten hours. We even smacked their faces a little when they started to complain. Then we took away their nickels and dimes and chewing gum and threw them out. Boy, we used to have fun in that fraternity house," he recalled peacefully, his corpulent cheeks aglow with the jovial, rubicund warmth of nostalgic recollection. "We used to ostracize everyone, even each other."

But Aarfy was no help to Nately now as the girl Nately had fallen so deeply in love with began swearing at him sullenly with rising, menacing resentment. Luckily, Hungry Joe burst in just then, and everything was all right again, except that Dunbar staggered in drunk a minute later and began embracing one of the other giggling girls at once. Now there were four men and three girls, and the seven of them left Aarfy in the apartment and climbed into a horse-drawn cab, which remained at the curb at a dead halt while the girls demanded their money in advance. Nately gave them ninety dollars with a gallant flourish, after borrowing twenty dollars from Yossarian, thirty-five dollars from Dunbar and seventeen dollars from Hungry Joe. The girls grew friendlier then and called an address to the driver, who drove them at a clopping pace halfway across the city into a section they had never visited before and stopped in front of an old, tall building on a dark street. The girls led them up four steep, very long flights of creaking wooden stairs and guided them through a doorway into their own wonderful and resplendent tenement apartment, which burgeoned miraculously with an infinite and proliferating flow of supple young naked girls and contained the evil and debauched ugly old man who irritated Nately constantly with his caustic laughter and the clucking, proper old woman in the ash-gray woolen sweater who disapproved of everything immoral that occurred there and tried her best to tidy up.

The amazing place was a fertile, seething cornucopia of female nipples and navels. At first, there were just their own three girls in the dimly-lit, drab brown sitting room that stood at the juncture of three murky hallways leading in separate directions to the distant recesses of the strange and marvelous bordello. The girls disrobed at once, pausing in different stages to point proudly to their garish underthings and bantering all the while with the gaunt and dissipated old man with the shabby long white hair and slovenly white unbuttoned shirt who sat cackling lasciviously in a musty blue armchair almost in the exact center of the room and bade Nately and his companions welcome with a mirthful and sardonic formality. Then the old woman trudged out to get a girl for Hungry Joe, dipping her captious head sadly, and returned with two big-bosomed beauties, one already undressed and the other in only a transparent pink half slip that she wiggled out of while sitting down. Three more naked girls sauntered in from a different direction and remained to chat, then two others. Four more girls passed through the room in an indolent group, engrossed in conversation; three were barefoot and one wobbled perilously on a pair of unbuckled silver dancing shoes that did not seem to be her own. One more girl appeared wearing only panties and sat down, bringing the total congregating there in just a few minutes to eleven, all but one of them completely unclothed.

There was bare flesh lounging everywhere, most of it plump, and Hungry Joe began to die. He stood stock still in rigid, cataleptic astonishment while the girls ambled in and made themselves comfortable. Then he let out a piercing shriek suddenly and bolted toward the door in a headlong dash back toward the enlisted men's apartment for his camera, only to be halted in his tracks with another frantic shriek by the dreadful, freezing premonition that this whole lovely, lurid, rich and colorful pagan paradise would be snatched away from him irredeemably if he were to let it out of his sight for even an instant. He stopped in the doorway and sputtered, the wiry veins and tendons in his face and neck pulsating violently. The old man watched him with victorious merriment, sitting in his musty blue armchair like some satanic and hedonistic deity on a throne, a stolen U.S. Army blanket wrapped around his spindly legs to ward off a chill. He laughed quietly, his sunken, shrewd eyes sparkling perceptively with a cynical and wanton enjoyment. He had been drinking. Nately reacted on sight with bristling enmity to this wicked, depraved and unpatriotic old man who was old enough to remind him of his father and who made disparaging jokes about America.

"America," he said, "will lose the war. And Italy will win it."

"America is the strongest and most prosperous nation on earth," Nately informed him with lofty fervor and dignity. "And the American fighting man is second to none."

"Exactly," agreed the old man pleasantly, with a hint of taunting amusement. "Italy, on the other hand, is one of the least prosperous nations on earth. And the Italian fighting man is probably second to all. And that's exactly why my country is doing so well in this war while your country is doing so poorly."

Nately guffawed with surprise, then blushed apologetically for his impoliteness. "I'm sorry I laughed at you," he said sincerely, and he continued in a tone of respectful condescension. "But Italy was occupied by the Germans and is now being occupied by us. You don't call that doing very well, do you?"

"But of course I do," exclaimed the old man cheerfully. "The Germans are being driven out, and we are still here. In a few years you will be gone, too, and we will still be here. You see, Italy is really a very poor and weak country, and that's what makes us so strong. Italian soldiers are not dying any more. But American and German soldiers are. I call that doing extremely well. Yes, I am quite certain that Italy will survive this war and still be in existence long after your own country has been destroyed."

Nately could scarcely believe his ears. He had never heard such shocking blasphemies before, and he wondered with instinctive logic why G-men did not appear to lock the traitorous old man up. "America is not going to be destroyed!" he shouted passionately.

"Never?" prodded the old man softly.

"Well . . ." Nately faltered.

The old man laughed indulgently, holding in check a deeper, more explosive delight. His goading remained gentle. "Rome was destroyed, Greece was destroyed, Persia was destroyed, Spain was destroyed. All great countries are destroyed. Why not yours? How much longer do you really think your own country will last? Forever? Keep in mind that the earth itself is destined to be destroyed by the sun in twenty-five million years or so."

Nately squirmed uncomfortably. "Well, forever is a long time, I guess."

"A million years?" persisted the jeering old man with keen, sadistic zest. "A half million? The frog is almost five hundred million years old. Could you really say with much certainty that America, with all its strength and prosperity, with its fighting man that is second to none, and with its standard of living that is the highest in the world, will last as long as . . . the frog?"

Nately wanted to smash his leering face. He looked about imploring for help in defending his country's future against the obnoxious calumnies of this sly and sinful assailant. He was disappointed. Yossarian and Dunbar were busy in a far corner pawing orgiastically at four or five frolicsome girls and six bottles of red wine, and Hungry Joe had long since tramped away down one of the mystic hallways, propelling before him like a ravening despot as many of the broadest-hipped young prostitutes as he could contain in his frail windmilling arms and cram into one double bed.

Nately felt himself at an embarrassing loss. His own girl sat sprawled out gracelessly on an overstuffed sofa with an expression of otiose boredom. Nately was unnerved by her torpid indifference to him, by the same sleepy and inert pose that he remembered so vividly, so sweetly, and so miserably from the first time she had seen him and ignored him at the packed penny-ante blackjack game in the living room of the enlisted men's apartment. Her lax mouth hung open in a perfect O, and God alone knew at what her glazed and smoky eyes were staring in such brute apathy. The old man waited tranquilly, watching him with a discerning smile that was both scornful and sympathetic. A lissome, blond, sinuous girl with lovely legs and honey-colored skin laid herself out contentedly on the arm of the old man's chair and began molesting his angular, pale, dissolute face languidly and coquettishly. Nately stiffened with resentment and hostility at the sight of such lechery in a man so old. He turned away with a sinking heart and wondered why he simply did not take his own girl and go to bed.

This sordid, vulturous, diabolical old man reminded Nately of his father because the two were nothing at all alike. Nately's father was a courtly white-haired gentleman who dressed impeccably; this old man was an uncouth bum. Nately's father was a sober, philosophical and responsible man; this old man was fickle and licentious. Nately's father was discreet and cultured; this old man was a boor. Nately's father believed in honor and knew the answer to everything; this old man believed in nothing and had only questions. Nately's father had a distinguished white mustache; this old man had no mustache at all. Nately's father—and everyone else's father Nately had ever met—was dignified, wise and venerable; this old man was utterly repellent, and Nately plunged back into debate with him, determined to repudiate his vile logic and insinuations with an ambitious vengeance that would capture the attention of the bored, phlegmatic girl he had fallen so intensely in love with and win her admiration forever.

"Well, frankly, I don't know how long America is going to last," he proceeded dauntlessly. "I suppose we can't last forever if the world itself is going to be destroyed someday. But I do know that we're going to survive and triumph for a long, long time."

"For how long?" mocked the profane old man with a gleam of malicious elation. "Not even as long as the frog?"

"Much longer than you or me," Nately blurted out lamely.

"Oh, is that all! That won't be very much longer then, considering that you're so gullible and brave and that I am already such an old, old man."

"How old are you?" Nately asked, growing intrigued and charmed with the old man in spite of himself.

"A hundred and seven." The old man chuckled heartily at Nately's look of chagrin. "I see you don't believe that either."

"I don't believe anything you tell me," Nately replied, with a bashful mitigating smile. "The only thing I do believe is that America is going to win the war."

"You put so much stock in *winning* wars," the grubby iniquitous old man scoffed. "The real trick lies in *losing* wars, in knowing which wars can be *lost*. Italy has been losing wars for centuries, and just see how splendidly we've done nonetheless. France wins wars and is in a continual state of crisis. Germany loses and prospers. Look at our own recent history. Italy won a war in Ethiopia and promptly stumbled into serious trouble. Victory gave us such insane delusions of grandeur that we helped start a world war we hadn't a chance of winning. But now that we are losing again, everything has taken a turn for the better, and we will certainly come out on top again if we succeed in being defeated."

Nately gaped at him in undisguised befuddlement. "Now I really don't understand what you're saying. You talk like a madman."

"But I live like a sane one. I was a fascist when Mussolini was on top, and I am an anti-fascist now that he has been deposed. I was fanatically pro-German when the Germans were here to protect us against the Americans, and now that the Americans are here to protect us against the Germans I am fanatically pro-American. I can assure you, my outraged young friend"—the old man's knowing, disdainful eyes shone even more effervescently as Nately's stuttering dismay increased—"that you and your country will have no more loyal partisan in Italy than me—but only as long as you *remain* in Italy."

"But," Nately cried out in disbelief, "you're a turncoat! A timeserver! A shameful, unscrupulous opportunist!"

"I am a hundred and seven years old," the old man reminded him suavely.

"Don't you have any principles?"

"Of course not."

"No morality?"

"Oh, I am a very moral man," the villainous old man assured him with satiric seriousness, stroking the bare hip of a buxom black-haired girl with pretty dimples who had stretched herself out seductively on the other arm of his chair. He grinned at Nately sarcastically as he sat between both naked girls in smug and threadbare splendor, with a sovereign hand on each.

"I can't believe it," Nately remarked grudgingly, trying stubbornly not to watch him in relationship to the girls. "I simply can't believe it."

"But it's all perfectly true. When the Germans marched into the city, I danced in the streets like a youthful ballerina and shouted, '*Heil* Hitler!' until my lungs were hoarse. I even waved a small Nazi flag that I had snatched away from a beautiful little girl while her mother was looking the other way. When the Germans left the city, I rushed out to welcome the Americans with a bottle of excellent brandy and a basket of flowers. The brandy was for myself, of course, and the flowers were to sprinkle upon our liberators. There was a very stiff and stuffy old major riding in the first car, and I hit him squarely in the eye with a red rose. A marvelous shot! You should have seen him wince."

Nately gasped and was on his feet with amazement, the blood draining from his cheeks. "Major —— de Coverley!" he cried.

"Do you know him?" inquired the old man with delight. "What a charming coincidence!"

Nately was too astonished even to hear him. "So *you're* the one who wounded Major —— de Coverley!" he exclaimed in horrified indignation. "How could you do such a thing?"

The fiendish old man was unperturbed. "How could I resist, you mean. You should have seen the arrogant old bore, sitting there so sternly in that car like the Almighty Himself, with his big, rigid head and his foolish, solemn face. What a tempting target he made! I got him in the eye with an American Beauty rose. I thought that was most appropriate. Don't you?"

"That was a *terrible* thing to do!" Nately shouted at him reproachfully. "A vicious and criminal thing! Major —— de Coverley is our squadron executive officer!"

"Is he?" teased the unregenerate old man, pinching his pointy jaw gravely in a parody of repentance. "In that case, you must give me credit for being impartial. When the Germans rode in, I almost stabbed a robust young *Oberstleutnant* to death with a sprig of edelweiss."

Nately was appalled and bewildered by the abominable old man's inability to perceive the enormity of his offense. "Don't you realize what you've done?" he scolded vehemently. "Major —— de Coverley is a noble and wonderful person, and everyone admires him."

"He's a silly old fool who really has no right acting like a silly young fool. Where is he today? Dead?"

Nately answered softly with somber awe. "Nobody knows. He seems to have disappeared."

"You see? Imagine a man his age risking what little life he has left for something so absurd as a country."

Nately was instantly up in arms again. "There is nothing so absurd about risking your life for your country!" he declared.

"Isn't there?" asked the old man. "What is a country? A country is a piece of land surrounded on all sides by boundaries, usually unnatural. Englishmen are dying for England, Americans are dying for America, Germans are dying for Germany, Russians are dying for Russia. There are now fifty or sixty countries fighting in this war. Surely so many countries can't *all* be worth dying for."

"Anything worth living for," said Nately, "is worth dying for."

"And anything worth dying for," answered the sacrilegious old man, "is certainly worth living for. You know, you're such a pure and naïve young man that I almost feel sorry for you. How old are you? Twenty-five? Twenty-six?"

"Nineteen," said Nately. "I'll be twenty in January."

"If you live." The old man shook his head, wearing, for a moment, the same touchy, meditating frown of the fretful and disapproving old woman. "They are going to kill you if you don't watch out, and I can see now that you are not going to watch out. Why don't you use some sense and try to be more like me? You might live to be a hundred and seven, too."

"Because it's better to die on one's feet than live on one's knee," Nately retorted with triumphant and lofty conviction. "I guess you've heard that saying before."

"Yes, I certainly have," mused the treacherous old man, smiling again. "But I'm afraid you have it backward. It is better to *live* on one's feet than die on one's knees. *That* is the way the saying goes."

"Are you sure?" Nately asked with sober confusion. "It seems to make more sense my way."

"No, it makes more sense my way. Ask your friends."

Nately turned to ask his friends and discovered they had gone. Yossarian and Dunbar had both disappeared. The old man roared with contemptuous merriment at Nately's look of embarrassed surprise. Nately's face darkened with shame. He vacillated helplessly for a few seconds and then spun himself around and fled inside the nearest of the hallways in search of Yossarian and Dunbar, hoping to catch them in time and bring them back to the rescue with news of the remarkable clash between the old man and Major —— de Coverley. All the doors in all the hallways were shut. There was light under none. It was already very late. Nately gave up his search forlornly. There was nothing left for him to do, he realized finally, but get the girl he was in love with and lie down with her somewhere to make tender, courteous love to her and plan their future together; but she had gone off to bed, too, by the time he returned to the sitting room for her, and there was nothing left for him to do then but resume his abortive discussion with the loathsome old man, who rose from his armchair with jesting civility and excused himself for the night, abandoning Nately there with two bleary-eyed girls who could not tell him into which room his own whore had gone and who padded off to bed several seconds later after trying in vain to interest him in themselves, leaving him to sleep alone in the sitting room on the small, lumpy sofa.

Nately was a sensitive, rich, good-looking boy with dark hair, trusting eyes, and a pain in his neck when he awoke on the sofa early the next morning and wondered dully where he was. His nature was invariably gentle and polite. He had lived for almost twenty years without trauma, tension, hate, or neurosis, which was proof to Yossarian of just how crazy he really was. His childhood had been a pleasant, though disciplined, one. He got on well with his brothers and sisters, and he did not hate his mother and father, even though they had both been very good to him.

Nately had been brought up to detest people like Aarfy, whom his mother characterized as climbers, and people like Milo, whom his father characterized as pushers, but he had never learned how, since he had never been permitted near them. As far back as he could recall, his homes in Philadelphia, New York, Maine, Palm Beach, Southampton, London, Deauville, Paris and the south of France had always been crowded only with ladies and gentlemen who were not climbers or pushers. Nately's mother, a descendant of the New England Thorntons, was a Daughter of the American Revolution. His father was a Son of a Bitch.

"Always remember," his mother had reminded him frequently, "that you are a Nately. You are not a Vanderbilt, whose fortune was made by a vulgar tugboat captain, or a Rockefeller, whose wealth was amassed through unscrupulous speculations in crude petroleum; or a Reynolds or Duke, whose income was derived from the sale to the unsuspecting public of products containing cancer-causing resins and tars; and you are certainly not an Astor, whose family, I believe, still lets rooms. You are a Nately, and the Natelys have never done *anything* for their money."

"What your mother means, son," interjected his father affably one time with that flair for graceful and economical expression Nately admired so much, "is that old money is better than new money and that the newly rich are never to be esteemed as highly as the newly poor. Isn't that correct, my dear?"

Nately's father brimmed continually with sage and sophisticated counsel of that kind. He was as ebullient and ruddy as mulled claret, and Nately liked him a great deal, although he did not like mulled claret. When war broke out, Nately's family decided that he would enlist in the armed forces, since he was too young to be placed in the diplomatic service, and since his father had it on excellent authority that Russia was going to collapse in a matter of weeks or months and that Hitler, Churchill, Roosevelt, Mussolini, Gandhi, Franco, Peron and the Emperor of Japan would then all sign a peace treaty and live together happily ever after. It was Nately's father's idea that he join the Air Corps, where he could train safely as a pilot while the Russians capitulated and the details of the armistice were worked out, and where, as an officer, he would associate only with gentlemen.

Instead, he found himself with Yossarian, Dunbar and Hungry Joe in a whore house in Rome, poignantly in love with an indifferent girl there with whom he finally did lie down the morning after the night he slept alone in the sitting room, only to be interrupted almost immediately by her incorrigible kid sister, who came bursting in without warning and hurled herself onto the bed jealously so that Nately could embrace her, too. Nately's whore sprang up snarling to whack her angrily and jerked her to her feet by the hair. The twelve-year-old girl looked to Nately like a plucked chicken or like a twig with the bark peeled off: her sapling body embarrassed everyone in her precocious attempts to imitate her elders, and she was always being chased away to put clothes on and ordered out into the street to play in the fresh air with the other children. The two sisters swore and spat at each other now savagely, raising a fluent, deafening commotion that brought a whole crowd of hilarious spectators swarming into the room. Nately gave up in exasperation. He asked his girl to get dressed and took her downstairs for breakfast. The kid sister tagged along, and Nately felt like the proud head of a family as the three of them ate respectably in a nearby open-air café. But Nately's whore was already bored by the time they started back, and she decided to go streetwalking with two other girls rather than spend more time with him. Nately and the kid sister followed meekly a block behind, the ambitious youngster to pick up valuable pointers, Nately to eat his liver in mooning frustration, and both were saddened when the girls were stopped by soldiers in a staff car and driven away.

Nately went back to the café and bought the kid sister chocolate ice cream until her spirits improved and then returned with her to the apartment, where Yossarian and Dunbar were flopped out in the sitting room with an exhausted Hungry Joe, who was still wearing on his battered face the blissful, numb, triumphant smile with which he had limped into view from his massive harem that morning like a person with numerous broken bones. The lecherous and depraved old man was delighted with Hungry Joe's split lips and black-and-blue eyes. He greeted Nately warmly, still wearing the same rumpled clothes of the evening before. Nately was profoundly upset by his seedy and disreputable appearance, and whenever he came to the apartment he wished that the corrupt, immoral old man would put on a clean Brooks Brothers shirt, shave, comb his hair, wear a tweed jacket, and grow a dapper white mustache so that Nately would not have to suffer such confusing shame each time he looked at him and was reminded of his father.

24

Milo

April had been the best month of all for Milo. Lilacs bloomed in April and fruit ripened on the vine. Heartbeats quickened and old appetites were renewed. In April a livelier iris gleamed upon the burnished dove. April was spring, and in the spring Milo Minderbinder's fancy had lightly turned to thoughts of tangerines.

"Tangerines?"

"Yes, sir."

"My men would love tangerines," admitted the colonel in Sardinia who commanded four squadrons of B-26s.

"There'll be all the tangerines they can eat that you're able to pay for with money from your mess fund," Milo assured him.

"Casaba melons?"

"Are going for a song in Damascus."

"I have a weakness for casaba melons. I've always had a weakness for casaba melons."

"Just lend me one plane from each squadron, just one plane, and you'll have all the casabas you can eat that you've money to pay for."

"We buy from the syndicate?"

"And everybody has a share."

"It's amazing, positively amazing. How can you do it?"

"Mass purchasing power makes the big difference. For example, breaded veal cutlets."

"I'm not so crazy about breaded veal cutlets," grumbled the skeptical B-25 commander in the north of Corsica.

"Breaded veal cutlets are very nutritious," Milo admonished him piously. "They contain egg yolk and bread crumbs. And so are lamb chops."

"Ah, lamb chops," echoed the B-25 commander. "Good lamb chops?"

"The best," said Milo, "that the black market has to offer."

"Baby lamb chops?"

"In the cutest little pink paper panties you ever saw. Are going for a song in Portugal."

"I can't send a plane to Portugal. I haven't the authority."

"I can, once you lend the plane to me. With a pilot to fly it. And don't forget—you'll get General Dreedle."

"Will General Dreedle eat in my mess hall again?"

"Like a pig, once you start feeding him my best white fresh eggs fried in my pure creamery butter. There'll be tangerines too, and casaba melons, honeydews, filet of Dover sole, baked Alaska, and cockles and mussels."

"And everybody has a share?"

"That," said Milo, "is the most beautiful part of it."

"I don't like it," growled the uncooperative fighter-plane commander, who didn't like Milo either.

"There's an uncooperative fighter-plane commander up north who's got it in for me," Milo complained to General Dreedle. "It takes just one person to ruin the whole thing, and then you wouldn't have your fresh eggs fried in my pure creamery butter any more."

General Dreedle had the uncooperative fighter-plane commander transferred to the Solomon Islands to dig graves and replaced him with a senile colonel with bursitis and a craving for litchi nuts who introduced Milo to the B-17 general on the mainland with a yearning for Polish sausage.

"Polish sausage is going for peanuts in Cracow," Milo informed him.

"Polish sausage," sighed the general nostalgically. "You know, I'd give just about anything for a good hunk of Polish sausage. Just about anything."

"You don't have to give *anything*. Just give me one plane for each mess hall and a pilot who will do what he's told. And a small down payment on your initial order as a token of good faith."

"But Cracow is hundreds of miles behind the enemy lines. How will you get to the sausage?"

"There's an international Polish sausage exchange in Geneva. I'll just fly the peanuts into Switzerland and exchange them for Polish sausage at the open market rate. They'll fly the peanuts back to Cracow and I'll fly the Polish sausage back to you. You buy only as much Polish sausage as you want through the syndicate. There'll be tangerines too, with only a little artificial coloring added. And eggs from Malta and Scotch from Sicily. You'll be paying the money to yourself when you buy from the syndicate, since you'll own a share, so you'll really be getting everything you buy for nothing. Doesn't that make sense?"

"Sheer genius. How in the world did you ever think of it?"

"My name is Milo Minderbinder. I am twenty-seven years old."

Milo Minderbinder's planes flew in from everywhere, the pursuit planes, bombers, and cargo ships streaming into Colonel Cathcart's field with pilots at the controls who would do what they were told. The planes were decorated with flamboyant squadron emblems illustrating such laudable ideals as Courage, Might, Justice, Truth, Liberty, Love, Honor and Patriotism that were painted out at once by Milo's mechanics with a double coat of flat white and replaced in garish purple with the stenciled name M & M ENTERPRISES, FINE FRUITS AND PRODUCE. The "M & M" in "M & M ENTERPRISES" stood for Milo & Minderbinder, and the & was inserted, Milo revealed candidly, to nullify any impression that the syndicate was a one-man operation. Planes arrived for Milo from airfields in Italy, North Africa and England, and from Air Transport Command stations in Liberia, Ascension Island, Cairo and Karachi. Pursuit planes were traded for additional cargo ships or retained for emergency invoice duty and small-parcel service; trucks and tanks were procured from the ground forces and used for short-distance road hauling. Everybody had a share, and men got fat and moved about tamely with toothpicks in their greasy lips. Milo supervised the whole expanding operation by himself. Deep otter-brown lines of preoccupation etched themselves permanently into his care-worn face and gave him a harried look of sobriety and mistrust. Everybody but Yossarian thought Milo was a jerk, first for volunteering for the job of mess officer and next for taking it so seriously. Yossarian also thought that Milo was a jerk; but he also knew that Milo was a genius.

One day Milo flew away to England to pick up a load of Turkish halvah and came flying back from Madagascar leading four German bombers filled with yams, collards, mustard greens and black-eyed Georgia peas. Milo was dumbfounded when he stepped down to the ground and found a contingent of armed M.P.s waiting to imprison the German pilots and confiscate their planes. *Confiscate!* The mere word was anathema to him, and he stormed back and forth in excoriating condemnation, shaking a piercing finger of rebuke in the guilt-ridden faces of Colonel Cathcart, Colonel Korn and the poor battle-scarred captain with the submachine gun who commanded the M.P.s.

"Is this Russia?" Milo assailed them incredulously at the top of his voice. "*Confiscate?*" he shrieked, as though he could not believe his own ears. "Since when is it the policy of the American government to confiscate the private property of its citizens? Shame on you! Shame on all of you for even thinking such a horrible thought."

"But Milo," Major Danby interrupted timidly, "we're at war with Germany, and those are German planes."

"They are no such thing!" Milo retorted furiously. "Those planes belong to the syndicate, and everybody has a share. *Confiscate?* How can you possibly confiscate your own private property? *Confiscate,* indeed! I've never heard anything so depraved in my whole life."

And sure enough, Milo was right, for when they looked, his mechanics had painted out the German swastikas on the wings, tails and fuselages with double coats of flat white and stenciled in the words M & M ENTERPRISES, FINE FRUITS AND PRODUCE. Right before their eyes he had transformed his syndicate into an international cartel.

Milo's argosies of plenty now filled the air. Planes poured in from Norway, Denmark, France, Germany, Austria, Italy, Yugoslavia, Romania, Bulgaria, Sweden, Finland, Poland—from everywhere in Europe, in fact, but Russia, with whom Milo refused to do business. When everybody who was going to had signed up with M & M Enterprises, Fine Fruits and Produce, Milo created a wholly owned subsidiary, M & M Enterprises, Fancy Pastry, and obtained more airplanes and more money from the mess funds for scones and crumpets from the British Isles, prune and cheese Danish from Copenhagen, eclairs, cream puffs, Napoleons and *petits fours* from Paris, Reims and Grenoble, *Kugelhopf,* pumpernickel and *Pfefferkuchen* from Berlin, *Linzer* and *Dobos Torten* from Vienna, *Strudel* from Hungary and *baklava* from Ankara. Each morning Milo sent planes aloft all over Europe and North Africa hauling long red tow signs advertising the day's specials in large square letters: "eye round, 79¢ . . . whiting, 21¢." He boosted cash income for the syndicate by leasing tow signs to Pet Milk, Gaines Dog Food, and Noxzema. In a spirit of civic enterprise, he regularly allotted a certain amount of free aerial advertising space to General Peckem for the propagation of such messages in the public interest as NEATNESS COUNTS, HASTE MAKES WASTE, and THE FAMILY THAT PRAYS TOGETHER STAYS TOGETHER. Milo purchased spot radio announcements on Axis Sally's and Lord Haw Haw's daily propaganda broadcasts from Berlin to keep things moving. Business boomed on every battlefront.

Milo's planes were a familiar sight. They had freedom of passage everywhere, and one day Milo contracted with the American military authorities to bomb the German-held highway bridge at Orvieto and with the German military authorities to defend the highway bridge at Orvieto with antiaircraft fire against his own attack. His fee for attacking the bridge for America was the total cost of the operation plus six percent, and his fee from Germany for defending the bridge was the same cost-plus-six agreement augmented by a merit bonus of a thousand dollars for every American plane he shot down. The consummation of these deals represented an important victory for private enterprise, he pointed out, since the armies of both countries were socialized institutions. Once the contracts were signed, there seemed to be no point in using the resources of the syndicate to bomb and defend the bridge, inasmuch as both governments had ample men and matériel right there to do so and were perfectly happy to contribute them, and in the end Milo realized a fantastic profit from both halves of his project for doing nothing more than signing his name twice.

The arrangements were fair to both sides. Since Milo did have freedom of passage everywhere, his planes were able to steal over in a sneak attack without alerting the German antiaircraft gunners; and since Milo knew about the attack, he was able to alert the German antiaircraft gunners in sufficient time for them to begin firing accurately the moment the planes came into range. It was an ideal arrangement for everyone but the dead man in Yossarian's tent, who was killed over the target the day he arrived.

"I didn't kill him!" Milo kept replying passionately to Yossarian's angry protest. "I wasn't even there that day, I tell you. Do you think I was down there on the ground firing an antiaircraft gun when the planes came over?"

"But you organized the whole thing, didn't you?" Yossarian shouted back at him in the velvet darkness cloaking the path leading past the still vehicles of the motor pool to the open-air movie theater.

"And I didn't organize anything," Milo answered indignantly, drawing great agitated sniffs of air in through his hissing, pale, twitching nose. "The Germans have the bridge, and we were going to bomb it, whether I stepped into the picture or not. I just saw a wonderful opportunity to make some profit out of the mission, and I took it. What's so terrible about that?"

"What's so terrible about it? Milo, a man in my tent was killed on that mission before he could even unpack his bags."

"But I didn't kill him."

"You got a thousand dollars extra for it."

"But I didn't kill him. I wasn't even there, I tell you. I was in

Barcelona buying olive oil and skinless and boneless sardines, and I've got the purchase orders to prove it. And I didn't get the thousand dollars. That thousand dollars went to the syndicate, and everybody got a share, even you." Milo was appealing to Yossarian from the bottom of his soul. "Look, I didn't start this war, Yossarian, no matter what that lousy Wintergreen is saying. I'm just trying to put it on a businesslike basis. Is anything wrong with that? You know, a thousand dollars ain't such a bad price for a medium bomber and a crew. If I can persuade the Germans to pay me a thousand dollars for every plane they shoot down, why shouldn't I take it?"

"Because you're dealing with the enemy, that's why. Can't you understand that we're fighting a war? People are dying. Look around you, for Christ's sake!"

Milo shook his head with weary forbearance. "And the Germans are not our enemies," he declared. "Oh, I know what you're going to say. Sure, we're at war with them. But the Germans are also members in good standing of the syndicate, and it's my job to protect their rights as shareholders. Maybe they did start the war, and maybe they are killing millions of people, but they pay their bills a lot more promptly than some allies of ours I could name. Don't you understand that I have to respect the sanctity of my contract with Germany? Can't you see it from my point of view?"

"No," Yossarian rebuffed him harshly.

Milo was stung and made no effort to disguise his wounded feelings. It was a muggy, moonlit night filled with gnats, moths, and mosquitoes. Milo lifted his arm suddenly and pointed toward the open-air theater, where the milky, dust-filled beam bursting horizontally from the projector slashed a conelike swath in the blackness and draped in a fluorescent membrane of light the audience tilted on the seats there in hypnotic sags, their faces focused upward toward the aluminized movie screen. Milos eyes were liquid with integrity, and his artless and uncorrupted face was lustrous with a shining mixture of sweat and insect repellent.

"Look at them," he exclaimed in a voice choked with emotion. "They're my friends, my countrymen, my comrades in arms. A fellow never had a better bunch of buddies. Do you think I'd do a single thing to harm them if I didn't have to? Haven't I got enough on my mind? Can't you see how upset I am already about all that cotton piling up on those piers in Egypt?" Milo's voice splintered into fragments, and he clutched at Yossarian's shirt front as though drowning. His eyes were throbbing visibly like brown caterpillars. "Yossarian, what am I going to do with so much cotton? It's all your fault for letting me buy it."

The cotton was piling up on the piers in Egypt, and nobody wanted any. Milo had never dreamed that the Nile Valley could be so fertile or that there would be no market at all for the crop he had bought. The mess halls in his syndicate would not help; they rose up in uncompromising rebellion against his proposal to tax them on a per capita basis in order to enable each man to own his own share of the Egyptian cotton crop. Even his reliable friends the Germans failed him in this crisis: they preferred ersatz. Milo's mess halls would not even help him store the cotton, and his warehousing costs skyrocketed and contributed to the devastating drain upon his cash reserves. The profits from the Orvieto mission were sucked away. He began writing home for the money he had sent back in better days; soon that was almost gone. And new bales of cotton kept arriving on the wharves at Alexandria every day. Each time he succeeded in dumping some on the world market for a loss it was snapped up by canny Egyptian brokers in the Levant, who sold it back to him at the original contract price, so that he was really worse off than before.

M & M Enterprises verged on collapse. Milo cursed himself hourly for his monumental greed and stupidity in purchasing the entire Egyptian cotton crop, but a contract was a contract and had to be honored, and one night, after a sumptuous evening meal, all Milo's fighters and bombers took off, joined in formation directly overhead and began dropping bombs on the group. He had landed another contract with the Germans, this time to bomb his own outfit. Milo's planes separated in a well-coordinated attack and bombed the fuel stocks and the ordnance dump, the repair hangars and the B-25 bombers resting on the lollipop-shaped hardstands at the field. His crews spared the landing strip and the mess halls so that they could land safely when their work was done and enjoy a hot snack before retiring. They bombed with their landing lights on, since no one was shooting back. They bombed all four squadrons, the officers' club and the Group Headquarters building. Men bolted from their tents in sheer terror and did not know in which direction to turn. Wounded soon lay screaming everywhere. A cluster of fragmentation bombs exploded in the yard of the officers' club and punched jagged holes in the side of the wooden building and in the bellies and backs of a row of lieutenants and captains standing at the bar. They doubled over in agony and dropped. The rest of the officers fled toward the two exits in panic and jammed up the doorways like a dense, howling dam of human flesh as they shrank from going farther.

Colonel Cathcart clawed and elbowed his way through the unruly, bewildered mass until he stood outside by himself. He stared up at the sky in stark astonishment and horror. Milo's planes, ballooning serenely in over the blossoming treetops with their bomb bay doors open and wing flaps down and with their monstrous, bug-eyed, blinding, fiercely flickering, eerie landing lights on, were the most apocalyptic sight he had ever beheld. Colonel Cathcart let go a stricken gasp of dismay and hurled himself headlong into his jeep, almost sobbing. He found the gas pedal and the ignition and sped toward the airfield as fast as the rocking car would carry him, his huge flabby hands clenched and bloodless on the wheel or blaring his horn tormentedly. Once he almost killed himself when he swerved with a banshee screech of tires to avoid plowing into a bunch of men running crazily toward the hills in their underwear with their stunned faces down and their thin arms pressed high around their temples as puny shields. Yellow, orange and red fires were burning on both sides of the road. Tents and trees were in flames, and Milo's planes kept coming around interminably with their blinking white landing lights on and their bomb bay doors open. Colonel Cathcart almost turned his jeep over when he slammed the brakes on at the control tower. He leaped from the car while it was still skidding dangerously and hurtled up the flight of steps inside, where three men were busy at the instruments and the controls. He bowled two of them aside in his lunge for the nickel-plated microphone, his eyes glittering wildly and his beefy face contorted with stress. He squeezed the microphone in a bestial grip and began shouting hysterically at the top of his voice,

"Milo, you son of a bitch! Are you crazy? What the hell are you doing? Come down! Come down!"

"Stop hollering so much, will you?" answered Milo, who was standing there right beside him in the control tower with a microphone of his own. "I'm right here." Milo looked at him with reproof and turned back to his work. "Very good, men, very good," he chanted into his microphone. "But I see one supply shed still standing. That will never do, Purvis—I've spoken to you about that kind of shoddy work before. Now, you go right back there this minute and try it again. And this time come in slowly . . . slowly. Haste makes waste, Purvis. Haste makes waste. If I've told you once, I must have told you a hundred times. Haste makes waste."

The loud-speaker overhead began squawking. "Milo, this is Alvin Brown. I've finished dropping my bombs. What should I do now?"

"Strafe," said Milo.

"Strafe?" Alvin Brown was shocked.

"We have no choice," Milo informed him resignedly. "It's in the contract."

"Oh, okay, then," Alvin Brown acquiesced. "In that case I'll strafe."

This time Milo had gone too far. Bombing his own men and planes was more than even the most phlegmatic observer could stomach, and it looked like the end for him. High-ranking government officials poured in to investigate. Newspapers inveighed against Milo with glaring headlines, and Congressmen denounced the atrocity in stentorian wrath and clamored for punishment. Mothers with children in the service organized into militant groups and demanded revenge. Not one voice was raised in his defense. Decent people everywhere were affronted, and Milo was all washed up until he opened his books to the public and disclosed the tremendous profit he had made. He could reimburse the government for all the people and property he had destroyed and still have enough money left over to continue buying Egyptian cotton. Everybody, of course, owned a share. And the sweetest part of the whole deal was that there really was no need to reimburse the government at all.

"In a democracy, the government is the people," Milo explained. "We're people, aren't we? So we might just as well keep the money and eliminate the middleman. Frankly, I'd like to see the government get out of war altogether and leave the whole field to private industry. If we pay the government everything we owe it, we'll only be encouraging government control and discouraging other individuals from bombing their own men and planes. We'll be taking away their incentive."

Milo was correct, of course, as everyone soon agreed but a few embittered misfits like Doc Daneeka, who sulked cantankerously and muttered offensive insinuations about the morality of the whole venture until Milo mollified him with a donation, in the name of the syndicate, of a lightweight aluminum collapsible garden chair that Doc Daneeka could fold up conveniently and carry outside his tent each time Chief White Halfoat came inside his tent and carry back inside his tent each time Chief White Halfoat came out. Doc Daneeka had lost his head during Milo's bombardment; instead of running for cover, he had remained out in the open and performed his duty, slithering along the ground through shrapnel, strafing and incendiary bombs like a furtive, wily lizard from casualty to casualty, administering tourniquets, morphine, splints and sulfanilamide with a dark and doleful visage, never saying one word more than he had to and reading in each man's bluing wound a dreadful portent of his own decay. He worked himself relentlessly into exhaustion before the long night was over and came down with a sniffle the next day that sent him hurrying querulously into the medical tent to have his temperature taken by Gus and Wes and to obtain a mustard plaster and vaporizer.

Doc Daneeka tended each moaning man that night with the same glum and profound and introverted grief he showed at the airfield the day of the Avignon mission when Yossarian climbed down the few steps of his plane naked, in a state of utter shock, with Snowden smeared abundantly all over his bare heels and toes, knees, arms and fingers, and pointed inside wordlessly toward where the young radio-gunner lay freezing to death on the floor beside the still younger tail-gunner who kept falling back into a dead faint each time he opened his eyes and saw Snowden dying.

Doc Daneeka draped a blanket around Yossarian's shoulders almost tenderly after Snowden had been removed from the plane and carried into an ambulance on a stretcher. He led Yossarian toward his jeep. McWatt helped, and the three drove in silence to the squadron medical tent, where McWatt and Doc Daneeka guided Yossarian inside to a chair and washed Snowden off him with cold wet balls of absorbent cotton. Doc Daneeka gave him a pill and a shot that put him to sleep for twelve hours. When Yossarian woke up and went to see him, Doc Daneeka gave him another pill and a shot that put him to sleep for another twelve hours. When Yossarian woke up again and went to see him, Doc Daneeka made ready to give him another pill and a shot.

"How long are you going to keep giving me those pills and shots?" Yossarian asked him.

"Until you feel better."

"I feel all right now."

Doc Daneeka's fragile suntanned forehead furrowed with surprise. "Then why don't you put some clothes on? Why are you walking around naked?"

"I don't want to wear a uniform any more."

Doc Daneeka accepted the explanation and put away his hypodermic syringe. "Are you sure you feel all right?"

"I feel fine. I'm just a little logy from all those pills and shots you've been giving me."

Yossarian went about his business with no clothes on all the rest of that day and was still naked late the next morning when Milo, after hunting everywhere else, finally found him sitting up a tree a small distance in back of the quaint little military cemetery at which Snowden was being buried. Milo was dressed in his customary business attire—olive-drab trousers, a fresh olive-drab shirt and tie, with one silver first lieutenant's bar gleaming on the collar, and a regulation dress cap with a stiff leather bill.

"I've been looking all over for you," Milo called up to Yossarian from the ground reproachfully.

"You should have looked for me in this tree," Yossarian answered. "I've been up here all morning."

"Come on down and taste this and tell me if it's good. It's very important."

Yossarian shook his head. He sat nude on the lowest limb of the tree and balanced himself with both hands grasping the bough directly above. He refused to budge, and Milo had no choice but to stretch both arms about the trunk in a distasteful hug and start climbing. He struggled upward clumsily with loud grunts and wheezes, and his clothes were squashed and crooked by the time he pulled himself up high enough to hook a leg over the limb and pause for breath. His dress cap was askew and in danger of falling. Milo caught it just when it began slipping. Globules of perspiration glistened like transparent pearls around his mustache and swelled like opaque blisters under his eyes. Yossarian watched him impassively. Cautiously Milo worked himself around in a half circle so that he could face Yossarian. He unwrapped tissue paper from something soft, round and brown and handed it out to Yossarian.

"Please taste this and let me know what you think. I'd like to serve it to the men."

"What is it?" asked Yossarian, and took a big bite.

"Chocolate-covered cotton."

Yossarian gagged convulsively and sprayed his big mouthful of chocolate-covered cotton right out into Milo's face. "Here, take it back!" he spouted angrily. "Jesus Christ! Have you gone crazy? You didn't even take the goddam seeds out."

"Give it a chance, will you?" Milo begged. "It can't be that bad. Is it really that bad?"

"It's even worse."

"But I've got to make the mess halls feed it to the men."

"They'll never be able to swallow it."

"They've got to swallow it," Milo ordained with dictatorial grandeur, and almost broke his neck when he let go with one arm to wave a righteous finger in the air.

"Come on out here," Yossarian invited him. "You'll be much safer, and you can see everything."

Gripping the bough above with both hands, Milo began inching his way out on the limb sideways with utmost care and apprehension. His face was rigid with tension, and he sighed with relief when he found himself seated securely beside Yossarian. He stroked the tree affectionately. "This is a pretty good tree," he observed admiringly with proprietary gratitude.

"It's the tree of life," Yossarian answered, waggling his toes, "and of knowledge of good and evil, too."

Milo squinted closely at the bark and branches. "No it isn't," he replied. "It's a chestnut tree. I ought to know. I sell chestnuts."

"Have it your way."

They sat in the tree without talking for several seconds, their legs dangling and their hands almost straight up on the bough above, the one completely nude but for a pair of crepe-soled sandals, the other completely dressed in a coarse olive-drab woolen uniform with his tie knotted tight. Milo studied Yossarian diffidently through the corner of his eye, hesitating tactfully.

"I want to ask you something," he said at last. "You don't have any clothes on. I don't want to butt in or anything, but I just want to know. Why aren't you wearing your uniform?"

"I don't want to."

Milo nodded rapidly like a sparrow pecking. "I see, I see," he stated quickly with a look of vivid confusion. "I understand perfectly. I heard Appleby and Captain Black say you had gone crazy, and I just wanted to find out." He hesitated politely again, weighing his next question. "Aren't you ever going to put your uniform on again?"

"I don't think so."

Milo nodded with spurious vim to indicate he still understood and then sat silent, ruminating gravely with troubled misgiving. A scarlet-crested bird shot by below, brushing sure dark wings against a quivering bush. Yossarian and Milo were covered in their bower by tissue-thin tiers of sloping green and largely surrounded by other gray chestnut trees and a silver spruce. The sun was high overhead in a vast sapphire-blue sky beaded with low, isolated, puffy clouds of dry and immaculate white. There was no breeze, and the leaves about them hung motionless. The shade was feathery. Everything was at peace but Milo, who straightened suddenly with a muffled cry and began pointing excitedly.

"Look at that!" he exclaimed in alarm. "Look at that! That's a funeral going on down there. That looks like the cemetery. Isn't it?"

Yossarian answered him slowly in a level voice. "They're burying that kid who got killed in my plane over Avignon the other day. Snowden."

"What happened to him?" Milo asked in a voice deadened with awe.

"He got killed."

"That's terrible," Milo grieved, and his large brown eyes filled with tears. "That poor kid. It really is terrible." He bit his trembling lip hard, and his voice rose with emotion when he continued. "And it will get even worse if the mess halls don't agree to buy my cotton. Yossarian, what's the matter with them? Don't they realize it's their syndicate? Don't they know they've all got a share?"

"Did the dead man in my tent have a share?" Yossarian demanded caustically.

"Of course he did," Milo assured him lavishly. "Everybody in the squadron has a share."

"He was killed before he even got into the squadron."

Milo made a deft grimace of tribulation and turned away. "I wish you'd stop picking on me about that dead man in your tent," he pleaded peevishly. "I told you I didn't have anything to do with killing him. Is it my fault that I saw this great opportunity to corner the market on Egyptian cotton and got us into all this trouble? Was I supposed to know there was going to be a glut? I didn't even know what a glut was in those days. An opportunity to corner a market doesn't come along very often, and I was pretty shrewd to grab the chance when I had it." Milo gulped back a moan as he saw six uniformed pallbearers lift the plain pine coffin from the ambulance and set it gently down on the ground beside the yawning gash of the freshly dug grave. "And now I can't get rid of a single penny's worth," he mourned.

Yossarian was unmoved by the fustian charade of the burial ceremony, and by Milo's crushing bereavement. The chaplain's voice floated up to him through the distance tenuously in an unintelligible, almost inaudible monotone, like a gaseous murmur. Yossarian could make out Major Major by his towering and lanky aloofness and thought he recognized Major Danby mopping his brow with a handkerchief.

Major Danby had not stopped shaking since his run-in with General Dreedle. There were strands of enlisted men molded in a curve around the three officers, as inflexible as lumps of wood, and four idle gravediggers in streaked fatigues lounging indifferently on spades near the shocking, incongruous heap of loose copper-red earth. As Yossarian stared, the chaplain elevated his gaze toward Yossarian beatifically, pressed his fingers down over his eyeballs in a manner of affliction, peered upward again toward Yossarian searchingly, and bowed his head, concluding what Yossarian took to be a climactic part of the funeral rite. The four men in fatigues lifted the coffin on slings and lowered it into the grave. Milo shuddered violently.

"I can't watch it," he cried, turning away in anguish. "I just can't sit here and watch while those mess halls let my syndicate die." He gnashed his teeth and shook his head with bitter woe and resentment. "If they had any loyalty, they would buy my cotton till it hurts so that they can keep right on buying my cotton till it hurts them some more. They would build fires and burn up their underwear and summer uniforms just to create a bigger demand. But they won't do a thing. Yossarian, try eating the rest of this chocolate-covered cotton for me. Maybe it will taste delicious now."

Yossarian pushed his hand away. "Give up, Milo. People can't eat cotton."

Milo's face narrowed cunningly. "It isn't really cotton," he coaxed. "I was joking. It's really cotton candy, delicious cotton candy. Try it and see."

"Now you're lying."

"I never lie!" Milo rejoindered with proud dignity.

"You're lying now."

"I only lie when it's necessary," Milo explained defensively, averting his eyes for a moment and blinking his lashes winningly. "This stuff is better than cotton candy, really it is. It's made out of real cotton. Yossarian, you've got to help me make the men eat it. Egyptian cotton is the finest cotton in the world."

"But it's indigestible," Yossarian emphasized. "It will make them sick, don't you understand? Why don't you try living on it yourself if you don't believe me?"

"I did try," admitted Milo gloomily. "And it made me sick."

The graveyard was yellow as hay and green as cooked cabbage. In a little while the chaplain stepped back, and the beige crescent of human forms began to break up sluggishly, like flotsam. The men drifted without haste or sound to the vehicles parked along the side of the bumpy dirt road. With their heads down disconsolately, the chaplain, Major Major and Major Danby moved toward their jeeps in an ostracized group, each holding himself friendlessly several feet away from the other two.

"It's all over," observed Yossarian.

"It's the end," Milo agreed despondently. "There's no hope left. And all because I left them free to make their own decisions. That should teach me a lesson about discipline the next time I try something like this."

"Why don't you sell your cotton to the government?" Yossarian suggested casually as he watched the four men in streaked fatigues shoveling heaping bladefuls of the copper-red earth back down inside the grave.

Milo vetoed the idea brusquely. "It's a matter of principle," he explained firmly. "The government has no business in business, and I would be the last person in the world to ever try to involve the government in a business of mine. But the business of government *is* business," he remembered alertly, and continued with elation. "Calvin Coolidge said that, and Calvin Coolidge was a President, so it must be true. And the government does have the responsibility of buying all the Egyptian cotton I've got that no one else wants so that I can make a profit, doesn't it?" Milo's face clouded almost as abruptly, and his spirits descended into a state of sad anxiety. "But how will I get the government to do it?"

"Bribe it," Yossarian said.

"Bribe it!" Milo was outraged and almost lost his balance and broke his neck again. "Shame on you!" he scolded severely, breathing virtuous fire down and upward into his rusty mustache through his billowing nostrils and prim lips. "Bribery is against the law, and you know it. But it's not against the law to make a profit, is it? So it can't be against the law for me to bribe someone in order to make a fair profit, can it? No, of course not!" He fell to brooding again, with a meek, almost pitiable distress. "But how will I know who to bribe?"

"Oh, don't you worry about that," Yossarian comforted him with a toneless snicker as the engines of the jeeps and ambulance fractured the drowsy silence and the vehicles in the rear began driving away backward. "You make the bribe big enough and they'll find you. Just make sure you do everything right out in the open. Let everyone know exactly what you want and how much you're willing to pay for it. The first time you act guilty or ashamed, you might get into trouble."

"I wish you'd come with me," Milo remarked. "I won't feel safe among people who take bribes. They're no better than a bunch of crooks."

"You'll be all right," Yossarian assured him with confidence. "If you run into trouble, just tell everybody that the security of the country requires a strong domestic Egyptian-cotton speculating industry."

"It does," Milo informed him solemnly. "A strong Egyptian-cotton speculating industry means a much stronger America."

"Of course it does. And if that doesn't work, point out the great number of American families that depend on it for income."

"A great many American families do depend on it for income."

"You see?" said Yossarian. "You're much better at it than I am. You almost make it sound true."

"It is true," Milo exclaimed with a strong trace of the old hauteur.

"That's what I mean. You do it with just the right amount of conviction."

"You're sure you won't come with me?"

Yossarian shook his head.

Milo was impatient to get started. He stuffed the remainder of the chocolate-covered cotton ball into his shirt pocket and edged his way back gingerly along the branch to the smooth gray trunk. He threw his arms about the trunk in a generous and awkward embrace and began shinnying down, the sides of his leather-soled shoes slipping constantly so that it seemed many times he would fall and injure himself. Halfway down, he changed his mind and climbed back up. Bits of tree bark stuck to his mustache, and his straining face was flushed with exertion.

"I wish you'd put your uniform on instead of going around naked that way," he confided pensively before he climbed back down again and hurried away. "You might start a trend, and then I'll never get rid of all this goldarned cotton."

25

The Chaplain

It was already some time since the chaplain had first begun wondering what everything was all about. Was there a God? How could he be sure? Being an Anabaptist minister in the American Army was difficult enough under the best of circumstances; without dogma, it was almost intolerable.

People with loud voices frightened him. Brave, aggressive men of action like Colonel Cathcart left him feeling helpless and alone. Wherever he went in the Army, he was a stranger. Enlisted men and officers did not conduct themselves with him as they conducted themselves with other enlisted men and officers, and even other chaplains were not as friendly toward him as they were toward each other. In a world in which success was the only virtue, he had resigned himself to failure. He was painfully aware that he lacked the ecclesiastical aplomb and *savoir-faire* that enabled so many of his colleagues in other faiths and sects to get ahead. He was just not equipped to excel. He thought of himself as ugly and wanted daily to be home with his wife.

Actually, the chaplain was almost good-looking, with a pleasant, sensitive face as pale and brittle as sandstone. His mind was open on every subject.

Perhaps he really was Washington Irving, and perhaps he really had been signing Washington Irving's name to those letters he knew nothing about. Such lapses of memory were not uncommon in medical annals, he knew. There was no way of really knowing anything, he knew, not even that there was no way of really knowing anything. He remembered very distinctly—or was under the impression he remembered very distinctly—his feeling that he had met Yossarian somewhere before the first time he *had* met Yossarian lying in bed in the hospital. He remembered experiencing the same disquieting sensation almost two weeks later when Yossarian appeared at his tent to ask to be taken off combat duty. By that time, of course, the chaplain *had* met Yossarian somewhere before, in that odd, unorthodox ward in which every patient seemed delinquent but the unfortunate patient covered from head to toe in white bandages and plaster who was found dead one day with a thermometer in his mouth. But the chaplain's impression of a prior meeting was of some occasion far more momentous and occult than that, of a significant encounter with Yossarian in some remote, submerged and perhaps even entirely spiritual epoch in which he had made the identical, foredooming admission that there was nothing, absolutely nothing, he could do to help him.

Doubts of such kind gnawed at the chaplain's lean, suffering frame insatiably. *Was* there a single true faith, or a life after death? How many angels *could* dance on the head of a pin, and with what matters *did* God occupy Himself in all the infinite aeons before the Creation? Why *was* it necessary to put a protective seal on the brow of Cain if there *were* no other people to protect him from? *Did* Adam and Eve produce daughters? These were the great, complex questions of ontology that tormented him. Yet they never seemed nearly as crucial to him as the question of kindness and good manners. He was pinched perspiringly in the epistemological dilemma of the skeptic, unable to accept solutions to problems he was unwilling to dismiss as unsolvable. He was never without misery, and never without hope.

"Have you ever," he inquired hesitantly of Yossarian that day in his tent as Yossarian sat holding in both hands the warm bottle of Coca-Cola with which the chaplain *had* been able to solace him, "been in a situation which you felt you had been in before, even though you knew you were experiencing it for the first time?" Yossarian nodded perfunctorily, and the chaplain's breath quickened in anticipation as he made ready to join his will power with Yossarian's in a prodigious effort to rip away at last the voluminous black folds shrouding the eternal mysteries of existence. "Do you have that feeling now?"

Yossarian shook his head and explained that *déjà vu* was just a momentary infinitesimal lag in the operation of two coactive sensory nerve centers that commonly functioned simultaneously. The chaplain scarcely heard him. He was disappointed, but not inclined to believe Yossarian, for he had been given a sign, a secret, enigmatic vision that he still lacked the boldness to divulge. There was no mistaking the awesome implications of the chaplain's revelation: it was either an insight of divine origin or a hallucination; he was either blessed or losing his mind. Both prospects filled him with equal fear and depression. It was neither *déjà vu*, *presque vu* nor *jamais vu*. It was possible that there were other *vus* of which he had never heard and that one of these other *vus* would explain succinctly the baffling phenomenon of which he had been both a witness and a part; it was even possible that none of what he thought had taken place, really *had* taken place, that he was dealing with an aberration of memory rather than of perception, that he never really *had* thought he had seen what he now thought he once did think he had seen, that his impression now that he once had thought so was merely the *illusion* of an illusion, and that he was only now imagining that he had ever once imagined seeing a naked man sitting in a tree at the cemetery.

It was obvious to the chaplain now that he was not particularly well suited to his work, and he often speculated whether he might not be happier serving in some other branch of the service, as a private in the infantry or field artillery, perhaps, or even as a paratrooper. He had no real friends. Before meeting Yossarian, there was no one in the group with whom he felt at ease, and he was hardly at ease with Yossarian, whose frequent rash and insubordinate outbursts kept him almost constantly on edge and in an ambiguous state of enjoyable trepidation. The chaplain felt safe when he was at the officers' club with Yossarian and Dunbar, and even with just Nately and McWatt. When he sat with them he had no need to sit with anyone else; his problem of where to sit was solved, and he was protected against the undesired company of all those fellow officers who invariably welcomed him with excessive cordiality when he approached and waited uncomfortably for him to go away. He made so many people uneasy. Everyone was always very friendly toward him, and no one was ever very nice; everyone spoke to him, and no one ever said anything. Yossarian and Dunbar were much more relaxed, and the chaplain was hardly uncomfortable with them at all. They even defended him the night Colonel Cathcart tried to throw him out of the officers' club again, Yossarian rising truculently to intervene and Nately shouting out, "*Yossarian!*" to restrain him. Colonel Cathcart turned white as a sheet at the sound of Yossarian's name, and, to everyone's amazement, retreated in horrified disorder until he bumped into General Dreedle, who elbowed him away with annoyance and ordered him right back to order the chaplain to start coming into the officers' club every night again.

The chaplain had almost as much trouble keeping track of his status at the officers' club as he had remembering at which of the ten mess halls in the group he was scheduled to eat his next meal. He would just as soon have remained kicked out of the officers' club, had it not been for the pleasure he was now finding there with his new companions. If the chaplain did not go to the officers' club at night, there was no place else he could go. He would pass the time at Yossarian's and Dunbar's table with a shy, reticent smile, seldom speaking unless addressed, a glass of thick sweet wine almost untasted before him as he toyed unfamiliarly with the tiny corncob pipe that he affected self-consciously and occasionally stuffed with tobacco and smoked. He enjoyed listening to Nately, whose maudlin, bittersweet lamentations mirrored much of his own romantic desolation and never failed to evoke in him resurgent tides of longing for his wife and children. The chaplain would encourage Nately with nods of comprehension or assent, amused by his candor and immaturity. Nately did not glory too immodestly that his girl was a prostitute, and the chaplain's awareness stemmed mainly from Captain Black, who never slouched past their table without a broad wink at the chaplain and some tasteless, wounding jibe about her to Nately. The chaplain did not approve of Captain Black and found it difficult not to wish him evil.

No one, not even Nately, seemed really to appreciate that he, Chaplain Albert Taylor Tappman, was not just a chaplain but a human being, that he *could* have a charming, passionate, pretty wife whom he loved almost insanely and three small blue-eyed children with strange, forgotten faces who would grow up someday to regard him as a freak and who might never forgive him for all the social embarrassment his vocation would cause them. Why couldn't anybody understand that he was not really a freak but a normal, lonely adult trying to lead a normal, lonely adult life? If they pricked him, didn't he bleed? And if he was tickled, didn't he laugh? It seemed never to have occurred to them that he, just as they, had eyes, hands, organs, dimensions, senses and affections, that he was wounded by the same kind of weapons they were, warmed and cooled by the same breezes and fed by the same kind of food, although, he was forced to concede, in a different mess hall for each successive meal. The only person who did seem to realize he had feelings was Corporal Whitcomb, who had just managed to bruise them all by going over his head to Colonel Cathcart with his proposal for sending form letters of condolence home to the families of men killed or wounded in combat.

The chaplain's wife was the one thing in the world he *could* be certain of, and it would have been sufficient, if only he had been left to live his life out with just her and the children. The chaplain's wife was a reserved, diminutive, agreeable woman in her early thirties, very dark and very attractive, with a narrow waist, calm intelligent eyes, and small, bright, pointy teeth in a childlike face that was vivacious and petite; he kept forgetting what his children looked like, and each time he returned to their snapshots it was like seeing their faces for the first time. The chaplain loved his wife and children with such tameless intensity that he often wanted to sink to the ground helplessly and weep like a castaway cripple. He was tormented inexorably by morbid fantasies involving them, by dire, hideous omens of illness and accident. His meditations were polluted with threats of dread diseases like Ewing's tumor and leukemia; he saw his infant son die two or three times every week because he had never taught his wife how to stop arterial bleeding; watched, in tearful, paralyzed silence, his whole family electrocuted, one after the other, at a baseboard socket because he had never told her that a human body would conduct electricity; all four went up in flames almost every night when the water heater exploded and set the two-story wooden house afire; in ghastly, heartless, revolting detail he saw his poor dear wife's trim and fragile body crushed to a viscous pulp against the brick wall of a market building by a half-witted drunken automobile driver and watched his hysterical five-year-old daughter being led away from the grisly scene by a kindly middle-aged gentleman with snow-white hair who raped and murdered her repeatedly as soon as he had driven her off to a deserted sandpit, while his two younger children starved to death slowly in the house after his wife's mother, who had been baby-sitting, dropped dead from a heart attack when news of his wife's accident was given to her over the telephone. The chaplain's wife was a sweet, soothing, considerate woman, and he yearned to touch the warm flesh of her slender arm again and stroke her smooth black hair, to hear her intimate, comforting voice. She was a much stronger person than he was. He wrote brief, untroubled letters to her once a week, sometimes twice. He wanted to write urgent love letters to her all day long and crowd the endless pages with desperate, uninhibited confessions of his humble worship and need and with careful instructions for administering artificial respiration. He wanted to pour out to her in torrents of self-pity all his unbearable loneliness and despair and warn her never to leave the boric acid or the aspirin in reach of the children or to cross a street against the traffic light. He did not wish to worry her. The chaplain's wife was intuitive, gentle, compassionate and responsive. Almost inevitably, his reveries of reunion with her ended in explicit acts of love-making.

The chaplain felt most deceitful presiding at funerals, and it would not have astonished him to learn that the apparition in the tree that day was a manifestation of the Almighty's censure for the blasphemy and pride inherent in his function. To simulate gravity, feign grief and pretend supernatural intelligence of the hereafter in so fearsome and arcane a circumstance as death seemed the most criminal of offenses. He recalled—or was almost convinced he recalled—the scene of the cemetery perfectly. He could still see Major Major and Major Danby standing somber as broken stone pillars on either side of him, see almost the exact number of enlisted men and almost the exact places in which they had stood, see the four unmoving men with spades, the repulsive coffin and the large, loose, triumphant mound of reddish-brown earth, and the massive, still, depthless, muffling sky, so weirdly blank and blue that day it was almost poisonous. He would remember them forever, for they were all part and parcel of the most extraordinary event that had ever befallen him, an event perhaps marvelous, perhaps pathological—the vision of the naked man in the tree. How could he explain it? It was not already seen or never seen, and certainly not almost seen; neither *déjà vu*, *jamais vu* nor *presque vu* was elastic enough to cover it. Was it a ghost, then? The dead man's soul? An angel from heaven or a minion from hell? Or was the whole fantastic episode merely the figment of a diseased imagination, his own, of a deteriorating mind, a rotting brain? The possibility that there really had been a naked man in the tree—two men, actually, since the first had been joined shortly by a second man clad in a brown mustache and sinister dark garments from head to toe who bent forward ritualistically along the limb of the tree to offer the first man something to drink from a brown goblet—never crossed the chaplain's mind.

The chaplain was sincerely a very helpful person who was never able to help anyone, not even Yossarian when he finally decided to seize the bull by the horns and visit Major Major secretly to learn if, as Yossarian had said, the men in Colonel Cathcart's group really were being forced to fly more combat missions than anyone else. It was a daring, impulsive move on which the chaplain decided after quarreling with Corporal Whitcomb again and washing down with tepid canteen water his joyless lunch of a Milky Way and Baby Ruth. He went to Major Major on foot so that Corporal Whitcomb would not see him leaving, stealing into the forest noiselessly until the two tents in his clearing were left behind, then dropping down inside the abandoned railroad ditch, where the footing was surer. He hurried along the fossilized wooden ties with accumulating mutinous anger. He had been browbeaten and humiliated successively that morning by Colonel Cathcart, Colonel

Korn and Corporal Whitcomb. He just *had* to make himself felt in some respect! His slight chest was soon puffing for breath. He moved as swiftly as he could without breaking into a run, fearing his resolution might dissolve if he slowed. Soon he saw a uniformed figure coming toward him between the rusted rails. He clambered immediately up the side of the ditch, ducked inside a dense copse of low trees for concealment and sped along in his original direction on a narrow, overgrown mossy path he found winding deep inside the shaded forest. It was tougher going there, but he plunged ahead with the same reckless and consuming determination, slipping and stumbling often and stinging his unprotected hands on the stubborn branches blocking his way until the bushes and tall ferns on both sides spread open and he lurched past an olive-drab military trailer on cinder blocks clearly visible through the thinning underbrush. He continued past a tent with a luminous pearl-gray cat sunning itself outside and past another trailer on cinder blocks and then burst into the clearing of Yossarian's squadron. A salty dew had formed on his lips. He did not pause, but strode directly across the clearing into the orderly room, where he was welcomed by a gaunt, stoop-shouldered staff sergeant with prominent cheekbones and long, very light blond hair, who informed him graciously that he could go right in, since Major Major was out.

The chaplain thanked him with a curt nod and proceeded alone down the aisle between the desks and typewriters to the canvas partition in the rear. He bobbed through the triangular opening and found himself inside an empty office. The flap fell closed behind him. He was breathing hard and sweating profusely. The office remained empty. He thought he heard furtive whispering. Ten minutes passed. He looked about in stern displeasure, his jaws clamped together indomitably, and then turned suddenly to water as he remembered the staff sergeant's exact words: he could go right in, since Major Major was out. *The enlisted men were playing a practical joke!* The chaplain shrank back from the wall in terror, bitter tears springing to his eyes. A pleading whimper escaped his trembling lips. Major Major was elsewhere, and the enlisted men in the other room had made him the butt of an inhuman prank. He could almost see them waiting on the other side of the canvas wall, bunched up expectantly like a pack of greedy, gloating omnivorous beasts of prey, ready with their barbaric mirth and jeers to pounce on him brutally the moment he reappeared. He cursed himself for his gullibility and wished in panic for something like a mask or a pair of dark glasses and a false mustache to disguise him, or for a forceful, deep voice like Colonel Cathcart's and broad, muscular shoulders and biceps to enable him to step outside fearlessly and vanquish his malevolent persecutors with an overbearing authority and self-confidence that would make them all quail and slink away cravenly in repentance. He lacked the courage to face them. The only other way out was the window. The coast was clear, and the chaplain jumped out of Major Major's office through the window, darted swiftly around the corner of the tent, and leaped down inside the railroad ditch to hide.

He scooted away with his body doubled over and his face contorted intentionally into a nonchalant, sociable smile in case anyone chanced to see him. He abandoned the ditch for the forest the moment he saw someone coming toward him from the opposite direction and ran through the cluttered forest frenziedly like someone pursued, his cheeks burning with disgrace. He heard loud, wild peals of derisive laughter crashing all about him and caught blurred glimpses of wicked, beery faces smirking far back inside the bushes and high overhead in the foliage of the trees. Spasms of scorching pains stabbed through his lungs and slowed him to a crippled walk. He lunged and staggered onward until he could go no farther and collapsed all at once against a gnarled apple tree, banging his head hard against the trunk as he toppled forward and holding on with both arms to keep from falling. His breathing was a rasping, moaning din in his ears. Minutes passed like hours before he finally recognized himself as the source of the turbulent roar that was overwhelming him. The pains in his chest abated. Soon he felt strong enough to stand. He cocked his ears craftily. The forest was quiet. There was no demonic laughter, no one was chasing him. He was too tired and sad and dirty to feel relieved. He straightened his disheveled clothing with fingers that were numb and shaking and walked the rest of the way to the clearing with rigid self-control. The chaplain brooded often about the danger of heart attack.

Corporal Whitcomb's jeep was still parked in the clearing. The chaplain tiptoed stealthily around the back of Corporal Whitcomb's tent rather than pass the entrance and risk being seen and insulted by him. Heaving a grateful sigh, he slipped quickly inside his own tent and found Corporal Whitcomb ensconced on his cot, his knees propped up. Corporal Whitcomb's mud-caked shoes were on the chaplain's blanket, and he was eating one of the chaplain's candy bars as he thumbed with a sneering expression through one of the chaplain's Bibles.

"Where've *you* been?" he demanded rudely and disinterestedly, without looking up.

The chaplain colored and turned away evasively. "I went for a walk through the woods."

"All right," Corporal Whitcomb snapped. "Don't take me into your confidence. But just wait and see what happens to my morale." He bit into the chaplain's candy bar hungrily and continued with a full mouth. "You had a visitor while you were gone. Major Major."

The chaplain spun around with surprise and cried: "Major Major? Major Major was *here?*"

"That's who we're talking about, isn't it?"

"Where did he go?"

"He jumped down into that railroad ditch and took off like a frightened rabbit." Corporal Whitcomb snickered. "What a jerk!"

"Did he say what he wanted?"

"He said he needed your help in a matter of great importance."

The chaplain was astounded. "Major Major said *that?*"

"He didn't *say* that," Corporal Whitcomb corrected with withering precision. "He wrote it down in a sealed personal letter he left on your desk."

The chaplain glanced at the bridge table that served as his desk and saw only the abominable orange-red pear-shaped plum tomato he had obtained that same morning from Colonel Cathcart, still lying on its side where he had forgotten it like an indestructible and incarnadine symbol of his own ineptitude. "Where is the letter?"

"I threw it away as soon as I tore it open and read it." Corporal Whitcomb slammed the Bible shut and jumped up. "What's the matter? Won't you take my word for it?" He walked out. He walked right back in and almost collided with the chaplain, who was rushing out behind him on his way back to Major Major. "You don't know how to delegate responsibility," Corporal Whitcomb informed him sullenly. "That's another one of the things that's wrong with you."

The chaplain nodded penitently and hurried past, unable to make himself take the time to apologize. He could feel the skillful hand of fate motivating him imperatively. Twice that day already, he realized now, Major Major had come racing toward him inside the ditch; and twice that day the chaplain had stupidly postponed the destined meeting by bolting into the forest. He seethed with self-recrimination as he hastened back as rapidly as he could stride along the splintered, irregularly-spaced railroad ties. Bits of grit and gravel inside his shoes and socks were grinding the tops of his toes raw. His pale, laboring face was screwed up unconsciously into a grimace of acute discomfort. The early August afternoon was growing hotter and more humid. It was almost a mile from his tent to Yossarian's squadron. The chaplain's summer-tan shirt was soaking with perspiration by the time he arrived there and rushed breathlessly back inside the orderly-room tent, where he was halted peremptorily by the same treacherous, soft-spoken staff sergeant with round eyeglasses and gaunt cheeks, who requested him to remain outside because Major Major was inside and told him he would not be allowed inside until Major Major went out. The chaplain looked at him in an uncomprehending daze. Why did the sergeant hate him? he wondered. His lips were white and trembling. He was aching with thirst. What was the *matter* with people? Wasn't there tragedy enough? The sergeant put his hand out and held the chaplain steady.

"I'm sorry, sir," he said regretfully in a low, courteous, melancholy voice. "But those are Major Major's orders. He never wants to see anyone."

"He wants to see me," the chaplain pleaded. "He came to my tent to see me while I was here before."

"Major Major did that?" the sergeant asked.

"Yes, he did. Please go in and ask him."

"I'm afraid I can't go in, sir. He never wants to see me either. Perhaps if you left a note."

"I don't want to leave a note. Doesn't he ever make an exception?"

"Only in extreme circumstances. The last time he left his tent was to attend the funeral of one of the enlisted men. The last time he saw anyone in his office was a time he was forced to. A bombardier named Yossarian forced—"

"Yossarian?" The chaplain lit up with excitement at this new coincidence. Was this another miracle in the making? "But that's exactly whom *I* want to speak to him about! Did they talk about the number of missions Yossarian has to fly?"

"Yes, sir, that's exactly what they did talk about. Captain Yossarian had flown fifty-one missions, and he appealed to Major Major to ground him so that he wouldn't have to fly four more. Colonel Cathcart wanted only fifty-five missions then."

"And what did Major Major say?"

"Major Major told him there was nothing he could do."

The chaplain's face fell. "Major Major said that?"

"Yes, sir. In fact, he advised Yossarian to go see you for help. Are you certain you wouldn't like to leave a note, sir? I have a pencil and paper right here."

The chaplain shook his head, chewing his clotted dry lower lip forlornly, and walked out. It was still so early in the day, and so much had already happened. The air was cooler in the forest. His throat was parched and sore. He walked slowly and asked himself ruefully what new misfortune could possibly befall him a moment before the mad hermit in the woods leaped out at him without warning from behind a mulberry bush. The chaplain screamed at the top of his voice.

The tall, cadaverous stranger fell back in fright at the chaplain's cry and shrieked, "Don't hurt me!"

"Who are you?" the chaplain shouted.

"Please don't hurt me!" the man shouted back.

"I'm the chaplain!"

"Then why do you want to hurt me?"

"I don't want to hurt you!" the chaplain insisted with a rising hint of exasperation, even though he was still rooted to the spot. "Just tell me who you are and what you want from me."

"I just want to find out if Chief White Halfoat died of pneumonia yet," the man shouted back. "That's all I want. I live here. My name is Flume. I belong to the squadron, but I live here in the woods. You can ask anyone."

The chaplain's composure began trickling back as he studied the queer, cringing figure intently. A pair of captain's bars ulcerated with rust hung on the man's ragged shirt collar. He had a hairy, tar-black mole on the underside of one nostril and a heavy rough mustache the color of poplar bark.

"Why do you live in the woods if you belong to the squadron?" the chaplain inquired curiously.

"I have to live in the woods," the captain replied crabbily, as though the chaplain ought to know. He straightened slowly, still watching the chaplain guardedly although he towered above him by more than a full head. "Don't you hear everybody talking about me? Chief White Halfoat swore he was going to cut my throat some night when I was fast asleep, and I don't dare lie down in the squadron while he's still alive."

The chaplain listened to the implausible explanation distrustfully. "But that's incredible," he replied. "That would be premeditated murder. Why didn't you report the incident to Major Major?"

"I did report the incident to Major Major," said the captain sadly, "and Major Major said *he* would cut my throat if I ever spoke to him again." The man studied the chaplain fearfully. "Are you going to cut my throat, too?"

"Oh, no, no, no," the chaplain assured him. "Of course not. Do you really live in the forest?"

The captain nodded, and the chaplain gazed at his porous, gray pallor of fatigue and malnutrition with a mixture of pity and esteem. The man's body was a bony shell inside rumpled clothing that hung on him like a disorderly collection of sacks. Wisps of dried grass were glued all over him; he needed a haircut badly. There were great, dark circles under his eyes. The chaplain was moved almost to tears by the harassed, bedraggled picture the captain presented, and he filled with deference and compassion at the thought of the many severe rigors the poor man had to endure daily. In a voice hushed with humility, he said,

"Who does your laundry?"

The captain pursed his lips in a businesslike manner. "I have it done by a washerwoman in one of the farmhouses down the road. I keep my things in my trailer and sneak inside once or twice a day for a clean handkerchief or a change of underwear."

"What will you do when winter comes?"

"Oh, I expect to be back in the squadron by then," the captain answered with a kind of martyred confidence. "Chief White Halfoat kept promising everyone that he was going to die of pneumonia, and I guess I'll just have to be patient until the weather turns a little colder and damper." He scrutinized the chaplain perplexedly. "Don't you know all this? Don't you hear all the fellows talking about me?"

"I don't think I've ever heard anyone mention you."

"Well, I certainly can't understand that." The captain was piqued, but managed to carry on with a pretense of optimism. "Well, here it is almost September already, so I guess it won't be too long now. The next time any of the boys ask about me, why, just tell them I'll be back grinding out those old publicity releases again as soon as Chief White Halfoat dies of pneumonia. Will you tell them that? Say I'll be back in the squadron as soon as winter comes and Chief White Halfoat dies of pneumonia. Okay?"

The chaplain memorized the prophetic words solemnly, entranced further by their esoteric import. "Do you live on berries, herbs and roots?" he asked.

"No, of course not," the captain replied with surprise. "I sneak into the mess hall through the back and eat in the kitchen. Milo gives me sandwiches and milk."

"What do you do when it rains?"

The captain answered frankly. "I get wet."

"Where do you sleep?"

Swiftly the captain ducked down into a crouch and began backing away. "You too?" he cried frantically.

"Oh, no," cried the chaplain. "I swear to you."

"You *do* want to cut my throat!" the captain insisted.

"I give you my word," the chaplain pleaded, but it was too late, for the homely hirsute specter had already vanished, dissolving so expertly inside the blooming, dappled, fragmented malformations of leaves, light and shadows that the chaplain was already doubting that he had even been there. So many monstrous events were occurring that he was no longer positive which events *were* monstrous and which *were* really taking place. He wanted to find out about the madman in the woods as quickly as possible, to check if there ever really *had* been a Captain Flume, but his first chore, he recalled with reluctance, was to appease Corporal Whitcomb for neglecting to delegate enough responsibility to him. He plodded along the zigzagging path through the forest listlessly, clogged with thirst and feeling almost too exhausted to go on. He was remorseful when he thought of Corporal Whitcomb. He prayed that Corporal Whitcomb would be gone when he reached the clearing so that he could undress without embarrassment, wash his arms and chest and shoulders thoroughly, drink water, lie down refreshed and perhaps even sleep for a few minutes; but he was in for still another disappointment and still another shock, for Corporal Whitcomb was *Sergeant* Whitcomb by the time he arrived and was sitting with his shirt off in the chaplain's chair sewing his new sergeant's stripes on his sleeve with the chaplain's needle and thread. Corporal Whitcomb had been promoted by Colonel Cathcart, who wanted to see the chaplain at once about the letters.

"Oh, no," groaned the chaplain, sinking down dumbfounded on his cot. His warm canteen was empty, and he was too distraught to remember the lister bag hanging outside in the shade between the two tents. "I can't believe it. I just can't believe that anyone would seriously believe that I've been forging Washington Irving's name."

"Not those letters," Corporal Whitcomb corrected, plainly enjoying the chaplain's chagrin. "He wants to see you about the letters home to the families of casualties."

"Those letters?" asked the chaplain with surprise.

"That's right," Corporal Whitcomb gloated. "He's really going to chew you out for refusing to let me send them. You should have seen him go for the idea once I reminded him the letters could carry his signature. That's why he promoted me. He's absolutely sure they'll get him into *The Saturday Evening Post.*"

The chaplain's befuddlement increased. "But how did he know we were even considering the idea?"

"I went to his office and told him."

"You did what?" the chaplain demanded shrilly, and charged to his feet in an unfamiliar rage. "Do you mean to say that you actually went over my head to the colonel without asking my permission?"

Corporal Whitcomb grinned brazenly with scornful satisfaction. "That's right, Chaplain," he answered. "And you better not try to do anything about it if you know what's good for you." He laughed quietly in malicious defiance. "Colonel Cathcart isn't going to like it if he finds out you're getting even with me for bringing him my idea. You know something, Chaplain?" Corporal Whitcomb continued, biting the chaplain's black thread apart contemptuously with a loud snap and buttoning on his shirt. "That dumb bastard really thinks it's one of the greatest ideas he's ever heard."

"It might even get me into *The Saturday Evening Post,*" Colonel Cathcart boasted in his office with a smile, swaggering back and forth convivially as he reproached the chaplain. "And you didn't have brains enough to appreciate it. You've got a good man in Corporal Whitcomb, Chaplain. I hope you have brains enough to appreciate *that.*"

"Sergeant Whitcomb," the chaplain corrected, before he could control himself.

Colonel Cathcart glared. "I *said* Sergeant Whitcomb," he replied. "I wish you'd try listening once in a while instead of always finding fault. You don't want to be a captain all your life, do you?"

"Sir?"

"Well, I certainly don't see how you're ever going to amount to anything else if you keep on this way. Corporal Whitcomb feels that you fellows haven't had a fresh idea in nineteen hundred and forty-four years, and I'm inclined to agree with him. A bright boy, that Corporal Whitcomb. Well, it's all going to change." Colonel Cathcart sat down at his desk with a determined air and cleared a large neat space in his blotter. When he had finished, he tapped his finger inside it. "Starting tomorrow," he said, "I want you and Corporal Whitcomb to write a letter of condolence for me to the next of kin of every man in the group who's killed, wounded or taken prisoner. I want those letters to be sincere letters. I want them filled up with lots of personal details so there'll be no doubt I mean every word you say. Is that clear?"

The chaplain stepped forward impulsively to remonstrate. "But, sir, that's impossible!" he blurted out. "We don't even know all the men that well."

"What difference does that make?" Colonel Cathcart demanded, and then smiled amicably. "Corporal Whitcomb brought me this basic form letter that takes care of just about every situation. Listen: 'Dear Mrs., Mr., Miss, or Mr. and Mrs.: Words cannot express the deep personal grief I experienced when your husband, son, father or brother was killed, wounded or reported missing in action.' And so on. I think that opening sentence sums up my sentiments exactly. Listen, maybe you'd better let Corporal Whitcomb take charge of the whole thing if you don't feel up to it." Colonel Cathcart whipped out his cigarette holder and flexed it between both hands like an onyx-and-ivory riding crop. "That's one of the things that's wrong with you, Chaplain. Corporal Whitcomb tells me you don't know how to delegate responsibility. He says you've got no initiative either. You're not going to disagree with me, are you?"

"No, sir." The chaplain shook his head, feeling despicably remiss because he did not know how to delegate responsibility and had no initiative, and because he really had been tempted to disagree with the colonel. His mind was a shambles. They were shooting skeet outside, and every time a gun was fired his senses were jarred. He could not adjust to the sound of the shots. He was surrounded by bushels of plum tomatoes and was almost convinced that he had stood in Colonel Cathcart's office on some similar occasion deep in the past and had been surrounded by those same bushels of those same plum tomatoes. *Déjà vu* again. The setting seemed so familiar; yet it also seemed so distant. His clothes felt grimy and old, and he was deathly afraid he smelled.

"You take things too seriously, Chaplain," Colonel Cathcart told him bluntly with an air of adult objectivity. "That's another one of the things that's wrong with you. That long face of yours gets everybody depressed. Let me see you laugh once in a while. Come on, Chaplain. You give me a belly laugh right now and I'll give you a whole bushel of plum tomatoes." He waited a second or two, watching, and then chortled victoriously. "You see, Chaplain, I'm right. You can't give me a belly laugh, can you?"

"No, sir," admitted the chaplain meekly, swallowing slowly with a visible effort. "Not right now. I'm very thirsty."

"Then get yourself a drink. Colonel Korn keeps some bourbon in his desk. You ought to try dropping around the officers' club with us some evening just to have yourself a little fun. Try getting lit once in a while. I hope you don't feel you're better than the rest of us just because you're a professional man."

"Oh, no, sir," the chaplain assured him with embarrassment. "As a matter of fact, I have been going to the officers' club the past few evenings."

"You're only a captain, you know," Colonel Cathcart continued, paying no attention to the chaplain's remark. "You may be a professional man, but you're still only a captain."

"Yes, sir. I know."

"That's fine, then. It's just as well you didn't laugh before. I wouldn't have given you the plum tomatoes anyway. Corporal Whitcomb tells me you took a plum tomato when you were in here this morning."

"This morning? But, sir! You gave it to me."

Colonel Cathcart cocked his head with suspicion. "I didn't say I didn't give it to you, did I? I merely said you took it. I don't see why you've got such a guilty conscience if you really didn't steal it. Did I give it to you?"

"Yes, sir. I swear you did."

"Then I'll just have to take your word for it. Although I can't imagine why I'd want to give you a plum tomato." Colonel Cathcart transferred a round glass paperweight competently from the right edge of his desk to the left edge and picked up a sharpened pencil. "Okay, Chaplain, I've got a lot of important work to do now if you're through. You let me know when Corporal Whitcomb has sent out about a dozen of those letters and we'll get in touch with the editors of *The Saturday Evening Post*." A sudden inspiration made his face brighten. "Say! I think I'll volunteer the group for Avignon again. That should speed things up!"

"For Avignon?" The chaplain's heart missed a beat, and all his flesh began to prickle and creep.

"That's right," the colonel explained exuberantly. "The sooner we get some casualties, the sooner we can make some progress on this. I'd like to get in the Christmas issue if we can. I imagine the circulation is higher then."

And to the chaplain's horror, the colonel lifted the phone to volunteer the group for Avignon and tried to kick him out of the officers' club again that very same night a moment before Yossarian rose up drunkenly, knocking over his chair, to start an avenging punch that made Nately call out his name and made Colonel Cathcart blanch and retreat prudently smack into General Dreedle, who shoved him off his bruised foot disgustedly and ordered him forward to kick the chaplain right back into the officers' club. It was all very upsetting to Colonel Cathcart, first the dreaded name *Yossarian!* tolling out again clearly like a warning of doom and then General Dreedle's bruised foot, and that was another fault Colonel Cathcart found in the chaplain, the fact that it was impossible to predict *how* General Dreedle would react each time he saw him. Colonel Cathcart would never forget the first evening General Dreedle took notice of the chaplain in the officers' club, lifting his ruddy, sweltering, intoxicated face to stare ponderously through the yellow pall of cigarette smoke at the chaplain lurking near the wall by himself.

"Well, I'll be damned," General Dreedle had exclaimed hoarsely, his shaggy gray menacing eyebrows beetling in recognition. "Is that a chaplain I see over there? That's really a fine thing when a man of God begins hanging around a place like this with a bunch of dirty drunks and gamblers."

Colonel Cathcart compressed his lips primly and started to rise. "I couldn't agree with you more, sir," he assented briskly in a tone of ostentatious disapproval. "I just don't know what's happening to the clergy these days."

"They're getting better, that's what's happening to them," General Dreedle growled emphatically.

Colonel Cathcart gulped awkwardly and made a nimble recovery. "Yes, sir. They are getting better. That's exactly what I had in mind, sir."

"This is just the place for a chaplain to be, mingling with the men while they're out drinking and gambling so he can get to understand them and win their confidence. How the hell else is he ever going to get them to believe in God?"

"That's exactly what I had in mind, sir, when I ordered him to come here," Colonel Cathcart said carefully, and threw his arm familiarly around the chaplain's shoulders as he walked him off into a corner to order him in a cold undertone to start reporting for duty at the officers' club every evening to mingle with the men while they were drinking and gambling so that he could get to understand them and win their confidence.

The chaplain agreed and did report for duty to the officers' club every night to mingle with men who wanted to avoid him, until the evening the vicious fist fight broke out at the Ping-Pong table and Chief White Halfoat whirled without provocation and punched Colonel Moodus squarely in the nose, knocking Colonel Moodus down on the seat of his pants and making General Dreedle roar with lusty, unexpected laughter until he spied the chaplain standing close by gawking at him grotesquely in tortured wonder. General Dreedle froze at the sight of him. He glowered at the chaplain with swollen fury for a moment, his good humor gone, and turned back toward the bar disgruntledly, rolling from side to side like a sailor on his short bandy legs. Colonel Cathcart cantered fearfully along behind, glancing anxiously about in vain for some sign of help from Colonel Korn.

"That's a fine thing," General Dreedle growled at the bar, gripping his empty shot glass in his burly hand. "That's really a fine thing. When a man of God begins hanging around a place like this with a bunch of dirty drunks and gamblers."

Colonel Cathcart sighed with relief. "Yes, sir," he exclaimed proudly. "It certainly is a fine thing."

"Then why the hell don't you do something about it?"

"Sir?" Colonel Cathcart inquired, blinking.

"Do you think it does you credit to have your chaplain hanging around here every night? He's in here every goddam time I come."

"You're right, sir, absolutely right," Colonel Cathcart responded. "It does me no credit at all. And I *am* going to do something about it, this very minute."

"Aren't you the one who ordered him to come here?"

"No, sir, that was Colonel Korn. I intend to punish him severely, too."

"If he wasn't a chaplain," General Dreedle muttered, "I'd have him taken outside and shot."

"He's not a chaplain, sir," Colonel Cathcart advised helpfully.

"Isn't he? Then why the hell does he wear that cross on his collar if he's not a chaplain?"

"He doesn't wear a cross on his collar, sir. He wears a silver leaf. He's a lieutenant colonel."

"You've got a chaplain who's a lieutenant colonel?" inquired General Dreedle with amazement.

"Oh, no, sir. My chaplain is only a captain."

"Then why the hell does he wear a silver leaf on his collar if he's only a captain?"

"He doesn't wear a silver leaf on his collar, sir. He wears a cross."

"Go away from me now, you son of a bitch," said General Dreedle. "Or I'll have *you* taken outside and shot!"

"Yes, sir."

Colonel Cathcart went away from General Dreedle with a gulp and kicked the chaplain out of the officers' club, and it was exactly the way it almost was two months later after the chaplain had tried to persuade Colonel Cathcart to rescind his order increasing the number of missions to sixty and had failed abysmally in that endeavor too, and the chaplain was ready now to capitulate to despair entirely but was restrained by the memory of his wife, whom he loved and missed so pathetically with such sensual and exalted ardor, and by the lifelong trust he had placed in the wisdom and justice of an immortal, omnipotent, omniscient, humane, universal, anthropomorphic, English-speaking, Anglo-Saxon, pro-American God, which had begun to waver. So many things were testing his faith. There was the Bible, of course, but the Bible was a book, and so were *Bleak House*, *Treasure Island*, *Ethan Frome* and *The Last of the Mohicans*. Did it indeed seem probable, as he had once overheard Dunbar ask, that the answers to the riddles of creation would be supplied by people too ignorant to understand the mechanics of rainfall? Had Almighty God, in all His infinite wisdom, really been afraid that men six thousand years ago would succeed in building a tower to heaven? Where the devil *was* heaven? Was it up? Down? There was no up or down in a finite but expanding universe in which even the vast, burning, dazzling, majestic sun was in a state of progressive decay that would eventually destroy the earth too. There were no miracles; prayers went unanswered, and misfortune tramped with equal brutality on the virtuous and the corrupt; and the chaplain, who had conscience and character, would have yielded to reason and relinquished his belief in the God of his fathers—would truly have resigned both his calling and his commission and taken his chances as a private in the infantry or field artillery, or even, perhaps, as a corporal in the paratroopers—had it not been for such successive mystic phenomena as the naked man in the tree at that poor sergeant's funeral weeks before and the cryptic, haunting, encouraging promise of the prophet Flume in the forest only that afternoon: *Tell them I'll be back when winter comes.*

26

Aarfy

In a way it was all Yossarian's fault, for if he had not moved the bomb line during the Big Siege of Bologna, Major —— de Coverley might still be around to save him, and if he had not stocked the enlisted men's apartment with girls who had no other place to live, Nately might never have fallen in love with his whore as she sat naked from the waist down in the room full of grumpy blackjack players who ignored her. Nately stared at her covertly from his overstuffed yellow armchair, marveling at the bored, phlegmatic strength with which she accepted the mass rejection. She yawned, and he was deeply moved. He had never witnessed such heroic poise before.

The girl had climbed five steep flights of stairs to sell herself to the group of satiated enlisted men, who had girls living there all around them; none wanted her at any price, not even after she had stripped without real enthusiasm to tempt them with a tall body that was firm and full and truly voluptuous. She seemed more fatigued than disappointed. Now she sat resting in vacuous indolence, watching the card game with dull curiosity as she gathered her recalcitrant energies for the tedious chore of donning the rest of her clothing and going back to work. In a little while she stirred. A little while later she rose with an unconscious sigh and stepped lethargically into her tight cotton panties and dark skirt, then buckled on her shoes and left. Nately slipped out behind her; and when Yossarian and Aarfy entered the officers' apartment almost two hours later, there she was again stepping into her panties and skirt, and it was almost like the chaplain's recurring sensation of having been through a situation before, except for Nately, who was moping inconsolably with his hands in his pockets.

"She wants to go now," he said in a faint, strange voice. "She doesn't want to stay."

"Why don't you just pay her some money to let you spend the rest of the day with her?" Yossarian advised.

"She gave me my money back," Nately admitted. "She's tired of me now and wants to go looking for someone else."

The girl paused when her shoes were on to glance in surly invitation at Yossarian and Aarfy. Her breasts were pointy and large in the thin white sleeveless sweater she wore that squeezed each contour and flowed outward smoothly with the tops of her enticing hips. Yossarian returned her gaze and was strongly attracted. He shook his head.

"Good riddance to bad rubbish," was Aarfy's unperturbed response.

"Don't say that about her!" Nately protested with passion that was both a plea and a rebuke. "I want her to stay with me."

"What's so special about her?" Aarfy sneered with mock surprise. "She's only a whore."

"And don't call her a whore!"

The girl shrugged impassively after a few more seconds and ambled toward the door. Nately bounded forward wretchedly to hold it open. He wandered back in a heartbroken daze, his sensitive face eloquent with grief.

"Don't worry about it," Yossarian counseled him as kindly as he could. "You'll probably be able to find her again. We know where all the whores hang out."

"Please don't call her that," Nately begged, looking as though he might cry.

"I'm sorry," murmured Yossarian.

Aarfy thundered jovially, "There are hundreds of whores just as good crawling all over the streets. That one wasn't even pretty." He chuckled mellifluously with resonant disdain and authority. "Why, you rushed forward to open that door as though you were in love with her."

"I think I am in love with her," Nately confessed in a shamed, far-off voice.

Aarfy wrinkled his chubby round rosy forehead in comic disbelief. "Ho, ho, ho, ho!" he laughed, patting the expansive forest-green sides of his officer's tunic prosperously. "That's rich. *You* in love with *her?* That's really rich." Aarfy had a date that same afternoon with a Red Cross girl from Smith whose father owned an important milk-of-magnesia plant. "Now, *that's* the kind of girl you ought to be associating with, and not with common sluts like that one. Why, she didn't even look clean."

"I don't care!" Nately shouted desperately. "And I wish you'd shut up. I don't even want to talk about it with you."

"Aarfy, shut up," said Yossarian.

"Ho, ho, ho, ho!" Aarfy continued. "I can just imagine what your father and mother would say if they knew you were running around with filthy trollops like that one. Your father is a very distinguished man, you know."

"I'm not going to tell him," Nately declared with determination. "I'm not going to say a word about her to him or Mother until after we're married."

"Married?" Aarfy's indulgent merriment swelled tremendously. "Ho, ho, ho, ho, ho! Now you're really talking stupid. Why, you're not even old enough to know what true love is."

Aarfy was an authority on the subject of true love because he had already fallen truly in love with Nately's father and with the prospect of working for him after the war in some executive capacity as a reward for befriending Nately. Aarfy was a lead navigator who had never been able to find himself since leaving college. He was a genial, magnanimous lead navigator who could always forgive the other men in the squadron for denouncing him furiously each time he got lost on a combat mission and led them over concentrations of antiaircraft fire. He got lost on the streets of Rome that same afternoon and never did find the eligible Red Cross girl from Smith with the important milk-of-magnesia plant. He got lost on the mission to Ferrara the day Kraft was shot down and killed, and he got lost again on the weekly milk run to Parma and tried to lead the planes out to sea over the city of Leghorn after Yossarian had dropped his bombs on the undefended inland target and settled back against his thick wall of armor plate with his eyes closed and a fragrant cigarette in his finger tips. Suddenly there was flak, and all at once McWatt was shrieking over the intercom. "Flak! Flak! Where the hell are we? What the hell's going on?"

Yossarian flipped his eyes open in alarm and saw the totally unexpected bulging black puffs of flak crashing down in toward them from high up and Aarfy's complacent melon-round, tiny-eyed face gazing out at the approaching cannon bursts with affable bemusement. Yossarian was flabbergasted. His leg went abruptly to sleep. McWatt had started to climb and was yelping over the intercom for instructions. Yossarian sprang forward to see where they were and remained in the same place. He was unable to move. Then he realized he was sopping wet. He looked down at his crotch with a sinking, sick sensation. A wild crimson blot was crawling upward rapidly along his shirt front like an enormous sea monster rising to devour him. He was hit! Separate trickles of blood spilled to a puddle on the floor through one saturated trouser leg like countless unstoppable swarms of wriggling red worms. His heart stopped. A second solid jolt struck the plane.

Yossarian shuddered with revulsion at the queer sight of his wound and screamed at Aarfy for help.

"I lost my balls! Aarfy, I lost my balls!" Aarfy didn't hear, and Yossarian bent forward and tugged at his arm. "Aarfy, help me," he pleaded, almost weeping. "I'm hit! I'm hit!"

Aarfy turned slowly with a blind, quizzical grin. "What?"

"I'm hit, Aarfy! Help me!"

Aarfy grinned again and shrugged amiably. "I can't hear you," he said.

"Can't you see me?" Yossarian cried incredulously, and he pointed to the deepening pool of blood he felt splashing down all around him and spreading out underneath. "I'm wounded! Help me, for God's sake! Aarfy, help me!"

"I still can't hear you," Aarfy complained tolerantly, cupping his podgy hand behind the blanched corolla of his ear. "What did you say?"

Yossarian answered in a collapsing voice, weary suddenly of shouting so much, of the whole frustrating, exasperating, ridiculous situation. He was dying, and no one took notice. "Never mind."

"What?" Aarfy shouted.

"I said I lost my balls! Can't you hear me? I'm wounded in the groin!"

"I still can't hear you," Aarfy chided.

"I said *never mind!*" Yossarian screamed with a trapped feeling of terror and began to shiver, feeling very cold suddenly and very weak.

Aarfy shook his head regretfully again and lowered his obscene, lactescent ear almost directly into Yossarian's face. "You'll just have to speak up, my friend. You'll just have to speak up."

"Leave me alone, you bastard! You dumb, insensitive bastard, leave me alone!" Yossarian sobbed. He wanted to pummel Aarfy, but lacked the strength to lift his arms. He decided to sleep instead and keeled over sideways into a dead faint.

He was wounded in the thigh, and when he recovered consciousness he found McWatt on both knees taking care of him. He was relieved, even though he still saw Aarfy's bloated cherub's face hanging down over McWatt's shoulder with placid interest. Yossarian smiled feebly at McWatt, feeling ill, and asked, "Who's minding the store?" McWatt gave no sign that he heard. With growing horror, Yossarian gathered in breath and repeated the words as loudly as he could.

McWatt looked up. "Christ, I'm glad you're alive!" he exclaimed, heaving an enormous sigh. The good-humored, friendly crinkles about his eyes were white with tension and oily with grime as he kept unrolling an interminable bandage around the bulky cotton compress Yossarian felt strapped burdensomely to the inside of one thigh. "Nately's at the controls. The poor kid almost started bawling when he heard you were hit. He still thinks you're dead. They knocked open an artery for you, but I think I've got it stopped. I gave you some morphine."

"Give me some more."

"It might be too soon. I'll give you some more when it starts to hurt."

"It hurts now."

"Oh, well, what the hell," said McWatt and injected another syrette of morphine into Yossarian's arm.

"When you tell Nately I'm all right . . ." said Yossarian to McWatt, and lost consciousness again as everything went fuzzy behind a film of strawberry-stained gelatin and a great baritone buzz swallowed him in sound. He came to in the ambulance and smiled encouragement at Doc Daneeka's weevillike glum and overshadowed countenance for the dizzy second or two he had before everything went rose-petal pink again and then turned really black and unfathomably still.

Yossarian woke up in the hospital and went to sleep. When he woke up in the hospital again, the smell of ether was gone and Dunbar was lying in pajamas in the bed across the aisle maintaining that he was not Dunbar but *a fortiori.* Yossarian thought he was cracked. He curled his lip skeptically at Dunbar's bit of news and slept on it fitfully for a day or two, then woke up while the nurses were elsewhere and eased himself out of bed to see for himself. The floor swayed like the floating raft at the beach and the stitches on the inside of his thigh bit into his flesh like fine sets of fish teeth as he limped across the aisle to peruse the name on the temperature card on the foot of Dunbar's bed, but sure enough, Dunbar was right: he was not Dunbar any more but Second Lieutenant Anthony F. Fortiori.

"What the hell's going on?"

A. Fortiori got out of bed and motioned to Yossarian to follow. Grasping for support at anything he could reach, Yossarian limped along after him out into the corridor and down the adjacent ward to a bed containing a harried young man with pimples and a receding chin. The harried young man rose on one elbow with alacrity as they approached. A. Fortiori jerked his thumb over his shoulder and said, "Screw." The harried young man jumped out of bed and ran away. A. Fortiori climbed into the bed and became Dunbar again.

"That was A. Fortiori," Dunbar explained. "They didn't have an empty bed in your ward, so I pulled my rank and chased him back here into mine. It's a pretty satisfying experience, pulling rank. You ought to try it sometime. You ought to try it right now, in fact, because you look like you're going to fall down."

Yossarian felt like he was going to fall down. He turned to the lantern-jawed, leather-faced middle-aged man lying in the bed next to Dunbar's, jerked his thumb over his shoulder and said, "Screw." The middle-aged man stiffened fiercely and glared.

"He's a major," Dunbar explained. "Why don't you aim a little lower and try becoming Warrant Officer Homer Lumley for a while? Then you can have a father in the state legislature and a sister who's engaged to a champion skier. Just tell him you're a captain."

Yossarian turned to the startled patient Dunbar had indicated. "I'm a captain," he said, jerking his thumb over his shoulder. "Screw."

The startled patient jumped down to the floor at Yossarian's command and ran away. Yossarian climbed up into his bed and became Warrant Officer Homer Lumley, who felt like vomiting and was covered suddenly with a clammy sweat. He slept for an hour and wanted to be Yossarian again. It did not mean so much to have a father in the state legislature and a sister who was engaged to a champion skier. Dunbar led the way back to Yossarian's ward, where he thumbed A. Fortiori out of bed to become Dunbar again for a while. There was no sign of Warrant Officer Homer Lumley. Nurse Cramer was there, though, and sizzled with sanctimonious anger like a damp firecracker. She ordered Yossarian to get right back into his bed and blocked his path so he couldn't comply. Her pretty face was more repulsive than ever. Nurse Cramer was a goodhearted, sentimental creature who rejoiced unselfishly at news of weddings, engagements, births and anniversaries even though she was unacquainted with any of the people involved.

"Are you crazy?" she scolded virtuously, shaking an indignant finger in front of his eyes. "I suppose you just don't care if you kill yourself, do you?"

"It's my self," he reminded her.

"I suppose you just don't care if you lose your leg, do you?"

"It's my leg."

"It certainly is not your leg!" Nurse Cramer retorted. "That leg belongs to the U.S. government. It's no different than a gear or a bedpan. The Army has invested a lot of money to make you an airplane pilot, and you've no right to disobey the doctor's orders."

Yossarian was not sure he liked being invested in. Nurse Cramer was still standing directly in front of him so that he could not pass. His head was aching. Nurse Cramer shouted at him some question he could not understand. He jerked his thumb over his shoulder and said, "Screw."

Nurse Cramer cracked him in the face so hard she almost knocked him down. Yossarian drew back his fist to punch her in the jaw just as his leg buckled and he began to fall. Nurse Duckett strode up in time to catch him. She addressed them both firmly.

"Just what's going on here?"

"He won't get back into his bed," Nurse Cramer reported zealously in an injured tone. "Sue Ann, he said something absolutely horrible to me. Oh, I can't even make myself repeat it!"

"She called me a gear," Yossarian muttered.

Nurse Duckett was not sympathetic. "Will you get back into bed," she said, "or must I take you by your ear and put you there?"

"Take me by my ear and put me there," Yossarian dared her.

Nurse Duckett took him by his ear and put him back in bed.

27

Nurse Duckett

Nurse Sue Ann Duckett was a tall, spare, mature, straight-backed woman with a prominent, well-rounded ass, small breasts and angular, ascetic New England features that came equally close to being very lovely and very plain. Her skin was white and pink, her eyes small, her nose and chin slender and sharp. She was able, prompt, strict and intelligent. She welcomed responsibility and kept her head in every crisis. She was adult and self-reliant, and there was nothing she needed from anyone. Yossarian took pity and decided to help her.

Next morning while she was standing bent over smoothing the sheets at the foot of his bed, he slipped his hand stealthily into the narrow space between her knees and, all at once, brought it up swiftly under her dress as far as it would go. Nurse Duckett shrieked and jumped into the air a mile, but it wasn't high enough, and she squirmed and vaulted and seesawed back and forth on her divine fulcrum for almost a full fifteen seconds before she wiggled free finally and retreated frantically into the aisle with an ashen, trembling face. She backed away too far, and Dunbar, who had watched from the beginning, sprang forward on his bed without warning and flung both arms around her bosom from behind. Nurse Duckett let out another scream and twisted away, fleeing far enough from Dunbar for Yossarian to lunge forward and grab her by the snatch again. Nurse Duckett bounced out across the aisle once more like a Ping-Pong ball with legs. Dunbar was waiting vigilantly, ready to pounce. She remembered him just in time and leaped aside. Dunbar missed completely and sailed by her over the bed to the floor, landing on his skull with a soggy, crunching thud that knocked him cold.

He woke up on the floor with a bleeding nose and exactly the same distressful head symptoms he had been feigning all along. The ward was in a chaotic uproar. Nurse Duckett was in tears, and Yossarian was consoling her apologetically as he sat beside her on the edge of a bed. The commanding colonel was wroth and shouting at Yossarian that he would not permit his patients to take indecent liberties with his nurses.

"What do you want from him?" Dunbar asked plaintively from the floor, wincing at the vibrating pains in his temples that his voice set up. "He didn't do anything."

"I'm talking about you!" the thin, dignified colonel bellowed as loudly as he could. "You're going to be punished for what you did."

"What do you want from him?" Yossarian called out. "All he did was fall on his head."

"And I'm talking about you too!" the colonel declared, whirling to rage at Yossarian. "You're going to be good and sorry you grabbed Nurse Duckett by the bosom."

"I didn't grab Nurse Duckett by the bosom," said Yossarian.

"*I* grabbed her by the bosom," said Dunbar.

"Are you both crazy?" the doctor cried shrilly, backing away in paling confusion.

"Yes, he really is crazy, Doc," Dunbar assured him. "Every night he dreams he's holding a live fish in his hands."

The doctor stopped in his tracks with a look of elegant amazement and distaste, and the ward grew still. "*He does what?*" he demanded.

"He dreams he's holding a live fish in his hand."

"What kind of fish?" the doctor inquired sternly of Yossarian.

"I don't know," Yossarian answered. "I can't tell one kind of fish from another."

"In which hand do you hold them?"

"It varies," answered Yossarian.

"It varies with the fish," Dunbar added helpfully.

The colonel turned and stared down at Dunbar suspiciously with a narrow squint. "Yes? And how come you seem to know so much about it?"

"I'm in the dream," Dunbar answered without cracking a smile.

The colonel's face flushed with embarrassment. He glared at them both with cold, unforgiving resentment. "Get up off the floor and into your bed," he directed Dunbar through thin lips. "And I don't want to hear another word about this dream from either one of you. I've got a man on my staff to listen to disgusting bilge like this."

"Just why do you think," carefully inquired Major Sanderson, the soft and thickset smiling staff psychiatrist to whom the colonel had ordered Yossarian sent, "that Colonel Ferredge finds your dream disgusting?"

Yossarian replied respectfully. "I suppose it's either some quality in the dream or some quality in Colonel Ferredge."

"That's very well put," applauded Major Sanderson, who wore squeaking GI shoes and had charcoal-black hair that stood up almost straight. "For some reason," he confided, "Colonel Ferredge has always reminded me of a sea gull. He doesn't put much faith in psychiatry, you know."

"You don't like sea gulls, do you?" inquired Yossarian.

"No, not very much," admitted Major Sanderson with a sharp, nervous laugh and pulled at his pendulous second chin lovingly as though it were a long goatee. "I think your dream is charming, and I hope it recurs frequently so that we can continue discussing it. Would you like a cigarette?" He smiled when Yossarian declined. "Just why do you think," he asked knowingly, "that you have such a strong aversion to accepting a cigarette from me?"

"I put one out a second ago. It's still smoldering in your ash tray."

Major Sanderson chuckled. "That's a very ingenious explanation. But I suppose we'll soon discover the true reason." He tied a sloppy double bow in his opened shoelace and then transferred a lined yellow pad from his desk to his lap. "This fish you dream about. Let's talk about that. It's always the same fish, isn't it?"

"I don't know," Yossarian replied. "I have trouble recognizing fish."

"What does the fish remind you of?"

"Other fish."

"And what do the other fish remind you of?"

"Other fish."

Major Sanderson sat back disappointedly. "Do you like fish?"

"Not especially."

"Just why do you think you have such a morbid aversion to fish?" asked Major Sanderson triumphantly.

"They're too bland," Yossarian answered. "And too bony."

Major Sanderson nodded understandingly, with a smile that was agreeable and insincere. "That's a very interesting explanation. But we'll soon discover the true reason, I suppose. Do you like this particular fish? The one you're holding in your hand?"

"I have no feelings about it either way."

"Do you dislike the fish? Do you have any hostile or aggressive emotions toward it?"

"No, not at all. In fact, I rather like the fish."

"Then you do like the fish."

"Oh, no. I have no feelings toward it either way."

"But you just said you liked it. And now you say you have no feelings toward it either way. I've just caught you in a contradiction. Don't you see?"

"Yes, sir, I suppose you have caught me in a contradiction."

Major Sanderson proudly lettered "Contradiction" on his pad with his thick black pencil. "Just why do you think," he resumed when he had finished, looking up, "that you made those two statements expressing contradictory emotional responses to the fish?"

"I suppose I have an ambivalent attitude toward it."

Major Sanderson sprang up with joy when he heard the words "ambivalent attitude." "You do understand!" he exclaimed, wringing his hands together ecstatically. "Oh, you can't imagine how lonely it's been for me, talking day after day to patients who haven't the slightest knowledge of psychiatry, trying to cure people who have no real interest in me or my work! It's given me such a terrible feeling of inadequacy." A shadow of anxiety crossed his face. "I can't seem to shake it."

"Really?" asked Yossarian, wondering what else to say. "Why do you blame yourself for gaps in the education of others?"

"It's silly, I know," Major Sanderson replied uneasily with a giddy, involuntary laugh. "But I've always depended very heavily on the good opinion of others. I reached puberty a bit later than all the other boys my age, you see, and it's given me sort of—well, all sorts of problems. I just know I'm going to enjoy discussing them with you. I'm so eager to begin that I'm almost reluctant to digress now to your problem, but I'm afraid I must. Colonel Ferredge would be cross if he knew we were spending all our time on me. I'd like to show you some ink blots now to find out what certain shapes and colors remind you of."

"You can save yourself the trouble, Doctor. Everything reminds me of sex."

"Does it?" cried Major Sanderson with delight, as though unable to believe his ears. "Now we're *really* getting somewhere! Do you ever have any good sex dreams?"

"My fish dream is a sex dream."

"No, I mean real sex dreams—the kind where you grab some naked bitch by the neck and pinch her and punch her in the face until she's all bloody and then throw yourself down to ravish her and burst into tears because you love her and hate her so much you don't know what else to do. *That's* the kind of sex dreams I like to talk about. Don't you ever have sex dreams like that?"

Yossarian reflected a moment with a wise look. "That's a fish dream," he decided.

Major Sanderson recoiled as though he had been slapped. "Yes, of course," he conceded frigidly, his manner changing to one of edgy and defensive antagonism. "But I'd like you to dream one like that anyway just to see how you react. That will be all for today. In the meantime, I'd also like you to dream up the answers to some of those questions I asked you. These sessions are no more pleasant for me than they are for you, you know."

"I'll mention it to Dunbar," Yossarian replied.

"Dunbar?"

"He's the one who started it all. It's his dream."

"Oh, Dunbar." Major Sanderson sneered, his confidence returning. "I'll bet Dunbar is that evil fellow who really does all those nasty things you're always being blamed for, isn't he?"

"He's not so evil."

"And yet you'll defend him to the very death, won't you?"

"Not that far."

Major Sanderson smiled tauntingly and wrote "Dunbar" on his pad. "Why are you limping?" he asked sharply, as Yossarian moved to the door. "And what the devil is that bandage doing on your leg? Are you mad or something?"

"I was wounded in the leg. That's what I'm in the hospital for."

"Oh, no, you're not," gloated Major Sanderson maliciously. "You're in the hospital for a stone in your salivary gland. So you're not so smart after all, are you? You don't even know what you're in the hospital for."

"I'm in the hospital for a wounded leg," Yossarian insisted.

Major Sanderson ignored his argument with a sarcastic laugh. "Well, give my regards to your friend Dunbar. And you will tell him to dream that dream for me, won't you?"

But Dunbar had nausea and dizziness with his constant headache and was not inclined to cooperate with Major Sanderson. Hungry Joe had nightmares because he had finished sixty missions and was waiting again to go home, but he was unwilling to share any when he came to the hospital to visit.

"Hasn't anyone got any dreams for Major Sanderson?" Yossarian asked. "I hate to disappoint him. He feels so rejected already."

"I've been having a very peculiar dream ever since I learned you were wounded," confessed the chaplain. "I used to dream every night that my wife was dying or being murdered or that my children were choking to death on morsels of nutritious food. Now I dream that I'm out swimming in water over my head and a shark is eating my left leg in exactly the same place where you have your bandage."

"That's a wonderful dream," Dunbar declared. "I bet Major Sanderson will love it."

"That's a horrible dream!" Major Sanderson cried. "It's filled with pain and mutilation and death. I'm sure you had it just to spite me. You know, I'm not even sure you belong in the Army, with a disgusting dream like that."

Yossarian thought he spied a ray of hope. "Perhaps you're right, sir," he suggested slyly. "Perhaps I ought to be grounded and returned to the States."

"Hasn't it ever occurred to you that in your promiscuous pursuit of women you are merely trying to assuage your subconscious fears of sexual impotence?"

"Yes, sir, it has."

"Then why do you do it?"

"To assuage my fears of sexual impotence."

"Why don't you get yourself a good hobby instead?" Major Sanderson inquired with friendly interest. "Like fishing. Do you really find Nurse Duckett so attractive? I should think she was rather bony. Rather bland and bony, you know. Like a fish."

"I hardly know Nurse Duckett."

"They why did you grab her by the bosom? Merely because she has one?"

"Dunbar did that."

"Oh, don't start that again," Major Sanderson exclaimed with vitriolic scorn, and hurled down his pencil disgustedly. "Do you really think that you can absolve yourself of guilt by pretending to be someone else? I don't like you, Fortiori. Do you know that? I don't like you at all."

Yossarian felt a cold, damp wind of apprehension blow over him. "I'm not Fortiori, sir," he said timidly. "I'm Yossarian."

"You're who?"

"My name is Yossarian, sir. And I'm in the hospital with a wounded leg."

"Your name is Fortiori," Major Sanderson contradicted him belligerently. "And you're in the hospital for a stone in your salivary gland."

"Oh, come on, Major!" Yossarian exploded. "I ought to know who I am."

"And I've got an official Army record here to prove it," Major Sanderson retorted. "You'd better get a grip on yourself before it's too late. First you're Dunbar. Now you're Yossarian. The next thing you know you'll be claiming you're Washington Irving. Do you know what's wrong with you? You've got a split personality, that's what's wrong with you."

"Perhaps you're right, sir," Yossarian agreed diplomatically.

"I know I'm right. You've got a bad persecution complex. You think people are trying to harm you."

"People *are* trying to harm me."

"You see? You have no respect for excessive authority or obsolete traditions. You're dangerous and depraved, and you ought to be taken outside and shot!"

"Are you serious?"

"You're an enemy of the people!"

"Are you nuts?" Yossarian shouted.

"No, I'm not nuts," Dobbs roared furiously back in the ward, in what he imagined was a furtive whisper. "Hungry Joe saw them, I tell you. He saw them yesterday when he flew to Naples to pick up some black-market air conditioners for Colonel Cathcart's farm. They've got a big replacement center there and it's filled with hundreds of pilots, bombardiers and gunners on the way home. They've got forty-five missions, that's all. A few with Purple Hearts have even less. Replacement crews are pouring in from the States into other bomber groups. They want everyone to serve overseas at least once, even administrative personnel. Don't you read the papers? We've got to kill him now!"

"You've got only two more missions to fly," Yossarian reasoned with him in a low voice. "Why take a chance?"

"I can get killed flying them, too," Dobbs answered pugnaciously in his rough, quavering voice. "We can kill him the first thing tomorrow morning when he drives back from his farm. I've got the gun right here."

Yossarian goggled with amazement as Dobbs pulled a gun out of his pocket and displayed it high in the air. "Are you crazy?" he hissed frantically. "Put it away. And keep your idiot voice down."

"What are you worried about?" Dobbs asked with offended innocence. "No one can hear us."

"Hey, knock it off down there," a voice rang out from the far end of the ward. "Can't you see we're trying to nap?"

"What the hell are you, a wise guy?" Dobbs yelled back and spun with clenched fists, ready to fight. He whirled back to Yossarian and, before he could speak, sneezed thunderously six times, staggering sideways on rubbery legs in the intervals and raising his elbow ineffectively to fend each seizure off. The lids of his watery eyes were puffy and inflamed. "Who does he think," he demanded, sniffing spasmodically and wiping his nose with the back of his sturdy wrist, "he is, a cop or something?"

"He's a C.I.D. man," Yossarian notified him tranquilly. "We've got three here now and more on the way. Oh, don't be scared. They're after a forger named Washington Irving. They're not interested in murderers."

"Murderers?" Dobbs was affronted. "Why do you call us murderers? Just because we're going to murder Colonel Cathcart?"

"Be quiet, damn you!" directed Yossarian. "Can't you whisper?"

"I am whispering. I—"

"You're still shouting."

"No, I'm not. I—"

"Hey, shut up down there, will you?" patients all over the ward began hollering at Dobbs.

"I'll fight you all!" Dobbs screamed back at them, and stood up on a rickety wooden chair, waving the gun wildly. Yossarian caught his arm and yanked him down. Dobbs began sneezing again. "I have an allergy," he apologized when he had finished, his nostrils running and his eyes streaming with tears.

"That's too bad. You'd make a great leader of men without it."

"Colonel Cathcart's the murderer," Dobbs complained hoarsely when he had shoved away a soiled, crumpled khaki handkerchief. "Colonel Cathcart's the one who's going to murder us all if we don't do something to stop him."

"Maybe he won't raise the missions any more. Maybe sixty is as high as he'll go."

"He always raises the missions. You know that better than I do." Dobbs swallowed and bent his intense face very close to Yossarian's, the muscles in his bronze, rocklike jaw bunching up into quivering knots. "Just say it's okay and I'll do the whole thing tomorrow morning. Do you understand what I'm telling you? I'm whispering now, ain't I?"

Yossarian tore his eyes away from the gaze of burning entreaty Dobbs had fastened on him. "Why the goddam hell don't you just go out and do it?" he protested. "Why don't you stop talking to me about it and do it alone?"

"I'm afraid to do it alone. I'm afraid to do anything alone."

"Then leave me out of it. I'd have to be crazy to get mixed up in something like this now. I've got a million-dollar leg wound here. They're going to send me home."

"Are you crazy?" Dobbs exclaimed in disbelief. "All you've got there is a scratch. He'll have you back flying combat missions the day you come out, Purple Heart and all."

"Then I really will kill him," Yossarian vowed. "I'll come looking for you and we'll do it together."

"Then let's do it tomorrow while we've still got the chance," Dobbs pleaded. "The chaplain says he's volunteered the group for Avignon again. I may be killed before you get out. Look how these hands of mine shake. I can't fly a plane. I'm not good enough."

Yossarian was afraid to say yes. "I want to wait and see what happens first."

"The trouble with you is that you just won't do anything," Dobbs complained in a thick, infuriated voice.

"I'm doing everything I possibly can," the chaplain explained softly to Yossarian after Dobbs had departed. "I even went to the medical tent to speak to Doc Daneeka about helping you."

"Yes, I can see." Yossarian suppressed a smile. "What happened?"

"They painted my gums purple," the chaplain replied sheepishly.

"They painted his toes purple, too," Nately added in outrage. "And then they gave him a laxative."

"But I went back again this morning to see him."

"And they painted his gums purple again," said Nately.

"But I did get to speak to him," the chaplain argued in a plaintive tone of self-justification. "Doctor Daneeka seems like such an unhappy man. He suspects that someone is plotting to transfer him to the Pacific Ocean. All this time he's been thinking of coming to *me* for help. When I told him I needed *his* help, he wondered if there wasn't a chaplain *I* couldn't go see." The chaplain waited in patient dejection when Yossarian and Dunbar both broke into laughter. "I used to think it was immoral to be unhappy," he continued, as though keening aloud in solitude. "Now I don't know what to think any more. I'd like to make the subject of immorality the basis of my sermon this Sunday, but I'm not sure I ought to give any sermon at all with these purple gums. Colonel Korn was very displeased with them."

"Chaplain, why don't you come into the hospital with us for a while and take it easy?" Yossarian invited. "You could be very comfortable here."

The brash iniquity of the proposal tempted and amused the chaplain for a second or two. "No, I don't think so," he decided reluctantly. "I want to arrange for a trip to the mainland to see a mail clerk named Wintergreen. Doctor Daneeka told me he could help."

"Wintergreen is probably the most influential man in the whole theater of operations. He's not only a mail clerk, but he has access to a mimeograph machine. But he won't help anybody. That's one of the reasons he'll go far."

"I'd like to speak to him anyway. There must be somebody who will help you."

"Do it for Dunbar, Chaplain," Yossarian corrected with a superior air. "I've got this million-dollar leg wound that will take me out of combat. If that doesn't do it, there's a psychiatrist who thinks I'm not good enough to be in the Army."

"I'm the one who isn't good enough to be in the Army," Dunbar whined jealously. "It was my dream."

"It's not the dream, Dunbar," Yossarian explained. "He likes your dream. It's my personality. He thinks it's split."

"It's split right down the middle," said Major Sanderson, who had laced his lumpy GI shoes for the occasion and had slicked his charcoal-dull hair down with some stiffening and redolent tonic. He smiled ostentatiously to show himself reasonable and nice. "I'm not saying that to be cruel and insulting," he continued with cruel and insulting delight. "I'm not saying it because I hate you and want revenge. I'm not saying it because you rejected me and hurt my feelings terribly. No, I'm a man of medicine and I'm being coldly objective. I have very bad news for you. Are you man enough to take it?"

"God, no!" screamed Yossarian. "I'll go right to pieces."

Major Sanderson flew instantly into a rage. "Can't you even do one thing right?" he pleaded, turning beet-red with vexation and crashing the sides of both fists down upon his desk together. "The trouble with you is that you think you're too good for all the conventions of society. You probably think you're too good for me too, just because I arrived at puberty late. Well, do you know what you are? You're a frustrated, unhappy, disillusioned, undisciplined, maladjusted young man!" Major Sanderson's disposition seemed to mellow as he reeled off the uncomplimentary adjectives.

"Yes, sir," Yossarian agreed carefully. "I guess you're right."

"Of course I'm right. You're immature. You've been unable to adjust to the idea of war."

"Yes, sir."

"You have a morbid aversion to dying. You probably resent the fact that you're at war and might get your head blown off any second."

"I more than resent it, sir. I'm absolutely incensed."

"You have deep-seated survival anxieties. And you don't like bigots, bullies, snobs or hypocrites. Subconsciously there are many people you hate."

"Consciously, sir, consciously," Yossarian corrected in an effort to help. "I hate them consciously."

"You're antagonistic to the idea of being robbed, exploited, degraded, humiliated or deceived. Misery depresses you. Ignorance depresses you. Persecution depresses you. Violence depresses you. Slums depress you. Greed depresses you. Crime depresses you. Corruption depresses you. You know, it wouldn't surprise me if you're a manic-depressive!"

"Yes, sir. Perhaps I am."

"Don't try to deny it."

"I'm not denying it, sir," said Yossarian, pleased with the miraculous rapport that finally existed between them. "I agree with all you've said."

"Then you admit you're crazy, do you?"

"Crazy?" Yossarian was shocked. "What are you talking about? Why am I crazy? You're the one who's crazy!"

Major Sanderson turned red with indignation again and crashed both fists down upon his thighs. "Calling me crazy," he shouted in a sputtering rage, "is a typically sadistic and vindictive paranoiac reaction! You really are crazy!"

"Then why don't you send me home?"

"And I'm going to send you home!"

"They're going to send me home!" Yossarian announced jubilantly as he hobbled back into the ward.

"Me too!" A. Fortiori rejoiced. "They just came to my ward and told me."

"What about me?" Dunbar demanded petulantly of the doctors.

"You?" they replied with asperity. "You're going with Yossarian. Right back into combat!"

And back into combat they both went. Yossarian was enraged when the ambulance returned him to the squadron, and he went limping for justice to Doc Daneeka, who glared at him glumly with misery and disdain.

"You!" Doc Daneeka exclaimed mournfully with accusing disgust, the egg-shaped pouches under both eyes firm and censorious. "All you ever think of is yourself. Go take a look at the bomb line if you want to see what's been happening since you went to the hospital."

Yossarian was startled. "Are we losing?"

"Losing?" Doc Daneeka cried. "The whole military situation has been going to hell ever since we captured Paris. I knew it would happen." He paused, his sulking ire turning to melancholy, and frowned irritably as though it were all Yossarian's fault. "American troops are pushing into German soil. The Russians have captured back all of Romania. Only yesterday the Greeks in the Eighth Army captured Rimini. The Germans are on the defensive everywhere!" Doc Daneeka paused again and fortified himself with a huge breath for a piercing ejaculation of grief. "There's no more Luftwaffe left!" he wailed. He seemed ready to burst into tears. "The whole Gothic line is in danger of collapsing!"

"So?" asked Yossarian. "What's wrong?"

"What's wrong?" Doc Daneeka cried. "If something doesn't happen soon, Germany may surrender. And then we'll all be sent to the Pacific!"

Yossarian gawked at Doc Daneeka in grotesque dismay. "Are you crazy? Do you know what you're saying?"

"Yeah, it's easy for you to laugh," Doc Daneeka sneered.

"Who the hell is laughing?"

"At least you've got a chance. You're in combat and might get killed. But what about me? I've got nothing to hope for."

"You're out of your goddam head!" Yossarian shouted at him emphatically, seizing him by the shirt front. "Do you know that? Now keep your stupid mouth shut and listen to me."

Doc Daneeka wrenched himself away. "Don't you dare talk to me like that. I'm a licensed physician."

"Then keep your stupid licensed physician's mouth shut and listen to what they told me up at the hospital. I'm crazy. Did you know that?"

"So?"

"Really crazy."

"So?"

"I'm nuts. Cuckoo. Don't you understand? I'm off my rocker. They sent someone else home in my place by mistake. They've got a licensed psychiatrist up at the hospital who examined me, and that was his verdict. I'm really insane."

"So?"

"So?" Yossarian was puzzled by Doc Daneeka's inability to comprehend. "Don't you see what that means? Now you can take me off combat duty and send me home. They're not going to send a crazy man out to be killed, are they?"

"Who else will go?"

28

Dobbs

McWatt went, and McWatt was not crazy. And so did Yossarian, still walking with a limp, and when Yossarian had gone two more times and then found himself menaced by the rumor of another mission to Bologna, he limped determinedly into Dobbs's tent early one warm afternoon, put a finger to his mouth and said, "Shush!"

"What are you shushing him for?" asked Kid Sampson, peeling a tangerine with his front teeth as he perused the dog-eared pages of a comic book. "He isn't even saying anything."

"Screw," said Yossarian to Kid Sampson, jerking his thumb back over his shoulder toward the entrance of the tent.

Kid Sampson cocked his blond eyebrows discerningly and rose to cooperate. He whistled upward four times into his drooping yellow mustache and spurted away into the hills on the dented old green motorcycle he had purchased secondhand months before. Yossarian waited until the last faint bark of the motor had died away in the distance. Things inside the tent did not seem quite normal. The place was too neat. Dobbs was watching him curiously, smoking a fat cigar. Now that Yossarian had made up his mind to be brave, he was deathly afraid.

"All right," he said. "Let's kill Colonel Cathcart. We'll do it together."

Dobbs sprang forward off his cot with a look of wildest terror. "Shush!" he roared. "Kill Colonel Cathcart? What are you talking about?"

"Be quiet, damn it," Yossarian snarled. "The whole island will hear. Have you still got that gun?"

"Are you crazy or something?" shouted Dobbs. "Why should I want to kill Colonel Cathcart?"

"*Why?*" Yossarian stared at Dobbs with an incredulous scowl. "*Why?* It was your idea, wasn't it? Didn't you come to the hospital and ask me to do it?"

Dobbs smiled slowly. "But that was when I had only fifty-eight missions," he explained, puffing on his cigar luxuriously. "I'm all packed now and I'm waiting to go home. I've finished my sixty missions."

"So what?" Yossarian replied. "He's only going to raise them again."

"Maybe this time he won't."

"He always raises them. What the hell's the matter with you, Dobbs? Ask Hungry Joe how many times he's packed his bags."

"I've got to wait and see what happens," Dobbs maintained stubbornly. "I'd have to be crazy to get mixed up in something like this now that I'm out of combat." He flicked the ash from his cigar. "No, my advice to you," he remarked, "is that you fly your sixty missions like the rest of us and then see what happens."

Yossarian resisted the impulse to spit squarely in his eye. "I may not live through sixty," he wheedled in a flat, pessimistic voice. "There's a rumor around that he volunteered the group for Bologna again."

"It's only a rumor," Dobbs pointed out with a self-important air. "You mustn't believe every rumor you hear."

"Will you stop giving me advice?"

"Why don't you speak to Orr?" Dobbs advised. "Orr got knocked down into the water again last week on that second mission to Avignon. Maybe he's unhappy enough to kill him."

"Orr hasn't got brains enough to be unhappy."

Orr had been knocked down into the water again while Yossarian was still in the hospital and had eased his crippled airplane down gently into the glassy blue swells off Marseilles with such flawless skill that not one member of the six-man crew suffered the slightest bruise. The escape hatches in the front and rear sections flew open while the sea was still foaming white and green around the plane, and the men scrambled out as speedily as they could in their flaccid orange Mae West life jackets that failed to inflate and dangled limp and useless around their necks and waists. The life jackets failed to inflate because Milo had removed the twin carbon-dioxide cylinders from the inflating chambers to make the strawberry and crushed-pineapple ice-cream sodas he served in the officers' mess hall and had replaced them with mimeographed notes that read: "What's good for M & M Enterprises is good for the country." Orr popped out of the sinking airplane last.

"You should have seen him!" Sergeant Knight roared with laughter as he related the episode to Yossarian. "It was the funniest goddam thing you ever saw. None of the Mae Wests would work because Milo had stolen the carbon dioxide to make those ice-cream sodas you bastards have been getting in the officers' mess. But that wasn't too bad, as it turned out. Only one of us couldn't swim, and we lifted that guy up into the raft after Orr had worked it over by its rope right up against the fuselage while we were all still standing on the plane. That little crackpot sure has a knack for things like that. Then the other raft came loose and drifted away, so that all six of us wound up sitting in one with our elbows and legs pressed so close against each other you almost couldn't move without knocking the guy next to you out of the raft into the water. The plane went down about three seconds after we left it and we were out there all alone, and right after that we began unscrewing the caps on our Mae Wests to see what the hell had gone wrong and found these goddam notes from Milo telling us that what was good for him was good enough for the rest of us. That bastard! Jesus, did we curse him, all except that buddy of yours Orr, who just kept grinning as though for all he cared what was good for Milo *might* be good enough for the rest of us.

"I swear, you should have seen him sitting up there on the rim of the raft like the captain of a ship while the rest of us just watched him and waited for him to tell us what to do. He kept slapping his hands on his legs every few seconds as though he had the shakes and saying 'All right now, all right,' and giggling like a crazy little freak, then saying 'All right now, all right' again and giggling like a crazy little freak some more. It was like watching some kind of a moron. Watching him was all that kept us from going to pieces altogether during the first few minutes, what with each wave washing over us into the raft or dumping a few of us back into the water so that we had to climb back in again before the next wave came along and washed us right back out. It was sure funny. We just kept falling out and climbing back in. We had the guy who couldn't swim stretched out in the middle of the raft on the floor, but even there he almost drowned, because the water inside the raft was deep enough to keep splashing in his face. Oh, boy!

"Then Orr began opening up compartments in the raft, and the fun really began. First he found a box of chocolate bars and he passed those around, so we sat there eating salty wet chocolate bars while the waves kept knocking us out of the raft into the water. Next he found some bouillon cubes and aluminum cups and made us some soup. Then he found some tea. Sure, he made it! Can't you see him serving us tea as we sat there soaking wet in water up to our ass? Now I was falling out of the raft because I was laughing so much. We were all laughing. And he was dead serious, except for that goofy giggle of his and that crazy grin. What a jerk! Whatever he found he used. He found some shark repellent and he sprinkled it right into the water. He found some marker dye and he threw it into the water. The next thing he finds is a fishing line and dried bait, and his face lights up as though the Air-Sea Rescue launch had just sped up to save us before we died of exposure or before the Germans sent a boat out from Spezia to take us prisoner or machine-gun us. In no time at all, Orr had that fishing line out into the water, trolling away as happy as a lark. 'Lieutenant, what do you expect to catch?' I asked him. 'Cod,' he told me. And he meant it. And it's a good thing he didn't catch any, because he would have eaten that codfish raw if he had caught any, and would have made us eat it, too, because he had found this little book that said it was all right to eat codfish raw.

"The next thing he found was this little blue oar about the size of a Dixie-cup spoon, and, sure enough, he began rowing with it, trying to move all nine hundred pounds of us with that little stick. Can you imagine? After that he found a small magnetic compass and a big waterproof map, and he spread the map open on his knees and set the compass on top of it. And that's how he spent the time until the launch picked us about thirty minutes later, sitting there with that baited fishing line out behind him, with the compass in his lap and the map spread out on his knees, and paddling away as hard as he could with that dinky blue oar as though he was speeding to Majorca. Jesus!"

Sergeant Knight knew all about Majorca, and so did Orr, because Yossarian had told them often of such sanctuaries as Spain, Switzerland and Sweden where American fliers could be interned for the duration of the war under conditions of utmost ease and luxury merely by flying there. Yossarian was the squadron's leading authority on internment and had already begun plotting an emergency heading into Switzerland on every mission he flew into northernmost Italy. He would certainly have preferred Sweden, where the level of intelligence was high and where he could swim nude with beautiful girls with low, demurring voices and sire whole happy, undisciplined tribes of illegitimate Yossarians that the state would assist through parturition and launch into life without stigma; but Sweden was out of reach, too far away, and Yossarian waited for the piece of flak that would knock out one engine over the Italian Alps and provide him with the excuse for heading for Switzerland. He would not even tell his pilot he was guiding him there. Yossarian often thought of scheming with some pilot he trusted to fake a crippled engine and then destroy the evidence of deception with a belly landing, but the only pilot he really trusted was McWatt, who was happiest where he was and still got a big boot out of buzzing his plane over Yossarian's tent or roaring in so low over the bathers at the beach that the fierce wind from his propellers slashed dark furrows in the water and whipped sheets of spray flapping back for seconds afterward.

Dobbs and Hungry Joe were out of the question, and so was Orr, who was tinkering with the valve of the stove again when Yossarian limped despondently back into the tent after Dobbs had turned him down. The stove Orr was manufacturing out of an inverted metal drum stood in the middle of the smooth cement floor he had constructed. He was working sedulously on both knees. Yossarian tried paying no attention to him and limped wearily to his cot and sat down with a labored, drawn-out grunt. Prickles of perspiration were turning chilly on his forehead. Dobbs had depressed him. Doc Daneeka depressed him. An ominous vision of doom depressed him when he looked at Orr. He began ticking with a variety of internal tremors. Nerves twitched, and the vein in one wrist began palpitating.

Orr studied Yossarian over his shoulder, his moist lips drawn back around convex rows of large buck teeth. Reaching sideways, he dug a bottle of warm beer out of his foot locker, and he handed it to Yossarian after prying off the cap. Neither said a word. Yossarian sipped the bubbles off the top and tilted his head back. Orr watched him cunningly with a noiseless grin. Yossarian eyed Orr guardedly. Orr snickered with a slight, mucid sibilance and turned back to his work, squatting. Yossarian grew tense.

"Don't start," he begged in a threatening voice, both hands tightening around his beer bottle. "Don't start working on your stove."

Orr cackled quietly. "I'm almost finished."

"No, you're not. You're about to begin."

"Here's the valve. See? It's almost all together."

"And you're about to take it apart. I know what you're doing, you bastard. I've seen you do it three hundred times."

Orr shivered with glee. "I want to get the leak in this gasoline line out," he explained. "I've got it down now to where it's only an ooze."

"I can't watch you," Yossarian confessed tonelessly. "If you want to work with something big, that's okay. But that valve is filled with tiny parts, and I just haven't got the patience right now to watch you working so hard over things that are so goddam small and unimportant."

"Just because they're small doesn't mean they're unimportant."

"I don't care."

"Once more?"

"When I'm not around. You're a happy imbecile and you don't

know what it means to feel the way I do. Things happen to me when you work over small things that I can't even begin to explain. I find out that I can't stand you. I start to hate you, and I'm soon thinking seriously about busting this bottle down on your head or stabbing you in the neck with that hunting knife there. Do you understand?"

Orr nodded very intelligently. "I won't take the valve apart now," he said, and began taking it apart, working with slow, tireless, interminable precision, his rustic, ungainly face bent very close to the floor, picking painstakingly at the minute mechanism in his fingers with such limitless, plodding concentration that he seemed scarcely to be thinking of it at all.

Yossarian cursed him silently and made up his mind to ignore him. "What the hell's your hurry with that stove, anyway?" he barked out a moment later in spite of himself. "It's still hot out. We're probably going swimming later. What are you worried about the cold for?"

"The days are getting shorter," Orr observed philosophically. "I'd like to get this all finished for you while there's still time. You'll have the best stove in the squadron when I'm through. It will burn all night with this feed control I'm fixing, and these metal plates will radiate the heat all over the tent. If you leave a helmet full of water on this thing when you go to sleep, you'll have warm water to wash with all ready for you when you wake up. Won't that be nice? If you want to cook eggs or soup, all you'll have to do is set the pot down here and turn the fire up."

"What do you mean, me?" Yossarian wanted to know. "Where are you going to be?"

Orr's stunted torso shook suddenly with a muffled spasm of amusement. "I don't know," he exclaimed, and a weird, wavering giggle gushed out suddenly through chattering buck teeth like an exploding jet of emotion. He was still laughing when he continued, and his voice was clogged with saliva. "If they keep on shooting me down this way, I don't know where I'm going to be."

Yossarian was moved. "Why don't you try to stop flying, Orr? You've got an excuse."

"I've only got eighteen missions."

"But you've been shot down on almost every one. You're either ditching or crash-landing every time you go up."

"Oh, I don't mind flying missions. I guess they're lots of fun. You ought to try flying a few with me when you're not flying lead. Just for laughs. Tee-hee." Orr gazed up at Yossarian through the corners of his eyes with a look of pointed mirth.

Yossarian avoided his stare. "They've got me flying lead again."

"When you're not flying lead. If you had my brains, do you know what you'd do? You'd go right to Piltchard and Wren and tell them you want to fly with me."

"And get shot down with you every time you go up? What's the fun in that?"

"That's just why you ought to do it," Orr insisted. "I guess I'm just about the best pilot around now when it comes to ditching or making crash landings. It would be good practice for you."

"Good practice for what?"

"Good practice in case you ever have to ditch or make a crash landing. Tee-hee-hee."

"Have you got another bottle of beer for me?" Yossarian asked morosely.

"Do you want to bust it down on my head?"

This time Yossarian did laugh. "Like that whore in that apartment in Rome?"

Orr sniggered lewdly, his bulging crab apple cheeks blowing outward with pleasure. "Do you really want to know why she was hitting me over the head with her shoe?" he teased.

"I do know," Yossarian teased back. "Nately's whore told me."

Orr grinned like a gargoyle. "No she didn't."

Yossarian felt sorry for Orr. Orr was so small and ugly. Who would protect him if he lived? Who would protect a warmhearted, simple-minded gnome like Orr from rowdies and cliques and from expert athletes like Appleby who had flies in their eyes and would walk right over him with swaggering conceit and self-assurance every chance they got? Yossarian worried frequently about Orr. Who would shield him against animosity and deceit, against people with ambition and the embittered snobbery of the big shot's wife, against the squalid, corrupting indignities of the profit motive and the friendly neighborhood butcher with inferior meat? Orr was a happy and unsuspecting simpleton with a thick mass of wavy polychromatic hair parted down the center. He would be mere child's play for them. They would take his money, screw his wife and show no kindness to his children. Yossarian felt a flood of compassion sweep over him.

Orr was an eccentric midget, a freakish, likable dwarf with a smutty mind and a thousand valuable skills that would keep him in a low income group all his life. He could use a soldering iron and hammer two boards together so that the wood did not split and the nails did not bend. He could drill holes. He had built a good deal more in the tent while Yossarian was away in the hospital. He had filed or chiseled a perfect channel in the cement so that the slender gasoline line was flush with the floor as it ran to the stove from the tank he had built outside on an elevated platform. He had constructed andirons for the fireplace out of excess bomb parts and had filled them with stout silver logs, and he had framed with stained wood the photographs of girls with big breasts he had torn out of cheesecake magazines and hung over the mantelpiece. Orr could open a can of paint. He could mix paint, thin paint, remove paint. He could chop wood and measure things with a ruler. He knew how to build fires. He could dig holes, and he had a real gift for bringing water for them both in cans and canteens from the tanks near the mess hall. He could engross himself in an inconsequential task for hours without growing restless or bored, as oblivious to fatigue as the stump of a tree, and almost as taciturn. He had an uncanny knowledge of wildlife and was not afraid of dogs or cats or beetles or moths, or of foods like scrod or tripe.

Yossarian sighed drearily and began brooding about the rumored mission to Bologna. The valve Orr was dismantling was about the size of a thumb and contained thirty-seven separate parts, excluding the casing, many of them so minute that Orr was required to pinch them tightly between the tips of his fingernails as he placed them carefully on the floor in orderly, catalogued rows, never quickening his movements or slowing them down, never tiring, never pausing in his relentless, methodical, monotonous procedure unless it was to leer at Yossarian with maniacal mischief. Yossarian tried not to watch him. He counted the parts and thought he would go clear out of his mind. He turned away, shutting his eyes, but that was even worse, for now he had only the sounds, the tiny, maddening, indefatigable, distinct clicks and rustles of hands and weightless parts. Orr was breathing rhythmically with a noise that was stertorous and repulsive. Yossarian clenched his fists and looked at the long bone-handled hunting knife hanging in a holster over the cot of the dead man in the tent. As soon as he thought of stabbing Orr, his tension eased. The idea of murdering Orr was so ridiculous that he began to consider it seriously with queer whimsy and fascination. He searched the nape of Orr's neck for the probable site of the medulla oblongata. Just the daintiest stick there would kill him and solve so many serious, agonizing problems for them both.

"Does it hurt?" Orr asked at precisely that moment, as though by protective instinct.

Yossarian eyed him closely. "Does what hurt?"

"Your leg," said Orr with a strange, mysterious laugh. "You still limp a little."

"It's just a habit, I guess," said Yossarian, breathing again with relief. "I'll probably get over it soon."

Orr rolled over sideways to the floor and came up on one knee, facing toward Yossarian. "Do you remember," he drawled reflectively, with an air of labored recollection, "that girl who was hitting me on the head that day in Rome?" He chuckled at Yossarian's involuntary exclamation of tricked annoyance. "I'll make a deal with you about that girl. I'll tell you why that girl was hitting me on the head with her shoe that day if you answer one question."

"What's the question?"

"Did you ever screw Nately's girl?"

Yossarian laughed with surprise. "Me? No. Now tell me why that girl hit you with her shoe."

"That wasn't the question," Orr informed him with victorious delight. "That was just conversation. She acts like you screwed her."

"Well, I didn't. How does she act?"

"She acts like she don't like you."

"She doesn't like anyone."

"She likes Captain Black," Orr reminded.

"That's because he treats her like dirt. Anyone can get a girl that way."

"She wears a slave bracelet on her leg with his name on it."

"He makes her wear it to needle Nately."

"She even gives him some of the money she gets from Nately."

"Listen, what do you want from me?"

"Did you ever screw my girl?"

"Your girl? Who the hell is your girl?"

"The one who hit me over the head with her shoe."

"I've been with her a couple of times," Yossarian admitted. "Since when is she your girl? What are you getting at?"

"She don't like you, either."

"What the hell do I care if she likes me or not? She likes me as much as she likes you."

"Did she ever hit you over the head with her shoe?"

"Orr, I'm tired. Why don't you leave me alone?"

"Tee-hee-hee. How about that skinny countess in Rome and her skinny daughter-in-law?" Orr persisted impishly with increasing zest. "Did you ever screw them?"

"Oh, how I wish I could," sighed Yossarian honestly, imagining, at the mere question, the prurient, used, decaying feel in his petting hands of their teeny, pulpy buttocks and breasts.

"They don't like you either," commented Orr. "They like Aarfy, and they like Nately, but they don't like you. Women just don't seem to like you. I think they think you're a bad influence."

"Women are crazy," Yossarian answered, and waited grimly for what he knew was coming next.

"How about that other girl of yours?" Orr asked with a pretense of pensive curiosity. "The fat one? The bald one? You know, that fat bald one in Sicily with the turban who kept sweating over us all night long? Is she crazy too?"

"Didn't she like me either?"

"How could you do it to a girl with no hair?"

"How was I supposed to know she had no hair?"

"I knew it," Orr bragged. "I knew it all the time."

"You knew she was bald?" Yossarian exclaimed in wonder.

"No, I knew this valve wouldn't work if I left a part out," Orr answered, glowing with cranberry-red elation because he had just duped Yossarian again. "Will you please hand me that small composition gasket that rolled over there? It's right near your foot."

"No it isn't."

"Right here," said Orr, and took hold of something invisible with the tips of his fingernails and held it up for Yossarian to see. "Now I'll have to start all over again."

"I'll kill you if you do. I'll murder you on the spot."

"Why don't you ever fly with me?" Orr asked suddenly, and looked straight into Yossarian's face for the first time. "There, that's the question I want you to answer. Why don't you ever fly with me?"

Yossarian turned away with intense shame and embarrassment. "I told you why. They've got me flying lead bombardier most of the time."

"That's not why," Orr said, shaking his head. "You went to Piltchard and Wren after the first Avignon mission and told them you didn't ever want to fly with me. That's why, isn't it?"

Yossarian felt his skin turn hot. "No, I didn't," he lied.

"Yes you did," Orr insisted equably. "You asked them not to assign you to any plane piloted by me, Dobbs or Huple because you didn't have confidence in us at the controls. And Piltchard and Wren said they couldn't make an exception of you because it wouldn't be fair to the men who did have to fly with us."

"So?" said Yossarian. "It didn't make any difference then, did it?"

"But they've never made you fly with me." Orr, working on both knees again, was addressing Yossarian without bitterness or reproach, but with injured humility, which was infinitely more painful to observe, although he was still grinning and snickering, as though the situation were comic. "You really ought to fly with me, you know. I'm a pretty good pilot, and I'd take care of you. I may get knocked down a lot, but that's not my fault, and nobody's ever been hurt in my plane. Yes, sir—if you had any brains, you know what you'd do? You'd go right to Piltchard and Wren and tell them you want to fly all your missions with me."

Yossarian leaned forward and peered closely into Orr's inscrutable mask of contradictory emotions. "Are you trying to tell me something?"

"Tee-hee-hee-hee," Orr responded. "I'm trying to tell you why that big girl with the shoe was hitting me on the head that day. But you just won't let me."

"Tell me."

"Will you fly with me?"

Yossarian laughed and shook his head. "You'll only get knocked down into the water again."

Orr did get knocked down into the water again when the rumored mission to Bologna was flown, and he landed his single-engine plane with a smashing jar on the choppy, wind-swept waves tossing and falling below the warlike black thunderclouds mobilizing overhead. He was late getting out of the plane and ended up alone in a raft that began drifting away from the men in the other raft and was out of sight by the time the Air-Sea Rescue launch came plowing up through the wind and splattering raindrops to take them aboard. Night was already falling by the time they were returned to the squadron. There was no word of Orr.

"Don't worry," reassured Kid Sampson, still wrapped in the heavy blankets and raincoat in which he had been swaddled on the boat by his rescuers. "He's probably been picked up already if he didn't drown in that storm. It didn't last long. I bet he'll show up any minute."

Yossarian walked back to his tent to wait for Orr to show up any minute and lit a fire to make things warm for him. The stove worked perfectly, with a strong, robust blaze that could be raised or lowered by turning the tap Orr had finally finished repairing. A light rain was falling, drumming softly on the tent, the trees, the ground. Yossarian cooked a can of hot soup to have ready for Orr and ate it all himself as the time passed. He hard-boiled some eggs for Orr and ate those too. Then he ate a whole tin of Cheddar cheese from a package of K rations.

Each time he caught himself worrying he made himself remember that Orr could do everything and broke into silent laughter at the picture of Orr in the raft as Sergeant Knight had described him, bent forward with a busy, preoccupied smile over the map and compass in his lap, stuffing one soaking-wet chocolate bar after another into his grinning, tittering mouth as he paddled away dutifully through the lightning, thunder and rain with the bright-blue useless toy oar, the fishing line with dried bait trailing out behind him. Yossarian really had no doubt about Orr's ability to survive. If fish could be caught with that silly fishing line, Orr would catch them, and if it was codfish he was after, then Orr would catch a codfish, even though no codfish had ever been caught in those waters before. Yossarian put another can of soup up to cook and ate that too when it was hot. Every time a car door slammed, he broke into a hopeful smile and turned expectantly toward the entrance, listening for footsteps. He knew that any moment Orr would come walking into the tent with big, glistening, rain-soaked eyes, cheeks and buck teeth, looking ludicrously like a jolly New England oysterman in a yellow oilskin rain hat and slicker numerous sizes too large for him and holding up proudly for Yossarian's amusement a great dead codfish he had caught. But he didn't.

29

Peckem

There was no word about Orr the next day, and Sergeant Whitcomb, with commendable dispatch and considerable hope, dropped a reminder in his tickler file to send a form letter over Colonel Cathcart's signature to Orr's next of kin when nine more days had elapsed. There was word from General Peckem's headquarters, though, and Yossarian was drawn to the crowd of officers and enlisted men in shorts and bathing trunks buzzing in grumpy confusion around the bulletin board just outside the orderly room.

"What's so different about *this* Sunday, I want to know?" Hungry Joe was demanding vociferously of Chief White Halfoat. "Why won't we have a parade *this* Sunday when we don't have a parade *every* Sunday? Huh?"

Yossarian worked his way through to the front and let out a long, agonized groan when he read the terse announcement there:

> *Due to circumstances beyond my control, there will be no big parade this Sunday afternoon.*
>
> COLONEL SCHEISSKOPF

Dobbs was right. They were indeed sending everyone overseas, even Lieutenant Scheisskopf, who had resisted the move with all the vigor and wisdom at his command and who reported for duty at General Peckem's office in a mood of grave discontent.

General Peckem welcomed Colonel Scheisskopf with effusive charm and said he was delighted to have him. An additional colonel on his staff meant that he could now begin agitating for two additional majors, four additional captains, sixteen additional lieutenants and untold quantities of additional enlisted men, typewriters, desks, filing cabinets, automobiles and other substantial equipment and supplies that would contribute to the prestige of his position and increase his striking power in the war he had declared against General Dreedle. He now had two full colonels; General Dreedle had only five, and four of those were combat commanders. With almost no intriguing at all, General Peckem had executed a maneuver that would eventually double his strength. And General Dreedle was getting drunk more often. The future looked wonderful, and General Peckem contemplated his bright new colonel enchantedly with an effulgent smile.

In all matters of consequence, General P. P. Peckem was, as he always remarked when he was about to criticize the work of some close associate publicly, a realist. He was a handsome, pink-skinned man of fifty-three. His manner was always casual and relaxed, and his uniforms were custom-made. He had silver-gray hair, slightly myopic eyes and thin, overhanging, sensual lips. He was a perceptive, graceful, sophisticated man who was sensitive to everyone's weaknesses but his own and found everyone absurd but himself. General Peckem laid great, fastidious stress on small matters of taste and style. He was always *augmenting* things. Approaching events were never *coming*, but always *upcoming*. It was not true that he wrote *memorandums* praising himself and recommending that his authority be *enhanced* to include all combat operations; he wrote *memoranda*. And the prose in the *memoranda* of other officers was always *turgid*, *stilted*, or *ambiguous*. The errors of others were inevitably *deplorable*. Regulations were *stringent*, and his data never *was* obtained from a reliable source, but always *were* obtained. General Peckem was frequently *constrained*. Things were often *incumbent* upon him, and he frequently acted with *greatest reluctance*. It never escaped his memory that neither black nor white was a color, and he never used *verbal* when he meant *oral*. He could quote glibly from Plato, Nietzsche, Montaigne, Theodore Roosevelt, the Marquis de Sade and Warren G. Harding. A virgin audience like Colonel Scheisskopf was grist for General Peckem's mill, a stimulating opportunity to throw open his whole dazzling erudite treasure house of puns, wisecracks, slanders, homilies, anecdotes, proverbs, epigrams, apothegms, bon mots and other pungent sayings. He beamed urbanely as he began orienting Colonel Scheisskopf to his new surroundings.

"My only fault," he observed with practiced good humor, watching for the effect of his words, "is that I have no faults."

Colonel Scheisskopf didn't laugh, and General Peckem was stunned. A heavy doubt crushed his enthusiasm. He had just opened with one of his most trusted paradoxes, and he was positively alarmed that not the slightest flicker of acknowledgment had moved across that impervious face, which began to remind him suddenly, in hue and texture, of an unused soap eraser. Perhaps Colonel Scheisskopf was tired,

General Peckem granted to himself charitably; he had come a long way, and everything was unfamiliar. General Peckem's attitude toward all the personnel in his command, officers and enlisted men, was marked by the same easy spirit of tolerance and permissiveness. He mentioned often that if the people who worked for him met him halfway, he would meet them more than halfway, with the result, as he always added with an astute chuckle, that there was never any meeting of the minds at all. General Peckem thought of himself as aesthetic and intellectual. When people disagreed with him, he urged them to be *objective.*

And it was indeed an objective Peckem who gazed at Colonel Scheisskopf encouragingly and resumed his indoctrination with an attitude of magnanimous forgiveness. "You've come to us just in time, Scheisskopf. The summer offensive has petered out, thanks to the incompetent leadership with which we supply our troops, and I have a crying need for a tough, experienced, competent officer like you to help produce the memoranda upon which we rely so heavily to let people know how good we are and how much work we're turning out. I hope you are a prolific writer."

"I don't know anything about writing," Colonel Scheisskopf retorted sullenly.

"Well, don't let that trouble you," General Peckem continued with a careless flick of his wrist. "Just pass the work I assign you along to somebody else and trust to luck. We call that delegation of responsibility. Somewhere down near the lowest level of this coordinated organization I run are people who do get the work done when it reaches them, and everything manages to run along smoothly without too much effort on my part. I suppose that's because I am a good executive. Nothing we do in this large department of ours is really very important, and there's never any rush. On the other hand, it is important that we let people know we do a great deal of it. Let me know if you find yourself shorthanded. I've already put in a requisition for two majors, four captains and sixteen lieutenants to give you a hand. While none of the work we do is very important, it is important that we do a great deal of it. Don't you agree?"

"What about the parades?" Colonel Scheisskopf broke in.

"What parades?" inquired General Peckem with a feeling that his polish just wasn't getting across.

"Won't I be able to conduct parades every Sunday afternoon?" Colonel Scheisskopf demanded petulantly.

"No. Of course not. What ever gave you that idea?"

"But they said I could."

"Who said you could?"

"The officers who sent me overseas. They told me I'd be able to march the men around in parades all I wanted to."

"They lied to you."

"That wasn't fair, sir.

"I'm sorry, Scheisskopf. I'm willing to do everything I can to make you happy here, but parades are out of the question. We don't have enough men in our own organization to make up much of a parade, and the combat units would rise up in open rebellion if we tried to make them march. I'm afraid you'll just have to hold back awhile until we get control. Then you can do what you want with the men."

"What about my wife?" Colonel Scheisskopf demanded with disgruntled suspicion. "I'll still be able to send for her, won't I?"

"Your wife? Why in the world should you want to?"

"A husband and wife should be together."

"That's out of the question also."

"But they said I could send for her!"

"They lied to you again."

"They had no right to lie to me!" Colonel Scheisskopf protested, his eyes wetting with indignation.

"Of course they had a right," General Peckem snapped with cold and calculated severity, resolving right then and there to test the mettle of his new colonel under fire. "Don't be such an ass, Scheisskopf. People have a right to do anything that's not forbidden by law, and there's no law against lying to you. Now, don't ever waste my time with such sentimental platitudes again. Do you hear?"

"Yes, sir," murmured Colonel Scheisskopf.

Colonel Scheisskopf wilted pathetically, and General Peckem blessed the fates that had sent him a weakling for a subordinate. A man of spunk would have been unthinkable. Having won, General Peckem relented. He did not enjoy humiliating his men. "If your wife were a Wac, I could probably have her transferred here. But that's the most I can do."

"She has a friend who's a Wac," Colonel Scheisskopf offered hopefully.

"I'm afraid that isn't good enough. Have Mrs. Scheisskopf join the Wacs if she wants to, and I'll bring her over here. But in the meantime, my dear Colonel, let's get back to our little war, if we may. Here, briefly, is the military situation that confronts us." General Peckem rose and moved toward a rotary rack of enormous colored maps.

Colonel Scheisskopf blanched. "We're not going into combat, are we?" he blurted out in horror.

"Oh, no, of course not," General Peckem assured him indulgently, with a companionable laugh. "Please give me *some* credit, won't you? That's why we're still down here in Rome. Certainly, I'd like to be up in Florence, too, where I could keep in closer touch with ex-P.F.C. Wintergreen. But Florence is still a bit too near the actual fighting to suit me." General Peckem lifted a wooden pointer and swept the rubber tip cheerfully across Italy from one coast to the other. "These, Scheisskopf, are the Germans. They're dug into these mountains very solidly in the Gothic Line and won't be pushed out till late next spring, although that isn't going to stop those clods we have in charge from trying. That gives us in Special Services almost nine months to achieve our objective. And that objective is to capture every bomber group in the U.S. Air Force. After all," said General Peckem with his low, well-modulated chuckle, "if dropping bombs on the enemy isn't a special service, I wonder what in the world is. Don't you agree?" Colonel Scheisskopf gave no indication that he did agree, but General Peckem was already too entranced with his own loquacity to notice. "Our position right now is excellent. Reinforcements like yourself keep arriving, and we have more than enough time to plan our entire strategy carefully. Our immediate goal," he said, "is right here." And General Peckem swung his pointer south to the island of Pianosa and tapped it significantly upon a large word that had been lettered on there with black grease pencil. The word was DREEDLE.

Colonel Scheisskopf, squinting, moved very close to the map, and for the first time since he entered the room a light of comprehension shed a dim glow over his stolid face. "I think I understand," he exclaimed. "Yes, I know I understand. Our first job is to capture Dreedle away from the enemy. Right?"

General Peckem laughed benignly, "No, Scheisskopf. Dreedle's on our side, and Dreedle *is* the enemy. General Dreedle commands four bomb groups that we simply must capture in order to continue our offensive. Conquering General Dreedle will give us the aircraft and vital bases we need to carry our operations into other areas. And that battle, by the way, is just about won." General Peckem drifted toward the window, laughing quietly again, and settled back against the sill with his arms folded, greatly satisfied by his own wit and by his knowledgeable, blasé impudence. The skilled choice of words he was exercising was exquisitely titillating. General Peckem liked listening to himself talk, liked most of all listening to himself talk about himself. "General Dreedle simply doesn't know how to cope with me," he gloated. "I keep invading his jurisdiction with comments and criticisms that are really none of my business, and he doesn't know what to do about it. When he accuses me of seeking to undermine him, I merely answer that my only purpose in calling attention to his errors is to strengthen our war effort by eliminating inefficiency. Then I ask him innocently if he's opposed to improving our war effort. Oh, he grumbles and he bristles and he bellows, but he's really quite helpless. He's simply out of style. He's turning into quite a souse, you know. The poor blockhead shouldn't even be a general. He has no tone, no tone at all. Thank God he isn't going to last." General Peckem chuckled with jaunty relish and sailed smoothly along toward a favorite learned allusion. "I sometimes think of myself as Fortinbras—ha, ha—in the play *Hamlet* by William Shakespeare, who just keeps circling and circling around the action until everything else falls apart, and then strolls in at the end to pick up all the pieces for himself. Shakespeare is—"

"I don't know anything about plays," Colonel Scheisskopf broke in bluntly.

General Peckem looked at him with amazement. Never before had a reference of his to Shakespeare's hallowed *Hamlet* been ignored and trampled upon with such rude indifference. He began to wonder with genuine concern just what sort of shithead the Pentagon had foisted on him. "What *do* you know about?" he asked acidly.

"Parades," answered Colonel Scheisskopf eagerly. "Will I be able to send out memos about parades?"

"As long as you don't schedule any." General Peckem returned to his chair still wearing a frown. "And as long as they don't interfere with your main assignment of recommending that the authority of Special Services be expanded to include combat activities."

"Can I schedule parades and then call them off?"

General Peckem brightened instantly. "Why, that's a wonderful idea! But just send out weekly announcements *postponing* the parades. Don't even bother to schedule them. That would be infinitely more disconcerting." General Peckem was blossoming spryly with cordiality again. "Yes, Scheisskopf," he said, "I think you've really hit on something. After all, what combat commander could possibly quarrel with us for notifying his men that there won't be a parade that coming

Sunday? We'd be merely stating a widely known fact. But the implication is beautiful. Yes, positively beautiful. We're implying that we *could* schedule a parade if we chose to. I'm going to like you, Scheisskopf. Stop in and introduce yourself to Colonel Cargill and tell him what you're up to. I know you two will like each other."

Colonel Cargill came storming into General Peckem's office a minute later in a furor of timid resentment. "I've been here longer than Scheisskopf," he complained. "Why can't I be the one to call off the parades?"

"Because Scheisskopf has experience with parades, and you haven't. You can call off U.S.O. shows if you want to. In fact, why don't you? Just think of all the places that won't be getting a U.S.O. show on any given day. Think of all the places each big-name entertainer won't be visiting. Yes, Cargill, I think you've hit on something. I think you've just thrown open a whole new area of operation for us. Tell Colonel Scheisskopf I want him to work along under your supervision on this. And send him in to see me when you're through giving him instructions."

"Colonel Cargill says you told him you want me to work along under his supervision on the U.S.O. project," Colonel Scheisskopf complained.

"I told him no such thing," answered General Peckem. "Confidentially, Scheisskopf, I'm not too happy with Colonel Cargill. He's bossy and he's slow. I'd like you to keep a close eye on what he's doing and see if you can't get a little more work out of him."

"He keeps butting in," Colonel Cargill protested. "He won't let me get any work done."

"There's something very funny about Scheisskopf," General Peckem agreed reflectively. "Keep a very close eye on him and see if you can't find out what he's up to."

"Now he's butting into *my* business!" Colonel Scheisskopf cried.

"Don't let it worry you, Scheisskopf," said General Peckem, congratulating himself on how adeptly he had fit Colonel Scheisskopf into his standard method of operation. Already his two colonels were barely on speaking terms. "Colonel Cargill envies you because of the splendid job you're doing on parades. He's afraid I'm going to put you in charge of bomb patterns."

Colonel Scheisskopf was all ears. "What are bomb patterns?"

"Bomb patterns?" General Peckem repeated, twinkling with self-satisfied good humor. "A *bomb pattern* is a term I dreamed up just several weeks ago. It means nothing, but you'd be surprised at how rapidly it's caught on. Why, I've got all sorts of people convinced I think it's important for the bombs to explode close together and make a neat aerial photograph. There's one colonel in Pianosa who's hardly concerned any more with whether he hits the target or not. Let's fly over and have some fun with him today. It will make Colonel Cargill jealous, and I learned from Wintergreen this morning that General Dreedle will be off in Sardinia. It drives General Dreedle insane to find out I've been inspecting one of his installations while he's been off inspecting another. We may even get there in time for the briefing. They'll be bombing a tiny undefended village, reducing the whole community to rubble. I have it from Wintergreen—Wintergreen's an ex-sergeant now, by the way—that the mission is entirely unnecessary. Its only purpose is to delay German reinforcements at a time when we aren't even planning an offensive. But that's the way things go when you elevate mediocre people to positions of authority." He gestured languidly toward his gigantic map of Italy. "Why, this tiny mountain village is so insignificant that it isn't even there."

They arrived at Colonel Cathcart's group too late to attend the preliminary briefing and hear Major Danby insist, "But it *is* there, I tell you. It's there, it's there."

"It's where?" Dunbar demanded defiantly, pretending not to see.

"It's right there on the map where this road makes this slight turn. Can't you see this slight turn on your map?"

"No, I can't see it."

"I can see it," volunteered Havermeyer, and marked the spot on Dunbar's map. "And here's a good picture of the village right on these photographs. I understand the whole thing. The purpose of the mission is to knock the whole village sliding down the side of the mountain and create a roadblock that the Germans will have to clear. Is that right?"

"That's right," said Major Danby, mopping his perspiring forehead with his handkerchief. "I'm glad somebody here is beginning to understand. These two armored divisions will be coming down from Austria into Italy along this road. The village is built on such a steep incline that all the rubble from the houses and other buildings you destroy will certainly tumble right down and pile up on the road."

"What the hell difference will it make?" Dunbar wanted to know, as Yossarian watched him excitedly with a mixture of awe and adulation. "It will only take them a couple of days to clear it."

Major Danby was trying to avoid an argument. "Well, it apparently makes some difference to Headquarters," he answered in a conciliatory tone. "I suppose that's why they ordered the mission."

"Have the people in the village been warned?" asked McWatt.

Major Danby was dismayed that McWatt too was registering opposition. "No, I don't think so."

"Haven't we dropped any leaflets telling them that this time we'll be flying over to hit them?" asked Yossarian. "Can't we even tip them off so they'll get out of the way?"

"No, I don't think so." Major Danby was sweating some more and still shifting his eyes about uneasily. "The Germans might find out and choose another road. I'm not sure about any of this. I'm just making assumptions."

"They won't even take shelter," Dunbar argued bitterly. "They'll pour out into the streets to wave when they see our planes coming, all the children and dogs and old people. Jesus Christ! Why can't we leave them alone?"

"Why can't we create the roadblock somewhere else?" asked McWatt. "Why must it be there?"

"I don't know," Major Danby answered unhappily. "I don't know. Look, fellows, we've got to have some confidence in the people above us who issue our orders. They know what they're doing."

"The hell they do," said Dunbar.

"What's the trouble?" inquired Colonel Korn, moving leisurely across the briefing room with his hands in his pockets and his tan shirt baggy.

"Oh, no trouble, Colonel," said Major Danby, trying nervously to cover up. "We're just discussing the mission."

"They don't want to bomb the village," Havermeyer snickered, giving Major Danby away.

"You prick!" Yossarian said to Havermeyer.

"You leave Havermeyer alone," Colonel Korn ordered Yossarian curtly. He recognized Yossarian as the drunk who had accosted him roughly at the officers' club one night before the first mission to Bologna, and he swung his displeasure prudently to Dunbar. "Why don't you want to bomb the village?"

"It's cruel, that's why."

"Cruel?" asked Colonel Korn with cold good humor, frightened only momentarily by the uninhibited vehemence of Dunbar's hostility. "Would it be any less cruel to let those two German divisions down to fight with our troops? American lives are at stake, too, you know. Would you rather see American blood spilled?"

"American blood is being spilled. But those people are living up there in peace. Why can't we leave them the hell alone?"

"Yes, it's easy for you to talk," Colonel Korn jeered. "You're safe here in Pianosa. It won't make any difference to you when these German reinforcements arrive, will it?"

Dunbar turned crimson with embarrassment and replied in a voice that was suddenly defensive. "Why can't we create the roadblock somewhere else? Couldn't we bomb the slope of a mountain or the road itself?"

"Would you rather go back to Bologna?" The question, asked quietly, rang out like a shot and created a silence in the room that was awkward and menacing. Yossarian prayed intensely, with shame, that Dunbar would keep his mouth shut. Dunbar dropped his gaze, and Colonel Korn knew he had won. "No, I thought not," he continued with undisguised scorn. "You know, Colonel Cathcart and I have to go to a lot of trouble to get you a milk run like this. If you'd sooner fly missions to Bologna, Spezia and Ferrara, we can get those targets with no trouble at all." His eyes gleamed dangerously behind his rimless glasses, and his muddy jowls were square and hard. "Just let me know."

"I would," responded Havermeyer eagerly with another boastful snicker. "I like to fly into Bologna straight and level with my head in the bombsight and listen to all that flak pumping away all around me. I get a big kick out of the way the men come charging over to me after the mission and call me dirty names. Even the enlisted men get sore enough to curse me and want to take socks at me."

Colonel Korn chucked Havermeyer under the chin jovially, ignoring him, and then addressed himself to Dunbar and Yossarian in a dry monotone. "You've got my sacred word for it. Nobody is more distressed about those lousy wops up in the hills than Colonel Cathcart and myself. *Mais c'est la guerre.* Try to remember that we didn't start the war and Italy did. That we weren't the aggressors and Italy was. And that we couldn't possibly inflict as much cruelty on the Italians, Germans, Russians and Chinese as they're already inflicting on themselves." Colonel Korn gave Major Danby's shoulder a friendly squeeze without changing his unfriendly expression. "Carry on with the briefing, Danby. And make sure they understand the importance of a tight bomb pattern."

"Oh, no, Colonel," Major Danby blurted out, blinking upward.

"Not for this target. I've told them to space their bombs sixty feet apart so that we'll have a roadblock the full length of the village instead of in just one spot. It will be a much more effective roadblock with a loose bomb pattern."

"We don't care about the roadblock," Colonel Korn informed him. "Colonel Cathcart wants to come out of this mission with a good clean aerial photograph he won't be ashamed to send through channels. Don't forget that General Peckem will be here for the full briefing, and you know how he feels about bomb patterns. Incidentally, Major, you'd better hurry up with these details and clear out before he gets here. General Peckem can't stand you."

"Oh, no, Colonel," Major Danby corrected obligingly. "It's General Dreedle who can't stand me."

"General Peckem can't stand you either. In fact, no one can stand you. Finish what you're doing, Danby, and disappear. I'll conduct the briefing."

"Where's Major Danby?" Colonel Cathcart inquired, after he had driven up for the full briefing with General Peckem and Colonel Scheisskopf.

"He asked permission to leave as soon as he saw you driving up," answered Colonel Korn. "He's afraid General Peckem doesn't like him. I was going to conduct the briefing anyway. I do a much better job."

"Splendid!" said Colonel Cathcart. "No!" Colonel Cathcart countermanded himself an instant later when he remembered how good a job Colonel Korn had done before General Dreedle at the first Avignon briefing. "I'll do it myself."

Colonel Cathcart braced himself with the knowledge that he was one of General Peckem's favorites and took charge of the meeting, snapping his words out crisply to the attentive audience of subordinate officers with the bluff and dispassionate toughness he had picked up from General Dreedle. He knew he cut a fine figure there on the platform with his open shirt collar, his cigarette holder, and his close-cropped, gray-tipped curly black hair. He breezed along beautifully, even emulating certain characteristic mispronunciations of General Dreedle's, and he was not the least bit intimidated by General Peckem's new colonel until he suddenly recalled that General Peckem detested General Dreedle. Then his voice cracked, and all confidence left him. He stumbled ahead through instinct in burning humiliation. He was suddenly in terror of Colonel Scheisskopf. Another colonel in the area meant another rival, another enemy, another person who hated him. And this one was tough! A horrifying thought occurred to Colonel Cathcart: Suppose Colonel Scheisskopf had already bribed all the men in the room to begin moaning, as they had done at the first Avignon mission. How could he silence them? What a terrible black eye that would be! Colonel Cathcart was seized with such fright that he almost beckoned to Colonel Korn. Somehow he held himself together and synchronized the watches. When he had done that, he knew he had won, for he could end now at any time. He had come through in a crisis. He wanted to laugh in Colonel Scheisskopf's face with triumph and spite. He had proved himself brilliantly under pressure, and he concluded the briefing with an inspiring peroration that every instinct told him was a masterful exhibition of eloquent tact and subtlety.

"Now, men," he exhorted. "We have with us today a very distinguished guest, General Peckem from Special Services, the man who gives us all our softball bats, comic books and U.S.O. shows. I want to dedicate this mission to him. Go on out there and bomb—for me, for your country, for God, and for that great American, General P. P. Peckem. And let's see you put all those bombs on a dime!"

30

Dunbar

Yossarian no longer gave a damn where his bombs fell, although he did not go as far as Dunbar, who dropped his bombs hundreds of yards past the village and would face a court-martial if it could ever be shown he had done it deliberately. Without a word even to Yossarian, Dunbar had washed his hands of the mission. The fall in the hospital had either shown him the light or scrambled his brains; it was impossible to say which.

Dunbar seldom laughed any more and seemed to be wasting away. He snarled belligerently at superior officers, even at Major Danby, and was crude and surly and profane even in front of the chaplain, who was afraid of Dunbar now and seemed to be wasting away also. The chaplain's pilgrimage to Wintergreen had proved abortive; another shrine was empty. Wintergreen was too busy to see the chaplain himself. A brash assistant brought the chaplain a stolen Zippo cigarette lighter as a gift and informed him condescendingly that Wintergreen was too deeply involved with wartime activities to concern himself with matters so trivial as the number of missions men had to fly. The chaplain worried about Dunbar and brooded more over Yossarian now that Orr was gone. To the chaplain, who lived by himself in a spacious tent whose pointy top sealed him in gloomy solitude each night like the cap of a tomb, it seemed incredible that Yossarian really preferred living alone and wanted no roommates.

As a lead bombardier again, Yossarian had McWatt for a pilot, and that was one consolation, although he was still so utterly undefended. There was no way to fight back. He could not even see McWatt and the co-pilot from his post in the nose. All he could ever see was Aarfy, with whose fustian, moon-faced ineptitude he had finally lost all patience, and there were minutes of agonizing fury and frustration in the sky when he hungered to be demoted again to a wing plane with a loaded machine gun in the compartment instead of the precision bombsight that he really had no need for, a powerful, heavy fifty-caliber machine gun he could seize vengefully in both hands and turn loose savagely against all the demons tyrannizing him: at the smoky black puffs of the flak itself; at the German antiaircraft gunners below whom he could not even see and could not possibly harm with his machine gun even if he ever did take the time to open fire; at Havermeyer and Appleby in the lead plane for their fearless straight and level bomb run on the third mission to Bologna where the flak from two hundred and twenty-four cannons had knocked out one of Orr's engines for the very last time and sent him down ditching into the sea between Genoa and La Spezia just before the brief thunderstorm broke.

Actually, there was not much he could do with that powerful machine gun except load it and test-fire a few rounds. It was no more use to him than the bombsight. He could really cut loose with it against attacking German fighters, but there were no German fighters any more, and he could not even swing it all the way around into the helpless faces of pilots like Huple and Dobbs and order them back down carefully to the ground, as he had once ordered Kid Sampson back down, which is exactly what he did want to do to Dobbs and Huple on the hideous first mission to Avignon the moment he realized the fantastic pickle he was in, the moment he found himself aloft in a wing plane with Dobbs and Huple in the flight headed by Havermeyer and Appleby. Dobbs and Huple? Huple and Dobbs? Who were they? What preposterous madness to float in thin air two miles high on an inch or two of metal, sustained from death by the meager skill and intelligence of two vapid strangers, a beardless kid named Huple and a nervous nut like Dobbs, who really did go nuts right there in the plane, running amuck over the target without leaving his co-pilot's seat and grabbing the controls from Huple to plunge them all down into that chilling dive that tore Yossarian's headset loose and brought them right back inside the dense flak from which they had almost escaped. The next thing he knew, another stranger, a radio-gunner named Snowden, was dying in back. It was impossible to be positive that Dobbs had killed him, for when Yossarian plugged his headset back in, Dobbs was already on the intercom pleading for someone to go up front and help the bombardier. And almost immediately Snowden broke in, whimpering, "Help me. Please help me. I'm cold. I'm cold." And Yossarian crawled slowly out of the nose and up on top of the bomb bay and wriggled back into the rear section of the plane—passing the first-aid kit on the way that he had to return for—to treat Snowden for the wrong wound, the yawning, raw, melon-shaped hole as big as a football in the outside of his thigh, the unsevered, blood-soaked muscle fibers inside pulsating weirdly like blind things with lives of their own, the oval, naked wound that was almost a foot long and made Yossarian moan in shock and sympathy the instant he spied it and nearly made him vomit. And the small, slight tail gunner was lying on the floor beside Snowden in a dead faint, his face as white as a handkerchief, so that Yossarian sprang forward with revulsion to help him first.

Yes, in the long run, he was much safer flying with McWatt, and he was not even safe with McWatt, who loved flying too much and went buzzing boldly inches off the ground with Yossarian in the nose on the way back from the training flight to break in the new bombardier in the whole replacement crew Colonel Cathcart had obtained after Orr was lost. The practice bomb range was on the other side of Pianosa, and, flying back, McWatt edged the belly of the lazing, slow-cruising plane just over the crest of mountains in the middle and then, instead of maintaining altitude, jolted both engines open all the way, lurched up on one side and, to Yossarian's astonishment, began following the falling land down as fast as the plane would go, wagging his wings gaily and skimming with a massive, grinding, hammering roar over each rocky rise and dip of the rolling terrain like a dizzy gull over wild brown waves. Yossarian was petrified. The new bombardier beside him sat demurely with a bewitched grin and kept whistling "Whee!" and Yossarian wanted to reach out and crush his idiotic face with one hand as he flinched and flung himself away from the boulders and hillocks and lashing branches of trees that loomed up above him out in front and rushed past just underneath in a sinking, streaking blur. No one had a right to take such frightful risks with his life.

"Go up, go up, go up!" he shouted frantically at McWatt, hating him venomously, but McWatt was singing buoyantly over the intercom and probably couldn't hear. Yossarian, blazing with rage and almost sobbing for revenge, hurled himself down into the crawlway and fought his way through against the dragging weight of gravity and inertia until he arrived at the main section and pulled himself up to the flight deck, to stand trembling behind McWatt in the pilot's seat. He looked desperately about for a gun, a gray-black .45 automatic that he could cock and ram right up against the base of McWatt's skull. There was no gun. There was no hunting knife either, and no other weapon with which he could bludgeon or stab, and Yossarian grasped and jerked the collar of McWatt's coveralls in tightening fists and shouted to him to go up, go up. The land was still swimming by underneath and flashing by overhead on both sides. McWatt looked back at Yossarian and laughed joyfully as though Yossarian were sharing his fun. Yossarian slid both hands around McWatt's bare throat and squeezed. McWatt turned stiff.

"Go up," Yossarian ordered unmistakably through his teeth in a low, menacing voice. "Or I'll kill you."

Rigid with caution, McWatt cut the motors back and climbed gradually. Yossarian's hands weakened on McWatt's neck and slid down off his shoulders to dangle inertly. He was not angry any more. He was ashamed. When McWatt turned, he was sorry the hands were his and wished there were someplace where he could bury them. They felt dead.

McWatt gazed at him deeply. There was no friendliness in his stare. "Boy," he said coldly, "you sure must be in pretty bad shape. You ought to go home."

"They won't let me," Yossarian answered with averted eyes, and crept away.

Yossarian stepped down from the flight deck and seated himself on the floor, hanging his head with guilt and remorse. He was covered with sweat.

McWatt set course directly back toward the field. Yossarian wondered whether McWatt would now go to the operations tent to see Piltchard and Wren and request that Yossarian never be assigned to his plane again, just as Yossarian had gone surreptitiously to speak to them about Dobbs and Huple and Orr and, unsuccessfully, about Aarfy. He had never seen McWatt look displeased before, had never seen him in any but the most lighthearted mood, and he wondered whether he had just lost another friend.

But McWatt winked at him reassuringly as he climbed down from the plane and joshed hospitably with the credulous new pilot and bombardier during the jeep ride back to the squadron, although he did not address a word to Yossarian until all four had returned their parachutes and separated and the two of them were walking side by side toward their own row of tents. Then McWatt's sparsely freckled tan Scotch-Irish face broke suddenly into a smile and he dug his knuckles playfully into Yossarian's ribs, as though throwing a punch.

"You louse," he laughed. "Were you really going to kill me up there?"

Yossarian grinned penitently and shook his head. "No, I don't think so."

"I didn't realize you got it so bad. Boy! Why don't you talk to somebody about it?"

"I talk to everybody about it. What the hell's the matter with you? Don't you ever hear me?"

"I guess I never really believed you."

"Aren't you ever afraid?"

"Maybe I ought to be."

"Not even on the missions?"

"I guess I just don't have brains enough." McWatt laughed sheepishly.

"There are so many ways for me to get killed," Yossarian commented, "and you had to find one more."

McWatt smiled again. "Say, I bet it must really scare you when I buzz your tent, huh?"

"It scares me to death. I've told you that."

"I thought it was just the noise you were complaining about." McWatt made a resigned shrug. "Oh, well, what the hell," he sang. "I guess I'll just have to give it up."

But McWatt was incorrigible, and, while he never buzzed Yossarian's tent again, he never missed an opportunity to buzz the beach and roar like a fierce and low-flying thunderbolt over the raft in the water and the secluded hollow in the sand where Yossarian lay feeling up Nurse Duckett or playing hearts, poker or pinochle with Nately, Dunbar and Hungry Joe. Yossarian met Nurse Duckett almost every afternoon that both were free and came with her to the beach on the other side of the narrow swell of shoulder-high dunes separating them from the area in which the other officers and enlisted men went swimming nude. Nately, Dunbar and Hungry Joe would come there, too. McWatt would occasionally join them, and often Aarfy, who always arrived pudgily in full uniform and never removed any of his clothing but his shoes and his hat; Aarfy never went swimming. The other men wore swimming trunks in deference to Nurse Duckett, and in deference also to Nurse Cramer, who accompanied Nurse Duckett and Yossarian to the beach every time and sat haughtily by herself ten yards away. No one but Aarfy ever made reference to the naked men sunbathing in full view farther down the beach or jumping and diving from the enormous white-washed raft that bobbed on empty oil drums out beyond the silt sand bar. Nurse Cramer sat by herself because she was angry with Yossarian and disappointed in Nurse Duckett.

Nurse Sue Ann Duckett despised Aarfy, and that was another one of the numerous fetching traits about Nurse Duckett that Yossarian enjoyed. He enjoyed Nurse Sue Ann Duckett's long white legs and supple, callipygous ass; he often neglected to remember that she was quite slim and fragile from the waist up and hurt her unintentionally in moments of passion when he hugged her too roughly. He loved her manner of sleepy acquiescence when they lay on the beach at dusk. He drew solace and sedation from her nearness. He had a craving to touch her always, to remain always in physical communication. He liked to encircle her ankle loosely with his fingers as he played cards with Nately, Dunbar and Hungry Joe, to lightly and lovingly caress the downy skin of her fair, smooth thigh with the backs of his nails or, dreamily, sensuously, almost unconsciously, slide his proprietary, respectful hand up the shell-like ridge of her spine beneath the elastic strap of the top of the two-piece bathing suit she always wore to contain and cover her tiny, long-nippled breasts. He loved Nurse Duckett's serene, flattered response, the sense of attachment to him she displayed proudly. Hungry Joe had a craving to feel Nurse Duckett up, too, and was restrained more than once by Yossarian's forbidding glower. Nurse Duckett flirted with Hungry Joe just to keep him in heat, and her round light-brown eyes glimmered with mischief every time Yossarian rapped her sharply with his elbow or fist to make her stop.

The men played cards on a towel, undershirt, or blanket, and Nurse Duckett mixed the extra deck of cards, sitting with her back resting against a sand dune. When she was not shuffling the extra deck of cards, she sat squinting into a tiny pocket mirror, brushing mascara on her curling reddish eyelashes in a birdbrained effort to make them longer permanently. Occasionally she was able to stack the cards or spoil the deck in a way they did not discover until they were well into the game, and she laughed and glowed with blissful gratification when they all hurled their cards down disgustedly and began punching her sharply on the arms or legs as they called her filthy names and warned her to stop fooling around. She would prattle nonsensically when they were striving hardest to think, and a pink flush of elation crept into her cheeks when they gave her more sharp raps on the arms and legs with their fists and told her to shut up. Nurse Duckett reveled in such attention and ducked her short chestnut bangs with joy when Yossarian and the others focused upon her. It gave her a peculiar feeling of warm and expectant well-being to know that so many naked boys and men were idling close by on the other side of the sand dunes. She had only to stretch her neck or rise on some pretext to see twenty or forty undressed males lounging or playing ball in the sunlight. Her own body was such a familiar and unremarkable thing to her that she was puzzled by the convulsive ecstasy men could take from it, by the intense and amusing need they had merely to touch it, to reach out urgently and press it, squeeze it, pinch it, rub it. She did not understand Yossarian's lust; but she was willing to take his word for it.

Evenings when Yossarian felt horny he brought Nurse Duckett to the beach with two blankets and enjoyed making love to her with most of their clothes on more than he sometimes enjoyed making love to all the vigorous bare amoral girls in Rome. Frequently they went to the beach at night and did not make love, but just lay shivering between the blankets against each other to ward off the brisk, damp chill. The ink-black nights were turning cold, the stars frosty and fewer. The raft swayed in the ghostly trail of moonlight and seemed to be sailing away. A marked hint of cold weather penetrated the air. Other men were just starting to build stoves and came to Yossarian's tent during the day to marvel at Orr's workmanship. It thrilled Nurse Duckett rapturously that Yossarian could not keep his hands off her when they were together, although she would not let him slip them inside her bathing shorts during the day when anyone was near enough to see, not even when the only witness was Nurse Cramer, who sat on the other side of her sand dune with her reproving nose in the air and pretended not to see anything.

Nurse Cramer had stopped speaking to Nurse Duckett, her best friend, because of her liaison with Yossarian, but still went everywhere with Nurse Duckett since Nurse Duckett was her best friend. She did not approve of Yossarian or his friends. When they stood up and went swimming with Nurse Duckett, Nurse Cramer stood up and went swimming, too, maintaining the same ten-yard distance between them, and maintaining her silence, snubbing them even in the water. When they laughed and splashed, she laughed and splashed; when they dived, she dived; when they swam to the sand bar and rested, Nurse Cramer swam to the sand bar and rested. When they came out, she came out, dried her shoulders with her own towel and seated herself aloofly in her own spot, her back rigid and a ring of reflected sunlight burnishing her light-blond hair like a halo. Nurse Cramer was prepared to begin talking to Nurse Duckett again if she repented and apologized. Nurse Duckett preferred things the way they were. For a long time she had wanted to give Nurse Cramer a rap to make her shut up.

Nurse Duckett found Yossarian wonderful and was already trying to change him. She loved to watch him taking short naps with his face down and his arm thrown across her, or staring bleakly at the endless tame, quiet waves breaking like pet puppy dogs against the shore, scampering lightly up the sand a foot or two and then trotting away. She was calm in his silences. She knew she did not bore him, and she buffed or painted her fingernails studiously while he dozed or brooded and the desultory warm afternoon breeze vibrated delicately on the surface of the beach. She loved to look at his wide, long, sinewy back with its bronzed, unblemished skin. She loved to bring him to flame instantly by taking his whole ear in her mouth suddenly and running her hand down his front all the way. She loved to make him burn and suffer till dark, then satisfy him. Then kiss him adoringly because she had brought him such bliss.

Yossarian was never lonely with Nurse Duckett, who really did know how to keep her mouth shut and was just capricious enough. He was haunted and tormented by the vast, boundless ocean. He wondered mournfully, as Nurse Duckett buffed her nails, about all the people who had died under water. There were surely more than a million already. Where were they? What insects had eaten their flesh? He imagined the awful impotence of breathing in helplessly quarts and quarts of water. Yossarian followed the small fishing boats and military launches plying back and forth far out and found them unreal; it did not seem true that there were full-sized men aboard, going somewhere every time. He looked toward stony Elba, and his eyes automatically searched overhead for the fluffy, white, turnip-shaped cloud in which Clevinger had vanished. He peered at the vaporous Italian skyline and thought of Orr. Clevinger and Orr. Where had they gone? Yossarian had once stood on a jetty at dawn and watched a tufted round log that was drifting toward him on the tide turn unexpectedly into the bloated face of a drowned man; it was the first dead person he had ever seen. He thirsted for life and reached out ravenously to grasp and hold Nurse Duckett's flesh. He studied every floating object fearfully for some gruesome sign of Clevinger and Orr, prepared for any morbid shock but the shock McWatt gave him one day with the plane that came blasting suddenly into sight out of the distant stillness and hurtled mercilessly along the shore line with a great growling, clattering roar over the bobbing raft on which blond, pale Kid Sampson, his naked sides scrawny even from so far away, leaped clownishly up to touch it at the exact moment some arbitrary gust of wind or minor miscalculation of McWatt's senses dropped the speeding plane down just low enough for a propeller to slice him half away.

Even people who were not there remembered vividly exactly what happened next. There was the briefest, softest *tsst!* filtering audibly through the shattering, overwhelming howl of the plane's engines, and then there were just Kid Sampson's two pale, skinny legs, still joined by strings somehow at the bloody truncated hips, standing stock-still on the raft for what seemed a full minute or two before they toppled over backward into the water finally with a faint, echoing splash and turned completely upside down so that only the grotesque toes and the plaster-white soles of Kid Sampson's feet remained in view.

On the beach, all hell broke loose. Nurse Cramer materialized out of thin air suddenly and was weeping hysterically against Yossarian's chest while Yossarian hugged her shoulders and soothed her. His other arm bolstered Nurse Duckett, who was trembling and sobbing against him, too, her long, angular face dead white. Everyone at the beach was screaming and running, and the men sounded like women. They scampered for their things in panic, stooping hurriedly and looking askance at each gentle, knee-high wave bubbling in as though some ugly, red, grisly organ like a liver or a lung might come washing right up against them. Those in the water were struggling to get out, forgetting in their haste to swim, wailing, walking, held back in their flight by the viscous, clinging sea as though by a biting wind. Kid Sampson had rained all over. Those who spied drops of him on their limbs or torsos drew back with terror and revulsion, as though trying to shrink away from their own odious skins. Everybody ran in a sluggish stampede, shooting tortured, horrified glances back, filling the deep, shadowy, rustling woods with their frail gasps and cries. Yossarian drove both stumbling, faltering women before him frantically, shoving them and prodding them to make them hurry, and raced back with a curse to help when Hungry Joe tripped on the blanket or the camera case he was carrying and fell forward on his face in the mud of the stream.

Back at the squadron everyone already knew. Men in uniform were screaming and running there too, or standing motionless in one spot, rooted in awe, like Sergeant Knight and Doc Daneeka as they gravely craned their heads upward and watched the guilty, banking, forlorn airplane with McWatt circle and circle slowly and climb.

"Who is it?" Yossarian shouted anxiously at Doc Daneeka as he ran up, breathless and limp, his somber eyes burning with a misty, hectic anguish. "Who's in the plane?"

"McWatt," said Sergeant Knight. "He's got the two new pilots with him on a training flight. Doc Daneeka's up there, too."

"I'm right here," contended Doc Daneeka, in a strange and troubled voice, darting an anxious look at Sergeant Knight.

"Why doesn't he come down?" Yossarian exclaimed in despair. "Why does he keep going up?"

"He's probably afraid to come down," Sergeant Knight answered, without moving his solemn gaze from McWatt's solitary climbing airplane. "He knows what kind of trouble he's in."

And McWatt kept climbing higher and higher, nosing his droning airplane upward evenly in a slow, oval spiral that carried him far out over the water as he headed south and far in over the russet foothills when he had circled the landing field again and was flying north. He was soon up over five thousand feet. His engines were soft as whispers. A white parachute popped open suddenly in a surprising puff. A second parachute popped open a few moments later and coasted down, like the first, directly in toward the clearing of the landing strip. There was no motion on the ground. The plane continued south for thirty seconds more, following the same pattern, familiar and predictable now, and McWatt lifted a wing and banked gracefully around into his turn.

"Two more to go," said Sergeant Knight. "McWatt and Doc Daneeka."

"I'm right here, Sergeant Knight," Doc Daneeka told him plaintively. "I'm not in the plane."

"Why don't they jump?" Sergeant Knight asked, pleading aloud to himself. "Why don't they jump?"

"It doesn't make sense," grieved Doc Daneeka, biting his lip. "It just doesn't make sense."

But Yossarian understood suddenly why McWatt wouldn't jump, and went running uncontrollably down the whole length of the squadron after McWatt's plane, waving his arms and shouting up at him imploringly to come down, McWatt, come down; but no one seemed to hear, certainly not McWatt, and a great, choking moan tore from Yossarian's throat as McWatt turned again, dipped his wings once in salute, decided oh, well, what the hell, and flew into a mountain.

Colonel Cathcart was so upset by the deaths of Kid Sampson and McWatt that he raised the missions to sixty-five.

31

Mrs. Daneeka

When Colonel Cathcart learned that Doc Daneeka too had been killed in McWatt's plane, he increased the number of missions to seventy.

The first person in the squadron to find out that Doc Daneeka was dead was Sergeant Towser, who had been informed earlier by the man in the control tower that Doc Daneeka's name was down as a passenger on the pilot's manifest McWatt had filed before taking off. Sergeant Towser brushed away a tear and struck Doc Daneeka's name from the roster of squadron personnel. With lips still quivering, he rose and trudged outside reluctantly to break the bad news to Gus and Wes, discreetly avoiding any conversation with Doc Daneeka himself as he moved by the flight surgeon's slight sepulchral figure roosting despondently on his stool in the late-afternoon sunlight between the orderly room and the medical tent. Sergeant Towser's heart was heavy; now he had *two* dead men on his hands—Mudd, the dead man in Yossarian's tent who wasn't even there, and Doc Daneeka, the new dead man in the squadron, who most certainly was there and gave every indication of proving a still thornier administrative problem for him.

Gus and Wes listened to Sergeant Towser with looks of stoic surprise and said not a word about their bereavement to anyone else until Doc Daneeka himself came in about an hour afterward to have his temperature taken for the third time that day and his blood pressure checked. The thermometer registered a half degree lower than his usual subnormal temperature of 96.8. Doc Daneeka was alarmed. The fixed, vacant, wooden stares of his two enlisted men were even more irritating than always.

"Goddammit," he expostulated politely in an uncommon excess of exasperation, "what's the matter with you two men anyway? It just isn't right for a person to have a low temperature all the time and walk around with a stuffed nose." Doc Daneeka emitted a glum, self-pitying sniff and strolled disconsolately across the tent to help himself to some aspirin and sulphur pills and paint his own throat with Argyrol. His downcast face was fragile and forlorn as a swallow's, and he rubbed the back of his arms rhythmically. "Just look how cold I am right now. You're sure you're not holding anything back?"

"You're dead, sir," one of his two enlisted men explained.

Doc Daneeka jerked his head up quickly with resentful distrust. "What's that?"

"You're dead, sir," repeated the other. "That's probably the reason you always feel so cold."

"That's right, sir. You've probably been dead all this time and we just didn't detect it."

"What the *hell* are you both talking about?" Doc Daneeka cried shrilly with a surging, petrifying sensation of some onrushing unavoidable disaster.

"It's true, sir," said one of the enlisted men. "The records show that you went up in McWatt's plane to collect some flight time. You didn't come down in a parachute, so you must have been killed in the crash."

"That's right, sir," said the other. "You ought to be glad you've got any temperature at all."

Doc Daneeka's mind was reeling in confusion. "Have you both gone crazy?" he demanded. "I'm going to report this whole insubordinate incident to Sergeant Towser."

"Sergeant Towser's the one who told us about it," said either Gus or Wes. "The War Department's even going to notify your wife."

Doc Daneeka yelped and ran out of the medical tent to remonstrate with Sergeant Towser, who edged away from him with repugnance and advised Doc Daneeka to remain out of sight as much as possible until some decision could be reached relating to the disposition of his remains.

"Gee, I guess he really is dead," grieved one of his enlisted men in a low, respectful voice. "I'm going to miss him. He was a pretty wonderful guy, wasn't he?"

"Yeah, he sure was," mourned the other. "But I'm glad the little fuck is gone. I was getting sick and tired of taking his blood pressure all the time."

Mrs. Daneeka, Doc Daneeka's wife, was not glad that Doc Daneeka was gone and split the peaceful Staten Island night with woeful shrieks of lamentation when she learned by War Department telegram that her husband had been killed in action. Women came to comfort her, and their husbands paid condolence calls and hoped inwardly that she would soon move to another neighborhood and spare them the obligation of continuous sympathy. The poor woman was totally distraught for almost a full week. Slowly, heroically, she found the strength to contemplate a future filled with dire problems for herself and her children. Just as she was growing resigned to her loss, the postman rang with a bolt from the blue—a letter from overseas that was signed with her husband's signature and urged her frantically to disregard any bad news concerning him. Mrs. Daneeka was dumbfounded. The date on the letter was illegible. The handwriting throughout was shaky and hurried, but the style resembled her husband's and the melancholy, self-pitying tone was familiar, although more dreary than usual. Mrs. Daneeka was overjoyed and wept irrepressibly with relief and kissed the crinkled, grubby tissue of V-mail stationery a thousand times. She dashed a grateful note off to her husband pressing him for details and sent a wire informing the War Department of its error. The War Department replied touchily that there had been no error and that she was undoubtedly the victim of some sadistic and psychotic forger in her husband's squadron. The letter to her husband was returned unopened, stamped KILLED IN ACTION.

Mrs. Daneeka had been widowed cruelly again, but this time her grief was mitigated somewhat by a notification from Washington that she was sole beneficiary of her husband's $10,000 GI insurance policy, which amount was obtainable by her on demand. The realization that she and the children were not faced immediately with starvation brought a brave smile to her face and marked the turning point in her distress. The Veterans Administration informed her by mail the very next day that she would be entitled to pension benefits for the rest of her natural life because of her husband's demise, and to a burial allowance for him of $250. A government check for $250 was enclosed. Gradually, inexorably, her prospects brightened. A letter arrived that same week from the Social Security Administration stating that, under the provisions of the Old Age and Survivors Insurance Act of 1935, she would receive monthly support for herself and her dependent children until they reached the age of eighteen, and a burial allowance of $250. With these government letters as proof of death, she applied for payment on three life insurance policies Doc Daneeka had carried, with a value of $50,000 each; her claim was honored and processed swiftly. Each day brought new unexpected treasures. A key to a safe-deposit box led to a fourth life insurance policy with a face value of $50,000, and to $18,000 in cash on which income tax had never been paid and need never be paid. A fraternal lodge to which he had belonged gave her a cemetery plot. A second fraternal organization of which he had been a member sent her a burial allowance of $250. His county medical association gave her a burial allowance of $250.

The husbands of her closest friends began to flirt with her. Mrs. Daneeka was simply delighted with the way things were turning out and had her hair dyed. Her fantastic wealth just kept piling up, and she had to remind herself daily that all the hundreds of thousands of dollars she was acquiring were not worth a single penny without her husband to share this good fortune with her. It astonished her that so many separate organizations were willing to do so much to bury Doc Daneeka, who, back in Pianosa, was having a terrible time trying to keep his head above the ground and wondered with dismal apprehension why his wife did not answer the letter he had written.

He found himself ostracized in the squadron by men who cursed his memory foully for having supplied Colonel Cathcart with provocation to raise the number of combat missions. Records attesting to his death were pullulating like insect eggs and verifying each other beyond all contention. He drew no pay or PX rations and depended for life on the charity of Sergeant Towser and Milo, who both knew he was dead. Colonel Cathcart refused to see him, and Colonel Korn sent word through Major Danby that he would have Doc Daneeka cremated on the spot if he ever showed up at Group Headquarters. Major Danby confided that Group was incensed with all flight surgeons because of Dr. Stubbs, the bushy-haired, baggy-chinned, slovenly flight surgeon in Dunbar's squadron who was deliberately and defiantly brewing insidious dissension there by grounding all men with sixty missions on proper forms that were rejected by Group indignantly with orders restoring the confused pilots, navigators, bombardiers and gunners to combat duty. Morale there was ebbing rapidly, and Dunbar was under surveillance. Group was glad Doc Daneeka had been killed and did not intend to ask for a replacement.

Not even the chaplain could bring Doc Daneeka back to life under the circumstances. Alarm changed to resignation, and more and more Doc Daneeka acquired the look of an ailing rodent. The sacks under his eyes turned hollow and black, and he padded through the shadows fruitlessly like a ubiquitous spook. Even Captain Flume recoiled when Doc Daneeka sought him out in the woods for help. Heartlessly, Gus and Wes turned him away from the medical tent without even a thermometer for comfort, and then, only then, did he realize that, to all intents and purposes, he really was dead, and that he had better do something damned fast if he ever hoped to save himself.

There was nowhere else to turn but to his wife, and he scribbled an impassioned letter begging her to bring his plight to the attention of the War Department and urging her to communicate at once with his group commander, Colonel Cathcart, for assurances that—no matter what else she might have heard—it was indeed he, her husband, Doc Daneeka, who was pleading with her, and not a corpse or some impostor. Mrs. Daneeka was stunned by the depth of emotion in the almost illegible appeal. She was torn with compunction and tempted to comply, but the very next letter she opened that day was from that same Colonel Cathcart, her husband's group commander, and began:

Dear Mrs., Mr., Miss, or Mr. and Mrs. Daneeka:

Words cannot express the deep personal grief I experienced when your husband, son, father or brother was killed, wounded or reported missing in action.

Mrs. Daneeka moved with her children to Lansing, Michigan, and left no forwarding address.

32

Yo-Yo's Roomies

Yossarian was warm when the cold weather came and whale-shaped clouds blew low through a dingy, slate-gray sky, almost without end, like the droning, dark, iron flocks of B-17 and B-24 bombers from the long-range air bases in Italy the day of the invasion of southern France two months earlier. Everyone in the squadron knew that Kid Sampson's skinny legs had washed up on the wet sand to lie there and rot like a purple twisted wishbone. No one would go to retrieve them, not Gus or Wes or even the men in the mortuary at the hospital; everyone made believe that Kid Sampson's legs were not there, that they had bobbed away south forever on the tide like all of Clevinger and Orr. Now that bad weather had come, almost no one ever sneaked away alone any more to peek through bushes like a pervert at the moldering stumps.

There were no more beautiful days. There were no more easy missions. There was stinging rain and dull, chilling fog, and the men flew at week-long intervals, whenever the weather cleared. At night the wind moaned. The gnarled and stunted tree trunks creaked and groaned and forced Yossarian's thoughts each morning, even before he was fully awake, back on Kid Sampson's skinny legs bloating and decaying, as systematically as a ticking clock, in the icy rain and wet sand all through the blind, cold, gusty October nights. After Kid Sampson's legs, he would think of pitiful, whimpering Snowden freezing to death in the rear section of the plane, holding his eternal, immutable secret concealed inside his quilted, armor-plate flak suit until Yossarian had finished sterilizing and bandaging the wrong wound on his leg, and then spilling it out suddenly all over the floor. At night when he was tying to sleep, Yossarian would call the roll of all the men, women and children he had ever known who were now dead. He tried to remember all the soldiers, and he resurrected images of all the elderly people he had known when a child—all the aunts, uncles, neighbors, parents and grandparents, his own and everyone else's, and all the pathetic, deluded shopkeepers who opened their small, dusty stores at dawn and worked in them foolishly until midnight. They were all dead, too. The number of dead people just seemed to increase. And the Germans were still fighting. Death was irreversible, he suspected, and he began to think he was going to lose.

Yossarian was warm when the cold weather came because of Orr's marvelous stove, and he might have existed in his warm tent quite comfortably if not for the memory of Orr, and if not for the gang of animated roommates that came swarming inside rapaciously one day from the two full combat crews Colonel Cathcart had requisitioned—and obtained in less than forty-eight hours—as replacements for Kid Sampson and McWatt. Yossarian emitted a long, loud, croaking gasp of protest when he trudged in tiredly after a mission and found them already there.

There were four of them, and they were having a whale of a good time as they helped each other set up their cots. They were horsing around. The moment he saw them, Yossarian knew they were impossible. They were frisky, eager and exuberant, and they had all been friends in the States. They were plainly unthinkable. They were noisy, overconfident, empty-headed kids of twenty-one. They had gone to college and were engaged to pretty, clean girls whose pictures were already standing on the rough cement mantelpiece of Orr's fireplace. They had ridden in speedboats and played tennis. They had been horseback riding. One had once been to bed with an older woman. They knew the same people in different parts of the country and had gone to school with each other's cousins. They had listened to the World Series and really cared who won football games. They were obtuse; their morale was good. They were glad that the war had lasted long enough for them to find out what combat was really like. They were halfway through unpacking when Yossarian threw them out.

They were plainly out of the question, Yossarian explained adamantly to Sergeant Towser, whose sallow equine face was despondent as he informed Yossarian that the new officers would have to be admitted. Sergeant Towser was not permitted to requisition another six-man tent from Group while Yossarian was living in one alone.

"I'm not living in this one alone," Yossarian said with a sulk. "I've got a dead man in here with me. His name is Mudd."

"Please, sir," begged Sergeant Towser, sighing wearily, with a sidelong glance at the four baffled new officers listening in mystified silence just outside the entrance. "Mudd was killed on the mission to Orvieto. You know that. He was flying right beside you."

"Then why don't you move his things out?"

"Because he never even got here. Captain, please don't bring that up again. You can move in with Lieutenant Nately if you like. I'll even send some men from the orderly room to transfer your belongings."

But to abandon Orr's tent would be to abandon Orr, who would have been spurned and humiliated clannishly by these four simple-minded officers waiting to move in. It did not seem just that these boisterous, immature young men should show up after all the work was done and be allowed to take possession of the most desirable tent on the island. But that was the law, Sergeant Towser explained, and all Yossarian could do was glare at them in baleful apology as he made room for them and volunteer helpful penitent hints as they moved inside his privacy and made themselves at home.

They were the most depressing group of people Yossarian had ever been with. They were always in high spirits. They laughed at everything. They called him "Yo-Yo" jocularly and came in tipsy late at night and woke him up with their clumsy, bumping, giggling efforts to be quiet, then bombarded him with asinine shouts of hilarious good-fellowship when he sat up cursing to complain. He wanted to massacre them each time they did. They reminded him of Donald Duck's nephews. They were afraid of Yossarian and persecuted him incessantly with nagging generosity and with their exasperating insistence on doing small favors for him. They were reckless, puerile, congenial, naïve, presumptuous, deferential and rambunctious. They were dumb; they had no complaints. They admired Colonel Cathcart and they found Colonel Korn witty. They were afraid of Yossarian, but they were not the least bit afraid of Colonel Cathcart's seventy missions. They were four clean-cut kids who were having lots of fun, and they were driving Yossarian nuts. He could not make them understand that he was a crotchety old fogey of twenty-eight, that he belonged to another generation, another era, another world, that having a good time bored him and was not worth the effort, and that they bored him, too. He could not make them shut up; they were worse than women. They had not brains enough to be introverted and repressed.

Cronies of theirs in other squadrons began dropping in unashamedly and using the tent as a hangout. There was often not room enough for him. Worst of all, he could no longer bring Nurse Duckett there to lie down with her. And now that foul weather had come, he had no place else! This was a calamity he had not foreseen, and he wanted to bust his roommates' heads open with his fists or pick them up, each in turn, by the seats of their pants and the scruffs of their necks and pitch them out once and for all into the dank, rubbery perennial weeds growing between his rusty soup-can urinal with nail holes in the bottom and the knotty-pine squadron latrine that stood like a beach locker not far away.

Instead of busting their heads open, he tramped in his galoshes and black raincoat through the drizzling darkness to invite Chief White Halfoat to move in with him, too, and drive the fastidious, clean-living bastards out with his threats and swinish habits. But Chief White Halfoat felt cold and was already making plans to move up into the hospital to die of pneumonia. Instinct told Chief White Halfoat it was almost time. His chest ached and he coughed chronically. Whiskey no longer warmed him. Most damning of all, Captain Flume had moved back into his trailer. Here was an omen of unmistakable meaning.

"He had to move back," Yossarian argued in a vain effort to cheer up the glum, barrel-chested Indian, whose well-knit sorrel-red face had degenerated rapidly into a dilapidated, calcareous gray. "He'd die of exposure if he tried to live in the woods in this weather."

"No, that wouldn't drive the yellowbelly back," Chief White Halfoat disagreed obstinately. He tapped his forehead with cryptic insight. "No, sirree. He knows something. He knows it's time for me to die of pneumonia, that's what he knows. And that's how I know it's time."

"What does Doc Daneeka say?"

"I'm not allowed to say anything," Doc Daneeka said sorrowfully from his seat on his stool in the shadows of a corner, his smooth, tapered, diminutive face turtle-green in the flickering candlelight. Everything smelled of mildew. The bulb in the tent had blown out several days before, and neither of the two men had been able to muster the initiative to replace it. "I'm not allowed to practice medicine, any more," Doc Daneeka added.

"He's dead," Chief White Halfoat gloated, with a hoarse laugh entangled in phlegm. "That's really funny."

"I don't even draw my pay any more."

"That's really funny," Chief White Halfoat repeated. "All this time he's been insulting my liver, and look what happened to him. He's dead. Killed by his own greed."

"That's not what killed me," Doc Daneeka observed in a voice that was calm and flat. "There's nothing wrong with greed. It's all that lousy Dr. Stubbs's fault, getting Colonel Cathcart and Colonel Korn stirred up against flight surgeons. He's going to give the medical profession a bad name by standing up for principle. If he's not careful, he'll be black-balled by his state medical association and kept out of the hospitals."

Yossarian watched Chief White Halfoat pour whiskey carefully into three empty shampoo bottles and store them away in the musette bag he was packing.

"Can't you stop by my tent on your way to the hospital and punch one of them in the nose for me?" he speculated aloud. "I've got four of them, and they're going to crowd me out of my tent altogether."

"You know, something like that once happened to my whole tribe," Chief White Halfoat remarked in jolly appreciation, sitting back on his cot to chuckle. "Why don't you get Captain Black to kick those kids out? Captain Black likes to kick people out."

Yossarian grimaced sourly at the mere mention of Captain Black, who was already bullying the new fliers each time they stepped into his intelligence tent for maps or information. Yossarian's attitude toward his roommates turned merciful and protective at the mere recollection of Captain Black. It was not their fault that they were young and cheerful, he reminded himself as he carried the swinging beam of his flashlight back through the darkness. He wished that he could be young and cheerful, too. And it wasn't their fault that they were courageous, confident and carefree. He would just have to be patient with them until one or two were killed and the rest wounded, and then they would all turn out okay. He vowed to be more tolerant and benevolent, but when he ducked inside his tent with his friendlier attitude a great yellow blaze was roaring in the fireplace, and he gasped in horrified amazement. *Orr's beautiful birch logs were going up in smoke!* His roommates had set fire to them! He gaped at the four insensitive overheated faces and wanted to shout curses at them. He wanted to bang their heads together as they greeted him with loud convivial cries and invited him generously to pull up a chair and eat their chestnuts and roasted potatoes. What could he do with them?

And the very next morning they got rid of the dead man in his tent! Just like that, they whisked him away! They carried his cot and all his belongings right out into the bushes and simply dumped them there, and then they strode back slapping their hands briskly at a job well done. Yossarian was stunned by their overbearing vigor and zeal, by their practical, direct efficiency. In a matter of moments they had disposed energetically of a problem with which Yossarian and Sergeant Towser had been grappling unsuccessfully for months. Yossarian was alarmed—they might get rid of him just as quickly, he feared—and he ran to Hungry Joe and fled with him to Rome the day before Nately's whore finally got a good night's sleep and woke up in love.

33

Nately's Whore

He missed Nurse Duckett in Rome. There was not much else to do after Hungry Joe left on his mail run. Yossarian missed Nurse Duckett so much that he went searching hungrily through the streets for Luciana, whose laugh and invisible scar he had never forgotten, or the boozy, blowzy, bleary-eyed floozy in the overloaded white brassiere and unbuttoned orange satin blouse whose naughty salmon-colored cameo ring Aarfy had thrown away so callously through the window of her car. How he yearned for both girls! He looked for them in vain. He was so deeply in love with them, and he knew he would never see either again. Despair gnawed at him. Visions beset him. He wanted Nurse Duckett with her dress up and her slim thighs bare to the hips. He banged a thin streetwalker with a wet cough who picked him up from an alley between hotels, but that was no fun at all and he hastened to the enlisted men's apartment for the fat, friendly maid in the lime-colored panties, who was overjoyed to see him but couldn't arouse him. He went to bed there early and slept alone. He woke up disappointed and banged a sassy, short, chubby girl he found in the apartment after breakfast, but that was only a little better, and he chased her away when he'd finished and went back to sleep. He napped till lunch and then went shopping for presents for Nurse Duckett and a scarf for the maid in the lime-colored panties, who hugged him with such gargantuan gratitude that he was soon hot for Nurse Duckett and ran looking lecherously for Luciana again. Instead he found Aarfy, who had landed in Rome when Hungry Joe returned with Dunbar, Nately and Dobbs, and who would not go along on the drunken foray that night to rescue Nately's whore from the middle-aged military big shots holding her captive in a hotel because she would not say uncle.

"Why should I risk getting into trouble just to help her out?" Aarfy demanded haughtily. "But don't tell Nately I said that. Tell him I had to keep an appointment with some very important fraternity brothers."

The middle-aged big shots would not let Nately's whore leave until they made her say uncle.

"Say uncle," they said to her.

"Uncle," she said.

"No, no. Say uncle."

"Uncle," she said.

"She still doesn't understand."

"You still don't understand, do you? We can't really make you say uncle unless you don't want to say uncle. Don't you see? Don't say uncle when I tell you to say uncle. Okay? Say uncle."

"Uncle," she said.

"No, don't say uncle. Say uncle."

She didn't say uncle.

"That's good!"

"That's very good."

"It's a start. Now say uncle."

"Uncle," she said.

"It's no good."

"No, it's no good that way either. She just isn't impressed with us. There's just no fun making her say uncle when she doesn't care whether we make her say uncle or not."

"No, she really doesn't care, does she? Say 'foot.'"

"Foot."

"You see? She doesn't care about anything we do. She doesn't care about us. We don't mean a thing to you, do we?"

"Uncle," she said.

She didn't care about them a bit, and it upset them terribly. They shook her roughly each time she yawned. She did not seem to care about anything, not even when they threatened to throw her out the window. They were utterly demoralized men of distinction. She was bored and indifferent and wanted very much to sleep. She had been on the job for twenty-two hours, and she was sorry that these men had not permitted her to leave with the other two girls with whom the orgy had begun. She wondered vaguely why they wanted her to laugh when they laughed, and why they wanted *her* to enjoy it when they made love to her. It was all very mysterious to her, and very uninteresting.

She was not sure what they wanted from her. Each time she slumped over with her eyes closed they shook her awake and made her say "uncle" again. Each time she said "uncle," they were disappointed. She wondered what "uncle" meant. She sat on the sofa in a passive, phlegmatic stupor, her mouth open and all her clothing crumpled in a corner on the floor, and wondered how much longer they would sit around naked with her and make her say uncle in the elegant hotel suite to which Orr's old girl friend, giggling uncontrollably at Yossarian's and Dunbar's drunken antics, guided Nately and the other members of the motley rescue party.

Dunbar squeezed Orr's old girl friend's fanny gratefully and passed her back to Yossarian, who propped her against the door jamb with both hands on her hips and wormed himself against her lasciviously until Nately seized him by the arm and pulled him away from her into the blue sitting room, where Dunbar was already hurling everything in sight out the window into the court. Dobbs was smashing furniture with an ash stand. A nude, ridiculous man with a blushing appendectomy scar appeared in the doorway suddenly and bellowed,

"What's going on here?"

"Your toes are dirty," Dunbar said.

The man covered his groin with both hands and shrank from view. Dunbar, Dobbs and Hungry Joe just kept dumping everything they could lift out the window with great, howling whoops of happy abandon. They soon finished with the clothing on the couches and the luggage on the floor, and they were ransacking a cedar closet when the door to the inner room opened again and a man who was very distinguished-looking from the neck up padded into view imperiously on bare feet.

"Here, you, stop that," he barked. "Just what do you men think you're doing?"

"Your toes are dirty," Dunbar said to him.

The man covered his groin as the first had done and disappeared. Nately charged after him, but was blocked by the first officer, who plodded back in holding a pillow in front of him, like a bubble dancer.

"Hey, you men!" he roared angrily. "Stop it!"

"Stop it," Dunbar replied.

"That's what I said."

"That's what I said," Dunbar said.

The officer stamped his foot petulantly, turning weak with frustration. "Are you deliberately repeating everything I say?"

"Are you deliberately repeating everything I say?"

"I'll thrash you." The man raised a fist.

"I'll thrash *you*," Dunbar warned him coldly. "You're a German spy, and I'm going to have you shot."

"German spy? I'm an American colonel."

"You don't look like an American colonel. You look like a fat man with a pillow in front of him. Where's your uniform, if you're an American colonel?"

"You just threw it out the window."

"All right, men," Dunbar said. "Lock the silly bastard up. Take the silly bastard down to the station house and throw away the key."

The colonel blanched with alarm. "Are you all crazy? Where's your badge? Hey, you! Come back in here!"

But he whirled too late to stop Nately, who had glimpsed his girl sitting on the sofa in the other room and had darted through the doorway behind his back. The others poured through after him right into the midst of the other naked big shots. Hungry Joe laughed hysterically when he saw them, pointing in disbelief at one after the other and clasping his head and sides. Two with fleshy physiques advanced truculently until they spied the look of mean dislike and hostility on Dobbs and Dunbar and noticed that Dobbs was still swinging like a two-handed club the wrought-iron ash stand he had used to smash things in the sitting room. Nately was already at his girl's side. She stared at him without recognition for a few seconds. Then she smiled faintly and let her head sink to his shoulder with her eyes closed. Nately was in ecstasy; she had never smiled at him before.

"Filpo," said a calm, slender, jaded-looking man who had not even stirred from his armchair. "You don't obey orders. I told you to get them out, and you've gone and brought them in. Can't you see the difference?"

"They've thrown our things out the window, General."

"Good for them. Our uniforms too? That *was* clever. We'll never be able to convince anyone we're superior without our uniforms."

"Let's get their names, Lou, and—"

"Oh, Ned, relax," said the slender man with practiced weariness. "You may be pretty good at moving armored divisions into action, but you're almost useless in a social situation. Sooner or later we'll get our uniforms back, and then we'll be their superiors again. Did they really throw our uniforms out? That was a splendid tactic."

"They threw everything out."

"The ones in the closet, too?"

"They threw the closet out, General. That was that crash we heard when we thought they were coming in to kill us."

"And I'll throw you out next," Dunbar threatened.

The general paled slightly. "What the devil is *he* so mad about?" he asked Yossarian.

"He means it, too," Yossarian said. "You'd better let the girl leave."

"Lord, take her," exclaimed the general with relief. "All she's done is make us feel insecure. At least she might have disliked or resented us for the hundred dollars we paid her. But she wouldn't even do that. Your handsome young friend there seems quite attached to her. Notice the way he lets his fingers linger on the inside of her thighs as he pretends to roll up her stockings."

Nately, caught in the act, blushed guiltily and moved more quickly through the steps of dressing her. She was sound asleep and breathed so regularly that she seemed to be snoring softly.

"Let's charge her now, Lou!" urged another officer. "We've got more personnel, and we can encircle—"

"Oh, no, Bill," answered the general with a sigh. "You may be a wizard at directing a pincer movement in good weather on level terrain against an enemy that has already committed his reserves, but you don't always think so clearly anywhere else. Why should we want to keep her?"

"General, we're in a very bad strategic position. We haven't got a stitch of clothing, and it's going to be very degrading and embarrassing for the person who has to go downstairs through the lobby to get some."

"Yes, Filpo, you're quite right," said the general. "And that's exactly why you're the one to do it. Get going."

"Naked, sir?"

"Take your pillow with you if you want to. And get some cigarettes, too, while you're downstairs picking up my underwear and pants, will you?"

"I'll send everything up for you," Yossarian offered.

"There, General," said Filpo with relief. "Now I won't have to go."

"Filpo, you nitwit. Can't you see he's lying?"

"Are you lying?"

Yossarian nodded, and Filpo's faith was shattered. Yossarian laughed and helped Nately walk his girl out into the corridor and into the elevator. Her face was smiling as though with a lovely dream as she slept with her head still resting on Nately's shoulder. Dobbs and Dunbar ran out into the street to stop a cab.

Nately's whore looked up when they left the car. She swallowed dryly several times during the arduous trek up the stairs to her apartment, but she was sleeping soundly again by the time Nately undressed her and put her to bed. She slept for eighteen hours, while Nately dashed about the apartment all the next morning shushing everybody in sight, and when she woke up she was deeply in love with him. In the last analysis, that was all it took to win her heart—a good night's sleep.

The girl smiled with contentment when she opened her eyes and saw him, and then, stretching her long legs languorously beneath the rustling sheets, beckoned him into bed beside her with that look of simpering idiocy of a woman in heat. Nately moved to her in a happy daze, so overcome with rapture that he hardly minded when her kid sister interrupted him again by flying into the room and flinging herself down onto the bed between them. Nately's whore slapped and cursed her, but this time with laughter and generous affection, and Nately settled back smugly with an arm about each, feeling strong and protective. They made a wonderful family group, he decided. The little girl would go to college when she was old enough, to Smith or Radcliffe or Bryn Mawr—he would see to that. Nately bounded out of bed after a few minutes to announce his good fortune to his friends at the top of his voice. He called to them jubilantly to come to the room and slammed the door in their startled faces as soon as they arrived. He had remembered just in time that his girl had no clothes on.

"Get dressed," he ordered her, congratulating himself on his alertness.

"*Perchè?*" she asked curiously.

"*Perchè?*" he repeated with an indulgent chuckle. "Because I don't want them to see you without any clothes on."

"*Perchè no?*" she inquired.

"*Perchè no?*" He looked at her with astonishment. "Because it isn't right for other men to see you naked, that's why."

"*Perchè no?*"

"Because I say so!" Nately exploded in frustration. "Now don't argue with me. I'm the man and you have to do whatever I say. From now on, I forbid you ever to go out of this room unless you have all your clothes on. Is that clear?"

Nately's whore looked at him as though he were insane. "Are you crazy? *Che succede?*"

"I mean every word I say."

"*Tu sei pazzo!*" she shouted at him with incredulous indignation, and sprang out of bed. Snarling unintelligibly, she snapped on panties and strode toward the door.

Nately drew himself up with full manly authority. "I forbid you to leave this room that way," he informed her.

"*Tu sei pazzo!*" she shot back at him, after she had left, shaking her head in disbelief. "*Idiota! Tu sei un pazzo imbecille!*"

"*Tu sei pazzo,*" said her thin kid sister, starting out after her in the same haughty walk.

"You come back here," Nately ordered her. "I forbid *you* to go out that way, too!"

"*Idiota!*" the kid sister called back at him with dignity after she had flounced past. "*Tu sei un pazzo imbecille.*"

Nately fumed in circles of distracted helplessness for several seconds and then sprinted out into the sitting room to forbid his friends to look at his girl friend while she complained about him in only her panties.

"Why not?" asked Dunbar.

"Why not?" exclaimed Nately. "Because she's my girl now, and it isn't right for you to see her unless she's fully dressed."

"Why not?" asked Dunbar.

"You see?" said his girl with a shrug. "*Lui è pazzo!*"

"*Sì, è molto pazzo,*" echoed her kid sister.

"Then make her keep her clothes on if you don't want us to see her," argued Hungry Joe. "What the hell do you want from us?"

"She won't listen to me," Nately confessed sheepishly. "So from now on you'll all have to shut your eyes or look in the other direction when she comes in that way. Okay?"

"*Madonn'!*" cried his girl in exasperation, and stamped out of the room.

"*Madonn'!*" cried her kid sister, and stamped out behind her.

"*Lui è pazzo,*" Yossarian observed good-naturedly. "I certainly have to admit it."

"Hey, you crazy or something?" Hungry Joe demanded of Nately. "The next thing you know you'll be trying to make her give up hustling."

"From now on," Nately said to his girl, "I forbid you to go out hustling."

"*Perchè?*" she inquired curiously.

"*Perchè?*" he screamed with amazement. "Because it's not nice, that's why!"

"*Perchè no?*"

"Because it just isn't!" Nately insisted. "It just isn't right for a nice girl like you to go looking for other men to sleep with. I'll give you all the money you need, so you won't have to do it any more."

"And what will I do all day instead?"

"Do?" said Nately. "You'll do what all your friends do."

"My friends go looking for men to sleep with."

"Then get new friends! I don't even want you to associate with girls like that, anyway. Prostitution is bad! Everybody knows that, even him." He turned with confidence to the experienced old man. "Am I right?"

"You're wrong," answered the old man. "Prostitution gives her an opportunity to meet people. It provides fresh air and wholesome exercise, and it keeps her out of trouble."

"From now on," Nately declared sternly to his girl friend, "I forbid you to have anything to do with that wicked old man."

"*Va fongul!*" his girl replied, rolling her harassed eyes up toward the ceiling. "What does he want from me?" she implored, shaking her fists. "*Lasciami!*" she told him in menacing entreaty. "*Stupido!* If you think my friends are so bad, go tell your friends not to ficky-fick all the time with my friends!"

"From now on," Nately told his friends, "I think you fellows ought to stop running around with her friends and settle down."

"*Madonn'!*" cried his friends, rolling their harassed eyes up toward the ceiling.

Nately had gone clear out of his mind. He wanted them all to fall in love right away and get married. Dunbar could marry Orr's whore, and Yossarian could fall in love with Nurse Duckett or anyone else he liked. After the war they could all work for Nately's father and bring up their children in the same suburb. Nately saw it all very clearly. Love had transmogrified him into a romantic idiot, and they drove him away back into the bedroom to wrangle with his girl over Captain Black. She agreed not to go to bed with Captain Black again or give him any more of Nately's money, but she would not budge an inch on her friendship with the ugly, ill-kempt, dissipated, filthy-minded old man, who witnessed Nately's flowering love affair with insulting derision and would not admit that Congress was the greatest deliberative body in the whole world.

"From now on," Nately ordered his girl firmly, "I absolutely forbid you even to speak to that disgusting old man."

"Again the old man?" cried the girl in wailing confusion. "*Perchè no?*"

"He doesn't like the House of Representatives."

"*Mamma mia!* What's the *matter* with you?"

"*È pazzo*," observed her kid sister philosophically. "That's what's the matter with him."

"*Sì,*" the older girl agreed readily, tearing at her long brown hair with both hands. "*Lui è pazzo.*"

But she missed Nately when he was away and was furious with Yossarian when he punched Nately in the face with all his might and knocked him into the hospital with a broken nose.

34

Thanksgiving

It was actually all Sergeant Knight's fault that Yossarian busted Nately in the nose on Thanksgiving Day, after everyone in the squadron had given humble thanks to Milo for providing the fantastically opulent meal on which the officers and enlisted men had gorged themselves insatiably all afternoon and for dispensing like inexhaustible largess the unopened bottles of cheap whiskey he handed out unsparingly to every man who asked. Even before dark, young soldiers with pasty white faces were throwing up everywhere and passing out drunkenly on the ground. The air turned foul. Other men picked up steam as the hours passed, and the aimless, riotous celebration continued. It was a raw, violent, guzzling saturnalia that spilled obstreperously through the woods to the officers' club and spread up into the hills toward the hospital and the antiaircraft-gun emplacements. There were fist fights in the squadron and one stabbing. Corporal Kolodny shot himself through the leg in the intelligence tent while playing with a loaded gun and had his gums and toes painted purple in the speeding ambulance as he lay on his back with the blood spurting from his wound. Men with cut fingers, bleeding heads, stomach cramps and broken ankles came limping penitently up to the medical tent to have their gums and toes painted purple by Gus and Wes and be given a laxative to throw into the bushes. The joyous celebration lasted long into the night, and the stillness was fractured often by wild, exultant shouts and by the cries of people who were merry or sick. There was the recurring sound of retching and moaning, of laughter, greetings, threats and swearing, and of bottles shattering against rock. There were dirty songs in the distance. It was worse than New Year's Eve.

Yossarian went to bed early for safety and soon dreamed that he was fleeing almost headlong down an endless wooden staircase, making a loud, staccato clatter with his heels. Then he woke up a little and realized someone was shooting at him with a machine gun. A tortured, terrified sob rose in his throat. His first thought was that Milo was attacking the squadron again, and he rolled off his cot to the floor and lay underneath in a trembling, praying ball, his heart thumping like a drop forge, his body bathed in a cold sweat. There was no noise of planes. A drunken, happy laugh sounded from afar. "Happy New Year, Happy New Year!" a triumphant familiar voice shouted hilariously from high above between the short, sharp bursts of machine gun fire, and Yossarian understood that some men had gone as a prank to one of the sandbagged machine gun emplacements Milo had installed in the hills after his raid on the squadron and staffed with his own men.

Yossarian blazed with hatred and wrath when he saw he was the victim of an irresponsible joke that had destroyed his sleep and reduced him to a whimpering hulk. He wanted to kill, he wanted to murder. He was angrier than he had ever been before, angrier even than when he had slid his hands around McWatt's neck to strangle him. The gun opened fire again. Voices cried "Happy New Year!" and gloating laughter rolled down from the hills through the darkness like a witch's glee. In moccasins and coveralls, Yossarian charged out of his tent for revenge with his .45, ramming a clip of cartridges up into the grip and slamming the bolt of the gun back to load it. He snapped off the safety catch and was ready to shoot. He heard Nately running after him to restrain him, calling his name. The machine gun opened fire once more from a black rise above the motor pool, and orange tracer bullets skimmed like low-gliding dashes over the tops of the shadowy tents, almost clipping the peaks. Roars of rough laughter rang out again between the short bursts. Yossarian felt resentment boil like acid inside him; they were endangering his life, the bastards! With blind, ferocious rage and determination, he raced across the squadron past the motor pool, running as fast as he could, and was already pounding up into the hills along the narrow, winding path when Nately finally caught up, still calling, "Yo-Yo! Yo-Yo!" with pleading concern and imploring him to stop. He grasped Yossarian's shoulders and tried to hold him back. Yossarian twisted free, turning. Nately reached for him again, and Yossarian drove his fist squarely into Nately's delicate young face as hard as he could, cursing him, then drew his arm back to hit him again, but Nately had dropped out of sight with a groan and lay curled up on the ground with his head buried in both hands and blood streaming between his fingers. Yossarian whirled and plunged ahead up the path without looking back.

Soon he saw the machine gun. Two figures leaped up in silhouette when they heard him and fled into the night with taunting laughter before he could get there. He was too late. Their footsteps receded, leaving the circle of sandbags empty and silent in the crisp and windless moonlight. He looked about dejectedly. Jeering laughter came to him again, from a distance. A twig snapped nearby. Yossarian dropped to his knees with a cold thrill of elation and aimed. He heard a stealthy rustle of leaves on the other side of the sandbags and fired two quick rounds. Someone fired back at him once, and he recognized the shot.

"Dunbar?" he called.

"Yossarian?"

The two men left their hiding places and walked forward to meet in the clearing with weary disappointment, their guns down. They were both shivering slightly from the frosty air and wheezing from the labor of their uphill rush.

"The bastards," said Yossarian. "They got away."

"They took ten years off my life," Dunbar exclaimed. "I thought that son of a bitch Milo was bombing us again. I've never been so scared. I wish I knew who the bastards were."

"One was Sergeant Knight."

"Let's go kill him." Dunbar's teeth were chattering. "He had no right to scare us that way."

Yossarian no longer wanted to kill anyone. "Let's help Nately first. I think I hurt him at the bottom of the hill."

But there was no sign of Nately along the path, even though Yossarian located the right spot by the blood on the stones. Nately was not in his tent either, and they did not catch up with him until the next morning when they checked into the hospital as patients after learning he had checked in with a broken nose the night before. Nately beamed in frightened surprise as they padded into the ward in their slippers and robes behind Nurse Cramer and were assigned to their beds. Nately's nose was in a bulky cast, and he had two black eyes. He kept blushing giddily in shy embarrassment and saying he was sorry when Yossarian came over to apologize for hitting him. Yossarian felt terrible; he could hardly bear to look at Nately's battered countenance, even though the sight was so comical he was tempted to guffaw. Dunbar was disgusted by their sentimentality, and all three were relieved when Hungry Joe came barging in unexpectedly with his intricate black camera and trumped-up symptoms of appendicitis to be near enough to Yossarian to take pictures of him feeling up Nurse Duckett. Like Yossarian, he was soon disappointed. Nurse Duckett had decided to marry a doctor —any doctor, because they all did so well in business—and would not take chances in the vicinity of the man who might someday be her husband. Hungry Joe was irate and inconsolable until—of all people!—the chaplain was led in wearing a maroon corduroy bathrobe, shining like a skinny lighthouse with a radiant grin of self-satisfaction too tremendous to be concealed. The chaplain had entered the hospital with a pain in his heart that the doctors thought was gas in his stomach and with an advanced case of Wisconsin shingles.

"What in the world are Wisconsin shingles?" asked Yossarian.

"That's just what the doctors wanted to know!" blurted out the chaplain proudly, and burst into laughter. No one had ever seen him so waggish, or so happy. "There's no such thing as Wisconsin shingles. Don't you understand? I lied. I made a deal with the doctors. I promised that I would let them know when my Wisconsin shingles went away if they would promise not to do anything to cure them. I never told a lie before. Isn't it wonderful?"

The chaplain had sinned, and it was good. Common sense told him that telling lies and defecting from duty were sins. On the other hand, everyone knew that sin was evil and that no good could come from evil. But he did feel good; he felt positively marvelous. Consequently, it followed logically that telling lies and defecting from duty could not be sins. The chaplain had mastered, in a moment of divine intuition, the handy technique of protective rationalization, and he was exhilarated by his discovery. It was miraculous. It was almost no trick at all, he saw, to turn vice into virtue and slander into truth, impotence into abstinence, arrogance into humility, plunder into philanthropy, thievery into honor, blasphemy into wisdom, brutality into patriotism, and sadism into justice. Anybody could do it; it required no brains at all. It merely required no character. With effervescent agility the chaplain ran through the whole gamut of orthodox immoralities, while Nately sat up in bed with flushed elation, astounded by the mad gang of companions of which he found himself the nucleus. He was flattered and apprehensive, certain that some severe official would soon appear and throw the whole lot of them out like a pack of bums. No one bothered them. In the evening they all trooped exuberantly out to see a lousy Hollywood extravaganza in Technicolor, and when they trooped exuberantly back in after the lousy Hollywood extravaganza, the soldier in white was there, and Dunbar screamed and went to pieces.

"He's back!" Dunbar screamed. "He's back! He's back!"

Yossarian froze in his tracks, paralyzed as much by the eerie shrillness in Dunbar's voice as by the familiar, white, morbid sight of the soldier in white covered from head to toe in plaster and gauze. A strange, quavering, involuntary noise came bubbling from Yossarian's throat.

"He's back!" Dunbar screamed again.

"He's back!" a patient delirious with fever echoed in automatic terror.

All at once the ward erupted into bedlam. Mobs of sick and injured men began ranting incoherently and running and jumping in the aisle as though the building were on fire. A patient with one foot and one crutch was hopping back and forth swiftly in panic crying, "What is it? What is it? Are we burning? Are we burning?"

"He's back!" someone shouted at him. "Didn't you hear him? He's back! He's back!"

"Who's back?" shouted someone else. "Who is it?"

"What does it mean? What should we do?"

"Are we on fire?"

"Get up and run, damn it! Everybody get up and run!"

Everybody got out of bed and began running from one end of the ward to the other. One C.I.D. man was looking for a gun to shoot one of the other C.I.D. men who had jabbed his elbow into his eye. The ward had turned into chaos. The patient delirious with the high fever leaped into the aisle and almost knocked over the patient with one foot, who accidentally brought the black rubber tip of his crutch down on the other's bare foot, crushing some toes. The delirious man with the fever and the crushed toes sank to the floor and wept in pain while other men tripped over him and hurt him more in their blind, milling, agonized stampede. "He's back!" all the men kept mumbling and chanting and calling out hysterically as they rushed back and forth. "He's back, he's back!" Nurse Cramer was there in the middle suddenly like a spinning policeman, trying desperately to restore order, dissolving helplessly into tears when she failed. "Be still, please be still," she urged uselessly through her massive sobs. The chaplain, pale as a ghost, had no idea what was going on. Neither did Nately, who kept close to Yossarian's side, clinging to his elbow, or Hungry Joe, who followed dubiously with his scrawny fists clenched and glanced from side to side with a face that was scared.

"Hey, what's going on?" Hungry Joe pleaded. "What the hell is going on?"

"It's the same one!" Dunbar shouted at him emphatically in a voice rising clearly above the raucous commotion. "Don't you understand? It's the same one."

"The same one!" Yossarian heard himself echo, quivering with a deep and ominous excitement that he could not control, and shoved his way after Dunbar toward the bed of the soldier in white.

"Take it easy, fellas," the short patriotic Texan counseled affably, with an uncertain grin. "There's no cause to be upset. Why don't we all just take it easy?"

"The same one!" others began murmuring, chanting and shouting.

Suddenly Nurse Duckett was there, too. "What's going on?" she demanded.

"He's back!" Nurse Cramer screamed, sinking into her arms. "He's back, he's back!"

It was, indeed, the same man. He had lost a few inches and added some weight, but Yossarian remembered him instantly by the two stiff arms and the two stiff, thick, useless legs all drawn upward into the air almost perpendicularly by the taut ropes and the long lead weights suspended from pulleys over him and by the frayed black hole in the bandages over his mouth. He had, in fact, hardly changed at all. There was the same zinc pipe rising from the hard stone mass over his groin and leading to the clear glass jar on the floor. There was the same clear glass jar on a pole dripping fluid into him through the crook of his elbow. Yossarian would recognize him anywhere. He wondered who he was.

"There's no one inside!" Dunbar yelled out at him unexpectedly.

Yossarian felt his heart skip a beat and his legs grow weak. "What are you talking about?" he shouted with dread, stunned by the haggard, sparking anguish in Dunbar's eyes and by his crazed look of wild shock and horror. "Are you nuts or something? What the hell do you mean, there's no one inside?"

"They've stolen him away!" Dunbar shouted back. "He's hollow inside, like a chocolate soldier. They just took him away and left those bandages there."

"Why should they do that?"

"Why do they do anything?"

"They've stolen him away!" screamed someone else, and people all over the ward began screaming, "They've stolen him away. They've stolen him away!"

"Go back to your beds," Nurse Duckett pleaded with Dunbar and Yossarian, pushing feebly against Yossarian's chest. "Please go back to your beds."

"You're crazy!" Yossarian shouted angrily at Dunbar. "What the hell makes you say that?"

"Did anyone see him?" Dunbar demanded with sneering fervor.

"You saw him, didn't you?" Yossarian said to Nurse Duckett. "Tell Dunbar there's someone inside."

"Lieutenant Schmulker is inside," Nurse Duckett said. "He's burned all over."

"Did she see him?"

"You saw him, didn't you?"

"The doctor who bandaged him saw him."

"Go get him, will you? Which doctor was it?"

Nurse Duckett reacted to the question with a startled gasp. "The doctor isn't even here!" she exclaimed. "The patient was brought to us that way from a field hospital."

"You see?" cried Nurse Cramer. "There's no one inside!"

"There's no one inside!" yelled Hungry Joe, and began stamping on the floor.

Dunbar broke through and leaped up furiously on the soldier in white's bed to see for himself, pressing his gleaming eye down hungrily against the tattered black hole in the shell of white bandages. He was still bent over staring with one eye into the lightless, unstirring void of the soldier in white's mouth when the doctors and the M.P.s came running to help Yossarian pull him away. The doctors wore guns at the waist. The guards carried carbines and rifles with which they shoved and jolted the crowd of muttering patients back. A stretcher on wheels was there, and the soldier in white was lifted out of bed skillfully and rolled out of sight in a matter of seconds. The doctors and M.P.s moved through the ward assuring everyone that everything was all right.

Nurse Duckett plucked Yossarian's arm and whispered to him furtively to meet her in the broom closet outside in the corridor. Yossarian rejoiced when he heard her. He thought Nurse Duckett finally wanted to get laid and pulled her skirt up the second they were alone in the broom closet, but she pushed him away. She had urgent news about Dunbar.

"They're going to disappear him," she said.

Yossarian squinted at her uncomprehendingly. "They're what?" he asked in surprise, and laughed uneasily. "What does that mean?"

"I don't know. I heard them talking behind a door."

"Who?"

"I don't know. I couldn't see them. I just heard them say they were going to disappear Dunbar."

"Why are they going to disappear him?"

"I don't know."

"It doesn't make sense. It isn't even good grammar. What the hell does it mean when they disappear somebody?"

"I don't know."

"Jesus, you're a great help!"

"Why are you picking on me?" Nurse Duckett protested with hurt feelings, and began sniffing back tears. "I'm only trying to help. It isn't my fault they're going to disappear him, is it? I shouldn't even be telling you."

Yossarian took her in his arms and hugged her with gentle, contrite affection. "I'm sorry," he apologized, kissing her cheek respectfully, and hurried away to warn Dunbar, who was nowhere to be found.

35

Milo the Militant

For the first time in his life, Yossarian prayed. He got down on his knees and prayed to Nately not to volunteer to fly more than seventy missions after Chief White Halfoat did die of pneumonia in the hospital and Nately had applied for his job. But Nately just wouldn't listen.

"I've got to fly more missions," Nately insisted lamely with a crooked smile. "Otherwise they'll send me home."

"So?"

"I don't want to go home until I can take her back with me."

"She means that much to you?"

Nately nodded dejectedly. "I might never see her again."

"Then get yourself grounded," Yossarian urged. "You've finished your missions and you don't need the flight pay. Why don't you ask for Chief White Halfoat's job, if you can stand working for Captain Black?"

Nately shook his head, his cheeks darkening with shy and regretful mortification. "They won't give it to me. I spoke to Colonel Korn, and he told me I'd have to fly more missions or be sent home."

Yossarian cursed savagely. "That's just plain meanness."

"I don't mind, I guess. I've flown seventy missions without getting hurt. I guess I can fly a few more."

"Don't do anything at all about it until I talk to someone," Yossarian decided, and went looking for help from Milo, who went immediately afterward to Colonel Cathcart for help in having himself assigned to more combat missions.

Milo had been earning many distinctions for himself. He had flown fearlessly into danger and criticism by selling petroleum and ball bearings to Germany at good prices in order to make a good profit and help maintain a balance of power between the contending forces. His nerve under fire was graceful and infinite. With a devotion to purpose above and beyond the line of duty, he had then raised the price of food in his mess halls so high that all officers and enlisted men had to turn over all their pay to him in order to eat. Their alternative—there was an alternative, of course, since Milo detested coercion and was a vocal champion of freedom of choice—was to starve. When he encountered a wave of enemy resistance to this attack, he stuck to his position without regard for his safety or reputation and gallantly invoked the law of supply and demand. And when someone somewhere said no, Milo gave ground grudgingly, valiantly defending, even in retreat, the historic right of free men to pay as much as they had to for the things they needed in order to survive.

Milo had been caught red-handed in the act of plundering his countrymen, and, as a result, his stock had never been higher. He proved good as his word when a rawboned major from Minnesota curled his lip in rebellious disavowal and demanded his share of the syndicate Milo kept saying everybody owned. Milo met the challenge by writing the words "A Share" on the nearest scrap of paper and handing it away with a virtuous disdain that won the envy and admiration of almost everyone who knew him. His glory was at a peak, and Colonel Cathcart, who knew and admired his war record, was astonished by the deferential humility with which Milo presented himself at Group Headquarters and made his fantastic appeal for more hazardous assignment.

"You want to fly more combat missions?" Colonel Cathcart gasped. "What in the world for?"

Milo answered in a demure voice with his face lowered meekly. "I want to do my duty, sir. The country is at war, and I want to fight to defend it like the rest of the fellows."

"But, Milo, you are doing your duty," Colonel Cathcart exclaimed with a laugh that thundered jovially. "I can't think of a single person who's done more for the men than you have. Who gave them chocolate-covered cotton?"

Milo shook his head slowly and sadly. "But being a good mess officer in wartime just isn't enough, Colonel Cathcart."

"Certainly it is, Milo. I don't know what's come over you."

"Certainly it isn't, Colonel," Milo disagreed in a somewhat firm tone, raising his subservient eyes significantly just far enough to arrest Colonel Cathcart's. "Some of the men are beginning to talk."

"Oh, is that it? Give me their names, Milo. Give me their names and I'll see to it that they go on every dangerous mission the group flies."

"No, Colonel, I'm afraid they're right," Milo said, with his head drooping again. "I was sent overseas as a pilot, and I should be flying more combat missions and spending less time on my duties as a mess officer."

Colonel Cathcart was surprised but cooperative. "Well, Milo, if you really feel that way, I'm sure we can make whatever arrangements you want. How long have you been overseas now?"

"Eleven months, sir."

"And how many missions have you flown?"

"Five."

"Five?" asked Colonel Cathcart.

"Five, sir."

"Five, eh?" Colonel Cathcart rubbed his cheek pensively. "That isn't very good, is it?"

"Isn't it?" asked Milo in a sharply edged voice, glancing up again.

Colonel Cathcart quailed. "On the contrary, that's very good, Milo," he corrected himself hastily. "It isn't bad at all."

"No, Colonel," Milo said, with a long, languishing, wistful sigh, "it isn't very good. Although it's very generous of you to say so."

"But it's really not bad, Milo. Not bad at all when you consider all your other valuable contributions. Five missions, you say? Just five?"

"Just five, sir."

"Just five." Colonel Cathcart grew awfully depressed for a moment as he wondered what Milo was really thinking, and whether he had already got a black eye with him. "Five is very good, Milo," he observed with enthusiasm, spying a ray of hope. "That averages out to almost one combat mission every two months. And I'll bet your total doesn't even include the time you bombed us."

"Yes, sir. It does."

"It does?" inquired Colonel Cathcart with mild wonder. "You didn't actually fly along on that mission, did you? If I remember correctly, you were in the control tower with me, weren't you?"

"But it was my mission," Milo contended. "I organized it, and we used my planes and supplies. I planned and supervised the whole thing."

"Oh, certainly, Milo, certainly, I'm not disputing you. I'm only checking the figures to make sure you're claiming all you're entitled to. Did you also include the time we contracted with you to bomb the bridge at Orvieto?"

"Oh, no, sir. I didn't think I should, since I was in Orvieto at the time directing the antiaircraft fire."

"I don't see what difference that makes, Milo. It was still your mission. And a damned good one, too, I must say. We didn't get the bridge, but we did have a beautiful bomb pattern. I remember General

Peckem commenting on it. No, Milo, I insist you count Orvieto as a mission, too."

"If you insist, sir."

"I do insist, Milo. Now, let's see—you now have a grand total of six missions, which is damned good, Milo, damned good, really. Six missions is an increase of twenty per cent in just a couple of minutes, which is not bad at all, Milo, not bad at all."

"Many of the other men have seventy missions," Milo pointed out.

"But they never produced any chocolate-covered cotton, did they? Milo, you're doing more than your share."

"But they're getting all the fame and opportunity," Milo persisted with a petulance that bordered on sniveling. "Sir, I want to get in there and fight like the rest of the fellows. That's what I'm here for. I want to win medals, too."

"Yes, Milo, of course. We all want to spend more time in combat. But people like you and me serve in different ways. Look at my own record." Colonel Cathcart uttered a deprecatory laugh. "I'll bet it's not generally known, Milo, that I myself have flown only four missions, is it?"

"No, sir," Milo replied. "It's generally known that you've flown only *two* missions. And that one of those occurred when Aarfy accidentally flew you over enemy territory while navigating you to Naples for a black-market water cooler."

Colonel Cathcart, flushing with embarrassment, abandoned all further argument. "All right, Milo. I can't praise you enough for what you want to do. If it really means so much to you, I'll have Major Major assign you to the next sixty-four missions so that you can have seventy, too."

"Thank you, Colonel, thank you, sir. You don't know what this means."

"Don't mention it, Milo, I know exactly what it means."

"No, Colonel, I don't think you do know what it means," Milo disagreed pointedly. "Someone will have to begin running the syndicate for me right away. It's very complicated, and I might get shot down at any time."

Colonel Cathcart brightened instantly at the thought and began rubbing his hands with avaricious zest. "You know, Milo, I think Colonel Korn and I might be willing to take the syndicate off your hands," he suggested in an offhand manner, almost licking his lips in savory anticipation. "Our experience in black-market plum tomatoes should come in very useful. Where do we begin?"

Milo watched Colonel Cathcart steadily with a bland and guileless expression. "Thank you, sir, that's very good of you. Begin with a salt-free diet for General Peckem and a fat-free diet for General Dreedle."

"Let me get a pencil. What's next?"

"The cedars."

"Cedars?"

"From Lebanon."

"Lebanon?"

"We've got cedars from Lebanon due at the sawmill in Oslo to be turned into shingles for the builder in Cape Cod. C.O.D. And then there's the peas."

"Peas?"

"That are on the high seas. We've got boatloads of peas that are on the high seas from Atlanta to Holland to pay for the tulips that were shipped to Geneva to pay for the cheeses that must go to Vienna M.I.F."

"M.I.F.?"

"Money in Front. The Hapsburgs are shaky."

"Milo."

"And don't forget the galvanized zinc in the warehouse at Flint. Four carloads of galvanized zinc from Flint must be flown to the smelters in Damascus by noon of the eighteenth, terms F.O.B. Calcutta two percent ten days E.O.M. One Messerschmitt full of hemp is due in Belgrade for a C-47 and a half full of those semi-pitted dates we stuck them with from Khartoum. Use the money from the Portuguese anchovies we're selling back to Lisbon to pay for the Egyptian cotton we've got coming back to us from Mamaroneck and to pick up as many oranges as you can in Spain. Always pay cash for *naranjas*."

"Naranjas?"

"That's what they call oranges in Spain, and these are Spanish oranges. And—oh, yes. Don't forget Piltdown Man."

"Piltdown Man?"

"Yes, Piltdown Man. The Smithsonian Institution is not in a position at this time to meet our price for a second Piltdown Man, but they are looking forward to the death of a wealthy and beloved donor and—"

"Milo."

"France wants all the parsley we can send them, and I think we might as well, because we'll need the francs for the lire for the pfennigs for the dates when they get back. I've also ordered a tremendous shipment of Peruvian balsa wood for distribution to each of the mess halls in the syndicate on a pro rata basis."

"Balsa wood? What are the mess halls going to do with balsa wood?"

"Good balsa wood isn't so easy to come by these days, Colonel. I just didn't think it was a good idea to pass up the chance to buy it."

"No, I suppose not," Colonel Cathcart surmised vaguely with the look of somebody seasick. "And I assume the price was right."

"The price," said Milo, "was outrageous—positively exorbitant! But since we bought it from one of our own subsidiaries, we were happy to pay it. Look after the hides."

"The hives?"

"The hides."

"The hides?"

"The hides. In Buenos Aires. They have to be tanned."

"Tanned?"

"In Newfoundland. And shipped to Helsinki N.M.I.F. before the spring thaw begins. Everything to Finland goes N.M.I.F. before the spring thaw begins."

"No Money in Front?" guessed Colonel Cathcart.

"Good, Colonel. You have a gift, sir. And then there's the cork."

"The cork?"

"That must go to New York, the shoes for Toulouse, the ham for Siam, the nails from Wales, and the tangerines for New Orleans."

"Milo."

"We have coals in Newcastle, sir."

Colonel Cathcart threw up his hands. "Milo, stop!" he cried, almost in tears. "It's no use. You're just like I am—*indispensable!*" He pushed his pencil aside and rose to his feet in frantic exasperation. "Milo, you can't fly sixty-four more missions. You can't even fly one more mission. The whole system would fall apart if anything happened to you."

Milo nodded serenely with complacent gratification. "Sir, are you forbidding me to fly any more combat missions?"

"Milo, I forbid you to fly any more combat missions," Colonel Cathcart declared in a tone of stern and inflexible authority.

"But that's not fair, sir," said Milo. "What about my record? The other men are getting all the fame and medals and publicity. Why should I be penalized just because I'm doing such a good job as mess officer?"

"No, Milo, it isn't fair. But I don't see anything we can do about it."

"Maybe we can get someone else to fly my missions for me."

"But maybe we can get someone else to fly your missions for you,"

Colonel Cathcart suggested. "How about the striking coal miners in Pennsylvania and West Virginia?"

Milo shook his head. "It would take too long to train them. But why not the men in the squadron, sir? After all, I'm doing all this for them. They ought to be willing to do something for me in return."

"But why not the men in the squadron, Milo?" Colonel Cathcart exclaimed. "After all, you're doing all this for them. They ought to be willing to do something for you in return."

"What's fair is fair."

"What's fair is fair."

"They could take turns, sir."

"They might even take turns flying your missions for you, Milo."

"Who gets the credit?"

"You get the credit, Milo. And if a man wins a medal flying one of your missions, you get the medal."

"Who dies if he gets killed?"

"Why, he dies, of course. After all, Milo, what's fair is fair. There's just one thing."

"You'll have to raise the number of missions."

"I might have to raise the number of missions again, and I'm not sure the men will fly them. They're still pretty sore because I jumped them to seventy. If I can get just one of the regular officers to fly more, the rest will probably follow."

"Nately will fly more missions, sir," Milo said. "I was told in strictest confidence just a little while ago that he'll do anything he has to in order to remain overseas with a girl he's fallen in love with."

"But Nately will fly more!" Colonel Cathcart declared, and he brought his hands together in a resounding clap of victory. "Yes, Nately will fly more. And this time I'm really going to jump the missions, right up to eighty, and really knock General Dreedle's eye out. And this is a good way to get that lousy rat Yossarian back into combat where he might get killed."

"Yossarian?" A tremor of deep concern passed over Milo's simple, homespun features, and he scratched the corner of his reddish-brown mustache thoughtfully.

"Yeah, Yossarian. I hear he's going around saying that he's finished his missions and the war's over for him. Well, maybe he has finished his missions. But he hasn't finished *your* missions, has he? Ha! Ha! Has *he* got a surprise coming to him!"

"Sir, Yossarian is a friend of mine," Milo objected. "I'd hate to be responsible for doing anything that would put him back in combat. I owe a lot to Yossarian. Isn't there anyway we could make an exception of him?"

"Oh, no, Milo." Colonel Cathcart clucked sententiously, shocked by the suggestion. "We must never play favorites. We must always treat every man alike."

"I'd give everything I own to Yossarian," Milo persevered gamely in Yossarian's behalf. "But since I don't own everything, I can't give everything to him, can I? So he'll just have to take his chances with the rest of the men, won't he?"

"What's fair is fair, Milo."

"Yes, sir, what's fair is fair," Milo agreed. "Yossarian is no better than the other men, and he has no right to expect any special privileges, has he?"

"No, Milo. What's fair is fair."

And there was no time for Yossarian to save himself from combat once Colonel Cathcart issued his announcement raising the missions to eighty late that same afternoon, no time to dissuade Nately from flying them or even to conspire again with Dobbs to murder Colonel Cathcart, for the alert sounded suddenly at dawn the next day and the men were rushed into the trucks before a decent breakfast could be prepared, and they were driven at top speed to the briefing room and then out to the airfield, where the clitter-clattering fuel trucks were still pumping gasoline into the tanks of the planes and the scampering crews of armorers were toiling as swiftly as they could at hoisting the thousand-pound demolition bombs into the bomb bays. Everybody was running, and engines were turned on and warmed up as soon as the fuel trucks had finished.

Intelligence had reported that a disabled Italian cruiser in drydock at La Spezia would be towed by the Germans that same morning to a channel at the entrance of the harbor and scuttled there to deprive the Allied armies of deepwater port facilities when they captured the city. For once, a military intelligence report proved accurate. The long vessel was halfway across the harbor when they flew in from the west, and they broke it apart with direct hits from every flight that filled them all with waves of enormously satisfying group pride until they found themselves engulfed in great barrages of flak that rose from guns in every bend of the huge horseshoe of mountainous land below. Even Havermeyer resorted to the wildest evasive action he could command when he saw what a vast distance he had still to travel to escape, and

Dobbs, at the pilot's controls in his formation, zigged when he should have zagged, skidded his plane into the plane alongside, and chewed off its tail. His wing broke off at the base, and his plane dropped like a rock and was almost out of sight in an instant. There was no fire, no smoke, not the slightest untoward noise. The remaining wing revolved as ponderously as a grinding cement mixer as the plane plummeted nose downward in a straight line at accelerating speed until it struck the water, which foamed open at the impact like a white water lily on the dark-blue sea, and washed back in a geyser of apple-green bubbles when the plane sank. It was over in a matter of seconds. There were no parachutes. And Nately, in the other plane, was killed too.

36

The Cellar

Nately's death almost killed the chaplain. Chaplain Tappman was seated in his tent, laboring over his paperwork in his reading spectacles, when his phone rang and news of the mid-air collision was given to him from the field. His insides turned at once to dry clay. His hand was trembling as he put the phone down. His other hand began trembling. The disaster was too immense to contemplate. Twelve men killed—how ghastly, how very, very awful! His feeling of terror grew. He prayed instinctively that Yossarian, Nately, Hungry Joe and his other friends would not be listed among the victims, then berated himself repentantly, for to pray for their safety was to pray for the death of other young men he did not even know. It was too late to pray; yet that was all he knew how to do. His heart was pounding with a noise that seemed to be coming from somewhere outside, and he knew he would never sit in a dentist's chair again, never glance at a surgical tool, never witness an automobile accident or hear a voice shout at night, without experiencing that same violent thumping in his chest and dreading that he was going to die. He would never watch another fist fight without fearing he was going to faint and crack his skull open on the pavement or suffer a fatal heart attack or cerebral hemorrhage. He wondered if he would ever see his wife again or his three small children. He wondered if he ever *should* see his wife again, now that Captain Black had planted in his mind such strong doubts about the fidelity and character of all women. There were so many other men, he felt, who could prove more satisfying to her sexually. When he thought of death now, he always thought of his wife, and when he thought of his wife he always thought of losing her.

In another minute the chaplain felt strong enough to rise and walk with glum reluctance to the tent next door for Sergeant Whitcomb. They drove in Sergeant Whitcomb's jeep. The chaplain made fists of his hands to keep them from shaking as they lay in his lap. He ground his teeth together and tried not to hear as Sergeant Whitcomb chirruped exultantly over the tragic event. Twelve men killed meant twelve more form letters of condolence that could be mailed in one bunch to the next of kin over Colonel Cathcart's signature, giving Sergeant Whitcomb hope of getting an article on Colonel Cathcart into *The Saturday Evening Post* in time for Easter.

At the field a heavy silence prevailed, overpowering motion like a ruthless, insensate spell holding in thrall the only beings who might break it. The chaplain was in awe. He had never beheld such a great, appalling stillness before. Almost two hundred tired, gaunt, downcast men stood holding their parachute packs in a somber and unstirring crowd outside the briefing room, their faces staring blankly in different angles of stunned dejection. They seemed unwilling to go, unable to move. The chaplain was acutely conscious of the faint noise his footsteps made as he approached. His eyes searched hurriedly, frantically, through the immobile maze of limp figures. He spied Yossarian finally with a feeling of immense joy, and then his mouth gaped open slowly in unbearable horror as he noted Yossarian's vivid, beaten, grimy look of deep, drugged despair. He understood at once, recoiling in pain from the realization and shaking his head with a protesting and imploring grimace, that Nately was dead. The knowledge struck him with a numbing shock. A sob broke from him. The blood drained from his legs, and he thought he was going to drop. Nately was dead. All hope that he was mistaken was washed away by the sound of Nately's name emerging with recurring clarity now from the almost inaudible babble of murmuring voices that he was suddenly aware of for the first time. Nately was dead: the boy had been killed. A whimpering sound rose in the chaplain's throat, and his jaw began to quiver. His eyes filled with tears, and he was crying. He started toward Yossarian on tiptoe to mourn beside him and share his wordless grief. At that moment a hand grabbed him roughly around the arm and a brusque voice demanded,

"Chaplain Tappman?"

He turned with surprise to face a stout, pugnacious colonel with a large head and mustache and a smooth, florid skin. He had never seen the man before. "Yes. What is it?" The fingers grasping the chaplain's arm were hurting him, and he tried in vain to squirm loose.

"Come along."

The chaplain pulled back in frightened confusion. "Where? Why? Who are you, anyway?"

"You'd better come along with us, Father," a lean, hawk-faced major on the chaplain's other side intoned with reverential sorrow. "We're from the government. We want to ask you some questions."

"What kind of questions? What's the matter?"

"Aren't you Chaplain Tappman?" demanded the obese colonel.

"He's the one," Sergeant Whitcomb answered.

"Go on along with them," Captain Black called out to the chaplain with a hostile and contemptuous sneer. "Go on into the car if you know what's good for you."

Hands were drawing the chaplain away irresistibly. He wanted to shout for help to Yossarian, who seemed too far away to hear. Some of the men nearby were beginning to look at him with awakening curiosity. The chaplain bent his face away with burning shame and allowed himself to be led into the rear of a staff car and seated between the fat colonel with the large, pink face and the skinny, unctuous, despondent major. He automatically held a wrist out to each, wondering for a moment if they wanted to handcuff him. Another officer was already in the front seat. A tall M.P. with a whistle and a white helmet got in behind the wheel. The chaplain did not dare raise his eyes until the closed car had lurched from the area and the speeding wheels were whining on the bumpy blacktop road.

"Where are you taking me?" he asked in a voice soft with timidity and guilt, his gaze still averted. The notion came to him that they were holding him to blame for the mid-air crash and the death of Nately. "What have I done?"

"Why don't you keep your trap shut and let us ask the questions?" said the colonel.

"Don't talk to him that way," said the major. "It isn't necessary to be so disrespectful."

"Then tell him to keep his trap shut and let us ask the questions."

"Father, please keep your trap shut and let us ask the questions," urged the major sympathetically. "It will be better for you."

"It isn't necessary to call me Father," said the chaplain. "I'm not a Catholic."

"Neither am I, Father," said the major. "It's just that I'm a very devout person, and I like to call all men of God Father."

"He doesn't even believe there are atheists in foxholes," the colonel mocked, and nudged the chaplain in the ribs familiarly. "Go on, Chaplain, tell him. Are there atheists in foxholes?"

"I don't know, sir," the chaplain replied. "I've never been in a foxhole."

The officer in front swung his head around swiftly with a quarrelsome expression. "You've never been in heaven either, have you? But you know there's a heaven, don't you?"

"Or do you?" said the colonel.

"That's a very serious crime you've committed, Father," said the major.

"What crime?"

"We don't know yet," said the colonel. "But we're going to find out. And we sure know it's very serious."

The car swung off the road at Group Headquarters with a squeal of tires, slackening speed only slightly, and continued around past the parking lot to the back of the building. The three officers and the chaplain got out. In single file, they ushered him down a wobbly flight of wooden stairs leading to the basement and led him into a damp, gloomy room with a low cement ceiling and unfinished stone walls. There were cobwebs in all the corners. A huge centipede blew across the floor to the shelter of a water pipe. They sat the chaplain in a hard, straight-backed chair that stood behind a small, bare table.

"Please make yourself comfortable, Chaplain," invited the colonel cordially, switching on a blinding spotlight and shooting it squarely into the chaplain's face. He placed a set of brass knuckles and a box of wooden matches on the table. "We want you to relax."

The chaplain's eyes bugged out incredulously. His teeth chattered and his limbs felt utterly without strength. He was powerless. They might do whatever they wished to him, he realized; these brutal men might beat him to death right there in the basement, and no one would intervene to save him, no one, perhaps, but the devout and sympathetic major with the sharp face, who set a water tap dripping loudly into a sink and returned to the table to lay a length of heavy rubber hose down beside the brass knuckles.

"Everything's going to be all right, Chaplain," the major said encouragingly. "You've got nothing to be afraid of if you're not guilty. What are you so afraid of? You're not guilty, are you?"

"Sure he's guilty," said the colonel. "Guilty as hell."

"Guilty of what?" implored the chaplain, feeling more and more bewildered and not knowing which of the men to appeal to for mercy. The third officer wore no insignia and lurked in silence off to the side. "What did I do?"

"That's just what we're going to find out," answered the colonel, and he shoved a pad and pencil across the table to the chaplain. "Write your name for us, will you? In your own handwriting."

"My own handwriting?"

"That's right. Anywhere on the page." When the chaplain had finished, the colonel took the pad back and held it up alongside a sheet of paper he removed from a folder. "See?" he said to the major, who had come to his side and was peering solemnly over his shoulder.

"They're not the same, are they?" the major admitted.

"I told you he did it."

"Did what?" asked the chaplain.

"Chaplain, this comes as a great shock to me," the major accused in a tone of heavy lamentation.

"What does?"

"I can't tell you how disappointed I am in you."

"For what?" persisted the chaplain more frantically. "What have I done?"

"For this," replied the major, and, with an air of disillusioned disgust, tossed down on the table the pad on which the chaplain had signed his name. "This isn't your handwriting."

The chaplain blinked rapidly with amazement. "But of course it's my handwriting."

"No it isn't, Chaplain. You're lying again."

"But I just wrote it!" the chaplain cried in exasperation. "You saw me write it."

"That's just it," the major answered bitterly. "I *saw* you write it. You can't deny that you did write it. A person who'll lie about his own handwriting will lie about anything."

"But who lied about my own handwriting?" demanded the chaplain, forgetting his fear in the wave of anger and indignation that welled up inside him suddenly. "Are you crazy or something? What are you both talking about?"

"We asked you to write your name in your own handwriting. And you didn't do it."

"But of course I did. In whose handwriting did I write it if not my own?"

"In somebody else's."

"Whose?"

"That's just what we're going to find out," threatened the colonel.

"Talk, Chaplain."

The chaplain looked from one to the other of the two men with rising doubt and hysteria. "That handwriting is mine," he maintained passionately. "Where else is my handwriting, if that isn't it?"

"Right here," answered the colonel. And looking very superior, he tossed down on the table a photostatic copy of a piece of V mail in which everything but the salutation "Dear Mary" had been blocked out and on which the censoring officer had written, "I long for you tragically. A. T. Tappman, Chaplain, U.S. Army." The colonel smiled scornfully as he watched the chaplain's face turn crimson. "Well, Chaplain? Do you know who wrote that?"

The chaplain took a long moment to reply; he had recognized Yossarian's handwriting. "No."

"You can read, though, can't you?" the colonel persevered sarcastically. "The author signed his name."

"That's my name there."

"Then you wrote it. Q.E.D."

"But I didn't write it. That isn't my handwriting, either."

"Then you signed your name in somebody else's handwriting again," the colonel retorted with a shrug. "That's all that means."

"Oh, this is ridiculous!" the chaplain shouted, suddenly losing all patience. He jumped to his feet in a blazing fury, both fists clenched. "I'm not going to stand for this any longer! Do you hear? Twelve men were just killed, and I have no time for these silly questions. You've no right to keep me here, and I'm just not going to stand for it."

Without saying a word, the colonel pushed the chaplain's chest hard and knocked him back down into the chair, and the chaplain was suddenly weak and very much afraid again. The major picked up the length of rubber hose and began tapping it menacingly against his open palm. The colonel lifted the box of matches, took one out and held it poised against the striking surface, watching with glowering eyes for the chaplain's next sign of defiance. The chaplain was pale and almost too petrified to move. The bright glare of the spotlight made him turn away finally; the dripping water tap was louder and almost unbearably irritating. He wished they would tell him what they wanted so that he would know what to confess. He waited tensely as the third officer, at a signal from the colonel, ambled over from the wall and seated himself on the table just a few inches away from the chaplain. His face was expressionless, his eyes penetrating and cold.

"Turn off the light," he said over his shoulder in a low, calm voice. "It's very annoying."

The chaplain gave him a small smile of gratitude. "Thank you, sir. And the drip, too, please."

"Leave the drip," said the officer. "That doesn't bother me." He tugged up the legs of his trousers a bit, as though to preserve their natty crease. "Chaplain," he asked casually, "of what religious persuasion are you?"

"I'm an Anabaptist, sir."

"That's a pretty suspicious religion, isn't it?"

"Suspicious?" inquired the chaplain in a kind of innocent daze. "Why, sir?"

"Well, I don't know a thing about it. You'll have to admit that, won't you? Doesn't that make it pretty suspicious?"

"I don't know, sir," the chaplain answered diplomatically, with an uneasy stammer. He found the man's lack of insignia disconcerting and was not even sure he had to say "sir." Who was he? And what authority had he to interrogate him?

"Chaplain, I once studied Latin. I think it's only fair to warn you of that before I ask my next question. Doesn't the word Anabaptist simply mean that you're not a Baptist?"

"Oh, no, sir. There's much more."

"Are you a Baptist?"

"No, sir."

"Then you *are* not a Baptist, aren't you?"

"Sir?"

"I don't see why you're bickering with me on that point. You've already admitted it. Now, Chaplain, to say you're not a Baptist doesn't really tell us anything about what you are, does it? You could be anything or anyone." He leaned forward slightly and his manner took on a shrewd and significant air. "You could even be," he added, "Washington Irving, couldn't you?"

"Washington Irving?" the chaplain repeated with surprise.

"Come on, Washington," the corpulent colonel broke in irascibly. "Why don't you make a clean breast of it? We know you stole that plum tomato."

After a moment's shock, the chaplain giggled with nervous relief. "Oh, is *that* it!" he exclaimed. "Now I'm beginning to understand. I didn't steal that plum tomato, sir. Colonel Cathcart gave it to me. You can even ask him if you don't believe me."

A door opened at the other end of the room and Colonel Cathcart stepped into the basement as though from a closet.

"Hello, Colonel. Colonel, he claims you gave him that plum tomato. Did you?"

"Why should I give him a plum tomato?" answered Colonel Cathcart.

"Thank you, Colonel. That will be all."

"It's a pleasure, Colonel," Colonel Cathcart replied, and he stepped back out of the basement, closing the door after him.

"Well, Chaplain? What have you got to say now?"

"He did give it to me!" the chaplain hissed in a whisper that was both fierce and fearful. "He did give it to me!"

"You're not calling a superior officer a liar, are you, Chaplain?"

"Why should a superior officer give you a plum tomato, Chaplain?"

"Is that why you tried to give it to Sergeant Whitcomb, Chaplain? Because it was a hot tomato?"

"No, no, no," the chaplain protested, wondering miserably why they were not able to understand. "I offered it to Sergeant Whitcomb because I didn't want it."

"Why'd you steal it from Colonel Cathcart if you didn't want it?"

"I didn't steal it from Colonel Cathcart!"

"Then why are you so guilty, if you didn't steal it?"

"I'm not guilty!"

"Then why would we be questioning you if you weren't guilty?"

"Oh, I don't know," the chaplain groaned, kneading his fingers in his lap and shaking his bowed and anguished head. "I don't know."

"He thinks we have time to waste," snorted the major.

"Chaplain," resumed the officer without insignia at a more leisurely pace, lifting a typewritten sheet of yellow paper from the open folder, "I have a signed statement here from Colonel Cathcart asserting you stole that plum tomato from him." He lay the sheet face down on one side of the folder and picked up a second page from the other side. "And here I have a notarized affidavit from Sergeant Whitcomb in which he states that he knew the tomato was hot just from the way you tried to unload it on him."

"I swear to God I didn't steal it, sir," the chaplain pleaded with distress, almost in tears. "I give you my sacred word it was not a hot tomato."

"Chaplain, do you believe in God?"

"Yes, sir. Of course I do."

"That's odd, Chaplain," said the officer, taking from the folder another typewritten yellow page, "because I have here in my hands now another statement from Colonel Cathcart in which he swears that you refused to cooperate with him in conducting prayer meetings in the briefing room before each mission."

After looking blank a moment, the chaplain nodded quickly with recollection. "Oh, that's not quite true, sir," he explained eagerly. "Colonel Cathcart gave up the idea himself once he realized enlisted men pray to the same God as officers."

"He did *what?*" exclaimed the officer in disbelief.

"What nonsense!" declared the red-faced colonel, and swung away from the chaplain with dignity and annoyance.

"Does he expect us to believe that?" cried the major incredulously.

The officer without insignia chuckled acidly. "Chaplain, aren't you stretching things a bit far now?" he inquired with a smile that was indulgent and unfriendly.

"But, sir, it's the truth, sir! I swear it's the truth."

"I don't see how that matters one way or the other," the officer answered nonchalantly, and reached sideways again toward the open folder filled with papers. "Chaplain, did you say you did believe in God in answer to my question? I don't remember."

"Yes, sir. I did say so, sir. I do believe in God."

"Then that really is very odd, Chaplain, because I have here another affidavit from Colonel Cathcart that states you once told him atheism was not against the law. Do you recall ever making a statement like that to anyone?"

The chaplain nodded without any hesitation, feeling himself on very solid ground now. "Yes, sir, I did make a statement like that. I made it because it's true. Atheism is not against the law."

"But that's still no reason to say so, Chaplain, is it?" the officer chided tartly, frowning, and picked up still one more typewritten, notarized page from the folder. "And here I have another sworn statement from Sergeant Whitcomb that says you opposed his plan of sending letters of condolence over Colonel Cathcart's signature to the next of kin of men killed or wounded in combat. Is that true?"

"Yes, sir, I did oppose it," answered the chaplain. "And I'm proud that I did. Those letters are insincere and dishonest. Their only purpose is to bring glory to Colonel Cathcart."

"But what difference does that make?" replied the officer. "They still bring solace and comfort to the families that receive them, don't they? Chaplain, I simply can't understand your thinking process."

The chaplain was stumped and at a complete loss for a reply. He hung his head, feeling tongue-tied and naïve.

The ruddy stout colonel stepped forward vigorously with a sudden idea. "Why don't we knock his goddam brains out?" he suggested with robust enthusiasm to the others.

"Yes, we could knock his goddam brains out, couldn't we?" the hawk-faced major agreed. "He's only an Anabaptist."

"No, we've got to find him guilty first," the officer without insignia cautioned with a languid restraining wave. He slid lightly to the floor and moved around to the other side of the table, facing the chaplain with both hands pressed flat on the surface. His expression was dark and very stern, square and forbidding. "Chaplain," he announced with magisterial rigidity, "we charge you formally with being Washington Irving and taking capricious and unlicensed liberties in censoring the letters of officers and enlisted men. Are you guilty or innocent?"

"Innocent, sir." The chaplain licked dry lips with a dry tongue and leaned forward in suspense on the edge of his chair.

"Guilty," said the colonel.

"Guilty," said the major.

"Guilty it is, then," remarked the officer without insignia, and wrote a word on a page in the folder. "Chaplain," he continued, looking up, "we accuse you also of the commission of crimes and infractions we don't even know about yet. Guilty or innocent?"

"I don't know, sir. How can I say if you don't tell me what they are?"

"How can we tell you if we don't know?"

"Guilty," decided the colonel.

"Sure he's guilty," agreed the major. "If they're his crimes and infractions, he must have committed them."

"Guilty it is, then," chanted the officer without insignia, and moved off to the side of the room. "He's all yours, Colonel."

"Thank you," commended the colonel. "You did a very good job." He turned to the chaplain. "Okay, Chaplain, the jig's up. Take a walk."

The chaplain did not understand. "What do you wish me to do?"

"Go on, beat it, I told you!" the colonel roared, jerking a thumb over his shoulder angrily. "Get the hell out of here."

The chaplain was shocked by his bellicose words and tone and, to his own amazement and mystification, deeply chagrined that they were turning him loose. "Aren't you even going to punish me?" he inquired with querulous surprise.

"You're damned right we're going to punish you. But we're certainly not going to let you hang around while we decide how and when to do it. So get going. Hit the road."

The chaplain rose tentatively and took a few steps away. "I'm free to go?"

"For the time being. But don't try to leave the island. We've got your number, Chaplain. Just remember that we've got you under surveillance twenty-four hours a day."

It was not conceivable that they would allow him to leave. The chaplain walked toward the exit gingerly, expecting at any instant to be ordered back by a peremptory voice or halted in his tracks by a heavy blow on the shoulder or the head. They did nothing to stop him. He found his way through the stale, dark, dank corridors to the flight of stairs. He was staggering and panting when he climbed out into the fresh air. As soon as he had escaped, a feeling of overwhelming moral outrage filled him. He was furious, more furious at the atrocities of the day than he had ever felt before in his whole life. He swept through the spacious, echoing lobby of the building in a temper of scalding and vindictive resentment. He was not going to stand for it any more, he told himself, he was simply not going to stand for it. When he reached the entrance, he spied, with a feeling of good fortune, Colonel Korn trotting up the wide steps alone. Bracing himself with a deep breath, the chaplain moved courageously forward to intercept him.

"Colonel, I'm not going to stand for it any more," he declared with vehement determination, and watched in dismay as Colonel Korn went trotting by up the steps without even noticing him. "Colonel Korn!"

The tubby, loose figure of his superior officer stopped, turned and came trotting back down slowly. "What is it, Chaplain?"

"Colonel Korn, I want to talk to you about the crash this morning. It was a terrible thing to happen, terrible!"

Colonel Korn was silent a moment, regarding the chaplain with a glint of cynical amusement. "Yes, Chaplain, it certainly was terrible," he said finally. "I don't know *how* we're going to write this one up without making ourselves look bad."

"That isn't what I meant," the chaplain scolded firmly without any fear at all. "Some of those twelve men had already finished their seventy missions."

Colonel Korn laughed. "Would it be any less terrible if they had all been new men?" he inquired caustically.

Once again the chaplain was stumped. Immoral logic seemed to be confounding him at every turn. He was less sure of himself than before when he continued, and his voice wavered. "Sir, it just isn't right to make the men in this group fly eighty missions when the men in other groups are being sent home with fifty and fifty-five."

"We'll take the matter under consideration," Colonel Korn said with bored disinterest, and started away. "*Adios*, Padre."

"What does that mean, sir?" the chaplain persisted in a voice turning shrill.

Colonel Korn stopped with an unpleasant expression and took a step back down. "It means we'll think about it, Padre," he answered with sarcasm and contempt. "You wouldn't want us to do anything without thinking about it, would you?"

"No, sir, I suppose not. But you have been thinking about it, haven't you?"

"Yes, Padre, we have been thinking about it. But to make you happy, we'll think about it some more, and you'll be the first person we'll tell if we reach a new decision. And now, *adios*." Colonel Korn whirled away again and hurried up the stairs.

"Colonel Korn!" The chaplain's cry made Colonel Korn stop once more. His head swung slowly around toward the chaplain with a look of morose impatience. Words gushed from the chaplain in a nervous torrent. "Sir, I would like your permission to take the matter to General Dreedle. I want to bring my protests to Wing Headquarters."

Colonel Korn's thick, dark jowls inflated unexpectedly with a suppressed guffaw, and it took him a moment to reply. "That's all right, Padre," he answered with mischievous merriment, trying hard to keep a straight face. "You have my permission to speak to General Dreedle."

"Thank you, sir. I believe it only fair to warn you that I think I have some influence with General Dreedle."

"It's good of you to warn me, Padre. And I believe it only fair to warn you that you won't find General Dreedle at Wing." Colonel Korn grinned wickedly and then broke into triumphant laughter. "General Dreedle is out, Padre. And General Peckem is in. We have a new wing commander."

The chaplain was stunned. "General Peckem!"

"That's right, Chaplain. Have you got any influence with him?"

"Why, I don't even know General Peckem," the chaplain protested wretchedly.

Colonel Korn laughed again. "That's too bad, Chaplain, because Colonel Cathcart knows him very well." Colonel Korn chuckled steadily with gloating relish for another second or two and then stopped abruptly. "And by the way, Padre," he warned coldly, poking his finger once into the chaplain's chest. "The jig is up between you and Dr. Stubbs. We know very well he sent you up here to complain today."

"Dr. Stubbs?" The chaplain shook his head in baffled protest. "I haven't seen Dr. Stubbs, Colonel. I was brought here by three strange officers who took me down into the cellar without authority and questioned and insulted me."

Colonel Korn poked the chaplain in the chest once more. "You know damned well Dr. Stubbs has been telling the men in his squadron they didn't have to fly more than seventy missions." He laughed harshly. "Well, Padre, they do have to fly more than seventy missions, because we're transferring Dr. Stubbs to the Pacific. So *adios*, Padre. *Adios*."

37

General Scheisskopf

Dreedle was out, and General Peckem was in, and General Peckem had hardly moved inside General Dreedle's office to replace him when his splendid military victory began falling to pieces around him.

"*General* Scheisskopf?" he inquired unsuspectingly of the sergeant in his new office who brought him word of the order that had come in that morning. "You mean *Colonel* Scheisskopf, don't you?"

"No, sir, General Scheisskopf. He was promoted to general this morning, sir."

"Well, that's certainly curious! Scheisskopf? A general? What grade?"

"Lieutenant general, sir, and—"

"Lieutenant general!"

"Yes, sir, and he wants you to issue no orders to anyone in your command without first clearing them through him."

"Well, I'll be dammed," mused General Peckem with astonishment, swearing aloud for perhaps the first time in his life. "Cargill, did you hear that? Scheisskopf was promoted way up to lieutenant general. I'll bet that promotion was intended for me and they gave it to him by mistake."

Colonel Cargill had been rubbing his sturdy chin reflectively. "Why is he giving orders to us?"

General Peckem's sleek, scrubbed, distinguished face tightened. "Yes, Sergeant," he said slowly with an uncomprehending frown. "Why is he issuing orders to us if he's still in Special Services and we're in combat operations?"

"That's another change that was made this morning, sir. All combat operations are now under the jurisdiction of Special Services. General Scheisskopf is our new commanding officer."

General Peckem let out a sharp cry. "Oh, my God!" he wailed, and all his practiced composure went up in hysteria. "Scheisskopf in charge? *Scheisskopf?*" He pressed his fists down on his eyes with horror. "Cargill, get me Wintergreen! *Scheisskopf?* Not *Scheisskopf!*"

All phones began ringing at once. A corporal ran in and saluted.

"Sir, there's a chaplain outside to see you with news of an injustice in Colonel Cathcart's squadron."

"Send him away, send him away! We've got enough injustices of our own. Where's Wintergreen?"

"Sir, General Scheisskopf is on the phone. He wants to speak to you at once."

"Tell him I haven't arrived yet. Good Lord!" General Peckem screamed, as though struck by the enormity of the disaster for the first time. "*Scheisskopf?* The man's a moron! I walked all over that blockhead, and now he's my superior officer. Oh, my Lord! Cargill! Cargill, don't desert me! Where's Wintergreen?"

"Sir, I have an ex-Sergeant Wintergreen on your telephone. He's been trying to reach you all morning."

"General, I can't get Wintergreen," Colonel Cargill shouted. "His line is busy."

General Peckem was perspiring freely as he lunged for the other telephone.

"Wintergreen!"

"Peckem, you son of a bitch—"

"Wintergreen, have you heard what they've done?"

"—what have you done, you stupid bastard?"

"They put Scheisskopf in charge of everything!"

Wintergreen was shrieking with rage and panic. "You and your goddam memorandums! They've gone and transferred combat operations to Special Services!"

"Oh, no," moaned General Peckem. "Is that what did it? My memoranda? Is that what made them put Scheisskopf in charge? Why didn't they put me in charge?"

"Because you weren't in Special Services any more. You transferred out and left him in charge. And do you know what he wants? Do you know what the bastard wants us all to do?"

"Sir, I think you'd better talk to General Scheisskopf," pleaded the sergeant nervously. "He insists on speaking to someone."

"Cargill, talk to Scheisskopf for me. I can't do it. Find out what he wants."

Colonel Cargill listened to General Scheisskopf for a moment and went white as a sheet. "Oh, my God!" he cried as the phone fell from his fingers. "Do you know what he wants? He wants us to march. He wants *everybody* to march!"

38

Kid Sister

Yossarian marched backward with his gun on his hip and refused to fly any more missions. He marched backward because he was continuously spinning around as he walked to make certain no one was sneaking up on him from behind. Every sound to his rear was a warning, every person he passed a potential assassin. He kept his hand on his gun butt constantly and smiled at no one but Hungry Joe. He told Captain Piltchard and Captain Wren that he was through flying. Captain Piltchard and Captain Wren left his name off the flight schedule for the next mission and reported the matter to Group Headquarters.

Colonel Korn laughed calmly. "What the devil do you mean, he won't fly more missions?" he asked with a smile as Colonel Cathcart crept away into a corner to brood about the sinister import of the name Yossarian popping up to plague him once again. "Why won't he?"

"His friend Nately was killed in the crash over Spezia. Maybe that's why."

"Who does he think he is—Achilles?" Colonel Korn was pleased with the simile and filed a mental reminder to repeat it the next time he found himself in General Peckem's presence. "He has to fly more missions. He has no choice. Go back and tell him you'll report the matter to us if he doesn't change his mind."

"We already did tell him that, sir. It made no difference."

"What does Major Major say?"

"We never see Major Major. He seems to have disappeared."

"I wish we could disappear *him!*" Colonel Cathcart blurted out from the corner peevishly. "The way they did that fellow Dunbar."

"Oh, there are plenty of other ways we can handle this one," Colonel Korn assured him confidently, and continued to Piltchard and Wren. "Let's begin with the kindest. Send him to Rome for a rest for a few days. Maybe this fellow's death really did hurt him a bit."

Nately's death, in fact, almost killed Yossarian too, for when he broke the news to Nately's whore in Rome she uttered a piercing heartbroken shriek and tried to stab him to death with a potato peeler.

"*Bruto!*" she howled at him in hysterical fury as he bent her arm up around behind her back and twisted gradually until the potato peeler dropped from her grasp. "*Bruto! Bruto!*" She lashed at him swiftly with the long-nailed fingers of her free hand and raked open his cheek. She spat in his face viciously.

"What's the matter?" he screamed in stinging pain and bewilderment, flinging her away from him all the way across the room to the wall. "What do you want from *me?*"

She flew back at him with both fists flailing and bloodied his mouth with a solid punch before he was able to grab her wrists and hold her still. Her hair tossed wildly. Tears were streaming in single torrents from her flashing, hate-filled eyes as she struggled against him fiercely in an irrational frenzy of maddened might, snarling and cursing savagely and screaming "*Bruto! Bruto!*" each time he tried to explain. Her great strength caught him off guard, and he lost his footing. She was nearly as tall as Yossarian, and for a few fantastic, terror-filled moments he was certain she would overpower him in her crazed determination, crush him to the ground and rip him apart mercilessly limb from limb for some heinous crime he had never committed. He wanted to yell for help as they strove against each other frantically in a grunting, panting stalemate, arm against arm. At last she weakened, and he was able to force her back and plead with her to let him talk, swearing to her that Nately's death had not been his fault. She spat in his face again, and he pushed her away hard in disgusted anger and frustration. She hurled herself down toward the potato peeler the instant he released her. He flung himself down after her, and they rolled over each other on the floor several times before he could tear the potato peeler away. She tried to trip him with her hand as he scrambled to his feet and scratched an excruciating chunk out of his ankle. He hopped across the room in pain and threw the potato peeler out the window. He heaved a huge sigh of relief once he saw he was safe.

"Now, please let me explain something to you," he cajoled in a mature, reasoning, earnest voice.

She kicked him in the groin. *Whoosh!* went the air out of him, and he sank down on his side with a shrill and ululating cry, doubled up over his knees in chaotic agony and retching for breath. Nately's whore ran from the room. Yossarian staggered up to his feet not a moment too soon, for she came charging back in from the kitchen carrying a long bread knife. A moan of incredulous dismay wafted from his lips as, still clutching his throbbing, tender, burning bowels in both hands, he dropped his full weight down against her shins and knocked her legs out from under her. She flipped completely over his head and landed on the floor on her elbows with a jarring thud. The knife skittered free, and he slapped it out of sight under the bed. She tried to lunge after it, and he seized her by the arm and yanked her up. She tried to kick him in the groin again, and he slung her away with a violent oath of his own. She slammed into the wall off balance and smashed a chair over into a vanity table covered with combs, hairbrushes and cosmetic jars that all went crashing off. A framed picture fell to the floor at the other end of the room, the glass front shattering.

"What do you *want* from me?" he yelled at her in whining and exasperated confusion. "I didn't kill him."

She hurled a heavy glass ash tray at his head. He made a fist and wanted to punch her in the stomach when she came charging at him again, but he was afraid he might harm her. He wanted to clip her very neatly on the point of the jaw and run from the room, but there was no clear target, and he merely skipped aside neatly at the last second and helped her along past him with a strong shove. She banged hard against the other wall. Now she was blocking the door. She threw a large vase at him. Then she came at him with a full wine bottle and struck him squarely on the temple, knocking him down half stunned on one knee. His ears were buzzing, his whole face was numb. More than anything else, he was embarrassed. He felt awkward because she was going to murder him. He simply did not understand what was going on. He had no idea *what to do.* But he did know he had to save himself, and he catapulted forward off the floor when he saw her raise the wine bottle to clout him again and barreled into her midriff before she could strike him. He had momentum, and he propelled her before him backward in his driving rush until her knees buckled against the side of the bed and she fell over onto the mattress with Yossarian sprawled on top of her between her legs. She plunged her nails into the side of his neck and gouged as he worked his way up the supple, full hills and ledges of her rounded body until he covered her completely and pressed her into submission, his fingers pursuing her thrashing arm persistently until they arrived at the wine bottle finally and wrenched it free. She was still kicking and cursing and scratching ferociously. She tried to bite him cruelly, her coarse, sensual lips stretched back over her teeth like an enraged omnivorous beast's. Now that she lay captive beneath him, he wondered how he would ever escape her without leaving himself vulnerable. He could feel the tensed, straddling inside of her buffeting thighs and knees squeezing and churning around one of his legs. He was stirred by thoughts of sex that made him ashamed. He was conscious of the voluptuous flesh of her firm, young-woman's body straining and beating against him like a humid, fluid, delectable, unyielding tide, her belly and warm, live, plastic breasts thrusting upward against him vigorously in sweet and menacing temptation. Her breath was scalding. All at once he realized—though the writhing turbulence beneath him had not diminished one whit—that she was no longer grappling with him, recognized with a quiver that she was not fighting him but heaving her pelvis up against him remorselessly in the primal, powerful, rhapsodic instinctual rhythm of erotic ardor and abandonment. He gasped in delighted surprise. Her face—as beautiful as a blooming flower to him now—was distorted with a new kind of torture, the tissues serenely swollen, her half-closed eyes misty and unseeing with the stultifying languor of desire.

"*Caro*," she murmured hoarsely as though from the depths of a tranquil and luxurious trance. "Ooooh, *caro mio.*"

He stroked her hair. She drove her mouth against his face with savage passion. He licked her neck. She wrapped her arms around him and hugged. He felt himself falling, falling ecstatically in love with her as she kissed him again and again with lips that were steaming and wet and soft and hard, mumbling deep sounds to him adoringly in an incoherent oblivion of rapture, one caressing hand on his back slipping deftly down inside his trouser belt while the other groped secretly and treacherously about on the floor for the bread knife and found it. He saved himself just in time. She still wanted to kill him! He was shocked and astounded by her depraved subterfuge as he tore the knife from her grasp and hurled it away. He bounded out of the bed to his feet. His face was agog with befuddlement and disillusion. He did not know whether to dart through the door to freedom or collapse on the bed to fall in love with her and place himself abjectly at her mercy again. She spared him from doing either by bursting unpredictably into tears. He was stunned again.

This time she wept with no other emotion than grief, profound, debilitating, humble grief, forgetting all about him. Her desolation was pathetic as she sat with her tempestuous, proud, lovely head bowed, her shoulders sagging, her spirit melting. This time there was no mistaking her anguish. Great, racking sobs choked and shook her. She was no longer aware of him, no longer cared. He could have walked from the room safely then. But he chose to remain and console and help her.

"Please," he urged her inarticulately with his arm about her shoulders, recollecting with pained sadness how inarticulate and enfeebled he had felt in the plane coming back from Avignon when Snowden kept whimpering to him that he was cold, he was cold, and all Yossarian could offer him in return was "There, there. There, there." "Please," he repeated to her sympathetically. "Please, please."

She rested against him and cried until she seemed too weak to cry any longer, and did not look at him once until he extended his handkerchief when she had finished. She wiped her cheeks with a tiny, polite smile and gave the handkerchief back, murmuring "*Grazie, grazie*" with meek, maidenly propriety, and then, without any warning whatsoever of a change in mood, clawed suddenly at his eyes with both hands. She landed with each and let out a victorious shriek.

"Ha! *Assassino!*" she hooted, and raced joyously across the room for the bread knife to finish him off.

Half blinded, he rose and stumbled after her. A noise behind him made him turn. His senses reeled in horror at what he saw. Nately's whore's kid sister, of all people, was coming after him with another long bread knife!

"Oh, no," he wailed with a shudder, and he knocked the knife out of her hand with a sharp downward blow on her wrist. He lost patience entirely with the whole grotesque and incomprehensible melee. There was no telling who might lunge at him next through the doorway with another long bread knife, and he lifted Nately's whore's kid sister off the floor, threw her at Nately's whore and ran out of the room, out of the apartment and down the stairs. The two girls chased out into the hall after him. He heard their footsteps lag farther and farther behind as he fled and then cease altogether. He heard sobbing directly overhead. Glancing backward up the stair well, he spied Nately's whore sitting in a heap on one of the steps, weeping with her face in both hands, while her pagan, irrepressible kid sister hung dangerously over the banister shouting "*Bruto! Bruto!*" down at him happily and brandished her bread knife at him as though it were an exciting new toy she was eager to use.

Yossarian escaped, but kept looking back over his shoulder anxiously as he retreated through the street. People stared at him strangely, making him more apprehensive. He walked in nervous haste, wondering what there was in his appearance that caught everyone's attention. When he touched his hand to a sore spot on his forehead, his fingers turned gooey with blood, and he understood. He dabbed his face and neck with a handkerchief. Wherever it pressed, he picked up new red smudges. He was bleeding everywhere. He hurried into the Red Cross building and down the two steep flights of white marble stairs to the men's washroom, where he cleansed and nursed his innumerable visible wounds with cold water and soap and straightened his shirt collar and combed his hair. He had never seen a face so badly bruised and scratched as the one still blinking back at him in the mirror with a dazed and startled uneasiness. What on earth had she wanted from *him?*

When he left the men's room, Nately's whore was waiting outside in ambush. She was crouched against the wall near the bottom of the staircase and came pouncing down upon him like a hawk with a glittering silver steak knife in her fist. He broke the brunt of her assault with his upraised elbow and punched her neatly on the jaw. Her eyes rolled. He caught her before she dropped and sat her down gently. Then he ran up the steps and out of the building and spent the next three hours hunting through the city for Hungry Joe so that he could get away from Rome before she could find him again. He did not feel really safe until the plane had taken off. When they landed in Pianosa, Nately's whore, disguised in a mechanic's green coveralls, was waiting with her steak knife exactly where the plane stopped, and all that saved him as she stabbed at his chest in her leather-soled high-heeled shoes was the gravel underfoot that made her feet roll out from under her. Yossarian, astounded, hauled her up into the plane and held her motionless on the floor in a double armlock while Hungry Joe radioed the control tower for permission to return to Rome. At the airport in Rome, Yossarian dumped her out of the plane on the taxi strip, and Hungry Joe took right off for Pianosa again without even cutting his engines. Scarcely breathing, Yossarian scrutinized every figure warily as he and Hungry Joe walked back through the squadron toward their tents. Hungry Joe eyed him steadily with a funny expression.

"Are you sure you didn't imagine the whole thing?" Hungry Joe inquired hesitantly after a while.

"Imagine it? You were right there with me, weren't you? You just flew her back to Rome."

"Maybe I imagined the whole thing, too. Why does she want to kill you for?"

"She never did like me. Maybe it's because I broke his nose, or maybe it's because I was the only one in sight she could hate when she got the news. Do you think she'll come back?"

Yossarian went to the officers' club that night and stayed very late. He kept a leery eye out for Nately's whore as he approached his tent. He stopped when he saw her hiding in the bushes around the side, gripping a huge carving knife and all dressed up to look like a Pianosan farmer. Yossarian tiptoed around the back noiselessly and seized her from behind.

"*Caramba!*" she exclaimed in a rage, and resisted like a wildcat as he dragged her inside the tent and hurled her down on the floor.

"Hey, what's going on?" queried one of his roommates drowsily.

"Hold her till I get back," Yossarian ordered, yanking him out of bed on top of her and running out. "Hold her!"

"Let me kill him and I'll ficky-fick you all," she offered.

The other roommates leaped out of their cots when they saw it was a girl and tried to make her ficky-fick them all first as Yossarian ran to get Hungry Joe, who was sleeping like a baby. Yossarian lifted Huple's cat off Hungry Joe's face and shook him awake. Hungry Joe dressed rapidly. This time they flew the plane north and turned in over Italy far behind the enemy lines. When they were over level land, they strapped a parachute on Nately's whore and shoved her out the escape hatch. Yossarian was positive that he was at last rid of her and was relieved. As he approached his tent back in Pianosa, a figure reared up in the darkness right beside the path, and he fainted. He came to sitting on the ground and waited for the knife to strike him, almost welcoming the mortal blow for the peace it would bring. A friendly hand helped him up instead. It belonged to a pilot in Dunbar's squadron.

"How are you doing?" asked the pilot, whispering.

"Pretty good," Yossarian answered.

"I saw you fall down just now. I thought something happened to you."

"I think I fainted."

"There's a rumor in my squadron that you told them you weren't going to fly any more combat missions."

"That's the truth."

"Then they came around from Group and told us that the rumor wasn't true, that you were just kidding around."

"That was a lie."

"Do you think they'll let you get away with it?"

"I don't know."

"What will they do to you?"

"I don't know."

"Do you think they'll court-martial you for desertion in the face of the enemy?"

"I don't know."

"I hope you get away with it," said the pilot in Dunbar's squadron, stealing out of sight into the shadows. "Let me know how you're doing."

Yossarian stared after him a few seconds and continued toward his tent.

"Pssst!" said a voice a few paces onward. It was Appleby, hiding in back of a tree. "How are you doing?"

"Pretty good," said Yossarian.

"I heard them say they were going to threaten to court-martial you for deserting in the face of the enemy. But that they wouldn't try to go through with it because they're not even sure they've got a case against you on that. And because it might make them look bad with the new commanders. Besides, you're still a pretty big hero for going around twice over the bridge at Ferrara. I guess you're just about the biggest hero we've got now in the group. I just thought you'd like to know that they'll only be bluffing."

"Thanks, Appleby."

"That's the only reason I started talking to you, to warn you."

"I appreciate it."

Appleby scuffed the toes of his shoes into the ground sheepishly. "I'm sorry we had that fist fight in the officers' club, Yossarian."

"That's all right."

"But I didn't start it. I guess that was all Orr's fault for hitting me in the face with his Ping-Pong paddle. What'd he want to do that for?"

"You were beating him."

"Wasn't I supposed to beat him? Isn't that the point? Now that he's dead, I guess it doesn't matter any more whether I'm a better Ping-Pong player or not, does it?"

"I guess not."

"And I'm sorry about making such a fuss about those Atabrine tablets on the way over. If you want to catch malaria, I guess it's your business, isn't it?"

"That's all right, Appleby."

"But I was only trying to do my duty. I was obeying orders. I was always taught that I had to obey orders."

"That's all right."

"You know, I said to Colonel Korn and Colonel Cathcart that I didn't think they ought to make you fly any more missions if you didn't want to, and they said they were very disappointed in me."

Yossarian smiled with rueful amusement. "I'll bet they are."

"Well, I don't care. Hell, you've flown seventy-one. That ought to be enough. Do you think they'll let you get away with it?"

"No."

"Say, if they do let you get away with it, they'll have to let the rest of us get away with it, won't they?"

"That's why they can't let me get away with it."

"What do you think they'll do?"

"I don't know."

"Do you think they will try to court-martial you?"

"I don't know."

"Are you afraid?"

"Yes."

"Are you going to fly more missions?"

"No."

"I hope you do get away with it," Appleby whispered with conviction. "I really do."

"Thanks, Appleby."

"I don't feel too happy about flying so many missions either now that it looks as though we've got the war won. I'll let you know if I hear anything else."

"Thanks, Appleby."

"Hey!" called a muted, peremptory voice from the leafless shrubs growing beside his tent in a waist-high clump after Appleby had gone. Havermeyer was hiding there in a squat. He was eating peanut brittle, and his pimples and large oily pores looked like dark scales. "How you doing?" he asked when Yossarian had walked to him.

"Pretty good."

"Are you going to fly more missions?"

"No."

"Suppose they try to make you?"

"I won't let them."

"Are you yellow?"

"Yes."

"Will they court-martial you?"

"They'll probably try."

"What did Major Major say?"

"Major Major's gone."

"Did they disappear him?"

"I don't know."

"What will you do if they decide to disappear you?"

"I'll try to stop them."

"Didn't they offer you any deals or anything if you did fly?"

"Piltchard and Wren said they'd arrange things so I'd only go on milk runs."

Havermeyer perked up. "Say, that sounds like a pretty good deal. I wouldn't mind a deal like that myself. I bet you snapped it up."

"I turned it down."

"That was dumb." Havermeyer's stolid, dull face furrowed with consternation. "Say, a deal like that wasn't so fair to the rest of us, was it? If you only flew on milk runs, then some of us would have to fly your share of the dangerous missions, wouldn't we?"

"That's right."

"Say, I don't like that," Havermeyer exclaimed, rising resentfully with his hands clenched on his hips. "I don't like that a bit. That's a real royal screwing they're getting ready to give me just because you're too goddam yellow to fly any more missions, isn't it?"

"Take it up with them," said Yossarian and moved his hand to his gun vigilantly.

"No, I'm not blaming you," said Havermeyer, "even though I don't like you. You know, I'm not too happy about flying so many missions any more either. Isn't there some way I can get out of it, too?"

Yossarian snickered ironically and joked, "Put a gun on and start marching with me."

Havermeyer shook his head thoughtfully. "Nah, I couldn't do that. I might bring some disgrace on my wife and kid if I acted like a coward. Nobody likes a coward. Besides, I want to stay in the reserves when the war is over. You get five hundred dollars a year if you stay in the reserves."

"Then fly more missions."

"Yeah, I guess I have to. Say, do you think there's any chance they might take you off combat duty and send you home?"

"No."

"But if they do and let you take one person with you, will you pick me? Don't pick anyone like Appleby. Pick me."

"Why in the world should they do something like that?"

"I don't know. But if they do, just remember that I asked you first, will you? And let me know how you're doing. I'll wait for you here in these bushes every night. Maybe if they don't do anything bad to you, I won't fly any more missions either. Okay?"

All the next evening, people kept popping up at him out of the darkness to ask him how he was doing, appealing to him for confidential information with weary, troubled faces on the basis of some morbid and clandestine kinship he had not guessed existed. People in the squadron he barely knew popped into sight out of nowhere as he passed and asked him how he was doing. Even men from other squadrons came one by one to conceal themselves in the darkness and pop out. Everywhere he stepped after sundown someone was lying in wait to pop out and ask him how he was doing. People popped out at him from trees and bushes, from ditches and tall weeds, from around the corners of tents and from behind the fenders of parked cars. Even one of his roommates popped out to ask him how he was doing and pleaded with him not to tell any of his other roommates he had popped out. Yossarian drew near each beckoning, overly cautious silhouette with his hand on his gun, never knowing which hissing shadow would finally turn dishonestly into Nately's whore or, worse, into some duly constituted governmental authority sent to club him ruthlessly into insensibility. It began to look as if they would have to do something like that. They did not want to court-martial him for desertion in the face of the enemy because a hundred and thirty-five miles away from the enemy could hardly be called the face of the enemy, and because Yossarian was the one who had finally knocked down the bridge at Ferrara by going around twice over the target and killing Kraft—he was always almost forgetting Kraft when he counted the dead men he knew. But they had to do something to him, and everyone waited grimly to see what horrible thing it would be.

During the day, they avoided him, even Aarfy, and Yossarian understood that they were different people together in daylight than they were alone in the dark. He did not care about them at all as he walked about backward with his hand on his gun and awaited the latest blandishments, threats and inducements from Group each time Captains Piltchard and Wren drove back from another urgent conference with Colonel Cathcart and Colonel Korn. Hungry Joe was hardly around, and the only other person who ever spoke to him was Captain Black, who called him "Old Blood and Guts" in a merry, taunting voice each time he hailed him and who came back from Rome toward the end of the week to tell him Nately's whore was gone. Yossarian turned sorry with a stab of yearning and remorse. He missed her.

"Gone?" he echoed in a hollow tone.

"Yeah, gone." Captain Black laughed, his bleary eyes narrow with fatigue and his peaked, sharp face sprouting as usual with a sparse reddish-blond stubble. He rubbed the bags under his eyes with both fists. "I thought I might as well give the stupid broad another boff just for old times' sake as long as I was in Rome anyway. You know, just to keep that kid Nately's body spinning in his grave, ha, ha! Remember the way I used to needle him? But the place was empty."

"Was there any word from her?" prodded Yossarian, who had been brooding incessantly about the girl, wondering how much she was suffering, and feeling almost lonely and deserted without her ferocious and unappeasable attacks.

"There's no one there," Captain Black exclaimed cheerfully, trying to make Yossarian understand. "Don't you understand? They're all gone. The whole place is busted."

"Gone?"

"Yeah, gone. Flushed right out into the street." Captain Black chuckled heartily again, and his pointed Adam's apple jumped up and down with glee inside his scraggly neck. "The joint's empty. The M.P.s busted the whole apartment up and drove the whores right out. Ain't that a laugh?"

Yossarian was scared and began to tremble. "Why'd they do that?"

"What difference does it make?" responded Captain Black with an exuberant gesture. "They flushed them right out into the street. How do you like that? The whole batch."

"What about the kid sister?"

"Flushed away," laughed. Captain Black. "Flushed away with the rest of the broads. Right out into the street."

"But she's only a kid!" Yossarian objected passionately. "She doesn't know anybody else in the whole city. What's going to happen to her?"

"What the hell do I care?" responded Captain Black with an indifferent shrug, and then gawked suddenly at Yossarian with surprise and with a crafty gleam of prying elation. "Say, what's the matter? If I knew this was going to make you so unhappy, I would have come right over and told you, just to make you eat your liver. Hey, where are you going? Come on back! Come on back here and eat your liver!"

39

The Eternal City

Yossarian was going absent without official leave with Milo, who, as the plane cruised toward Rome, shook his head reproachfully and, with pious lips pursed, informed Yossarian in ecclesiastical tones that he was ashamed of him. Yossarian nodded. Yossarian was making an uncouth spectacle of himself by walking around backward with his gun on his hip and refusing to fly more combat missions, Milo said. Yossarian nodded. It was disloyal to his squadron and embarrassing to his superiors. He was placing Milo in a very uncomfortable position, too. Yossarian nodded again. The men were starting to grumble. It was not fair for Yossarian to think only of his own safety while men like Milo, Colonel Cathcart, Colonel Korn and ex-P.F.C. Wintergreen were willing to do everything they could to win the war. The men with seventy missions were starting to grumble because they had to fly eighty, and there was a danger some of them might put on guns and begin walking around backward, too. Morale was deteriorating and it was all Yossarian's fault. The country was in peril; he was jeopardizing his traditional rights of freedom and independence by daring to exercise them.

Yossarian kept nodding in the co-pilot's seat and tried not to listen as Milo prattled on. Nately's whore was on his mind, as were Kraft and Orr and Nately and Dunbar, and Kid Sampson and McWatt, and all the poor and stupid and diseased people he had seen in Italy, Egypt and North Africa and knew about in other areas of the world, and Snowden and Nately's whore's kid sister were on his conscience, too. Yossarian thought he knew why Nately's whore held him responsible for Nately's death and wanted to kill him. Why the hell shouldn't she? It was a man's world, and she and everyone younger had every right to blame him and everyone older for every unnatural tragedy that befell them; just as she, even in her grief, was to blame for every man-made misery that landed on her kid sister and on all other children behind her. Someone had to do something sometime. Every victim was a culprit, every culprit a victim, and somebody had to stand up sometime to try to break the lousy chain of inherited habit that was imperiling them all. In parts of Africa little boys were still stolen away by adult slave traders and sold for money to men who disemboweled them and ate them. Yossarian marveled that children could suffer such barbaric sacrifice without evincing the slightest hint of fear or pain. He took it for granted that they did submit so stoically. If not, he reasoned, the custom would certainly have died, for no craving for wealth or immortality could be so great, he felt, as to subsist on the sorrow of children.

He was rocking the boat, Milo said, and Yossarian nodded once more. He was not a good member of the team, Milo said. Yossarian nodded and listened to Milo tell him that the decent thing to do if he did not like the way Colonel Cathcart and Colonel Korn were running the group was go to Russia, instead of stirring up trouble. Yossarian refrained from pointing out that Colonel Cathcart, Colonel Korn and Milo could all go to Russia if they did not like the way he was stirring up trouble. Colonel Cathcart and Colonel Korn had both been very good to Yossarian, Milo said; hadn't they given him a medal after the last mission to Ferrara and promoted him to captain? Yossarian nodded. Didn't they feed him and give him his pay every month? Yossarian nodded again. Milo was sure they would be charitable if he went to them to apologize and recant and promised to fly eighty missions. Yossarian said he would think it over, and held his breath and prayed for a safe landing as Milo dropped his wheels and glided in toward the runway. It was funny how he had really come to detest flying.

Rome was in ruins, he saw, when the plane was down. The airdrome had been bombed eight months before, and knobby slabs of white stone rubble had been bulldozed into flat-topped heaps on both sides of the entrance through the wire fence surrounding the field. The Colosseum was a dilapidated shell, and the Arch of Constantine had fallen. Nately's whore's apartment was a shambles. The girls were gone, and the only one there was the old woman. The windows in the apartment had been smashed. She was bundled up in sweaters and skirts and wore a dark shawl about her head. She sat on a wooden chair near an electric hot plate, her arms folded, boiling water in a battered aluminum pot. She was talking aloud to herself when Yossarian entered and began moaning as soon as she saw him.

"Gone," she moaned before he could even inquire. Holding her elbows, she rocked back and forth mournfully on her creaking chair. "Gone."

"Who?"

"All. All the poor young girls."

"Where?"

"Away. Chased away into the street. All of them gone. All the poor young girls."

"Chased away by who? Who did it?"

"The mean tall soldiers with the hard white hats and clubs. And by our *carabinieri.* They came with their clubs and chased them away. They would not even let them take their coats. The poor things. They just chased them away into the cold."

"Did they arrest them?"

"They chased them away. They just chased them away."

"Then why did they do it if they didn't arrest them?"

"I don't know," sobbed the old woman. "I don't know. Who will take care of me? Who will take care of me now that all the poor young girls are gone. Who will take care of me?"

"There must have been a reason," Yossarian persisted, pounding his fist into his hand. "They couldn't just barge in here and chase everyone out."

"No reason," wailed the old woman. "No reason."

"What right did they have?"

"Catch-22."

"*What?*" Yossarian froze in his tracks with fear and alarm and felt his whole body begin to tingle. "*What* did you say?"

"Catch-22," the old woman repeated, rocking her head up and down. "Catch-22. Catch-22 says they have a right to do anything we can't stop them from doing."

"What the hell are you talking about?" Yossarian shouted at her in bewildered, furious protest. "How did you know it was Catch-22? Who the hell told you it was Catch-22?"

"The soldiers with the hard white hats and clubs. The girls were crying. 'Did we do anything wrong?' they said. The men said no and pushed them away out the door with the ends of their clubs. 'Then why are you chasing us out?' the girls said. 'Catch-22,' the men said. 'What right do you have?' the girls said. 'Catch-22,' the men said. All they kept saying was 'Catch-22, Catch-22.' What does it mean, Catch-22? What is Catch-22?"

"Didn't they show it to you?" Yossarian demanded, stamping about in anger and distress. "Didn't you even make them read it?"

"They don't have to show us Catch-22," the old woman answered. "The law says they don't have to."

"What law says they don't have to?"

"Catch-22."

"Oh, God damn!" Yossarian exclaimed bitterly. "I bet it wasn't even really there." He stopped walking and glanced about the room disconsolately. "Where's the old man?"

"Gone," mourned the old woman.

"Gone?"

"Dead," the old woman told him, nodding in emphatic lament, pointing to her head with the flat of her hand. "Something broke in here. One minute he was living, one minute he was dead."

"But he can't be dead!" Yossarian cried, ready to argue insistently. But of course he knew it was true, knew it was logical and true: once again the old man had marched along with the majority.

Yossarian turned away and trudged through the apartment with a gloomy scowl, peering with pessimistic curiosity into all the rooms. Everything made of glass had been smashed by the men with the clubs. Torn drapes and bedding lay dumped on the floor. Chairs, tables and dressers had been overturned. Everything breakable had been broken. The destruction was total. No wild vandals could have been more thorough. Every window was smashed, and darkness poured like inky clouds into each room through the shattered panes. Yossarian could imagine the heavy, crashing footfalls of the tall M.P.s in the hard white hats. He could picture the fiery and malicious exhilaration with which they had made their wreckage, and their sanctimonious, ruthless sense of right and dedication. All the poor young girls were gone. Everyone was gone but the weeping old woman in the bulky brown and gray sweaters and black head shawl, and soon she too would be gone.

"Gone," she grieved, when he walked back in, before he could even speak. "Who will take care of me now?"

Yossarian ignored the question. "Nately's girl friend—did anyone hear from her?" he asked.

"Gone."

"I know she's gone. But did anyone hear from her? Does anyone know where she is?"

"Gone."

"The little sister. What happened to her?"

"Gone." The old woman's tone had not changed.

"Do you know what I'm talking about?" Yossarian asked sharply, staring into her eyes to see if she were not speaking to him from a coma. He raised his voice. "What happened to the kid sister, to the little girl?"

"Gone, gone," the old woman replied with a crabby shrug, irritated by his persistence, her low wail growing louder. "Chased away with the rest, chased away into the street. They would not even let her take her coat."

"Where did she go?"

"I don't know. I don't know."

"Who will take care of her?"

"Who will take care of me?"

"She doesn't know anybody else, does she?"

"Who will take care of me?"

Yossarian left money in the old woman's lap—it was odd how many wrongs leaving money seemed to right—and strode out of the apartment, cursing Catch-22 vehemently as he descended the stairs, even though he knew there was no such thing. Catch-22 did not exist, he was positive of that, but it made no difference. What did matter was that everyone thought it existed, and that was much worse, for there was no object or text to ridicule or refute, to accuse, criticize, attack, amend, hate, revile, spit at, rip to shreds, trample upon or burn up.

It was cold outside, and dark, and a leaky, insipid mist lay swollen in the air and trickled down the large, unpolished stone blocks of the houses and the pedestals of monuments. Yossarian hurried back to Milo and recanted. He said he was sorry and, knowing he was lying, promised to fly as many more missions as Colonel Cathcart wanted if Milo would only use all his influence in Rome to help him locate Nately's whore's kid sister.

"She's just a twelve-year-old virgin, Milo," he explained anxiously, "and I want to find her before it's too late."

Milo responded to his request with a benign smile. "I've got just the twelve-year-old virgin you're looking for," he announced jubilantly. "This twelve-year-old virgin is really only thirty-four, but she was brought up on a low-protein diet by very strict parents and didn't start sleeping with men until—"

"Milo, I'm talking about a little girl!" Yossarian interrupted him with desperate impatience. "Don't you understand? I don't want to sleep with her. I want to help her. You've got daughters. She's just a little kid, and she's all alone in this city with no one to take care of her. I want to protect her from harm. Don't you know what I'm talking about?"

Milo did understand and was deeply touched. "Yossarian, I'm proud of you," he exclaimed with profound emotion. "I really am. You don't know how glad I am to see that everything isn't always just sex with you. You've got principles. Certainly I've got daughters, and I know exactly what you're talking about. We'll find that girl. Don't you worry. You come with me and we'll find that girl if we have to turn this whole city upside down. Come along."

Yossarian went along in Milo Minderbinder's speeding M & M staff car to police headquarters to meet a swarthy, untidy police commissioner with a narrow black mustache and unbuttoned tunic who was fiddling with a stout woman with warts and two chins when they entered his office and who greeted Milo with warm surprise and bowed and scraped in obscene servility as though Milo were some elegant marquis.

"Ah, Marchese Milo," he declared with effusive pleasure, pushing the fat, disgruntled woman out the door without even looking toward her. "Why didn't you tell me you were coming? I would have a big party for you. Come in, come in, Marchese. You almost never visit us any more."

Milo knew that there was not one moment to waste. "Hello, Luigi," he said, nodding so briskly that he almost seemed rude. "Luigi, I need your help. My friend here wants to find a girl."

"A girl, Marchese?" said Luigi, scratching his face pensively. "There are lots of girls in Rome. For an American officer, a girl should not be too difficult."

"No, Luigi, you don't understand. This is a twelve-year-old virgin that he has to find right away."

"Ah, yes, now I understand," Luigi said sagaciously. "A virgin might take a little time. But if he waits at the bus terminal where the young farm girls looking for work arrive, I—"

"Luigi, you still don't understand," Milo snapped with such brusque impatience that the police commissioner's face flushed and he jumped to attention and began buttoning his uniform in confusion. "This girl is a friend, an old friend of the family, and we want to help her. She's only a child. She's all alone in this city somewhere, and we have to find her before somebody harms her. Now do you understand? Luigi, this is very important to me. I have a daughter the same age as that little girl, and nothing in the world means more to me right now than saving that poor child before it's too late. Will you help?"

"*Sì*, Marchese, now I understand," said Luigi. "And I will do everything in my power to find her. But tonight I have almost no men. Tonight all my men are busy trying to break up the traffic in illegal tobacco."

"Illegal tobacco?" asked Milo.

"Milo," Yossarian bleated faintly with a sinking heart, sensing at once that all was lost.

"*Sì,* Marchese," said Luigi. "The profit in illegal tobacco is so high that the smuggling is almost impossible to control."

"Is there really that much profit in illegal tobacco?" Milo inquired with keen interest, his rust-colored eyebrows arching avidly and his nostrils sniffing.

"Milo," Yossarian called to him. "Pay attention to *me,* will you?"

"*Sì,* Marchese," Luigi answered. "The profit in illegal tobacco is very high. The smuggling is a national scandal, Marchese, truly a national disgrace."

"Is that a fact?" Milo observed with a preoccupied smile and started toward the door as though in a spell.

"Milo!" Yossarian yelled, and bounded forward impulsively to intercept him. "Milo, you've got to help me."

"Illegal tobacco," Milo explained to him with a look of epileptic lust, struggling doggedly to get by. "Let me go. I've got to smuggle illegal tobacco."

"Stay here and help me find her," pleaded Yossarian. "You can smuggle illegal tobacco tomorrow."

But Milo was deaf and kept pushing forward, nonviolently but irresistibly, sweating, his eyes, as though he were in the grip of a blind fixation, burning feverishly, and his twitching mouth slavering. He moaned calmly as though in remote, instinctive distress and kept repeating, "Illegal tobacco, illegal tobacco." Yossarian stepped out of the way with resignation finally when he saw it was hopeless to try to reason with him. Milo was gone like a shot. The commissioner of police unbuttoned his tunic again and looked at Yossarian with contempt.

"What do you want here?" he asked coldly. "Do you want me to arrest you?"

Yossarian walked out of the office and down the stairs into the dark, tomblike street, passing in the hall the stout woman with warts and two chins, who was already on her way back in. There was no sign of Milo outside. There were no lights in any of the windows. The deserted sidewalk rose steeply and continuously for several blocks. He could see the glare of a broad avenue at the top of the long cobblestone incline. The police station was almost at the bottom; the yellow bulbs at the entrance sizzled in the dampness like wet torches. A frigid, fine rain was falling. He began walking slowly, pushing uphill. Soon he came to a quiet, cozy, inviting restaurant with red velvet drapes in the windows and a blue neon sign near the door that said: TONY'S RESTAURANT. FINE FOOD AND DRINK. KEEP OUT. The words on the blue neon sign surprised him mildly for only an instant. Nothing warped seemed bizarre any more in his strange, distorted surroundings. The tops of the sheer buildings slanted in weird, surrealistic perspective, and the street seemed tilted. He raised the collar of his warm woolen coat and hugged it around him. The night was raw. A boy in a thin shirt and thin tattered trousers walked out of the darkness on bare feet. The boy had black hair and needed a haircut and shoes and socks. His sickly face was pale and sad. His feet made grisly, soft, sucking sounds in the rain puddles on the wet pavement as he passed, and Yossarian was moved by such intense pity for his poverty that he wanted to smash his pale, sad, sickly face with his fist and knock him out of existence because he brought to mind *all* the pale, sad, sickly children in Italy that same night who needed haircuts and needed shoes and socks. He made Yossarian think of cripples and of cold and hungry men and women, and of all the dumb, passive, devout mothers with catatonic eyes nursing infants outdoors that same night with chilled animal udders bared insensibly to that same raw rain. Cows. Almost on cue, a nursing mother padded past holding an infant in black rags, and Yossarian wanted to smash her too, because she reminded him of the barefoot boy in the thin shirt and thin, tattered trousers and of all the shivering, stupefying misery in a world that never yet had provided enough heat and food and justice for all but an ingenious and unscrupulous handful. What a lousy earth! He wondered how many people were destitute that same night even in his own prosperous country, how many homes were shanties, how many husbands were drunk and wives socked, and how many children were bullied, abused or abandoned. How many families hungered for food they could not afford to buy? How many hearts were broken? How many suicides would take place that same night, how many people would go insane? How many cockroaches and landlords would triumph? How many winners were losers, successes failures, rich men poor men? How many wise guys were stupid? How many happy endings were unhappy endings? How many honest men were liars, brave men cowards, loyal men traitors, how many sainted men were corrupt, how many people in positions of trust had sold their souls to blackguards for petty cash, how many had never had souls? How many straight-and-narrow paths were crooked paths? How many best families were worst families and how many good people were bad people? When you added them all up and then subtracted, you might be left with only the children, and perhaps with Albert Einstein and an old violinist or sculptor somewhere. Yossarian walked in lonely torture, feeling estranged, and could not wipe from his mind the excruciating image of the barefoot boy with sickly cheeks until he turned the corner into the avenue finally and came upon an Allied soldier having convulsions on the ground, a young lieutenant with a small, pale, boyish face. Six other soldiers from different countries wrestled with different parts of him, striving to help him and hold him still. He yelped and groaned unintelligibly through clenched teeth, his eyes rolled up into his head. "Don't let him bite his tongue off," a short sergeant near Yossarian advised shrewdly, and a seventh man threw himself into the fray to wrestle with the ill lieutenant's face. All at once the wrestlers won and turned to each other undecidedly, for now that they held the young lieutenant rigid they did not know what to do with him. A quiver of moronic panic spread from one straining brute face to another. "Why don't you lift him up and put him on the hood of that car?" a corporal standing in back of Yossarian drawled. That seemed to make sense, so the seven men lifted the young lieutenant up and stretched him out carefully on the hood of a parked car, still pinning each struggling part of him down. Once they had him stretched out on the hood of the parked car, they stared at each other uneasily again, for they had no idea what to do with him next. "Why don't you lift him up off the hood of that car and lay him down on the ground?" drawled the same corporal behind Yossarian. That seemed like a good idea, too, and they began to move him back to the sidewalk, but before they could finish, a jeep raced up with a flashing red spotlight at the side and two military policemen in the front seat.

"What's going on?" the driver yelled.

"He's having convulsions," one of the men grappling with one of the young lieutenant's limbs answered. "We're holding him still."

"That's good. He's under arrest."

"What should we do with him?"

"Keep him under arrest!" the M.P. shouted, doubling over with raucous laughter at his jest, and sped away in his jeep.

Yossarian recalled that he had no leave papers and moved prudently past the strange group toward the sound of muffled voices emanating from a distance inside the murky darkness ahead. The broad, rain-blotched boulevard was illuminated every half-block by short, curling lampposts with eerie, shimmering glares surrounded by smoky brown mist. From a window overhead he heard an unhappy female voice pleading, "Please don't. Please don't." A despondent young woman in a black raincoat with much black hair on her face passed with her eyes lowered. At the Ministry of Public Affairs on the next block, a drunken lady was backed up against one of the fluted Corinthian columns by a drunken young soldier, while three drunken comrades in arms sat watching nearby on the steps with wine bottles scantling between their legs. "Pleeshe don't," begged the drunken lady. "I want to go home now. Pleeshe don't." One of the three sitting men cursed pugnaciously and hurled a wine bottle down at Yossarian when he turned to look up. The bottle shattered harmlessly far away with a brief and muted noise. Yossarian continued walking away at the same listless, unhurried pace, hands buried in his pockets. "Come on, baby," he heard the drunken soldier urge determinedly. "Its my turn now." "Pleeshe don't," begged the drunken lady. "Pleeshe don't." At the very next corner, deep inside the dense, impenetrable shadows of a narrow, winding side street, he heard the mysterious, unmistakable sound of someone shoveling snow. The measured, labored, evocative scrape of iron shovel against concrete made his flesh crawl with terror as he stepped from the curb to cross the ominous alley and hurried onward until the haunting, incongruous noise had been left behind. Now he knew where he was; soon, if he continued without turning, he would come to the dry fountain in the middle of the boulevard, then to the officers' apartment seven blocks beyond. He heard snarling, inhuman voices cutting through the ghostly blackness in front suddenly. The bulb on the corner lamppost had died, spilling gloom over half the street, throwing everything visible off balance. On the other side of the intersection, a man was beating a dog with a stick like the man who was beating the horse with a whip in Raskolnikov's dream. Yossarian strained helplessly not to see or hear. The dog whimpered and squealed in brute, dumbfounded hysteria at the end of an old Manila rope and groveled and crawled on its belly without resisting, but the man beat it and beat it anyway with his heavy, flat stick. A small crowd watched. A squat woman stepped out and asked him please to stop. "Mind your own business," the man barked gruffly, lifting his stick as though he might beat her too, and the woman retreated sheepishly with an abject and humiliated air. Yossarian quickened his pace to get away, almost ran. The night was filled with horrors, and he thought he knew how Christ must have felt as he walked through the world, like a psychiatrist through a ward full of nuts, like a victim through a prison full of thieves. What a welcome sight a leper must have been! At the next corner a man was beating a small boy brutally in the midst of an immobile crowd of adult spectators who made no effort to intervene. Yossarian recoiled with sickening recognition. He was certain he had witnessed that same horrible scene sometime before. *Déjà vu?* The sinister coincidence shook him and filled him with doubt and dread. It was the same scene he had witnessed a block before, although everything in it seemed quite different. What in the world was happening? Would a squat woman step out and ask the man to please stop? Would he raise his hand to strike her and would she retreat? Nobody moved. The child cried steadily as though in drugged misery. The man kept knocking him down with hard, resounding open-palm blows to the head, then jerking him up to his feet in order to knock him down again. No one in the sullen, cowering crowd seemed to care enough about the stunned and beaten boy to interfere. The child was no more than nine. One drab woman was weeping silently into a dirty dish towel. The boy was emaciated and needed a haircut. Bright-red blood was streaming from both ears. Yossarian crossed quickly to the other side of the immense avenue to escape the nauseating sight and found himself walking on human teeth lying on the drenched, glistening pavement near splotches of blood kept sticky by the pelting raindrops poking each one like sharp fingernails. Molars and broken incisors lay scattered everywhere. He circled on tiptoe the grotesque debris and came near a doorway containing a crying soldier holding a saturated handkerchief to his mouth, supported as he sagged by two other soldiers waiting in grave impatience for the military ambulance that finally came clanging up with amber fog lights on and passed them by for an altercation on the next block between a single civilian Italian with books and a slew of civilian policemen with armlocks and clubs. The screaming, struggling civilian was a dark man with a face white as flour from fear. His eyes were pulsating in hectic desperation, flapping like bat's wings, as the many tall policemen seized him by the arms and legs and lifted him up. His books were spilled on the ground. "Help!" he shrieked shrilly in a voice strangling in its own emotion, as the policemen carried him to the open doors in the rear of the ambulance and threw him inside. "Police! Help! Police!" The doors were shut and bolted, and the ambulance raced away. There was a humorless irony in the ludicrous panic of the man screaming for help to the police while policemen were all around him. Yossarian smiled wryly at the futile and ridiculous cry for aid, then saw with a start that the words were ambiguous, realized with alarm that they were not, perhaps, intended as a call for police but as a heroic warning from the grave by a doomed friend to everyone who was *not* a policeman with a club and a gun and a mob of other policemen with clubs and guns to back him up. "Help! Police!" the man had cried, and he could have been shouting of danger. Yossarian responded to the thought by slipping away stealthily from the police and almost tripped over the feet of a burly woman of forty hastening across the intersection guiltily, darting furtive, vindictive glances behind her toward a woman of eighty with thick, bandaged ankles doddering after her in a losing pursuit. The old woman was gasping for breath as she minced along and muttering to herself in distracted agitation. There was no mistaking the nature of the scene; it was a chase. The triumphant first woman was halfway across the wide avenue before the second woman reached the curb. The nasty, small, gloating smile with which she glanced back at the laboring old woman was both wicked and apprehensive. Yossarian knew he could help the troubled old woman if she would only cry out, knew he could spring forward and capture the sturdy first woman and hold her for the mob of policemen nearby if the second woman would only give him license with a shriek of distress. But the old woman passed by without even seeing him, mumbling in terrible, tragic vexation, and soon the first woman had vanished into the deepening layers of darkness and the old woman was left standing helplessly in the center of the thoroughfare, dazed, uncertain which way to proceed, alone. Yossarian tore his eyes from her and hurried away in shame because he had done nothing to assist her. He darted furtive, guilty glances back as he fled in defeat, afraid the old woman might now start following him, and he welcomed the concealing shelter of the drizzling, drifting, lightless, nearly opaque gloom. Mobs . . . mobs of policemen—everything but England was in the hands of mobs, mobs, mobs. Mobs with clubs were in control everywhere.

The surface of the collar and shoulders of Yossarian's coat was soaked. His socks were wet and cold. The light on the next lamppost was out, too, the glass globe broken. Buildings and featureless shapes flowed by him noiselessly as though borne past immutably on the surface of some rank and timeless tide. A tall monk passed, his face buried entirely inside a coarse gray cowl, even the eyes hidden. Footsteps sloshed toward him steadily through a puddle, and he feared it would be another barefoot child. He brushed by a gaunt, cadaverous, tristful man in a black raincoat with a star-shaped scar in his cheek and a glossy mutilated depression the size of an egg in one temple. On squishing straw sandals, a young woman materialized with her whole face disfigured by a God-awful pink and piebald burn that started on her neck and stretched in a raw, corrugated mass up both cheeks past her eyes! Yossarian could not bear to look, and shuddered. No one would ever love her. His spirit was sick; he longed to lie down with some girl he could love who would soothe and excite him and put him to sleep. A mob with a club was waiting for him in Pianosa. The girls were all gone. The countess and her daughter-in-law were no longer good enough; he had grown too old for fun, he no longer had the time. Luciana was gone, dead, probably; if not yet then soon enough. Aarfy's buxom trollop had vanished with her smutty cameo ring, and Nurse Duckett was ashamed of him because he had refused to fly more combat missions and would cause a scandal. The only girl he knew nearby was the plain maid in the officers' apartment, whom none of the men had ever slept with. Her name was Michaela, but the men called her filthy things in dulcet, ingratiating voices, and she giggled with childish joy because she understood no English and thought they were flattering her and making harmless jokes. Everything wild she watched them do filled her with enchanted delight. She was a happy, simple-minded, hard-working girl who could not read and was barely able to write her name. Her straight hair was the color of retting straw. She had sallow skin and myopic eyes, and none of the men had ever slept with her because none of the men had ever wanted to, none but Aarfy, who had raped her once that same evening and had then held her prisoner in a clothes closet for almost two hours with his hand over her mouth until the civilian curfew sirens sounded and it was unlawful for her to be outside.

Then he threw her out the window. Her dead body was still lying on the pavement when Yossarian arrived and pushed his way politely through the circle of solemn neighbors with dim lanterns, who glared with venom as they shrank away from him and pointed up bitterly toward the second-floor windows in their private, grim, accusing conversations. Yossarian's heart pounded with fright and horror at the pitiful, ominous, gory spectacle of the broken corpse. He ducked into the hallway and bolted up the stairs into the apartment, where he found Aarfy pacing about uneasily with a pompous, slightly uncomfortable smile. Aarfy seemed a bit unsettled as he fidgeted with his pipe and assured Yossarian that everything was going to be all right. There was nothing to worry about.

"I only raped her once," he explained.

Yossarian was aghast. "But you killed her, Aarfy! You killed her!"

"Oh, I had to do that after I raped her," Aarfy replied in his most condescending manner. "I couldn't very well let her go around saying bad things about us, could I?"

"But why did you have to touch her at all, you dumb bastard?" Yossarian shouted. "Why couldn't you get yourself a girl off the street if you wanted one? The city is full of prostitutes."

"Oh, no, not me," Aarfy bragged. "I never paid for it in my life."

"Aarfy, are you insane?" Yossarian was almost speechless. "You *killed* a girl. They're going to put you in jail!"

"Oh, no," Aarfy answered with a forced smile. "Not me. They aren't going to put good old Aarfy in jail. Not for killing *her.*"

"But you threw her out the window. She's lying there dead in the street."

"She has no right to be there," Aarfy answered. "It's after curfew."

"Stupid! Don't you realize what you've done?" Yossarian wanted to grab Aarfy by his well-fed, caterpillar-soft shoulders and shake some sense into him. "You've murdered a human being. They *are* going to put you in jail. They might even *hang* you!"

"Oh, I hardly think they'll do that," Aarfy replied with a jovial chuckle, although his symptoms of nervousness increased. He spilled tobacco crumbs unconsciously as his short fingers fumbled with the bowl of his pipe. "No, sirree. Not to good old Aarfy" He chortled again. "She was only a servant girl. I hardly think they're going to make too much of a fuss over one poor Italian servant girl when so many thousands of lives are being lost every day. Do you?"

"Listen!" Yossarian cried, almost in joy. He pricked up his ears and watched the blood drain from Aarfy's face as sirens mourned far away, police sirens, and then ascended almost instantaneously to a howling, strident, onrushing cacophony of overwhelming sound that seemed to crash into the room around them from every side. "Aarfy, they're coming for you," he said in a flood of compassion, shouting to be heard above the noise. "They're coming to arrest you. Aarfy, don't you understand? You can't take the life of another human being and get away with it, even if she is just a poor servant girl. Don't you see? Can't you understand?"

"Oh, no," Aarfy insisted with a lame laugh and a weak smile. "They're not coming to arrest me. Not good old Aarfy."

All at once he looked sick. He sank down on a chair in a trembling stupor, his stumpy, lax hands quaking in his lap. Cars skidded to a stop outside. Spotlights hit the windows immediately. Car doors slammed and police whistles screeched. Voices rose harshly. Aarfy was green. He kept shaking his head mechanically with a queer, numb smile and repeating in a weak, hollow monotone that they were not coming for him, not for good old Aarfy, no sirree, striving to convince himself that this was so even as heavy footsteps raced up the stairs and pounded across the landing, even as fists beat on the door four times with a deafening, inexorable force. Then the door to the apartment flew open, and two large, tough, brawny M.P.s with icy eyes and firm, sinewy, unsmiling jaws entered quickly, strode across the room, and arrested Yossarian.

They arrested Yossarian for being in Rome without a pass.

They apologized to Aarfy for intruding and led Yossarian away between them, gripping him under each arm with fingers as hard as steel manacles. They said nothing at all to him on the way down. Two more tall M.P.s with clubs and hard white helmets were waiting outside at a closed car. They marched Yossarian into the back seat, and the car roared away and weaved through the rain and muddy fog to a police station. The M.P.s locked him up for the night in a cell with four stone walls. At dawn they gave him a pail for a latrine and drove him to the airport, where two more giant M.P.s with clubs and white helmets were waiting at a transport plane whose engines were already warming up when they arrived, the cylindrical green cowlings oozing quivering beads of condensation. None of the M.P.s said anything to each other either. They did not even nod. Yossarian had never seen such granite faces. The plane flew to Pianosa. Two more silent M.P.s were waiting at the landing strip. There were now eight, and they filed with precise, wordless discipline into two cars and sped on humming tires past the four squadron areas to the Group Headquarters building, where still two more M.P.s were waiting at the parking area. All ten tall, strong, purposeful, silent men towered around him as they turned toward the entrance. Their footsteps crunched in loud unison on the cindered ground. He had an impression of accelerating haste. He was terrified. Every one of the ten M.P.s seemed powerful enough to bash him to death with a single blow. They had only to press their massive, toughened, boulderous shoulders against him to crush all life from his body. There was nothing he could do to save himself. He could not even see which two were gripping him under the arms as they marched him rapidly between the two tight single-file columns they had formed. Their pace quickened, and he felt as though he were flying along with his feet off the ground as they trotted in resolute cadence up the wide marble staircase to the upper landing, where still two more inscrutable military policemen with hard faces were waiting to lead them all at an even faster pace down the long, cantilevered balcony overhanging the immense lobby. Their marching footsteps on the dull tile floor thundered like an awesome, quickening drum roll through the vacant center of the building as they moved with even greater speed and precision toward Colonel Cathcart's office, and violent winds of panic began blowing in Yossarian's ears when they turned him toward his doom inside the office, where Colonel Korn, his rump spreading comfortably on a corner of Colonel Cathcart's desk, sat waiting to greet him with a genial smile and said,

"We're sending you home."

40

Catch-22

There was, of course, a catch.

"Catch-22?" inquired Yossarian.

"Of course," Colonel Korn answered pleasantly, after he had chased the mighty guard of massive M.P.s out with an insouciant flick of his hand and a slightly contemptuous nod—most relaxed, as always, when he could be most cynical. His rimless square eyeglasses glinted with sly amusement as he gazed at Yossarian. "After all, we can't simply send you home for refusing to fly more missions and keep the rest of the men here, can we? That would hardly be fair to them."

"You're goddam right!" Colonel Cathcart blurted out, lumbering back and forth gracelessly like a winded bull, puffing and pouting angrily. "I'd like to tie him up hand and foot and throw him aboard a plane on every mission. That's what I'd like to do."

Colonel Korn motioned Colonel Cathcart to be silent and smiled at Yossarian. "You know, you really have been making things terribly difficult for Colonel Cathcart," he observed with flip good humor, as though the fact did not displease him at all. "The men are unhappy and morale is beginning to deteriorate. And it's all your fault."

"It's your fault," Yossarian argued, "for raising the number of missions."

"No, it's your fault for refusing to fly them," Colonel Korn retorted. "The men were perfectly content to fly as many missions as we asked as long as they thought they had no alternative. Now you've given them hope, and they're unhappy. So the blame is all yours."

"Doesn't he know there's a war going on?" Colonel Cathcart, still stamping back and forth, demanded morosely without looking at Yossarian.

"I'm quite sure he does," Colonel Korn answered. "That's probably why he refuses to fly them."

"Doesn't it make any difference to him?"

"Will the knowledge that there's a war going on weaken your decision to refuse to participate in it?" Colonel Korn inquired with sarcastic seriousness, mocking Colonel Cathcart.

"No, sir," Yossarian replied, almost returning Colonel Korn's smile.

"I was afraid of that," Colonel Korn remarked with an elaborate sigh, locking his fingers together comfortably on top of his smooth, bald, broad, shiny brown head. "You know, in all fairness, we really haven't treated you too badly, have we? We've fed you and paid you on time. We gave you a medal and even made you a captain."

"I never should have made him a captain," Colonel Cathcart exclaimed bitterly. "I should have given him a court-martial after he loused up that Ferrara mission and went around twice."

"I told you not to promote him," said Colonel Korn, "but you wouldn't listen to me."

"No you didn't. You told me to promote him, didn't you?"

"I told you *not* to promote him. But you just wouldn't listen."

"I should have listened."

"You never listen to me," Colonel Korn persisted with relish. "That's the reason we're in this spot."

"All right, gee whiz. Stop rubbing it in, will you?" Colonel Cathcart burrowed his fists down deep inside his pockets and turned away in a slouch. "Instead of picking on me, why don't you figure out what we're going to do about him?"

"We're going to send him home, I'm afraid." Colonel Korn was chuckling triumphantly when he turned away from Colonel Cathcart to face Yossarian. "Yossarian, the war is over for you. We're going to send you home. You really don't deserve it, you know, which is one of the reasons I don't mind doing it. Since there's nothing else we can risk doing to you at this time, we've decided to return you to the States. We've worked out this little deal to—"

"What kind of deal?" Yossarian demanded with defiant mistrust.

Colonel Korn tossed his head back and laughed. "Oh, a thoroughly despicable deal, make no mistake about that. It's absolutely revolting. But you'll accept it quickly enough."

"Don't be too sure."

"I haven't the slightest doubt you will, even though it stinks to high heaven. Oh, by the way. You haven't told any of the men you've refused to fly more missions, have you?"

"No, sir," Yossarian answered promptly.

Colonel Korn nodded approvingly. "That's good. I like the way you lie. You'll go far in this world if you ever acquire some decent ambition."

"Doesn't he know there's a war going on?" Colonel Cathcart yelled out suddenly, and blew with vigorous disbelief into the open end of his cigarette holder.

"I'm quite sure he does," Colonel Korn replied acidly, "since you brought that identical point to his attention just a moment ago." Colonel Korn frowned wearily for Yossarian's benefit, his eyes twinkling swarthily with sly and daring scorn. Gripping the edge of Colonel Cathcart's desk with both hands, he lifted his flaccid haunches far back on the corner to sit with both short legs dangling freely. His shoes kicked lightly against the yellow oak wood, his sludge-brown socks, garterless, collapsed in sagging circles below ankles that were surprisingly small and white. "You know, Yossarian," he mused affably in a manner of casual reflection that seemed both derisive and sincere, "I really do admire you a bit. You're an intelligent person of great moral character who has taken a very courageous stand. I'm an intelligent person with no moral character at all, so I'm in an ideal position to appreciate it."

"These are very critical times," Colonel Cathcart asserted petulantly from a far corner of the office, paying no attention to Colonel Korn.

"Very critical times indeed," Colonel Korn agreed with a placid nod. "We've just had a change of command above, and we can't afford a situation that might put us in a bad light with either General Scheisskopf or General Peckem. Isn't that what you mean, Colonel?"

"Hasn't he got any patriotism?"

"Won't you fight for your country?" Colonel Korn demanded, emulating Colonel Cathcart's harsh, self-righteous tone. "Won't you give up your life for Colonel Cathcart and me?"

Yossarian tensed with alert astonishment when he heard Colonel Korn's concluding words. "What's that?" he exclaimed. "What have you and Colonel Cathcart got to do with my country? You're not the same."

"How can you separate us?" Colonel Korn inquired with ironical tranquility.

"That's right," Colonel Cathcart cried emphatically. "You're either for us or against us. There's no two ways about it."

"I'm afraid he's got you," added Colonel Korn. "You're either *for* us or against your country. It's as simple as that."

"Oh, no, Colonel. I don't buy that."

Colonel Korn was unruffled. "Neither do I, frankly, but everyone else will. So there you are."

"You're a disgrace to your uniform!" Colonel Cathcart declared with blustering wrath, whirling to confront Yossarian for the first time. "I'd like to know how you ever got to be a captain, anyway."

"You promoted him," Colonel Korn reminded sweetly, stifling a snicker. "Don't you remember?"

"Well, I never should have done it."

"I told you not to do it," Colonel Korn said. "But you just wouldn't listen to me."

"Gee whiz, will you stop rubbing it in?" Colonel Cathcart cried. He furrowed his brow and glowered at Colonel Korn through eyes narrow with suspicion, his fists clenched on his hips. "Say, whose side are you on, anyway?"

"Your side, Colonel. What other side could I be on?"

"Then stop picking on me, will you? Get off my back, will you?"

"I'm on your side, Colonel. I'm just loaded with patriotism."

"Well, just make sure you don't forget that." Colonel Cathcart turned away grudgingly after another moment, incompletely reassured, and began striding the floor again, his hands kneading his long cigarette holder. He jerked a thumb toward Yossarian. "Let's settle with him. I know what I'd like to do with him. I'd like to take him outside and shoot him. That's what I'd like to do with him. That's what General Dreedle would do with him."

"But General Dreedle isn't with us any more," said Colonel Korn, "so we can't take him outside and shoot him." Now that his moment of tension with Colonel Cathcart had passed, Colonel Korn relaxed again and resumed kicking softly against Colonel Cathcart's desk. He returned to Yossarian. "So we're going to send you home instead. It took a bit of thinking, but we finally worked out this horrible little plan for sending you home without causing too much dissatisfaction among the friends you'll leave behind. Doesn't that make you happy?"

"What kind of plan? I'm not sure I'm going to like it."

"I know you're not going to like it." Colonel Korn laughed, locking his hands contentedly on top of his head again. "You're going to loathe it. It really is odious and certainly will offend your conscience. But you'll agree to it quickly enough. You'll agree to it because it will send you home safe and sound in two weeks, and because you have no choice. It's that or a court-martial. Take it or leave it."

Yossarian snorted. "Stop bluffing, Colonel. You can't court-martial me for desertion in the face of the enemy. It would make you look bad and you probably couldn't get a conviction."

"But we can court-martial you now for desertion from duty, since you went to Rome without a pass. And we could make it stick. If you think about it a minute, you'll see that you'd leave us no alternative. We can't simply let you keep walking around in open insubordination without punishing you. All the other men would stop flying missions, too. No, you have my word for it. We will court-martial you if you turn our deal down, even though it would raise a lot of questions and be a terrible black eye for Colonel Cathcart."

Colonel Cathcart winced at the words "black eye" and, without any apparent premeditation, hurled his slender onyx-and-ivory cigarette holder down viciously on the wooden surface on his desk. "Jesus Christ!" he shouted unexpectedly. "I hate this goddam cigarette holder!" The cigarette holder bounced off the desk to the wall, ricocheted across the window sill to the floor and came to a stop almost where he was standing. Colonel Cathcart stared down at it with an irascible scowl. "I wonder if it's really doing me any good."

"It's a feather in your cap with General Peckem, but a black eye for you with General Scheisskopf," Colonel Korn informed him with a mischievous look of innocence.

"Well, which one am I supposed to please?"

"Both."

"How can I please them both? They hate each other. How am I ever going to get a feather in my cap from General Scheisskopf without getting a black eye from General Peckem?"

"March."

"Yeah, march. That's the only way to please him. March. March." Colonel Cathcart grimaced sullenly. "Some generals! They're a disgrace to their uniforms. If people like those two can make general, I don't see how I can miss."

"You're going to go far," Colonel Korn assured him with a flat lack of conviction, and turned back chuckling to Yossarian, his disdainful merriment increasing at the sight of Yossarian's unyielding expression of antagonism and distrust. "And there you have the crux of the situation. Colonel Cathcart wants to be a general and I want to be a colonel, and that's why we have to send you home."

"Why does he want to be a general?"

"Why? For the same reason that I want to be a colonel. What else have we got to do? Everyone teaches us to aspire to higher things. A general is higher than a colonel, and a colonel is higher than a lieutenant colonel. So we're both aspiring. And you know, Yossarian, it's a lucky thing for you that we are. Your timing on this is absolutely perfect, but I suppose you took that factor into account in your calculations."

"I haven't been doing any calculating," Yossarian retorted.

"Yes, I really do enjoy the way you lie," Colonel Korn answered. "Won't it make you proud to have your commanding officer promoted to general—to know you served in an outfit that averaged more combat missions per person than any other? Don't you want to earn more unit citations and more oak leaf clusters for your Air Medal? Where's your *'sprit de corps?* Don't you want to contribute further to this great record by flying more combat missions? It's your last chance to answer yes."

"No."

"In that case, you have us over a barrel—" said Colonel Korn without rancor.

"He ought to be ashamed of himself!"

"—and we have to send you home. Just do a few little things for us, and—"

"What sort of things?" Yossarian interrupted with belligerent misgiving.

"Oh, tiny, insignificant things. Really, this is a very generous deal we're making with you. We will issue orders returning you to the States—really, we will—and all you have to do in return is . . ."

"What? What must I do?"

Colonel Korn laughed curtly. "Like us."

Yossarian blinked. "Like you?"

"Like us."

"Like you?"

"That's right," said Colonel Korn, nodding, gratified immeasurably by Yossarian's guileless surprise and bewilderment. "Like us. Join us. Be our pal. Say nice things about us here and back in the States. Become one of the boys. Now, that isn't asking too much, is it?"

"You just want me to like you? Is that all?"

"That's all."

"That's all?"

"Just find it in your heart to like us."

Yossarian wanted to laugh confidently when he saw with amazement that Colonel Korn was telling the truth. "That isn't going to be too easy," he sneered.

"Oh, it will be a lot easier than you think," Colonel Korn taunted in return, undismayed by Yossarian's barb. "You'll be surprised at how easy you'll find it to like us once you begin." Colonel Korn hitched up the waist of his loose, voluminous trousers. The deep black grooves isolating his square chin from his jowls were bent again in a kind of jeering and reprehensible mirth. "You see, Yossarian, we're going to put you on easy street. We're going to promote you to major and even give you another medal. Captain Flume is already working on glowing press releases describing your valor over Ferrara, your deep and abiding loyalty to your outfit and your consummate dedication to duty. Those phrases are all actual quotations, by the way. We're going to glorify you and send you home a hero, recalled by the Pentagon for morale and public-relations purposes. You'll live like a millionaire. Everyone will lionize you. You'll have parades in your honor and make speeches to raise money for war bonds. A whole new world of luxury awaits you once you become our pal. Isn't it lovely?"

Yossarian found himself listening intently to the fascinating elucidation of details. "I'm not sure I want to make speeches."

"Then we'll forget the speeches. The important thing is what you say to people here." Colonel Korn leaned forward earnestly, no longer smiling. "We don't want any of the men in the group to know that we're sending you home as a result of your refusal to fly more missions. And we don't want General Peckem or General Scheisskopf to get wind of any friction between us, either. That's why we're going to become such good pals."

"What will I say to the men who asked me why I refused to fly more missions?"

"Tell them you had been informed in confidence that you were being returned to the States and that you were unwilling to risk your life for another mission or two. Just a minor disagreement between pals, that's all."

"Will they believe it?"

"Of course they'll believe it, once they see what great friends we've become and when they see the press releases and read the flattering things you have to say about me and Colonel Cathcart. Don't worry about the men. They'll be easy enough to discipline and control when you've gone. It's only while you're still here that they may prove troublesome. You know, one good apple can spoil the rest," Colonel Korn concluded with conscious irony. "You know—this would really be wonderful—you might even serve as an inspiration to them to fly more missions."

"Suppose I denounce you when I get back to the States?"

"After you've accepted our medal and promotion and all the fanfare? No one would believe you, the Army wouldn't let you, and why in the world should you want to? You're going to be one of the boys, remember? You'll enjoy a rich, rewarding, luxurious, privileged existence. You'd have to be a fool to throw it all away just for a moral principle, and you're not a fool. Is it a deal?"

"I don't know."

"It's that or a court-martial."

"That's a pretty scummy trick I'd be playing on the men in the squadron, isn't it?"

"Odious," Colonel Korn agreed amiably, and waited, watching Yossarian patiently with a glimmer of private delight.

"But what the hell!" Yossarian exclaimed. "If they don't want to fly more missions, let them stand up and do something about it the way I did. Right?"

"Of course," said Colonel Korn.

"There's no reason I have to risk my life for them, is there?"

"Of course not."

Yossarian arrived at his decision with a swift grin. "It's a deal!" he announced jubilantly.

"Great," said Colonel Korn with somewhat less cordiality than Yossarian had expected, and he slid himself off Colonel Cathcart's desk to stand on the floor. He tugged the folds of cloth of his pants and undershorts free from his crotch and gave Yossarian a limp hand to shake. "Welcome aboard."

"Thanks, Colonel. I—"

"Call me Blackie, John. We're pals now."

"Sure, Blackie. My friends call me Yo-Yo. Blackie, I—"

"His friends call him Yo-Yo," Colonel Korn sang out to Colonel Cathcart. "Why don't you congratulate Yo-Yo on what a sensible move he's making?"

"That's a real sensible move you're making, Yo-Yo," Colonel Cathcart said, pumping Yossarian's hand with clumsy zeal.

"Thank you, Colonel, I—"

"Call him Chuck," said Colonel Korn.

"Sure, call me Chuck," said Colonel Cathcart with a laugh that was hearty and awkward. "We're all pals now."

"Sure, Chuck."

"Exit smiling," said Colonel Korn, his hands on both their shoulders as the three of them moved to the door.

"Come on over for dinner with us some night, Yo-Yo," Colonel

Cathcart invited hospitably. "How about tonight? In the Group dining room."

"I'd love to, sir."

"Chuck," Colonel Korn corrected reprovingly.

"I'm sorry, Blackie. Chuck. I can't get used to it."

"That's all right, pal."

"Sure, pal."

"Thanks, pal."

"Don't mention it, pal."

"So long, pal."

Yossarian waved goodbye fondly to his new pals and sauntered out onto the balcony corridor, almost bursting into song the instant he was alone. He was home free: he had pulled it off; his act of rebellion had succeeded; he was safe, and he had nothing to be ashamed of to anyone. He started toward the staircase with a jaunty and exhilarated air. A private in green fatigues saluted him. Yossarian returned the salute happily, staring at the private with curiosity. He looked strangely familiar. When Yossarian returned the salute, the private in green fatigues turned suddenly into Nately's whore and lunged at him murderously with a bone-handled kitchen knife that caught him in the side below his upraised arm. Yossarian sank to the floor with a shriek, shutting his eyes in overwhelming terror as he saw the girl lift the knife to strike him again. He was already unconscious when Colonel Korn and Colonel Cathcart dashed out of the office and saved his life by frightening her away.

41

Snowden

"Cut," said a doctor.

"You cut," said another.

"No cuts," said Yossarian with a thick, unwieldy tongue.

"Now look who's butting in," complained one of the doctors. "Another county heard from. Are we going to operate or aren't we?"

"He doesn't need an operation," complained the other. "It's a small wound. All we have to do is stop the bleeding, clean it out and put a few stitches in."

"But I've never had a chance to operate before. Which one is the scalpel? Is this one the scalpel?"

"No, the other one is the scalpel. Well, go ahead and cut already if you're going to. Make the incision."

"Like this?"

"Not there, you dope!"

"No incisions," Yossarian said, perceiving through the lifting fog of insensibility that two strangers were ready to begin cutting him.

"Another county heard from," complained the first doctor sarcastically. "Is he going to keep talking that way while I operate on him?"

"You can't operate on him until I admit him," said a clerk.

"You can't admit him until I clear him," said a fat, gruff colonel with a mustache and an enormous pink face that pressed down very close to Yossarian and radiated scorching heat like the bottom of a huge frying pan. "Where were you born?"

The fat, gruff colonel reminded Yossarian of the fat, gruff colonel who had interrogated the chaplain and found him guilty. Yossarian stared up at him through a glassy film. The cloying scents of formaldehyde and alcohol sweetened the air.

"On a battlefield," he answered.

"No, no. In what state were you born?"

"In a state of innocence."

"No, no, you don't understand."

"Let me handle him," urged a hatchet-faced man with sunken acrimonious eyes and a thin, malevolent mouth. "Are you a smart aleck or something?" he asked Yossarian.

"He's delirious," one of the doctors said. "Why don't you let us take him back inside and treat him?"

"Leave him right here if he's delirious. He might say something incriminating."

"But he's still bleeding profusely. Can't you see? He might even die."

"*Good* for him!"

"It would serve the finky bastard right," said the fat, gruff colonel. "All right, John, let's speak out. We want to get to the truth."

"Everyone calls me Yo-Yo."

"We want you to cooperate with us, Yo-Yo. We're your friends and we want you to trust us. We're here to help you. We're not going to hurt you."

"Let's jab our thumbs down inside his wound and gouge it," suggested the hatchet-faced man.

Yossarian let his eyes fall closed and hoped they would think he was unconscious.

"He's fainted," he heard a doctor say. "Can't we treat him now before it's too late? He really might die."

"All right, take him. I hope the bastard does die."

"You can't treat him until I admit him," the clerk said.

Yossarian played dead with his eyes shut while the clerk admitted him by shuffling some papers, and then he was rolled away slowly into a stuffy, dark room with searing spotlights overhead in which the cloying smell of formaldehyde and sweet alcohol was even stronger. The pleasant, permeating stink was intoxicating. He smelled ether too and heard glass tinkling. He listened with secret, egotistical mirth to the husky breathing of the two doctors. It delighted him that they thought he was unconscious and did not know he was listening. It all seemed very silly to him until one of the doctors said,

"Well, do you think we should save his life? They might be sore at us if we do."

"Let's operate," said the other doctor. "Let's cut him open and get to the inside of things once and for all. He keeps complaining about his liver. His liver looks pretty small on this X ray."

"That's his pancreas, you dope. This is his liver."

"No it isn't. That's his heart. I'll bet you a nickel this is his liver. I'm going to operate and find out. Should I wash my hands first?"

"No operations," Yossarian said, opening his eyes and trying to sit up.

"Another county heard from," scoffed one of the doctors indignantly. "Can't we make him shut up?"

"We could give him a total. The ether's right here."

"No totals," said Yossarian.

"Another county heard from," said a doctor.

"Let's give him a total and knock him out. Then we can do what we want with him."

They gave Yossarian total anesthesia and knocked him out. He woke up thirsty in a private room, drowning in ether fumes. Colonel Korn was there at his bedside, waiting calmly in a chair in his baggy, wool, olive-drab shirt and trousers. A bland, phlegmatic smile hung on his brown face with its heavy-bearded cheeks, and he was buffing the facets of his bald head gently with the palms of both hands. He bent forward chuckling when Yossarian awoke, and assured him in the friendliest tones that the deal they had made was still on if Yossarian didn't die. Yossarian vomited, and Colonel Korn shot to his feet at the first cough and fled in disgust, so it seemed indeed that there was a silver lining in every cloud, Yossarian reflected, as he drifted back into a suffocating daze. A hand with sharp fingers shook him awake roughly. He turned and opened his eyes and saw a strange man with a mean face who curled his lip at him in a spiteful scowl and bragged,

"We've got your pal, buddy. We've got your pal."

Yossarian turned cold and faint and broke into a sweat.

"Who's my pal?" he asked when he saw the chaplain sitting where Colonel Korn had been sitting.

"Maybe I'm your pal," the chaplain answered.

But Yossarian couldn't hear him and closed his eyes. Someone gave him water to sip and tiptoed away. He slept and woke up feeling great until he turned his head to smile at the chaplain and saw Aarfy there instead. Yossarian moaned instinctively and screwed his face up with excruciating irritability when Aarfy chortled and asked how he was feeling. Aarfy looked puzzled when Yossarian inquired why he was not in jail. Yossarian shut his eyes to make him go away. When he opened them, Aarfy was gone and the chaplain was there. Yossarian broke into laughter when he spied the chaplain's cheerful grin and asked him what in the hell he was so happy about.

"I'm happy about you," the chaplain replied with excited candor and joy. "I heard at Group that you were very seriously injured and that you would have to be sent home if you lived. Colonel Korn said your condition was critical. But I've just learned from one of the doctors that your wound is really a very slight one and that you'll probably be able to leave in a day or two. You're in no danger. It isn't bad at all."

Yossarian listened to the chaplain's news with enormous relief. "That's good."

"Yes," said the chaplain, a pink flush of impish pleasure creeping into his cheeks. "Yes, that is good."

Yossarian laughed, recalling his first conversation with the chaplain. "You know, the first time I met you was in the hospital. And now I'm in the hospital again. Just about the only time I see you lately is in the hospital. Where've you been keeping yourself?"

The chaplain shrugged. "I've been praying a lot," he confessed. "I try to stay in my tent as much as I can, and I pray every time Sergeant Whitcomb leaves the area, so that he won't catch me."

"Does it do any good?"

"It takes my mind off my troubles," the chaplain answered with another shrug. "And it gives me something to do."

"Well, that's good, then, isn't it?"

"Yes," agreed the chaplain enthusiastically, as though the idea had not occurred to him before. "Yes, I guess that is good." He bent forward impulsively with awkward solicitude. "Yossarian, is there anything I can do for you while you're here, anything I can get you?"

Yossarian teased him jovially. "Like toys, or candy, or chewing gum?"

The chaplain blushed again, grinning self-consciously, and then turned very respectful. "Like books, perhaps, or anything at all. I wish there *was* something I could do to make you happy. You know, Yossarian, we're all very proud of you."

"Proud?"

"Yes, of course. For risking your life to stop that Nazi assassin. It was a very noble thing to do."

"What Nazi assassin?"

"The one that came here to murder Colonel Cathcart and Colonel Korn. And you saved them. He might have stabbed you to death as you grappled with him on the balcony. It's a lucky thing you're alive."

Yossarian snickered sardonically when he understood. "That was no Nazi assassin."

"Certainly it was. Colonel Korn said it was."

"That was Nately's girl friend. And she was after me, not Colonel

Cathcart and Colonel Korn. She's been trying to kill me ever since I broke the news to her that Nately was dead."

"But how could that be?" the chaplain protested in livid and resentful confusion. "Colonel Cathcart and Colonel Korn both saw him as he ran away. The official report says you stopped a Nazi assassin from killing them."

"Don't believe the official report," Yossarian advised dryly. "It's part of the deal."

"What deal?"

"The deal I made with Colonel Cathcart and Colonel Korn. They'll let me go home a big hero if I say nice things about them to everybody and never criticize them to anyone for making the rest of the men fly more missions."

The chaplain was appalled and rose halfway out of his chair. He bristled with bellicose dismay. "But that's terrible! That's a shameful, scandalous deal, isn't it?"

"Odious," Yossarian answered, staring up woodenly at the ceiling with just the back of his head resting on the pillow. "I think 'odious' is the word we decided on."

"Then how could you agree to it?"

"It's that or a court-martial, Chaplain."

"Oh," the chaplain exclaimed with a look of stark remorse, the back of his hand covering his mouth. He lowered himself into his chair uneasily. "I shouldn't have said anything."

"They'd lock me in prison with a bunch of criminals."

"Of course. You must do whatever you think is right, then." The chaplain nodded to himself as though deciding the argument and lapsed into embarrassed silence.

"Don't worry," Yossarian said with a sorrowful laugh after several moments had passed. "I'm not going to do it."

"But you must do it," the chaplain insisted, bending forward with concern. "Really, you must. I had no right to influence you. I really had no right to say anything."

"You didn't influence me." Yossarian hauled himself over onto his side and shook his head in solemn mockery. "Christ, Chaplain! Can you imagine that for a sin? Saving Colonel Cathcart's life! That's the one crime I don't want on my record."

The chaplain returned to the subject with caution. "What will you do instead? You can't let them put you in prison."

"I'll fly more missions. Or maybe I really will desert and let them catch me. They probably would."

"And they'd put you in prison. You don't want to go to prison."

"Then I'll just keep flying missions until the war ends, I guess. Some of us have to survive."

"But you might get killed."

"Then I guess I won't fly any more missions."

"What will you do?"

"I don't know."

"Will you let them send you home?"

"I don't know. Is it hot out? It's very warm in here."

"It's very cold out," the chaplain said.

"You know," Yossarian remembered, "a very funny thing happened—maybe I dreamed it. I think a strange man came in here before and told me he's got my pal. I wonder if I imagined it."

"I don't think you did," the chaplain informed him. "You started to tell me about him when I dropped in earlier."

"Then he really did say it. 'We've got your pal, buddy,' he said. 'We've got your pal.' He had the most malignant manner I ever saw. I wonder who my pal is."

"I like to think that I'm your pal, Yossarian," the chaplain said with humble sincerity. "And they certainly have got me. They've got my number and they've got me under surveillance, and they've got me right where they want me. That's what they told me at my interrogation."

"No, I don't think it's you he meant," Yossarian decided. "I think it must be someone like Nately or Dunbar. You know, someone who was killed in the war, like Clevinger, Orr, Dobbs, Kid Sampson or McWatt." Yossarian emitted a startled gasp and shook his head. "I just realized it," he exclaimed. "They've got all my pals, haven't they? The only ones left are me and Hungry Joe." He tingled with dread as he saw the chaplain's face go pale. "Chaplain, what is it?"

"Hungry Joe was killed."

"God, no! On a mission?"

"He died in his sleep while having a dream. They found a cat on his face."

"Poor bastard," Yossarian said, and began to cry, hiding his tears in the crook of his shoulder. The chaplain left without saying goodbye. Yossarian ate something and went to sleep. A hand shook him awake in the middle of the night. He opened his eyes and saw a thin, mean man in a patient's bathrobe and pajamas who looked at him with a nasty smirk and jeered,

"We've got your pal, buddy. We've got your pal."

Yossarian was unnerved. "What the *hell* are you talking about?" he pleaded in incipient panic.

"You'll find out, buddy. You'll find out."

Yossarian lunged for his tormentor's throat with one hand, but the man glided out of reach effortlessly and vanished into the corridor with a malicious laugh. Yossarian lay there trembling with a pounding pulse. He was bathed in icy sweat. He wondered who his pal was. It was dark in the hospital and perfectly quiet. He had no watch to tell him the time. He was wide-awake, and he knew he was a prisoner in one of those sleepless, bedridden nights that would take an eternity to dissolve into dawn. A throbbing chill oozed up his legs. He was cold, and he thought of Snowden, who had never been his pal but was a vaguely familiar kid who was badly wounded and freezing to death in the puddle of harsh yellow sunlight splashing into his face through the side gunport when Yossarian crawled into the rear section of the plane over the bomb bay after Dobbs had beseeched him on the intercom to help the gunner, please help the gunner. Yossarian's stomach turned over when his eyes first beheld the macabre scene; he was absolutely revolted, and he paused in fright a few moments before descending, crouched on his hands and knees in the narrow tunnel over the bomb bay beside the sealed corrugated carton containing the first-aid kit. Snowden was lying on his back on the floor with his legs stretched out, still burdened cumbersomely by his flak suit, his flak helmet, his parachute harness and his Mae West. Not far away on the floor lay the small tail gunner in a dead faint. The wound Yossarian saw was in the outside of Snowden's thigh, as large and deep as a football, it seemed. It was impossible to tell where the shreds of his saturated coveralls ended and the ragged flesh began.

There was no morphine in the first-aid kit, no protection for Snowden against pain but the numbing shock of the gaping wound itself. The twelve syrettes of morphine had been stolen from their case and replaced by a cleanly lettered note that said: "What's good for M & M Enterprises is good for the country. Milo Minderbinder." Yossarian swore at Milo and held two aspirins out to ashen lips unable to receive them. But first he hastily drew a tourniquet around Snowden's thigh because he could not think what else to do in those first tumultuous moments when his senses were in turmoil, when he knew he must act competently at once and feared he might go to pieces completely. Snowden watched him steadily, saying nothing. No artery was spurting, but Yossarian pretended to absorb himself entirely into the fashioning of a tourniquet, because applying a tourniquet was something he did know how to do. He worked with simulated skill and composure, feeling Snowden's lackluster gaze resting upon him. He recovered possession of himself before the tourniquet was finished and loosened it immediately to lessen the danger of gangrene. His mind was clear now, and he knew how to proceed. He rummaged through the first-aid kit for scissors.

"I'm cold," Snowden said softly. "I'm cold."

"You're going to be all right, kid," Yossarian reassured him with a grin. "You're going to be all right."

"I'm cold," Snowden said again in a frail, childlike voice. "I'm cold."

"There, there," Yossarian said, because he did not know what else to say. "There, there."

"I'm cold," Snowden whimpered. "I'm cold."

"There, there. There, there."

Yossarian was frightened and moved more swiftly. He found a pair of scissors at last and began cutting carefully through Snowden's coveralls high up above the wound, just below the groin. He cut through the heavy gabardine cloth all the way around the thigh in a straight line. The tiny tail gunner woke up while Yossarian was cutting with the scissors, saw him, and fainted again. Snowden rolled his head to the other side of his neck in order to stare at Yossarian more directly. A dim, sunken light glowed in his weak and listless eyes. Yossarian, puzzled, tried not to look at him. He began cutting downward through the coveralls along the inside seam. The yawning wound—was that a tube of slimy bone he saw running deep inside the gory scarlet flow behind the twitching, startling fibers of weird muscle?—was dripping blood in several trickles, like snow melting on eaves, but viscous and red, already thickening as it dropped. Yossarian kept cutting through the coveralls to the bottom and peeled open the severed leg of the garment. It fell to the floor with a plop, exposing the hem of khaki undershorts that were soaking up blotches of blood on one side as though in thirst. Yossarian was stunned at how waxen and ghastly Snowden's bare leg looked, how loathsome, how lifeless and esoteric the downy, fine, curled blond hairs on his odd, white shin and calf. The wound, he saw now, was not nearly as large as a football, but as long and wide as his hand, and too raw and deep to see into clearly. The raw muscles inside twitched like live hamburger meat. A long sigh of relief escaped slowly through Yossarian's mouth when he saw that Snowden was not in danger of dying. The blood was already coagulating inside the wound, and it was simply a matter of bandaging him up and keeping him calm until the plane landed. He removed some packets of sulfanilamide from the first-aid kit. Snowden quivered when Yossarian pressed against him gently to turn him up slightly on his side.

"Did I hurt you?"

"I'm cold," Snowden whimpered. "I'm cold."

"There, there," Yossarian said. "There, there."

"I'm cold. I'm cold."

"There, there. There, there."

"It's starting to hurt me," Snowden cried out suddenly with a plaintive, urgent wince.

Yossarian scrambled frantically through the first-aid kit in search of morphine again and found only Milo's note and a bottle of aspirin. He cursed Milo and held two aspirin tablets out to Snowden. He had no water to offer. Snowden rejected the aspirin with an almost imperceptible shake of his head. His face was pale and pasty. Yossarian removed Snowden's flak helmet and lowered his head to the floor.

"I'm cold," Snowden moaned with half-closed eyes. "I'm cold."

The edges of his mouth were turning blue. Yossarian was petrified. He wondered whether to pull the rip cord of Snowden's parachute and cover him with the nylon folds. It was very warm in the plane. Glancing up unexpectedly, Snowden gave him a wan, cooperative smile and shifted the position of his hips a bit so that Yossarian could begin salting the wound with sulfanilamide. Yossarian worked with renewed confidence and optimism. The plane bounced hard inside an air pocket, and he remembered with a start that he had left his own parachute up front in the nose. There was nothing to be done about that. He poured envelope after envelope of the white crystalline powder into the bloody oval wound until nothing red could be seen and then drew a deep, apprehensive breath, steeling himself with gritted teeth as he touched his bare hand to the dangling shreds of drying flesh to tuck them up inside the wound. Quickly he covered the whole wound with a large cotton compress and jerked his hand away. He smiled nervously when his brief ordeal had ended. The actual contact with the dead flesh had not been nearly as repulsive as he had anticipated, and he found excuse to caress the wound with his fingers again and again to convince himself of his own courage.

Next he began binding the compress in place with a roll of gauze. The second time around Snowden's thigh with the bandage, he spotted the small hole on the inside through which the piece of flak had entered, a round, crinkled wound the size of a quarter with blue edges and a black core inside where the blood had crusted. Yossarian sprinkled this one with sulfanilamide too and continued unwinding the gauze around Snowden's leg until the compress was secure. Then he snipped off the roll with the scissors and slit the end down the center. He made the whole thing fast with a tidy square knot. It was a good bandage, he knew, and he sat back on his heels with pride, wiping the perspiration from his brow, and grinned at Snowden with spontaneous friendliness.

"I'm cold," Snowden moaned. "I'm cold."

"You're going to be all right, kid," Yossarian assured him, patting his arm comfortingly. "Everything's under control."

Snowden shook his head feebly. "I'm cold," he repeated, with eyes as dull and blind as stone. "I'm cold."

"There, there," said Yossarian, with growing doubt and trepidation. "There, there. In a little while we'll be back on the ground and Doc Daneeka will take care of you."

But Snowden kept shaking his head and pointed at last, with just the barest movement of his chin, down toward his armpit. Yossarian bent forward to peer and saw a strangely colored stain seeping through the coveralls just above the armhole of Snowden's flak suit. Yossarian felt his heart stop, then pound so violently he found it difficult to breathe. Snowden was wounded inside his flak suit. Yossarian ripped open the snaps of Snowden's flak suit and heard himself scream wildly as Snowden's insides slithered down to the floor in a soggy pile and just kept dripping out. A chunk of flak more than three inches big had shot into his other side just underneath the arm and blasted all the way through, drawing whole mottled quarts of Snowden along with it through the gigantic hole in his ribs it made as it blasted out. Yossarian screamed a second time and squeezed both hands over his eyes. His teeth were chattering in horror. He forced himself to look again. Here was God's plenty, all right, he thought bitterly as he stared—liver, lungs, kidneys, ribs, stomach and bits of the stewed tomatoes Snowden had eaten that day for lunch. Yossarian hated stewed tomatoes and turned away dizzily and began to vomit, clutching his burning throat. The tail gunner woke up while Yossarian was vomiting, saw him, and fainted again. Yossarian was limp with exhaustion, pain and despair when he finished. He turned back weakly to Snowden, whose breath had grown softer and more rapid, and whose face had grown paler. He wondered how in the world to begin to save him.

"I'm cold," Snowden whimpered. "I'm cold."

"There, there," Yossarian mumbled mechanically in a voice too low to be heard. "There, there."

Yossarian was cold, too, and shivering uncontrollably. He felt goose pimples clacking all over him as he gazed down despondently at the grim secret Snowden had spilled all over the messy floor. It was easy to read the message in his entrails. Man was matter, that was Snowden's secret. Drop him out a window and he'll fall. Set fire to him and he'll burn. Bury him and he'll rot, like other kinds of garbage. The spirit gone, man is garbage. That was Snowden's secret. Ripeness was all.

"I'm cold," Snowden said. "I'm cold."

"There, there," said Yossarian. "There, there." He pulled the rip cord of Snowden's parachute and covered his body with the white nylon sheets.

"I'm cold."

"There, there."

42

Yossarian

"Colonel Korn says," said Major Danby to Yossarian with a prissy, gratified smile, "that the deal is still on. Everything is working out fine."

"No it isn't."

"Oh, yes, indeed," Major Danby insisted benevolently. "In fact, everything is much better. It was really a stroke of luck that you were almost murdered by that girl. Now the deal can go through perfectly."

"I'm not making any deals with Colonel Korn."

Major Danby's effervescent optimism vanished instantly, and he broke out all at once into a bubbling sweat. "But you do have a deal with him, don't you?" he asked in anguished puzzlement. "Don't you have an agreement?"

"I'm breaking the agreement."

"But you shook hands on it, didn't you? You gave him your word as a gentleman."

"I'm breaking my word."

"Oh, dear," sighed Major Danby, and began dabbing ineffectually at his careworn brow with a folded white handkerchief "But why, Yossarian? It's a very good deal they're offering you."

"It's a lousy deal, Danby. It's an odious deal."

"Oh, dear," Major Danby fretted, running his bare hand over his dark, wiry hair, which was already soaked with perspiration to the tops of the thick, close-cropped waves. "Oh, dear."

"Danby, don't you think it's odious?"

Major Danby pondered a moment. "Yes, I suppose it is odious," he conceded with reluctance. His globular, exophthalmic eyes were quite distraught. "But why did you make such a deal if you didn't like it?"

"I did it in a moment of weakness," Yossarian wisecracked with glum irony. "I was trying to save my life."

"Don't you want to save your life now?"

"That's why I won't let them make me fly more missions."

"Then let them send you home and you'll be in no more danger."

"Let them send me home because I flew more than fifty missions," Yossarian said, "and not because I was stabbed by that girl, or because I've turned into such a stubborn son of a bitch."

Major Danby shook his head emphatically in sincere and bespectacled vexation. "They'd have to send nearly every man home if they did that. Most of the men have more than fifty missions. Colonel Cathcart couldn't possibly requisition so many inexperienced replacement crews at one time without causing an investigation. He's caught in his own trap."

"That's his problem."

"No, no, no, Yossarian," Major Danby disagreed solicitously. "It's your problem. Because if you don't go through with the deal, they're going to institute court-martial proceedings as soon as you sign out of the hospital."

Yossarian thumbed his nose at Major Danby and laughed with smug elation. "The hell they will! Don't lie to me, Danby. They wouldn't even try."

"But why wouldn't they?" inquired Major Danby, blinking with astonishment.

"Because I've really got them over a barrel now. There's an official report that says I was stabbed by a Nazi assassin trying to kill them. They'd certainly look silly trying to court-martial me after that."

"But, Yossarian!" Major Danby exclaimed. "There's another official report that says you were stabbed by an innocent girl in the course of extensive black-market operations involving acts of sabotage and the sale of military secrets to the enemy."

Yossarian was taken back severely with surprise and disappointment. "Another official report?"

"Yossarian, they can prepare as many official reports as they want and choose whichever ones they need on any given occasion. Didn't you know that?"

"Oh, dear," Yossarian murmured in heavy dejection, the blood draining from his face. "Oh, dear."

Major Danby pressed forward avidly with a look of vulturous well-meaning. "Yossarian, do what they want and let them send you home. It's best for everyone that way."

"It's best for Cathcart, Korn and me, not for everyone."

"For everyone," Major Danby insisted. "It will solve the whole problem."

"Is it best for the men in the group who will have to keep flying more missions?"

Major Danby flinched and turned his face away uncomfortably for a second. "Yossarian," he replied, "it will help nobody if you force Colonel Cathcart to court-martial you and prove you guilty of all the crimes with which you'll be charged. You will go to prison for a long time, and your whole life will be ruined."

Yossarian listened to him with a growing feeling of concern. "What crimes will they charge me with?"

"Incompetence over Ferrara, insubordination, refusal to engage the enemy in combat when ordered to do so, and desertion."

Yossarian sucked his cheeks in soberly. "They could charge me with all that, couldn't they? They gave me a medal for Ferrara. How could they charge me with incompetence now?"

"Aarfy will swear that you and McWatt lied in your official report."

"I'll bet the bastard would!"

"They will also find you guilty," Major Danby recited, "of rape, extensive black-market operations, acts of sabotage and the sale of military secrets to the enemy."

"How will they prove any of that? I never did a single one of those things."

"But they have witnesses who will swear you did. They can get all the witnesses they need simply by persuading them that destroying you is for the good of the country. And in a way, it *would* be for the good of the country."

"In what way?" Yossarian demanded, rising up slowly on one elbow with bridling hostility.

Major Danby drew back a bit and began mopping his forehead again. "Well, Yossarian," he began with an apologetic stammer, "it would not help the war effort to bring Colonel Cathcart and Colonel Korn into disrepute now. Let's face it, Yossarian—in spite of everything, the group does have a very good record. If you were court-martialed and found innocent, other men would probably refuse to fly missions, too. Colonel Cathcart would be in disgrace, and the military efficiency of the unit might be destroyed. So in that way it *would* be for the good of the country to have you found guilty and put in prison, even though you *are* innocent."

"What a sweet way you have of putting things!" Yossarian snapped with caustic resentment.

Major Danby turned red and squirmed and squinted uneasily. "Please don't blame me," he pleaded with a look of anxious integrity. "You know it's not my fault. All I'm doing is trying to look at things objectively and arrive at a solution to a very difficult situation."

"I didn't create the situation."

"But you can resolve it. And what else can you do? You don't want to fly more missions."

"I can run away."

"Run away?"

"Desert. Take off. I can turn my back on the whole damned mess and start running."

Major Danby was shocked. "Where to? Where could you go?"

"I could get to Rome easily enough. And I could hide myself there."

"And live in danger every minute of your life that they would find you? No, no, no, no, Yossarian. That would be a disastrous and ignoble thing to do. Running away from problems never solved them. Please believe me. I am only trying to help you."

"That's what that kind detective said before he decided to jab his thumb into my wound," Yossarian retorted sarcastically.

"I am not a detective," Major Danby replied with indignation, his cheeks flushing again. "I'm a university professor with a highly developed sense of right and wrong, and I wouldn't try to deceive you. I wouldn't lie to anyone."

"What would you do if one of the men in the group asked you about this conversation?"

"I would lie to him."

Yossarian laughed mockingly, and Major Danby, despite his blushing discomfort, leaned back with relief, as though welcoming the respite Yossarian's changing mood promised. Yossarian gazed at him with a mixture of reserved pity and contempt. He sat up in bed with his back resting against the headboard, lit a cigarette, smiled slightly with wry amusement, and stared with whimsical sympathy at the vivid, pop-eyed horror that had implanted itself permanently on Major Danby's face the day of the mission to Avignon, when General Dreedle had ordered him taken outside and shot. The startled wrinkles would always remain, like deep black scars, and Yossarian felt sorry for the gentle, moral, middle-aged idealist, as he felt sorry for so many people whose shortcomings were not large and whose troubles were light.

With deliberate amiability he said, "Danby, how can you work along with people like Cathcart and Korn? Doesn't it turn your stomach?"

Major Danby seemed surprised by Yossarian's question. "I do it to help my country," he replied, as though the answer should have been obvious. "Colonel Cathcart and Colonel Korn are my superiors, and obeying their orders is the only contribution I can make to the war effort. I work along with them because it's my duty. And also," he added in a much lower voice, dropping his eyes, "because I am not a very aggressive person."

"Your country doesn't need your help any more," Yossarian reasoned without antagonism. "So all you're doing is helping them."

"I try not to think of that," Major Danby admitted frankly. "I try to concentrate on only the big result and to forget that they are succeeding, too. I try to pretend that they are not significant."

"That's my trouble, you know," Yossarian mused sympathetically, folding his arms. "Between me and every ideal I always find Scheisskopfs, Peckems, Korns and Cathcarts. And that sort of changes the ideal."

"You must try not to think of them," Major Danby advised affirmatively. "And you must never let them change your values. Ideals are good, but people are sometimes not so good. You must try to look up at the big picture."

Yossarian rejected the advice with a skeptical shake of his head. "When I look up, I see people cashing in. I don't see heaven or saints or angels. I see people cashing in on every decent impulse and every human tragedy."

"But you must try not to think of that," Major Danby insisted. "And you must try not to let it upset you."

"Oh, it doesn't really upset me. What does upset me, though, is that they think I'm a sucker. They think that they're smart, and that the rest of us are dumb. And, you know, Danby, the thought occurs to me right now, for the first time, that maybe they're right."

"But you must try not to think of that too," argued Major Danby. "You must think only of the welfare of your country and the dignity of man."

"Yeah," said Yossarian.

"I mean it, Yossarian. This is not World War One. You must never forget that we're at war with aggressors who would not let either one of us live if they won."

"I know that," Yossarian replied tersely, with a sudden surge of scowling annoyance. "Christ, Danby, I earned that medal I got, no matter what their reasons were for giving it to me. I've flown seventy goddam combat missions. Don't talk to me about fighting to save my country. I've been fighting all along to save my country. Now I'm going to fight a little to save myself. The country's not in danger any more, but I am."

"The war's not over yet. The Germans are driving toward Antwerp."

"The Germans will be beaten in a few months. And Japan will be beaten a few months after that. If I were to give up my life now, it wouldn't be for my country. It would be for Cathcart and Korn. So I'm turning my bombsight in for the duration. From now on I'm thinking only of me."

Major Danby replied indulgently with a superior smile, "But, Yossarian, suppose everyone felt that way."

"Then I'd certainly be a damned fool to feel any other way, wouldn't I?" Yossarian sat up straighter with a quizzical expression. "You know, I have a queer feeling that I've been through this exact conversation before with someone. It's just like the chaplain's sensation of having experienced everything twice."

"The chaplain wants you to let them send you home," Major Danby remarked.

"The chaplain can jump in the lake."

"Oh, dear." Major Danby sighed, shaking his head in regretful disappointment. "He's afraid he might have influenced you."

"He didn't influence me. You know what I might do? I might stay right here in this hospital bed and vegetate. I could vegetate very comfortably right here and let other people make the decisions."

"You must make decisions," Major Danby disagreed. "A person can't live like a vegetable."

"Why not?"

A distant warm look entered Major Danby's eyes. "It must be nice to live like a vegetable," he conceded wistfully.

"It's lousy," answered Yossarian.

"No, it must be very pleasant to be free from all this doubt and pressure," insisted Major Danby. "I think I'd like to live like a vegetable and make no important decisions."

"What kind of vegetable, Danby?"

"A cucumber or a carrot."

"What kind of cucumber? A good one or a bad one?"

"Oh, a good one, of course."

"They'd cut you off in your prime and slice you up for a salad."

Major Danby's face fell. "A poor one, then."

"They'd let you rot and use you for fertilizer to help the good ones grow."

"I guess I don't want to live like a vegetable, then," said Major Danby with a smile of sad resignation.

"Danby, must I really let them send me home?" Yossarian inquired of him seriously.

Major Danby shrugged. "It's a way to save yourself."

"It's a way to lose myself, Danby. You ought to know that."

"You could have lots of things you want."

"I don't want lots of things I want," Yossarian replied, and then beat his fist down against the mattress in an outburst of rage and frustration. "Goddammit, Danby! I've got friends who were killed in this war. I can't make a deal now. Getting stabbed by that bitch was the best thing that ever happened to me."

"Would you rather go to jail?"

"Would you let them send *you* home?"

"Of course I would!" Major Danby declared with conviction. "Certainly I would," he added a few moments later, in a less positive manner. "Yes, I suppose I would let them send me home if I were in your place," he decided uncomfortably, after lapsing into troubled contemplation. Then he threw his face sideways disgustedly in a gesture of violent distress and blurted out, "Oh, yes, of course I'd let them send me home! But I'm such a terrible coward I couldn't really be in your place."

"But suppose you weren't a coward?" Yossarian demanded, studying him closely. "Suppose you did have the courage to defy somebody?"

"Then I *wouldn't* let them send me home," Major Danby vowed emphatically with vigorous joy and enthusiasm. "But I certainly wouldn't let them court-martial me."

"Would you fly more missions?"

"No, of course not. That would be total capitulation. And I might be killed."

"Then you'd run away?"

Major Danby started to retort with proud spirit and came to an abrupt stop, his half-opened jaw swinging closed dumbly. He pursed his lips in a tired pout. "I guess there just wouldn't be any hope for me, then, would there?"

His forehead and protuberant white eyeballs were soon glistening nervously again. He crossed his limp wrists in his lap and hardly seemed to be breathing as he sat with his gaze drooping toward the floor in acquiescent defeat. Dark, steep shadows slanted in from the window. Yossarian watched him solemnly, and neither of the two men stirred at the rattling noise of a speeding vehicle skidding to a stop outside and the sound of racing footsteps pounding toward the building in haste.

"Yes, there's hope for you," Yossarian remembered with a sluggish flow of inspiration. "Milo might help you. He's bigger than Colonel Cathcart, and he owes me a few favors."

Major Danby shook his head and answered tonelessly. "Milo and Colonel Cathcart are pals now. He made Colonel Cathcart a vice-president and promised him an important job after the war."

"Then ex-P.F.C. Wintergreen will help us," Yossarian exclaimed. "He hates them both, and this will infuriate him."

Major Danby shook his head bleakly again. "Milo and ex-P.F.C. Wintergreen merged last week. They're all partners now in M & M Enterprises."

"Then there is no hope for us, is there?"

"No hope."

"No hope at all, is there?"

"No, no hope at all," Major Danby conceded. He looked up after a while with a half-formed notion. "Wouldn't it be nice if they could disappear us the way they disappeared the others and relieve us of all these crushing burdens?"

Yossarian said no. Major Danby agreed with a melancholy nod, lowering his eyes again, and there was no hope at all for either of them until footsteps exploded in the corridor suddenly and the chaplain, shouting at the top of his voice, came bursting into the room with the electrifying news about Orr, so overcome with hilarious excitement that he was almost incoherent for a minute or two. Tears of great elation were sparkling in his eyes, and Yossarian leaped right out of bed with an incredulous yelp when he finally understood.

"*Sweden?*" he cried.

"Orr!" cried the chaplain.

"Orr?" cried Yossarian.

"Sweden!" cried the chaplain, shaking his head up and down with gleeful rapture and prancing about uncontrollably from spot to spot in a grinning, delicious frenzy. "It's a miracle, I tell you! A miracle! I believe in God again. I really do. Washed ashore in Sweden after so many weeks at sea! It's a miracle."

"Washed ashore, hell!" Yossarian declared, jumping all about also and roaring in laughing exultation at the walls, the ceiling, the chaplain and Major Danby. "He didn't *wash* ashore in Sweden. He *rowed* there! He *rowed* there, Chaplain, he *rowed* there."

"Rowed there?"

"He *planned* it that way! He went to Sweden deliberately."

"Well, I don't care!" the chaplain flung back with undiminished zeal. "It's still a miracle, a miracle of human intelligence and human endurance. Look how much he accomplished!" The chaplain clutched his head with both hands and doubled over in laughter. "Can't you just picture him?" he exclaimed with amazement. "Can't you just picture him in that yellow raft, paddling through the Straits of Gilbraltar at night with that tiny little blue oar—"

"With that fishing line trailing out behind him, eating raw codfish all the way to Sweden, and serving himself tea every afternoon—"

"I can just see him!" cried the chaplain, pausing a moment in his celebration to catch his breath. "It's a miracle of human perseverance, I tell you. And that's just what I'm going to do from now on! I'm going to persevere. Yes, I'm going to persevere."

"He knew what he was doing every step of the way!" Yossarian rejoiced, holding both fists aloft triumphantly as though hoping to squeeze revelations from them. He spun to a stop facing Major Danby. "Danby, you dope! There is hope, after all. Can't you see? Even Clevinger might be alive somewhere in that cloud of his, hiding inside until it's safe to come out."

"What are you talking about?" Major Danby asked in confusion. "What are you both talking about?"

"Bring me apples, Danby, and chestnuts too. Run, Danby, run. Bring me crab apples and horse chestnuts before it's too late, and get some for yourself."

"Horse chestnuts? Crab apples? What in the world for?"

"To pop into our cheeks, of course." Yossarian threw his arms up into the air in a gesture of mighty and despairing self-recrimination. "Oh, why didn't I listen to him? Why wouldn't I have some faith?"

"Have you gone crazy?" Major Danby demanded with alarm and bewilderment. "Yossarian, will you please tell me what you are talking about?"

"Danby, Orr planned it that way. Don't you understand—he planned it that way from the beginning. He even practiced getting shot down. He rehearsed for it on every mission he flew. And I wouldn't go with him! Oh, why wouldn't I listen? He invited me along, and I wouldn't go with him! Danby, bring me buck teeth too, and a valve to fix and a look of stupid innocence that nobody would ever suspect of any cleverness. I'll need them all. Oh, why wouldn't I listen to him. Now I understand what he was trying to tell me. I even understand why that girl was hitting him on the head with her shoe."

"Why?" inquired the chaplain sharply.

Yossarian whirled and seized the chaplain by the shirt front in an importuning grip. "Chaplain, help me! Please help me. Get my clothes. And hurry, will you? I need them right away."

The chaplain started away alertly. "Yes, Yossarian, I will. But where are they? How will I get them?"

"By bullying and browbeating anybody who tries to stop you. Chaplain, get me my uniform! It's around this hospital somewhere. For once in your life, succeed at something."

The chaplain straightened his shoulders with determination and tightened his jaw. "Don't worry, Yossarian. I'll get your uniform. But why was that girl hitting Orr over the head with her shoe? Please tell me."

"Because he was paying her to, that's why! But she wouldn't hit him hard enough, so he had to row to Sweden. Chaplain, find me my uniform so I can get out of here. Ask Nurse Duckett for it. She'll help you. She'll do anything she can to be rid of me."

"Where are you going?" Major Danby asked apprehensively when the chaplain had shot from the room. "What are you going to do?"

"I'm going to run away," Yossarian announced in an exuberant, clear voice, already tearing open the buttons of his pajama tops.

"Oh, no," Major Danby groaned, and began patting his perspiring face rapidly with the bare palms of both hands. "You can't run away. Where can you run to? Where can you go?"

"To Sweden."

"To Sweden?" Major Danby exclaimed in astonishment. "You're going to run to Sweden? Are you crazy?"

"Orr did it."

"Oh, no, no, no, no, no," Major Danby pleaded. "No, Yossarian, you'll never get there. You can't run away to Sweden. You can't even row."

"But I can get to Rome if you'll keep your mouth shut when you leave here and give me a chance to catch a ride. Will you do it?"

"But they'll find you," Major Danby argued desperately, "and bring you back and punish you even more severely."

"They'll have to try like hell to catch me this time."

"They will try like hell. And even if they don't find you, what kind of way is that to live? You'll always be alone. No one will ever be on your side, and you'll always live in danger of betrayal."

"I live that way now."

"But you can't just turn your back on all your responsibilities and run away from them," Major Danby insisted. "It's such a negative move. It's escapist."

Yossarian laughed with buoyant scorn and shook his head. "I'm not running *away* from my responsibilities. I'm running *to* them. There's nothing negative about running away to save my life. You know who the escapists are, don't you, Danby? Not me and Orr."

"Chaplain, please talk to him, will you? He's deserting. He wants to run away to Sweden."

"Wonderful!" cheered the chaplain, proudly throwing on the bed a pillowcase full of Yossarian's clothing. "Run away to Sweden, Yossarian. And I'll stay here and persevere. Yes. I'll persevere. I'll nag and badger Colonel Cathcart and Colonel Korn every time I see them. I'm not afraid. I'll even pick on General Dreedle."

"General Dreedle's out," Yossarian reminded, pulling on his trousers and hastily stuffing the tails of his shirt inside. "It's General Peckem now."

The chaplain's babbling confidence did not falter for an instant. "Then I'll pick on General Peckem, and even on General Scheisskopf. And do you know what else I'm going to do? I'm going to punch Captain Black in the nose the very next time I see him. Yes, I'm going to punch him in the nose. I'll do it when lots of people are around so that he may not have a chance to hit me back."

"Have you both gone crazy?" Major Danby protested, his bulging eyes straining in their sockets with tortured awe and exasperation. "Have you both taken leave of your senses? Yossarian, listen—"

"It's a miracle, I tell you," the chaplain proclaimed, seizing Major Danby about the waist and dancing him around with his elbows extended for a waltz. "A real miracle. If Orr could row to Sweden, then I can triumph over Colonel Cathcart and Colonel Korn, if I only persevere."

"Chaplain, will you please shut up?" Major Danby entreated politely, pulling free and patting his perspiring brow with a fluttering motion. He bent toward Yossarian, who was reaching for his shoes. "What about Colonel—"

"I couldn't care less."

"But this may actua—"

"To hell with them both!"

"This may actually help them," Major Danby persisted stubbornly. "Have you thought of that?"

"Let the bastards thrive, for all I care, since I can't do a thing to stop them but embarrass them by running away. I've got responsibilities of my own now, Danby. I've got to get to Sweden."

"You'll never make it. It's impossible. It's almost a geographical impossibility to get there from here."

"Hell, Danby, I know that. But at least I'll be trying. There's a young kid in Rome whose life I'd like to save if I can find her. I'll take her to Sweden with me if I can find her, so it isn't all selfish, is it?"

"It's absolutely insane. Your conscience will never let you rest."

"God bless it." Yossarian laughed. "I wouldn't want to live without strong misgivings. Right, Chaplain?"

"I'm going to punch Captain Black right in the nose the next time I see him," gloried the chaplain, throwing two left jabs in the air and then a clumsy haymaker. "Just like that."

"What about the disgrace?" demanded Major Danby.

"What disgrace? I'm in more disgrace now." Yossarian tied a hard knot in the second shoelace and sprang to his feet. "Well, Danby, I'm ready. What do you say? Will you keep your mouth shut and let me catch a ride?"

Major Danby regarded Yossarian in silence, with a strange, sad smile. He had stopped sweating and seemed absolutely calm. "What would you do if I did try to stop you?" he asked with rueful mockery. "Beat me up?"

Yossarian reacted to the question with hurt surprise. "No, of course not. Why do you say that?"

"I will beat you up," boasted the chaplain, dancing up very close to Major Danby and shadowboxing. "You and Captain Black, and maybe even Corporal Whitcomb. Wouldn't it be wonderful if I found I didn't have to be afraid of Corporal Whitcomb any more?"

"Are you going to stop me?" Yossarian asked Major Danby, and gazed at him steadily.

Major Danby skipped away from the chaplain and hesitated a moment longer. "No, of course not!" he blurted out, and suddenly was waving both arms toward the door in a gesture of exuberant urgency.

"Of course I won't stop you. Go, for God's sake, and hurry! Do you need any money?"

"I have some money."

"Well, here's some more." With fervent, excited enthusiasm, Major Danby pressed a thick wad of Italian currency upon Yossarian and clasped his hand in both his own, as much to still his own trembling fingers as to give encouragement to Yossarian. "It must be nice to be in Sweden now," he observed yearningly. "The girls are so sweet. And the people are so advanced."

"Goodbye, Yossarian," the chaplain called. "And good luck. I'll stay here and persevere, and we'll meet again when the fighting stops."

"So long, Chaplain. Thanks, Danby."

"How do you feel, Yossarian?"

"Fine. No, I'm very frightened."

"That's good," said Major Danby. "It proves you're still alive. It won't be fun."

Yossarian started out. "Yes it will."

"I mean it, Yossarian. You'll have to keep on your toes every minute of every day. They'll bend heaven and earth to catch you."

"I'll keep on my toes every minute."

"You'll have to jump."

"I'll jump."

"Jump!" Major Danby cried.

Yossarian jumped. Nately's whore was hiding just outside the door. The knife came down, missing him by inches, and he took off.

History, Context, and Criticism

Edited by Jonathan R. Eller

CONTENTS

PART ONE

The Story of *Catch-22*

THE STORY OF *CATCH-22*

by Jonathan R. Eller

It shouldn't have survived the first printing. It was a first novel by a part-time writer who had published very little since the 1940s. It was a book that captured the feelings of helplessness and horror generated by the darker side of the American dream at a time when the general reading public still expected fiction to reflect a positive view of contemporary America and its hallowed institutions. The title was changed twice during presswork; as if that weren't enough, someone who thought he was portrayed in the book threatened to sue, prompting a name change for one of the main characters after almost a year in print.

But for a number of editors, advertisers, writers, and critics, reading the book echoed the opening line of the novel: "It was love at first sight." This core of avid supporters kept the novel alive in the East Coast book market until word-of-mouth praise (and overnight bestseller status in Great Britain) took it to international prominence. In time, the title *Catch-22* became a part of the English language, and Joseph Heller's novel became an enduring part of American culture.

Heller was not unknown in publishing circles prior to *Catch-22*. His first published work appeared in the fall 1945 issue of *Story*, an issue dedicated to short fiction by returning servicemen. For several years after the war, he wrote what he called "*New Yorker*–type" stories about Jewish life in Depression-era Brooklyn. Several of these formula pieces were published in *Esquire* and the *Atlantic Monthly* while Heller was completing undergraduate work in English at NYU. These publications gained him some attention as a promising new writer, but he published no new stories after 1948—partly because they weren't selling anymore, but primarily because he was ready to move on to more universal material:

> By the time I was a senior in college, I'd done a little more reading and I began to suspect that literature was more serious, more interesting than analyzing an endless string of Jewish families in the Depression. I could see that type of writing was going out of style. I wanted to write something that was very good and I had nothing good to write. So I wrote nothing.[1]

Instead, he began graduate studies in English at Columbia, which he would complete with an M.A. in 1949, followed by an additional year at Oxford on a Fulbright Scholarship. After two years teaching expository writing at Pennsylvania State University, Heller moved back to New York in 1952 and took a job writing for a small advertising agency, and later for Remington Rand. Graduate work provided the insight required to attempt serious literature, and Heller wanted to write a novel. The drive developed tentatively and without much outside inspiration. He was generally disappointed by the new novels of the early postwar years: "There was a terrible sameness about books being published and I almost stopped reading as well as writing." He considered the war novels of Jones, Miller, Shaw, and others quite good, but he did not at first consider his own wartime experiences as subject for fiction. Nearly thirty typescripts accumulated by 1952, but only one—the never-published "Crippled Phoenix"—offered a hint of the wartime traumas that would surface in *Catch-22*.

In 1953, he began a series of notecards outlining characters and a military scenario for what would become *Catch-22*. Certainly his wartime experiences, and those of boyhood friends like George Mandel, formed a basis for the new project. Mandel, who had been seriously

A photograph from Joseph Heller's copy of the 488th Squadron's unofficial scrapbook. Heller is on the right.

wounded as an infantryman in Europe, would eventually write *The Wax Boom* (1962), a tough war novel that also questioned traditional army chain-of-command responses to combat situations. Mandel remained a responsive and insightful reader for Heller during the seven years that *Catch-22* evolved.

But in 1953, Heller was still searching for the right form and style of expression. In literature, he found himself attracted to the innovative work of Waugh, Nabokov, and Céline for their successes in achieving the kind of effect Heller wanted. In an early post-publication interview, Heller used Nabokov's work to describe the effect he himself was searching for: "Nabokov in *Laughter in the Dark* takes an extremely flippant approach to situations deeply tragic and pathetic, and I began to try for a similar blending of the comic and the tragic so that everything that takes place seems to be grotesque yet plausible."[2]

From a publishing perspective, however, it was Heller's interest in Céline that finally sparked a marketable product. Heller had read Céline's *Journey to the End of the Night* while teaching at Penn State; sometime later, probably in 1954, he read Céline's *Death on the Installment Plan.* Céline's experimentation with time, structure, and colloquial speech profoundly affected him, and triggered a crucial burst of creative energy. Heller recalled the event for his 1975 *Playboy* interview with Sam Merrill:

> I was lying in bed, thinking about Céline, when suddenly the opening lines of *Catch-22* came to me: "It was love at first sight. The first time he saw the chaplain, Blank fell madly in love with him." I didn't come up with the name Yossarian until later, and the chaplain wasn't necessarily an Army chaplain. He could have been a prison chaplain. Ideas of plot, pace, character, style, and tone all tumbled out that night, pretty much the way they finally appeared in the book. The next morning, at work, I wrote out the whole first chapter and sent it to my agent, Candida Donadio, who sold it to *New World Writing.*

Donadio offered "Catch-18" to Arabel Porter at New American Library's Mentor Books, and immediately found another enthusiastic fan; Porter wanted "Catch-18" for the Seventh Mentor Selection of *New World Writing*, an NAL series dedicated to publishing the best new literature and criticism. Other NAL editors concurred in superlative terms; Walter Freeman believed that "Of all the recommended pieces lately, this stands out. It seems like part of a really exciting, amusing novel." Founding editor Victor Weybright was convinced that "Catch-18" was the "funniest thing we have ever had for *NWW*."[3]

Although Heller was already referring to his initial experiment as a prospective novel, it would be a year before he completed the next chapter, and two years before he finished enough material to send out the story for further review. The main problem was time: between business and family responsibilities, Heller was only able to work on *Catch-18* in the evenings, and never very late. He worked slowly and revised extensively at the kitchen table in his West End Avenue apartment, completing about three handwritten pages each night on yellow legal tablets. By day he continued in advertising, moving to successively better-paying positions at *Time* in 1955 and *Look* in 1956. In 1957 he moved into the Advertising-Promotion Department at *McCall's*, where he would remain until *Catch-22* changed his life forever.

By the summer of 1957, Heller had completed enough to make a seventy-five-page typescript. In August, Candida Donadio circulated the typescript and received offers from Bob Gottlieb at Simon and Schuster and Tom Ginsberg at Viking. Each offered options to draw a contract when the book was complete; author and agent passed on both, opting to develop more of the book and then ask for an immediate contract.

In February 1958, Donadio sent a longer typescript to Bob Gottlieb, who had shown a very strong interest the previous summer. By this time, Heller had finished seven handwritten chapters and revised them into a 259-page typescript. This typescript eventually became the first third of the book, evolving into the first sixteen chapters of the final novel. Gottlieb, at twenty-six the youngest editor at Simon and Schuster, loved what he saw of the book and arranged a contract for Heller, but not without a struggle.

Four members of the editorial board reported on the manuscript: Gottlieb, administrative editor Peter Schwed, Justin Kaplan (then an executive assistant to Henry Simon and Max Schuster), and Henry Simon, younger brother of founder Richard Simon and by 1958 a vice president. In his report, Gottlieb wrote:

> I still love this crazy book and very much want to do it. It is a very rare approach to the war—humor that slowly turns to horror. The funny parts are wildly funny, the serious parts are excellent. The whole certainly suffers somewhat by the two attitudes, but this can be partly overcome by revisions. The central character, Yossarian,

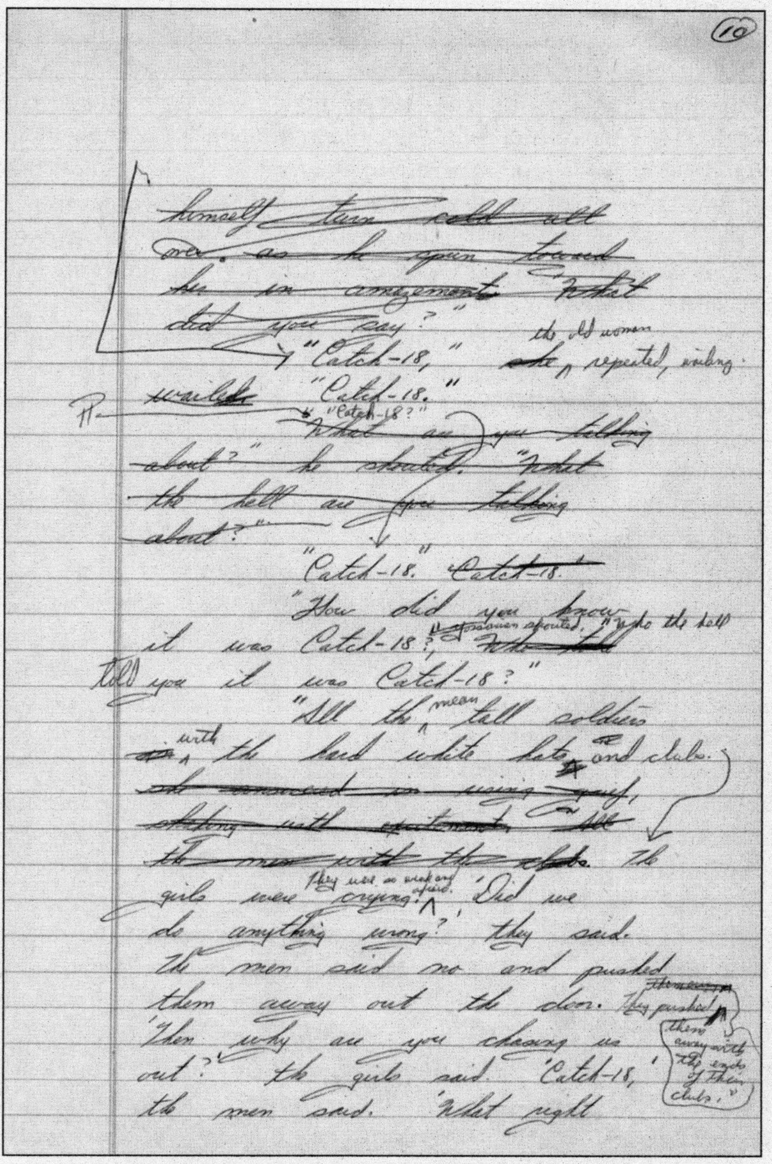

(10)

~~himself turn cold all over. as he spun toward her in amazement. "What did you say?"~~

"Catch-18," the old woman repeated, ~~wailing~~. "Catch-18."

"Catch-18?" ~~"What are you talking about?" he shouted. "What the hell are you talking about?"~~

"Catch-18." ~~"Catch-18."~~

"How did you know it was Catch-18?" Yossarian shouted. "Who the hell told you it was Catch-18?"

"All the mean tall soldiers with the hard white hats and clubs. ~~...~~ The girls were crying. They were so weak and afraid. 'Did we do anything wrong?' they said. The men said no and pushed them away out the door. They pushed them away with the ends of their clubs. 'Then why are you chasing us out?' the girls said. 'Catch-18,' the men said. 'What right

A page from the early manuscript, with revisions by Heller.

> must be strengthened somewhat—his single-minded drive to survive is both the comic and the serious center of the story.[4]

Gottlieb was the strongest advocate, and both Schwed and Kaplan found it wildly funny but at times repetitive. Even Gottlieb conceded that the book would not be a big seller, although he felt that it was "bound to find real admirers in certain literary sets." Henry Simon, however, found Yossarian's escapades repetitive and at times offensive, and recommended against publication. In the end, Heller's willingness to make revisions, and Gottlieb's willingness to work with him, convinced the board to contract the book.

The 1955 appearance of chapter 1 in *New World Writing* had introduced the publishing world to *Catch-18*, and by the end of the decade news about the novel had spread by word of mouth from Heller's agent, his publisher, and his own circle of friends and advertising associates. His contract had originally called for 1960 publication, but Heller needed all of 1960 to finish the manuscript and work it into shape for publication. By this time the 259-page typescript of 1958 had more than doubled in length; Heller had extended the existing episodes by interleaving handwritten pages of the familiar legal-sized yellow paper into the typescript, thus expanding it from seven to sixteen chapters (through "Luciana," chapter 16 of the final work) without altering the order and basic structure of the earlier draft. But a major new manuscript section picked up where the original circulating typescript left off, adding another twenty-eight chapters to the increasingly complex narrative. Chapter 39, "The Eternal City," had proven most troublesome; it took months to refine the dark tones of Yossarian's final trip to Rome and create a smooth transition into the revelations of the novel's concluding chapters.

During 1960, Heller prepared a new 758-page typescript from this conflation, and made revisions that included deletion of the original manuscript chapter 18, "Rosoff." This chapter provided a chronological bridge between the "Soldier in White" chapter, set in the hospital on Pianosa, and "The Soldier Who Saw Everything Twice" chapter, a flashback into Yossarian's earlier hospital episodes at Lowry Air Base in Denver, Colorado. The deleted chapter included an overlong but delightful digression into "PT" and team sports at Lowry, but Heller soon sensed that this interlude impeded the progress of the narrative. Other digressive episodes would have to be cut as well before the book would go to press.

With the newly revised typescript in hand, Heller and Gottlieb made further revisions in the text. After a series of editorial sessions, Heller

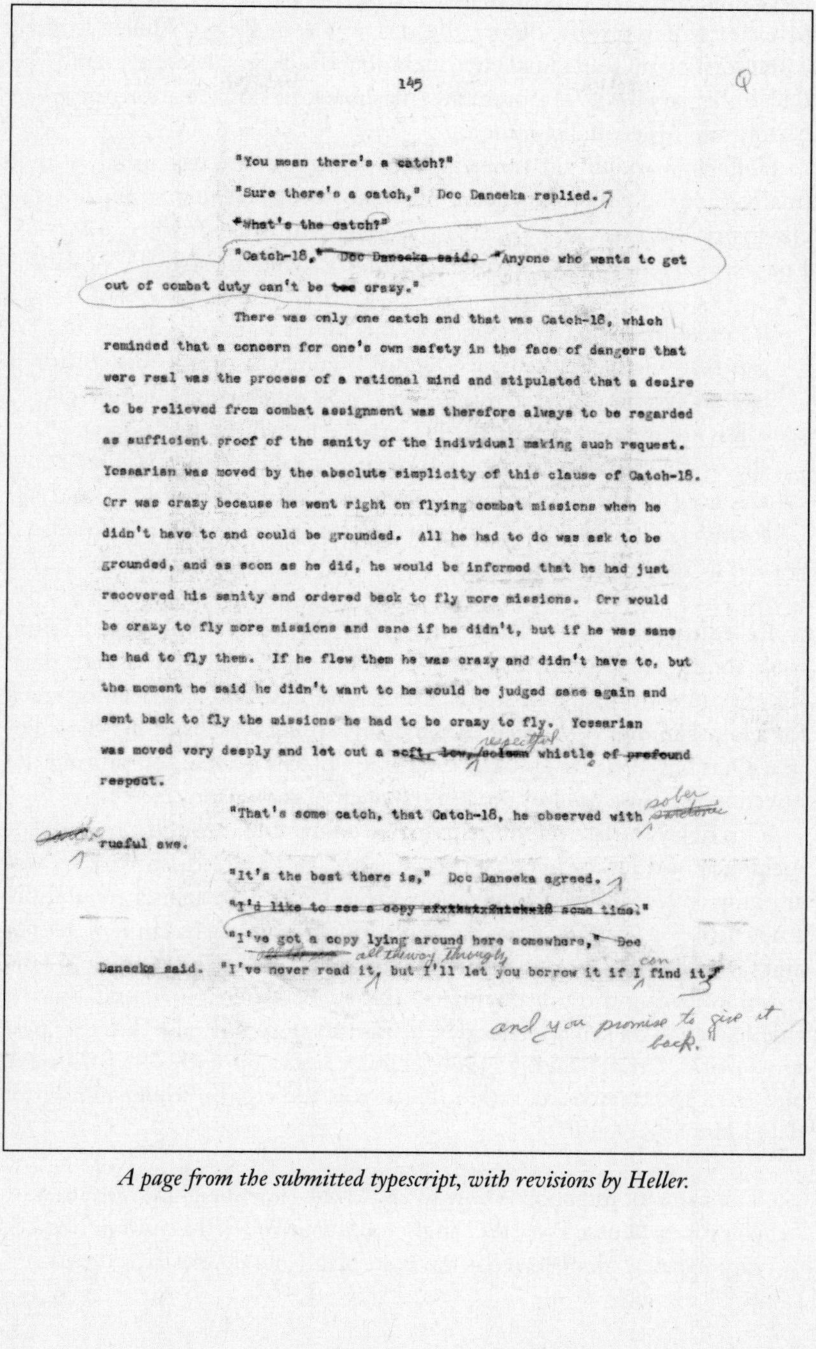

145

"You mean there's a catch?"

"Sure there's a catch," Doc Daneeka replied.

"What's the catch?"

"Catch-18," Doc Daneeka said. "Anyone who wants to get out of combat duty can't be too crazy."

There was only one catch and that was Catch-18, which reminded that a concern for one's own safety in the face of dangers that were real was the process of a rational mind and stipulated that a desire to be relieved from combat assignment was therefore always to be regarded as sufficient proof of the sanity of the individual making such request. Yossarian was moved by the absolute simplicity of this clause of Catch-18. Orr was crazy because he went right on flying combat missions when he didn't have to and could be grounded. All he had to do was ask to be grounded, and as soon as he did, he would be informed that he had just recovered his sanity and ordered back to fly more missions. Orr would be crazy to fly more missions and sane if he didn't, but if he was sane he had to fly them. If he flew them he was crazy and didn't have to, but the moment he said he didn't want to he would be judged sane again and sent back to fly the missions he had to be crazy to fly. Yossarian was moved very deeply and let out a soft, low, solemn whistle of profound respect.

"That's some catch, that Catch-18, he observed with rueful awe.

"It's the best there is," Doc Daneeka agreed.

"I'd like to see a copy some time."

"I've got a copy lying around here somewhere," Doc Daneeka said. "I've never read it, but I'll let you borrow it if I find it."

A page from the submitted typescript, with revisions by Heller.

shortened the typescript by about 150 pages. The typescript, now heavily revised and partially retyped, became printer's copy for the Simon and Schuster galley proofs. Before the text was actually set, Heller worked with Gottlieb on some final cuts, including the original chapter 23 ("The Old Folks at Home"), a digressive flashback to conversations between Nately and his capitalist father.

Heller's working relationship with Gottlieb was the catalyst that finally reduced the complex narrative to a manageable scale; but the chemistry did not carry over to the copy editor assigned to *Catch-18*. For weeks, Heller found himself locked in a syntactic struggle of wills:

> [Gottlieb] assigned the book to a copy editor who immediately began rearranging my sentences and paragraphs. . . . She apparently had an aversion to what I think might be called compound predicates. For example, if I wrote "He struck a match and lit a cigarette," she would change it to "He struck a match and he lit a cigarette." It was even worse when she got to sentences like "'Get out,' he said, foaming at the mouth." This she would change to "'Get out,' he said, and he foamed at the mouth."[5]

Re-editing the book back into Heller's own conversational idiom took about six weeks in early 1961, and led to a delayed release date. Before the copyediting problem, Heller and Gottlieb had been on track for a late-summer release; after the delay, Heller was given his choice of mid-October 1961 or January 1962. He opted for October, putting the novel on the threshold of the holiday marketing season.

This delay led to even more unexpected trouble through a bizarre coincidence of titles. In January 1961, Leon Uris's new novel, *Mila 18*, was announced for summer publication; given Uris's best-selling reputation, a new title for *Catch-18* was inevitable. For two weeks in January, Heller and Gottlieb tried a number of new titles. *Catch-11* was promising—the vowel following the consonants in "Catch" had the right sound, but the title had an extra syllable; besides, it was too close to Frank Sinatra's new movie title, *Ocean's Eleven* (1960). Heller came up with *Catch-14* next, and tried to convince Gottlieb that it was the right number in a letter dated January 29, 1961:

> The name of the book is now CATCH-14. (Forty-eight hours after you resign yourself to the change, you'll find yourself almost preferring this new number. It has the same bland and nondescript signifi-

cance of the original. It is far enough away from Uris for the book to establish an identity of its own, I believe, yet close enough to the original title to still benefit from the word of mouth publicity we have been giving it.)

Gottlieb was not happy with 14—the central concept of the novel was "Catch-18," and for everyone at Simon and Schuster, it had been "Catch-18" for more than three years. After a halfhearted attempt at accepting *Catch-14*, Gottlieb had a late-night flash of conviction and came up with the title which has long since passed into the language: "22, it's 22! And I remember calling up Joe and saying, 'It's funnier than 18!' But of course the fact is that no number is funnier than any other number, it's complete self-delusion. But once we were convinced it was funnier, then it became funny."[6] Both Heller and Gottlieb soon realized just how well the new title represented the structure of events in the novel—the soldier who saw everything twice, Yossarian's disastrous second target pass during the Bologna mission, and the chaplain's déjà vu are key examples of the novel's doubling structure. But all this came later—as Gottlieb observes, "We were just desperate publishers looking for a title."

Catch-22 was published on October 10, 1961, but an aggressive marketing campaign was already reaching beyond reviewers to a wide circle of writers, literary critics, and even to competing publishers. The day after publication, advertising manager Nina Bourne and Bob Gottlieb published "What's the Catch?" a full-page five-column ad in *The New York Times* recapping the intellectual fan mail that was streaming into Bourne's office. A second, full-length two-column ad appeared in the November 3 *Times*, and after Christmas short, eye-catching bullets by Morris West, Kenneth Tynan, and Nelson Algren appeared every few days under the paper soldier logo designed for the dust jacket by Paul Bacon. Six months after release, a status report on the emerging "*Catch* Craze" appeared across an entire page and a facing column of the April 29, 1962, *New York Times Book Review*. But this ad was different—most of the columns documented a new wave of letters from grassroots American readers who discovered *Catch-22* through the word-of-mouth endorsements that were beginning to create a long-term market for the novel.

In spite of praise from an ever-increasing number of critics, writers, and mainstream readers, Heller was about to face a Yossarian-like challenge that would soon force a major change in the text of his novel. He had relied on his own wartime experiences in a Mediterranean-based B-25 bomber squadron for plot elements, but his use of fictitious charac-

October 11, 1961

What's the CATCH?

It's **JOSEPH HELLER'S** indescribably wonderful novel, *Catch-22*, just published, in a ferment of advance excitement, after eight years in work. If you have acquaintances in the book world, you have been hearing that *Catch-22* is one of the great serious-comic creations of our era, shocking, moving . . . that a few days ago Simon and Schuster got the following cable from Paris:

> PLEASE CONGRATULATE JOSEPH HELLER ON MASTERPIECE CATCH 22 STOP I THINK IT IS ONE OF THE GREATEST WARBOOKS STOP SO DO IRWIN SHAW AND JAMES JONES
> BUCHWALD

. . . that the book's vigorous partisans include S. J. Perelman, Robert Brustein (who says "it is beyond question one of the funniest works in the language"), Merle Miller and Alexander King . . . that Harper Lee, whose *To Kill a Mockingbird* is one of the gentlest and most loving books of our time, loves *Catch-22*.

. . . that it was originally called *Catch-18* until the magic number was innocently appropriated by Leon Uris . . . that the Editor-in-Chief of Anchor Books is so devoted to *Catch-22* that he is spreading the word as if he were its publisher . . . that Seymour Epstein, author of *The Successor*, likens Heller to a collaboration among Dante and Abbott & Costello and Kafka . . . that *Catch-22* is Editor's-Choice-of-the-Month in the book trade publication, *Book Buyer's Guide* . . . that Professor Oscar Cargill of New York University says "Heller writes the freshest dialogue since the advent of Hemingway thirty years ago" . . .

. . . that John Armstrong of the Doubleday Book Shops says "in 25 years as a writer and bookseller, I have never been as excited about any novel as I am about *Catch-22*"

. . . that indications are that reviews will be split right down the middle between the conservatives who have never seen anything like *Catch-22* before and never want to again — and discoverers who, like the Anchor man, feel about it as if they were its parents and publishers . . . that among the latter is *The Book-of-the-Month-Club News* . . .

. . . that a 3rd printing has been ordered before publication

. . . that Muriel Rukeyser wrote us "*Catch-22* is appalling, frightfully funny, and amazing in its beauty" . . . that Ed and Pegeen Fitzgerald have been talking about it and reading aloud from it on the radio two days running (Mr. F. says he doesn't remember when a novel has made him laugh so hysterically and predicts "it's going to be way up there on top of the bestseller list in no time at all") . . .

. . . that the Book Find Club has found it . . . that the publishers are so determined to make the world aware of *Catch-22*, they are contemplating skywriting . . .

. . . and that *Catch-22* is, in sum, a funny, tragic, tonic novel in which an American airforce base on a small island off Italy becomes a microcosm of the modern world as it might look to someone dangerously sane. We predict that Heller's totally original manner will affect our generation's way of talking.

First reviews, just in—*Newsweek:* "One of the very best novels to come out of the Second World War." Maurice Dolbier in the *N. Y. Herald Tribune:* "A wild, moving, shocking, hilarious, raging, exhilarating, giant roller-coaster of a book." Don't miss it.

"**Heralds a talent** of so much wit, grace, and intellectual awareness that one enthusiastic reader is strongly tempted to burst into loud hurzahs. In *Catch-22*, Joseph Heller has endowed World War II with a vital, somewhat more sophisticated Good Soldier Schweik. His anti-hero is an American Air Force Captain and his name, for all generations to come, is Yossarian. A truly mordant satire. Even if Mr. Heller never writes another line, his reputation is high and secure." —*Alexander King*

"**Catch-22** is the only war novel I've ever read that makes any sense." —*Harper Lee*

"**I have read** *Catch-22* with ever blossoming wonder, admiration, and pleasure. I do not know when I have encountered an American novel which evoked from me such immediate sympathy and assent. It is beyond question one of the funniest works in the language, possessing a grotesque nightmare humor which, like that of Kingsley Amis and J. P. Donleavy, is animated by the author's unrelenting hatred of cant and hypocrisy." —*Robert Brustein*

"**Catch-22 is a gut-area book;** it grabbed me there along about Page 9, and it has not yet let go, although I finished it more than a week ago; I doubt that it will ever completely let go. It is one of the funniest books I have ever read, one of the saddest, in every way the truest, and the most sensible. All of it. To quote from it — and I've been doing that incessantly—'suddenly it all made sense. It made sense to cry out in pain every night.' . . . I am a big believer in civil liberties, but if I were President I would get Congress to pass a law requiring that every adult person read *Catch-22*. At least twice." —*Merle Miller*

"**An effective and savagely funny** diatribe against man's inhumanity to man." —*Book-of-the-Month Club News*

"**They're going to say** that this book is rowdy, ferocious, full of soldiers and whores, and against matriotism. It is more than that: *Catch-22* is appalling, frightfully funny, and amazing in its beauty. I was never in the army, but I was brought up in the building business, and arrested in Alabama, I have been in hospitals, taught in colleges, seen poetry centers and wartime domestic services, and been baited by the American Legion. They were all made of this wild mixture, so I suppose the Army is, too." —*Muriel Rukeyser*

"**A remarkable** comedy. At once amusing and harshly satirical. Joseph Heller has the mean bite of the dedicated satirist. He is a writer to watch." —*Harry T. Moore*

"**If Dante** made a second, 20th-century, descent with Franz Kafka and Abbott & Costello along for company, they might come up with a collaboration bearing some resemblance to *Catch-22*. On second thought, perhaps not. Joseph Heller has a homogeneous lunacy all his own. In the purgatory of things as they are, were, and probably will be, Heller has come shudderingly close to the exact dialect. Reading this book was nothing less than a fantastic experience." —*Seymour Epstein*

"**A devastatingly** comic war novel. The preposterous morality of the world passes in review. Read it and weep!" —*Selden Rodman*

"**Here is** a novel like no other you have ever read. It will almost certainly shock you now and then, but it will never bore you. It is a riotous, preposterous mixture of humor and terror, of bawdiness and a ruthless common sense and a sublime insanity. It's wonderful!" —*Book Buyer's Guide*

CATCH-22

By JOSEPH HELLER

$5.95 SIMON AND SCHUSTER

November 3, 1961

What a CATCH!

We can't reel it in fast enough — the praise, the news, the rumor, the excitement about **Joseph Heller's** indescribably hilarious & wonderful novel **CATCH-22** . . .

On Monday (Oct. 23), a dazzling review from Orville Prescott . . . on Tuesday, a long, brilliant, serious critique in *Time* . . . on Wednesday, a rave from *Associated Press* . . . In the mail: letters from James Jones, Irwin Shaw, Nelson Algren . . . In the *Times:* a note that Graham Greene tried to buy British rights for Bodley Head. Too late; Cape will publish . . . On the phone: news that bookstores on the coast as well as in town are selling out . . .

All this and more—details in a minute—in *addition* to the first rush of praise (the huge ad we ran day after publication didn't have enough room for all of it) from the *Herald Tribune's* Maurice Dolbier ("A wild, moving, shocking, hilarious, raging, exhilarating, giant roller coaster of a book") . . . from Harper Lee, Harry T. Moore, Seymour Epstein, Oscar Cargill ("Freshest dialogue since the advent of Hemingway"), S. J. Perelman, Robert Brustein, *Newsweek*, Book-of-the-Month-Club *News*, Muriel Rukeyser, Ed and Pegeen Fitzgerald, Alexander King, Merle Miller, Art Buchwald . . .

So much for the headlines, on to the news itself:

☛ **First printing sold out** in first 10 days; 2nd and 3rd, fortunately ordered in good time, just in and almost out.

☛ "It is not simply the best American novel to come out of World War II" says **Nelson Algren** in the *Nation*. "It is simply the best American novel that has come out of anywhere in years."

☛ Prescott, in *The New York Times* calls *Catch* "Wildly original, brutally gruesome. **A dazzling performance** that will outrage nearly as many readers as it delights. It is realistic in its powerful accounts of bombing missions with men screaming and dying and planes crashing. But most of Mr. Heller's story rises above mere realism and soars into the stratosphere of satire, grotesque exaggeration, fantasy, farce and sheer lunacy. Those who are interested may be reminded of the Voltaire who wrote *Candide* and of the Kafka who wrote *The Trial*. *Catch-22* is a funny book — vulgarly, bitterly, savagely funny. [Its characters] make certain it will not be forgotten by those who can take it."

☛ **Irwin Shaw writes from Paris:** "My congratulations to the author. An uproarious and horrifying book."

☛ **Travel Note.** William Holden (according to the *Philadelphia Inquirer*) "flew from Switzerland to New York to nab screen rights to *Catch-22*. Bill plans starring in the movie version of Joe Heller's hell-bent-for-bestsellerdom novel."

☛ **James Jones** writes us: "Its weird comedy is marvelous, and underneath this, on an entirely different level, its pathos for the tragic situation of the men is equally fine. It is a book that should be read and roared over by anyone who was caught up in the late war."

☛ **Life says** it's uproarious. **Time says** "magnificent illogic whips like a mistral all through the novel, blowing both sequence and motivation into a rubble of farcical shocks and grisly surprises. Heller's Yossarian might have been the creature of a benign Kafka." And after some reservations *Time* sums up by saying "they are not enough to extinguish the real fire of *Catch-22*."

☛ *Newsday* calls *Catch:* **"A crazy, wonderful,** yet cruelly sane story, written with wit and wonder."

☛ **Another Essandess author** is buying 12 copies at bookstores and getting her brother who has a print shop to make stickers saying "Better Yossarian than Rotarian." (Y. is the hero of *Catch*.)

☛ **Heller has, to date, been compared** by leading writers and critics to (1) Kingsley Amis (2) a collaboration among Dante, Abbott and Costello and Kafka (3) J. D. Salinger (4) Swift (5) a collaboration of Lewis Carroll and Hieronymous Bosch, according to *Associated Press*, and (6) so many times to *Good Soldier Schweik* that some enterprising bookstore should display *G. S. S.* in its window.

☛ **"A combination of Minsky's burlesque,** Dante's purgatory, Chaplin's slapstick and Al Capone's gangster headquarters," says the *Cincinnati Enquirer*. "True, the insanities of army life are exaggerated to the nth power, but enough of the blinding light of truth is focused thereon to sting and pain the reader and at the same time make him laugh aloud."

☛ Gladwyn Hill in the *Los Angeles Mirror* says **"It may become a classic of this era.** Absorbing, entertaining, thought provoking, fraught with humor, pathos, tragedy and even an element of triumph. It is hard to imagine any reader with breadth of imagination failing to get exhilaration from it."

As this goes to press: ☛ Nov. 3 issue of *Time* (a week after the review quoted above) lists *Catch* under Best Reading: ". . . this apocalyptic burlesque of war is written with brilliance and echoes with mad laughter." ☛ The *Nashville Tennessean* says, "Page after page, Heller, depending upon his mood, will pull your leg, goose you in the ribs, or kick you in the guts, all with Rabelaisian gusto." ☛ 1,131 copies sold in last 2 days alone. ☛ Brentano's reports that *Catch* is its newest fiction bestseller.

CATCH-22

By JOSEPH HELLER

$5.95 SIMON AND SCHUSTER

April 29, 1962

Report on CATCH-22

The first six months in the life of a novel that is showing signs of living forever

JOSEPH HELLER'S "wild, moving, shocking, hilarious, raging, exhilarating giant roller-coaster of a book" (we quote the *Herald Tribune*) was published on October 10, 1961. Now, half a year later, it is one of the most talked about novels in America. It has just gone to press for the 5th time. The cheers of delight that first greeted it have multiplied into a non-stop ovation.

Immediately on publication NELSON ALGREN called it "the best American novel that has come out of anywhere in years."... For Christmas, KENNETH TYNAN said: "the most striking debut in American fiction since The Catcher in the Rye."... No week has passed without new praise for its extraordinary wit and power... Just this month (in the April issue of "Show") NORMAN PODHORETZ tells why, in his opinion, Catch-22 "has provoked more enthusiasm than any first novel in years."

Impossible, in this page-and-1/5th, to do more than capsule the wave upon wave of critical acclaim. For a partial list of distinguished enthusiasts already on record see the panel at the left. Celebrated novelists have responded with spontaneous applause to *Catch-22*. The Book Find Club has found it – and just called for a new supply. Hollywood and Broadway producers are circling in for the final swoop.

Most exciting of all: the rush of wonderfully expressive letters that are coming in from readers everywhere. For instance:

From a college instructor:

"At first I wouldn't go into the next room without it. Then I wouldn't go outside without it. I read it everywhere – on the buses, subways, grocery lines. If I *did* leave it out of my sight for a moment, I panicked. '*Catch-22*' was all I could say when my wife found me on the living room floor doubled over with laughter; '*Catch-22*' was all I could or would answer when my worried friends called; '*Catch-22*' I nodded like an idiot to people on the grocery line, to strangers I was meeting for the first time. *Catch-22, Catch-22* . . . until last night I finally finished it and burst out crying.

"I don't think I'll ever recover . . . But before I die of *Catch-22*, I will do everything to keep it alive. I will change ads on subways to: 'Promise her anything but give her *Catch-22*.' I'll write *Catch-22* on every surface I can find. I'll pirate and organize a *Catch-22* Freedom Bus . . . I'm a happier person today for *Catch-22*. Happier, sadder, crazier, saner, clearer, better, wiser, braver. Just for knowing it exists. Thank you."

JOSEPH HELLER

Photograph of the author by Seymour Linden

From a Put-and-Call broker:

"Fabulous. Found New York dealers all sold out. Had to buy it in Dallas. Made me laugh all the way from Dallas to New York on the plane."

From a 15-year-old boy in Eugene, Oregon:

"The last chapter left me with such an overflowing of relief I felt I must let you know of my gratitude to you for writing it."

From a New Jersey die-casting manufacturer:

"I couldn't believe that it had really happened to me until I read your book. I was unsure of the events that took place during my six years as G.I. and officer. Now I know that it all did happen. *You done it!* You've made the war understandable. I would say that you are the greatest author alive – but you'd think I was nuts. So think I'm nuts. I loved it."

From a housewife:

"The damn thing seems to have a chain reaction. I am now getting phone calls in the middle of the night from people I've given the book to who want to read bits aloud to *me*."

From a man who got a copy as a gift from Darryl Zanuck:

"Of compelling interest. A new style of writing and presentation wacky enough to make for solid entertainment."

From an ex-cook 3-C:

"I laughed until I was sick. I sat stunned at the enormousness of your insight and the magnitude of your understanding. To say that it moved me would be to nominate myself for the Understatement Team in the next Olympics. In short, may I congratulate you, thank you, praise you. If I could, I would hug you. But I can't because I have a wife and children and a dog, and men who hug other men are censured and ostracized and looked upon with arched eyebrows. Again thank you for a wonderful experience."

From a New York grandmother:

"Wonderful, wonderful, wonderful, wonderful, wonderful. Only one novel has been written in the U.S.A. in the 20th century that I think deserves to be compared with yours – and that is *The Great Gatsby*."

From the total stranger in Pennsylvania who bullied us into running this ad:

"Dear Sir (or Madam): What are you doing about the wittiest book since *Beowulf*, the cleverest since *Paradise Lost*, the most remarkable since the *Talmud*, the greatest since Judah Ben Ezra wrote Shakespeare? This is the *Alice in Wonderland* of the Sixties. Why are you hiding it? Why are you holding-back? Are you some kind of subversive? Let's get cracking. Advertise!"

There seems to be no doubt that those who bought Heller's novel back in October now possess first edition copies of a new American classic that will be read, loved, roared over, quoted from, discussed and written about for years and years to come. If you are still un-*Catched*, don't put off a moment longer the incomparable pleasure of reading Joseph Heller's *Catch-22*.

5th printing. $5.95 at all bookstores. SIMON AND SCHUSTER, Publishers

ter names, unit designations, and base locations minimized the potential for lawsuit. In fact, none of the aviators who inspired the characters in *Catch-22* ever voiced objection. But in the late spring of 1962 someone *not* portrayed in the novel threatened a lawsuit because he *thought* he was. He shared the name of Heller's "Anabaptist" chaplain, Robert Oliver Shipman, referred to for the most part throughout the novel simply as R. O. Shipman.

The Shipman character had already developed a literary identity, and Heller did not want readers to be confused by different versions of the book. Heller had never known the real Shipman, but the coincidence of name and certain background similarities led to a name change to A. T. Tappman—another seven-letter name that avoided resetting the entire book. This significant change appears in the sixth and subsequent printings of the Simon and Schuster text, and in all printings of the Dell mass-market paperback edition released in the fall of 1962. Later printings of Jonathan Cape's British first edition also picked up the change, but the Transworld mass-market British paperback has continued to use the original name for decades.

This controversy remained a private matter, and the Simon and Schuster staff soon turned to more public marketing milestones. The house advertising effort culminated a year after release with a full-page eight-column "Happy Birthday *Catch-22*" ad in the daily *New York Times*. As with the other ads, it had the unique style that Nina Bourne had learned from Richard Simon himself—the idea of bringing the reader inside the publishing house to learn the story of the novel. It was a personal approach, like writing a letter to a friend, or, as Bob Gottlieb observed, like "bringing the public—bringing the reader in on it. You were talking to people instead of inventing things, coming out with real feelings about a particular book." The ads—an impossible undertaking at today's costs—were more heartfelt than calculated, but in the end, the Catch caught on.

And as the word spread, public and academic interest in the novel continued to grow. The postmodern experimental structure was worthy of critical investigation, and the satire engaged students (and professors) who were skeptical of the postwar military establishment. But the chance for *Catch-22* to become a contemporary classic, and for the "Catch" phrase to pass into our culture, grew from universal aspects of the plot. As Nelson Algren noted in his June 23, 1962, *Chicago Daily News* review, Heller's burlesque of the military leader is also a burlesque of the business leader, or the leader of any bureaucratic machine. Syndicated columnists beyond the book world also came on board for *Catch-22*, including Richard Starnes, Murray Kempton, and Ralph Gleason. Starnes—a conservative political columnist writing for the conservative *New York World Telegram*—offered proof enough that the novel's universal relevance could break through ideological biases. In fact, by overcoming the odds of the publishing business, Heller fulfilled Starnes's early prognosis for literary immortality: "Yossarian will, I think, live a very long time."

JONATHAN R. ELLER is professor of English and senior textual editor in the Institute for American Thought, Indiana University School of Liberal Arts (IUPUI). Portions of this essay appeared in his article "Catching a Market: The Publishing History of *Catch-22*," *Prospects* 17 (1992), 475–525.

Notes

1 Sam Merrill, "Playboy Interview: Joseph Heller," *Playboy* (June 1975): 59ff.

2 W. J. Weatherby, "The Joy Catcher," *Manchester Guardian*, Nov. 20, 1962.

3 Kenneth C. Davis, *Two-Bit Culture: The Paperbacking of America* (Boston: Houghton-Mifflin, 1984), 200.

4 A copy of Gottlieb's editorial report, dated Feb. 12, 1958, is in the *Catch-22* Papers, Brandeis University.

5 Richard Greeman, "Joseph Heller Lionized by Critics for His Novel of War and Mankind," *Fire Island News*, July 14, 1962.

6 Robert Gottlieb, interview with the author, New York, June 12, 1991. Heller's slightly different version appears in Josh Greenfield, "22 Was Funnier Than 14," *New York Times Book Review*, Mar. 3, 1968. Subsequent quotations by Gottlieb are from the same interview.

Reeling in *Catch-22*

by Joseph Heller

The concept of the novel came to me as a seizure, a single inspiration. I'd come to the conclusion that I wanted to write a novel, and moving back to New York after two years of teaching college in Pennsylvania sent the ambition coursing again. I had no idea what it would be about, however. Then one night the opening lines of *Catch-22*—all but the character's name, Yossarian—came to me: "It was love at first sight. The first time he saw the chaplain he fell madly in love with him."

My mind flooded with verbal images. I got up in the night and walked around, just thinking about it. The next day I returned to the small ad agency where I worked, wrote the first chapter in longhand, spent the week touching it up, and then sent it to my literary agent. It took a year more to plan the book and seven years to write it, but it remained pretty much the same inspiration that came to me that night.

I don't know where it came from. I know that it was a conscious assembling of factors, but the unconscious element was very strong, too. Almost immediately I invented the phrase "Catch-18," which would later be changed to "Catch-22" when it was discovered that Leon Uris's *Mila 18* would be coming out at about the same time as my book. Initially Catch-22 required that every censoring officer put his name on every letter he censored. Then as I went on, I deliberately looked for self-contradictory situations, and artistic contrivance came in. I began to expand each application of Catch-22 to encompass more and more of the social system. Catch-22 became a law: "they" can do anything to us we can't stop "them" from doing. The very last use is philosophical: Yossarian is convinced that there is no such thing as Catch-22, but it doesn't matter as long as people believe there is.

Virtually none of the attitudes in the book—the suspicion and distrust of the officials in the government, the feelings of helplessness and victimization, the realization that most government agencies would lie—coincided with my experiences as a bombardier in World War II. The antiwar and antigovernment feelings in the book belong to the period following World War II: the Korean War, the cold war of the fifties. A general disintegration of belief took place then, and it affected *Catch-22* in that the form of the novel became almost disintegrated. *Catch-22* was a collage; if not in structure, then in the ideology of the novel itself.

Without being aware of it, I was part of a near-movement in fiction. While I was writing *Catch-22*, J. P. Donleavy was writing *The Ginger Man*, Jack Kerouac was writing *On the Road*, Ken Kesey was writing *One Flew Over the Cuckoo's Nest*, Thomas Pynchon was writing *V.*, and Kurt Vonnegut was writing *Cat's Cradle*. I don't think any one of us even knew any of the others. Certainly I didn't know them. Whatever forces were at work shaping a trend in art were affecting not just me, but all of us. The feelings of helplessness and persecution in *Catch-22* are very strong in Pynchon and in *Cat's Cradle*.

Catch-22 was more political than psychological. In the book, opposition to the war against Hitler was taken for granted. The book dealt instead with conflicts existing between a man and his own superiors, between him and his own institutions. The really difficult struggle happens when one does not even know who it is that's threatening him, grinding him down—and yet one does know that there is a tension, an antagonist, a conflict with no conceivable end to it.

Catch-22 came to the attention of college students at about the same time that the moral corruption of the Vietnam War became evident. The treatment of the military as corrupt, ridiculous, and asinine could be applied literally to that war. Vietnam was a lucky coincidence—lucky for me, not for the people. Between the mid and late Sixties, the paperback of *Catch-22* went from twelve printings to close to thirty.

There was a change in spirit, a new spirit of healthy irreverence. There was a general feeling that the platitudes of Americanism were horseshit. Number one, they didn't work. Number two, they weren't true. Number three, the people giving voice to them didn't believe them either. The phrase "Catch-22" began appearing more and more frequently in a wide range of contexts. I began hearing from people who believed that I'd named the book after the phrase.

One way or another, everybody is at the mercy of some context in the novel. I move from situations in which the individual is against his own society, to those in which the society itself is the product of something impenetrable, something that either has no design or has a design which escapes the boundaries of reason.

There is a dialogue early in the book between Lieutenant Dunbar and Yossarian. They are discussing the chaplain, and Yossarian says, "Wasn't he sweet? Maybe they should give him three votes." Dunbar says, "Who's they?" And a page or two later, Yossarian tells Clevinger "They're trying to kill me," and Clevinger wants to know "Who's they?"

It is the anonymous "they," the enigmatic "they," who are in charge. Who is "they"? I don't know. Nobody knows. Not even "they" themselves.

From *The Sixties*, ed. Lynda Rosen Obst (New York: Random House/Rolling Stone Press, 1977), pp. 50, 52.

Preface to the 1994 Edition of *Catch-22*

by Joseph Heller

In 1961, *The New York Times* was a newspaper with eight columns. And on October 11 of that year, one day after the official publication date of *Catch-22*, the page with the book review carried an unusual advertisement that ran from top to bottom and was five columns wide. To the eye the effect was stupendous. The book review that day, of a work by somebody else, was squeezed aside to the fold of the page, as were the crossword puzzle and all else. The ad had this caption: WHAT'S THE CATCH? And displayed at the top in silhouette was the comic cartoon of a uniformed figure in flight, glancing off to the side at some unspecified danger with an expression of panic.

It was an announcement ad for *Catch-22*. Interwoven with the text were mentions of praise from twenty-one individuals and groups of some public standing, most connected to literature and the publishing world, who had received the novel before publication and had already reviewed it or commented about it favorably.

Within days after publication, there was a review in *The Nation* by Nelson Algren (a client of my own literary agent, who had urged him to read it), who wrote of *Catch-22* that it "was the best novel to come out of anywhere in years." And there was a review by Studs Terkel in a Chicago daily newspaper that recommended it about as highly.

So much attention to the work at publication was in large part the result of the industrious zeal and appreciation of my literary agent, Candida Donadio, and my editor, Robert Gottlieb, and I embrace the opportunity afforded now to dedicate this new edition to both of them, as colleagues and allies with talents that were of immeasurable value.

The work was not reviewed in the *Times* that day. However, it was reviewed in the *Herald Tribune* by Maurice Dolbier, and Mr. Dolbier said of it: "A wild, moving, shocking, hilarious, raging, exhilarating, giant roller-coaster of a book."

That the reviewer for the *Herald Tribune* came to review at all this war novel by someone unknown was almost entirely the product of coincidence. S. J. Perelman, much better known and the subject of an interview by Mr. Dolbier, was publishing his own book at just about that time. His publisher was Simon and Schuster, mine too, and the editor in charge of his work there was also the same, Bob Gottlieb. In answer to a question put to him by Dolbier about his own reading, Mr. Perelman replied that he was very much engrossed in a novel pressed upon him by his editor, a novel called *Catch-22.* Returning to his office, Mr. Dolbier later confessed to me, he found the book already in the pile with others he had decided he would not have time to study as prospects to write about. Had it not been for Gottlieb, there would have been no Perelman, and had it not been for Perelman, there would have been no review by Dolbier.

And had it not been for Dolbier, there might not have been the *Times.* Two weeks afterward, and probably only because of Mr. Dolbier, the book was described with approbation in the daily *Times* by the reviewer Orville Prescott, who predicted it would not be forgotten by those who could take it and called it: "A dazzling performance that will outrage nearly as many readers as it delights."

The rest, one might say, is history, but it's a history easily misconstrued.

The novel won no prizes and was not on any bestseller list. And, as Mr. Prescott foresaw, for just about every good report, there seemed to appear one that was negative. Looking back at this novel after twenty-five years, John Aldridge, to my mind the most perceptive and persistent commentator on American literature over the decades, lauded Robert Brustein for his superbly intelligent review in *The New Republic,* which contained "essential arguments that much of later criticism has done little to improve on," and Mr. Aldridge recognized that many in the early audience of *Catch-22* "liked the book for just the reasons that caused others to hate it."

The disparagements were frequently venomous. In the Sunday *Times,* in a notice in back so slender that the only people seeing it were those awaiting it, the reviewer (a novelist who also by chance was a client of my own agent, Candida) decided that the "novel gasps for want of craft and sensibility," "is repetitious and monotonous," "fails," "is an emotional hodgepodge," and was no novel; and in the esteemed *The New Yorker,* the reviewer, a staff writer who normally writes about jazz, compared the book unfavorably with a novel of similar setting by Mitchell Goodman and decided that *Catch-22* "doesn't even seem to have been written; instead, it gives the impression of having been shouted onto paper," "what remains is a debris of sour jokes," and that in the end Heller "wallows in his own laughter and finally drowns in it." (I am tempted now to drown in laughter as I set this down.)

I do not recall that the novel was included in the several hundred books in the Christmas roundup of recommended reading of the *Times* that year or in the several hundred others picked out in the spring for summer reading.

But in late summer of 1962, Raymond Walters, on the bestseller page of the Sunday *Times*, which then carried regularly the column "In and Out of Books," reported that the underground book New Yorkers seemed to be talking about most was *Catch-22*. (The novel probably was more heavily advertised than any other that year, but it was still underground.) Not much later, *Newsweek* carried a story to the same effect in a space more than a page wide. And late that same summer, I was invited to my first television interview. The program was the *Today* show, then a variety show as much as anything else. The interim host was John Chancellor. Mr. Chancellor had recently returned from his newsman's post in the Kremlin, and he had agreed to accept the position on condition that he interview only those people he himself chose to.

After the show, in a bar close by the studio where I found myself drinking martinis at an earlier hour than ever in my life, he handed me a packet of stickers he'd had printed privately. They read: YOSSARIAN LIVES. And he confided he'd been pasting these stickers secretly on the walls of the corridors and in the executive rest rooms of the NBC building.

Then came September and the paperback edition and with it, finally, an expansion in popular appeal that seemed to take the publishers, Dell, by surprise, despite elaborate promotion and distribution strategies. It seemed for a while that the people there could not fully bring themselves to believe the sales figures and that they would never catch up.

Paperback publishers print in the hundreds of thousands. For this, after an initial release of 300,000 copies, they went back to press five more times between September and the end of the year, twice each in October and December, and by the end of 1963, there were eleven printings. In England, under the auspices of the enterprising young editor there, Tom Maschler, it was that way from the start. Bestseller lists there were new and rudimentary then, but *Catch-22* was quickly at the head of them.

For me, the history of *Catch-22* begins back in 1953, when I started writing it. In 1953, I was employed as a copywriter at a small advertising agency in New York, after two years as an instructor in English composition at Pennsylvania State University, which then was a college. Early on, in anxious need of an approving opinion, I sent the opening chapter off to the literary agents I had managed to obtain after publishing a few short stories in magazines, in *Esquire* and *The Atlantic*. The agents were

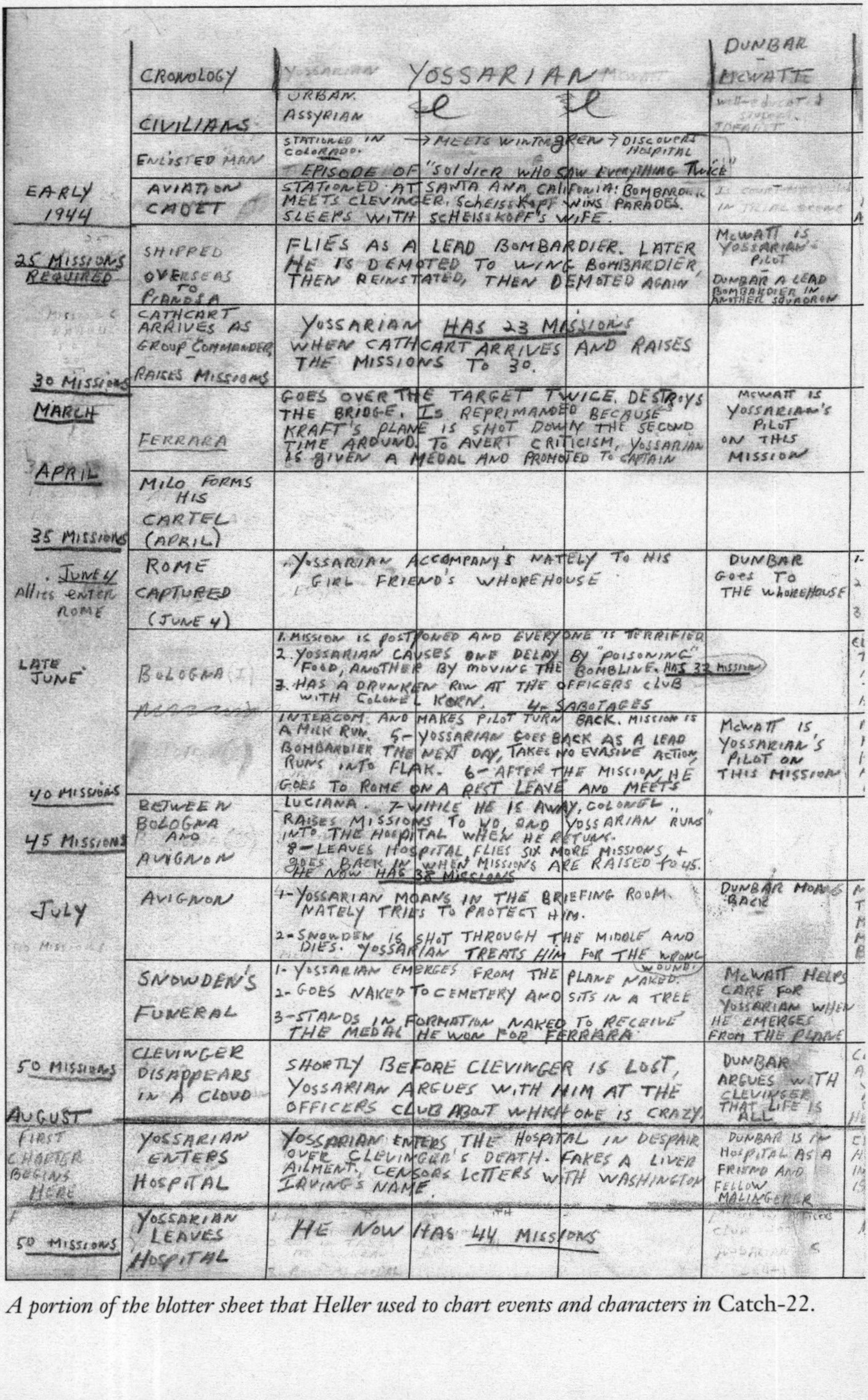

	CRONOLOGY	YOSSARIAN	DUNBAR – McWATT
	CIVILIANS	URBAN. ASSYRIAN	
	ENLISTED MAN	STATIONED IN COLORADO. → MEETS WINTERGREEN → DISCOVERS HOSPITAL. EPISODE OF "SOLDIER WHO SAW EVERYTHING TWICE"	
EARLY 1944	AVIATION CADET	STATIONED AT SANTA ANA CALIFORNIA: BOMBARDIER. MEETS CLEVINGER. SCHEISSKOPF WINS PARADES. SLEEPS WITH SCHEISSKOPF'S WIFE.	
25 MISSIONS REQUIRED	SHIPPED OVERSEAS TO PIANOSA	FLIES AS A LEAD BOMBARDIER. LATER HE IS DEMOTED TO WING BOMBARDIER, THEN REINSTATED, THEN DEMOTED AGAIN	McWATT IS YOSSARIAN'S PILOT. DUNBAR A LEAD BOMBARDIER IN ANOTHER SQUADRON
30 MISSIONS	CATHCART ARRIVES AS GROUP COMMANDER – RAISES MISSIONS	YOSSARIAN HAS 23 MISSIONS WHEN CATHCART ARRIVES AND RAISES THE MISSIONS TO 30.	
MARCH	FERRARA	GOES OVER THE TARGET TWICE, DESTROYS THE BRIDGE. IS REPRIMANDED BECAUSE KRAFT'S PLANE IS SHOT DOWN THE SECOND TIME AROUND. TO AVERT CRITICISM, YOSSARIAN IS GIVEN A MEDAL AND PROMOTED TO CAPTAIN	McWATT IS YOSSARIAN'S PILOT ON THIS MISSION
APRIL / 35 MISSIONS	MILO FORMS HIS CARTEL (APRIL)		
JUNE 4 Allies enter Rome	ROME CAPTURED (JUNE 4)	YOSSARIAN ACCOMPANY'S NATELY TO HIS GIRL FRIEND'S WHOREHOUSE	DUNBAR GOES TO THE WHOREHOUSE
LATE JUNE	BOLOGNA (I)	1. MISSION IS POSTPONED AND EVERYONE IS TERRIFIED. 2. YOSSARIAN CAUSES ONE DELAY BY "POISONING" FOOD, ANOTHER BY MOVING THE BOMBLINE. HAS 32 MISSIONS. 3. HAS A DRUNKEN ROW AT THE OFFICERS CLUB WITH COLONEL KORN. 4– SABOTAGES INTERCOM AND MAKES PILOT TURN BACK. MISSION IS A MILK RUN. 5– YOSSARIAN GOES BACK AS A LEAD BOMBARDIER THE NEXT DAY, TAKES NO EVASIVE ACTION, RUNS INTO FLAK. 6– AFTER THE MISSION, HE GOES TO ROME ON A REST LEAVE AND MEETS	McWATT IS YOSSARIAN'S PILOT ON THIS MISSION
40 MISSIONS / 45 MISSIONS	BETWEEN BOLOGNA AND AVIGNON	LUCIANA. 7– WHILE HE IS AWAY, COLONEL " RAISES MISSIONS TO 40, AND YOSSARIAN "RUNS" INTO THE HOSPITAL WHEN HE RETURNS. 8– LEAVES HOSPITAL, FLIES SIX MORE MISSIONS + GOES BACK IN WHEN MISSIONS ARE RAISED TO 45. HE NOW HAS 38 MISSIONS	
JULY	AVIGNON	1– YOSSARIAN MOANS IN THE BRIEFING ROOM. NATELY TRIES TO PROTECT HIM. 2– SNOWDEN IS SHOT THROUGH THE MIDDLE AND DIES. YOSSARIAN TREATS HIM FOR THE WRONG WOUND.	DUNBAR MOANS BACK
	SNOWDEN'S FUNERAL	1– YOSSARIAN EMERGES FROM THE PLANE NAKED. 2– GOES NAKED TO CEMETERY AND SITS IN A TREE. 3– STANDS IN FORMATION NAKED TO RECEIVE THE MEDAL HE WON FOR FERRARA	McWATT HELPS CARE FOR YOSSARIAN WHEN HE EMERGES FROM THE PLANE
50 MISSIONS	CLEVINGER DISAPPEARS IN A CLOUD	SHORTLY BEFORE CLEVINGER IS LOST, YOSSARIAN ARGUES WITH HIM AT THE OFFICERS CLUB ABOUT WHICH ONE IS CRAZY.	DUNBAR ARGUES WITH CLEVINGER THAT LIFE IS ALL
AUGUST – FIRST CHAPTER BEGINS HERE	YOSSARIAN ENTERS HOSPITAL	YOSSARIAN ENTERS THE HOSPITAL IN DESPAIR OVER CLEVINGER'S DEATH. FAKES A LIVER AILMENT, CENSORS LETTERS WITH WASHINGTON IRVING'S NAME.	DUNBAR IS IN HOSPITAL AS A FRIEND AND FELLOW MALINGERER
50 MISSIONS	YOSSARIAN LEAVES HOSPITAL	HE NOW HAS 44TH MISSIONS	

A portion of the blotter sheet that Heller used to chart events and characters in Catch-22.

CLEVINGER — NATELY	HUNGRY JOE — DOBBS	ORR	MILO	AARFY — CAPTAIN BLACK	CHAPLAIN
NATELY RICH CLEVINGER AN IDEALISTIC STUDENT	HUNGRY JOE A PHOTOGRAPHER	POOR AND RUSTIC	MARRIED; A FAITHFUL HUSBAND	AARFY A COLLEGE ALUMNUS	MARRIED: WI YOUNG CHILDRE
CLEVINGER FACES TRIAL AS A CADET AND IS FOUND GUILTY.			MILO IS A PILOT		
NATELY IS A CO-PILOT — CLEVINGER A BOMBARDIER	HUNGRY JOE AND DOBBS ARE BOTH PILOTS.	ORR IS A PILOT IN A WING PLANE AND IS ALWAYS BEING SHOT DOWN	VOLUNTEERS FOR MESS OFFICER AS SOON AS HE ARRIVES OVERSEAS	AARFY IS YOSSARIAN'S NAVIGATOR. BLACK IS THE SQUADRON INTELLIGENCE OFFICER	THE CHAPLAIN DOES NOT FIT IN AND HAS NO FRIENDS
	HUNGRY JOE HAS 25 MISSIONS AND IS WAITING TO GO HOME. HE IS PUT BACK ON COMBAT DUTY		HE PRODUCES FRESH EGGS AND BEGINS ORGANIZING HIS BUYING SYNDICATE		HE FEARS BOTH COLONELS AND IS BULLIED BY THEM.
	HUNGRY JOE HAS WRECKED A PLANE NEEDLESSLY. HE WAS GIVEN A MEDAL TO COVER UP HIS MISTAKE			AARFY MISLEADS YOSSARIAN, MAKING IT NECESSARY FOR THEM TO GO AROUND TWICE	
		ORR GOES ALONG ON THE TRIP TO EGYPT TO BUY COTTON.	MILO FLIES TO EGYPT AND BUYS THE WHOLE COTTON CROP	BLACK STARTS HIS LOYALTY OATH CRUSADE AGAINST MAJOR MAJOR	HE LOVES HIS WIFE AND MISSES HER.
1. NATELY FALLS IN LOVE 2. NATELY FINDS HIS GIRL AGAIN 3. THEY GO TO HER APARTMENT	HUNGRY JOE IS AMAZED BY ALL THE NAKED GIRLS IN THE APARTMENT		MILO ARRANGES THE MISSION TO ORVIETO AS A BUSINESS DEAL, WORKING FOR BOTH SIDES	AARFY SPEAKS OF NATELY'S GIRL WITH SMUG CONTEMPT	
CLEVINGER ARGUES THAT YOSSARIAN HAS NO RIGHT TO TRY TO SAVE HIS OWN LIFE	HUNGRY JOE HAS NIGHTMARES BECAUSE HE IS NOT SCHEDULED FOR THE MISSION TO BOLOGNA		MILO HAS DISPOSED OF THE LOYALTY OATH CRUSADE BECAUSE IT DISRUPTED BUSINESS	BLACK REJOICES THAT MEN ARE GOING TO BOLOGNA AND HANGS THE MORBID SIGN ON THE CLOSED MEDICAL TENT	
NATELY IS IN ROME COURTING HIS WHORE AND RUNS OUT OF MONEY	HUNGRY JOE TRIES TO TAKE PICTURES OF YOSSARIAN IN BED WITH LUCIANA	ORR HAS AN ENGINE AND HIS LANDING GEAR SHOT OUT BUT CRASH LANDS SAFELY.		AARFY GETS EVERYTHING WRONG ON THE BOLOGNA MISSION + DOESN'T HEAR WHEN YOSSARIAN SHOUTS AT HIM TO GET OUT OF THE NOSE	
			MILO BOMBS HIS OWN SQUADRON WHEN PAID TO DO SO BY THE GERMANS	BLACK SLEEPS WITH NATELY'S GIRL JUST TO TAUNT HIM	HE WORRIES CONSTANTLY ABOUT THE HEALTH AND SAFETY OF HIS WIFE AND CHILDREN
NATELY SUCCUMBS TO YOSSARIAN'S MISCHIEF AND MOANS IN THE BRIEFING ROOM	DOBBS PANICS, SEIZES CONTROLS, AND PLUNGES PLANE DOWN INTO FLAK		MILO HAS REMOVED THE MORPHINE FROM THE FIRST AID KIT, AND THERE IS NOTHING TO EASE SNOWDEN'S PAIN		
			MILO SEEKS YOSSARIAN OUT DURING SNOWDEN'S FUNERAL FOR HELP IN DISPOSING OF COTTON		CHAPLAIN SPIES YOSSARIAN NAKED IN A TREE AND THINKS IT IS A MYSTICAL VISION.
CLEVINGER ARGUES THAT YOSSARIAN IS CRAZY JUST BEFORE HE IS KILLED					
CLEVINGER'S PLANE HAS DISAPPEARED IN A CLOUD + HE IS GIVEN UP FOR DEAD	HUNGRY JOE KEEPS FINISHING MISSIONS AND KEEPS BEING RETURNED TO COMBAT DUTY	ORR IS YOSSARIAN'S ROOMMATE + KEEPS IMPROVING TENT	MILO TRUSTS YOSSARIAN BECAUSE HE WILL NOT STEAL FROM THE COUNTRY HE LOVES	AARFY IS YOSSARIAN'S INCOMPETENT LEAD NAVIGATOR	THE CHAPLAIN MEETS YOSSARIAN IN THE HOSPITAL.
NATELY IS AWAY IN ROME COURTING HIS WHORE		ORR HAS STARTED TO WINTERIZE THE TENT WHILE YOSSARIAN WAS IN THE HOSPITAL	MILO IS AWAY BUYING FIGS		

not impressed, but a young assistant there, Ms. Candida Donadio, was, and she secured permission to submit that chapter to a few publications that regularly published excerpts from "novels in progress."

In 1955 the chapter appeared in a paperback quarterly *New World Writing #7* (an anthology that also contained, under a pseudonym, an extract from another novel in progress—Jack Kerouac's *On the Road*). There came complimentary letters of interest from a few editors at established book publishers, and I was encouraged to continue with a work I now saw realistically was going to take me a good many years longer than I at first had guessed.

In 1957, when I had about 270 pages in typescript, I was employed at *Time* magazine, writing advertising-sales presentations by day when not furtively putting thoughts down on paper for my work on the novel at home that evening. And Candida Donadio was establishing herself as a preeminent agent in her own right, with a list of American authors as clients as impressive as any. We agreed it made sense to submit the partial manuscript to some publishers, mainly to obtain a practical idea of the potential for publication of this novel we both thought so much of. She was drawn toward a new young editor she knew of at Simon and Schuster, one she thought might prove more receptive to innovation than most. His name was Robert Gottlieb, and she was right.

While Gottlieb busied himself with those pages, I, with a four-week summer vacation from bountiful *Time* magazine, began rewriting them. Gottlieb and I met for lunch, mainly for him to gauge my temperament and ascertain how amenable I would be as an author to work with. After I listened to him allude with tact to certain broad suggestions he thought he eventually might be compelled to make, I handed him my new pages with the boastful response that I believed I had already taken care of nearly all of them.

He surprised me with concern that I might take exception to working with someone so young—he was twenty-six, I think, and I was thirty-four. I was more greatly surprised to learn from him later that both he and his closest colleague at Simon and Schuster, Nina Bourne, were intimidated at first by an air of suspicion I projected that I did not know I even possessed. I have not been suspicious of him since, and I doubt very much that Gottlieb, who went on to become the head of Alfred A. Knopf and then editor of *The New Yorker* magazine, has ever again been intimidated by anybody.

And what I still remember most agreeably about him is that he did not ask for an outline or once seek for even a hint of where this one-third of a novel he'd seen was going to go. The contract I received called for an advance of fifteen hundred dollars, half on signing, which I did not need, and the remainder on completion and acceptance.

Probably, I was his first novelist, but not his first to be published; other authors with completed manuscripts came to him in the three more years I needed to finish mine. Probably, I was Candida's earliest client too. Both were as delighted as I was with the eventual success of *Catch-22*, and the three of us have been reveling in our recollections of the experience ever since.

On February 28, 1962, the journalist Richard Starnes published a column of unrestrained praise in his newspaper, *The New York World-Telegram*, that opened with these words:

"Yossarian will, I think, live a very long time."

His tribute was unexpected, because Mr. Starnes was a newspaperman in the hard-boiled mode whose customary beat was local politics, and the *World-Telegram* was widely regarded as generally conservative.

To this day, I am grateful to Mr. Starnes for his unqualified and unsolicited approval and bless him for the accuracy of his prediction. Yossarian has indeed lived a long time. The *World-Telegram* has passed on. Many of the people mentioned in that first advertisement have died, and most of the rest of us are on the way.

But Yossarian is alive when the novel ends. Because of the motion picture, even close readers of the novel have a final, lasting image of him at sea, paddling toward freedom in a yellow inflated lifeboat. In the book he doesn't get that far; but he is not captured and he isn't dead. At the end of the successor volume I've just completed, *Closing Time* (that fleeing cartoon figure is again on the book jacket, but wearing a businessman's chapeau and moving with a cane), he is again still alive, more than forty years older but definitely still there. "Everyone has got to go," his physician friend in that novel reminds him with emphasis. "Everyone!" But should I ever write another sequel, he would still be around at the end.

Sooner or later, I must concede, Yossarian, now seventy, will have to pass away too. But it won't be by my hand.

Joseph Heller, 1994
East Hampton, New York

PART TWO

Other Voices

ROBERT BRUSTEIN (1927–) was one of the first prominent critics to weigh in on the literary significance of *Catch-22*. Nearly a month before the book's release, he wrote to Simon and Schuster's Nina Bourne to praise Heller's masterful dark humor and his ability to penetrate the surface illusions protecting the fundamental evils of our time. Brustein, writing during the early years of his long tenure as theater critic for *The New Republic*, published the following review in the November 13, 1961, issue.

THE LOGIC OF SURVIVAL IN A LUNATIC WORLD

by Robert Brustein

> The man who declares that survival at all costs is the end of existence is morally dead, because he's prepared to sacrifice all other values which give life its meaning.
>
> —SIDNEY HOOK

> ". . . It's better to die on one's feet than live on one's knees," Nately retorted with triumphant and lofty conviction. "I guess you've heard that saying before." "Yes, I certainly have," mused the treacherous old man, smiling again. "But I'm afraid you have it backward. It is better to live on one's feet than die on one's knees. That is the way the saying goes."
>
> —*CATCH-22*

Like all superlative works of comedy—and I am ready to argue that this is one of the most bitterly funny works in the language—*Catch-22* is based on an unconventional but utterly convincing internal logic. In the very opening pages, when we come upon a number of Air Force officers malingering in a hospital—one censoring all the modifiers out of enlisted men's letters and signing the censor's name "Washington Irving," another pursuing tedious conversations with boring Texans in order to increase his life span by making time pass slowly, still another storing horse chestnuts in his cheeks to give himself a look of innocence—it seems obvious that an inordinate number of Joseph Heller's characters are, by all conventional standards, mad. It is a triumph of Mr. Heller's skill that he is so quickly able to persuade us 1) that the most lunatic are the most logical, and 2) that it is our conventional standards which lack any logical consistency. The sanest looney of them all is the apparently harebrained central character, an American bombardier of Syrian extraction named Captain John Yossarian, who is based on a mythical Italian island (Pianosa) during World War II. For while many of his fellow officers seem indifferent to their own survival, and most of his superior officers are overtly hostile to his, Yossarian is animated solely by a desperate determination to stay alive:

> It was a vile and muddy war, and Yossarian could have lived without it—lived forever, perhaps. Only a fraction of his countrymen would give up their lives to win it, and it was not his ambition to be among them. . . . That men would die was a matter of necessity; which men would die, though, was a matter of circumstance, and Yossarian was willing to be the victim of anything but circumstance.

The single narrative thread in this crazy patchwork of anecdotes, episodes, and character portraits traces Yossarian's herculean efforts—through caution, cowardice, defiance, subterfuge, strategem, and subversion, through feigning illness, goofing off, and poisoning the company's food with laundry soap—to avoid being victimized by circumstance, a force represented in the book as Catch-22. For Catch-22 is the unwritten law which empowers the authorities to revoke your rights whenever it suits their cruel whims; it is, in short, the principle of absolute evil in a malevolent, mechanical, and incompetent world. Because of Catch-22, justice is mocked, the innocent are victimized, and Yossarian's squadron is forced to fly more than double the number of missions prescribed by Air Force code. Dogged by Catch-22, Yossarian becomes the anguished witness to the ghoulish slaughter of his crew members and the destruction of all his closest friends, until finally his fear of death becomes so intense that he refuses to wear a uniform, after his own has been besplattered with the guts of his dying gunner, and receives a medal standing naked in formation. From this point on, Yossarian's logic becomes so pure that everyone thinks him mad, for it is the logic of sheer survival, dedicated to keeping him alive in a world noisily clamoring for his annihilation.

According to this logic, Yossarian is surrounded on all sides by hostile forces: his enemies are distinguished less by their nationality than by their ability to get him killed. Thus, Yossarian feels a blind, electric rage against the Germans whenever they hurl flak at his easily penetrated plane; but he feels an equally profound hatred for those of his own countrymen who exercise an arbitrary power over his life and well-being. Heller's huge cast of characters, therefore, is dominated by a large number of comic malignities, *genus Americanus*, drawn with a grotesqueness so audacious that they somehow transcend caricature entirely and become vividly authentic. These include: Colonel Cathcart, Yossarian's commanding officer, whose consuming ambition to get his picture in the *Saturday Evening Post* motivates him to volunteer his command for every dangerous mission, and to initiate prayers during briefing sessions ("I don't want any of this Kingdom of God or Valley of Death stuff. That's all too negative. . . . Couldn't we pray for a tighter bomb pattern?"), an idea he abandons only when he learns enlisted men pray to the same God; General Peckem, head of Special Services, whose strategic objective is to replace General Dreedle, the wing commander, capturing every bomber group in the U.S. Air Force ("If dropping bombs on the enemy isn't a special service, I wonder what in the world is"); Captain Black, the squadron intelligence officer, who inaugurates the Glorious Loyalty Oath Crusade in order to discomfort a rival, forcing all officers (except the rival, who is thereupon declared a Communist) to sign a new oath whenever they get their flak suits, their paychecks, or their haircuts; Lieutenant Scheisskopf, paragon of the parade ground, whose admiration for efficient formations makes him scheme to screw nickel-alloy swivels into every cadet's back for perfect ninety-degree turns; and cadres of sadistic officers, club-happy MPs, and muddleheaded agents of the CID, two of whom, popping in and out of rooms like farcical private eyes, look for Washington Irving throughout the action, finally pinning the rap on the innocent chaplain.

These are Yossarian's antagonists, all of them reduced to a single exaggerated humor, and all identified by their totally mechanical attitude towards human life. Heller has a profound hatred for this kind of military mind, further anatomized in a wacky scene before the Action Board which displays his (and their) animosity in a manner both hilarious and scarifying. But Heller, at war with much larger forces than the army, has provided his book with much wider implications than a war novel. For the author (apparently sharing the Italian belief that vengeance is a dish which tastes best cold) has been nourishing his grudges for so long that they have expanded to include the postwar American world. Through the agency of grotesque comedy, Heller has found a way to confront the humbug, hypocrisy, cruelty, and sheer stupidity of our mass society—qualities which have made the few other Americans who care almost speechless with baffled rage—and through some miracle of prestidigitation, Pianosa has become a satirical microcosm for many of the macrocosmic idioicies of our time. Thus, the author flourishes his Juvenalian scourge at government-subsidized agriculture (and farmers, one of whom "spent every penny he didn't earn on new land to increase the amount of alfalfa he did not grow"); at the exploitation of American Indians, evicted from their oil-rich land; at smug psychiatrists; at bureaucrats and patriots; at acquisitive war widows; at high-spirited American boys; and especially, and most vindictively, at war profiteers.

This last satirical flourish, aimed at the whole mystique of corporation capitalism, is embodied in the fantastic adventures of Milo Minderbinder, the company mess officer, and a paradigm of good-natured Jonsonian cupidity. Anxious to put the war on a businesslike basis, Milo has formed a syndicate designed to corner the world market on all available foodstuffs, which he then sells to army mess halls at huge profits. Heady with success (his deals have made him mayor of every town in Sicily, Vice-Shah of Oran, Caliph of Baghdad, Imam of Damascus, and the Sheik of Araby), Milo soon expands his activities, forming a private army which he hires out to the highest bidder. The climax of Milo's career comes when he fulfills a contract with the Germans to bomb and strafe his own outfit, directing his planes from the Pianosa control tower and justifying the action with the stirring war cry: "What's good for the syndicate is good for the country." Milo has almost succeeded in his ambition to preempt the field of war for private enterprise when he makes a fatal mistake: he has cornered the entire Egyptian cotton market and is unable to unload it anywhere. Having failed to pass it off to his own mess hall in the form of chocolate-covered cotton, Milo is finally persuaded by Yossarian to bribe the American government to take it off his hands: "If you run into trouble, just tell everybody that the security of the country requires a strong domestic Egyptian cotton speculating industry." The Minderbinder sections—in showing the basic incompatibility of idealism and economics by satirizing the patriotic cant which usually accompanies American greed—illustrate the procedure of the entire book: the ruthless ridicule of hypocrisy through a technique of farce-fantasy, beneath which the demon of satire lurks, prodding fat behinds with a red-hot pitchfork.

It should be abundantly clear, then, that *Catch-22*, despite some of the most outrageous sequences since *A Night at the Opera*, is an intensely serious work. Heller has certain technical similarities to the Marx Brothers, Max Schulman, Kingsley Amis, Al Capp, and S. J. Perelman, but his mordant intelligence, closer to that of Nathanael West, penetrates the surface of the merely funny to expose a world of ruthless self-advancement, gruesome cruelty, and flagrant disregard for human life—a world, in short, very much like our own as seen through a magnifying glass, distorted for more perfect accuracy. Considering his indifference to surface reality, it is absurd to judge Heller by standards of psychological realism (or, for that matter, by conventional artistic standards at all, since his book is as formless as any picaresque epic). He is concerned entirely with that thin boundary of the surreal, the borderline between hilarity and horror, which, much like the apparent formlessness of the unconscious, has its own special integrity and coherence. Thus, Heller will never use comedy for its own sake; each joke has a wider significance in the intricate pattern, so that laughter becomes a prologue for some grotesque revelation. This gives the reader an effect of surrealistic dislocation, intensified by a weird, rather flat, impersonal style, full of complicated reversals, swift transitions, abrupt shifts in chronological time, and manipulated identities (e.g., if a private named Major Major Major is promoted to Major by a faulty IBM machine, or if a malingerer, sitting out a doomed mission, is declared dead through a bureaucratic error, then this remains their permanent fate), as if all mankind was determined by a mad and merciless mechanism.

Thus, Heller often manages to heighten the macabre obscenity of total war much more effectively through its gruesome comic aspects than if he had written realistic descriptions. And thus, the most delicate pressure is enough to send us over the line from farce into phantasmagoria. In the climactic chapter, in fact, the book leaves comedy altogether and becomes an eerie nightmare of terror. Here, Yossarian, walking through the streets of Rome as though through an Inferno, observes soldiers molesting drunken women, fathers beating ragged children, policemen clubbing innocent bystanders until the whole world seems swallowed up in the maw of evil:

> The night was filled with horrors, and he thought he knew how Christ must have felt as he walked through the world, like a psychiatrist through a ward of nuts, like a victim through a prison of thieves. . . . Mobs . . . mobs of policemen. . . . Mobs with clubs were in control everywhere.

Here, as the book leaves the war behind, it is finally apparent that Heller's comedy is his artistic response to his vision of transcendent evil, as if the escape route of laughter were the only recourse from a malignant world.

It is this world, which cannot be divided into boundaries or ideologies, that Yossarian has determined to resist. And so when his fear and disgust have reached the breaking point, he simply refuses to fly another mission. Asked by a superior what would happen if everybody felt the same way, Yossarian exercises his definitive logic, and answers, "Then I'd be a damned fool to feel any other way." Having concluded a separate peace, Yossarian maintains it in the face of derision, ostracism, psychological pressure, and the threat of court-martial. When he is finally permitted to go home if he will only agree to a shabby deal whitewashing Colonel Cathcart, however, he finds himself impaled on two impossible alternatives. But his unique logic, helped along by the precedent of an even more logical friend, makes him conclude that desertion is the better part of valor; and so (after an inspirational sequence which is the weakest thing in the book) he takes off for neutral Sweden—the only place left in the world, outside of England, where "mobs with clubs" are not in control.

Yossarian's expedient is not very flattering to our national ideals, being defeatist, selfish, cowardly, and unheroic. On the other hand, it is one of those sublime expressions of anarchic individualism without which all national ideals are pretty hollow anyway. Since the mass State, whether totalitarian or democratic, has grown increasingly hostile to Falstaffian irresponsibility, Yossarian's antiheroism is, in fact, a kind of inverted heroism which we would do well to ponder. For, contrary to the armchair pronouncements of patriotic ideologues, Yossarian's obsessive concern for survival makes him not only not morally dead, but one of the most morally vibrant figures in recent literature—and a giant of the will beside those wary, wise, and wistful prodigals in contemporary novels who always accommodate sadly to American life. I believe that Joseph Heller is one of the most extraordinary talents now among us. He has Mailer's combustible radicalism without his passion for violence and self-glorification; he has Bellow's gusto with his compulsion to affirm the unaffirmable; and he has Salinger's wit without his coquettish self-consciousness. Finding his absolutes in the freedom to be, in a world dominated by cruelty, carnage, inhumanity, and a rage to destroy itself, Heller has come upon a new morality based on an old ideal, the morality of refusal. Perhaps—now that *Catch-22* has found its most deadly nuclear form—we have reached the point where even the logic of survival is unworkable. But at least we can still contemplate the influence of its liberating honesty on a free, rebellious spirit in this explosive, bitter, subversive, brilliant book.

NELSON ALGREN (1909–1981) advanced *Catch-22*'s grassroots popularity in the Midwest with an influential assessment of the novel's staying power in the June 23, 1962, issue of the *Chicago Daily News*. Algren's abiding love of outsiders and nonconformists and his hatred of corruption made him an early fan of *Catch-22;* the following review presented his first assessment of the novel in the November 4, 1961, issue of *The Nation*.

THE CATCH

by Nelson Algren

There was only one catch and that was Catch-22, which specified that a concern for one's own safety in the face of dangers that were real and immediate was the process of a rational mind. Orr was crazy and could be grounded. All he had to do was ask; and as soon as he did, he would no longer be crazy and would have to fly more missions. He would be crazy to fly more missions and sane if he didn't, but if he was sane he had to fly them. Yossarian was moved very deeply by the absolute simplicity of this clause and let out a respectful whistle:

> "That's some catch, that Catch-22," he observed.
> "It's the best there is," Doc Daneeka agreed.

Yossarian was moved deeply day and night and what moved him more deeply than anything else was the fact that they were trying to murder him.

> "Who's '*they*'?" Clevenger wanted to know. "Who, specifically, is trying to murder you?"
> "Every one of them," Yossarian told him.
> "Every one of *whom*?"
> "Every one of whom do you think?"
> "I haven't any idea."
> "Then how do you know they aren't?"

Yossarian had proof, because strangers he didn't know shot at him with cannons every time he flew up into the air to drop bombs on them, so it was of no use for Clevenger to say "No one is trying to kill you."

"Then why are they shooting at me?"

"They're shooting at everyone."

"And what difference does that make?"

"I'm not going to argue with you," Clevenger decided, "you don't know who you hate."

"Whoever is trying to poison me."

"Nobody is trying to poison you."

"They poisoned my food twice, didn't they? Didn't they put poison in my food at Ferrara and during the Great Big Siege of Bologna?"

"They put poison in everybody's food," Clevenger explained.

"And what difference does that make?"

There was no established procedure for evasive action. All you needed was fear, and Yossarian had plenty of that. He bolted wildly for his life on each mission the instant his bombs were away. When he fufilled the thirty-five missions required of each man of his group, he asked to be sent home.

Colonel Cathcart had by then raised the missions required to forty. When Yossarian had flown forty he asked to be sent home. Colonel Cathcart had raised the missions required to forty-five—there *did* seem to be a catch *somewhere*. Yossarian went into the hospital with a pain in his liver that fell just short of being jaundice. If it became jaundice the doctors could treat it. If it didn't become jaundice and went away they could discharge him. Yossarian decided to spend the rest of the war in bed by running a daily temperature of 101. He had found a catch of his own.

To preserve his sanity against the formalized lunacy of the military mind in action, Yossarian had to turn madman. Yet even Yossarian is more the patriot than Sgt. Minderbinder, the business mind in action. Even Yossarian has to protest when Minderbinder arranges with the Germans to let them knock American planes down at a thousand dollars per plane. Minderbinder is horrified—"Have you no respect for the sanctity of a business contract?" he demands of Yossarian, and Yossarian feels ashamed of himself.

Below its hilarity, so wild that it hurts, *Catch-22* is the strongest repudiation of our civilization, in fiction, to come out of World War II. *The Naked and the Dead* and *From Here to Eternity* are lost within it. That the horror and the hypocrisy, the greed and the complacency, the endless cunning and the endless stupidity which now go to constitute what we term Christianity are dealt with here in absolutes, does not lessen the truth of its repudiation. Those happy few who hit upon Terry Southern's *The Magic Christian* will find that what Southern said with some self-doubt, Heller says with no doubt whatsoever. To compare *Catch-22* favorably with *The Good Soldier Schweik* would be an injustice, because this novel is not merely the best American novel to come out of World War II; it is the best American novel that has come out of anywhere in years.

STUDS TERKEL (1912–2008) had not yet developed the literary prominence that marked the final decades of his long career when he wrote one of the first Midwest reviews of *Catch-22*. He was a prominent Chicago radio interview host, and his fascination with characters and human interaction is apparent in his review, which appeared in the November 26, 1961, *Chicago Sun-Times*.

There's Always a Catch, Especially 22

by Studs Terkel

As the old Italian woman wailed at Yossarian, the bombardier, "Catch-22 says they have a right to do anything we can't stop them from doing." Yossarian, a bad soldier Schweik, tries in wondrous ways to stop them. "Them" is the Military Mind. "Them" is the nutty world of war.

Yossarian, dangerously sane, is scared equally of those crazy strangers who keep firing flak at him just because he's dropping bombs on them and of Col. Cathcart, who keeps raising the number of combat missions. Yossarian seeks to endure in bewildering manner and fashion: inventing a mysterious liver complaint, seeing everything twice, walking backwards, standing in formation quite naked, deserting.

You will meet in this astonishing novel, certainly one of the most original in years, madmen of every rank: Major Major Major, on whose unwilling frame the gold leaf is pinned because of his unfortunate resemblance to Henry Fonda; Doc Daneeka, who is declared dead despite his high temperature; Hungry Joe and his fistfights with Huple's cat; ex-Pfc. Wintergreen, who has more power than almost anybody.

Most remarkable of all performers in this circus of hilarity and horror is Milo Minderbinder, the mess officer. He is the classic apostle of private enterprise. He bombs his own airfield when the Germans make him a civilized offer of cost plus 6 percent.

Things look bad for Milo what with everybody accusing him of treachery and things like that until he opens his books. There's a reasonable profit for everybody. You see, everybody shares because everybody is a member of Milo's syndicate. Even the enemy.

Anyway, there is such a thing as sanctity of contract and when Milo becomes righteously indignant, who can blame him? He is a revolutionary thinker who seeks to take war out of the hands of government. He believes private enterprise can do it better.

Page after page, you will howl, you will roar. You may even fall off your chair as I did. Suddenly you will sit up and mumble: "What's so funny?" To call it the finest comic novel of our day is faulting it.

To call it a surrealistic commentary of our time won't do either. Is it any more surrealistic than the neutron bomb, guaranteed to damage neither brick nor metal and merely kill man?

Kafka, Schweik, the Marx Brothers, all these come to mind. Lewis Carroll may be even closer. Alice's adventures were no more outrageous than Yossarian's.

If Joseph Heller writes no other book, he will be well remembered for this apocalyptic masterpiece. There is only one catch . . . and that's "Catch-22."

PHILIP TOYNBEE (1916–1981), son of the historian Arnold Toynbee, was a prominent mid-century British intellectual and a longtime literary critic for the London *Observer*. His early anti-establishment views and his own success with experimental forms of fiction underlie his June 17, 1962, *Observer* review of *Catch-22*, which traces Heller's satire all the way to the tragicomic core of the human condition.

HERE'S GREATNESS—IN SATIRE

by Philip Toynbee

When I began reading *Catch-22* I thought it was a farcical satire on life in the United States Army Air Force. Later I believed that Mr. Heller's target was modern war and all those who are responsible for waging it. Still later it seemed that he was attacking social organization and anyone who derives power from it. But by the end of the book it had become plain to me that it is—no other phrase will do—the human condition itself which is the object of Mr. Heller's outraged fury and disgust.

A reviewer must always keep an anxious eye on the state of his currency. If he announces too many masterpieces he risks inflation (though it is sometimes forgotten by some of us that the cowardice of perpetual crabbing receives its own kind of punishment). It does not seem many weeks since I was proclaiming that Malcolm Lowry's *Under the Volcano* is one of the great English novels of the century; and not long before that I was urging that attention should be paid to the magnificent and neglected talent of William Gerhardi.

But at the risk of inflation I cannot help writing that *Catch-22* is the greatest satirical work in English since *Erewhon*. For the fact is that all my successive interpretations of this book now seem to me to have been accurate, even if the earlier ones were also incomplete. The book has an immense and devastating theme, but this theme is illustrated, as it should be, by means of an observed reality.

Reality Inflated

I am not suggesting that *Catch-22* is a realistic account of life in the wartime air force of America or any other country. The method of satire is to inflate reality so that all its partially concealed blemishes turn into monstrous and apparent deformations. The effect of good satire is to make us laugh with horror. And this means that the social and personal evils which are being satirized must have been *there*, and must be felt by the reader to be there even while he is laughing at the results of the satirist's inflating imagination.

Here is an example. Among the vast number of hallucinatory characters in *Catch-22* there is an officer called Milo Minderbinder who devotes all his time to infinitely elaborate commercial enterprises in the Mediterranean field of operations. At one point he bombs his own airfield in exchange for a promise from the Germans of the cost of the operation plus 6 percent. Several of his friends are killed, but Milo is much too valuable to be reprimanded, let alone punished, by the American authorities.

Murderous

Utterly impossible? No doubt; yet when I was stationed on the northeast coast in 1941 the new concrete dragon's teeth on the beach began to corrode away after only three months. It was found that the contractor had built brittle shells of concrete and filled them with sand. Yet when I expressed outrage at this murderous piece of cheating it was explained that the man was of too much local importance for any action to be taken against him. His behavior had, indeed, been less dramatic than Milo's; but was it any less flagrant or appalling?

In the same way the frightful Colonel Cathcart of *Catch-22* cares about nothing except keeping in well with his superiors at any price. To do so he continually increases the quota of missions which his men must fly before being sent home on leave. The original number was forty, but by the end of the book it has reached eighty.

We may reasonably guess that higher authorities would have prevented this from happening, even if the flyers themselves had not achieved some sort of resistance. Yet I haven't the least doubt that many a colonel in the armies involved would have behaved like Colonel Cathcart if he had believed that he could get away with it. Was Haig's behavior very different at the third battle of Ypres?

If *Catch-22* has any continuous theme it lies in the tireless efforts of Yossarian, the Assyrian-American hero, to evade combat duties. The book defends the right, indeed almost the moral obligation, of men to be physical cowards. It is pointed out, for example, that the brave almost always involve others in their senseless and unfeeling cooperation with the forces of war. The man who has the courage of his physical cowardice is the only kind of man who will eventually make war impossible by refusing to play any part in it at all.

This is, in fact, the position which Yossarian—one of the most sympathetic heroes in modern literature—finally arrives at:

> "From now on I'm thinking only of me."
>
> Major Danby replied indulgently with a superior smile, "But, Yossarian, suppose everyone felt that way."
>
> "Then I'd certainly be a damned fool to feel any other way, wouldn't I?"

Exactly; and it is clearly Mr. Heller's fervent hope that everyone will, in the end, feel that way.

Raging Pity

This is an arguable attitude, I suppose, though I have never been able to think of much to be said against it. But though it places Mr. Heller in a very strong satirical position it would not, by itself, have enabled him to write a great book. He has done this because he is a man of deep and urgent compassion whose raging pity is concerned with the nature of human existence itself no less than with specific and curable iniquities.

> "And don't tell me God works in a mysterious way," Yossarian continued, hurtling on over her objection. "There's nothing mysterious about it. He's not working at all. He's playing. Or else He's forgotten all about us. That's the kind of God you people talk about—a country bumpkin, a clumsy, bungling, brainless, conceited, uncouth hayseed. Good God, how much reverence can you have for a Supreme Being who finds it necessary to include such phenomena as phlegm and tooth decay in His divine system of creation? What in the world was running through that warped, evil, scatological mind of His when He robbed old people of the power to control their bowel movements? Why in the world did He ever create pain?"
>
> "Pain?" Lieutenant Scheisskopf's wife pounced upon the word victoriously. "Pain is a useful symptom. Pain is a warning to us of bodily dangers."
>
> "And who created the dangers?" Yossarian demanded.

But it is death itself which is the principal target of this book, the principal object of Mr. Heller's horrified resentment. Unlike that old philistine, Carlyle, he does not find it necessary to accept the universe. This comparatively early passage is confirmed in the magnificent sustained horror of Yossarian's nightmare peregrination of the streets of Rome. And this is placed near enough the end of the book to act as a peroration.

Yet it can hardly be too much insisted that *Catch-22* is a very, very funny book and by no means a depressing one. To counter his horror of death Mr. Heller celebrates sexuality in a richly comic tone which is blessedly unLawrentian. What is so remarkable, and perhaps unique, is that Mr. Heller can move us from farce into tragedy within a page or two, and that we accept the transition without demur.

In *Candide* the hero suffers the most drastic physical injuries, yet we are never tempted to take them seriously. Candide's mutilations are a convention of the satirical genre, and nothing more. But when, for example, Kid Sampson is suddenly cut in two while bathing we share the horror and shock of the onlookers.

Subversive

I suppose the book has faults. It is a little too long and repetitive. Very occasionally the humor turns into a rather brittle and slick form of verbal wit. ("He advocated thrift and hard work and disapproved of loose women who turned him down.") There is rather too much Lewis Carroll nonsense humour, and sometimes the passages of "straight" horror or pity sound a little raucous. If anything Mr. Heller tends to be overexplanatory, and to ram home his messages beyond the point where they have been well taken. But I mean these complaints to be trivial, for this is a book that I could wish everyone to read. It is a genuinely subversive book in the best sense—written, incidentally, by a thirty-nine-year-old New York "promotion executive," whatever that may be—but it sounds deplorable. It is a book which should really help us to feel more clearly.

And Catch-22?

> Yossarian looked at him soberly and tried another approach. "Is Orr crazy?"
>
> "He sure is," Doc Daneeka said.
>
> "Can you ground him?"
>
> "I sure can. But first he has to ask me to. That's part of the rule."
>
> "Then why doesn't he ask you to?"
>
> "Because he's crazy," Doc Daneeka said. "He has to be crazy to

keep flying combat missions after all the close calls he's had. Sure I can ground Orr. But first he has to ask me."

"And then you can ground him?" Yossarian asked.

"No. Then I can't ground him."

"You mean there's a catch?"

"Sure there's a catch," Doc Daneeka replied. "Catch-22. Anyone who wants to get out of combat duty isn't really crazy. . . ."

"That's some catch, that Catch-22," Yossarian observed.

"It's the best there is," Doc Daneeka agreed.

NORMAN MAILER (1923–2007) included a significant assessment of Heller and *Catch-22* in "Some Children of the Goddess—Norman Mailer Vs. Nine Writers," a controversial essay intended as an emotional response to the work of selected contemporaries rather than a conventional piece of literary criticism. Heller, along with Saul Bellow and William S. Burroughs, received higher marks than other authors; the Heller section is extracted in its entirety from the July 1963 issue of *Esquire*.

An Excerpt from "Some Children of the Goddess—Norman Mailer Vs. Nine Writers"

by Norman Mailer

Now beyond a doubt, of all the books discussed here, the one which most cheats evaluation is Joseph Heller's *Catch-22*. It was the book which took me longest to finish, and I almost gave it up. Yet I think that a year from now I may remember it more vividly than *The Thin Red Line*. Because it is an original. There's no book like it anyone has read. Yet it's maddening. It reminds one of a Jackson Pollock painting, eight feet high, twenty feet long. Like yard goods, one could cut it anywhere. One could take out a hundred pages anywhere from the middle of *Catch-22*, and not even the author could be certain they were gone. Yet the length and similarity of one page to another gives a curious meat-and-potatoes to the madness; building upon itself the book becomes substantial until the last fifty pages grow suddenly and surprisingly powerful, only to be marred by an ending over the last five pages which is hysterical, sentimental and wall-eyed for Hollywood.

This is the skin of the reaction. If I were a major critic, it would be a virtuoso performance to write a definitive piece on *Catch-22*. It would take ten thousand words or more. Because Heller is carrying his reader on a more consistent voyage through Hell than any American writer before him (except Burroughs who has already made the trip and now sells choice seats in the auditorium), and so the analysis of Joseph H.'s Hell would require a discussion of other varieties of inferno and whether they do more than this author's tour.

Catch-22 is a nightmare about an American bomber squadron on a made-up island off Italy. Its hero is a bombardier named Yossarian who has flown fifty missions and wants out. On this premise is tattooed the events of the novel, fifty characters, two thousand frustrations (an average of four or five to the page) and one simple motif: more frustration. Yossarian's colonel wants to impress his general and so raises the number of missions to fifty-five. When the pilots have fifty-four, the figure is lifted to sixty. They are going for eighty by the time the book has been done. On the way every character goes through a routine *on every page* which is as formal as a little peasant figure in a folk dance. Back in school, we had a joke we used to repeat. It went:

> "Whom are you talking about?"
> "Herbert Hoover."
> "Never heard of him."
> "Never heard of whom?"
> "Herbert Hoover."
> "Who's he?"
> "He's the man you mentioned."
> "Never heard of Herbert Hoover."

So it went. So goes *Catch-22*. It's the rock and roll of novels. One finds its ancestor in Basic Training. We were ordered to have clean sheets for Saturday inspection. But one week we were given no clean sheets from the Post laundry so we slept on mattress covers, which got dirty. After inspection, the platoon was restricted to quarters. "You didn't have clean sheets," our sergeant said.

"How could we have clean sheets if the clean sheets didn't come?"

"How do I know?" said the sergeant. "The regulation says you gotta have clean sheets."

"But we can't have clean sheets if there are no clean sheets."

"That," said the sergeant, "is tough shit."

Which is what *Catch-22* should have been called. The army is a village of colliding bureaucracies whose colliding orders cook up impossibilities. Heller takes this one good joke and exploits it into two thousand variations of the same good joke, but in the act he somehow creates a rational vision of the modern world. Yet the crisis of reason is that it can no longer comprehend the modern world. Heller demonstrates that a rational man devoted to reason must arrive at the conclusion that either the world is mad and he is the only sane man in it, or (and this is the weakness of *Catch-22*—it never explores this possibility) the sane man is not really sane because his rational propositions are without existential reason.

On page 179, there is a discussion about God.

> ". . . how much reverence can you have for a Supreme Being who finds it necessary to include such phenomena as phlegm and tooth decay in His divine system of creation . . . Why in the world did He ever create pain?"
>
> "Pain?" Lieutenant Scheisskopf's wife pounced upon the word victoriously. "Pain is a useful symptom. Pain is a warning to us of bodily dangers."
>
> . . . "Why couldn't He have used a doorbell instead, to notify us, or one of His celestial choirs?"

Right there is planted the farthest advance of the flag of reason in his cosmology. Heller does not look for any answer, but there is an answer which might go that God gave us pain for the same reason the discovery of tranquilizers was undertaken by the Devil: if we have an immortal soul some of us come close to it only through pain. A season of sickness can be preferable to a flight from disease for it discourages the onrush of a death which begins in the center of oneself.

Give talent its due. *Catch-22* is the debut of a writer with merry gifts. Heller may yet become Gogol. But what makes one hesitate to call his first novel great or even major is that he has only grasped the inferior aspect of Hell. What is most unendurable is not the military world of total frustration so much as the midnight frustration of the half-world, Baldwin's other country, where a man may have time to hear his soul, and time to go deaf, even be forced to contemplate himself as he becomes deadened before his death. (Much as Hemingway may have been.) That is when one becomes aware of the anguish, the existential *angst*, which wars enable one to forget. It is that other death—without war—where one dies by a failure of nerve, which opens the bloodiest vents of Hell. And that is a novel none of us has yet come back alive to write.

ALFRED KAZIN (1915–1998) was one of the most influential literary historians and critics of the twentieth century. *On Native Grounds* (1942) established a dominant view of the fiction of the previous four decades; Kazin's sequel, *Bright Book of Life* (1973), continued his assessment through the intervening decades. His evaluation of *Catch-22*, along with Kazin's brief framing comments about midcentury war literature, are reprinted below from the "Decline of War" chapter of *Bright Book of Life*.

AN EXCERPT FROM *BRIGHT BOOK OF LIFE*

by Alfred Kazin

World War II turned into a very different war over the twenty-five years in which we have been forced to think of Hiroshima, Auschwitz, Dresden, the thirty million dead, the returning Soviet soldiers imprisoned by their own government for having been captured by the Germans, the threat of universal nuclear destruction. Of *this* war, opposed to the war described in *A Bell for Adano*, *The Young Lions*, *The Caine Mutiny*, *The Gallery*—war as liberal tourism—one can only say what Whitman said of the Civil War—"the real war will never get into the books." No individual experience, as reported in literature, can do justice to it, and the most atrocious common experiences will always seem unreal as we read about them. When the British liberated Belsen on April 15, 1945, they came upon forty thousand sick, starving and dying prisoners, over ten thousand corpses stacked in heaps. Belsen was not the worst Nazi camp, merely the first to be exposed to the world. *The* (London) *Times* correspondent began his dispatch—"It is my duty to describe something beyond the imagination of mankind." This became the only serious and honest view of World War II as, by the Fifties, the liberal intellectual's image of it was demolished by so many uncovered horrors, so many new wars on the horizon, such a continued general ominousness, that "*the* war" soon became War anywhere, anytime—War that has never ended. War as the continued experience of twentieth-century man.

Realism about war, observation from the literary sidelines, even one's own unvarnished experience in a concentration camp, could no longer express "War" as they did "*the* war." War as an actuality, bound by space and time, an event that literature "could do justice to," soon yielded to an apocalyptic sense of the possible destruction of mankind, the boundlessness of its enmities. Above all, we had the sense of a world made totally the same, which it wasn't, and "absurd," that glib term for the rejection of society by those living tolerably in it. Albert Camus in *Le Mythe de Sisyphe* had meant by the absurd no more than what modern writers in the tradition of romantic individualism have always meant: the superiority of man to his naturally limited and frustrating existence. As D. H. Lawrence said, man has his excess always on his hands. It is natural for man to be rebellious against the terms of his life and his death, to be dissatisfied with everything but his own mind, to be an outsider and an overreacher—and thus to feel "absurd" to himself. But now society became "absurd," an untenable term but natural to a period in which the power of the state to make war, to destroy life on the planet, seemed more and more unmanageable. "War" had come to seem the normal, omnipresent condition of daily living, dominating a whole generation by the terror of its weapons and by the visible undoing, in the preparations for war, of those human loyalties and common values in the name of which war used to be fought.

The essence of such novels as Joseph Heller's *Catch-22* and Kurt Vonnegut's *Slaughterhouse-Five, or The Children's Crusade* is that though both are ostensibly about the 1941–1945 war, in which both writers served, they are really about The Next War, and thus about a war which will be without limits and without meaning, a war that will end only when no one is alive to fight it. The theme of *Catch-22* in particular is the total craziness of war, the craziness of all those who submit to it, and the struggle to survive by the one man, Yossarian, who knows the difference between his sanity and the insanity of the system. But how can one construct fictional meaning, narrative progression, out of a system in which virtually everyone but the hero assents to madness, willingly falls into the role of the madman-who-pretends-to-be-sane? The answer is that *Catch-22* is about the hypothesis of a totally rejectable world, a difficult subject, perhaps impossible so long as the "world" is undifferentiated, confused with man's angry heart itself—but expressive of the political uselessness many Americans have felt about themselves since World War II. So Heller, who combines the virtuousness of a total pacifist with the mocking pseudo-rationality of traditional Jewish humor, has to fetch up one sight gag after another. "The dead man in Yossarian's tent was simply not easy to live with." "General Dreedle was incensed by General Peckem's recent directive requiring all tents in the Mediterranean theater of operations to be pitched along parallel lines with entrances facing back proudly toward the Washington monument." The book moves by Yossarian's asking sensible, human, logical questions about war to which the answers are madly inconsequent. Heller himself is the straight man on this lunatic stage, Yossarian the one human being in this farcically antihuman setup. The jokes are variations on the classic Yiddish story of the totally innocent recruit who pokes his head over the trench, discovers that everyone is firing away, and cries out in wonder—"One can get killed here!"

Yet the impressive emotion in *Catch-22* is not "black humor," the "totally absurd," those current articles of liberal politics, but horror. Whenever the book veers back to its primal scene, a bombardier's evisceration in a plane being smashed by flak, a scene given us directly and piteously, we recognize what makes *Catch-22* disturbing. The gags are a strained effort to articulate the imminence of *anyone's* death now by violence, and it is just this that makes it impossible to "describe war" in traditional literary ways. Despite the running gags, the telltale quality of *Catch-22* is that it doesn't move, it can't. The buried-alive feeling of being caught in a plane under attack, of seeing one's partner eviscerated, produces the total impotence of being unable to move, to escape. And this horror-cold immobility is reproduced not in the static, self-conscious distortion of the gags but in the violence of the straight "serious" passages:

> The forward bombardier would have liked to be a ball turret gunner. That was where he wanted to be if he had to be there at all, instead of hung out there in front like some goddamned cantilevered goldfish bowl while the goddam foul black tiers of flak were bursting and booming and billowing all around and above and below him in a climbing, cracking, staggered, banging, phantasmagorical, cosmological wickedness that jarred and tossed and shivered, clattered and pierced, and threatened to annihilate them all in one splinter of a second in one vast flash of fire.

The urgent emotion in Heller's book is thus every individual's sense today of being directly in the line of fire, of being trapped, of war not as an affair of groups in which *we* may escape, but as my and your nemesis. The psychology in *Catch-22* is that of a man being led to execution, of a gallows humor in which the rope around one's neck feels all too real (and is plainly stamped General Issue). This sense of oneself not as a soldier in a large protective group but as an isolated wretch doomed to die *unaccountably* is more and more a feature of literature about World War II. It haunts all fiction by Jews since the war, even novels which do not deal with the war, like Edward Lewis Wallant's *The Pawnbroker,* Saul Bellow's *Mr. Sammler's Planet,* Mordecai Richler's *St. Urbain's Horseman.* As the Holocaust becomes more and more unreal to every new generation, Jewish writers who were stamped by it turn it into the only Jewish version of Original Sin—evil unredeemed, unexplained, unpunished, even unbelieved by most of mankind. So every account of it by Jewish writers, no matter how dim and remote from 1933–1945 the attempt to pass the story on, turns into one man's account of insupportable and inexplicable evil—into the seeming fantasy of a "world" coming down on the single and often insignificant witness who is telling the story. Just as traditional Christian poetry and epic helped to create a postclassical literature founded on the individual's relation to original sin, so much of contemporary fiction is founded on a struggle with evil "intolerable" because of the inability of liberal politics to explain and of the liberal imagination to represent. There is no politics in our contemporary war novels, for it is impossible to posit any aim to destruction on such a scale as the thirty million who died in World War II. Destruction was committed at Hiroshima, Nagasaki, Dresden because the weapons for it were available, because these cities were on the timetable.

JOHN W. ALDRIDGE (1922–2007) was considered by many postwar writers to be the most insightful scholarly critic of midcentury American fiction. His seminal 1951 study, *After the Lost Generation*, was reissued in 1985, and was soon followed by his twenty-fifth-anniversary assessment of *Catch-22*, reprinted here from the October 26, 1986, *New York Times Book Review*.

THE LOONY HORROR OF IT ALL—*CATCH-22* TURNS 25

by John W. Aldridge

Looking back today at *Catch-22*—which was published twenty-five years ago this month—we are able to see that it has had a remarkable, if not altogether unclouded, literary history. It has passed from relatively modest initial success with readers and critics—many of whom liked the book for just the reasons that caused others to hate it—through massive best-sellerdom and early canonization as a youth-cult sacred text to its current status as a monumental artifact of contemporary American literature, almost as assured of longevity as the statues on Easter Island.

Yet it is only in recent years that we have begun to learn how to read this curious book and, as is the case with those statues, to understand how and why it got here and became what it is instead of what we may once have believed it to be. The history of *Catch-22* is, in effect, also a significant chapter in the history of contemporary criticism—its steady growth in sophistication, its evolving archeological intelligence, above all its realization that not only is the medium of fiction the message but that the medium *is* a fiction capable of sending a fair number of frequently discrete but interlocking messages, depending of course on the complexity of the imagination behind it and the sensibility of the receiver.

The truth of this last is attested to in perhaps a meretricious sort of way by the large diversity of responses *Catch-22* received in the first year or two following its publication in 1961. They ranged from the idiotically uncomprehending at the lowest end of the evaluative scale to the prophetically perceptive at the highest, and in between there were the reservedly appreciative, the puzzled but enthusiastic, the ambivalent and annoyed, and more than a few that were rigid with moral outrage.

One of the best examples of the many mixed responses was Richard G. Stern's brief but eloquent review that appeared in these pages on October 22, 1961. Mr. Stern saw the book as "a portrait gallery, a collection of anecdotes, some of them wonderful, a parade of scenes" presented with "much passion, comic and fervent." But "it gasps for want of craft and sensibility" and finally it is not a novel. "Joseph Heller is like a brilliant painter who decides to throw all the ideas in his sketchbooks onto one canvas, relying on their charm and shock to compensate for the lack of design."

Way over at the other end of the critical combat zone were those who were extravagant in their praise of the book and entirely untroubled by its eccentricities of form. Most notable among these were Nelson Algren and Robert Brustein. Algren, writing in *The Nation*, called *Catch-22* "not merely the best American novel to come out of World War II; it is the best American novel to come out of anywhere in years." Mr. Brustein, in his *New Republic* review, was so superbly intelligent about the book that much of the later criticism has done little to improve his essential argument. He saw at once, for example, that the air force setting in World War II is only the ostensible subject of the book and that Mr. Heller's achievement lies in his brilliant use of that setting as a metaphor or "a satirical microcosm for many of the macrocosmic idiocies" afflicting the postwar era in general. Mr. Brustein was also able to foresee what later critics, after considerable equivocation, came to acknowledge: that the descent into phantasmagoric horror, which occurs in the concluding chapters of the book, is not a violation of the comic mode but a plausible vindication of it, since, as he put it, "the escape route of laughter [is] the only recourse from a malignant world."

Finally, following the same pioneering logic, Mr. Brustein recognized that, given the premises Mr. Heller had established, Yossarian's decision to desert, which has been much debated by critics, far from being a poorly justified conclusion for the novel, is in fact a meticulously prepared-for conclusion. It represents an act of "invested heroism," "one of those sublime expressions of anarchic individualism without which all natural ideals are pretty hollow anyway," if only because it is proof that Yossarian, alone of them all, has managed to remain morally alive and able to take responsibility for his life in a totally irresponsible world.

If responses as appreciative as Mr. Brustein's were a rarity in 1961, one reason may be that most reviewers were locked into a conventional and—as shortly became evident—an outmoded assumption about what war fiction should be. They had, after all, been conditioned by the important novels of World War I and reconditioned by the World War II novels of Norman Mailer, Irwin Shaw, John Horne Burns, James Jones and others to expect that the authentic technique for treating war experience is harshly documentary realism. The exceptions, of course, were the sweetly hygienic productions of Marion Hargrove and Thomas Heggen, which were comic in an entirely innocuous way and depicted military life—mostly well behind the combat zone—as being carried on with all the prankish exuberance of a fraternity house beer party.

Coming into this context, *Catch-22* clearly seemed anomalous and more than a trifle ominous. It was a work of consummate zaniness populated by squadrons of madly eccentric, cartoonographic characters whose antics were far loonier than anything ever seen before in war fiction—or, for that matter, in any fiction. Yet the final effect of the book was neither exhilarating nor palliative. This was a new kind of comedy, one that disturbed and subverted before it delighted and was ultimately as deadly in earnest, as savagely bleak and ugly, as the most dissident war fiction of Erich Maria Remarque, Dos Passos or Mr. Mailer. In fact, many readers must have sensed that beneath the comic surfaces Mr. Heller was saying something outrageous, unforgivably outrageous, not just about the idiocy of war but about our whole way of life and the system of false values on which it is based. The horror he exposed was not confined to the battlefield or the bombing mission but permeated the entire labyrinthine structure of establishment power. It found expression in the most completely inhumane exploitation of the individual for trivial, self-serving ends and the most extreme indifference to the official objectives that supposedly justified the use of power.

It was undoubtedly this recognition that the book was something far broader in scope than a mere indictment of war—a recognition perhaps arrived at only subconsciously by most readers in 1961—that gave it such pertinence to readers who discovered it over the next decade. For with the seemingly eternal and mindless escalation of the war in Vietnam, history had at last caught up with the book and caused it to be more and more widely recognized as a deadly accurate metaphorical portrait of the nightmarish conditions in which the country appeared to be engulfed.

Ironically, in the same year that *Catch-22* came out, Philip Roth published in *Commentary* his famous essay "Writing American Fiction," in which he expressed his feelings of bafflement and frustration when confronted with the grotesque improbability of most of the events of contemporary life. In a frequently quoted paragraph he said that "the American writer in the middle of the twentieth century has his hands full in trying to understand, and then describe, and then make credible much of the American reality. It stupefies, it sickens, it infuriates, and finally it is even a kind of embarrassment to one's meager imagination. The actuality is continually outdoing our talents."

Mr. Roth then proceeded to discuss the work of certain of his contemporaries (most notably, Norman Mailer, J. D. Salinger, Bernard Malamud, William Styron and Herbert Gold) and to find in much of it evidence of a failure to engage the American reality—an inevitable failure, he believed, because "what will be the [writer's] subject? His landscape? It is the tug of reality, its mystery and magnetism, that leads one into the writing of fiction—what then when one is not mystified but stupefied? Not drawn but repelled? It would seem that what we might get would be a high proportion of historical novels or contemporary satire—or perhaps just nothing. No books."

Mr. Roth was, of course, writing out of an era that was particularly notable for unbelievable and often quite repellent happenings. There had been the fiascoes of the Eisenhower Presidency, the costly Korean War, the sordid inquisitions of the McCarthy era, the Rosenberg executions, the Nixon-Kennedy debates. But then, Mr. Heller was writing out of the same era, and what makes Mr. Roth's essay historically interesting is that nowhere in it does he show an awareness or even imagine the possibility that the effort to come to terms with the unreality of the American reality might already have begun to be made by such writers as William Gaddis and John Barth, whose first works had been published by 1961, and would continue to be made by Thomas Pynchon, whose *V.* came out two years later, as well as by Joseph Heller in *Catch-22.*

These writers were all, in their different ways, seeking to create a fiction that would assimilate the difficulties Mr. Roth described. And they achieved this by creating an essentially new kind of fiction that represented an abdication of traditional realism—a form rendered mostly ineffectual because of those very difficulties—and that made use of the techniques of black humor, surrealism and grotesque metaphor to dramatize unreality, most often by making it seem even more unreal than it actually was.

The complexity and originality of the work these and other writers have produced imposed demands upon criticism that have forced it to grow in sophistication and have obviously contributed to such growth in the criticism of *Catch-22.* As evidence of this, we need only observe that most of the questions that perplexed or annoyed critics of the novel in the years immediately following its publication have now been answered, and as this has occurred, the size of Mr. Heller's achievement has been revealed to be far larger than it was first thought to be.

Recent studies have shown, for example, that two initially worrisome aspects of the novel are in fact quite adequately prepared for in the development of the action. The first is Yossarian's decision to desert, for which Mr. Brustein's early explanation remains the most convincing and widely shared. The second is the ostensibly sudden transition in the closing chapters from hilarious comedy to scenes of the blackest horror. The more sensitive of later critics have demonstrated—again following Mr. Brustein's lead—that the horror has actually been present from the beginning, but its force has been blunted and, in effect, evaded by the comedy. Through a complicated process, involving countless repetitions of references and details and a looping and straightening inchworm progression, the moment is finally reached in the *Walpurgisnacht* "Eternal City" chapter when the humor is stripped away and the terrified obsession with death, from which the humor has been a hysterical distraction, is revealed in full nakedness.

It has also been demonstrated that the tangled, excessively repetitive structure is a perfectly convincing formal statement of the novel's theme, even of the reiterated double bind of the central symbol, Catch-22. The opening figure of the soldier in white, whose bodily fluids are endlessly drained back into him, the soldier who sees everything twice, the constant raising of the required number of bombing missions, the massive incremental enumeration of detail—all these come together to suggest a world based upon a principle of quantitative evaluation in which more is better and most is best. Yet it is a world in which the accumulated excess of any one element may at any moment be neutralized by the greater accumulated excess of an antithetical element, as the comedy is finally neutralized by the weightier force of terror and death, as the fateful ubiquity of Catch-22 finally eclipses all demands for logic and sanity.

As is the case with many original works of art, *Catch-22* is a novel that reminds us once again of all that we have taken for granted in our world and should not, the madness we try not to bother to notice, the deceptions and falsehoods we lack the will to try to distinguish from truth. Twenty-five years later, we can see that the situation Mr. Heller describes has, during those years, if anything grown more complicated, deranging and perilous than it was in 1944 or 1961. The comic fable that ends in horror has become more and more clearly a reflection of the altogether uncomic and horrifying realities of the world in which we live and hope to survive.

ANTHONY BURGESS (1917–1993) was immediately attracted by the full-throttle satire of *Catch-22* and proclaimed it a "brilliantly contrived book" in his June 28, 1962, review for the *Yorkshire Evening Post.* In 1972, he held a distinguished visiting professorship at City College of New York, where he began a close friendship with his colleague Joseph Heller. Burgess prepared the following twenty-fifth-anniversary introduction for the British trade paperback reissue of *Catch-22* (London: Transworld, 1986).

An Introduction

by Anthony Burgess

The Second World War was a long, painful and debilitating experience for the British, and one consolation should have been the eventual emergence of a literary masterpiece about it. But all we have is Evelyn Waugh's *Sword of Honour,* a brilliant and witty performance with a severely limited point of view, presenting the military odyssey of a man of Waugh's own class and religious faith. We read about a war fought by patricians, in which the British lower orders are permitted to intrude and die on sufferance. To the Americans, World War II was a more democratic experience. It also represented a release of energy which was to ensure American domination of the West when the struggle was over, while the British were to accept complacently the loss of an empire and a world role and pretend that there was a certain virtue in exhaustion.

It is not surprising that the democratic energy of America was to find literary expression and produce the really important fictional writings about the war. This has to be a source of chagrin to the British, who fought longer and endured more, but the muses have no true sense of justice. Whether we like it or not, the novels which really tell us what the war was like for ordinary people, as opposed to upper-class Catholics, are Herman Wouk's *The Caine Mutiny,* Norman Mailer's *The Naked and the Dead,* and Joseph Heller's *Catch-22.* It may or may not be significant that all these authors are Jews, though not one of them limited himself to the experience of Jewish serving men.

We can take the matter beyond the recording of a particular war and affirm that the masterpieces which state what twentieth-century war in general is about—in, at least, its impact on the ordinary participant—

have come from America, a traditionally most unwarlike nation. Thomas Pynchon's novel *Gravity's Rainbow* has as much to say about the First World War as the Second, and it found its technique of expression in a region which was not historically denied to the literary recorders who served in what we may still term the Great War, but was antipathetic to their literary temperaments. Pynchon employs symbolism, surrealism and, above all, obscenity of language and image to express the madness of the conflict—something that Robert Graves, Siegfried Sassoon and R. C. Sheriff were unable to do. *Catch-22*, which is about World War II but is prophetic about Korea and Vietnam, uses a special technique of satire which finds in the breakdown of language an analog to the breakdown of reason and ordinary human decency.

We're aware in the very first chapter that words are no longer adequate to express the dementia which has overtaken the organization of American civilians into faceless elements of the military machine. Yossarian is censoring soldiers' letters, and to break the monotony of the task he invents games. "Death to all modifiers, he declared one day, and out of every letter that passed through his hands went every adverb and every adjective. The next day he made war on articles. He reached a much higher plane of creativity the following day when he blocked out everything in the letters but *a*, *and* and *the*." Personal names lose their meanings: "What kind of a name is Yossarian?" a high-ranking officer wants to know. But the real madness is expressed in the very title, where logic becomes circular and A equals not-A. The term "Catch-22" has passed into the language and is used by people who have never read the book.

The other day I was writing about the situation of nineteenth-century philologists. They could not teach their subject in universities without possessing a degree in it, but degrees in it would never exist until they taught the subject in universities. This, rightly I think, I designated a Catch-22 situation. But it is a genuinely deadly matter in its text of origin. Doc Daneeka can ground fliers if they are crazy, but they have to ask him first. But if they ask him they are not really crazy, since it is no mark of sanity to be prepared to go on suicide missions. This is Catch-22, says Doc Daneeka. What is the punishment for cowardice? Death. What is cowardice? The desire to avoid death. Wherever you look in the U.S. Air Force you are up against anomaly, the subversion of logic which is nevertheless a form of logic.

The Americans are fighting the Nazis in Italy, but the Nazis are not permitted to be the targets of the comic bitterness. The enemy is on this side of the fence. Any veteran serving man will recognize the truth beneath Heller's mad satire. There was always enough to hate in one's own army; there was no space left to feel abhorrence of the enemy, which was primarily the concern of newspaper-fed civilians. Our detestation of the Nazi system we were trying to overthrow has been very much a retrospective business, as has been the discovery of the incredible horrors the Nazis perpetrated. Soldiers sympathize with soldiers, whatever side they are on, and reserve their loathing for professional top brass and jingoistic civilians. It was always like that. Nevertheless, the reader of *Catch-22* has to feel a little uncomfortable when an American airman bombs his base on behalf of the Nazis, and the squeamish may question whether satire is appropriate to a book about a war waged for the ridding of humanity of the worst scourge of the century. It is best to transfer the action to some mythical zone where war is gratuitous and unjust, and then to accept the wild comedy as the only possible literary response to a stupid and coldblooded military machine.

The cynicisms are well chosen. A mess officer steals the carbon dioxide capsules from the fliers' Mae Wests to make ice cream sodas for the officers' mess. A stock letter is sent out to next of kin: "Dear Mrs, Mr, Miss or Mr and Mrs—; Words cannot express the deep personal grief I experienced when your husband, son, father or brother was killed, wounded, or reported missing in action (cross out whatever is inapplicable)." The victimization of the conscripts and the monstrous egotism of the high command are treated with a lightness which in itself is a mode of heroism. Yossarian only wishes to survive, and, quite as much as *La Chartreuse de Parme* or *War and Peace*, Heller's hilarious novel is dedicated to the desire of the ordinary man to live through the madness and come through alive. The curious and heartening thing about *Catch-22* is that the *vis comica* does not get in the way of the presentation of real human beings. Even the monsters of the top brass are all too horribly human.

Mike Nichols made an unsuccessful film of *Catch-22*—unsuccessful because it had to portray horrors in full bloodinesses, exploiting the visual to the limit and forgetting that Heller offers us a verbal experience. The horror of the book is expressed less through images than through the perversion of thought and language: there is no horror worse than madness. I was a colleague of Heller's at City College in New York—we were both Distinguished Professors—when Nichols's film and Kubrick's film of my novel *A Clockwork Orange* appeared, and we were both able to point to the unfilmability of works based on the impact of literary style. At that time Heller seemed to be suffering from the very American ailment of Writer's Block (which European writers locate only in film studios) and seemed unready to attach his satirical technique to postwar civilian America. With *Something Happened* and *Good As Gold*, Heller has demonstrated superbly that his chief theme as a novelist is the universal twentieth-century madness which can only be expressed in the absurdist collapse of verbal communication. One would have thought that so metaphysical a mind and so subtle a technician could never achieve wide popularity, but the immense success of *Catch-22* has shown that a distinguished work of literature can sometimes reach a very wide audience indeed. The twenty-fifth anniversary of the first publication of this remarkable novel is worthy of celebration, and I am happy and proud to be one of the celebrants.

CHRISTOPHER HITCHENS (1949–), a prolific and wide-ranging Anglo-American journalist, valued the prescient cultural insights of *Catch-22* in much the same way that he has always valued the show-trial revelations of Arthur Koestler's *Darkness at Noon* and the geopolitical extrapolations of George Orwell's *Nineteen Eighty-Four*. His salute to Joseph Heller's powerful gift of satire and enduring stoicism, published just after Heller's death, is reprinted from the December 15, 1999, issue of *The Nation*.

JOSEPH HELLER

by Christopher Hitchens

Joe Heller once told me the following. Having submitted the manuscript of his first novel, he was invited to a meeting by his editor, Robert Gottlieb, who lost no time in telling him that it had been accepted. There was, however, a problem with the title. The same publishing house was already scheduled to bring out Leon Uris's *Mila 18*. Two books, both about World War II, both by Jewish authors and both with 18 on the cover, wouldn't do. "So I'm very much afraid, Mr. Heller, that your *Catch-18* title will need to be changed." "Whaddaya suggest?" was Joe's approximate response. "Well, I've given it considerable thought, and I believe that the alliteration of Catch-22 would be an apt one."

Is it thinkable that America's ludic Kafka would have scored so massively with any phrase other than the numinously hieroglyphic 22? I like to believe that he might. As it was, the book didn't get much of a reception (except from Nelson Algren in *The Nation*, who called it "the best American novel to come out of World War II") and achieved most of its effect by bush telegraph. And the timing had an unusual felicity, helping to curtain-raise what nobody knew would be The Sixties. By the time I read, in an AP dispatch from Vietnam in 1968, that the village of Ben Tre had had to be destroyed in order to save it, I and countless others had been well prepared for such news from the dark frontiers of Absurdistan, and prepared by reading Heller. Having endless times been asked, by schoolmasters, military cadet instructors and other purveyors of the literal and banal: "Look here, Hitchens, what would happen if everyone thought like you?" I came across Yossarian's riposte to this eternal interrogatory (which was roughly, Why, then, I'd be a damn fool to think any other way, wouldn't I?) and sent the book hurtling skywards with a yell of triumph. Yes! That's the stuff to give them! And who didn't think of Milo Minderbinder when they read about the Oliver North network; trading with the enemy to furnish the goods and services to finance treason and terrorism?

Heller's underrated later works, especially *Good as Gold* and *Something Happened*, can be treasured for their persisting stoicism and wit in the face of the random and the capricious. Heller never became a *Commentary* kvetch like so many of his peers; his hatred for men like Nixon and Kissinger had a nice purity and integrity to it. A gruesome recent memoir, Norman Podhoretz's *Ex-Friends*, pays Heller a handsome compliment. Podhoretz generally reserved the right to be the one to end a connection, dropping Norman Mailer here and Allen Ginsberg there. Heller, however, as Podhoretz ruefully records, got in first by dropping him. Good work. After Clinton went husky at Nixon's funeral in 1996, Heller decided he had heard enough, and had no further use for him. Snap judgments are so often the best.

Amazingly handsome and sexy (and greedy) right up to the end, Joe probably benefited from the enlivening thought that he could so easily have been dead. He might well have snuffed it during the Italian campaign that taught him military logic; he was dead lucky (as he might have phrased it) to pull through his hellish encounter with Guillain-Barré syndrome. He was luckier still to meet Valerie as a consequence of surviving that second dress rehearsal for the ineluctable. His *Catch* by any other name would have been as resonant, and, not that he cared for theories of immortality, his reservation in the Pantheon of the ironic was always confirmed.

CREDITS

The publisher wishes to thank Jonathan R. Eller of Indiana University, Sarah Shoemaker of Brandeis University, and Jack Begg of the *New York Times* for their help with the supplementary material for this edition of *Catch-22*.

"Some Children of the Goddess" by Norman Mailer, originally published in *Esquire*. Copyright © 1963 by the Norman Mailer Estate, reprinted by permission of The Wylie Agency LLC.

Excerpt from *Bright Book of Life: American Novelists and Storytellers from Hemingway to Mailer* by Alfred Kazin. Copyright © 1973 by the Estate of Alfred Kazin, reprinted by permission of The Wylie Agency LLC.

"The Loony Horror of It All—*Catch-22* Turns 25" by John W. Aldridge, *The New York Times Book Review*, October 26, 1986. Reprinted by permission of John W. Aldridge papers, Bentley Historical Library, University of Michigan.

"An Introduction" by Anthony Burgess. Copyright © The Estate of Anthony Burgess. Reprinted with permission.

"Joseph Heller" by Christopher Hitchens, *The Nation*, January 3, 2000. Reprinted with permission from *The Nation*. For subscription information, call 1-800-333-8536. Portions of each week's *Nation* magazine can be accessed at http://www.thenation.com.